PRAISE FOR THE WRITING OF DAVID BRIN

The Uplift Saga

"The Uplift books are as compulsive reading as anything ever published in the genre." —*The Encyclopedia of Science Fiction*

Startide Rising

"One of the outstanding SF novels of recent years." —*Publishers Weekly*

"One hell of a novel . . . *Startide Rising* has what SF readers want these days; intelligence, action, and an epic scale." —*Isaac Asimov's Science Fiction Magazine*

"*Startide Rising* is one of the books that I remember most fondly, out of all I have read, and rereading it thirty years later proved just as enjoyable as the first time. I remain amazed at how many different characters and subplots Brin juggles without a misstep, and the way he keeps the tension and suspense high throughout."
—Alan Brown, Tor.com

The Uplift War

"An exhilarating read that encompasses everything from breathless action to finely drawn moments of quiet intimacy. There is no way we can avoid coming back as many times as Brin wants us to, until his story is done." —*Locus*

"With a plot that takes unexpected, and often quite uplifting (forgive the pun), twists, especially for animal lovers, a compelling cast of characters, and a fast, expanding pace, this is a science fiction classic." —Fantasy Book Review

Brightness Reef

"A captivating read." —*Star Tribune*

"Tremendously inventive, ambitious work." —*Kirkus Reviews*

"Brin is a skillful storyteller . . . There is more than enough action to keep the book exciting, and like all good serials, the first volume ends with a bang."
—*The Plain Dealer*

"Brin has shown beyond doubt that he is a master of plot and character and incident, of sheer storytelling, while he is also thoughtful enough to satisfy anyone's craving for meat on those literary bones. Don't miss this one, folks, or the next."
—*Analog Science Fiction and Fact*

Infinity's Shore

"Well paced, immensely complex, highly literate . . . On full display here is Brin's extraordinary capacity to handle a wide-range narrative and to create convincingly complex alien races . . . Superior SF." —*Publishers Weekly*

"This was a really amazing book in its own right, with alien, awesomely evil villains, a range of shocks to the system, and characters you really come to care about."
—Fantasy Book Review

Heaven's Reach

"Brin fans will find plenty to gorge themselves on here, including Niss Machines, Galactic Library cubes and Zang ship-entities." —*Publishers Weekly*

"Extremely entertaining books because of the sheer richness of the background information."
—SF Site

"*Heaven's Reach* was a massive ringing conclusion to a truly epic saga with more of the strange and alien than ever before." —Fantasy Book Review

"A brilliant author whose science and style are perfect matches, both believable and gripping, Brin has written masterfully yet again of races and individuals, histories and prophecies that will give readers suspenseful chills and send desperate hearts racing." —*Curled Up With a Good Book*

HEAVEN'S REACH

DAVID BRIN

INTEGRATED MEDIA
NEW YORK

To

Terren Jacob Brin, our unlimited explorer
and crowning work in our trilogy

ISBN: 978-1-5040-6475-0

This edition published in 2021 by Open Road Integrated Media, Inc.
180 Maiden Lane
New York, NY 10038
www.openroadmedia.com

CONTENTS

Cast of Characters *vii*

Cast of Sapient Species *x*

Glossary of Terms *xii*

PART I: The Five Galaxies *1*

PART II: The Orders of Life *61*

PART III: The Great Harrower *141*

PART IV: Candidates for Transcendence *193*

PART V: The Time of Changes *301*

Afterword *337*

"Civilization" . . . A Hoonish Denouement! *339*

A Timeline of the Uplift Universe *343*

Acknowledgments *347*

*About the Autho*r 348

CAST OF CHARACTERS

Akeakemai—a dolphin member of *Streaker*'s bridge crew.

Alvin—the humicker (human-mimicking) nickname of Hph-wayuo, an adolescent hoon from Jijo.

Asx—a member of the Jijo Council of High Sages, representing the traeki race. See Ewasx.

Baskin, Gillian—a Terragens Agent assigned as physician to the dolphin survey vessel *Streaker.* In command since the debacle at Kithrup.

Creideiki—a male dolphin, former captain of the dolphin-crewed Earth vessel *Streaker.* Left behind on Kithrup, along with several other members of the crew, with just a space "skiff" to make their way across the Five Galaxies.

D'Anite, Emerson—a human engineer, once assigned to the Terragens spacecraft *Streaker.*

Dor-hinuf—a young female hoon. Twaphu-anuph's daughter.

Dwer—the son of the papermaker Nelo Koolhan, brother of Sara and Lark, chief tracker of the Commons of Six Races of Jijo.

Ewasx—a Jophur ring-stack entity made mostly from components of the Jijoan sage Asx, plus a master ring.

Gillian—see Baskin, Gillian.

Harms, Harry—a neo-chimpanzee scout for the Institute of Navigation.

Huck—the humicker (human-mimicking) nickname of a g'Kek orphan raised by a hoonish family on Jijo. Alvin's closest friend.

Huphu—Alvin's pet noor beast.

Kaa—second pilot of *Streaker.* Formerly "Lucky Kaa."

Karkaett—a male dolphin and engineering mate on *Streaker.*

Keepiru—former chief pilot of *Streaker.* Left behind on Kithrup.

Kiwei Ha'aoulin—a Synthian trader.

Lark—brother of Sara and Dwer, a lesser sage of the Commons of Jijo.

Ling—a Danik (human heretic) biologist.

Makanee—a female dolphin, the ship's surgeon on *Streaker.* Left on Jijo to tend mentally reverted members of *Streaker*'s crew.

Mudfoot—a wild noor beast, named by Dwer Koolhan.

Niss—pseudosapient computer lent to *Streaker* by a Tymbrimi spy.

Old Ones—a term given to the "retired" races of the Fractal World.

Orley, Thomas—a genetically engineered Terragens Agent assigned to *Streaker.* Married to Gillian, left on Kithrup with Creideiki's group.

Peepoe—a geneticist and nurse on *Streaker.* Kidnapped on Jijo.

Pincer-Tip—a red qheuen friend of Alvin's who carved the hull for the bathyscaphe *Wuphon's Dream* out of the trunk of a garu tree.

Prity—a female neo-chimpanzee; Sara's servant, skilled at certain aspects of mathematical imagery.

Rann—leader of the Danik humans.

Rety—a human sooner, she fled her savage band's hidden offshoot colony in the Gray Hills of Jijo.

Ro-kenn—a Rothen overlord.

Sara—daughter of the papermaker Nelo Koolhan, sister of Dwer and Lark, mathematician and language scholar.

Suessi, Hannes—a human engineer on *Streaker,* converted into a cyborg by the Old Ones.

Twaphu-anuph—a hoonish customs official at Kazzkark Base.

Tsh't—a female dolphin, originally *Streaker*'s fifth in command. Later shared command with Gillian.

Tyug—the traeki alchemist of Mount Guenn Forge. A new crew member on *Streaker.*

Uriel—urrish Master Smith of the Mount Guenn Forge on Jijo.

Ur-ronn—Alvin's urrish friend and member of the *Wuphon's Dream* expedition. Uriel's niece.

Wer'Q'quinn—Harry's boss at the Institute of Navigation.

yee—an urrish male ejected from his pouch-home by his former mate. Later "married" the sooner girl Rety.

* See the end of this book for a *Glossary of Species and Terms,* plus a *TIMELINE* of the Uplift Universe.

CAST OF SAPIENT SPECIES

g'Keks—the first sooner race to arrive on Jijo, some two thousand years ago. Originally uplifted by the Drooli, the g'Kek have biomagnetically driven wheels and four eyestalks rising from a combined torso-braincase. Due to vendettas by enemies, the g'Kek are extinct throughout the Five Galaxies, except on Jijo.

glavers—the third sooner race to reach Jijo. Uplifted by the Tunuctyur, who were themselves uplifted by the Buyur. Glavers are partly bipedal with opalescent skin and large, bulging eyes. Roughly a meter tall, they have a prehensile forked tail to assist their inefficient hands. Since illegally settling Jijo they devolved to a state of presapience, dropping out of the Commons of Six Races. To some, glavers seem to be shining examples, having shown the way down the Path of Redemption.

hoons—the fifth wave of settlers to arrive on Jijo, bipedal omnivores, with pale scaly skin and woolly white leg fur. Their spines are massive, hollow structures that form part of their circulatory system. Hoons' inflatable throat sacs, originally for mating displays, are now used for "umbling." Since their Uplift by the Guthatsa, this race have found widespread service as dour, officious bureaucrats in Galactic culture.

humans—the youngest sooner race arrived on Jijo less than three hundred years ago. Human "wolflings" evolved on Earth, apparently achieving technological civilization and crude interstellar travel on their own, or else assisted by some unknown patron. Passionate debates rage over this issue.

Jophur—semicommunal organisms resembling cones of stacked donuts. Like their traeki cousins, Jophur consist of interchangeable spongy "sap-rings," each with limited intelligence, but combining to form a sapient community being. Specialized rings give the stack its senses, manipulative organs, and sometimes exotic chemosynthetic abilities. As traeki, this unique species was originally gentle and unaspiring when first uplifted by the Poa. The zealous Oallie later reinvented them by providing "master rings," transforming the traeki into Jophur, willful and profoundly ambitious beings.

qheuens—the fourth sooner race on Jijo. Originally uplifted by the Zhosh, qheuens are radially symmetric exo-skeletal beings with five legs and claws. Their brain is partly contained in a retractable central dome or "cupola." A rebel band of qheuens settled Jijo attempting to hold on to their ancient caste system, with the gray variety providing royal matriarchs while red and blue types were servants and artisans.

Conditions on Jijo—including later human intervention—provoked the breakdown of this system.

Rothen—a mysterious Galactic race. One human group (the dakkins or Daniks) believe the Rothen to be Earth's lost patrons. Rothen are bipeds, somewhat larger than humans but with similar proportions and charismatic features. Believed to be carnivores.

traeki—second illicit settler race to arrive on Jijo. Traeki are a throwback variant of Jophur, who fled the imposition of master rings.

urs—the sixth sooner race on Jijo. Carnivorous, centauroid plains dwellers; they have long, flexible necks, narrow heads, and shoulderless arms ending in dexterous hands. Urs start life as tiny, six-limbed grubs, turned out of their mothers' pouches to fend for themselves. Any that survive to "childhood" may be accepted into an urrish band. Urrish females reach the size of a large deer, and possess twin brood pouches where they keep diminutive mates, who are smaller than a house cat. A female with prelarval young ejects one or both husbands to make room for the brood. Urs have an aversion to water in its pure form.

GLOSSARY OF TERMS

allaphor—the metaphorical interpretation made by sentient minds of certain features in E-Level hyperspace.

Anglic—a human language created in the Twenty-First century, using many English words, but influenced by other pre-Contact tongues and modified according to new understandings of linguistic theory.

Buyur—former legal tenants of Jijo, froglike appearance, known for wit, foresight, and gene-crafting of specialized animal-tools. Departed when Jijo was declared fallow half a million years ago.

client—a race still working out a period of servitude to the patrons that uplifted it from presapient animal status.

criswell structures—fractal shells designed to surround small red suns, utilizing all light energy. The fractal shape allows maximum possible "window area," unlike a simple Dyson sphere.

Daniks—a vulgarized term for "Danikenite," a cultural movement dating from humanity's first contact with Galactic Civilization. Daniks believe Earthlings were uplifted by a Galactic patron race that chose to remain hidden for unknown reasons. An offshoot cult believes Rothen are this race of wise, enigmatic guides.

dura—approximately one-third of a minute.

E-Level hyperspace—a dangerous hyperspatial region in which the distinctions between consciousness and reality become blurred. Self-consistent concepts may exist without a host brain or computer to contain or contemplate them. See allaphor.

Earthclan—a small, eccentric Galactic "family" of sapient races consisting of neo-chimpanzee and neo-dolphin clients, along with their human patrons.

Egg—see Holy Egg.

Embrace of Tides—a quasi addiction that causes elder races to seek the sensation of gravitational tides, close to very dense stars.

er—genderless pronoun, sometimes used when referring to a traeki.

fen—plural of "fin," Anglic shorthand for a neo-dolphin.

Fractal World—a place of retirement for races that have nearly transcended the Civilization of the Five Galaxies. (See criswell structures.)

Galactic—a person, race, concept, or technology deriving from the aeons-old Civilization of the Five Galaxies.

Galactic Institutes—vast, powerful academies, purportedly neutral and above interclan politics. The Institutes regulate various aspects of Galactic Civilization. Some are over a billion years old.

Galactic Library—a fantastically capacious collection of knowledge gathered over the course of hundreds of millions of years. Quasi-sapient "Branch Libraries" are found in most Galactic starships and settlements.

Gronin Collapse—historical name given to the last time in Galactic history when the expansion of the universe caused transfer points between galaxies to "pull apart," thus fragmenting Galactic society.

Holy Egg—a mysterious mass of psi-active stone that emerged from a Jijoan volcano a century ago, accompanied by widespread visions.

humicker—slang term for someone who mimics humans, because Earthling texts dominated literate life on Jijo after the Great Printing.

Ifni—a vulgarization of "Infinity." In spacer tradition, a name given to the goddess of luck. Personification of chance or Murphy's Law.

Izmunuti—a red giant star close to Jijo's sun; spews a carbon wind masking Jijo from supervision by the Institute for Migration.

jadura—approximately forty-three hours.

Jijo—a planet in Galaxy Four. Home of seven sooner races: humans, hoons, qheuen, urs, g'Kek, the devolved glavers, and "demodified" Jophur known as traeki.

Kazzkark—a space station operated by the several major Galactic Institutes, including the Institute of Navigation.

kidura—approximately one-half second.

Kiqui—an amphibious presapient race native to Kithrup.

Kithrup—a water world rich in heavy metals.

Midden—a vast undersea crevasse, or subduction zone, formed by plate tectonics, running alongside the Slope on Jijo. All dross generated by the inhabitant races—from skeletal remains to the hulls of sooner spacecraft—is dumped into the Midden, where natural forces will carry it below Jijo's crust for melting.

midura—a unit of time, approximately seventy-one minutes.

Morgran—a transfer point where *Streaker* was first attacked by warships of the most fanatic religious clans.

neo-chimpanzee—humanity's first clients. Fully uplifted neo-chimps can speak; the "unfinished" variety that accompanied humans to Jijo are mute, but able to communicate with sign language.

neo-dolphin—uplifted dolphins; clients of humanity.

noor—a Jijoan term for tytlal, a Galactic species uplifted by the Tymbrimi, and living on Jijo in secret sapient form. To Jijoans, noor are bright, dexterous, mischievous otterlike creatures. Noor cannot be tamed, but the patient, good-natured hoon are able to employ some on their ships. Noor are considered pests by other sooner races.

NuDawn Colony—a world colonized by the Terragens before contact was made with Galactic Civilization, in unknowing violation of migration laws. The inhabitants were forcibly and violently evicted by hoonish bureaucrats, supported by Jophur and other vigilantes.

Oakka—a regional headquarters of the Institute of Migration.

Orders of Life—seven types of sapient life are known among the Five Galaxies:

1. oxygen breathers—members of Galactic culture, including humans.

2. hydrogen breathers—utilize "reducing" atmospheres, having slower metabolisms. Most inhabit giant gas planets, drifting among the clouds, performing internal simulations of the world.

3. the retired order—former patron races that have reached senescence and "retired" from Galactic affairs, taking residence in fractal structures, amif the gravitational tides close to red dwarf suns.

4. machine—self-replicating sentient machines. Generally confine themselves to high-radiation areas or zones of deep space unwanted by either hydrogen or oxygen civilizations, though a few types are tolerated for their usefulness.

5. *transcendents* — even older than "retired," these are races that have "passed on" to a higher plane, having melded or merged with other orders. Mere Galactics are riven by many beliefs about this stage of life. The first to transcend (it is assumed) were the Progenitors.

6. *memetic*—bizarre "thought" organisms residing primarily in E-Level hyperspace.

7. *quantum*—organisms discovered only during the last 100 million years, existing between the interstices of the universe, making scant contact with Galactic society. Their way of life seems to depend on macroquantum uncertainty.

There is widespread disagreement over whether the number of life orders should equal eight. Even more are suspected. Contact between life orders is dangerous, and widely discouraged.

patron—a Galactic race that has uplifted at least one animal species to full sapience.

pidura—six to the eighth power duras, or approximately four hundred days.

Polkjhy—the name of the Jophur battleship that landed on Jijo in search of the fugitive Earthship *Streaker.*

Primal Delphin—semilanguage used by natural, nonuplifted dolphins on Earth.

Progenitors—the legendary first spacefaring race, who began the cycle of Uplift two billion years ago, establishing Galactic society.

rewq—quasifungal symbionts that help the Six Races "read" each other's emotions and body language.

sooners—outlaws who colonize worlds designated fallow by the Galactic Institute of Migration. On Jijo, the term means those who try to make new illegal settlements, beyond the confines of the Slope.

Streaker—a dolphin-crewed Terran starship. The *Streaker*'s discoveries led to unprecedented pursuit by dozens of Galactic factions, each seeking advantage by possessing the dolphins' secrets.

stress atavism—a condition found among newly uplifted species, which tend to lose their higher cognitive functions under stress.

Terragens Council—the ruling body of humanity's interstellar government, in charge of matters directly affecting relations between Earthclan and Galactic society.

toporgic—pseudomaterial substrate made of organically folded time.

transfer point—an area of twisted spacetime that allows faster-than-light travel for vessels entering at a precise angle and velocity.

Tymbrimi—a humanoid species allied with Earthclan, known for cleverness and devilish humor.

Tytlal—see *noor*.

Uplift—process of turning a presapient animal species into a fully sapient race ready to join Galactic society. Performed by a "patron."

wolfling—a derogatory Galactic term for a race that appears to have uplifted itself to spacefaring status without help, or else to have been abandoned by its patron.

ylem—the underlying fabric of reality itself.

Zang—a phylum of hydrogen breathers consisting of single cells, often spherical or blobby but sometimes organized to resemble huge squids. They live in the atmospheres of gas giants. Jijo's entire region (Galaxy Four) has been leased to hydrogen breathers by the Institute of Migration.

PART ONE

THE FIVE GALAXIES

What emblems grace the fine prows of our fast ships?

How many spirals swirl on the bow of each great vessel, turning round and round, symbolizing our connections? How many are the links that form our union?

ONE spiral represents the fallow worlds, slowly brewing, steeping, stewing—where life begins its long, hard climb.

Struggling out of that fecundity, new races emerge, ripe for Uplift.

TWO is for starfaring culture, streaking madly in our fast ships, first as clients, then as patrons, vigorously chasing our young interests—trading, fighting, and debating—

Straining upward, till we hear the call of beckoning tides.

THREE portrays the Old Ones, graceful and serene, who forsake starships to embrace a life of contemplation. Tired of manic rushing. Cloistering for self-improvement, they prepare to face the Great Harrower.

FOUR depicts the High Transcendents, too majestic for us to perceive. But they exist. They must! Making plans that encompass all levels of space, and all times.

FIVE is for the galaxies—great whirls of shining light—our islands in a sterile cosmos, surrounded by enigmatic silence.

On and on they spin, nurturing all life's many orders, linked perpetually, everlasting.

Or so we are assured. . . .

HARRY

ALARMS SING A VARIETY OF MELODIES.

Some shriek for attention, yanking you awake from deathlike repose. Others send your veins throbbing with adrenaline. Aboard any space vessel there are sirens and wails that portend collision, vacuum leaks, or myriad other kinds of impending death.

But the alarm tugging at Harry Harms wasn't like that. Its creepy ratchet scraped lightly along the nerves.

"No rush," the soft buzzer seemed to murmur. *"I can wait."*

"But don't even think about going back to sleep."

Harry rolled over to squint blearily at the console next to his pillow. Glowing symbols beckoned meaningfully. But the parts of his brain that handled reading weren't perfectly designed. They took a while to warm up.

"Guh. . . ." he commented. "Wuh?"

Drowsiness clung to his body, still exhausted after another long, solitary watch. How many duras had passed since he tumbled into the bunk, vowing to quit his commission when this tour of duty ended?

Sleep had come swiftly, but not restfully. Dreams always filled Harry's slumber, here in E Space.

In fact, dreaming was part of the job.

In REM state, Harry often revisited the steppes of Horst, where a dusty horizon had been his constant background in childhood. A forlorn world, where ponderous dark clouds loomed and flickered, yet held tightly to their moisture, sharing little with the parched ground. He usually woke from such visions with a desiccated mouth, desperate for water.

Other dreams featured *Earth*—jangling city-planet, brimming with tall humans—its skyscrapers and lush greenery stamped in memory by one brief visit, ages ago, in another life.

Then there were nightmares about ships—great battlecraft and moonlike invasion arks—glistening by starlight or cloaked in the dark glow of their terrible fields. Wraithlike frigates, looming more eerie and terrifying than real life.

Those were the more *normal* dream images to come creeping in, whenever his mind had room between far stranger apparitions. For the most part, Harry's night thoughts were filled with spinning, dizzying *allaphors,* which billowed and muttered in the queer half-logic of E Space. Even his shielded quarters weren't impervious to tendrils of counterreality, penetrating the bulkheads, groping through his sleep. No wonder he woke disoriented, shaken by the grating alarm.

Harry stared at the glowing letters—each twisting like some manic, living hieroglyph, gesticulating in the ideogrammatic syntax of Galactic Language Number Seven. Concentrating, he translated the message into the Anglic of his inner thoughts.

"Great," Harry commented in a dry voice.

Apparently, the patrol vessel had run aground again.

"Oh, that's just fine."

The buzzer increased its tempo. Pushing out of bed, Harry landed barefoot on the chill deck plates, shivering.

"And to think . . . they tell me I got an *aptitude* for this kind of work."

In other words, you had to be at least partway crazy to be suited for his job.

Shaking lethargy, he clambered up a ladder to the observing platform just above his quarters—a hexagonal chamber, ten meters across, with a control panel in the center. Groping toward the alarm cutoff, Harry somehow managed not to trigger any armaments, or purge the station's atmosphere into E Space, before slapping the right switch. The maddening noise abruptly ceased.

"Ah . . ." he sighed, and almost fell asleep again right there, standing behind the padded command chair.

But then . . . if sleep did come, he might start dreaming again.

I never understood Hamlet till they assigned me here. Now I figure, Shakespeare must've glimpsed E Space before writing that "to be or not to be" stuff.

. . . perchance to dream . . .

Yup, ol' Willie must've known there's worse things than death.

Scratching his belly, Harry scanned the status board. No red lights burned. The station appeared functional. No major reality leaks were evident. With a sigh, he moved around to perch on the seat.

"Monitor mode. Report station status."

The holo display lit up, projecting a floating blue M, sans serif. A melodious voice emanated from the slowly revolving letter.

"Monitor mode. Station integrity is nominal. An alarm has been acknowledged by station superintendent Harry Harms at 4:48:52 internal subjective estimate time. . . ."

"*I'm* Harry Harms. Why don't you tell me something I don't know, like what the alarm's *for,* you shaggy excuse for a baldie's toup . . . ah . . . ah . . ."

A sneeze tore through Harry's curse. He wiped his eyes with the back of a hirsute wrist.

"The alarm denoted an interruption in our patrol circuit of E Level hyperspace," the monitor continued, unperturbed. *"The station has apparently become mired in an anomaly region."*

"You mean we're grounded on a reef. I already knew that much. But what *kind* of . . ." he muttered. "Oh, never mind. I'll go see for myself."

Harry ambled over to a set of vertical louvered blinds—one of six banks that rimmed the hexagonal chamber—and slipped a fingertip between two of the slats, prying them apart to make a narrow slit opening. He hesitated, then brought one eye forward to peer outside.

The station appeared to be *shaped* in its standard format, at least. Not like a whale, or jellyfish, or amorphous blob, thank Ifni. Sometimes this continuum had effects on physical objects that were gruesomely bizarre, or even fatal.

On this occasion the control chamber still perched like a glass cupola atop an oblate white spheroid, commanding a 360-degree view of a vast metaphorical realm—a dubious, dangerous, but seldom monotonous domain.

Jagged black mountains bobbed in the distance, like ebony icebergs, majestically traversing what resembled an endless sea of purple grass. The "sky" was a red-blue shade that could only be seen on E Level. It had holes in it.

So far so good.

Harry spread the slats wider to take in the foreground and blinked in surprise at what he saw. The station rested on a glistening, slick brown surface. Spread across this expanse, for what might seem a kilometer in all directions, lay a thick scattering of giant yellow starfish!

At least that was his first impression. Harry rushed to another bank of curtains and peeked again. More "starfish" lay on that side as well, dispersed randomly, but thickly enough to show no easy route past.

"Damn." From experience he knew it would be useless to try *flying over* the things. If they represented two-dimensional obstacles, they must be overcome in a two-dimensional way. That was how allaphorical logic worked in this zone of E Space.

Harry went back to the control board and touched a button. All the blinds retracted, revealing an abrupt panoramic view. Mountains and purple grass in the distance. Brown slickness closer in.

And yes, the station was completely surrounded by starfish. Yellow starfish everywhere.

"Pfeh." Harry shivered. Most of the jaundiced monsters had six arms, though some had five or seven. They didn't appear to be moving. That, at least, was a relief. Harry hated ambulatory allaphors.

"Pilot mode!" he commanded.

With a faint crackling, the floating helvetica M was replaced by a jaunty, cursive *P*.

"Aye aye, o' Person-Commander. Where to now, Henry?"

"Name's Harry," he grunted. The perky tones used by pilot mode might have been cheery and friendly in Anglic, but they came across as just plain silly in Galactic Seven.

Yet the only available alternative meant substituting a voice chip programmed in whistle-clicking GalTwo. A Gubru dialect, even. He wasn't desperate enough to try that yet.

"Prepare to ease us along a perceived-flat course trajectory of two forty degrees, ship centered," he told the program. "Dead slow."

"Whatever you say, Boss-Sentient. Adapting interface parameters now."

Harry went back to the window, watching the station *grow* four huge wheels, bearing giant balloon tires with thick treads. Soon they began to turn. A squeaky whine, like rubbing your hand on a soapy countertop, penetrated the thick crystal panes.

As he had feared, the tires found little traction on the slick brown surface. Still, he held back from overruling the pilot's choice of countermeasures. Better see what happened first.

Momentum built gradually. The station approached the nearest yellow starfish.

Doubt spread in Harry's mind.

"Maybe I should try looking this up first. They might have the image listed somewhere."

Once upon a time, back when he was inducted as Earth's first volunteer-recruit in the Navigation Institute survey department—full of tape-training and idealism—he used to consult the records every time E Space threw another weird symbolism at him. After all, the Galactic civilization of oxygen-breathing races had been exploring, cataloging, and surveying this bizarre continuum for half a billion years. The amount of information contained in even his own tiny shipboard Library unit exceeded the sum of all human knowledge before contact was made with extraterrestrials.

An impressive store . . . and as it turned out, nearly useless. Maybe he wasn't very good at negotiating with the Library's reference persona. Or perhaps the problem came from being born of Earth-simian stock. Anyway, he soon took to trusting his own instincts during missions to E Space.

Alas, that approach had one drawback. You have only yourself to blame when things blow up in your face.

Harry noticed he was slouching. He straightened and brought his hands together to prevent scratching. But nervous energy had to express itself, so he tugged on his thumbs, instead. A Tymbrimi he knew had once remarked that many of Harry's species had that habit, perhaps a symptom from the long, hard process of Uplift.

The forward tires reached the first starfish. There was no way around the things. No choice but to try climbing over them.

Harry held his breath as contact was made. But touching drew no reaction. The obstacle just lay there, six long, flat strips of brown-flecked yellow, splayed from a nubby central hump. The first set of tires skidded, and the station rode up the yellow strip, pushed by the back wheels.

The station canted slightly. Harry rumbled anxiously in his chest, trying to tease loose a tickling thread of recognition. Maybe "starfish" wasn't the best analogy for these things. They looked familiar though.

The angle increased. A troubled whine came from the spinning rear wheels until they, too, reached the yellow.

In a shock of recognition, Harry shouted—"No! Reverse! They're *ban*—"

Too late. The back tires whined as slippery yellow strips flew out from under the platform, sending it flipping in a sudden release of traction. Harry tumbled, struck the ceiling, then slid across the far wall, shouting as the scout platform rolled, skidded, and rolled again . . . until it dropped with a final, bone-jarring thud. Fetching up against a bulkhead, Harry clutched a wall rail with his toes until the jouncing finally stopped.

"Oh . . . my head . . ." he moaned, picking himself up.

At least things had settled right side up. He shuffled back to the console in a crouch and read the main display. The station had suffered little damage, thank Ifni. But Harry must have put off housecleaning chores too long, for dust balls now coated his fur from head to toe. He slapped them off, raising clouds and triggering violent sneezes.

The shutters had closed automatically the instant things went crazy, protecting his eyes against potentially dangerous allaphors.

He commanded gruffly, "Open blinds!" Perhaps the violent action had triggered a local phase change, causing all the nasty obstacles to vanish. It had happened before.

No such luck, he realized as the louvers slid into pillars between the wide viewing panes. Outside, the general scenery had not altered noticeably. The same reddish blue, swisscheese sky rolled over a mauve pampas, with black mountains bobbing biliously in the distance. And a slick mesa still had his scoutship mired, hemmed on all sides by yellow, multiarmed shapes.

"Banana peels," he muttered. "Goddamn *banana peels.*"

One reason why these stations were manned by only a single observer . . . allaphors tended to get even weirder with more than one mind perceiving them at the same time. The "objects" he saw were images his own mind pasted over a reality that no living brain could readily fathom. A reality that mutated and transformed under influence *by* his thoughts and perceptions.

All that was fine, in theory. He ought to be used to it by now. But what bothered Harry in particular about the banana allaphor was that it seemed gratuitously personal. Like others of his kind, Harry hated being trapped by stereotypes.

He sighed, scratching his side. "Are all systems stable?"

"Everything is stable, Taskmaster-Commander Harold," the pilot replied. *"We are stuck for the moment, but we appear to be safe."*

He considered the vast open expanse beyond the plateau. Actually, visibility was excellent from here. The holes in the sky, especially, were all clear and unobstructed. A thought occurred to him.

"Say, do we really have to move on right away? We can observe all the assigned transit routes from this very spot, until our cruise clock runs out, no?"

"That appears to be correct. For the moment, no illicit traffic can get by our watch area undetected."

"Hmmph. Well then . . ." He yawned. "I guess I'll just go back to bed! I have a feelin' I'm gonna need my wits to get outta this one."

"Very well. Good night, Employer-Observer Harms. Pleasant dreams."

"Fat chance o' that," he muttered in Anglic as he left the observation deck. "And close the friggin' blinds! Do I have to think of everything around here? Don't answer that! Just . . . never mind."

Even closed, the louvers would not prevent all leakage. Flickering archetypes slipped between the slats, as if eager to latch into his mind during REM state, tapping his dreams like little parasites.

It could not be helped. When Harry got his first promotion to E Space, the local head of patrollers for the Navigation Institute told him that susceptibility to allaphoric images was a vital part of the job. Waving a slender, multijointed arm, that Galactic official confessed his surprise, in Nahalli-accented GalSix, at Harry's qualifications.

"Skeptical we were, when first told that your race might have traits useful to us.

"Repudiating our doubts, this you have since achieved, Observer Harms.

"To full status, we now advance you. First of your kind to be so honored."

Harry sighed as he threw himself under the covers again, tempted by the sweet stupidity of self-pity.

Some honor! He snorted dubiously.

Still, he couldn't honestly complain. He had been warned. And this wasn't Horst. At least he had escaped the dry, monotonous wastes.

Anyway, only the mad lived for long under illusions that the cosmos was meant for their convenience.

There were multitudes of conflicting stories about whoever designed this crazy universe, so many billions of years ago. But even before he ever considered dedicating his life to Institute work—or even heard of E Space—Harry had reached one conclusion about metatheology.

For all His power and glory, the Creator must not have been a very sensible person.

At least, not as sensible as a neo-chimpanzee.

SARA

There is a word-glyph.

It names a locale where three states of matter coincide—two that are fluid, swirling past a third that is adamant as coral.

A kind of froth can form in such a place. Dangerous, deceptive foam, beaten to a head by fate-filled tides. No one enters such a turmoil voluntarily.

But sometimes a force called desperation drives prudent sailors to set course for ripping shoals.

A slender shape plummets through the outer fringes of a mammoth star. Caterpillar-ribbed, with rows of talon-like protrusions that bite into spacetime, the vessel claws its way urgently against a bitter gale.

Diffuse flames lick the scarred hull of ancient cerametal, adding new layers to a strange soot coating. Tendrils of plasma fire seek entry, thwarted (so far) by wavering fields.

In time, though, the heat will find its way through.

Midway along the vessel's girth, a narrow wheel turns, like a wedding band that twists around a nervous finger. Rows of windows pass by as the slim ring rotates. Unlit from within, most of the dim panes only reflect stellar fire.

Then, rolling into view, a single rectangle shines with artificial color.

A pane for viewing in two directions. A universe without, and within.

Contemplating the maelstrom, Sara mused aloud.

"My criminal ancestors took their sneakship through this same inferno on their way to Jijo . . . covering their tracks under the breath of Great Izmunuti."

Pondering the forces at work just a handbreadth away, she brushed her fingertips against a crystal surface that kept actinic heat from crossing the narrow gap. One part of her—book-weaned and tutored in mathematics—could grasp the physics of a star whose radius was bigger than her homeworld's yearly orbit. A red giant, in its turgid final stage, boiling a stew of nuclear-cooked atoms toward black space.

Abstract knowledge was fine. But Sara's spine also trembled with a superstitious shiver, spawned by her upbringing as a savage sooner on a barbarian world. The Earthship *Streaker* might be hapless prey—desperately fleeing a titanic hunter many times its size—but this dolphin-crewed vessel still struck Sara as godlike and awesome, carrying more mass than all the wooden dwellings of the Slope. In her wildest dreams, dwelling in a treehouse next to a groaning water mill, she had never imagined that destiny might take her on such a ride, swooping through the fringes of a hellish star.

Especially Izmunuti, whose very name was fearsome. To the Six Races, huddling in secret terror on Jijo, it stood for the downward path. A door that swung just one way, toward exile.

For two thousand years, emigrants had slinked past the giant star to find shelter on Jijo. First the wheeled g'Kek race, frantically evading genocide. Then came traekis—gentle stacks of waxy rings who were fleeing their own tyrannical cousins—followed by qheuens, hoons, urs, and humans, all settling in a narrow realm between the Rimmer Mountains and a surf-stained shore. Each wave of new arrivals abandoned their starships, computers, and other high-tech implements, sending every god-machine down to the sea, tumbling into Jijo's deep midden of forgetfulness. Breaking with their past, all six clans of former sky lords settled down to rustic lives, renouncing the sky forever.

Until the Civilization of the Five Galaxies finally stumbled on the commonwealth of outcasts.

The day had to come, sooner or later; the Sacred Scrolls had said so. No band of trespassers could stay hidden perpetually. Not in a cosmos that had been cataloged for over a billion years, where planets such as Jijo were routinely declared fallow, set aside for rest and restoration. Still, the sages of the Commons of Jijo had hoped for more time.

Time for the exile races to prepare. To purify themselves. To seek redemption. To forget the galactic terrors that made them outcasts in the first place.

The Scrolls foresaw that august magistrates from the Galactic Migration Institute would alight to judge the descendants of trespassers. But instead, the starcraft that pierced Jijo's veil this fateful year carried several types of *outlaws.* First gene raiders, then murderous opportunists, and finally a band of Earthling refugees even more ill-fated than Sara's hapless ancestors.

I used to dream of riding a starship, she thought, pondering the plasma storm outside. But no fantasy was ever like this—leaving behind my world, my teachers, my father and brothers—fleeing with dolphins through a fiery night, chased by a battleship full of angry Jophur.

Fishlike cousins of humans, pursued through space by egotistical cousins of traeki.

The coincidence beggared Sara's imagination.

Anglic words broke through her musing, in a voice that Sara always found vexingly sardonic.

"I have finished calculating the hyperspatial tensor, oh, Sage.

"It appears you were right in your earlier estimate.

"The mysterious beam that emanated from Jijo a while ago did more than cause disruptions in this giant star. It also triggered a state-change in a fossil dimension-nexus that lay dormant just half a mictaar away."

Sara mentally translated into terms she was used to, from the archaic texts that had schooled her.

Half a mictaar. In flat space, that would come to roughly a twentieth of a light-year.

Very close, indeed.

"So, the beam reactivated an old transfer point." She nodded. "I knew it."

"Your foresight would be more impressive if I understood your methods. Humans are noted for making lucky guesses."

Sara turned away from the fiery spectacle outside. The office they had given her seemed like a palace, roomier than the reception hall in a qheuen rookery, with lavish fixtures she had only seen described in books two centuries out of date. This suite once belonged to a man named Ignacio Metz, an expert in the genetic uplifting of dolphins—killed during one of *Streaker*'s previous dire encounters—a true scientist, not a primitive with academic pretensions, like Sara.

And yet, here she was—fearful, intimidated . . . and yet proud in a strange way, to be the first Jijoan in centuries who returned to space.

From the desk console, a twisted blue blob drifted closer—a languid, undulating shape she found as insolent as the voice it emitted.

"Your so-called wolfling mathematics hardly seem up to the task of predicting such profound effects on the continuum. Why not just admit that you had a hunch?"

Sara bit her lip. She would not give the Niss Machine the satisfaction of a hot response.

"Show me the tensor," she ordered tersely. "And a chart . . . a *graphic* . . . that includes all three gravity wells."

The billowing holographic creature managed to imply sarcasm with an obedient bow.

"As you wish."

A cubic display, two meters on a side, lit up before Sara, far more vivid than the flat, unmoving diagrams-on-paper she had grown up with.

A glowing mass roiled in the center, representing Izmunuti, a fireball radiating the color of wrath. Tendrils of its engorged corona waved like Medusan hair, reaching beyond the limits of any normal solar system. But those lacy filaments were fast being drowned under a new disturbance. During the last few miduras, something had stirred the star to an abnormal fit of rage. Abrupt cyclonic storms began throwing up gouts of dense plasma, tornadolike funnels, rushing far into space.

And we're going to pass through some of the worst of it, she thought.

How strange that all this violent upheaval might have originated in a boulder of psi-active stone, back home on primitive Jijo. Yet she felt sure it all was triggered somehow by the Holy Egg.

Already half-immersed in this commotion, a green pinpoint was depicted plunging toward Izmunuti at frantic speed, aimed at a glancing near-passage, its hyperbolic orbit marked by a line that bent sharply around the giant star. In one direction, that slim trace led all the way back to Jijo, where *Streaker*'s escape attempt had begun two exhausting days earlier, breaking for liberty amid a crowd of ancient derelicts—ocean-bottom junk piles reactivated for one last, glorious, screaming run through space.

One by one, those decoys had failed, or dropped out, or were snared by the pursuing enemy's clever capture-boxes, until only *Streaker* remained, plummeting for the brief shelter of stormy Izmunuti.

As for the *forward* direction . . . Instrument readings sent by the bridge crew helped the Niss Machine calculate their likely heading. Apparently, Gillian Baskin had ordered a course change, taking advantage of a gravitational slingshot around the star to fling *Streaker* toward galactic north and east.

Sara swallowed hard. The destination had originally been her idea. But as time passed, she grew less certain.

"The new transfer-point doesn't look very stable," she commented, following the ship's planned trajectory to the top left corner of the holo unit, where a tight mesh of curling lines funneled through an empty-looking zone of interstellar space.

Reacting to her close regard, the display monitor enhanced that section. Rows of glowing symbols described the local hyperspatial matrix.

She had predicted this wonder—the reawakening of something old. Something marvelous. For a brief while, it had seemed like just the miracle they needed. A gift from the Holy Egg. An escape route from a terrible trap.

But on examining the analytical profiles, Sara concluded that the cosmos was not being all that helpful after all.

"There *are* connection tubes opening up to other spacetime locales. But they seem rather . . . scanty."

"Well, what can you expect from a nexus that is only a few hours old? One that was only recently yanked from slumber by a force neither of us can grasp?"

After a pause, the Niss unit continued. "Most of the transfer threads leading away from this nexus are still on the order of a Planck width. Some promising routes do seem to be coalescing, and may be safely traversable by starship in a matter of weeks. Of course, that will be of little use to us."

Sara nodded. The pursuing Jophur battleship would hardly give *Streaker* that much time. Already the mighty *Polkjhy* had abandoned its string of captured decoys in order to focus all its attention on the real *Streaker*, keeping the Earthship bathed in long-range scanning rays.

"Then what does Gillian Baskin hope to accomplish by heading toward a useless . . ."

She blinked, as realization lurched within her rib cage.

"Oh. I see."

Sara stepped back, and the display resumed its normal scale. Two meters away, at the opposite corner, neat curves showed the spatial patterns of another transfer point. The familiar, reliably predictable one that every sneakship had used to reach Izmunuti during the last two millennia. The only quick way in or out of this entire region of Galaxy Four.

But not always. Once, when Jijo had been a center of commerce and civilization under the mighty Buyur, traffic used to flux through *two* hyperdimensional nexi. One of them shut down when Jijo went fallow, half a million years ago, coincidentally soon after the Buyur departed.

Sara and her mentor, Sage Purofsky, had nursed a suspicion. That shutdown was no accident.

"Then we concur," said the Niss Machine. "Gillian Baskin clearly intends to lead the Jophur into a suicidal trap."

Sara looked elsewhere in the big display, seeking the enemy. She found it several stellar radii behind Izmunuti, a yellow glow representing the hunter—a Jophur dreadnought whose crew coveted the Earthship and its secrets. Having abandoned the distraction of all the old dross ship decoys, the *Polkjhy* had been racing toward the *regular* t-point, confident of cutting off *Streaker*'s sole escape route.

Only now, the sudden reopening of another gateway must have flummoxed the giant sap-rings who commanded the great warship. The yellow trace turned sharply, as the *Polkjhy* frantically shed momentum, aiming to chase *Streaker* past Izmunuti's flames toward the new door in spacetime.

A door that's not ready for use, Sara thought. Surely the Jophur must also have instruments capable of reading probability flows. They must realize how dangerous it would be to plunge into a newborn—or newly re-awakened—transfer point.

Yet, could the *Polkjhy* commanders afford to dismiss it? *Streaker* was small, maneuverable, and had dolphin pilots, reputed to be among the best in all five galaxies.

And the Earthlings were desperate.

The Jophur have to assume we know something about this transfer point that they do not. From their point of view, it seems as if we called it into existence with a wave of our hands—or fins. If we plunge inside, it must be because we know a tube or thread we can latch on to and follow to safety.

They're obliged to give chase, or risk losing Streaker forever.

Sara nodded.

"Gillian and the dolphins . . . they're sacrificing themselves, for Jijo."

The tightly meshed Niss hologram appeared to shrug in agreement.

"It does seem the best choice out of a wretched set of options.

"Suppose we turn and fight? The only likely outcomes are capture or death, with your Jijoan civilization lost in the bargain. After extracting *Streaker*'s secrets, the Jophur will report to their home clan, then take their time organizing a systematic program for Jijo, first annihilating every g'Kek, then turning the planet into their own private breeding colony, developing new types of humans, traekis, and hoons to suit their perverted needs.

"By forcing the *Polkjhy* to follow us into the new transfer point, Dr. Baskin makes it likely that no report will ever reach the Five Galaxies about your Six Races. Your fellow exiles may continue wallowing in sublime, planet-bound squalor for a while longer, chasing vague notions of redemption down the muddy generations."

How very much like the Niss it was, turning a noble gesture into an excuse for insult. Sara shook her head. Gillian's plan was both grand and poignant.

It also meant Sara's own hours were numbered.

"What a waste," the Niss commented. "This vessel and crew appear to have made the discovery-of-the-age, and now it may be lost."

Things had been so hectic since the rushed departure from Jijo that Sara was still unclear about the cause of all this ferment—what the *Streaker* crew had done to provoke such ire and pursuit by some of the great powers of the known universe.

"It began when Captain Creideiki took this ship poking through a seemingly unlikely place, looking for relics or anomalies that had been missed by the Great Library," the artificial intelligence explained. "It was a shallow globular cluster, lacking planets or singularities. Creideiki never told his reasons for choosing such a spot. But his hunch paid off when Streaker came upon a great fleet of derelict ships, drifting in splendid silence through open space. Samples and holos taken of this mystery armada seemed to hint at possible answers to our civilization's most ancient mystery.

"Of course, our findings should have been shared openly by the institutes of the Civilization of Five Galaxies, in the name of all oxygen-breathing life. Immense credit would have come to your frail, impoverished Earthclan, as well as my Tymbrimi makers. But every other race and alliance might have shared as well, gaining new insight into the origins of our billion-year-old culture.

"Alas, several mighty coalitions interpreted Streaker's initial beamcast as fulfillment of dire prophecy. They felt the news presaged a fateful time of commotion and upheaval, in which a decisive advantage would go to anyone monopolizing our discovery. Instead of celebratory welcome, Streaker returned from the Shallow Cluster to find battle fleets lying in wait, eager to secure our secrets before we reached neutral ground. Several times, we were cornered, and escaped only because hordes of fanatics fought savagely among themselves over the right of capture.

"Alas, that compensation seems lacking in our present situation."

That was an understatement. The Jophur could pursue *Streaker* at leisure, without threat of interference. As far as the rest of civilization was concerned, this whole region was empty and off-limits.

"Was poor Emerson wounded in one of those earlier space battles?"

Sara felt concern for her friend, the silent star voyager, whose cryptic injuries she had treated in her treehouse, before taking him on an epic journey across Jijo, to be reunited with his crewmates.

"No. Engineer D'Anite was captured by members of the Retired Caste, at a place we call the Fractal World. That event—"

The blue blob halted its twisting gyration. Hesitating a few seconds, it trembled before resuming.

"The detection officer reports something new! A phenomenon heretofore masked by the flames of Izmunuti."

The display rippled. Abruptly, swarms of orange pinpoints sparkled amid the filaments and stormy prominences of Izmunuti's roiling atmosphere.

Sara leaned forward. "What are they?"

"Condensed objects.

"Artificial, self-propelled spacial motiles.

"In other words, starships."

Sara's jaw opened and closed twice before she could manage speech.

"Ifni, there must be hundreds! How could we have overlooked them before?"

The Niss answered defensively.

"Oh, great Sage, one normally does not send probing beams through a red giant's flaming corona in search of spacecraft. Our attention was turned elsewhere. Besides, these vessels only began using gravitic engines moments ago, applying gravi-temporal force to escape the new solar storms."

Sara stared in amazement. Hope whirled madly.

"These ships, could they help us?"

Again, Niss paused, consulting remote instruments.

"It seems doubtful, oh Sage. They will scarcely care about our struggles. These beings belong to another order on the pyramid of life, completely apart from yours . . . though one might call them distant cousins of mine."

Sara shook her head, at first confused. Then she cried out.

"Machines!"

Even Jijo's fallen castaways could recite the Eight Orders of Sapience, with oxygen-based life being only one of the most flamboyant. Among the other orders, Jijo's sacred scrolls spoke darkly of synthetic beings, coldly cryptic, who designed and built each other in the farthest depths of space, needing no ground to stand on or wind to breathe.

"Indeed. Their presence here surely involves matters beyond our concern. Most likely, the mechanoids will avoid contact with us out of prudent caution."

The voice paused.

"Fresh data is coming in. It seems that the flotilla is having a hard time with those new tempests. Some mechaniforms may be more needy of rescue than we are."

Sara pointed at one of the orange dots.

"Show me!"

Using data from long-range scans, the display unit swooped giddily inward. Swirling stellar filaments seemed to heave around Sara as her point of view plunged toward the chosen speck—one of the mechanoid vessels—which began taking form against a backdrop of irate gas.

Stretching the limits of magnification, the blurry enhancement showed a glimmering trapezoidal shape, almost mirrorlike, that glancingly reflected solar fire. The mechanoid's outline grew slimmer as it turned to flee a plume of hot ions, fast rising toward it from Izmunuti's whipped convection zones. The display software compensated for perspective as columns of numbers estimated the vessel's actual measurements—a square whose edges were hundreds of kilometers in length, with a third dimension that was vanishingly small.

Space seemed to ripple just beneath the mechaniform vessel. Though still inexperienced, Sara recognized the characteristic warping effects of a gravi-temporal field. A modest one, according to the display. Perhaps sufficient for interplanetary speeds, but not to escape the devastation climbing toward it. She could only watch with helpless sympathy as the mechanoid struggled in vain.

The first shock wave ripped the filmy object in half . . . then into shreds that raveled quickly, becoming a swarm of bright, dissolving streamers.

"This is not the only victim. Observe, as fate catches up with other stragglers."

The display returned to its former scale. As Sara watched, several additional orange glitters were overwhelmed by waves of accelerating dense plasma. Others continued climbing, fighting to escape the maelstrom.

"Whoever they are, I hope they get away," Sara murmured.

How strange it seemed that machine-vessels would be less sturdy than *Streaker*, whose protective fields could stand full immersion for several miduras in the red star's chromosphere, storm or no storm.

If they can't take on a plasma surge, they'd be useless against Jophur weapons.

Disappointment tasted bitter after briefly raised hope. Clearly, no rescue would come from that direction.

Sara perceived a pattern to her trials and adventures during the last year—swept away from her dusty study to encounter aliens, fight battles, ride fabled horses, submerge into the sea, and then join a wild flight aboard a starship. The universe seemed bent on revealing wonders at the edge of her grasp or imagining—giant stars, transfer points, talking computers, universal libraries . . . and now glimpses of a different *life order.* A mysterious phylum, totally apart from the vast, encompassing Civilization of Five Galaxies.

Such marvels lay far beyond her old life as a savage intellectual on a rustic world.

And yet, a glimpse was clearly all the cosmos planned to give her.

Go ahead and look, it seemed to say. But you can't touch.

For you, time has almost run out.

Saddened, Sara watched orange pinpoints flee desperately before tornadoes of stellar heat. More laggards were swept up by the rising storm, their frail light quenched like drowned embers.

Gillian and the dolphins seem sure we can stand a brief passage through that hell. But the vanishing sparks made Sara's confidence waver. After all, weren't machines supposed to be stronger than mere flesh?

She was about to ask the Niss about it when, before her eyes, the holo display abruptly changed once more. Izmunuti flickered, and when the image reformed, something new had come into view. Below the retreating orange glimmers, there now appeared *three sparkling forms,* rising with complacent grace, shining a distinct shade of imperial purple as they emerged from the flames toward *Streaker*'s path.

"What now?" she asked. "More mechanoids?"

"No," the Niss answered in a tone that seemed almost awed. *"These appear to be something else entirely. I believe they are . . ."* The computer's hologram deformed into jagged shapes, like nervous icicles. *"I believe they are Zang."*

Sara's skin crawled. That name was fraught with fear and legend. On Jijo, it was never spoken above a whisper. "But . . . how . . . what could *they* be doing. . . ?"

Before she finished her question, the Niss spoke again.

"Excuse me for interrupting, Sara. Our acting captain, Dr. Gillian Baskin, has called an urgent meeting of the ship's council to consider these developments. You are invited to attend.

"Do you wish me to make excuses on your behalf?"

Sara was already hurrying toward the exit.

"Don't you dare!" she cried over one shoulder as the door folded aside to let her pass.

The hallway beyond curved up and away in both directions, like a segment of tortured spacetime, rising toward vertical in the distance. The sight always gave Sara qualms. Nevertheless, this time she ran.

GILLIAN

For some reason, the tumultuous red star reminded her of Venus.

Naturally, that brought Tom to mind.

Everything reminded Gillian of Tom. After two years, his absence was still a wound that left her reflexively turning for his warmth each night. By day, she kept expecting his strong voice, offering to help take on the worries. All the damned decisions.

Isn't it just like a hero, to die saving the world?

A little voice pointed out—*that's what heroes are for.*

Yes, she answered. *But the world goes on, doesn't it? And it keeps needing to be saved.*

Ever since the universe sundered them apart at Kithrup, Gillian told herself that Tom couldn't be dead. *I'd know it,* she would think repeatedly, convincing herself by force of will. *Across galaxies and megaparsecs, I could tell if he were gone. Tom must be out there somewhere still, with Creideiki and Hikahi and the others we were forced to leave behind.*

He'll find a way to get safely home . . . or else back to me.

That certainty helped Gillian bear her burdens during *Streaker*'s first distraught fugitive year . . . until the last few months of steady crisis finally cracked her assurance.

Then, without realizing when it happened, she began thinking of Tom in the past tense.

He loved Venus, she pondered, watching the raging solar vista beyond *Streaker*'s hull. Of course Izmunuti's atmosphere was bright, while Earth's sister world was dim beneath perpetual acid clouds. Yet, both locales shared essential traits. Harsh warmth, unforgiving storms, and scant moisture.

Both provoked extremes of hope and despair.

She could see him now, spreading both spacesuited arms to encompass the panorama below Aphrodite Pinnacle, gesturing toward stark lowlands. Lightning danced about a phalanx of titanic structures that stretched to a warped horizon—one shadowy behemoth after another—vast new devices freshly engaged in the labor of changing Venus. Transforming hell, one step at a time.

"Isn't it tremendous?" Tom asked. "This endeavor proves that our species is capable of thinking long thoughts."

Even with borrowed Galactic technology, the task would take more time to complete than humans had known writing or agriculture. Ten thousand years must pass before seas rolled across the sere plains. It was a bold project for poor wolflings to engage in, especially when Sa'ent and Kloornap bookies gave Earthclan slim odds of surviving more than another century or two.

"We have to show the universe that we trust ourselves," Tom added. "Or else who will believe in us?"

His words sounded fine. Noble and grand. At the time, Tom almost convinced Gillian.

Only things changed.

Half a year ago, during *Streaker*'s brief, terrified refuge at the Fractal World, Gillian had managed to pick up rumors about the Siege of Terra, taking place in faraway Galaxy Two. Apparently, the Sa'ent touts were now taking bets on human extinction in mere years or piduras, not centuries.

In retrospect, the Venus terraforming project seemed moot.

We'd have been better off as farmers, Tom and me. Or teaching school. Or helping settle Calafia. We should never have listened to Jake Demwa and Creideiki. This mission has brought ruin on everyone it touched.

Including the poor colonists of Jijo—six exile races who deserved a chance to find their own strange destinies undisturbed. In seeking shelter on that forbidden world, *Streaker* only brought disaster to Jijo's tribes.

There seemed one way to redress the harm.

Can we lure the Jophur after us into the new transfer point? Kaa must pilot a convincing trajectory, as if he can sense a perfect thread to latch on to. A miracle path leading toward safety. If we do it right, the Jophur will assume our dolphin pilots sense a route—one that our pursuers can't see. The big ugly sap rings will have to follow! They'll have no choice.

Saving Jijo justified that option, since there seemed no way to bring *Streaker*'s cargo safely home to Earth.

Another reason tasted acrid, vengeful.

At least we'll take enemies with us.

Some say that impending death clarifies the mind, but in Gillian it only stirred regret.

I hope Creideiki and Tom aren't too disappointed in me, she pondered at the door of the conference room.

I did my best.

The ship's council had changed since Gillian reluctantly took over the captain's position, where Creideiki presided in happier times. At the far end of the long table, *Streaker*'s last surviving dolphin officer, Lieutenant Tsh't, expertly piloted a six-legged walker apparatus carrying her sleek gray form into the same niche where Takkata-Jim once nestled his great bulk, before he was killed near Kithrup.

Tsh't greeted the human chief engineer, though Hannes Suessi's own mother wouldn't recognize him now, with so many body parts replaced by cyborg components, and a silver dome where his head used to be. Much of that gleaming surface was now covered with pre-Contact-era motorcycle decals—an irreverent touch that endeared Hannes to the crew. At least someone had kept a sense of humor through years of relentless crisis.

Gillian felt acutely the absence of one council member, her friend and fellow physician Makanee, who remained behind on Jijo with several dozen dolphins—those suffering from devolution fever or who were unessential for the breakout attempt. In effect, dolphins had established a seventh illegal colony on that fallow world—another secret worth defending with the lives of those left aboard.

Secrets. There are other enigmas, less easily protected.

Gillian's thoughts slipped past the salvaged objects in her office, some of them worth a stellar ransom. Mere hints at their existence had already knocked civilization teetering across five galaxies.

Foremost was a corpse, nicknamed Herbie. An alien cadaver so ancient, its puzzling smile might be from a joke told a billion years ago. Other relics were scarcely less provocative—or cursed. Trouble had followed *Streaker* ever since its crew began picking up objects they didn't understand.

"Articles of Destiny." That was how one of the Old Ones referred to *Streaker*'s cargo of mysteries when they visited the Fractal World.

Maybe this will be fitting. All those irksome treasures will get smashed down to a proton's width after we dive into the new transfer point.

At least then she'd get the satisfaction of seeing Herbie's expression finally change, at the last instant, when the bounds of reality closed in rapidly from ten dimensions.

A holo of Izmunuti took up one wall of the conference room, an expanse of swirling clouds wider than Earth's orbit, surging and shifting as the Niss Machine relayed the latest intelligence in Tymbrimi-accented Galactic Seven.

"The Jophur battleship was speeding toward the first transfer point, the one via which we arrived, hurrying to cut us off. Now the Jophur have changed goals. The *Polkjhy* has jettisoned the last of the decoy vessels it seized, letting them drift through space. Freed of their momentum-burden, *Polkjhy* is more agile, turning its frightful bulk toward the *new* transfer point. They aim to reach the reborn nexus before *Streaker* does."

"Can they beat us there?" Gillian asked in Anglic.

The Niss hologram whirled thoughtfully. "It seems unlikely, unless they use some risky type of probability drive, which is not typical of Jophur. They wasted a lot of time dashing ahead toward the older t-point. Our tight swing past Izmunuti should help *Streaker* to arrive first . . . for whatever good it will do."

Gillian ignored the machine's sarcasm. Most of the crew seemed in accord with her decision. Lacking other options, death was more bearable if you took an enemy with you.

The Jophur situation appeared stable, so she changed subject. "What can you report about the other ships?"

"The two mysterious flotillas we recently detected in Izmunuti's atmosphere? After consulting tactical archives, I conclude they must have been operating jointly. Nothing else could explain their close proximity, fleeing together to escape unexpected plasma storms."

Hannes Suessi objected, his voice wavering low and raspy from the silver dome. "Mechanoids and hydrogen breathers cooperating? That sounds odd."

The whirling blob made a gesture like a nod. "Indeed. The various orders of life seldom interact. But according to our captured Library unit, it does happen, especially when some vital project requires the talents of two or more orders, working together."

The newest council member whistled for attention. Kaa, the chief pilot, did not ride a walker, since he might have to speed back to duty any moment. The young dolphin commented from a fluid-filled tunnel that passed along a wall near one side of the table.

• *Can any purpose*
  • *Under tide-pulled moons explain*
    • *Such anomalies?* •

For emphasis, Kaa slashed his tail flukes through water that fizzed with bubbles. Gillian translated the popping whistle-poem for Sara Koolhan, who had never learned Trinary.

"Kaa asks what project could be worth the trouble and danger of diving into a star."

Sara replied with an eager nod. "I may have a partial answer." The young Jijoan stroked a black cube in front of her—the personal algorithmic engine Gillian had lent her when she came aboard.

"Ever since we first spotted these strange ships, I've wondered what trait of Izmunuti might attract folks here from some distant system. For instance, my own ancestors. After passing through the regular t-point, they took a path through this giant star's outer atmosphere. All the sneakships of Jijo used the same method to cover their tracks."

We thought of it too, Gillian pondered, unhappily. *But I must have done something wrong, since the Rothen were able to follow us, betraying our hiding place and the Six Races.*

Gillian noticed Lieutenant Tsh't was looking at her. With reproach for getting *Streaker* into this fix? The dolphin's eye remained fixed for a long, appraising moment, then turned away as Sara continued.

"According to this teaching unit, stars like Izmunuti pour immense amounts of heavy atoms from their bloated atmospheres. Carbon is especially rich, condensing on anything solid that happens nearby. All our ancestor ships arrived at Jijo black with the stuff. *Streaker* may be the first vessel ever to try the trick *twice,* both coming and going. I bet the stuff is causing you some problems."

"No bet!" boomed Suessi's amplified voice. Hannes had been battling the growing carbon coating. "The stuff is heavy, it has weird properties, and it's been gumming up the verity flanges."

Sara nodded. "But consider—what if somebody has a *use* for such coatings? What would be their best way to accumulate it?"

She stroked her black cube again, transferring data to the main display. Though Sara had been aboard just a few days, she was adapting to the convenience of modern tools.

A mirrorlike rectangle appeared before the council, reflecting fiery prominences from a broad, planar surface.

"I may be an ignorant native," Sara commented. "But it seems one could collect atoms out of a stellar wind using something with high surface area and small initial mass, such a vehicle might not even have to expend energy departing, if it rode outward on the pressure of both light and particle waves."

Lieutenant Tsh't murmured.

"A sssolar sail!"

"Is that what you call it?" Sara nodded. "Imagine machines arriving through the transfer point as compact objects, plummeting down to Izmunuti, then unfurling such sails and catching a free ride back to the t-point, gaining layers of this molecularly unique carbon, and other stuff along the way. Energy expenditures per ton of yield would be minimal!"

The whirling Niss hologram edged forward.

"Your hypothesis suggests an economical resource-gathering technique, providing the mechanoids needn't make more than one simple hyperspatial transfer, coming or going. There are cheap alternatives in industrialized regions of the Five Galaxies, but here in Galaxy Four, industry is currently minimal or nil, due to the recent fallow-migration—" The Niss paused briefly.

"Mechanoids would be ideal contractors for such a harvesting chore, creating special versions to do the job swiftly, with minimal mass. It explains why their drives and shields seem frail before the rising storms. They had no margin for the unexpected."

Gillian saw that just half of the orange glitters remained, struggling to flee Izmunuti's gravity before more plasma surges caught them.

"What about the Zang?" she asked. The three purple dots had already climbed toward the mechanoid convoy, ascending with graceful ease.

"I surmise they are the mechanoids employers. Our Library says Zang groups sometimes hire special services from the Machine Order. Great clans of oxygen breathers also do it, now and then"

"Well, it seems their plans have been ripped," commented Suessi. "Not much cargo getting home, this time."

Pensive whistle ratchets escaped the gray dolphin in the water-filled tunnel—not Trinary, but the scattered clicks a cetacean emits when pondering deeply. Gillian still felt guilty about asking Kaa to volunteer for this mission, since it meant abandoning his lover to danger on Jijo. But *Streaker* needed a first-class pilot for this desperate ploy.

"I concur," the whirling Niss hologram concluded. "The Zang will be in a foul mood after this setback."

"Because they suffered economic loss?" Tsh't asked.

"That and more. According to the Library, hydrogen breathers react badly to surprise. They have slower metabolisms than oxy-life. Anything unpredictable is viscerally unpleasant to them.

"Of course, this attitude is strange to an entity like me, programmed by the Tymbrimi to seek novelty! Without surprise, how can you tell there is an objective world? You might as well presume the whole universe is one big sim—"

"Wait a minute," Gillian interrupted, before the Niss got sidetracked in philosophy. "We're all taught to avoid Zang as dangerous, leaving any contact to experts from the Great Institutes."

"That is right."

"But now you're saying they may be especially angry? Possibly short-tempered?"

The Niss hologram coiled tensely.

"After three years together, Dr. Baskin—amid growing familiarity with your voice tones and thought patterns—your latest inquiry provokes uneasy feelings.

"Am I justified to be wary?

"Do you find the notion of short-tempered Zang . . . appealing?"

Gillian kept silent. But she allowed a grim, enigmatic smile.

HARRY

Five earth years had passed on his personal duration clock since he took the irrevocable step, standing amid volunteers from fifty alien races, laboriously mouthing polyglottal words of a memorized oath that had been written ages ago, by some species long extinct. Upon joining the Observer Corps, Harry's life didn't simply shift—it leaped from the riverbed of his genetic lineage, transferring loyalty from his family and species and birth planet to an austere bureaucracy that was old when his distant ancestors still scurried under Triassic jungle canopies, hiding from dinosaurs.

Yet, during training he was struck by how often other students sought him out with questions about Earthclan, whose struggles were the latest riveting interstellar penny-drama. Would the newest band of unprotected, sponsorless "wolflings" catch up with starfaring civilization in time to forestall the normal fate of upstarts? Despite Terra's puny unimportance, this provoked much speculation and wagering.

What was it like—his fellow acolytes asked—to have patrons like humans, who *taught themselves* such basic arts as speech, spaceflight, and eugenics? As a neo-chimp, Harry was junior in status to every other client-citizen at the base, yet he was almost a celebrity, getting hostility from some, admiration from others, and curiosity from nearly all.

In fact, he couldn't tell his classmates much about Terragens Civilization, having spent just a year among the talky neo-chimpanzees of Earth before dropping out of university to sign on with the Navigation Institute. His life was already one of exile.

He had been born in space, aboard a Terragens survey vessel. Harry's vague memories of TSS *Pelenor* were of a misty paradise lost, filled with high-tech comforts and warm places to play. The crew had seemed like gods—human officers, neo-chim and neo-dolphin ratings . . . plus a jolly, treelike Kanten advisor—all moving about their tasks so earnestly, except when he needed to be cuddled or tickled or tossed in the air.

Then, one awful day, his parents chose to debark and study the strange human tribes on a desolate colony world—Horst. That ended Harry's part in the epochal voyage of the *Pelenor,* and began his simmering resentment.

Memories of starscapes and humming engines became muzzy, idealized. Throughout childhood on that dusty world, the notion of space travel grew more magical. By the time Harry finally left Horst, he was shocked by the true sterile bleakness that stretched between rare stellar oases.

I remember it differently, he thought, during the voyage to Earth. Of course that earlier memory was a fantasy, formed by an impressionable toddler. At university, instructors taught that subjective impressions are untrustworthy, biased by the mind's fervent wish to believe.

Still, the thirst would not be slaked. An ambition to seek paradise in other versions of reality.

* * *

The bananas held him trapped for days.

If the allaphor had been less personal, Harry might have fought harder. But the image was too explicitly pointed to ignore. After the first debacle, when the station nearly foundered, he decided to wait before challenging the reef again.

Anyway, this wasn't a bad site to observe from. In a synergy between this strange continuum and his own mind, the local region manifested itself as a high plateau, overlooking a vast, undulating sea of purple tendrils. Black mountains still bobbed in the distance, though some of the "holes" in the red-blue sky became drooping dimples, as if the celestial dome had decided to melt or slump.

There were also life-forms—mostly creatures of the Memetic Order. Shapes that fluttered, crawled, or shimmered past Harry's octagonal platform, grazing and preying on each other, or else merging or undergoing eerie transformations before his eyes. On all other dimensional planes, memes could only exist as parasites, dwelling in the host brains or mental processors of physical beings. But here in E Space, they roamed free, in a realm of palpable ideas.

"Your imagination equips you to perform the duties of a scout," Wer'Q'quinn explained during Harry's training. "But do not succumb to the lure of solipsism, believing you can make something happen in E Space simply by willing it. E Space can sever your life path, if you grow obstinate or unwary."

Harry never doubted that. Watching memiforms slither across the purple steppe, he passed the time speculating what concepts they contained. Probably, none of the creatures were sapient, since true intelligence was rare on any level of reality. Yet, each of the memes crossing before him manifested a *single thought,* unconstrained by any organic or electronic brain—a self-contained idea with as much structured complexity as Harry held in his organs and genetic code.

That one over there, prancing like a twelve-legged antelope—was it an abstraction distantly related to *freedom?* When a jagged-edged flying thing swooped down to chase it, Harry wondered if the hunter might be an intricate version of *craving.* Or was he typically trying to cram complex and ineffable concepts into simple niches, in order to satisfy the pattern-needs of his barely sapient mind?

Well, it is "human nature" to trivialize. To make stereotypes. To pretend you can eff the ineffable.

Local meme organisms were fascinating, but now and then something else appeared beneath his vantage point, demanding closer attention.

He could always tell an interloper. Outsiders moved awkwardly, as if their allaphorical shapes were clumsy costumes. Often, predatory memes would approach, sniffing for a savory conceptual meal, only to retreat quickly from the harsh taste of solid matter. Metal-hulled ships or organic life-forms. Intruders from some other province of reality, not pausing or staring, but hastening past the floating mountains to seek refuge in the Swiss cheese sky.

Harry welcomed these moments when he earned his pay. Speaking clearly, he would describe each newcomer for his partner, the station computer, which lay below his feet, shielded against the hostile effects of E Space. At headquarters, experts would decipher his eyewitness account to determine what kind of vessel had made transit before Harry's eyes, and where it may have been bound. Meanwhile, he and the computer collaborated to make the best guess they could.

"Onboard memory files are familiar with this pattern," said the floating **M** at one point, after Harry described an especially bizarre newcomer, rushing by atop myriad stiff, glimmering stalks, like a striding sunburst. *"It appears to be a member of the Quantum Order of Sapiency."*

"Really?" Harry pressed against the glass. The object looked as fragile as a feathery zilm spore, carried on the wind to far corners of Horst. Delicate stems kept breaking off and vaporizing as the thing—(was it a ship? or a single being?)—hurried toward a sky hole that lay near the horizon.

"I've never seen a quant anywhere near that big before. What's it doing here? I thought they didn't like E Space."

"Try to imagine how you organics feel about hard vacuum—you shrivel and perish unless surrounded by layers of protective technology. So the fluctuating subjectivities of this domain imperil some other kinds of life. E Space is even more distasteful to quantum beings than it is to members of the Machine Order."

"Hm. Then why's it here?"

"I am at a loss to speculate what urgent errand impels it. Most quantum beings reside in the foam interstices of the cosmos, out of sight from other life variants—like bacteria on your homeworld who live in solid rock. Explicit contact with the Quantum Order was only established by experts of the Library Institute less than a hundred million years ago.

"What I can suggest is that you should politely avert your gaze, Scout Harms. The quant is clearly having difficulties. You needn't add to its troubles by staring."

Harry winced at the reminder.

"Oh, right. The Uncertainty Principle!" He turned away. His job in E Space was to watch, but you could do harm by watching too closely.

Anyway, his real task was to look for less exotic interlopers.

Most of his ship sightings were of hydrogen breathers, easily identified because their balloonlike vessels looked the same in any continuum. For some reason, members of that order liked taking shortcuts through E Space on their way from one Jupiter-type world to another, even though A and B levels of hyperspace were more efficient, and transfer points much faster.

On those rare occasions when Harry spotted anyone from his own order of oxygen breathers—the great and mighty Civilization of Five Galaxies—none of them approached his sentry position, defending a proscribed route to a forbidden place.

No wonder they hired a low-class chim for this job. Even criminals, trying to sneak into a fallow zone, would be fools to use allaphor space as a back door.

As I'm a fool, to be stuck guarding it.

Still, it beat the dry, windy steppes of Horst.

Anything was better than Horst.

He and his parents were the only members of their species on the planet, which meant the long process of learning speech, laborious for young neo-chimps, came doubly hard. With Marko and Felicity distracted by research,

Harry had to practice with wild-eyed Probsher kids, who mocked him for his long, furry arms and early stammer. With painted faces and short tempers, they showed none of the dignified patience he'd been taught to expect from the elder race. By the time he learned how different humans were on Horst, it didn't matter. He vowed to leave, not only Horst, but Terragens society. To seek the strange and unfamiliar.

Years later, Harry realized a similar ambition must have driven his parents. In youthful anger, he had spurned their pleas for patience, their awkward affections, even their parting blessing.

Still, regret was just a veneer, forgiveness a civilized abstraction, devoid of pang or poignancy.

Other memories still had power to make his veins tense with emotion. Growing up listening to botbian night wolves howl across dry lakes under patch-gilt moons. Or holding his knees by firelight while a Probsher shaman chanted eerie tales—fables that Marko and Felicity avidly studied as venerable folk legends, although these tribes had roamed Horst for less than six generations.

His own sapient race wasn't much older! Only a few centuries had passed since human beings began genetic meddling in chimpanzee stock.

Who gave them the right?

No permission was needed. Galactics had followed the same pattern for aeons—each "generation" of starfarers spawning the next in a rippling bootstrap effect called Uplift.

On the whole, humans were better masters than most . . . and he would rather be sapient than not.

No. What drove him away from Earthclan was not resentment but a kind of detachment. The mayfly yammerings of Probsher mystics mattered no more or less than the desperate moves of the Terragens Council, against grinding forces of an overwhelming universe. One might as well compare sparks rising from a campfire to the stars wheeling by overhead. They looked similar, at a glance. But what did another incandescent cinder really matter on the grand scale of things?

Did the cosmos care if humans or chims survived?

Even at university this notion threaded his thoughts. Harry's natural links elongated till they parted one by one. All that remained was a nebulous desire to seek out something lasting. Something that deserved to last.

Joining Wer'Q'quinn and the Navigation Institute, he found something enduring, a decision he never regretted.

Still, it puzzled Harry years later that his dreams kept returning to the desolate world of his youth. Horst ribbed his memory. Its wind in the dry grass. Smells that assailed your nose, sinking claws into your sinuses. And images the shaman painted in your mind, like arcs of multicolored sand, falling in place to convey *deer,* or *loper-beast,* or *spearhunter.*

Even as an official of Galactic civilization, representing the oxygen order on a weird plane of reality where allaphors shimmered in each window like reject Dali images, Harry still saw funnels of sparkling heat rising from smoky campfires, vainly seeking union with aloof stars.

LARK

"Not that way!" Ling shouted.

Her cry made Lark stumble to a halt, a few meters down a new corridor.

"But I'm sure this is the best route back to our nest." Lark pointed along a dim, curved aisle, meandering between gray ceramic walls. Strong odors wafted from each twisty, branching passageway aboard the maze-like Jophur ship. This one beckoned with distinct flavors of GREEN and SANCTUARY.

"I believe you." Ling nodded. "That's why we mustn't go there. In case we're still being followed."

She didn't look much like a star god anymore, with her dark hair hacked short and pale skin covered with soot. Wearing just a torn undertunic from her once shiny uniform, Ling now seemed far wilder than the Jijoan natives she once called "savages." In a cloth sling she carried a crimson torus that leaked gore like a wounded sausage.

Lark saw her meaning. Ever since they had tried sabotaging the dreadnought's control chamber, giant Jophur and their robot servants had chased them across the vast vessel. As fugitives, the humans mustn't lead pursuers to the one place offering food and shelter.

"Where to then?" Lark hated being in the open. He grasped their only weapon, a circular purple tube. Larger and healthier than the red one, it was their sole key to get past locked doors and unwary guardians.

Ling knew starships far better than he. But this behemoth warship was different. She peered up one shadowy tunnel, a curled shaft that seemed more organic than artificial.

"Just pick a direction. Quickly. I hear someone coming."

With a wistful glance in the general direction of their "nest," Lark took her hand and plunged away at right angles, into another passageway.

These walls glistened with an oily sheen, each passage or portal emitting its own distinct aroma, partly making up for the lack of written signs. Although he was just a primitive sooner, Lark did know traeki. Those cousins of the Jophur had different personalities, but shared many physical traits. As a Jijoan native, he could grasp many nuances in the shipboard scent language.

Despite the eerie hall curvature, he was starting to get a mental picture of the huge vessel—an oblate spheroid, studded with aggressive weaponry and driven by engines mighty enough to warp space in several ways. The remaining volume was a labyrinth of workshops, laboratories, and enigmatic chambers that puzzled even the star sophisticate, Ling. Since barely escaping the Jophur command center, they had worked their way inward, back toward the tiny eden where they had hidden after escaping their prison cell.

The place where they first made love.

Only now the greasy ring stacks had shut down all the axial drop tubes, blocking easy access along the *Polkjhy*'s north-south core.

"It makes the whole ship run inefficiently," Ling had explained earlier, with some satisfaction. "They can't shift or reassign crew for different tasks. We're still hurting them, Lark, as long as we're free!"

He appreciated her effort to see a bright side to their predicament. Even if the future seemed bleak, Lark felt content to be with her for as much time as they had left.

Glancing backward, Ling gripped his arm. Heightened rustling sounds suggested pursuit was drawing near. Then Lark also heard something from the opposite direction, closing in beyond the next sharp bend. "We're trapped!" Ling cried.

Lark rushed to the nearest sealed door. Its strong redolence reminded him of market days back home, when traeki torus breeders brought their fledglings for sale in mulch-lined pens.

He aimed the purple ring at a nearby scent plate and a thin mist shot from the squirming creature. *Come on. Do your stuff,* he silently urged.

Their only hope lay in this gift from the former traeki sage, Asx, who had struggled free of mental repression by a Jophur master ring just long enough to pop out two infant tubes. The human fugitives had no idea what the wounded red one was for, but the purple marvel had enabled them to stay free for several improbable days, ever since the battleship took off from Jijo on its manic errand through outer space.

Of course we knew it couldn't last.

The door lock accepted the coded chemical key with a soft click, and the portal slid open, letting them rush through acrid fumes into a dim chamber, divided by numerous tall, glass partitions. Lark had no time to sort impressions, however, before the corridor behind them echoed with *human* shouts and a staccato of running feet.

"Stop! Don't you stupid skins know you're just making things worse? Come out, before they start using—"

The closing door cut off angry threats by Ling's former commander. Lark pushed the purple traeki against the inner sense-plate, where it oozed aromatic scramblers—chemicals tuned to randomize the lock's coding. From experience, he realized it could take half a midura for their pursuers to get through—unless they brought heavy cutting tools to bear.

Why should they bother? They can tell we're trapped inside.

He found it especially galling to be cornered by Rann.

The third human prisoner had thrown in his lot with the Jophur, perhaps currying favor for release of his Rothen patron gods from frozen internment on Jijo. It left Lark with no options, since the purple ring would have nil effect on the big Danik warrior.

Turning around, Lark saw that the glass walls—stretching from floor to a high ceiling—made up giant vivariums holding row after row of wriggling, squirming things.

Midget toruses!

Clear tubes carried brown, sludgelike material to each niche.

Refined liquid mulch. Baby food.

We're in their nursery!

By itself, no traeki ring was intelligent. Back on the world where they evolved, slithering through fetid swamps as wormlike scavengers, they never amounted to much singly. Only when traeki began stacking together and specializing did there emerge a unique kind of presapient life, ripe for adoption and Uplift by their snail-like Poa patrons.

This was where the *Polkjhy* crew grew special kinds of rings, packed with the right skills to be new members of the team.

A potent kind of reproduction. No doubt some of the pulsing doughnut shapes were *master rings,* designed millennia ago to transform placid, contemplative traeki into adamant, alarming Jophur.

Lark jumped as a human scream clamored down the narrow aisles. Pulse pounding, he ran, shouting Ling's name.

Her voice echoed off glass walls. "Hurry! They've got me cornered!"

Lark burst around a vivarium to find her at last, backing away from two huge Jophur workers, toward a niche in the far wall. The nursery staff, Lark realized. Each tapered pile consisted of at least thirty component toruses—swaying and hissing—two meters wide at the bottom and massing almost a ton. Their waxy flanks gleamed with an opulent vitality one never saw in traeki back home on Jijo, flickering with meaningful patterns of light and dark. Colored stenches vented from chemsynth pores, as manipulator tendrils stretched toward Ling.

She moved lithely, darting left and right. Seeking an opening or else something to use as a weapon. There was no panic in her eyes, nor did she give Lark away in her relief to see him.

Of course, Jophur vision sensors faced all directions at once. But with that advantage came a handicap—slow reaction time. The first stack was still swaying toward its victim when Lark dashed up from behind. Somehow, Asx's gift knew to send a jet of sour spray, striking a gemlike organ that quickly spasmed and went dim.

The whole stack shuddered, slumping to quiescence.

Lark wasted no time spinning toward the other foe—

—only to find his right arm suddenly pinned by an adamant tentacle! An odious scent of TRIUMPH swirled as the second Jophur pulled him close, coiling tendrils and commencing to squeeze.

The purple ring spasmed in Lark's hand, but the chemical spray could not hit its mark at this impossible angle, past the Jophur's bulging midriff. The master torus drove its lesser tubes with a malice and intensity Lark had never seen in serene traekis back home. The constriction grew unbearable, expelling his breath in a choking cry of agony.

A shattering crash filled his ears, as a rain of wetness and needlelike shards fell across his back.

The Jophur emitted a shrill ululation. Then someone shouted a fierce warning in the clicking whistles of staccato Galactic Two.

"To let the human go—this you must.

"Or else other young ones—to ruin shall fall!"

The harsh pressure eased off Lark's rib cage just as consciousness appeared about to waver and blow out. His captor huffed and teetered uncertainly. Peering blearily, Lark saw that slivers of glass dusted the big stack, and moisture lay everywhere. Then he caught sight of Ling, crouching several meters away with a crooked metal bar, brandishing it threateningly in front of another vivarium. Where she had found the tool, he couldn't guess. But the floor was already strewn with flopping infant rings decanted violently from one of the nurturing mulch towers. Some struggled on vague flippers or undeveloped legs. Midget master rings waved neural feelers, seeking other toroids to dominate.

Lark felt the nursery worker tremble with hesitation.

Noises beyond the doorway indicated that the *Polkjhy* crew were already at work, unscrambling the door.

Clearly, the two fugitive humans weren't going anywhere.

The Jophur stack decided. It released Lark.

He managed to keep from slumping to the floor, teetering on wobbly knees, feebly raising the purple torus for a clean shot at the pheromone sensors.

In moments, the second worker joined the first in estivation stupor.

Sheesh, Lark pondered. *If this was just a tender nurse, I'd hate to meet one of their fighters.*

Ling grabbed his arm to keep him from buckling.

"Come on," she urged. "There's no time to rest. We've got lots to do."

"What're you talking about?" Lark tried asking. The question emerged as a gurgling sigh. But Ling refused to let him sink down and rest.

"I think I know a way out of here," she said urgently. "But it's going to be an awful tight fit."

True to her prediction, the cargo container was tiny. Even by scrunching over double, Lark could barely cram himself inside. The purple ring squirmed in the hollow between his rib cage and a wall.

"I still think you should go first," he complained. Ling hurriedly punched commands on a complex keypad next to the little supply shuttle. "Do *you* know how to program one of these things?"

She had a point, though Lark didn't like it much.

"Besides, we're heading somewhere unknown. Shouldn't our best fighter lead the way?"

Now Ling was teasing. Whoever went first would overcome opposition by using Asx's purple gift, or else fail. Physical strength was nearly useless against a robot or a full-size Jophur.

He glanced past her toward the far door of the nursery, where the red glow of a cutting torch could be seen, slicing an arched opening from the other side. Apparently, Rann and the Jophur had given up unscrambling the lock and decided on a brute-force approach.

"You'll hurry after me?"

For an answer, she bent and kissed him—once on the forehead in benediction, and again, passionately, on the mouth. "How is that for a promise?" she asked, mingling her breath with his.

As Ling backed away, a transparent hatch slid over the little cab—built to carry equipment and samples between workstations throughout the Jophur ship. There had been a crude version of such a system back at Biblos, the Jijoan archive, where cherished paper books and messages shuttled between the libraries in narrow tubes of boo.

"Hey!" he called. "Where are you sending m—"

A noise and brilliant flash cut off his question and made Ling spin around. The torch cutter was accelerating, as if the enemy somehow sensed a need to hurry. To Lark's horror, the arc was over half finished.

"Let me out!" he demanded. "We're switching places!"

Ling shook her head as she resumed programming the console. "Not an option. Get ready. This will be wrenching."

Before Lark could protest a second time, the wall section abruptly fell with a crash. Curt billowings of sparks and dense smoke briefly filled the vestibule. But soon, Jophur warriors would come pouring through . . . and Ling didn't even have a weapon!

Lark hammered on the clear panel as several things happened in rapid succession.

Ling knelt to the floor, where scores of infant traeki rings still squirmed in confusion amid shards of their broken vivarium. She emptied her cloth sling, gently spilling Asx's second gift—the wounded crimson torus—to mingle among the others.

A tall silhouette passed through the roiling cloud to stand in the glowing doorway. The wedgelike torso was unmistakably Rann, leader of the Danik tribe of human renegades sworn to Rothen lords.

Ling stood. She glanced over her shoulder at Lark, who pounded the hatch, moaning frustration and fear for her.

Calmly, she reached for the keypad.

"No! Let me out! I'll—"

Acceleration kicked suddenly. Lark's folded body slammed one wall of the little car.

Ling's face vanished in a blur as he was swept away toward Ifni-knew-where.

DWER

"Are they really gone?"

Dwer bent close to an ancient, pitted window. He peered at a glittering starscape, feeling some of the transmitted chill of outer space, just a finger's breadth away.

"I don't see any sign of 'em over here," he called back to Rety. "Is it clear on your side?"

His companion—a girl about fourteen, with a scarred face and stringy hair—pressed against another pane at the opposite end of the dusty chamber, once the control room of a sleek vessel, but now hardly more than a grimy ruin.

"There's nothin'—unless you count the bits an' pieces floatin' out there, that keep fallin' off this rusty ol' bucket."

Her hand slammed the nearest bulkhead. Streams of dust trickled from crevices in prehistoric metal walls.

The starship's original owners must have been oddly shaped, since the viewing ports were arrayed at knee height to a standing human, while corroded instruments perched on tall pillars spread around the oblong room. Whatever race once piloted this craft, they eventually abandoned it as junk, over half a million years ago, when it was dumped onto a great pile of discarded hulks in the dross midden that lay under Jijo's ocean.

Immersion in subicy water surely had preserving effects. Still, the *Streaker* crew had accomplished a miracle, reviving scores of these wrecks for one final voyage. It made Rety's remark seem unfair, all considered.

There is air in here, Dwer thought. *And a machine that spits out a paste we can eat . . . sort of. We're holding death at bay. For the moment.*

Not that he felt exactly happy about their situation. But after all the narrow escapes of the last few days, Dwer found continued life and health cause for surprised pleasure, not spiteful complaint.

Of course, Rety had her own, unique way of looking at things. Her young life had been a lot harder than his, after all.

"i sniff every corner of this old boat," a small voice piped, speaking Anglic with a hissing accent and a note of triumph, "no sign of metal monsters, none! we scare them off!"

The speaker trotted across the control room on four miniature hooves—a quadruped with two slim centauroid arms and an agile, snakelike neck. Holding his head up proudly, little 'yee' clattered over to Rety, leaped into her arms and slipped into her belt pouch. The two called each other "husband and wife," an interspecies union that made some sense to another Jijoan but would have stunned any citizen of the Civilization of Five Galaxies. The verbose little urrish male and an unbathed, prepubescent human female made quite a pairing.

Dwer shook his head.

"Those robots didn't leave on account of our fierce looks. We were hiding in a closet, scared out of our wits, remember?" He shrugged. "I bet they didn't search the ship because they saw it for an empty shell right away."

Almost a hundred ancient derelict ships had been resurrected from the subsea graveyard by Hannes Suessi and his clever dolphin engineers in order to help mask *Streaker*'s breakout, giving the Earthlings a slim chance against the overpowering Jophur dreadnought. Dwer's presence aboard one of the decoys resulted from a series of rude accidents. Right now he was supposed to be landing a hot-air balloon in Jijo's Gray Hills, fulfilling an old obligation, not plummeting into the blackness away from the wilderness he knew best.

But Rety had planned to be here! A scheme to hijack her very own starship must have been stewing in that devious brain for weeks, Dwer now realized.

"The sap-rings cut us loose so they can go dolphin hunting somewhere else! I knew this'd happen," Rety exulted. "Now all we gotta do is head for the Five Galaxies. Make it to someplace with a lot of traffic, flag down some passing trading ship, an' strike a deal. This old hulk oughta be worth something. You watch, Dwer. Meetin' me was the best thing that ever happened to you! You'll thank me when you're a star god, livin' high for three hunnerd years."

Her enthusiasm forced him to smile. How easily Rety looked past their immediate problems! Such as the fact that all three of them were primitive Jijoans. Learning to pilot a space vessel would have been a daunting task for Dwer's brilliant siblings—Lark or Sara—who were junior sages of the Commons of Six Races. *But I'm just a simple forester! How is skill at tracking beasts going to help us navigate from star to star?*

As for Rety, brought up by a savage band of exile sooners, she could not even read until a few months ago, when she began picking up the skill.

"Hey, teacher!" Rety called. "Show us where we are!"

Four gray boxes lay bolted to the floor, linked by cable to an ancient control pillar. Three had been left by the dolphins, programmed to guide this vessel through the now completed breakout maneuver. Last was a portable "advisor"—a talking machine—given to Rety by the *Streaker* crew. She had shown Dwer her toy earlier, before the Jophur robots came.

"Passive sensors are operating at just seven percent efficiency," the unit answered. *"Active sensors are disabled. For those reasons, this representation will be commensurately imprecise."*

A picture suddenly erupted between Rety and Dwer . . . one of those magical holo images that moved and had the texture of solidity. It showed a fiery ball in one low corner—*Great Izmunuti,* Dwer realized with a superstitious shiver—prodigiously grown from what he had known as a bright, red spark in Jijo's night sky. A yellow dot in the exact center represented this hapless vessel. Several other bits of yellow glimmered nearby, drifting slowly toward the upper right.

The Jophur have cut loose all the captured decoys. I guess that means they know where Streaker is.

He thought of Gillian Baskin, so sad and so beautiful, carrying burdens he could never hope to understand. During his brief time aboard the Earth vessel he had a feeling . . . an impression that she did not expect to carry the burdens much longer.

Then what was it all for? If escape was hopeless, why did Gillian lead her poor crew through so much pain and struggle?

"Behold the Jophur battleship," said Rety's teacher. A blurry dot appeared toward the top right corner, now moving rapidly leftward, retracing its path at a close angle toward Izmunuti.

"It has changed course dramatically, moving at maximum C-Level pseudospeed."

"Can you see *Streaker*?" Dwer asked.

"I cannot. But judging from the Polkjhy's *angle of pursuit, the Terran ship may be masked by the red giant star."*

He sensed Rety sitting cross-legged on the floor next to him, her eyes shining in light from the hologram.

"Forget the Earthers," she demanded. "Show us where we're headin'!"

The display changed, causing Izmunuti and the Jophur frigate to drift out of view. A fuzzy patch moved in from the top edge, slippery to look at. Rows of symbols and numbers flickered alongside—information that might have meant something to his sister but just seemed frightening to Dwer.

"That's the . . . *transfer point,* right?" Rety asked, her voice growing hushed. "The *hole* thing that'll take us to the Five Galaxies?"

"It is a hole, in a manner of speaking. But this transfer point cannot serve as a direct link out of Galaxy Four—the galaxy we are in—to any of the others. In order to

accomplish that, we must follow transition threads leading to some other hyperspatial nexi. Much bigger ones, capable of longer-range jumps."

"You mean we'll have to portage from stream to stream, a few times?" Dwer asked, comparing the voyage to a canoe trip across a mountain range.

"Your metaphor has some limited relevance. According to recent navigation data, a route out of this galaxy to more populated regions can be achieved by taking a series of five transfers, or three transfers plus two long jumps through A-Level hyperspace, or two difficult transfers plus one A-Level jump and three B-Level cruises, or—"

"That's okay," Rety said, clapping her hands to quiet the machine. "Right now all I want to know is, will we get to the point all right?"

There followed a brief pause while the machine pondered.

"I am a teaching unit, not a starship navigator. All I can tell is that our C-Level pseudomomentum appears adequate to reach the periphery of the nexus. This vessel's remaining marginal power may be sufficient to then aim toward one of the simpler transfer threads."

Rety did not have to speak. Her smug expression said it all. Everything was going according to her devious plan.

But Dwer would not be fooled.

She may be brilliant, he thought. *But she's also crazier than a mulc spider.*

He had known it ever since the two of them almost died together, months ago in the Rimmer Mountains, seized in the clutches of a mad antiquarian creature called One-of-a-Kind. Rety's boldness since then had verged on reckless mania. Dwer figured she survived only because Ifni favors the mad with a special, warped set of dice.

He had no idea what a transfer point was, but it sounded more dangerous than poking a ruoul shambler in the face with a fetor worm.

Ah, well. Dwer sighed. There was nothing to be done about it right now. As a tracker, he knew when to just sit back and practice patience, letting nature take its course. "Whatever you say, Rety. Only now let's turn the damn thing off. Show me that food machine again. Maybe we can teach it to give us something better than greasy paste to eat."

HARRY

He reconfigured the station to look something like a Martian arachnite, a black oval body perched on slender, stalklike legs. It was all part of Harry's plan to deal with the problem of those transumptive banana peels.

After pondering the matter, and consulting the symbolic reference archive, he decided the screwy yellow things must be allaphorical representations of short-scale time warps, each one twisting around itself through several subspace dimensions. Encountering one, you would meet little resistance at first. Then, without warning, you'd slam into a slippery, repulsive field that sent you tumbling back toward your point of origin at high acceleration.

If this theory was true, he'd been lucky to survive that first brush with the nasty things. Another misstep might be much more . . . energetic.

Since flight seemed memetically untenable in this part of E Level, a spider morphology was the best idea Harry could come up with, offering an imaginative way to maneuver past the danger, using stilt legs to pick carefully from one stable patch to the next. It would be risky, though, so he delayed the attempt for several days, hoping the anomaly reef would undergo another phase shift. At any moment, the irksome "peels" might just evaporate or transform into a less lethal kind of insult. As long as he had a good view of his appointed watch area, it seemed best to just sit and wait.

Of course, he knew why a low-class Earthling recruit was assigned to this post. Wer'Q'quinn had said Harry's test scores showed an ideal match of cynicism and originality, suiting him for lookout duty in allaphor space. But in truth, E Level was unappealing to most oxygen breathers. The great clans of the Civilization of Five Galaxies thought it a quaint oddity at best. Dangerous and unpredictable. Unlike Levels A, B, and C, it offered few shortcuts around the immense vacuum deserts of normal space. Anyone in a hurry—or with a strong sense of self-preservation—chose transfer points, hyperdrive, or soft-quantum tunneling, instead of braving a realm where fickle subjectivity reigned.

Of course, oxygen breathers only made up the most gaudy and frenetic of life's eight orders. Harry kept notes whenever he sighted hydros, quantals, memoids, and other exotic types, with their strange insouciance about the passage of time. *They don't see it as quite the enemy we oxy-types do.*

His bosses at the Navigation Institute craved data about those strange comings and goings, though he could hardly picture why. The orders of sapiency so seldom interacted, they might as well occupy separate universes.

Still, you could hide a lot in all this weirdness, a trait that sometimes drew oxy-based life down here. On occasion, some faction or alliance would try sending a battle fleet through E Space, suffering its disadvantages in order to take rivals by surprise. Or else criminals might hope to move by a secret path through this treacherous realm. Harry was trained to look out for sooners, gene raiders, smugglers, syntac thieves, and others trying to cheat the strict rules of migration and Uplift. Rules that so far kept the known cosmos from dissolving into chaos and ruin.

He nursed no illusions about his status. Harry knew this job was just the sort of dangerous, tedious duty the great institutes assigned to lowly clients of an unimportant clan. Yet he took seriously his vow to Wer'Q'quinn and NavInst. He planned to show all the doubters what a neo-chimp could do.

That determination was put to the test when he roused from his next rest break to peer through the louvered blinds, blinking with groggy surprise at an endless row of serrated green ridges that had erupted while he slept. Undulating sinusoidally across the foreground, they resembled the half-submerged spiny torso of some gigantic, lazy sea serpent that seemed to stretch toward both horizons, blocking his panorama of the purple plane.

Maybe it *was* some kind of giant serpent, or viewed itself as such. At its slothful rate of passage, several pseudodays might pass before Harry's view was unobstructed once again. He stared for some time at the coils' slow rise and fall, wondering what combination of reality and his own mental processes could have evoked such a thing. If a memoid—another self-sustaining, living abstraction—it was huge enough to engulf most of the more modest animated idealizations grazing nearby.

When a concept grows big enough, does it become part of the landscape? Will it merge with the underpinnings of E Level? Will this "idea" take part in motivating the entire cosmos?

One thing was for sure, he could hardly survey his assigned area with something like this in the way!

Unfortunately, the damned banana peels still surrounded his station with a deadly allaphorical minefield. But clearly the time had come to move on.

The station swayed at first when he tried controlling the stilt legs by hand. Apparently, his spindly tower pushed the limits of verticality in this region, where flight was forbidden by local laws of physics. The structure teetered and nearly fell three times before he started getting the hang of things.

Alas, he had no option of handing supervision over to the computer. "Pilot mode" was often useless on E Level, where machines could be deaf and blind to allaphors that lay right in front of them.

"Well, here goes," he murmured, gingerly navigating the scout platform ahead, raising one spidery stem, maneuvering it skittishly past a yellow and brown "peel," and planting it on the best patch of open ground within reach. Testing its footing, he shifted the station's center of gravity, transferring more weight forward until it felt safe to try again with another.

The process was a lot like chess—you had to think at least a dozen moves ahead, for there could be no going back. "Reversibility" was a meaningless term in this continuum, where *death* might take on the attributes of a physical creature, and *entropy* was just another predatory concept prowling a savannah of ideas.

It became a slow, tense process of exertion, tedious and utterly demanding. Harry grew to despise the banana peel symbols, even more than before. He *used* his hatred to reinforce concentration, picking slowly amid the yellow emblems of slipperiness, knowing that any misstep might send the little scoutship flipping violently toward gaudy oblivion.

Somehow—he could tell—the peels sensed his loathing. Their boundaries seemed to shrink a little and solidify under his gaze.

"We do not require passionless observers for this kind of duty," Wer'Q'quinn had explained when Harry joined the Observer Corps at Kazzkark Base.

"There are many others we could choose, whose minds are more disciplined. More detached, cautious, and in most ways more intelligent. Those volunteers are needed elsewhere. But on E Level, we are better served by someone like you."

"Gee, thanks," Harry had replied. "So, are you saying you don't want me to be skeptical when I'm out on a mission?"

The squadron leader bowed a great, wormlike head. Rustling segment plates crafted words in ratchety Galactic Five.

"Only those who start with skepticism can open themselves to true adventure," Wer'Q'quinn continued. "But there are many types of skeptical outlook. Yours is gritty, visceral. You take things personally, young Earthling, as if the cosmos has a particular interest in your inconvenience. On most planes of reality, that is an egregious error of solipsistic pride. But on E Level, it may be the only appropriate way of dealing with an idiosyncratic cosmos."

Harry came away from that interview with oddly mixed feelings—as if he had just received the worst insult—and highest praise—of his life. The effect was to make him more determined than ever.

Perhaps Wer'Q'quinn had intended that, all along.

I hate you, he thought at the ridiculous, offensive yellow peels. On some level, they might be neutral twists of space, described by cold equations. But they seemed to taunt him by appearing the way they did, provoking an intimate abhorrence that Harry used to his advantage, piloting around the traps as if each success humiliated a real enemy.

His body grew sweaty and warm. A musty odor filled the cupola as one tense, cautious hour passed into the next.

Finally, with a nimble hop, he stepped his spindly vehicle away from the last obstacle, breathing a deep sigh, feeling tired, smelly, and victorious. Perhaps at some level the reef allaphors knew they had lost, for at that moment the "peels" began transforming from yellow and brown starfish forms into another shape, one with curls and spikes. . . .

Harry didn't wait to see what they would become. He ordered the pilot program to hurry away from there.

It took a while to get past the green "sea monster," ducking through a gap between two of its slowly undulating coils. The passage made Harry nervous, staring up at portions of that mammoth, living conceptual torso. But then he was free at last to race for open territory. The purple plain swept by as he aimed for the most promising vantage point—a stable-looking brown hillock, too barren and mundane to attract any hungry memoids. A place where he might settle down to watch his assigned patrol zone in peace.

The prominence lay quite some distance away—several miduras of subjective duration, at least. Meanwhile, the surrounding tableland appeared placid. The few allaphorical beings he did spy moved quickly out of the way. Most types of predatory memes disliked the simplistic scents of metal and other hard stuff intruding from other levels of reality.

Harry deemed it safe to go below and take a shower. Then, while combing knots out of his fur, he ordered something to eat from the autochef. He considered taking a nap, but found he was still too keyed up. Sleep, under such conditions, would be dream-racked and hardly restful. Anyway, it might be wiser to supervise while the ship was in motion. Pilot mode could not be counted on to notice everything.

The decision proved fortuitous. He returned upstairs to find his trusty vessel already much closer to its destination than expected. *That's quick progress. We're already halfway up the hill, he thought, surveying the view from each window. This should offer an ideal surveillance site.*

Several instruments on Harry's console suddenly began whirring and chirping excitedly. Checking the telltales, he saw that something made mostly of solid matter lay just ahead, over the ridge top. It did not seem to be from any of the other sapiency orders, but showed all the suspicious-familiar signs he was trained to look for in a ship from the Civilization of Five Galaxies.

Oxies, he realized.

Gotcha!

Harry felt a thrill while checking his weapon systems. This was what he had trained for. An encounter with his own kind of life, moving through a realm of space where protoplasmic beings did not belong. He relished the prospect of stopping and inspecting a ship from some highfalutin clan, like the Soro or Tandu. They might even gag on the disgrace of being caught and fined by a mere chimpanzee from the wolfling clan of Terra.

You aren't really here to fight, Harry reminded himself as the station's armaments reported primed and ready.

Your primary mission is to observe and report.

Still, he was an officer of the law, empowered to question oxy-beings who passed this way. Anyway, preparing weapons seemed a wise precaution. Scouts often disappeared during missions to E Level. Being attacked by some band of criminals might seem mundane, compared to getting gobbled by a rampant, self-propagating idea . . . but it could get you just as dead.

The bogey's not moving, Harry noted with some surprise. *It's just sitting there, a little beyond the hillcrest. Perhaps they've broken down, or run into trouble. Or else . . .*

Among the worries flashing through his mind was the thought of ambush. The bogey might be lying in wait.

In fact, though, Harry's sensors were specially designed for E-Level use, while the interlopers, whoever they were, probably had a starship's generalized instruments. There was a good chance they hadn't even detected him yet!

I might take 'em by surprise.

And yet, he began rethinking how good an idea that was, as more duras passed and pseudodistance to the target shrank. This continuum made most oxy-types edgy. Perhaps trigger-happy. Surprise might be an overrated virtue. Too late, he recalled that the station was still formatted like an arachnite! Spindle-legged and fierce looking as it took giant footsteps. The design offered a good view of his surroundings . . . and exposed him to crippling fire if things came down to a firefight.

Well, it's too late to change now. Ready or not, here we go!

As he crested the metaphorical hill, Harry triggered the recognition transponder, boldly beaming symbolic references to his official status, commissioned by one of the high institutes of Galactic culture.

The intruder entered line-of-sight, filling a forward viewing panel—a squat oblong shape, resembling a fierce armored beetle, with formidable claws. Those tearing pincers swiveled toward Harry. Spindly emitter arrays waved like antenna-feelers above the beetle's browridge, hurling aggressive symbolic replies to Harry's challenge.

Those writhing blobs of corporeal meaning sped rapidly across the narrowing gap between the two vessels. When the first one struck his forward pane, it made a splatting sound that resonated loudly, smearing and transforming into a shout that filled the little chamber.

"SURRENDER, EARTHLING! RESISTANCE IS USELESS. CAPITULATE OR DIE!"

Harry blinked. He stared for two or three duras, hand poised over the weapons panel while new threats pounded the window in quick succession.

"HEAVE TO AND SUBMIT! PREPARE TO MEET THY MAKER! DROP YOUR SHORTS! CRY UNCLE! GIVE UP, IN THE NAME OF THE LAW!"

Abruptly, Harry let out a low moan.

It must be Zasusazu . . . my replacement. Can it be time already?

Besides, who else would squat on a hillock in E Level, just hanging around in the open, but another damn fool recruit of Wer'Q'quinn?

More horrid clichés smacked against his windshield, making the cupola resound painfully until he answered with volleys of his own, serving Zasusazu salvo after salvo of rich Terran curses, satisfying his colleague's appetite for colorful wolfling invective.

"Laugh while you can, frog face! Take that, you overgrown slimeball! Moldy Jack cheese!" He laughed, half out of relief, and half because Zasusazu's obsession seemed so silly.

Well, everyone who works for Wer'Q'quinn is more than a little weird, Harry thought, trying to feel charitable. Zasusazu's not as bad as some. At least he likes a little surprise now and then.

Still, even after they both ran out of insults, then exchanged reports with his replacement, and finally left Zasusazu in command over the realm of ideas, Harry wondered about his own reaction to being relieved. After all, this had been a wearying mission and he certainly deserved time off. Yet, despite the frustration, danger, and loneliness of E Space, it always came as a bit of a letdown for a mission to end. To head back home.

Home? Maybe the problem lay in that term.

He mused on the word, as if it were a conceptual creature, wandering the purple plain.

It can't mean Horst, since I hated nearly every minute there. Or Earth, where I spent just a year, lonely and confused.

Can Kazzkark Base be "home," if it lacks any others of my kind?

Does the Navigation Institute fill that role, now that I've given it the same loyalty others devote to kin and country?

Harry realized he didn't really know how to define the word.

All the superficial landmarks and reference points had changed since he first set out from Kazzkark. Still, there was an underlying familiarity to the main route. He never worried about getting lost.

Harry wasn't much surprised when the red-blue sky overhead gradually angled downward to meet "ground," like a vast, descending wall. He took over from the autopilot. Gingerly, maneuvering by hand, he sent the station striding daintily through a convenient perforation in heaven.

SARA

The High Sages tell us that a special kind of peace comes with resignation.

With letting go of life's struggles.

With releasing hope.

Now, for the first time, Sara understood that ancient teaching as she watched Gillian Baskin decide whether to live or die.

No one doubted that the Terragens Agent had the right, duty, and wisdom to make that choice, for herself and everyone aboard. Not the dolphin crew, nor Hannes Suessi, nor the Niss Machine. Sara's mute friend Emerson seemed to agree—though she wondered how much the crippled former engineer comprehended from those manic lights in the holo display, glimmering frantically near Izmunuti's roiling flame.

Even the kids from Wuphon Port—Alvin, Huck, Ur-ronn, and Pincer—accepted the commander's authority. If Gillian thought it best to send *Streaker* diving toward an unripe t-point—in order to lure the enemy after them in an attempt to save Jijo—few aboard this battered ship would curse the decision. At least it would bring an end to ceaseless troubles.

We were resigned. I was at peace, and so was Dr. Baskin.

Only now things aren't so simple anymore. She sees a possible alternative . . . and it's painful as hell.

Sara found most of the crew's activities confusing, in both the water-filled bridge and the dry Plotting Room nearby, where dolphins moved about on wheeled or six-legged contraptions.

Of course, Sara's knowledge about Galactic technology was two centuries out of date, acquired by reading Jijo's sparse collection of paper books. Despite that, her theoretical underpinnings worked surprisingly well when it came to grasping conditions in local spacetime. But she remained utterly dazed by the way crew members dealt with practical matters—conveying status reports along brain-linked cables, or sending each other info-packets consisting of tiny self-contained gobbets of semi-intelligent light. When dolphins spoke aloud, it was often in a terse argot of clicks and overlapping cries that had little in common with any standard Galactic tongue. Still, nothing awed Sara quite as much as when Dr. Baskin invited her along to watch an attempt to pry information from a captured unit of the Galactic Library.

The big cube lay in its own chamber, swaddled by a chill fog, one face emblazoned with a rayed-spiral sign that was notorious even to Jijo's savage tribes. Within its twelve edges and six boundary planes lay an amassment of knowledge so huge that comparing it to the Biblos archive was like matching the great sea against a single teardrop.

Gillian Baskin approached the Library unit clothed in a ghostlike mantle of illusion, her slim human form cloaked behind the computer-generated image of a monstrous, leathery creature called a "Thennanin." Observing from nearby shadows, Sara could only blink in apprehensive awe as the older woman used this uncanny ruse, speaking a guttural dialect of Galactic Six, making urgent inquiries about enigmatic creatures known as Zang.

The topic was not well received.

"Beware mixing the orders of life," droned the cube's frigid voice, in what Sara took to be a ritualized warning.

"Prudent contact is best achieved in the depths of the Majestic Bowl, where those who were born separated may safely combine.

"In that deep place, differences merge and unity is born.

"But here in black vacuum—where space is flat and light rays cut straight trails—young races should not readily mingle with other orders. In this outer realm, they behave like hostile gases. Fraternization can lead to conflagration."

Impressed by the archive's vatic tone, Sara pondered how its parabolic language resembled the Sacred Scrolls that devout folks read aloud on holidays, back home on Jijo. The same obliqueness could be found in many other priestly works she had sampled in the Biblos archive, inherited from Earth's long night of isolation. Those ancient tomes, differing in many ways, all shared that trait of allegorical obscurity.

In science—real science—there was always a way to improve a good question, making it harder to dismiss with prevarication. Nature might not give explicit answers right away, but you could tell when someone gave you the old runaround. In contrast, mystical ambiguity sounded grand and striking—it could send chills down your spine. But in the end, it boiled down to evasion.

Ah, but ancient Earthlings—and early Jijoan sages—had an excuse. Ignorance. Vagueness and parables are only natural among people who know no other way. *I just never expected it from the Galactic Library.*

From an early age, Sara had dreamed of facing a unit like this one, posing all the riddles that baffled her, diving into clouds of distilled acumen collected by the great thinkers of a million races for over a billion years. Now she felt like Dorothy, betrayed by a charlatan in the chamber of Oz.

Oh, the knowledge must be there, all right—crammed in deep recesses of that chilled cube. But the Library wasn't sharing readily, even to Dr. Baskin's feigned persona as a warlord of a noble clan.

"Gr-tuthuph-manikhochesh, zangish torgh mph," Gillian demanded, wearing the mask of a Thennanin admiral. *"Manik-hophtupf mph!"*

A button in Sara's ear translated the eccentric dialect.

"We understand that Zang, by nature, dislike surprise," Dr. Baskin inquired. "Tell me how they typically react when one rude shock is followed by several more."

This time, the Library was only slightly more forthcoming.

"The term Zang refers to just one subset of hydrogen-breathing forms—the variant encountered most often by oxy-life in open-space situations. The vast majority of hydro breathers seldom leave the comfort of dense circulation storms on their heavy worlds . . ."

The lecture ran on, relating information Sara would normally find mesmerizing. But time was short. A crucial decision loomed in less than a midura.

Should *Streaker* continue her headlong drive for the resurrected transfer point? After lying dormant for half a million years—ever since Galaxy Four was declared fallow to sapient life—it was probably unripe for safe passage. Still, its uncanny rebirth offered *Streaker*'s crew a dour opportunity.

The solution of Samson. To bring the roof down on our enemies, and ourselves.

Only now fate proffered another daring possibility. The presence of collector machines and Zang ships still lacked clear explanation. The harvesting armada seemed weak, scattering in confusion before Izmunuti's unexpected storms. *And yet—Might they somehow help us defeat the Jophur without it costing our lives?*

Orders from the Terragens Council made Gillian's top priority clear. This ship carried treasure—relics of great consequence that might destabilize the Five Galaxies, especially if they were seized by a single fanatic clan. Poor little Earth could not afford to be responsible for one zealot alliance gaining advantage over all the others. There was no surer formula for Terran annihilation. Far better that both ship and cargo should be lost than some malign group like the Jophur seize a monopoly. Especially if a prophesied Time of Changes was at hand.

But what if *Streaker* could somehow deliver her burdens to the proper authorities? Ideally, that would force the Great Institutes and "moderate" clans to end their vacillation and take responsibility. So far, relentless pursuit and a general breakdown of law had made that seemingly simple step impossible. Neutral forces proved cowardly or unwilling to help *Streaker* come in out of the cold. Still, if it were done just right, success could win Earthclan a triumph of epic proportions.

Unfortunately, the passing duras weren't equipping Gillian any better for her decision. Listening in growing frustration to the Library's dry oration, she finally interrupted.

"You don't have to tell me again that Zang hate surprise! I want practical advice! Does that mean they'll shoot right away, if we approach? Or will they give us a chance to talk?

"I need contact protocols!"

Still, the Library unit seemed bent on remaining vague, or else inundating Gillian with useless details. Standing where the Thennanin disguise did not block her view, Sara watched Gillian grow craggy with tense worry.

There is another source, Sara thought. *Someone else aboard who might be able to help with the Zang.*

She had been hesitant to mention the possibility before. After all, her "source" was suspect. Fallen beings whose ancestors had turned away from sapiency and lacked any knowledge of spatial dilemmas. But now, as precious duras passed and Gillian's frustration grew, Sara knew she must intervene.

If the Great Library can't help us, maybe we should look to an unlikely legend.

ALVIN'S JOURNAL

Ever since we brave volunteers joined the Earthlings on their forlorn quest, I've compared it to our earlier trip aboard a handmade submarine—a little summer outing that wound up taking four settler kids all the way to the bottom of the sea, and from there to the stars.

Of course, our little *Wuphon's Dream* was just a hollowed-out log with a glass nose, hardly big enough for an urs, a hoon, a qheuen, and a g'Kek to squeeze inside, providing we took turns breathing. In contrast, *Streaker* is so roomy you could fit all the khutas of Port Wuphon inside. It has comforts I never imagined, even after a youth spent reading crates of Terran novels about spacefaring days.

And yet, the trips have similarities.

In each case, we took a willing chance, plunging into a lightless abyss to face unexpected wonders.

On both expeditions, my friends and I had different assigned tasks.

And sure enough, aboard *Streaker,* just like *Wuphon's Dream,* I got the worst job to do.

Keeper of Animals. That's me.

Ur-ronn gets to follow her passion for machinery, helping Suessi's gang down in engineering.

Pincer runs errands for the bridge crew. He's having a grand time dashing amphibiously from dry to watery parts of the ship and back again, with flashing claws and typical qheuen enthusiasm.

Huck spins her wheels happily. She gets to play *spy,* waving all four eyestalks to taunt the Jophur captives in their cell below, enraging them with the sight of a living g'Kek, provoking them into revealing more information than they would by other means. The *nyah-nyah* school of interrogation, I call it.

All three of them get to interact with the dolphin crew, helping in ways that matter. Even if we all get blown to bits soon, at least Huck and the others got to do interesting things.

But me? I'm stuck in the hold, keeping herd on twenty bleating glavers and a pair of cranky noors, with the combined conversational abilities of a qheuen larva.

According to the Niss Machine, one of these noors ought to be quite a conversationalist. It's *not* a noor, you see, but a *tytlal*—from a starfaring race that look like noor, smell like noor, and have the same knavish temperament. Somehow, they hid among us on Jijo all these years without ever being recognized. A seventh race of sooners—illegal settlers—who benefited from our Commons, but never bothered to formally join.

That'd take some cleverness, I admit. But Mudfoot acts just like my pet noor, Huphu. Lounging around, eating anything that isn't bolted down, and licking his sleek black pelt all the way to the discolored paws that give him his name. Everyone thinks I'm an expert at coaxing noor, just because hoonish mariners hire some of them to help on our sailing ships, scooting deftly along the spars and rigging, working for umbles and sourballs. But I say that only shows how easy it is to fool a hoon. A thousand years. That's how long we worked with the nimble creatures, and we never caught on.

Now they're counting on me to get Mudfoot to speak once more.

Yeah, right. And this journal of mine is going to be published when we reach Earth, and win a Sheldon Award.

Huphu and Mudfoot still glare at each other, hissing jealously—not unusual for two noor who haven't worked out their mutual status yet. Meanwhile, I try to keep my *other* wards comfortable.

We never saw very many glavers in my hometown, down along the Slope's volcanic coast. They love rooting through garbage piles and rotten logs for tasty bugs, but such things are in short supply aboard *Streaker.*

Dr. Baskin worked out an exchange with Uriel the Smith, swapping this little herd for several dozen crew members who stayed behind to form a new dolphin colony on Jijo. It hardly seems an even trade. Watching the glavers mewl and jostle in a corner of the hold, I can scarcely picture their ancestors as mighty starfarers. Those bulging, chameleon eyes—swiveling independently, searching the sterile metal hold for crawling things—hold no trace of sapient light. According to Jijo's Sacred Scrolls, that makes the opal-skinned quadrupeds sacred beings. They've attained the highest goal of any sooner race—reaching simplicity by crossing the Path of Redemption.

Renewed, cleansed of ancestral sin, they face the universe with reborn innocence, ready for a fresh start. Or so the sages say.

Forgive me for being unimpressed. You see, I have to clean up after the smelly things. If some patron race ever takes on the honored task of reuplifting glavers, they had better make housebreaking their first priority.

At first sight, you wouldn't think the filthy wretches had much in common with fastidious noor. But they both seem to like it when I puff out my throat sac and give a low, booming umble-song. Ever since my adult vertebroids erupted, I've acquired a deep resonance that I'm rather proud of. It helps keep the critters calm whenever *Streaker* makes a sudden maneuver and her gravity fields waver.

I try not to think about where the ship is right now, tearing along at incredible speed, diving through the flames of a giant, angry star.

Fortunately, I can umble while editing and updating my diary on a little teacher-scribe device that Dr. Baskin provided. By now I'm used to working with letters that float before me, instead of lying fixed on an ink-stained page. It's convenient to be able to reach into my work, shifting and nudging sentences by hand or voice command. Still, I wish the machine would stop trying to fix my grammar and syntax! I may not be human, but I'm one of Jijo's best experts on the Anglic language, and I don't need a smart-aleck computer telling me my dialect's "archaic." If my journal ever gets published on a civilized world, I'm sure my colonial style will enhance its charm, like the old-time appeal of works by Defoe and Swift.

It grows harder to stave off frustration, knowing my friends are in the thick of things, and me stuck below, staring at blank walls, with just dumb beasts for company. I know, by doing this I freed a member of *Streaker*'s understaffed crew to do important work. Still, it sometimes feels like the bulkheads are closing in.

"Who do you think *you're* looking at?" I snapped, when I caught Mudfoot glancing alternately at me and the floating lines of my journal. "You want to read it?"

I swiveled the autoscribe so hovering words swarmed toward the sleek creature.

"If you tytlal are so brainy, maybe you know where I should take the story next. Hrm?"

Mudfoot peered at the glyph symbols. His expression made my spines prickle. I wondered.

Just how much memory do they retain—this secret clan of supernoor? When did the Tymbrimi plant a clandestine colony of their clients on Jijo, masked by a surrounding, larger population of non-uplifted cousins? It must have been before we hoons came. Perhaps they predate even the g'Kek.

I had heard many legends of the clever Tymbrimi, of course—a spacefaring race widely disliked by conservative Galactics for their scamplike natures. The same trait made them befriend Earthlings, when that naïve clan first stumbled onto the star lanes. Ignorance can be fatal in this dangerous universe, and Terra might have quickly suffered the typical Wolflings' Fate, if not for Tymbrimi sponsorship and advice.

Only now crisis convulses the Five Galaxies. Mighty alliances are wreaking vengeance for past grievances. Earth and her friends may have reached the end of their luck, after all.

Even before meeting humans, the Tymbrimi must have known a day might come when all their enemies would converge against them. They must have been tempted to stash a small population group in some secluded place, before war, accident, or betrayal extinguished their main racial stock.

Did they consider taking the sooners' path themselves?

I'm no expert, but from what I've read, it seems unlikely that their natures would ever let Tymbrimi settle down to quiet pastoral lives on a hick world like Jijo. *Humans* barely accomplished it, and they are much more down to earth.

But if the Tymbrimi couldn't hide out as sooners, it wasn't too late for their beloved clients. The tytlal were still largely unknown. Still close to their animal roots. A small gene pool might be safely cached on far-off Jijo. It all made eerie sense. Including the notion of a race within a race—a band of undevolved noor, hidden among them. Guardians, keeping twin black eyes open for danger . . . or opportunity.

Watching Mudfoot, I recalled stories told by Dwer Koolhan—during his brief time aboard this ship, when *Streaker* hid beneath Jijo's sea—about how this wild animal kept snooping and meddling, following Dwer across half a continent. Ever mysterious, infuriating, and unhelpful. The behavior seemed to combine noorish recklessness with an attention span worthy of a hoon.

Intelligent irony now seemed to dominate Mudfoot's snub-nosed, carnivorous face while he scanned my most recent lines of prose—the very musings about tytlal nature that lay just above. His black-pelted form coiled tightly, in an expression that I mistook for studious interest. I could almost imagine mute noorish whimsy transforming into eloquent speech—witty commentary perhaps, or else a brutal putdown of my dense composition style.

Then, with an abrupt display of unleashed energy, Mudfoot leaped into the crowd of floating words, flailing left and right with agile forepaws, slashing sentences to ribbons, knocking whole paragraphs awry before *Streaker*'s artificial g-field yanked him to a crouched landing on the metal deck. At once, he swiveled with a hunter's delighted yowl and readied another pounce.

"Don't save those changes!" I shouted at the autoscribe with unaccustomed haste. "Make all text intangible!"

My command made Mudfoot's second leap less satisfying. Robbed of semi-solidity, the words of my journal were now mere visual holograms, unaffected by physical touch. His second assault slashed uselessly while he passed through ghostly symbols, barking with disappointment.

Moments later, though, Mudfoot perched once more on my right shoulder, as Huphu glared at him lazily from the left. Both of them preened for a while, then began rubbing my throat, begging for an umble.

"You don't fool me for a dura," I muttered. But there seemed little else to do except repair the damage, finish up this journal entry, and then give them what they wanted.

I was doing that—singing for two noor and a herd of mesmerized glaver—when the Niss Machine barged in with a message.

I still have no idea why the snide robotic mind keeps interrupting this way, without preamble or greeting, despite my complaints that it grates against a hoon's nature. And the tornado of spinning, twisted lines somehow hurts my eyes. Ifni, it's hard enough getting used to the idea of talking computers, even though I used to read about them in classics by Nagata and Ecklar and Devenport. Can it be that the Niss has some sort of family relationship with Mudfoot? A connection via the Tymbrimi, would be my guess. You can tell by their disdain for courtesy and knack for putting people off balance.

"I bring a message from the bridge crew," announced the whirling shape. "Although I see little good coming out of it, they want to see one or two of your charges up there. You must bring the creatures along at once. A crew member is already coming to replace you here."

Gently putting Huphu down on the metal deck, I gathered Mudfoot in a carrying hold, comfortably cradling him in the crook of one arm, so he could not writhe free. He seemed content, but I was taking no chances. The last thing I needed was for him to dash off in some random direction on our way to the bridge, wreaking havoc in the galley, or hiding in some storeroom till *Streaker* was blasted to smithereens.

"Won't you tell me what it's all about?" I asked.

The abstract lines appeared to shrug.

"For some reason, Dr. Baskin and Sage Sara Koolhan seem to think the beast may speak up, at an opportune moment, helping us deal with potentially hostile aliens."

I umbled a deep, rolling laugh.

"Well they got hopes! This Ifni-slucking tytlal is gonna talk when it wants to, and the universe can go to hell till then, for all it cares."

The lines twisted tighter than ever.

"I am not referring to the tytlal, Alvin. Please put the little rascal down and pay attention."

"But . . ." I shook my head, human style, confused. "Then, who. . . ?"

The Niss hologram bent toward the far wall, making an effort to point.

"You are requested to bring up one or two of those."

I stared at a crowd of goggle-eyed cretins. Mewling, nosing through their own revolting feces . . . "blessed" with sacred forgetfulness, immune to worry.

So, this hurried journal entry ends on a note of blank surprise.

They want me to bring *glavers* to the bridge.

LARK

He stumbled down twisty, intestinelike corridors, fleeing almost randomly through the vast ship, pausing occasionally to rest his head against a squishy bulkhead and sob. Cloying Jophur scentomeres mingled with his own stench of self-disgust and grief.

I should have stayed with her.

Lark's unwashed body, still sticky with juices from that dreadful nursery, kept moving despite fatigue and hunger, driven on by occasional sounds of pursuit. But his mind seemed mired, with all its fine edges dulled by regret.

Repeatedly, he tried to rouse from this depression and come up with a way to fight back.

You've got to think. Ling is counting on you!

In fact, Lark wasn't even sure where to go looking for his lover. His mental image of the *Polkjhy* was a blur of tangled passages linking odd-shaped chambers, more chaotic than the hivelike innards of a qheuen dam. Anyway, suppose he did find his way back to the prison section, the vault where he and Ling had made their getaway just a few days ago. By now the place would be triply guarded. By Jophur ring stacks, robots, and the tall human renegade.

Rann will be expecting me. He knows exactly what I'm thinking . . . that I want to go charging to her rescue.

Alas, Lark was no man of action like his brother, Dwer. The odds paralyzed him. He was too good at envisioning drawbacks and potential flaws in each tentative plan.

As long as I'm free, Ling can still hope. I have no right to throw that away by rushing into a trap. First priority has to be a place where I can rest . . . maybe find something to eat . . . then come up with a plan.

Using the purple ring as a universal passkey, Lark inspected various rooms along his meandering path, hoping to find a tool or information he could use against the enemy. Some compartments were empty. Others were occupied by Jophur crew, but these paid little heed to the distraction of an opening or closing door. Like their traeki cousins on Jijo, Jophur tended to be task-focused, reacting slowly to interruptions.

Only once did Lark fail to duck out of sight in time.

He was poking through a laboratory filled with coiled, transparent glassy tubes that flickered and hissed with roiling vapors. Abruptly Lark found his path blocked by a massive ring stack. It had just turned away from an instrument console, and all sensor toruses were active.

Flatulent smoke bursts vented from the Jophur's peak, indignant to spy an intruding human. Fatty toruses flickered with shadowy patterns of light and dark, expressing surprised rage.

If he had paused to think, Lark would never have had the courage to lunge toward that intimidating mass, thrusting his only weapon past a dozen reaching tentacles. Tendrils converged to surround him, slapping his shoulders.

Master rings make Jophur ambitious and decisive, thought a bookish corner of his mind. *But thank Ifni they're like traeki in other ways. Their sluggish nerves were never tested by carnivores on a savannah.*

But Jophur had other advantages. Throbbing feelers coiled around his neck and arms, even as soporific juices sprayed from the throbbing torus in his hands, the final gift of gentle Asx.

This time there was no reaction from the huge, tapered tower. Its grippers tightened, drawing Lark toward glistening, oily flanks.

He felt the purple ring flex and emit three more sprays, each one a different pungent fetor that made his eyes sting and his throat gag . . . till constricting pressure round his chest made it impossible to breathe at all.

The trick . . . may not work anymore. They may have spread . . . word. Distributed . . . counteragents . . .

All at once, the greasy titan shivered. The nooses tensed . . . then slackened, going limp as the Jophur settled its great mass to the floor, discharging a low sigh and rank smells. Lark nearly strangled on his first ragged breath. Shrugging free of the horrid embrace, he stumbled away, sucking for fresh air.

They're catching on. Each time the purple ring fools one of them, they share information and antidotes. Even Asx couldn't anticipate every possible scent code the Jophur might use.

The big stack seemed quiescent now, but Lark worried it might have put out an alarm. Swiftly, he scanned the rest of the chamber for co-workers. But the creature was alone.

Lark was about to head back to the corridor when he stopped, intrigued to see that the Jophur's console was still active. Holo displays flickered, tuned to spectral bands his eyes found murky at best. Still, he approached one in curiosity—then growing excitement.

It's a map! He recognized the battle cruiser's oblate shape, cut open to expose the ship's mazelike interior. It turned slowly. Varied shadings changed slowly while he watched.

I wish I knew more about Galactic tech. Before the Rothen-Danik expedition came to Jijo, computers had been legendary things one read about in dusty tomes within the Biblos archive. Even now, he saw them partly through two centuries of fear and half-superstition. Of course, even the star-sophisticate Ling would have trouble with this unit, designed for Jophur use. So Lark chose not to touch any buttons or sense plates.

Anyway, sometimes you can learn a lot just by observing.

This bright box over here . . . I know I'm in that quadrant of the ship. Could it signify this room?

The symbols were in efficient Galactic Two, though he found the specific subdialect technical and hard to interpret. Still, he managed to locate the security section where he and Ling had been imprisoned when they were first brought aboard on Jijo. A deep, festering blue rippled outward from that area and spread gradually "northward" along the ship's main axis, filling one deck at a time.

A search pattern. They've been driving me into an ever smaller volume . . . back toward the control room.

And away from Ling.

From their slow, methodical progress, he estimated that the hunter robots would reach this chamber in less than a midura. Though it was a daunting prospect, that realization actually made Lark feel much better, just knowing where he stood. It also gave him time to seek a flaw in their strategy by studying the map for a while.

If hunger pangs don't muddle my brain first. Unfortunately, the pursuers were also herding him farther from the one place he knew of where a human could find food.

Looking around the laboratory, he found a sink with a water tap. Ling had called it a constant on almost any vessel of an oxygen-breathing species. The fluid was distilled to utter purity, and so tasted weird. But Lark slurped greedily—trying to wash myriad complex ship flavors out of his mouth—before returning once more to peruse the data screens.

Other than the ship map, most of the displays were enigmatic—flickering graphs or cascades of hurtful color, impossible to comprehend. Except for one showing a black field speckled with glittering points of light.

Ling and I saw something like this in the Jophur command center. She called it a star chart, showing where we are in space, and what's going on around us.

It still made Lark queasy to picture himself hurtling at multiples of lightspeed through an airless void. Unlike Sara, he had never dreamed of leaving Jijo, where his life's work was to study the life-forms of a richly varied world. Only war and chaos could have torn him away from there. Only his growing ardor for Ling compensated for the loss and alienation.

And now she was gone from his side. It felt like being amputated.

Staring at the display—a black vista broken by a few sparkling motes—he felt utterly daunted by the distance scales, in which vast Jijo would be lost like a floating speck of dust.

One pinpoint glowed steady in the center—the Jophur dreadnought, he guessed. And a great, yarnlike ball in the lower left must be a flaming star. But without his cosmopolitan friend to interpret, Lark was at a loss to decipher other colored objects shifting and darting in between. GalTwo symbols flashed, but he lacked the experience to make sense of them.

In frustration, Lark was about to turn away when he noticed one slim fact.

That big dot over there, near the star . . . it seems to be heading straight for us.

I wonder if it's going to be friendly.

EMERSON

Nothing could feel more natural or familiar than looking at a spatial chart. It was like regarding his own face in the mirror.

More familiar than that, since Emerson had just spent a dazed year on a primitive world, gaping blankly at his reflection in water pools or on crude slabs of polished metal, wondering about that person staring back at him, with the gaping hole above one ear and the dazed look in his eyes. Even his own name was a mystery till a few weeks ago, when some pieces of his past began falling together.

. . . scattered memories of wondrous Earth, and a youth spent targeting himself, with a solemn firmness that awed his parents, toward the glittering lure of five galaxies.

. . . his life as an engineer, privileged to receive the very best training, learning to make starships plunge between mysterious folds of spacetime.

. . . the lure of adventure—a deep voyage with the famous Captain Creideiki—an offer he could never refuse, even knowing it might lead past the jaws of Hades.

All that, and much more, was restored when Emerson learned how to beat down the savage pain that kept memory imprisoned, regaining much that had been robbed from him.

But not the best part. Not the rich, textured power of speech. Not the river of words that used to lubricate each subtle thought and bear knowledge on graceful boats of syntax. Without speech, his mind was a desert realm, devastated by agnosia as deep as the crippling wound in the left side of his skull.

At least now Emerson understood his maiming had been deliberate, an act so malicious he could scarcely grasp its boundaries or encompass the scale of revenge needed to make things right.

Then, unasked and unexpected, it happened once again. Some mix of sense and emotion triggered a shift inside, releasing a sudden outpouring. All at once he imagined an enveloping swirl of soft sound—reverberations that stroked his skin, rather than his ears. Echoes that he felt, rather than heard.

• *With each turning*
  • *Of the cycloid,*
• *In dimensions*
  • *Beyond number*
• *Comes a tumble*
  • *Of those cuboids,*
• *Many sided,*
  • *Countless faces—*
 • *Ever unfair . . . never nice.*

• *Watch them spin on,*
  • *So capricious,*
• *White and spotted,*
  • *Always loaded,*
• *Yet you, hopeless,*
  • *Reach to gamble,*
• *Tossing for a*
  • *Risky payback—*
 • *Smack the haughty! Ifni's dice. . . .*•

Emerson smiled faintly as the Trinary ode played out, using circuits in his battered brain that even the vicious Old Ones never touched with their knives. Like the groaning melody of a Great Dreamer, it resonated whole, with tones of cetacean wisdom.

And yet, he knew its promise was but a slender reed. Hardly much basis for hope. As if the universe would ever really give him a chance at vengeance! Life was seldom so accommodating. Especially to the weak, the harried and pursued.

Still, Emerson felt grateful for the gift of strange poetry. Though it wasn't an engineer's language, Trinary excelled at conveying irony.

He watched through a broad crystal window as neo-dolphins raced back and forth, traversing *Streaker*'s water-filled bridge with powerful tail thrusts, leaving trails of fizzing, hyper-oxygenated water in their wake. Other crewfins lay at ramplike control stations, their sleek heads inserted in airdomes while neural cables linked their large brains to computers and distant instrumentalities.

The crystal pane vibrated against his fingertips, carrying sonar clicks and rapid info-bursts from the other side. The music of cooperative skill. A euphony of craft. These were the finest members of a select crew. The *Tursiops amicus* elite. The pride of Earth's Uplift campaign, recruited and trained by the late Captain Creideiki to be pilots without peer.

The dolphin lieutenant, Tsh't, crisply handled routine decisions and relayed orders to the bridge crew. Beside her, chief helmsman Kaa lay shrouded by cables, his narrow jaw open and sunken eyes closed. Kaa's flukes slashed as he steered the starship like an extended part of his own body. Thirty million years of instinct assisted Kaa—intuition accumulated ever since his distant ancestors ceded land for a fluid realm of three dimensions.

Behind Emerson, the Plotting Room was equally abuzz. Here dolphins moved on rollers or walkers—machines that offered agility in dry terrain, making them seem even more massively bulky next to a pair of slender bipeds. And yet, those humans called the tune, directing all this furious activity. Two women whose lives had been utterly different, until circumstances brought them together.

The two women whom Emerson loved, though he could never tell them.

Thrumming engine sounds changed pitch as he sensed the nimble ship brake harder to fight its hyperbolic plunge, clawing against the drag of a giant star, changing course in another of Gillian Baskin's daring ventures.

Emerson had paid a dear price for one of her earlier hunches, in that huge, intricately structured place called the *Fractal World*—a realm of snowy icicles whose smallest branchlets spread wider than a planet. But he had resented Gillian's mistake. Who else could have kept *Streaker* free for three years, eluding the armadas of a dozen fanatical alliances? He only regretted that his sacrifice had been in vain.

Above all, Emerson wanted to help right now. To go below, toward those distant humming motors, and help Hannes Suessi nurse more pseudovelocity from the laboring gravistators. But his handicap was too severe. His torn cortex could not read sense from the symbols on flashing displays, and there was only so much you could do by touch or instinct alone. His comrades had been kind, giving him make-work tasks, but he soon realized it was better just to get out of their way.

Anyway, Sara and Gillian were clearly up to something. Tension filled the Plotting Room as both women argued with the spinning apparition of the Niss Machine.

Its spiral lines coiled tightly. Clearly, a moment of drama was approaching.

So Emerson played spectator, watching as a chart portrayed *Streaker*'s tight maneuver, slewing past giant Izmunuti's stubborn grasp, threading hurricanes of ionized heat that strained the laboring shields, changing course to climb aggressively toward a cluster of pale, flickering lights.

A convoy of ships . . . or things that acted like ships, moving about the cosmos at the volition of thinking minds.

He overheard Sara utter buzzing glottal stops to frame a strange GalSix term. One seldom heard, except in tones of muted awe.

Zang.

Despite his handicap, Emerson abruptly knew what advice Gillian was receiving from the young Jijoan mathematician. He shivered. Of all the chances taken by *Streaker*'s crew, none was like this. Even daring the throat of a newly roused transfer point might have been better. Just thinking about it provoked a reply from some recess of his sundered brain. Precious as a jewel, a single word glittered hot and hopeless.

Desperation . . .

It didn't take long for *Streaker*'s tactic to be noticed.

The Jophur enemy—just twenty paktaars away—began slewing at once, shedding pseudovelocity to intercept the Earthship's new course.

A crowd of others lay even nearer at hand.

Blue glimmers represented frail harvesting machines—Emerson had seen graphic images and recognized the gossamer sails. By now half the luckless convoy were already consumed by rapidly expanding solar storms. The rest gathered light frantically, pulsing with inadequate engines, struggling to find refuge at the older transfer point.

Among those frail sparks, four bright yellow dots had been cruising imperviously, speeding to assist some of the beleaguered mechanicals. But this effort was disrupted by *Streaker*'s sudden, hard turn.

Two of the yellow glows continued their rescue efforts, darting from one harvester to the next, plucking a glittering nucleus unit out of the swelling flames and leaving the broad sail to burn.

A third yellow dot swung toward the Jophur ship.

The last one moved to confront *Streaker.*

Everyone in the Plotting Room stopped what they were doing when a shrill, crackling sound erupted over the comm speakers. Though Emerson had lost function in his normal speech centers, his ears worked fine, and he could tell at once that it was unlike any Galactic language—or wolfling tongue—he had ever heard.

The noise sounded bellicose, nervous, and angry.

The Niss hologram shivered with each staccato burst of screeching pops. Dolphins slashed their flukes, loosing unhappy moans. Sara covered her ears and closed her eyes.

But Gillian Baskin spoke calmly, soothing her companions with a wry tone of voice. In moments, chirps of dolphin laughter filled the chamber. Sara grinned, lowering her hands, and even the Niss straightened its mesh of jagged lines.

Emerson burned inside, wishing he could know what Gillian had said—what well-timed humor swiftly roused her crewmates from their alarmed funk. But all he made out were "wah-wah" sounds, nearly as foreign as those sent by a different order of life.

The Niss Machine made rasping noises of its own. Emerson guessed it must be trying to communicate with the yellow dot. Or rather, what the dot represented . . . one of those legendary, semifluid globes that served as "ships" for mighty, cryptic hydrogen breathers. He recalled being warned repeatedly, back in training, to avoid all contact with the unpredictable Zang. Even the Tymbrimi curbed their rash natures when it came to such deadly enigmas. If this particular Zang perceived *Streaker* as a threat—or if it were merely touchy at the moment—any chance of survival was practically nil. The Earthship's fragments would soon join the well-cooked atoms of Izmunuti's seething atmosphere.

Soon, long-range scans revealed the face of the unknown. An image wavered at highest magnification, refracted by curling knots of stormy plasma heat, revealing a vaguely spherical object with flanks that rippled eerily. The effect didn't remind Emerson of a soap bubble as much as a tremendous gobbet of quivering grease, surrounded by dense evaporative haze.

A small bulge distended outward from the parent body as he watched. It separated and seemed briefly to float, glistening, alongside.

The detached blob abruptly exploded.

From the actinic fireball a needle of blazing light issued straight toward *Streaker*!

Klaxons erupted warnings in both the bridge and Plotting Room. The spatial chart revealed a slender line, departing the yellow emblem to spear rapidly across a distance as wide as Earth's orbit. As a weapon, it was unlike any Emerson had seen.

He braced for annihilation . . .

. . . only to resume breathing when the destructive ray passed just ahead of *Streaker*'s bow.

Lieutenant Tsh't commented wryly.

• *As warning shots go,*
  • *(Acts speak much louder than words!)*
    • *That was a doozy.* •

While Emerson labored to make sense of her Trinary haiku, the door of the Plotting Room hissed open and three figures slipped inside. One was a shaggy biped, nearly as tall as a dolphin is long, with a spiky backbone and flapping folds of scaly skin under his chin. Two pale, shambling forms followed, knuckle-walking like proto-chimpanzees, with big round heads and chameleon eyes that tried to stare in all directions at once. Emerson had seen hoons and glavers before, so he spared their entrance little thought. Everyone was watching Gillian and Sara exchange whispers as tension built.

No order was given to turn aside. Sara's lips pressed grimly, and Emerson understood. At this point, they were committed. The second transfer point was no longer an option. Its dubious refuge could not be reached now before the Jophur got there first. Nor could *Streaker* flee toward deep space, or try her luck on one of the varied levels of hyperspace. The dreadnought's engines—the best affordable by a wealthy clan—could outrun poor *Streaker* in any long chase.

The Zang did not have to destroy the Earthship. They need only ignore her, leaving the filthy oxygen breathers to settle their squabbles among themselves.

Perhaps that might have happened . . . or else the orb-ship might have finished them off with another volley. Except that something else happened then, taking Emerson completely off guard.

The Niss hologram popped into place near the tall hoon—Alvin was the youngster's name, Emerson recalled—and then drifted lower, toward the bewildered glavers. Mewling with animal-like trepidation, they quailed back from the floating mesh of spiral curves . . . until the Niss began emitting a noisome racket. The same that had come over the loudspeakers minutes ago.

Blinking rapidly, the pair of glavers began reflexively swaying. Emerson could swear they seemed just as surprised as he was, and twice as frightened. Yet, they must have found the clamor somehow compelling, for soon they began responding with cries of their own—at first muted and uncertain, then with increasing force and vigor.

To the crew, it came as a rude shock. The master-at-arms—a burly male dolphin with mottled flanks—sent his six-legged walker stomping toward the beasts, intent on clearing the room. But Gillian countermanded the move, watching with enthralled interest.

Sara clapped her hands, uttering a satisfied oath, as if she had hoped for something like this.

On the face of the young hoon, surprise gave way to realization. A subdued, rolling sound escaped Alvin's vibrating throat sac. Emerson made out a single phrase—

"*. . . the legend . . .*"

—but its significance was slippery, elusive. Concentrating hard, he almost pinned down a meaning before it was lost amid resumed howls from the loudspeakers. More caterwauled threats beamed by the Zang, objecting to *Streaker*'s rapid approach.

At long range, he saw the great globule pulsate menacingly. Another liquid bulge began separating from the main body, bigger than the first, already glowing with angry heat.

The glavers clamored louder. They seemed different from the ones he had seen back on Jijo, which always behaved like grunting beasts. Now Emerson saw something new. A light. A *knowing*. The impression of a task long deferred, now being performed at last.

The Zang globe rippled. Its rasping threats merged with the glaver bedlam, forming a turbulent pas de deux. Meanwhile, the new bud fully detached from its flank, pulsating with barely constrained wrath.

This one might not be a warning shot.

RETY

"I guess there's more to using one of these transfer point things than I thought."

Rety meant her words as a peace offering. A rare admission of fault. But Dwer wasn't going to let her off that easy.

"I can't believe you thought a couple of savages could just go zooming about the heavens like star gods. *This* was your plan? To grab a wrecked ship, still dripping seaweed from the dross piles of the Great Midden, and ride along while it *falls into a hole in space?*"

For once, Rety quashed her normal, fiery response. True, she had never invited Dwer to join her aboard her hijacked vessel in the first place. Nor was *he* offering any bright ideas about what to do with a million-year-old hulk that could barely hold air, let alone fly.

Still, she kind of understood why he was upset. With death staring him in the face, the Slopie could be expected to get a bit testy.

"When Besh and Rann talked about it, they made it sound simple. You just aim your ship to dive inside—"

Dwer snorted. "Yeah, well you just said a mouthful there, Rety. *Aim* into a transfer point? Did you ever think how many generations it took our ancestors to learn how to pull that off? A trick we've got to figure out in just a midura or two?"

This time, Rety didn't have to reply. Little yee snaked his long neck from her belt pouch, reaching out to nip Dwer's arm.

"Hey!" he shouted, drawing back.

"see?" the little urs chided in a lisping voice, "no good come from snip-snapping each other, use midura to study! or just complain till you die."

Dwer rubbed a three-sided weal, glaring at the miniature male. But yee's teeth had left the skin unbroken.

Any Jijoan human knew enough about urrish bites to recognize when one was just a warning.

"All right then," he muttered to Rety. "You're the apprentice star god. Talk that smug computer of yours into saving us."

Rety sighed. In the wilderness back home, Dwer had always been the one with clever solutions to every problem, never at a loss. She liked him better that way, not cowed by the mere fact that he was trapped in a metal coffin, hurtling toward crushing death and ruin. *I hope this don't mean I'm gonna have to nursemaid him all the way across space to some civilized world. When we're all set up—with nice apart'mints and slave machines doin' anything we want—he sure is gonna owe me!*

Rety squatted before the little black box Gillian Baskin had given her aboard the *Streaker*—a teaching unit programmed for very young human children. It functioned well at its intended purpose—explaining the basics of modern society to a wild girl from the hicks of Jijo. To her surprise, she had even started picking up the basics of reading and writing. But when it came to instructing them how to pilot a starship . . . well, that was another matter.

"Tutor," she said.

A tiny cubic hologram appeared just above the box, showing a pudgy male face—with a pencil mustache and a cheery smile.

"Well, hello again! Have we been keeping our spirits up? Tried any of those games I taught you? Remember, it's important to stay busy-busy and think positive until help arrives!"

Rety lashed with her left foot, but it passed through the face without touching anything solid.

"Look, you. I told ya there's nobody gonna come help us, even if you did get out a distress call, which I doubt, since the dolphins only fixed the parts they needed to, to make this tub fly."

The hologram pursed simulated lips, disapproving of Rety's attitude.

"Well, that's no excuse for pessimism! Remember, whenever we're in a rough spot, it is much better to seek ways of turning adversity into opportunity! So why don't we—"

"Why don't we go back to talking about how we'll *control* this here piece of dross," Rety interrupted. "I already asked you for lessons how to steer it through the t-point just ahead. Let's get on with it!"

The tutor frowned.

"As I tried to explain before, Rety, this vessel is in no condition to attempt an inter-spatial transfer at this time. Navigation systems are minimal and incapable of probing the nexus ahead for information about thread status. The drive is balky and seems only capable of operating at full thrust, or not at all. It may simply give up the next time we turn it on. The supervisory computer has degraded to mentation level six. That is below what's normally needed to calculate hyperspatial tube trajectories. For all of these reasons, attempting to cross the transfer point is simply out of the question."

"But there's no place else to go! The Jophur battleship was dragging us there when it flung us loose. You already said we don't have the engine juice to break away before falling in. So we got nothin' to lose by trying!"

The tutor shook its simulated head.

"Standard wisdom dictates that any maneuver we tried now would only make it harder for friends/relatives/parents to find you—"

This time, Rety flared.

"How many times do I gotta tell you, no one's coming for us! Nobody knows we're here. Nobody would care, if they knew. And nobody could reach us if they cared!"

The teaching unit looked perplexed. Its ersatz gaze turned toward Dwer, who looked more adult with his week-old stubble. Of course, that irritated Rety even more.

"Is this true, sir? There is no help within reach?"

Dwer nodded. Though he too had spent time aboard *Streaker,* he never found it easy speaking to a ghost.

"Well then," the tutor replied. *"I suppose there is just one thing to do."*

Rety sighed relief. At last the jeekee thing was going to start getting practical.

"I must withdraw and get back to work talking to the ship's computer, no matter what state it is in. I am not designed or programmed for this kind of work, but it is of utmost importance to try harder."

"Right!" Rety murmured.

"Indeed. Somehow, we must find a way to boost power to communications systems, and get out a stronger message for help!"

Rety bolted to her feet.

"What? Didn't you hear me, you pile o' glaver dreck?

I just said—"

"Don't worry while I am out of touch. Try to be brave. I'll be back just as soon as I can!"

With that, the little cube vanished, leaving Rety shaking, frustrated, and angry.

It didn't help that old Dwer broke up, laughing. He guffawed, hissing and snorting a bit like an urs. Since nothing funny had happened, she figured he must be doing it out of spite. Or else this might be another example of that thing called *irony* people sometimes talked about, when they wanted an excuse for acting stupid.

I'll slap some irony across your jeekee head, Dwer, if you don't shut up.

But he was bigger and stronger . . . and he had saved her life at least three times in the past few months. So Rety just clenched her fists instead, waiting till he finally stopped chuckling and wiped tears from his eyes.

The tutor remained silent for a long time, leaving both human castaways with no way to deal with the ship on their own.

There were makeshift controls, left in place by *Streaker*'s dolphin crew when they had resurrected this ancient Buyur hulk from a pile of discarded spacecraft on Jijo's sea bottom. Mysterious boxes had been spliced by cable to the hulk's control circuits, programmed to send it erupting skyward along with a swarm of other revived decoys, confusing Jophur instruments and masking *Streaker*'s breakout attempt. But since the dolphins had never expected stowaways, there were only minimal buttons and dials. Without the tutor, there'd be no chance of making the ship budge from its current unguided plummet.

Lacking anything better to do, Rety and Dwer went forward and stared ahead through the bow windows, pitted from immersion in the Great Midden for half a million years. Together, they tried to spot the mysterious "spinning hole in space" that Jijo's fallen races still recalled in sagas about ancestral days—the mighty doorway each sneakship passed through when it brought a new wave of refugee-settlers to a forbidden world in a fallow galaxy.

At first, Rety saw nothing special in the glittering starscape. Then Dwer pointed.

"Over there. See? The *Frog* is all bent out of shape."

Rety had grown up amid a primitive tribe, hiding in a grubby wilderness without even the rough comforts of Dwer's homeland, the Slope. Living in crude huts, with just campfires to ward off chill and darkness, she had constellations overhead nearly every night of her life. But while her cousins made up elaborate hunters' tales about those twinkling patterns, her only interest lay in their practical use as signposts, pointing the westward path she might someday use to escape her wretched clan.

Dwer, on the other hand, was chief scout of the Commons of Jijo, trained to know every quirk of the sky—from which the Six Races always expected doom and judgment to arrive. He would notice if something was out of place.

"I don't see . . ." She peered toward the cluster of glimmering pinpoints he indicated. "Oh! Some of the stars . . . they're clumped in a circle and—"

"And there's nothing inside," he finished for her. "Nothing at all."

They stared silently for a while. Rety couldn't help comparing the disklike blackness to a predator's open maw, looming rapidly to swallow the ship and all its contents.

"The stars seem t'be smearing out around it," she added.

Dwer nodded, making hoonish umbling sounds.

"Hr-rm. My sister called this thing a sort of *twist in the universe,* where space gets all wound up in knots."

Rety sniffed.

"Space is *empty,* dummy. I learned that back when I lived with the Daniks, in their underground station. There's nothin' out here to *get* twisted."

"Fine. Then *you* explain what we're about to fall into."

Little yee chose to speak up then.

"no problem to explain, big man-boy.

"what is life?

"is going from one hole to another, then another!

"is better this way. go in! yee will sniff good burrow for us.

"good, comfy burrow is happiness."

Dwer glanced sourly at the urrish male, but Rety smiled and stroked yee's tiny head.

"You tell him, husban'. We'll slide on through this thing, slick as a mud skink, an' come out in the main spiral arcade of Galaxy Number One, where the lights are bright an' ships are thicker than ticks on a ligger's back. Where the stars are close enough to gossip with each other, an' everyone's so rich they need computers to count their computers!

"Folks like that'll need folks like us, Dwer," she assured. "They'll be soft, while we're tough an' savvy, ready for adventure! We'll take on jobs the star gods are too prissy for—an' get paid more'n your whole Commons of Jijo is worth.

"Soon we'll be livin' high, you watch. You'll bless the day you met me."

Dwer stared back at her. Then, clearly against his will, a smile broke out. This time the laugh was friendlier.

"Honestly, Rety. I'd rather just go home and keep some promises I made. But I guess that's unlikely now, so—" He glanced ahead at the dark circle. It had grown noticeably as they watched. "So maybe you're right. We'll make the best of things. Somehow."

She could tell he was putting up a front. Dwer figured they would be torn apart soon, by forces that could demolish all of Jijo in moments.

He oughta have more faith, she thought. *Somethin'll come along. It always does.*

With nothing better to do, they counted the passing duras, commenting to each other about the strange way stars stretched and blurred around the rim of the monstrous thing ahead. It doubled in size, filling a quarter of the window by the time Rety's "tutor" popped back into existence above the black box. The tiny face had triumph in its eyes.

"Success!" it exulted.

Rety blinked.

"You mean you found a way to control this tub?"

"Better than that! I managed to coax more power and bandwidth from the communications system!"

"Yes?" Dwer moved forward. "And?"

"And I got a response, at last!"

The two humans looked at each other, sharing confusion. Then Rety cursed.

"You didn't pull the bloody-damn *Jophur* back to us, did you?"

That might help the *Streaker* crew. But she had no interest in resuming her former role as bait. Rety would rather risk the transfer point than surrender to those stacks of stinky rings.

"The battleship is beyond effective range as it dives toward the red giant star, where other mighty vessels are dimly perceived engaging in energetic activity that I cannot make out very well.

"The rescuers I refer to are entirely different parties."

The tutor paused.

"Go on," Dwer prompted warily.

"The active scanners were balky and difficult at first. But I finally got them online. At which point I spotted several ships nearby, fleeing toward the transfer point just as we are! After some further effort, I managed to flag the attention of the closest . . . whereupon it changed course slightly to head this way!"

Rety and Dwer nearly stumbled over each other rushing to the aft viewing ports. They stared for some time, but even with coaxing from the tutor, Rety saw nothing at first except the great red sun. Even at this long range, it looked larger than her thumbnail held at arm's reach. And angry storms extended farther still, with tornadolike tendrils.

Dwer pointed.

"There! Three points up from Izmunuti and two points left. You can't miss it."

Rety tried looking where he pointed, but despite his promise, she found it hard to make out anything different. Stars glittered brightly. . . .

Some of them shifted slightly, moving in unison, like a flock of birds. First they jogged a little left, then a little right, but always together, as if a section of the sky itself were sliding around, unable to keep still.

Finally, she realized—the moving stars all lay in an area shaped like a slightly canted *square.*

"Those aren't real stars . . . she began, hushed.

"They're reflections," Dwer finished. "Like off a mirror. But how?"

The tutor seemed happiest explaining something basic.

"The image you see is caused by a tremendous reflector-and-energy-collector. In Galactic Seven the term is ntove tunictun. Or in Earthling tradition—a solar sail.

"The method is used chiefly by sapients who perceive time as less a factor than do oxygen breathers. But right now, they are using a supplementary gravitic engine to hasten progress, fleeing unexpected chaos in this stellar system. At these pseudovelocities, the vessel should be able to pick us up and still reposition itself for optimal transfer point encounter toward its intended destination."

Dwer held up both hands.

"Whoa! Are you saying the creatures piloting that thing don't breathe oxygen? You mean they aren't even part of the, um—"

"The Civilization of Five Galaxies? No sir, they are not. These are machines, with their own spacefaring culture, quite unlike myself, or the robot soldier devices of the Jophur. Their ways are strange. Nevertheless, they seem quite willing to take us with them through the transfer point. That is a much better situation than we faced a while ago."

Rety watched the "sail" uneasily. Soon she made out a glittering nest of complex shapes that lay at the very center of the smooth, mirrorlike surface. As the t-point burgeoned on one side and the machine-vessel on the other, she couldn't stave off a wild sensation—like being cornered between a steep cliff and a predator.

"This thing . . ." she began asking, with a dry mouth. "This thing comin' to *save* us. Do you know what it was doin' here, before Izmunuti blew up?"

"It is seldom easy understanding other life orders," the tutor explained. *"But in this case the answer is simple. It is a class of device called a Harvester/Salvager. Such machines collect raw materials to be used in various engineering or construction projects. It must have been using the sail to gather metal atoms from the star's rich wind when the storm struck. But given an opportunity, a harvester will collect the material it needs from any other source of accumulated or condensed . . ."*

The artificial voice trailed off as the tutor's face froze.

The pause lasted several duras.

"Any other source," Dwer repeated the phrase in a low mutter. "Like a derelict ship, drifting through space, maybe?"

Rety felt numb.

The tutor did not say *"oops."*

Not exactly.

It wasn't necessary.

Two young humans watched claws, grapplers, and scythe-like blades unfurl as strong fields seized their vessel, drawing it toward a dark opening at the center of a broad expanse of filmy light.

LARK

Something was happening.

The deck shuddered and vibrated. Muffled thuds penetrated through the spongy walls, puzzling him at first.

Then Lark recalled the first time he had heard such sounds—just after he and Ling were captured, when the Six Races of Jijo had surprised their tormentors by attacking this battle cruiser with crude rockets.

On a monitor screen he had watched explosive-filled tree trunks blaze like avenging spirits through the sky above the Slope, hundreds of them, handmade by the finest artisans of the Six Races and dispatched on a mission of vengeance. He remembered praying that some of the fiery missiles would get through—to end his life along with all the loathsome Jophur invaders aboard this cruel ship.

Then came that muted rumbling.

"Defensive counterfire." Ling had identified the sound as Jophur weapons spoke.

One by one, the natives' proud missiles had evaporated, well short of their target . . . and Lark had to reconcile himself with remaining alive.

This time, the tempo of jarring quivers rattled the ship ten times as fast.

It sounds pretty frantic. I wonder who the greasy stacks are fighting this time.

Alas, his pursuers gave Lark no time to ponder it. Whatever was going on in space beyond, the hunter robots kept up their relentless and systematic search through twisty corridors, blocking every effort to sneak past them, constantly hemming him northward along the great ship's axis.

Hissing Jophur soldiery accompanied the posse, operating in groups of three or more. And on several occasions he also heard a human voice, male, shouting suggestions to help chase down one of his own kind.

Rann.

Lark had few options. With the traitor taking part, he didn't dare try his luck again with the purple ring, whose usefulness was probably finished anyway. So, he fled back toward the place where he and Ling had once made their brief attempt at sabotage, throwing a pathetic little bomb at the Jophur nerve center, then fleeing together in triumph amid clouds of smoke, running and laughing as they played spy, using their purple pass-ring to go almost anywhere, defying the enemy to catch them.

Of course it hadn't felt like that much fun at the time. Only in contrast to Lark's present misery did it seem a carefree episode. A frolic. He'd give anything to go back to that time. Even creeping about as half-naked vermin in an alien ship, he had been happy with Ling at his side.

More than a day must have passed since he'd last had any rest. Food became a fading memory, and there was no leisure anymore to explore chambers along the way—only the tense wariness of a prey animal, fighting desperately to stave off the inevitable.

Mysterious vibrations intensified, punctuated by other noises that boomed or crackled faintly in the distance. The normal pungency of Jophur hallway aromatics thickened with new scentomeres, wafting through the ventilation system. Some were too strange or complex for him to decipher, but *fear* and *revulsion* were almost identical to traeki versions he knew from growing up on Jijo.

Something had the crew very upset.

Queasy sensations warned Lark of shifts in the ship's artificial gravity, making the floor seem to tilt, then briefly lose pressure against the soles of his feet. The steady background hum of engines increased pitch and intensity. Lark was tempted to duck into a nearby chamber and try to activate a view screen, just to find out what was going on. But any room might become a trap while his pursuers were so close.

A few duras later, he felt a nervous shiver on the back of his neck that warned him of approaching robots—a fey sensitivity to their suspensor fields that had saved him more than once so far. The scent of approaching Jophur soldiery reinforced his decision.

Back the other way, quickly!

Though weary, he sped up, trying to reach one of the ramps leading to the next level. Of course, with each move north the width of his domain narrowed, leaving him fewer options. Soon, they would harry him into a corner with no escape. . . .

Lark scurried around a bend, only to brake sharply, with a grunt of dismayed surprise.

Just a few meters ahead of him, Rann let out a shout. The tall Danik warrior yelled at a golden bracelet on his wrist. "I've got the son of a bitch!"

Lark spun about and fled, seeking the only remaining branch tunnel that seemed free of foes. Behind him, Rann could be heard switching to GalTwo—more useful at communicating with Jophur than vulgar Anglic cursing.

"To this locale, speed quickly and urgently. The quarry, it is near!"

Lark considered halting. Finding a corner to hide behind and ambush Rann as he hurried after. Better to face the human traitor alone, and possibly do Rann harm, than wind up facing a swarm of Jophur and their robots, who would be invulnerable to his fists.

But he chose to stay free, if only for a few moments longer, dashing down the sole remaining escape path—a narrow corridor, probably leading nowhere.

Sure enough, exultant cries followed, and Lark knew he was cornered when he saw the dead end, no more than forty meters ahead.

He halted by a closed doorway, fumbling with shaky hands to bring the purple ring up against the lock plate. It sprayed a soft mist, but either the torus was tired or the Jophur commanders had learned their lesson. The door stayed adamantly shut.

Lark heard a cry of satisfaction as Rann spied him from the far intersection. But the Danik waited for others—Jophur and their machines—to join him before approaching any closer. For several duras the two of them just stared at each other in mutual loathing. Then Rann smiled as a Jophur and two robots joined him. They started to advance.

Suddenly, from Lark's other side, there came a low reverberation and a growing sense of heat. He turned around, backing away from the bulkhead where the hallway ended. That blank wall began glowing and bowing outward. Molten droplets oozed from the edges of an oval that blazed brightly, forcing him to raise both hands and shield his eyes. Lark gagged on an odor he recalled from visits to the laboratory of the Explosers Guild, in Tarek Town—hydrogen sulfide gas.

As the oval slumped inward, he briefly glimpsed another twisty corridor beyond, glowing with an eerie light. Lark turned to flee, but a wave of hot vapors slammed his back, knocking him down. His forearms struck the deck painfully hard while a surge of baked air passed overhead and on down the hall, toward Rann and his companions.

For an instant, Lark's senses were in such an uproar that he felt swaddled by numbness. No information could get through, except pain . . . and the fact that he still lived. When he managed to open his eyes once more, Lark blinked in disbelief.

Down the corridor, where moments ago his hunters had been marching confidently to capture him, he now glimpsed the last of them fleeing round the corner. Rann glanced back, terror in his pale eyes, and Jophur warriors heaved their bulky forms out of sight. Only two robots remained at the intersection, taking up defensive stances, but not firing—as if loath to try.

Lark knew he should be happy of anything that put his enemies to flight. Yet, he felt reluctant to roll over and see what had arrived. *I just know I'm not gonna like this,* he thought.

The rotten egg smell was almost overpowering, and a faint luminance filled the hall, coming from above and behind his prone form, along with a faint, whispering hum.

Gathering his courage, Lark pushed off the floor with his scalded right arm, rolling onto his back.

It stood a few paces behind him, just this side of the hole it had made in the bulkhead. A glowing ball, roughly three meters across, barely able to squeeze through the corridor. Though it had the color of bronze metal, the intruder seemed to ooze and ripple as it rolled slowly forward, more like a fluid-filled bag than a balloon. Lark recalled the living cells he used to watch through his beloved microscope, back when he and other sages had the time to pursue knowledge, doing what passed for science on the primitive Slope.

A cell, many times his size. Living.

And yet, all at once, Lark knew—

This is like no life I ever saw before.

The thing made sloshing sounds as it crept languidly toward Lark, swarming over his foot, climbing upward, rendering him immobile, then causing a chill numbness to spread along his bones.

PART TWO

THE ORDERS OF LIFE

For ages—ever since the blessed Progenitors departed—some contemplative oxygen-breathing races have wondered about the question of "plenitude."

If life is so common and vibrant here in the Five Linked Galaxies, they ask, should we not expect to see signs of it elsewhere? Astronomers have counted seven hundred billion other galactic pinwheels, ovals, and other vast conglomerations of stars out there, some of them even bigger than our own Galaxy One. It seems to defy all logic that ours would be the only nexus where sapiency has arisen.

What a waste of potential, if it were so!

Of course, this opinion is not universally shared. Among the many social-religious alliances making up our diverse civilization, some insist that we must be unique, since any other situation would only mock the ultimate greatness of the Progenitors. Others perceive those billions of other galaxies as heavenly abodes where the august Transcendents go, once they complete the long process of perfecting themselves on this plane of reality.

Many have tried to pierce the veil with scientific instruments, such as vast telescopes, aimed at studying our silent neighbors. Indeed, some anomalies have been found. For instance, several targets emit rhythmic noise pulsations of towering complexity. Other galaxies seem burned out, as if a recent conflagration tore through them, destroying nearly every planetary system at the same time.

And yet, the data always seems ambiguous, allowing a variety of interpretations. The Great Library is filled with arguments that have raged for aeons.

Are other galactic groups linked together by hyperspatial transfer points, the way our own five spirals are, despite huge separations in flat spacetime? Our best models and calculations do not give definitive answers.

From time to time, some young race gets impatient and tries posing these questions to the Old Ones—those sage species who have surrendered starships to develop their souls within the Embrace of Tides, passing on to the next order of life.

Depending on their mood, the ancients either ignore such entreaties or reply in frustrating ways.

We are alone, answered one community of venerable ones.

No, we are not, countered a second. Other galaxies are just like ours, teeming with multitudinous sapient species, taking turns uplifting each other as a sacred duty, then turning their attention toward the duties of transcendence . . . as we are doing now.

One cluster of Old Ones claimed to know a different answer—that most island universes are settled quite suddenly, by the first race to achieve spaceflight. These first races then proceed to fill every star system, annihilating or enslaving all succeeding life-forms. Such galaxies are poor in diversity or insight, having lacked the wisdom that our blessed Progenitors showed, when they began the great chain of Uplift.

That is wrong, claimed yet another assembly of venerables in their spiky habitat, huddled amid contemplative tides. The unity of purpose that we sense in such galaxies only means that they have already evolved toward united oneness! A high state wherein all sapient beings participate in a grand overmind . . .

Finally, it grew clear that these conflicting stories must mean just one of two things.

Either the Old Ones really have no idea what they are talking about, or else . . .

Or else their varied answers together comprise a sermon. A basic lesson.

Other galaxies are none of our business! That is what they are teaching. We should get back to the proper tasks of young races—struggling, learning, uplifting, and striving with each other, gathering experience and strength for the next phase.

Answers will be forthcoming to each of us who survives the testing, when we ultimately face the bright light of the Great Harrower.

HARRY

It seemed that E space was not the only realm where *ideas* had a life of their own. On his return, Harry found Kazzkark Base teeming with hearsay. Strange rumors roamed like ravenous parasites, springing from one nervous being to the next, thriving in an atmosphere of contagious anxiety.

Steering his scoutcraft to the planetoid's north pole, Harry docked at a slip reserved for the Navigation Institute and cut power with a sense of relief. All he wanted now was to sleep for several days without having to endure relentless exhausting dreams. But no sooner did he debark and begin the protocols of reentry than he found himself immersed in a maelstrom of dubious gossip.

"It is said that the Abdicator Alliance has broken into several heretical factions that are fighting among themselves," murmured a tourmuj trade representative standing in line ahead of Harry at immigration, chattering in hasty Galactic Four. "And the League of Prudent Neutral Clans are said to have begun mobilizing at last, combining their fleets under pargi command!"

Harry stared at the tourmuj—a lanky, sallow-skinned being that seemed all elbows and knees—before responding in the same language.

"Said? It is said by whom? In which medium? With what veracity?"

"With no veracity at all!" This came from an oulomin diplomat whose tentacle fringes bore colored caps to prevent inadvertent pollen emission. Slithering just behind Harry, the oulomin expressed disdain toward the stooped tourmuj with sprays of orange saliva that barely missed Harry's arm.

"I have it on good authority that the eminent and much respected pargi intend to withdraw from the League—and from Galactic affairs entirely—out of disgust with the present state of chaos. That noble race will shortly move on to blessed retirement, joining their ancestral patrons in the fortunate realm of tides. Only a regressed fool would believe otherwise."

It was hardly the sort of speech that Harry would associate with "diplomacy." The tourmuj reacted by irately unfolding its long legs and both sets of arms so swiftly that its knobby head bumped the ceiling. Wincing in pain, the trader stomped off, sacrificing its place in line.

Oh, I get it, Harry thought, glancing once more at the being behind him, whose grasp of other-species psychology was evident.

Just don't try the same on me, he thought. *I'm not budging, even if you call me a dolphin's uncle.*

The diplomat seemed to recognize this and merely waved two tendrils in a universal gesture of placid goodwill, as they both moved forward.

Harry took out his portable data plaque and stroked its command knobs, swiftly accessing the planetoid's Galactic Library unit for news. It was an excellent branch, since Kazzkark housed local headquarters for several important institutes. Yet, the master index claimed to know nothing about an Abdicator schism. Moreover, according to official sources, the influential pargi were still active in Galactic councils, calling for peace and restraint, urging all militant alliances to withdraw their armadas and settle the present crisis through mediation, not war.

Were both rumormongers wrong, then? During normal times, Harry would scarcely doubt the master index. In the Civilization of Five Galaxies, it was commonly said that nothing ever *really* happened until it was logged by the Great Library. A planet might explode before your eyes, but it wasn't a certified fact without the rayed spiral glyph, flashing in a corner of a readout screen.

Clearly these weren't "normal times."

While taking his turn at the customs kiosk, Harry overheard a talpu'ur seed merchant complain to a guldingar pilgrim about how many nauseating thread changes she had had to endure during the crossing from Galaxy Three. Harry found it hard to follow the talpu'ur's dialect—a syncopated ratchet-rubbing of her vestigial wing cases—but it seemed that several traditional transfer points had shifted their oscillation patterns, either losing coherence or going off-line completely.

The slight, spiderlike guldingar answered in the same rhythmic idiom, speaking through a mechanical device strapped to one leg.

"Those explanations seem dubious. In fact, they are excuses given by great powers, as each attempts to seize and monopolize valuable hyperspatial links for its own strategic purposes."

Harry frowned. Worry made the fur itch beneath his uniform. If something was happening to the viability of t-points, the matter was of vital interest to the Navigation Institute. Once again, he referred to the Branch Library but found little information—just routine travel advisories and warnings of detours along some routes.

I'm sure Wer'Q'quinn will fill me in. The old serpent oughta know what's goin' on, if anybody does.

One topic Harry wanted to hear about, but none of the gossipers mentioned, was the Siege of Terra. Weeks ago, when he departed to patrol E Space, the noose around Earth and the Canaan Colonies had been drawing gradually tighter. Despite welcome assistance from the Tymbrimi and Thennanin, battle fleets from a dozen fanatical alliances had ceased their mutual bickering for a time, joining cause and pressing the blockade ever closer, choking off trade and communication to Harry's ancestral world.

Though tempted, he refrained from querying the Library about that. Given the present political situation—while his status was still probationary—it wouldn't be wise to make too many inquiries about his old clan. *I'm not supposed to care about that anymore. Navigation is my home now.*

After clearing customs, his next obstacle was all-too-unpleasantly familiar—a tall sour-faced hoon wearing the glossy robe of a senior patron. With a magisterial badge of the Migration Institute on one shoulder, Inspector Twaphu-anuph gripped a plaque flowing with data while scanners probed Harry's vessel. Every time Harry returned from a mission, he had to endure the big male biped's humorless black eyes scrutinizing his ship's bio-manifest for any sign of illicit genetic cargo, while that prodigious hoonish throat sac throbbed low rumblings of pompous scorn.

So, it rocked Harry back a bit when the brawny bureaucrat spoke up this time, using rolling undertones that seemed positively affable!

"I note that you have just returned from E Space," the inspector murmured in GalSeven, the spacer dialect most favored by Earthlings. "Hr-rm. Welcome home. I trust you had a pleasant, interesting voyage?"

Harry blinked, startled by the tone of informal friendliness. *What happened to the usual snub?* he wondered.

It was normal for Migrationists to act high and mighty. After all, their institute supervised matters of cosmic importance, such as where oxygen-breathing starfarers might colonize, and which oxy-worlds must lay fallow for a time, untouched by sapient hands. In contrast, Harry's organization was a "little cousin," with duties resembling the old-time coastal guardians of Earth's oceans—surveying hyperlink routes, monitoring spacetime conditions, and safeguarding lanes of travel for Galactic commerce.

"E Space is a realm of surprises," Harry responded cautiously. "But my mission went as well as can be expected. Thank you for asking."

A small, furry *rousit*—a servant-client of the hoon—moved alongside its master, aiming a recorder unit at Harry, making him increasingly nervous. The inspector meanwhile towered closer, pressing his inquiry.

"Of course I am asking purely out of personal curiosity, but would you mind enlightening me on one matter? Would you happen to have noticed any especially large memoid beings while you patrolled E Space? Hrrrm. Perchance a conceptual entity capable of extending beyond its native continuum, into . . . hrr-rr . . . other levels of reality?"

Almost instinctively, Harry grew guarded. Like many oxy-races, hoons could not bear the ambiguous conditions of E Space or the thronging allaphors inhabiting that weird realm. Small surprise, given their notorious lack of humor or imagination.

But then why this sudden interest?

Clearly, the awkward situation called for a mix of formal flattery and evasion. Harry fell back on the old *yes bwana* tactic.

"It is well known that meme organisms throng E Space like vacuum barnacles infesting a slow freighter," he said, switching to GalSix. "But alas <oh senior-patron-level entity> I saw only those creatures that my poor, half-uplifted brain allowed me subjectively to perceive. No doubt those impressions were too crude to interest an exalted being like yourself."

Harry hoped the warden would miss his sarcasm. In theory, all those who swore fealty to the Great Institutes were supposed to leave behind their old loyalties and prejudices. But ever since the disaster at NuDawn, everyone knew how hoons felt toward the upstarts of Earthclan. As a neo-chimpanzee—from a barely fledged client race, indentured to humans—Harry expected only snobbery from Twaphu-anuph.

"You are probably right about that <oh precocious-but-promising infant>" came the hoon's response. "Still, I remain <casually> interested in your observations. Might you have sighted any <exceptionally large or complex> memoids traveling in <close> company with transcendent life-forms?"

The inspector's data plaque was turned away, but its glow reflected off a patch of glossy chest scales, flashing familiar blue shades of approval. All checks on Harry and his vessel were complete. There was no legal excuse to hold him anymore.

He switched languages again, this time to Anglic, the tongue of wolflings.

"I'll tell you what, Twaphu-anuph. I'll do you a favor and make an official inquiry about that . . . in your name, of course."

Harry aimed his own plaque and pointedly took an ident-print before the warden could object.

"That is not necessary! I only asked informally, in order—"

Harry enjoyed interrupting.

"Oh, you needn't thank me. We are all sworn to mutual cooperation, after all. So, shall I arrange for the usual inter-institute discount and forward the report to you in care of Migration HQ? Will that do?"

Before the flustered hoon could respond, Harry continued.

"Good! Then according to the protocols of entry, and by your exalted leave, I guess I'll be going."

The little rousit scurried out of the way as Harry moved forward, silently daring the barrier to prevent him.

It swished aside, opening his path onto the avenues of Kazzkark.

Perhaps perversely, Harry found it exciting to live in a time of danger and change.

For almost half a galactic rotation—millions of years—this drifting, hollowed-out stone had been little more than a sleepy outpost for Galactic civil servants, utilizing but a fraction of the prehistoric shafts that some extinct race once tunneled through a hundred miles of spongy rock. Then, in just the fifteen kaduras since Harry was assigned here, the planetoid transformed. Catacombs that had lain silent since the *Ch'th'turn* Epoch hummed again as more newcomers arrived every day. Over the course of a couple of Earth years, a cosmopolitan city came to life where each cavity and corridor offered a melange for the senses—a random sampling of the full range of oxy-life culture.

Some coincidence, Harry thought sardonically. *It's almost as if all this was waiting to happen, until I came to Kazzkark.*

Of course, the truth was a little different. In fact, he was one of the least important free sapients walking around these ancient halls.

Walking . . . and scooting, slithering, creeping, ambling . . . name a form of locomotion and you could see it being used. Those too frail to stand in half an Earth gravity rolled everywhere on graceful carts, some with the sophistication of miniature spaceships. Harry even saw a dozen or so members of a long-armed species that looked something like gibbons—with purple, upside-down faces—leaping and brachiating from convenient bars and handholds set in the high ceiling. He wanted to laugh and hoot at their antics, but their race had probably been piloting starcraft back when humans lived in caves. Galactics seldom had what he would call a sense of humor.

Not long ago, a majority of those living on Kazzkark wore uniforms of MigrInst, NavInst, WarInst, or the Great Library. But now those dressed in livery made a small minority, lost amid a throng. The rest sported wildly varied costumes, from full body enviro suits and formal robes bearing runes describing their race genealogy and patronymics, all the way to beings who strode unabashedly naked—or with just an excretory-restraint cloth—revealing a maximum of skin, scale, feather, or torg.

When he first entered service, most Galactics seemed unable to tell a neo-chimpanzee from a plush recliner, so obscure and unimportant was the small family of Terra. But that had changed lately. Quite a few faces turned and stared as Harry walked by. Beings nudged each other to point, sharing muted utterances—a sure sign that the *Streaker* crisis hadn't been solved while he was away. Clearly Earthclan was still gaining a renown it never sought.

A venerable Galactic expression summed up the problem.

"Look ye to peril—in attracting unplanned notice from the mighty."

Still, for the most part it was easy enough to feel lost in the crowd as he took a long route back to headquarters, entranced by how much busier things had become since he left on patrol.

Using his plaque to scan immigration profiles, Harry knew that many of these sophonts were emissaries and commercial delegates, sent by their race, alliance, or corporation to seek some advantage as the staid routines of civilization dissolved in an age of rising misgivings. There were opportunities to be gained from chaos, so agents and proxies maneuvered, playing venerable games of espionage. Compacts were made and broken. Bribes were offered and loyalties compromised in double-cross gambits so ornate that the court intrigues of the Medicis might have occurred in a sandbox. Small clans, without any stake in galacto-politics or the outcome of fleet engagements, nevertheless swarmed about, endeavoring to make themselves useful to great powers like the Klesh, Soro, or Jophur, who in turn spent lavishly, seeking an edge over their foes.

With so much portable wealth being passed around, an economy flourished serving the needs of each emissary, deputy, merchant or spy. Almost a million free sophonts and servitor machines saw to the visitors' biotic needs, from distinct atmospheric preferences to exotic foodstuffs and intoxicants.

It's a good thing we chims had to give up some of our sense of smell, trading the brain tissue for use in sapience, Harry thought as he sauntered along the Great Way—a mercantile avenue near the surface of Kazzkark, stretching from pole to pole, where bubble domes interrupted the rocky ceiling every few kilometers to show dazzling views of an inner spiral arm of Galaxy Five. This passage had been a ghostly corridor when he first came from training at Navigation Central. Now shops and restaurants filled every niche, casting an organic redolence so thick that any species would surely find something toxic in the air. Most visitors underwent thorough antiallergic treatments to prepare their immune systems before leaving quarantine. And even so, many walked the Great Way wearing respirators.

Harry found the experience heady. Every few meters, fresh aromatics assailed his nostrils and sinuses. Some provoked waves of delight or overpowering hunger. Others brought him to the brink of nausea.

It kind of reminds me of New York, he pondered, recalling that brief time on Earth.

His ears also verged on sensory overload. The dozen or so standard Galactic tongues came in countless dialects, depending on how each race made signals. Sound was the most frequent carrier of negotiation or gossip, and the buzzing, clicking, groaning clamor of several hundred species types made the Great Way seem to throb with physical waves of intrigue. Those preferring visual gestures made things worse by waving, dancing, or flashing message displays that Harry found at once both beautiful and intimidating.

Then there's psi.

Stern rules limited how adepts might use the "vivid spectrum" indoors. Vigilant detectors caught the most egregious offenders. Still, Harry figured part of his tension came from a general background of psychic noise.

Fortunately, most neo-chims are deaf to psi stuff. Some of the same traits that made a good observer in E Space also kept him semi-immune to the cacophony of mental vibrations filling Kazzkark right now.

Of course, many of the "restaurants" were actually shielded sites of rendezvous, where informal meetings could take place, sometimes between star clans registered as enemies under edicts of the Institute for Civilized Warfare. Harry glimpsed a haughty, lizard-like Soro, accompanied by a minimal retinue of Pila and Paha clients, slip into a shrouded establishment whose proprietor at once turned off the flashing "Available" sign . . . but left the door ajar, as if expecting one more customer.

It might have been interesting to stand around and see who entered next to parley with the Soro matriarch, but Harry spotted at least a dozen loiterers who were already doing that very thing, pretending to read info-plaques or sample wares from street vendors, while always keeping clear line of sight to the dimmed entranceway.

Harry recalled the clumsy effort of the hoon inspector to probe him about E Space. As trust in the Institutes unraveled, everyone seemed eager for supplementary data, perhaps hoping a little extra might make a crucial difference.

He couldn't afford to be mistaken for another spy. Especially not in uniform. Some of the other great services might be showing signs of strain, losing their trustworthiness and professionalism, but Navigation had an unsullied reputation to uphold.

Passing a busy intersection, Harry glimpsed a pair of racoonish Synthian traders, whose folk had a known affinity for Terran art and culture. They were too far away to make eye contact, but he was distracted by the sight and moments later carelessly bumped into the bristly, crouched form of a Xatinni.

Oh, hell, he thought as the ocelot face whirled toward him with a twist of sour hatred. Wasting no time, Harry ducked his head and crossed both arms before him in the stance of a repentant client, backing away as the creature launched into a tirade, berating him in shrill patronizing tonal clefts of GalFour.

"To explain this insolent interruption! To abase thyself and apologize with groveling sincerity! To mark this affront on the long list of debts accumulated by your clan of worthless—"

Not a great power, the Xatinni routinely picked on Earthlings for the oldest reason of bullies anywhere—because they could.

"To report in three miduras at my apartment for further rebukes, at the following address! Forty-seven by fifty-two Corridor of the—"

Fortunately, at that moment a bulky Vriiilh came gallumping down the avenue, grunting ritual apologies to all who had to scoot aside before the amiable behemoth's two-meter footsteps. The Xatinni fell back with an angry yowl as the Vriiilh pushed between them.

Harry took advantage of the interruption to escape by melting through the crowd.

So long, pussycat, he thought, briefly wishing he could psi cast an insult as he fled. Instead of shameful abasement, he would much rather have smacked the Xatinni across the kisser—and maybe removed a few excess limbs to improve the eatee's aerodynamics. *I hope we meet again sometime, in a dark alley with no one watching.*

Alas, self-control was the first criterion looked for by the Terragens Council, before letting any neo-chim head unsupervised into the cosmos at large. Small and weak, Earthclan could not afford incidents.

Yeah . . . and a fat lotta good that policy did us in the long run.

They gave dolphins a starship of their own, and look what the clever fishies went and did. They stirred up the worst crisis in Ifni-knows-how-many millions of years.

If the honest truth be told, it made Harry feel just a little jealous.

Beyond those coming to Kazzkark on official business, the streets and warrens supported a drifting population of others—refugees from places disrupted by the growing chaos, plus opportunists, altruists, and mystics.

The lattermost seemed especially plentiful, these days.

On most worlds, matters of philosophy or religion were discussed at a languid pace, with arguments spanning slow generations and even being passed from a patron race to the clients of its clients, over the course of aeons. But here and now, Harry detected something frenetic about the speeches being given by missionaries who had set up shop beneath Dome Sixty-Seven. While clusters and nebulae shimmered overhead, envoys of the best-known denominations offered ancient wisdom from perfumed pavilions—among them the Inheritors, the Awaiters, the Transcenders . . . and the Abdicators, showing no apparent sign of fragmentation as red-robed acolytes from a dozen species hectored passersby with their orthodox interpretations of the Progenitors' Will.

Harry knew there were many aspects of Galactic Civilization he would never understand, no matter how long or hard he tried. For instance, how could great alliances of sapient races feud for whole epochs over minute differences in dogma?

He wasn't alone in this confusion. Many of Earth's greatest minds stumbled over such issues as whether the fabled First Race began the cycle of Uplift two billion years ago as a manifestation of predetermined physical law—or as an emergent property of self-organizing systems in a pseudovolutionary universe. All Harry ever figured out was that most disputes revolved around how oxy-life became sapient, and what its ultimate destiny might be as the cosmos evolved.

"Not exactly worth killing anybody over," he snorted. "Or *gettin'* killed, for that matter."

Then again, humans could hardly claim complete innocence. They had slaughtered countless numbers of their own kind over differences even more petty and obscure during Earth's long dark isolation before Contact. Before bringing light to Harry's kind.

"Now *this* is new," he mused, pausing at the far end of the dome.

Beyond the glossy pavilions of the main sects, an aisle had opened featuring proselytes of a shabbier sort, preaching from curtained alcoves and stony niches, or even wandering the open Way, proclaiming unconventional beliefs.

"Go ye hence from this place!" screeched a dour-looking pee'oot with a spiral neck and goggle eyes. *"For each of you, but one place offers safety from the upheavals to come. That is the wellspring where you began!"*

Harry had to decode the heretical creed from highly inflected Galactic Three. Use of the Collective-Responsive case meant that the Pee'oot was referring to salvation of *species,* of course, not individuals. Even heresy had its limits.

Is he saying each race should return to its homeworld? The mudball where its presapient ancestors evolved and were first adopted by some patron for Uplift?

Or did the preacher refer to something more allegorical?

Perhaps he means that each chain of Uplift is supposed to seek knowledge of its own legacy, distinct from the others. That would call for breaking up the Institutes and letting every oxy-life clan go its own way.

Of course, Harry wasn't equipped to parse out the fine points of Galactic theology, nor did he really care. Anyway, the next zealot was more interesting to watch.

A komahd evangelist—with a tripod lower torso but humanoid trunk and arms—looked jovial and friendly. Its lizard-like head featured a broad mouth that seemed split by a permanent happy grin, while long eyelashes made the face seem almost beguiling. But a single, fat rear leg thumped a morose beat while the komahd chanted in GalSix. Its sullen tale belied those misleadingly cheerful features.

"All our <current, lamentable> social disruptions have their roots in a <despicable, nefarious> plot by the enemies of all oxygen-breathing life!

"See how our great powers and alliances bleed each other, wasting their armed might, struggling and striving in search of <vague> hints and clues to a <possible, though unlikely> return of the <long-gone> Progenitors!

"This can only serve the interests of <inscrutable, inimical> hydrogen breathers! Jealous of our <quick, agile> speed and <high> metabolisms, they have feared us for aeons, plotting <long, slow, vile> schemes. Now, at last, they are ready. See how the <wicked> hydros maneuver <malignly> for our <collective> end!

"Who does not recall how <very> recently we had to give up one of our Five Galaxies! Just half a million years ago, <the entirety of> Galaxy Four was declared 'fallow' and emptied of all <starfaring> oxy-life culture. Never before has the Migration Institute agreed to such a <wholesale, traitorous> ceding of territory, whose resettlement repercussions are still being felt!

"We are told that the hydros <in return> abandoned <all of> Galaxy Five, but do we not <daily> hear reports of strange sightings and perturbations in normal space that can only be work of the <perfidious> Zang? "What of the <disrupted> transfer points? What of <vast> tracts in <level-A and Level-B> hyperspace that now turn sluggish and unusable? Why do the <great but suspiciously silent> Institutes not tell us the truth?"

* * *

The komahd finished by pointing an all-too-humanlike finger straight at Harry, who in his uniform seemed a convenient representative of NavInst. Blushing under his fur, Harry backed away quickly.

Too bad. That was starting to get interesting.

At least someone's complaining about the stupid way the Soro and other powers are acting. And the komahd's message was about the future, instead of the regular obsession with the past. All right, it's a bit paranoid. But if more sophonts believed it, they might ease the pressure off Earth and give those poor dolphins a chance to come home.

Harry found it ironic then that the freethinking Komahd generally disliked Terrans. For his own part, Harry rather fancied their looks, and thought they smelled pretty good, too. What a pity the admiration wasn't reciprocal.

A ruckus from behind made him swivel around—just in time to join a crowd scooting hurriedly toward the nearest wall! Harry felt a shiver course his spine when he saw what was coming. A squadron of twenty frightening, mantis-like Tandu warriors, unarmed but still equipped with deadly, razor-sharp claws, trooped single file down the middle of the boulevard, the tops of their waving eye pods almost brushing the corrugated ceiling. Everyone who saw them coming scurried aside. No one argued right of way with a Tandu, nor did any vendors try to hawk wares at the spiky-limbed beings.

Before departing on his latest mission, Harry had seen a Tandu bite off the head of an obstinate Paha who had proudly refused to give way. Almost at once, the leader of that Tandu group had reproved the assailant by casually chopping its brother to bits. By that act, a simple tit-for-tat justice was served, preventing any action by authorities. And yet, the chief lesson was clear to all and sundry.

Don't mess with us.

No inquiry was ever held. Even the Paha's commanders had to admit that its bravado and demise amounted to a case of suicide.

Harry's pulse raced till the terrifying squadron entered a side avenue and passed out of sight.

I . . . better not dawdle anymore, he thought, suddenly feeling drained and oppressed by all the clamorous crowding. Wer'Q'quinn is gonna spit bile if I don't hand in my mission report soon.

He also wanted to ask the old snake about things he had heard and seen since landing—about hoons interested in E Space, and t-points going on the blink, and komahd preachers who claimed—

Harry's heart almost did a back flip when his shoulder was suddenly engulfed by a bony hand bigger than his forearm. Slim white fingers—tipped with suckers—gripped softly but adamantly.

He pivoted, only to stare up past an expanse of silver robe at a tall biped who must surely mass half a metric ton.

Its head was cast like a sea ship's prow, but where an ancient boat might have a single eye painted on each side, this creature had *two* pairs, one atop the other. A flat jaw extended beneath, resembling the ram of a Greek trireme.

It's . . . a Skiano . . . Harry recalled from the endless memory drills during training. He had never expected to encounter this race on the street, let alone have one accost him personally.

What've I done now? he worried, preparing to go through another humiliating kowtow and repentance. *At least the walking skyscraper can't accuse me of blocking his light.*

A colorful birdlike creature perched on one of the Skiano's broad shoulders, resembling an Earthly parrot.

"I beg your pardon for startling you, brother," the titan said mellowly, preempting Harry's apology. It spoke through a vodor device held in its other mammoth hand. The mouth did not move or utter sound. Instead, soft light flashed from its lower pair of eyes. The vodor translated this into audible sound.

"It seemed to me that you looked rather lost."

Harry shook his head. "Apologies for contradiction, elder patron. Your concern warms this miserable client-spawn. But I do know where I'm going. So, with thanks, I'll just be on my—"

The bird interrupted, squawking derisively.

"Idiot! Fool! Not your *body.* It's your soul. Your soul! Your soul!"

Only then did Harry realize—the conversation was taking place in Anglic, the wolfling tongue of his birth. He took a second squint at the bird.

Given the stringent requirements of flight, feathered avians had roughly similar shapes, no matter what oxy-world they originated on. Still, in this case there could be no mistake. It *was* a parrot. A real one. The yo-ho-ho and a bottle of rum kind . . . which made the Skiano seem even stranger than before.

Wrong number of eyes, Harry thought numbly. You should be wearing a patch over one—or even three! Also oughta have a peg leg . . . and a hook instead of a hand . . .

"Indeed, my good ape," the buzzing voice from the vodor went on, agreeing with the talking bird. "It is your soul that seems in jeopardy. Have you taken the time to consider its salvation?"

Harry blinked. He had never heard of a Skiano proselyte before, let alone one that preached in Anglic, wearing a smartass Terran bird as an accessory.

"You're talking about me," he prompted.

"Yes, you."

Harry blinked, incredulous.

"Me . . . personally?"

The parrot let out an exasperated raspberry, but the Skiano's eyes seemed to carry a satisfied twinkle. The machine sounds were joyous.

"At last, someone who quickly grasps the concept! But indeed, I should not be surprised that one of your noble lineage comprehends."

"Uh, noble lineage?" Harry repeated. No one had ever accused him of that before.

"Of course. You are from *Earth*! Blessed home of Moses, Jesus, Buddha, Mohammed, Tipler, and Weimberg-Chang! The abode where wolflings burst to sapience in a clear case of virgin birth, without intervention by any other race of Galactic sinners, but as an immaculate gift from the Cosmos itself!"

Harry stepped back, staring in blank amazement. But the Skiano followed.

"The world whence comes a notion that will change the universe forever. A concept that *you,* dear brother, must come help us share!"

The huge evangelist leaned toward Harry, projecting intense fervor through both sound and an ardent light in its eyes.

"The idea of a God who loves each *person!* Who finds importance not in your race or clan, or any grand abstraction, but every particular entity who is self-aware and capable of improvement.

"The Creator of All, who promises bliss when we join Him at the Omega Point.

"The One who offers salvation, not collectively, but to each individual soul."

Harry could do nothing but blink, flabbergasted, as his brain and throat locked in a rigor from which no speech could break free.

"Amen!" squawked the parrot. "Amen and hallelujah!"

ALVIN'S JOURNAL

For once *I* had the best view of what was going on. My pals—Ur-ronn, Huck, and Pincer—were all in other parts of the ship where they had to settle for what they could see on monitors. But I stood just a few arm's lengths from Dr. Baskin, sharing the commander's view while we made our escape from Izmunuti.

It all happened right in front of me.

Officially, I was in the Plotting Room to take care of the smelly glavers. But that job didn't amount to much more than feeding them an occasional snack of synthi pellets I kept in a pouch . . . and cleaning up when they made a mess. Beyond that, I was content to watch, listen, and wonder how I'd ever describe it all in my journal.

Nothing in my experience—either growing up in a little hoonish fishing port or reading books from the human past—prepared me for what happened during those miduras of danger and change.

I took some inspiration from Sara Koolhan. She's another sooner—a Jijo native like me, descended from criminal settlers. Like me, she never saw a starship or computer before this year. And yet, the young human's suggestions are heeded. Her advice is sought by those in authority. She doesn't seem lost when they discuss "circumferential thread boundaries" and "quantum reality layers." (My little autoscribe is handling the spelling, in case you wonder.) Anyway, I tell myself that if one fellow citizen of the Slope can handle all this strangeness, I should too.

Ah, but Sara was a sage and a wizard back home, so I'm right back where I started, hoping to narrate the actions of star gods and portray sights far stranger than we saw in the deepest Midden, relying on language that I barely understand.

(On Jijo, we use Anglic to discuss technical matters, since most books from the Great Printing were in that tongue. But it's different aboard *Streaker.* When scientific details have to be precise, they switch to GalSeven or GalTwo, using word-glyphs I find impenetrable . . . showing how much our Jijoan dialects have devolved.)

The caterwauling of the glavers was something else entirely. It resembled no idiom I had ever heard before! Enhanced and embellished by the Niss Machine, their noise reached out across the heavens, while a terrifying Zang vessel bore down toward *Streaker,* intent on blasting our atoms through the giant star's whirling atmosphere.

Even if the approaching golden globule was bluffing—if it veered aside at the last moment and let us pass—we would only face another deadly force. The Jophur battleship that had chased *Streaker* from Jijo now hurtled to cut us off from the only known path out of this storm-racked system.

Without a doubt, Gillian Baskin had set us on course past a gauntlet of demons.

Still, the glavers bayed and moaned while tense duras passed.

Until, finally, the hydrogen breathers replied!

That screeching racket was even worse. Yet, Sara slapped the plotting table and exulted.

"So the legend is true!"

All right, I should have known the story too. I admit, I spent too much of my youth devouring ancient Earthling novels instead of works by our own Jijoan scholars. Especially the collected oral myths and sagas that formed our cultural heritage before humans joined the Six Races and gave us back literacy.

Apparently, the first generation of glaver refugees who came to our world spoke to the g'Keks who were already there, and told them something about their grounds for fleeing the Civilization of Five Galaxies. Centuries before their kind trod the Path of Redemption, the glavers explained something of their reason for self-banishment.

It seems they used to have a talent that gave them some importance long ago, among the starfaring clans. In olden times, they were among the few races with a knack for conversing with hydrogen breathers! It made them rich, serving as middlemen in complex trade arrangements . . . till they grew arrogant and careless. Something you should never do when dealing with Zang.

One day, their luck ran out. Maybe they betrayed a confidence, or took a bribe, or failed to make a major debt payment. Anyway, the consequences looked pretty grim.

In compensation, the Zang demanded the one thing glavers had left.

Themselves.

At least that's how Sara relayed the legend to Gillian and the rest of us, speaking breathlessly while time bled away and the glavers howled and we plunged ever closer to a vast, threatening space leviathan.

Piecing together what was happening, I realized the glavers weren't actually *talking* to the Zang. After all, they've reached redemption and are now presapient beings, nearly bereft of speech.

But the Zang have long memories, and our glavers seemed instinctively—maybe at some genetically programmed level—to know how to yowl just one meaningful thing. One phrase to let their ancient creditors know.

Hey! It is us! We're here! It's us!

To this identifying ululation, all the Niss Machine had to add/overlay was a simple request.

Kindly get those Jophur bastards off our butts.

Help us get away from here.

Anxious moments passed. My spines frickled as we watched the Zang loom closer. I felt nervous as an urs on a beach, playing tag with crashing waves.

Then, just as it seemed to be swooping for the kill, our would-be destroyer abruptly swerved! A climactic screech came over the loudspeakers. It took the Niss several duras, consulting with the Library unit, to offer a likely translation.

Come with us now.

Just like that, our nemesis changed into an escort, showing us the way. Leading *Streaker* out of Izmunuti's angry chaos.

We took our place in convoy as the Zang ship gathered the surviving harvester machines, fleeing toward the old transfer point.

Meanwhile, one of its companion vessels turned to confront our pursuers.

Long-distance sensors depicted a face-off between omnipotent titans.

The showdown was awesome to behold, even at a range that made it blurry. I listened to Lieutenant Tsh't describe the action for Sara.

"Those are hellfire missiles-s-s," the dolphin officer explained as the Jophur battleship accelerated, firing glittering pinpoints at its new adversary.

The sap-rings must want the dolphins awful bad, I thought. If they're willing to fight their way past that monster to get at *Streaker*.

The Zang globule was even bigger than the Jophur . . . a quivering shape that seemed more like gelatin, or something oozing from a wounded traeki, than solid matter. Once, I thought I glimpsed shadowy figures moving within, like drifting clouds or huge living creatures swimming through an opaque fluid.

Small bits of the main body split off, like droplets spraying from a gobbet of grease on a hot griddle. These did not hasten with the same lightning grace as the Jophur missiles. They seemed more massive. And relentless.

One by one, each droplet swelled like an inflating balloon, interposing its expanding surface between the two warships. Jophur weapons maneuvered agilely, striving to get past the obstructions, but nearly all the missiles were caught by one bubble or another, triggering brilliant explosions.

From her massive walking machine, watching the fight with one cool gray eye, Tsh't commented. "The Zang throws parts of its own substance ahead, in order to defend itself-f-f. So far, it has taken no offensive action of its own."

I recall thinking hopefully that this meant the hydros were of a calm nature, less prone to savage violence than we are told by the sagas. Perhaps they only meant to delay the Jophur long enough for us to get away.

Then I reconsidered.

Let's say this help from hydrogen breathers lets *Streaker* make good her escape. That's great for the Earthlings—and maybe for the Five Galaxies—but it still leaves Jijo in a mess. The Jophur will be able to call reinforcements and do anything they want to the people of the Slope. Slaughter all the g'Kek. Transform all the poor traeki. Burn down the archive at Biblos and turn the Slope into their private genetic farm, breeding the other races into pliable little client life-forms. . . .

Gillian's earlier plan, to draw the battleship after us into a deadly double suicide, would have caused my own death, and that of everyone else aboard—but my homeworld might then have been safe.

The trade-offs were stark and bitter. I found myself resenting the older woman for making a choice that spared my life.

I also changed my mind about the Zang.

Well? What're you waiting for? Shoot back!

The Jophur were oxygen beings like myself, distant relatives, sharing some of the same DNA that had spread around the galaxies during a predawn era before Progenitors arose to begin the chain of Uplift.

Nevertheless, right then I was cheering for their annihilation by true aliens. Beings from a strange, incomprehensible order of life.

Come on, Zang. Fry the big ugly ring stacks!

But things went on pretty much the same as distance narrowed between the two giants. The globule spent itself prodigiously to block missiles and gouts of deadly fire from the great dreadnought. Yet despite this, some rays and projectiles got through, impacting the parent body with bitter violence. Fountains of gooey material spewed across the black background, sparkling gorgeously as they burned. Waves rippled and convulsed across the Zang ship. Still it forged on while the glavers yowled, seeming to urge the hydros on.

"*T-point insertion approaching,*" announced a dolphin's amplified voice. It had a fizzing quality that meant the speaker was breathing oxygen-charged water, so it must be coming from the bridge. "*All hands prepare for transition. Kaa says our guides are acting strange. They're choosing an unconventional approach pattern, so this may get rough!*"

Gillian and Sara gripped their armrests. The dolphins in the Plotting Room caused their walkers' feet to splay out and magnetize, gripping the floor. But there was little for me and the glavers to do except stare about with wild, feral eyes. In the forward viewer, I now saw the starscape interrupted by a twist of utter blackness. Computer-generated lines converged while figures and glyphs made Sara murmur with excitement.

I watched the ship ahead of us, the first Zang globule, shiver almost eagerly as it plunged at a steep angle toward the twist. . . .

Then it *fell* in a direction I could not possibly describe if my life depended on it.

A direction that I never, till that moment, knew existed.

I glanced quickly at the rearward display. It showed the other hydro vessel shaking asunder before repeated fierce blows as the Jophur battle cruiser fired desperately with short-range weapons. The two behemoths were almost next to each other now, matched in velocity, still racing after us.

A final, frantic hammering ripped through the Zang ship, tearing it into several unraveling gobs.

For a moment, I thought it was over.

I thought the Jophur had won.

Then two of those huge gobs *curled,* almost like living tendrils, and settled across the gleaming metal hull. They clung to its surface. Spreading. Oozing.

Somehow, despite the distance and flickering haze, I had the sense, of something probing for a way *in.*

Then the image vanished.

I turned back to the main viewer. Transition had begun.

KAA

There was a fine art to piloting a starship through the stretched geometries of a transfer point. No machine or logical algorithm could manage the feat alone.

Part of it involved playing hunches, knowing when to release the flange fields holding you to one shining thread and choosing just the right moment to make a leap—lasting both seconds and aeons—across an emptiness deeper than vacuum . . . then clamping nimbly to another slender discontinuity (without actually touching its deadly rim) and riding that one forward to your goal.

Even a well-behaved t-point was a maelstrom. A spaghetti tangle of shimmering arcs and folds, bending the cosmic fabric through multiple—and sometimes partial—dimensions.

A maze of dazzling, filamentary imperfections.

Stringlike cracks in the mirror of creation.

For those wise enough to use them well, the glowing strands offered a great boon. A way to travel safely from galaxy to linked galaxy, much faster than using hyperspace.

But to the foolish, or inattentive, their gift was a quick and flashy end.

Kaa loved thread-jumping more than any other part of spaceflight. Something about it meshed with both sides of neo-dolphin nature.

The new brain layers, added by human genecrafters, let him regard each strand as a *flaw* in the quantum metric, left behind when the universe first cooled from an inflating superheated froth, congealing like a many-layered cake to form the varied levels of real and hyperspace. That coalescence left defects behind—boundaries and fractures—where physical laws bent and shortcuts were possible. He could ponder all of that with the disciplined mental processes Captain Creideiki used to call the Engineer's Mind.

Meanwhile, in parallel, Kaa picked up different textures and insights through older organs, deep within his skull. Ancient bits of gray matter tuned for *listening*—to hear the swishing structure of a current, or judge the cycloid rhythms of a wave. Instruments probed the dense tangle of fossil topological boundaries, feeding him data in the form of *sonar images*. Almost by intuition, he could sense when a transfer thread was about to play out, and which neighboring cord he should clamp on to, sending *Streaker* darting along a new gleaming path toward her next goal.

Thomas Orley had once compared the process to "leaping from one roller coaster to another, in the middle of a thunderstorm."

Creideiki expressed it differently.

- *Converging nature*
    - *Begins and ends, lives and dies,*

• *Where tide meets shoal and sky . . .* •

Even during the expedition's early days—when the captain was still with them and *Streaker*'s brilliant chief pilot Keepiru handled all the really tough maneuvers—everyone had nevertheless agreed that there was nothing quite like a t-point ride with Kaa at the helm—an exuberance of daring, flamboyant maneuvers that never seemed to go wrong. Once, after a series of absurdly providential thread jumps let him break a million-year-old record, taking the crossing from Tanith to Calafia in five and a quarter mictaars, the crew bestowed on him a special nickname.

"Lucky."

In Trinary, the word-phrase meant much more than it did in Anglic. It connoted special favor in the fortune sea, the deep realm of chance where Ifni threw her dice and ancient dreamers crooned songs that were old before the stars were born.

It was a great honor. But some also say that such titles, once won, are hard to keep.

He started losing his during the fiasco at Oakka, that awful green world of betrayal, and things went rapidly downhill after that. By the time *Streaker* fled to a murky trash heap beneath Jijo's forlorn ocean, few called him Lucky Kaa anymore.

Then, in a matter of days, fate threw him the best and cruelest turns of all. He found love . . . and quickly lost it again when duty yanked Kaa away from his heart, sending him hurtling parsecs farther from Peepoe with each passing minute.

At the very moment she needed me most.

So he took little joy from this flight through a labyrinth of shimmering threads. Only grim professionalism sustained him.

Kaa had learned not to count on luck.

Behind him, the water-filled control room seemed eerily silent. Without opening his eyes or breaking concentration, Kaa felt the other crewfins holding tense rein over their reflex sonar clicking, in order not to disturb him.

They had cause for taut nerves. This transfer was like no other.

The reason gleamed ahead of *Streaker*—a vast object that Kaa perceived one moment as a gigantic jellyfish . . . then like a mammoth squid, with tentacles bigger than any starship he had ever seen. Its fluid profile, transformed for travel through the t-point's twisted bowels, gave him shivers. Instinct made Kaa yearn to get away—to cut the flanges and hop any passing thread, no matter where in the universe it might lead—just to elude that dreadful shape.

But it's our guide. And if we tried to get away, the Zang would surely kill us.

Kaa heard a faint caterwauling cry, coming from the dry chamber next door—the plotting room. By now he recognized the wailing sound of glavers, those devolved creatures from Jijo who had voluntarily returned to animal presapience. That alone would be enough to give him the utter willies, even without this bizarre affinity the bulge-eyed beasts seemed to have with a completely different order of life. That understanding offered *Streaker* a way clear of the dreaded Jophur, but at what cost?

Saved from one deadly foe, he pondered. *Only to face another that's feared all across Galactic Civilization.*

In fact, such dilemmas were becoming routine to the dolphin crew. The whole universe seemed filled with nothing but frying pans and fires.

They're getting ready, Kaa contemplated as a gentle throbbing passed along the tentacles of the squid-like shape ahead. Twice before, this had just preceded a jump maneuver. On both occasions, it had taken all his skill to follow without slamming *Streaker* into a nearby string singularity. The hydros used a thread-riding style unlike any he had seen before, following world lines that were more timelike than spacelike, triggering micro causality waves that nauseated everyone aboard. Nothing about the Zang method was any more efficient. Each jarring maneuver—and churning neural reflex—made Kaa want to swerve back and do it in a way that made more sense.

I could probably get you there in half the time, he thought resentfully toward the squishy, squid-shaped thing. *If you just told me where we're going.*

True, the resonances had changed since he last used this t-point, back when *Streaker* fled the horrid Fractal World, attempting Gillian's last desperate gamble . . . the "sooner's path," seeking a hiding place on far-off Jijo. When that second singularity nexus reopened near Izmunuti, it must have jiggered this one as well. Still, there *must* be an easier way to get where the Zang wanted to go than—

Sonar images merged into focus. He perceived a bright cluster of threads just ahead . . . a Gordian tangle with no spacelike strands at all.

Ugh! That ghastly clutter has got to be where the hydros are aiming, damn them.

And yet, listening carefully to the transposed sound portrait, he thought he could sense something about the knotty mess. . . .

You know, I'll bet I can guess which thread they're gonna take.

Kaa's attention riveted. This was important to him. More than duty and survival were at stake. Or the vaunted reputation neo-dolphin pilots had begun to earn among the Five Galaxies. Even regaining his nickname held little attraction anymore.

Only one thing really mattered to Kaa. Getting the job done. Delivering Gillian Baskin and her cargo safely. And then finding a way back to Jijo. Back to Peepoe. Even if it meant never piloting again. He triggered an alarm to warn the others.

Here we go!

The "squid" uncoiled, preparing for its final leap.

ALVIN'S JOURNAL

I am at a loss to describe even a single moment of our time inside the t-point.

Comparisons come to mind. Like a Founders' Day fireworks display. Or watching a clever urrish tinker throw sparkling exploser dust during a magic show, or . . .

Give up, Alvin.

All I really recall from that nauseating passage is a blur of dazzling ribbons waving across every monitor screen. While Sara Koolhan shouted ecstatically, watching her beloved mathematics come alive before her eyes, the more experienced Gillian Baskin kept grunting in dismayed surprise—a sound I found worrisome.

The gravity fields pitched and fluxed. Sparks flew from nearby instrument banks. Crew-fen stomped their walker machines close, dousing hot spots with inert gas. All told, this first-time space traveler figured we were experiencing no typical passage.

In fact, I soon felt too miserable to notice much of anything. I just spread my arms in a wide circle so the glavers could huddle inside, mewling pathetically. But the shrieking cry of *Streaker*'s engines tore through all my efforts to umble reassuringly.

Without any doubt, it was among the worst couple of miduras in my life, even when I compare it to the awful time when my friends and I fell off the edge of a subsea cliff in our broken *Wuphon's Dream*, with icy water jetting at my face as we tumbled toward the cold hell of Jijo's Midden.

At one point a dolphin cried out—*"Here we go!"*—and things rapidly got a whole lot worse. My second bowel did a lurch against my heart-spine. Then I found I couldn't breathe, as every sound around me abruptly ceased!

For a long, extended moment it felt like being swaddled in a dense bale of bec cotton, as if I were being torn from the universe, looking back at it from the end of a long tunnel, or from the bottom of a deep, deep well.

Then, just as suddenly, I was back! The cosmos swarmed around me again. A great weight seemed to lift off my vertebral spines, allowing me to inhale sharply.

We Jijoan hoons love our sailing ships, I thought, fighting off waves of queasiness. We never get sick at sea. But our star traveling ancestors must've been throwing up all the time, if this was how they had to get about. No wonder legends say they were such grouches.

Glancing up, I saw that Gillian and Sara were already on their feet, moving tensely toward the big display. Tsh't and the dolphin staff piloted their walkers to crowd just behind the humans, peering over their shoulders.

A bit shaky, I stood and joined them. On the main screen, all the roiling colors were dissipating fast. *Streaker*'s roaring engines dropped to a soft mutter as the ripple-swirls parted like folds of a curtain, revealing . . .

. . . stars.

I gazed at strange constellations.

Stars that are some damn Ifni-incalculable distance from the ones I know.

How is one supposed to feel when a long-held, impossible dream comes true?

Alvin, you are now a long, long way from home.

While I mused on that marvel, *Streaker* slowly turned. The shining skyscape flowed past our gaze—strange clusters, nebulae, and spiral arms whose light might not reach Jijo for thousands or millions of years—until at last we caught sight of our escort, the huge Zang ship-entity.

And the place where it was leading us.

A gasp shuddered through the Plotting Room, as every Earthling expressed the same emotion at once.

"Oh, no," groaned Lieutenant Tsh't. "It c-can't be!"

Dr. Gillian Baskin sighed.

"I don't believe it! All that misery . . . just to wind up *back here?*"

Before me, starting to fill the forward screen, there stretched yet another sight I could barely describe at first. A *structure* of some kind, nearly as black as space. Only when Gillian ordered further image enhancement did it stand forth from the background, glowing a deep shade of umber.

It looked roughly spherical, but *spiky* all around, like one of those burr seeds that stick to your leg fur when you go tramping through undergrowth. I thought it must be another mammoth starship, looming frightfully close.

Then I realized—we were still barreling along at great speed, but its apparent size was changing only very slowly.

It must be really huge, I realized, *shifting my imagination. Even bigger than the Zang ship!*

That jaundiced globule cruised alongside *Streaker,* shivering in a way that made me nervous. Scratchy noises assailed us again through the loudspeakers, making the glavers sway their big heads, rolling bulbous eyes and moaning.

"They say that we must follow," translated the Niss Machine.

Lieutenant Tsh't stuttered.

"Sh-shall we try for the t-transfer point? We could turn quickly. Dive back in. Trust Kaa to—"

Gillian shook her head.

"The Zang wouldn't let us get two meters."

Her shoulders hunched in a human expression of misery that no hoon could mimic. Clearly, this jagged place was a familiar sight that no one aboard *Streaker* would have chosen to visit again.

I caught the eye of Sara Koolhan. For the first time, my fellow Jijoan seemed just as much at a loss as I. She blinked in apparent confusion, unable to grasp the immensity of this thing ahead of us.

A strange sound came from the only male human present. The mute one who never speaks—Emerson d'Anite. He had been especially quiet during the trip from Izmunuti, silently studying the strange colors of t-space, as if they carried more meaning than the words of his own kind.

Now, staring at the huge, prickly ball, his face expressed the same astonishment as his crewmates' faces, intense emotion twisting the dark man's wounded features. Sara moved quickly to Emerson's side, taking his arm and speaking gently.

I recall thinking, If this place made the Terrans desperate enough to flee to Jijo, I'm not surprised they're upset finding themselves right back here.

A familiar voice cried out behind me, in tones of awed delight.

"Uttergloss!"

I turned in time to see Huck come wheeling into the Plotting Room, waving all four of her agile g'Kek eyes toward the big screen.

"That thing looks so cool. What is it?"

Another pal reached the open door not far behind her. An urrish head snaked through at the end of a long, sinuous neck, its single nostril flaring at the unpleasant reek of Earthling fear.

Arriving from another direction, a red qheuen lunged his armored bulk rudely past Ur-ronn while she hesitated. Pincer-Tip's vision cupola spun and he snapped his claws in excitement.

I should have expected it, of course. They weren't invited, but if my friends share one instinct across all species boundaries, it's a knack for finding trouble and charging straight for it.

"Hey, furry legs!" Huck snapped, nudging my flank with two waving eyestalks while the other pair strained to peer past the crowd. "Make your overstuffed carcass useful. Clear a way through these fishy things so I can see!"

Wincing, I hoped the dolphins were too busy to note her impertinence. Rather than disturb the crew, I bent down and grabbed Huck's axle rims, grunting as I lifted her above the crowd for a better view. (A young g'Kek doesn't weigh much, though at the time my back was still healing. It twinged each time she squirmed and spun from excitement.)

"What *is* that thing?" Huck repeated, gesturing toward the huge spiky ball.

Lieutenant Tsh't raised her glossy head from the soft platform of her mechanical walker, aiming one dark eye at my g'Kek friend.

"It'ssss a place where we *fishy things* suffered greatly, before coming to your world."

Had I been human, my ears would have burned with embarrassment. Being a hoon, my throat sac puffed with apologetic umbles. But Huck barged on without noticing.

"Sheesh, it looks big!"

The dolphin emitted snorting laughter from her moist blowhole.

"You c-could say that. That spiky shell encloses a volume of approximately thirty astrons, or a trillionth of a cubic parsec."

Huck's stalks expressed a blithe shrug.

"Huh! Whatever that means. I'll tell you what it reminds me of. It looks like the spiny armor covering a desert clam!"

"Lookssss can be deceiving, young Jijoan," Tsh't answered. "That shell is soft enough to cut with a wooden spoon. If you approached and exhaled on it, the patch touched by your breath would boil away. Its average density is like a cloud in a snowstorm."

That doesn't sound too threatening, I pondered. Then I caught the startled look on Sara Koolhan's face. Our young human sage frowned as her eyes darted back and forth, from data panels to the main screen, then to Tsh't.

"The infrared . . . the reemission profiles . . . You're not saying that thing actually *contains*—"

She stopped, unable to finish her sentence. The dolphin officer snickered.

"Indeed it does. A *star* resides at the heart of that soft confffection. That deceptive puff of p-poison ssssnow.

"Welcome, dear Jijoan friends. Welcome to the Fractal World."

LARK

He didn't feel cold. Not exactly. Even though, logically, he ought to.

A cloying mist surrounded Lark as membranes pressed against him from all sides, keeping his body bent nearly double, with knees up near his chin.

Lark felt as he imagined he might if someone crammed him back into the womb.

Soon another similarity grew apparent.

He wasn't breathing anymore.

In fact, his mouth was sealed shut and swollen plugs filled both nostrils. The rhythmic expansion of his chest, the soft sigh of sweet air, these notable portions of life's usual background . . . were gone!

With this realization, panic nearly engulfed Lark. A red haze obscured vision, narrowing to a tunnel as he struggled and thrashed. Though his body seemed reluctant at first, he obliged it to try inhaling . . . and achieved nothing.

He tried harder, *commanding* effort from his sluggish diaphragm and rib cage. Lark's spine arched as he strained, until at last a scant trickle of gas slipped by one nose plug—perhaps only a few molecules—

—carrying an acrid stench!

Sudden paroxysms contorted Lark. Limbs churned and bowels convulsed as he tried voiding himself into the turbid surroundings.

Fortunately, his gut was empty—he had eaten little for days. A cottony feeling spread through his extremities like a drug, filling them with soothing numbness as the fit soon passed, leaving behind a lingering foul taste in his mouth.

Lark had learned a valuable lesson.

Next time you find yourself wrapped up in fetal position, crammed inside a stinking bag without an instinct to breathe, take a hint. Go with the flow.

Lark felt for a pulse and verified that his heart, at least, was still functioning. The persistent stinging in his sinuses—a noxious-familiar stench—was enough all by itself to verify that life went on, painful as it was.

Turning his head to look around, Lark soon noticed that his bag of confinement was just one of many floating in a much larger volume. Through the obscuring mist he made out other membranous sacks. Most held big, conical-shaped Jophur—tapered stacks of fatty rings that throbbed feebly while their basal leg segments pushed uselessly, without any solid surface for traction. Some of the traeki-like beings looked whole, but others had clearly been broken down to smaller stacks, or even individual rings.

Knotty cables, like the throbbing tendrils of a mulc spider, led away from each cell . . . including his own. In fact, one penetrated the nearby translucent wall, snaking around Lark's left leg and terminating finally at his inner thigh, just below the groin.

The sight triggered a second wave of panic, which he fought this time by drawing on his best resource, his knowledge as a primitive scientist. Jijo might be a backwater, lacking the intellectual resources of the Five Galaxies, but you could still train a working mind from the pages of paper books.

Use what you know. Figure this out!

All right.

First thing . . . the cable piercing his leg appeared to target the femoral artery. Perhaps it was feeding *on* him, like some space-leech in a garish, pre-Contact scifi yarn. But that horror image seemed so silly that Lark suspected the truth was quite different.

Basic life support. I'm floating in a poison atmosphere, so they can't let me breathe or eat or drink. They must be sending oxygen and nutrients directly to my blood.

Whoever "they" were.

As for the jiggling containers, Lark was enough of a field biologist to know *sampling bags* when he saw them. Although he could not laugh, a sense of ironic justice helped him put a wry perspective on the situation. He had put more than enough hapless creatures in confinement during his career as a naturalist, dissecting the complex interrelationships of living species on Jijo.

If nature passed out karma for such acts, Lark's burden might merit a personal purgatory that looked something like this.

He strained harder to see through the mist, hoping not to find Ling among the captives. And yet, a pall of loneliness settled when he verified she was nowhere in sight.

Maybe she escaped from Rann and the Jophur, when these yellow monsters invaded the Polkjhy. *If she made it to the Life Core, she might clamber through the jungle foliage and be safe in our old nest.* For a while, at least.

He glimpsed walls beyond the murk, estimating this chamber to be larger than the meeting tree back in his home village. From certain visible furnishings and wall-mounted data units, he could tell it was still the Jophur dreadnought, but invaders had taken over this portion, filling it with their own nocuous atmosphere.

That ought to be a clue. The familiar-horrid scent. A toxicity that forbade inhaling. But Lark's bruised mind drew no immediate conclusions. To a Jijoan—even a so-called "scientist"—all of space was a vast realm of terrible wonders.

Have they seized the whole vessel?

It seemed farfetched, given the power of mighty Jophur skygods, but Lark looked for some abstract solace in that prospect. Those traeki-cousins meant only bad news to all the Six Races of Jijo, especially the poor g'Kek. The best thing that could happen to his homeworld would be if battleship *Polkjhy* never reached its home to report what it had found in an obscure corner of Galaxy Four.

And yet, this situation could hardly be expected to make him glad, or grateful to his new captors.

It took a while, but eventually Lark realized—some of them were nearby!

At first, he mistook the quivering shapes for lumps in the overall fog, somewhat denser than normal. But these particular patches remained compact and self-contained, though fluid in outline. He likened them to shifting heaps of pond scum . . . or else succinct thunderheads, cruising imperiously among lesser clouds. Several of these amorphous-looking bodies clustered around a nearby sample bag, inspecting the Jophur prisoner within.

Inspecting? What makes you think that? Do you see any eyes? Or sensory organs of any kind?

The floating globs moved languidly, creeping through the dense medium by extending or writhing temporary arms or pseudopods. There did not seem to be any permanent organs or structures within their translucent skins, but a rhythmic movement of small, blobby subunits that came together, merged, or divided with a complexity he could only begin to follow.

He recalled an earlier amoebalike creature, much bigger than these—the invader who had burst through a ship's bulkhead, scaring away Rann and the other pursuers who had Lark cornered. That one had seemed to look right at Lark, before swarming ahead rapidly to swallow him up.

What could they be? Did Ling ever mention anything like this? I don't remember. . . .

All at once Lark knew where he had encountered the foul smell before. At Biblos . . . the Hall of Science . . . in a part of the great archive that had been cleared of bookshelves in order to set up a chemistry lab, where a small band of sages labored to recreate ancient secrets, financed and subsidized by the Jijoan Explosers Guild.

Trying to recover old skills, or even learn new things. The guild must have been full of heretics like Sara. Believers in "progress."

I never thought of it before, but the Slope was rife with renegade thinking even weirder than my own. In time, we'd probably have had a religious schism—even civil war—if gods hadn't come raining from the sky this year.

He thought about Harullen and Uthen, his chitinous friends, laid low by alien treachery. And about Dwer and Sara—safe at home, he hoped. For their sake alone, he would blow up this majestic vessel, if that meant Jijo could be shrouded once more in blessed obscurity.

Lark's dour contemplations orbited from the melancholy past, around the cryptic present, and through a dubious future.

Time advanced, though he had no way of measuring it except by counting heartbeats. That grew tedious, after a while, but he kept at it, just to keep his hand in.

I'm alive! The creatures in charge here must find me interesting, in some way.

Lark planned on stoking that interest, whatever it took.

ALVIN'S JOURNAL

"Welcome, Dear Jijoan Friends. Welcome to the Fractal World."

That line would have been a great place to finish this journal entry.

The moment had an eerie, intense drama. I could sense the tragic letdown of the *Streaker* crew, having fled all the way to Jijo's hellish deeps, and lost many comrades, only to wind up back at the very spot that had caused them so much pain in the first place.

But what happened next made all that seem to pale, like a shadow blasted by lightning.

"Maybe it'sss a different criswell structure," suggested Akeakemai, one of the dolphin technical officers, calling from the bridge. "After all, there's supposed to be millions of them, in just this galaxy alone."

But that wishful hope shattered when Tsh't confirmed the star configurations.

"Besides. What are the chances another criswell would sit this close to a transfer point? Most lie in remote globular clusters.

"No," the lieutenant went on. "Our Zang friends have brought us back for s-sssome bloody reason . . . may they vaporize and burn for it."

We four kids from Wuphon gathered at one end of the Plotting Room to compare notes. Ur-ronn communicated with her friends in Engineering. Her urrish lisp grew stronger as she became more excited, explaining what she had learned about the spiky ball.

"It is *hollow*, with a radius avout three tines as wide as Jijo's *orvit*, centered on a little red dwarf star. It is all jagged vecause that creates the highest surface area to radiate heat to space. And it's just like that on the inside too, where the uneven surface catches every ray of light from the star!"

"Actually, a simple sphere would accomplish that," explained the Niss Machine in professorial tones. A pictorial image appeared, showing a hollow shell surrounding a bright crimson pinpoint.

"Some pre-Contact Earthlings actually prophesied such things, calling them—"

"Dyson spheres!" Huck shouted.

We all stared at her. She twisted several vision-stalks in a shrug.

"C'mon guys. Catch up on your classic scifi."

Hoons think more slowly than g'Keks, but I nodded at last.

"Hr-rm, yes. I recall seeing them mentioned in novels by . . . hr-r . . . Shaw and Steele and Foster. But the idea seemed too fantastic ever to take serious . . ."

My voice trailed off. Of course, seeing is believing.

"As I was about to explain," the Niss continued, somewhat huffily, "the simple Dyson sphere concept missed an essential geometric requirement of a stellar enclosure. Allow me to illustrate."

A new pictorial replaced the smooth ball with a prickly one—like a knob of quill-coral dredged up by a fishing scoop. The computer-generated image split open before our eyes, exposing a wide central void where the tiny star shone. Only now a multitude of knifelike protrusions jutted *inward* as well, crisscrossing like the competing branches of a riotous rain forest.

"Latter-day Earthlings call this a criswell structure. The spikiness creates a fractal shape, of dimension approximately two point four. The interior has a bit more folding, where the purpose is to maximize total surface area getting some exposure to sunlight, even if it comes at a glancing angle."

"Why?" Pincer-Tip asked.

"To maximize the number of windows, of course," answered the Niss, as if that explained everything.

"Energy is the chief limiting factor here. This small sun puts out approximately ten to the thirty ergs per second. By capturing all of that, and allowing each inhabitant a generous megawatt of power to use, this abode can adequately serve a population exceeding one hundred thousand billion sapient beings. At lower per capita power use, it would support more than ten quadrillions."

We all stared. For once, even Huck was stunned to complete silence.

I struggled for some way to wrap my poor, slow thoughts around such numbers.

Put it this way. If every citizen of the Six Races of Jijo were suddenly to have each *cell* of his or her body transformed into a full-sized sapient being, the total would still fall short of the kind of census the Niss described. It far surpassed the count of every star and life-bearing planet in all five galaxies.

(I figured all this out later, of course. At the time, it taxed my stunned brain to do more than stare.)

Ur-ronn recovered first.

"It sounds . . . *crowded,*" she suggested.

"Actually, population levels are constrained by energy and sun-facing surface area. By contrast, volume for living space is not a serious limitation. Accommodations would be fairly roomy. Each sovereign entity could have a private chamber larger than the entire volcano you Jijoans call Mount Guenn."

"Uh-uh-uh-uh-uh . . ." Pincer-Tip stuttered from five leg vents at once, summing up my own reaction at the time." P-p-people *made* this thing . . . t-t-to live in?"

The Niss hologram curled into a spinning abstraction of meshed lines that somehow conveyed amusement.

"These inhabitants might consider the term 'people' insultingly pejorative, my dear young barbarian. In fact, most of them are classified as higher entities than you or me. Fractal colonies are primarily occupied by members of the Retired Order of Life. In this place—and about fifty million other structures like it, scattered across the Five Galaxies—elder races live out their quiet years in relative peace, freed from the bickering noise and fractious disputes of younger clans."

A nearby dolphin snorted derisively, though at that moment I did not grasp the bitter irony of the Niss Machine's words.

Sara Koolhan wandered back to join our group.

"But what is it *made of*?" the young sage asked. "What kind of materials could possibly support anything so huge?"

The pictorial image zoomed, focusing our view on one small segment of a cutaway edge. From a basically circular arc, craggy shapes projected both toward the star and away from it, splitting into branches, then sub-branches, and so on till the eye lost track of the smallest. Faceted chambers filled every enclosed volume.

"The inner surface is built largely of spun carbon, harvested from various sources, like the star itself. Hydrogen-helium fusion reactors produced more, over the course of many millions of years. Carbon can withstand direct sunlight. Moreover, it is strong in centrifugal tension.

"The outer portions of this huge structure, on the other hand, are in sub-Keplerian dynamic conditions. Because they feel a net inward pull, they must be strong against compression. Much of the vast honeycomb structure therefore consists of field-stabilized metallic hydrogen, the most plentiful element in the cosmos, mixed into a ceramic-carbon polymorph. This building material was stripped from the star long ago by magnetic induction, removing roughly a tenth of its overall mass—along with oxygen and other components needed for protoplasmic life. That removal had an added benefit of allowing the sun to burn in a slower, more predictable fashion.

"The external shell of the criswell structure is so cold that it reradiates heat to space at a temperature barely above the universal background . . ."

My ears kind of switched off at that point. I guess the Niss must have thought it was making sense. But even when me and my friends labored through recordings of the lecture later, consulting the autoscribe one word at a time, only Ur-ronn claimed to grasp more than a fraction of the explanation.

Truly, we had arrived at the realm of gods.

I drifted away, since the one question foremost in my mind wasn't being addressed. It had nothing to do with technical details.

I wanted to know *why*!

If this monstrous thing was built to house millions of millions of millions of occupants, then who lived there? Why gather so many beings into a giant snowball, surrounding a little star? A "house" so soft and cold that I could melt portions with my own warm breath?

All that hydrogen made me wonder—did the Zang live here?

Above all, what had happened to make the *Streaker* crew fear this place so?

I observed Gillian Baskin standing alone before two big displays. One showed the Fractal World in real light—a vast disk of blackness. A jagged mouth, biting off whole constellations.

The other screen depicted the same panorama in "shifted infrared," resembling the head of a garish medieval mace, glowing a shade like hoonish blood. It grew larger and slowly turned as *Streaker* moved across the night, approaching the monstrous thing at a shallow angle. I wondered how many sets of eyes were watching from vast chill windows, regarding us with a perspective of experience going back untold aeons. At best such minds would consider my species a mere larval form. At worst, they might see us no more worthy than insects.

Our escort, the giant Zang vessel, started spitting smaller objects from its side—the harvester machines it had managed to salvage from the chaos at Izmunuti, carrying their crumpled sails. These began spiraling ahead of us, orbiting more rapidly toward the vast sphere, as if hastening on some urgent errand.

It occurred to me that I was privileged at that moment to witness four of the great Orders of Life in action at the same instant. Hydrogen breathers, machine intelligences, oxy-creatures like myself, and the "retired" phylum—beings who built on such a scale that they thought nothing of husbanding a *star* like their own personal hearth fire. As a Jijo native, I knew my tribe was crude compared to the august Civilization of Five Galaxies. But now it further dawned on me that even the Great Galactic Institutes might be looked on as mere anthills by others who were even higher on the evolutionary pyramid.

I guess I know where that puts me.

The dark human male joined Dr. Baskin before the twin screens, sharing a glance with her that must have communicated more than words.

"You can feel it too, Emerson?" she said in a low voice. "Something is different. I'm getting a real creepy feeling."

The mute man rubbed his scarred head, then abruptly grinned and started whistling a catchy melody. I did not recognize the tune. But it made her laugh.

"Yeah. Life is full of changes, all right. And we might as well be optimistic.

Perhaps the Old Ones have grown up a bit since we've been away." Her mirthless smile made that seem unlikely. "Or maybe something else distracted them enough to forget all about little us."

I yearned to follow up on that—to step forward and press her for explanations. But somehow it felt improper to interrupt their poignant mood. So I kept my peace and watched nearby as the harvester robots circled ahead and vanished beyond the limb of the Fractal World.

A little while later, a worried voice spoke over the intercom. It was Olelo, the ship's detection officer, calling from the bridge.

"For some time we've been picking up substantially higher systemwide gas and particulate signaturesss," the dolphin reported. "Now we're seeing reflections from larger grain sizes, just ahead, plus entrained ionic flows characteristic of sssolar wind." Dr. Baskin looked puzzled.

"Reflections? Reflecting what? Starlight?"

There was a brief pause.

"No ma'am. Spectral profiles match direct illumination by a nearby class M8 dwarf."

This time, Emerson d'Anite and I shared a baffled look. Neither of us understood a word—he due to his injury, and me because of my savage birth. But the information must have meant plenty to the other human.

"Direct . . . but that can only mean . . ." Her eyes widened in a combination of fear and realization. "Oh dear sweet—"

She was cut off by a sudden alarm blare. Across the Plotting Room, all conversation stopped. The image on the main screen zoomed forward, concentrating directly ahead of *Streaker*'s path, to the limb of the great sphere that was now rotating into view.

Huck spread all her eyestalks and uttered a hushed oath.

"Ifni!"

Neo-dolphins rocked their walkers in nervous agitation. Ur-ronn clattered her hooves and Pincer-Tip kept repeating—"Gosh-osh-osh-osh-osh!"

I had no comment, but reflexively began umbling to calm the nervous beings around me. As usual, I was probably the last one to comprehend what lay before my ogling gaze.

An indentation, interrupting the curved-serrated contour of the sphere.

A wide streamer of faint reddish light, wafting toward the stars.

A scattering of myriad soft glints and twinkling points, like embers blowing from a burning house.

Our Jijoan sage, Sara Koolhan, stepped forward.

"The sphere . . . it's ruptured!"

Olelo's anxious voice reported again from the bridge.

"Confirmed . . . We've got-t a breach in the Criswell structure! It'sss . . . a big hole, at least an astron or two acrosss. Can't tell yet-t, but I think . . ."

There was another long pause. No one spoke a word or dared even breathe while we waited.

"Yes, it's verified," Olelo resumed. "The collapse is continuing as we ssspeak.

"Whatever happened to this place . . . it's still going on."

GILLIAN

A panorama of death had her riveted.

"I will grant you one thing," remarked the voice from the spinning hologram. "Wherever you Terrans travel in the universe, you do tend to leave a mark."

She had no reply for the Niss Machine. Gillian hoped if she kept silent it would go away.

But the tornado of whirling lines moved closer instead. Sidling by her left ear, it spoke her native tongue in soft, natural tones.

"Two million centuries.

"That is how long the Library says this particular structure existed, calmly orbiting the galaxy, a refuge of peace.

"Then, one day, some wolflings came by for a brief visit."

Gillian slashed, but her hand swept through the hologram without resistance. The abstract pattern kept spinning. Its mesh of fine lines cast ghost-flickers across her face. Of course the damned Niss was right. *Streaker* carried a jinx, bringing ruin everywhere it went. Only here, the consequent misfortune surpassed any scale she could grasp with heart or mind.

Instruments highlighted grim symptoms of devastation as, escorted by the huge Zang globule-vessel, *Streaker* entered a ragged gap in the tremendous fractal shell, bathed in reddish sunlight that was escaping confinement for the first time in aeons. A storm of atoms and particles blew out through the same hole, so dense that at one point the word "vacuum" lost pertinence. A noticeable pressure appeared on instruments, faintly resisting the Earthship's progress.

There was larger debris. Chunks that Kaa moved nimbly to avoid. Some were great wedges, revealing hexagonal, comblike rooms the size of asteroids. Tumbling outward, each evaporating clump wore shimmering tails of dust and ions. Thousands of these artificial comets lit up the broad aperture . . . a cavity so wide that Earth would take a month in its orbit to cross it.

"Albeit reluctantly, Dr. Baskin," the Niss concluded, "I admit I am impressed. Congratulations."

Nearby, a throng of walker-equipped neo-dolphins jostled among the passengers. The Plotting Room grew crowded as off-duty personnel came to gawk at the spectacle. But a gap surrounded Gillian, like a moat none dared cross, except the sardonic Tymbrimi machine-mind. No one exulted. This place had caused the crew great pain, but the havoc was too immense, too overwhelming for gloating.

Nor would it be fair. Just a few factions of Old Ones had been responsible for the betrayal that sent *Streaker* fleeing almost a year ago, while some other blocs actually helped the Earthship get away. Anyway, should hundreds of billions die because of the greed of a few?

Don't get carried away, she thought. *There's no proof this disaster has anything to do with us. It could be something completely unrelated.*

But that seemed unlikely. Sheer coincidence of timing beggared any other explanation.

She recalled how their previous visit ended—with a final backward glimpse during *Streaker*'s narrow getaway.

We saw violence erupting behind us, even as someone opened up a door, letting us make a break for the transfer point. I saw a couple of nearby fractal branches get damaged, and some windows broken, while sects clashed over Emerson's little scout-ship, seizing and preventing him from following us.

Gillian's friend paid dearly for his brave rearguard action, suffering unimaginably cruel torture and abuse before somehow, mysteriously, being transported to Jijo right after *Streaker*. The speechless former engineer was never able to explain.

Amid the guilt of abandoning him, and our hurry fleeing this place, who would have guessed the Old Ones would keep on fighting after we escaped! Why? What purpose could an apocalypse serve, after we took our cursed cargo away?

But a horrible tribulation must have followed. Ahead lay ample testimony. Plasma streamers and red-tinged dust plumes . . . along with countless long black shadows trailing from bits of dissolving rubble, some larger than a moon, but all of them as frail as snowflakes.

She pondered the ultimate cause—the treasures *Streaker* carried, like Herbie, the ancient cadaver that had taken over her study, like Poe's raven, or Banquo's ghost. Prizes lusted after by fanatical powers hoping to seize and monopolize their secrets, winning some advantage in a Time of Changes.

It was imperative to prevent that. The Terragens Council had made their orders clear—first to Creideiki and later to Gillian when she assumed command. *Streaker*'s discoveries must be shared openly, according to ancient Galactic custom, or not at all. Mighty races and alliances might violate that basic rule and think they could get away with it. But frail Earthclan dared not show even a hint of partiality.

In an age of rising chaos, sometimes the weak and friendless have no sanctuary but the law. Humans and their clients had to keep faith with Galactic institutions. To do less would be to risk losing everything. Unfortunately, Gillian's quest for a neutral power to take over the relics had proved worse than futile.

It wasn't for lack of trying. After the Great Institutes proved untrustworthy at Oakka, Gillian had what seemed (at the time) an inspired notion.

Why not pass the buck even higher?

She decided to bring the relics *here*, to a citadel for species that had "moved on" from the mundane, petty obsessions plaguing the Civilization of Five Galaxies. At one of the legendary Fractal Worlds, harassed Earthlings might at last find dispassionate advice and mediation from beings who were revered enough to intercede, halting the spasmodic madness of younger clans. These respected elder sapients would assume responsibility for the burden, relieve *Streaker* of its toxic treasures, and force the bickering oxygen alliances to share.

Then, at long last, the weary dolphins could go home.

And I could go searching for Tom, wherever he and Creideiki and the others have drifted since Kithrup.

That had been the theory, the hope.

Too bad the Old Ones turned out to be as fretful, desperate, and duplicitous as their younger cousins who still dwelled amid blaring hot stars.

It's as if we were a plague ship, carrying something contagious from the distant past. Wherever we go, rational beings start acting like they've gone mad.

Monitors focused on the nearest edge of the great wound, revealing a shell several thousand kilometers thick, not counting the multipronged spikes jutting both in and out. Dense haze partly shrouded the continuing tragedy but could not mask a sparkle of persistent convulsions. Structural segments buckled and tore as Gillian watched. Fractal branches broke and went spinning through space, colliding with others, setting off further chain reactions.

The massive spikes on the sunward side glittered in a way that reminded Gillian.

Windows. When we first came here . . . after they opened a slim door to let us through . . . the first thing I noticed was how much of the inner face seemed to be made of glass. And beneath those immense panes—

She closed her eyes, recalling how the telescope had revealed each branchlet was its own separate world. Some greenhouses—larger than her home state of Minnesota—sheltered riotous jungles. Others shone with city lights, or floating palaces adrift on rippled seas, or plains of sparkling sand. It would take many millions of Earths, unrolled flat, to cover so much surface, and that would not begin to express the diversity. She might have spent years magnifying one habitat after another and still routinely found something distinct or new.

It was the most majestic and beautiful place Gillian had ever seen.

Now it was unraveling before her eyes.

That haze, she realized, aghast. *It isn't just structural debris and subliming gas. It's people. Their furniture and pets and clothes and houseplants and family albums . . . Or whatever comprised the equivalent for Old Ones. What human could guess the wishes, interests, and obsessions that became important to species who long ago had seen everything there was to see in the Five Galaxies, and had done everything there was to do?*

However abstruse or obscure those hopes, they were dissolving fast. Just during *Streaker*'s brief passage through the gaping wound, more sapient beings must have died than the whole population of Earth.

Her mind quailed from that thought. To personalize the tragedy invited madness.

"Is anyone trying to stop this?" she asked in a hoarse voice.

The Niss Machine paused before answering.

"Some strive hard. Behold their efforts."

The monitor view shifted forward as *Streaker* finally arrived at the habitat's vast interior space.

Just like the last time, Gillian abruptly felt as if she had entered a vast domed chamber of bright corrugated stalactites and measureless shadows. Although the farthest portions of the vault were a hundred million kilometers away, she could nevertheless make out fine details. The imaging system monitored her eyes to track the cone of her attention, highlighting and amplifying whatever she chose to regard.

Directly ahead—like a glowing lamp in the center of a basilica—a dwarf star cast its warming glow. The visible disk was dimmer and redder than the spendthrift kind of sun where nursery worlds like Terra spun and flourished. By stripping the outer layers for construction material, the makers of this place had created a perfect hearth fire, whose fuel ought to last a hundred billion years. To stare straight at the disk caused no physical pain. But its plasma skin, placid during their first visit, now seemed covered by livid sores. Dazzling pinpoints flared as planet-sized gobs of debris tumbled to the roiling surface.

Yet, Gillian soon realized such collisions were exceptional. Most of the jagged chunks were being intercepted and burned by narrow beams of searing blue energy, long before they reached the solar photosphere.

"Of course, even when they succeed in pulverizing rubble, the mass still settles downward as gas, eventually rejoining the sun from which it was stripped so long ago. The star's thermonuclear and atmospheric resonances will be adversely affected. Still, it reduces the number of large ablative impacts, and thus many actinic flares."

"So, the maintenance system functions," Gillian commented, with rising hope.

"Yes, but it is touch and go. Worse yet, parts of the system are being abused."

The monitor went blurry as it sped to focus on a point along a far quadrant of the criswell sphere, where one of the blue scalpel-rays was busy with less altruistic work, carving a brutal path across the jagged landscape, severing huge fractal branchlets, shattering windows and raising mighty gouts of steam.

Gillian cried an oath and stepped back. "My God. It's genocide!"

"We have learned a sad lesson during this expedition," the Niss Machine conceded. "One that should very much interest my Tymbrimi makers, if we ever get a chance to report it.

"When an oxygen-breathing race retires from Galactic affairs to seek repose in one of these vast shells, it does not always leave behind the prejudices and loyalties of youth. While many do seek enlightenment, or insights needed for transcendence, others stay susceptible to temptation, or remain steadfast to alliances of old."

In other words, Gillian had been naive to expect detachment and impartiality from the species living here.

Some were patrons—or great-grandpatrons—of Earth's persecutors.

She watched in horror as some faction misused a defensive weapon—designed to protect the whole colony—against a stronghold of its opponents.

"Ifni. What's to keep them from doing that to us!"

"Dr. Baskin, I haven't any idea," the spinning hologram confided. "Perhaps the locals are too busy in their struggles to notice our arrival.

"Or else, it could be because of the company we keep."

A screen showed the great Zang ship—floating just ninety kilometers away, quivering as the grim, sooty wind brushed its semiliquid flanks. Clouds of smaller objects fluttered nearby. Some were machine entities. Others qualified as living portions of the massive vessel, detached to do errands outside, then quietly reabsorbed when their tasks were done.

"I've confirmed my earlier conjecture. The hydrogen beings are coordinating efforts by the harvester robots and other machine beings to help shore up and stabilize the Fractal World."

Gillian nodded. "That's why they were at Izmunuti. To fetch construction material. It's an easy source of carbon just one t-point jump away."

"Under normal conditions, yes. Until unforeseen storms erupted, precipitated by that psi wave from Jijo. The harvesters we saw there were apparently just a small fraction of those involved in this massive effort."

"It's a repair contract, then. A commercial deal."

"I assume so. Since Galaxy Four has been evacuated by oxygen-breathing starfarers, it would be logical for Old Ones to seek help from the nearest available source. Shall I confirm these suppositions by tapping into the Fractal World's data nexus?"

"Do no such thing! I don't want to draw attention. If no one has noticed us, let's leave it that way."

"May I point out that some groups within the retired order weren't inimical? Without their assistance we could never have eluded capture the first time. Perhaps those groups would help again, if we make contact."

Gillian shook her head firmly.

"I'm still worried the Jophur may show up any minute, hot on our heels. Let's just settle our business with the Zang and get away. Have you heard anything from them?"

Sara Koolhan thought the hydrogen breathers had some ancient claim on the glaver race . . . a debt to be paid now that glavers had regained presapient innocence. But even so, how would the transaction take place? Was it proper or moral for the *Streaker* crew to hand over another oxy-species without formal sanction by appropriate institutes? Would the creatures be safe aboard a craft built to support a completely different chemistry of life?

More to the point, would the Zang let *Streaker* go afterward? According to sketchy Library accounts, hydros did have concepts of honor and obligation, but their logic was skewed. They might reward the Earthlings . . . or blast them to get rid of a residual nuisance.

At least they didn't drag us here for prosecution, as I feared. They haven't handed us over to the Old Ones. Not yet.

A small voice of conscience chided Gillian. Here she was, worried about how to skulk away in her tiny starship, saving less than a hundred lives, while around them nation-sized populations were dying each moment that she breathed.

One more reason not to let the Niss contact the Fractal World's comm net. She needed to keep the calamity as abstract as possible. A gaudy special-effects show. A vast collision of impersonal forces. Right now, any confirmation of the real death toll might push her to despair.

It's not our fault.

We came here seeking help within the law. Within our rights.

True, Streaker brought curses from the Shallow Cluster. But how could we know madness would strike the eminent and wise?

This isn't our fault!

TSH'T

It would be the perfect time, while everyone else was preoccupied with the spectacle outside. *Streaker* seemed likely to be motionless for a while, so Tsh't didn't have to be at Dr. Baskin's beck and call, pretending to share command when everyone knew who gave the orders anyway.

Many crew members ignored the chance to go off duty when their shifts ended, finding excuses to hang around. They stared, wide-eyed, at the shattered glory of the Fractal World, commenting to each other with rapid clicks, exchanging bets whether the frantic efforts by a myriad hireling robots would save the giant wounded habitat. After a couple of hours, several gawkers had to be ordered below to rest. But when her own watch period finished, Tsh't quickly took advantage of the excuse to leave.

This might be her only chance to go below and check out her suspicions.

I know Gillian snuck somebody or something aboard, she thought. Back in that little Jijoan village, where hoons happily sail crude boats, even though they can't swim a stroke. It was a stormy night, and I was busy discussing technical matters with that urrish blacksmith. But I know Akeakemai. He's a regular teacher's pet, and would do anything Gillian asked.

He's lying or hiding something.

Something he smuggled in the back way when I wasn't looking.

It worried Tsh't to be left in the dark like this. She was supposed to be Gillian's close confidant and co-commander. The show of distrust disturbed her. Especially since she deserved it.

I've seen no sign that anyone has connected me to the dead humans.

Nevertheless. Tsh't worried as she sent her walker stomping down one of *Streaker*'s main corridors. The hallway felt deserted, emptied by attrition after three years on the run.

Of course it's always possible that Gillian picked up something with that psi talent of hers. She may suspect the demise of Kunn and Jass was no case of double suicide.

Tsh't fought to suppress the disturbing image of those two human corpses. She quelled a nervous tremor that coursed her dorsal nerves, making the moist skin shiver and her flukes thrash on the rear portion of the walker's soft suspension hammock.

How badly she yearned for a real swim! But nearly all the water had been flushed out to lighten *Streaker*'s frantic breakout from Jijo. Dragging a heavy coat of carbon soot from smoldering Izmunuti, the Earth vessel needed every bit of agility, so nearly all the residence and recreation areas were now bone-dry. Soon, long queues would form at sick bay, as neo-dolphins reported skin sores and bruised ribs. After too much time spent lying prone atop jarring machines, even the softest field-effect cushion made you feel like you had been beached and stranded on a shore covered with sharp pebbles.

Now Dr. Makanee is gone, along with three aides—left behind to take care of the

Jijo colonists—and I'm the one who has to figure out how to stretch our remaining med staff and cover the inevitable complaints. Somehow, despite everything, team efficiency and morale have got to be kept up.

That's what the high and mighty Dr. Baskin leaves to me—all the grungy details of running a ship and crew—while she ponders vast issues of policy and destiny, leading us hither and yon across the Five Galaxies, trying this and then trying that, fleeing from one disaster to the next.

The bitterness was not unmixed with affection. Tsh't genuinely loved Gillian, whose skill at getting *Streaker out* of jams had proved nearly as impressive as her affinity for getting into them. Nor did Tsh't resent human beings as patrons. Without their awkward, well-meaning efforts at genetic engineering, the Tursiops race might never have taken the final step from bright, innocent animals to promising starfarers . . . and Tsh't would not have seen the Starbow, or Hercules Arch—or the Shallow Cluster.

Terragens culture granted neo-dolphins more rights and respect than a new client race normally received in the Civilization of Five Galaxies. Most clients spent a hundred millennia in servitude to their patrons. Humans were doing about as well as they could, under the circumstances.

But there are limits to what you can expect from wolflings, she thought, entering a double airlock to pass into Streaker's Dry Wheel.

The latest pathetic episode proved this point. Just hours after arriving inside the Fractal World, Gillian Baskin had decided to see whether they were prisoners or guests. Waiting till the Zang seemed preoccupied—supervising a swarm of machine entities doing repair work—she had ordered Kaa to gently nudge *Streaker's* engines, easing the ship through the opening toward a beckoning glitter of starlight.

The Zang dropped what it was doing, scattering robot attendants, racing with astonishing agility to cut off the Earthlings' escape.

Still covered with several meters of star soot, *Streaker* could not outrun the giant globule. Gillian acquiesced, turning the ship back into the immense habitat. She then ordered a general stand-down. Except for watch crew, everyone was told to get some rest. The Zang vessel returned to work, without evident rancor. And yet Tsh't felt a hard-won lesson was reinforced.

Humans were sapient for only a few thousand years longer than us dolphins—a mere eyeblink in the story of life in the universe. It's not their fault they are ignorant and clumsy.

That only means they need help. Even if they are too obstinate to ask for it.

An elevator ride took her to the rim of the wide centrifugal wheel, where rooms lined a long hallway that seemed to curve up and away in both directions. The great hoop straddled *Streaker* halfway along its length and could be spun up to provide weight on those occasions when the crew needed to turn off floor gravity for some reason—if they were doing sensor scans in deep space, for instance . . . or evading fleets of pursuers by hiding in an asteroid belt. There was a drawback, though. Whenever they had to land on a planet's surface—as happened at Kithrup, Oakka, and Jijo—most of the Dry Wheel's rooms were out of reach.

To anyone except a biped who's a skilled climber, that is.

Tsh't strode past the sealed door to Dr. Baskin's office, where layers of security devices guarded Creideiki's treasure—the relics responsible for so much grief. This part of the Dry Wheel was always "bottom," whenever *Streaker* lay grounded. Dolphins routinely used nearby suites and workshops, but those on the opposite side were often inaccessible. In fact, the crew seldom thought of them at all.

That's where I'd hide something, if I were Gillian.

The Wheel was spinning right now, so Tsh't had no trouble striding around its wide circumference, passing laboratories once used by scientists like Ignacio Metz, Dennie Sudman, and the neo-chimpanzee geologist Charles Dart. She kept lifting her jaw to listen, as if nervously expecting to hear ghost footsteps of the bright young Calafian midshipman Toshio Iwashika . . . or the strong, confident gait of Gillian's lost Tom Orley.

But they were gone. All of them, along with Creideiki and Hikahi. Dead, or else abandoned on poisonous Kithrup—which was almost the same as being dead.

They were the best of us, taken away before our trials really began. How much would have been different if the captain and the others were still aboard? Instead command fell to Gillian and me . . . a physician-healer and the ship's most junior lieutenant . . . who never imagined we'd have to carry such a burden, year after dreary year.

Fatigue wore at Tsh't. During sleep shifts she would cast her clicking sonar song toward the Whale Dream, praying for someone to come take away the hardship, the responsibility.

We Streakers are in way over our heads. All of Earth-clan is! Gillian was right about one thing. We need help and advice. But we won't get it from eatees. Not from the Great Institutes, or the Old Ones.

She's forgotten one of life's great truths, known by almost every human and dolphin from childhood. When you're in real bad trouble, the place to turn is your own family.

Using her neural tap, Tsh't called up the ship's maintenance system and ordered a trace of atmospheric pollutants, concentrating room by room on the section of the Dry Wheel directly opposite from Dr. Baskin's office—the sector routinely left on "top" when *Streaker* lay on a planet's surface. The part that dolphins were likely to ignore, even when it was accessible.

Aha! Just as I thought. An elevated profile of carbon dioxide, plus several ketones, a touch of methane, and a strange pair of alcohols. Sure signs of respiration by an oxygen-breathing life-form . . . though clearly not an Earthling.

And it's all centered . . . here.

She made her walker halt before a door labeled HAZARDOUS ORGANIC MATERIALS—and chuckled at Gillian's little joke.

A slight nudge of volition caused a work-arm to swing forward from her tool harness, aiming a slim drill at the door, near the jamb, where a hole might not be noticed right away. A fine whirring was the only sound. Her cutter penetrated, vaporized, and vac-disposed debris as it moved ahead.

Tsh't mused on how she was now compounding her own felony. Her growing record of treason. It all started the last time *Streaker* visited the Fractal World, when everyone grew aware that the Old Ones were going to disappoint them. As crew morale sank, Tsh't decided it was time to act on her own. To send a message, contacting the one source whose help could be relied on.

Fortunately, the Fractal World had regular commercial mail taps. Even while Gillian parried increasing threats and imprecations from various factions of the Retired Order, Tsh't found it fairly simple to dispatch a secret message packet, programmed to go bouncing across the Five Galaxies, paranoically covering its own tracks and randomly rerouting before heading for its final destination—a time-drop capsule whose coordinates she had memorized as a youth, long ago. One tuned to respond to just one species in the universe.

By then, Gillian had already decided to flee the Criswell structure and try the "sooner option"—absconding through forbidden Galaxy Four, sneaking past a blaring giant star, then taking shelter on a proscribed world called Jijo.

A clandestine rendezvous seemed easy enough for Tsh't to arrange. . . .

The drill bit broke through. She commanded the arm back and sent a fiber communicator snaking through the hole, rearing like a cobra inside the sealed room.

It scanned left and right until a lanky bipedal figure came into view, seated on a bench before a small table.

The head lifted, as if reacting to a sound. When the creature turned halfway around, Tsh't gasped at the sight.

A slanted, narrow face with a jutting, chinless jaw and large, bared teeth.

Yet, the eyes and brow seemed uncannily human, squinting as they caught sight of the spy probe.

Hurriedly, the head turned away again. Shoulders hunched to block her view. Tsh't saw both arms grope for a box—a bio-support unit designed for maintaining small animals sampled from an ecosystem. Deft hands pulled out something squirmy. She couldn't follow what was happening, but it seemed as if the biped was *eating* the wriggly creature, or embracing it.

The shoulders relaxed, arms settling to the tall being's side as it stood up and gracefully turned around.

The face was transformed. Now it looked more noble than human. More genially amused than a Tymbrimi. More patient and understanding than a god.

Well, well. It is him. The very one.

The Rothen's face quivered in a few places, where its mask-symbiont was still nestling in—a living creature crafted to become *part* of his features, providing fine cheekbones, a regal chin, and lips that both covered the teeth and drew a tender, gracious smile.

The Missionary.

Tsh't remembered his visit to Earth, long ago, when she was still half grown and barely able to speak. It was like yesterday, the image of him preaching in a hidden undersea grotto to a tiny gathering of dolphin converts.

"The universe is a lonely place," he had said then. "But not as dangerous as it seems. The present government of Earth may consist of Darwinists and unbelievers, but that does not matter. Remember, despite the propaganda of those preaching wolfling pride, that you are not alone. We who crafted the genes of humanity in secret, guiding them toward a great destiny, remain steadfast to that dream. The same glorious goal. We still act behind the scenes, protecting, preserving, preparing for the Day.

"And as we love our human clients, so we also love you. For ours is a special clan, with a future more splendid than any other. Dolphins will play a great role when the time comes. Especially those of you who choose the Danik Way."

It had felt singular to grow up as a member of an exclusive sect, knowing a great and reassuring Truth. Of course the Terragens Constitution promised religious freedom, but in practice it would only bring on ridicule to reveal too much, too soon. Most dolphins believed the myth that humans must have evolved sapience without intervention from above. An absurd notion, but too strong a current for dissenters to fight openly.

Even among humans and chimps, where Danikenite beliefs were more common, debates raged between conflicting cults. Many had their own candidates for the *secret patrons* . . . the mystery race said to have up lifted Homo sapiens long ago. Several Galactic races were called "more likely" than the obscure, secretive Rothen.

So Tsh't had kept it to herself, through school, training, and early assignments for the TAASF. She bided her time through the disasters at Morgran, Kithrup, and Oakka. Until one day she realized humans just weren't up to the task. Gillian Baskin was among the best . . . and could do no more.

It was time to seek help higher up the family tree.

The Rothen would know what to do.

Now her emotions roiled with conflict, complexity, and confusion. She had come here uncertain what to expect.

I knew about the symbiont. The Jijoans saw a Rothen unmasked. It's all in the reports. And yet, to see that bared face for myself—

The glimpse of Ro-kenn's natural features had been shocking. And yet, Tsh't now felt warmed by the same reassuring smile she recalled from childhood.

I can understand the need for a mask. It isn't necessarily dishonest. Not if it helps them do their work better, guiding Earthlings toward our destiny.

It's what's inside that counts.

"Well?" Ro-kenn said, taking a step toward the door. He brought both hands together, his long arms sticking out from the sleeves of a bathrobe made for a tall human. The captive must have been sent in secret by the Sages of Jijo, after capturing him in the highland place they called Festival Glade—perhaps the sole survivor of a mixed Rothen-human expedition that had met treachery and disaster, first from the Six Races and then the crew of the Jophur battleship.

Everything came together in Tsh't's heart. The longing she had carried since childhood. The frustration of three horrible years. Guilt over having acted against Gillian's wishes. The far larger guilt of assassinating two humans—even if it was in the interest of a greater cause.

She had come here intending to confront Ro-kenn. To demand an explanation of what had happened.

The message I sent . . . tuned to be picked up by a Rothen mind. It told you about Gillian's destination. You were supposed to come in secret to Jijo . . . to help us. To rescue us.

Now they say you persecuted the sooners, including Jijo's human settlers. They say your people sold Jijo to the Jophur for pocket change. They say you are swindlers, who convert gullible Earthlings to follow you, in order to use them as shills and petty thieves.

One of the men I killed—the pilot Kunn—I did it to protect our secret. But how can I be sure. . . .

None of that came out. The words would not come.

Instead, all the streams coursing through her suddenly combined in an emotional confluence. Despair, which had dominated for so long, cracked and gave way to its only true enemy.

Hope.

Tsh't had to take several deep breaths, then found the will to speak.

"Masssster . . . there is something I have come to confesssssss."

A look of surprise briefly crossed the Rothen's face, and his left cheek quivered.

Then a warm smile spread, and with a deep, gentle voice he spoke.

"Indeed, child of the warm seas. I am here. Take your time and I will listen. Be assured that redemption is found in telling all."

LARK

I wonder how long I've been in here. Is there any way to tell if it's been hours, days . . . or months?

If they understand my body chemistry well enough to keep me alive, these beings could turn my consciousness on and off like a lamp. They might change the way I perceive duration, simply by adjusting my metabolism.

That, too, felt like a clue. Lark yearned to compare notes with somebody.

With Ling, the way they used to, when they were wary adversaries, then allies, and finally lovers. He missed her terribly. Her warm skin and rich scent, but most of all her vivid mind. Amid all their ups and downs, it was her unpredictable wit that most fascinated Lark. He would give anything now, just to talk to her.

I was supposed to find a way to rescue her from Rann and the Jophur. Now all I can do is spin fantasies of a space-suited Ling blasting her way through that far wall, lasers in both hands, yanking me out of this awful vault so we can fly off together in some hijacked . . .

The enticing daydream dissolved as he realized that something had changed. His spine crawled with an uneasy sensation . . . a feeling of being watched. Lark turned his head . . . and shuddered reflexively.

A large blobby . . . thing floated near the membrane barrier, roughly spherical, but with bulges and ripples that swelled rhythmically, in ways that somehow conveyed *life* . . . and perhaps even intent. Currents of yellow mist flowed past, but it maintained position with a blur of tiny waving tendrils, as numerous as hairs on the leg of a hoon.

Cilia, Lark thought, recognizing a form of locomotion used by tiny organisms you might see under a microscope. He had never heard of this means occurring on a macro-entity anywhere near this size. As a biologist, he found it quite odd.

But curiosity turned to amazement when the creature abruptly *sucked in* all the waving cilia. Ballooning outward to the left, it elongated into a cylinder. Depressions at both ends deepened, penetrating along its length until they met, forming a hollow tube that began flexing longitudinally. Jets of yellow fluid compressed and shot out one opening, propelling the beast rapidly around Lark's little transparent cell.

Three times it circumnavigated this way. Lark had an impression it was looking him over from all angles.

That's not any normal gas or vapor out there, he thought. *But it doesn't seem like liquid, either.*

He had a feeling that the medium might have something to do with the creature's flexibility—its knack for switching from tendrils to siphon-jet propulsion.

Wherever it evolved, the environment must be stranger than anything I ever read about in the archives. That is . . . except . . .

Lark's eyes opened in sudden realization, so wide that the lids nudged small, clear cups that arched over them. Till that moment he hadn't even been aware of the protective coverings, but when his action let a few harsh molecules sneak past, he paid with stinging tears and deep, laryngial moans.

Yet, that hardly interrupted the rapid flow of Lark's thoughts.

Hydrogen breathers! The ancient scrolls call them one of the great orders of life. Sharing the Five Galaxies with oxy-types, but completely separate from our civilization, sticking to their own worlds and interests as we keep to ours.

Of course that oversimplified matters. Even in the few Biblos texts to mention hydro-life, it was clear that danger stalked each uneasy interaction between the two different molecular heritages. Minimizing contact made up a large part of the duties of the Migration Institute, which designed its leasehold rules partly to protect fallow worlds, but also to lessen the shared space where accidental encounters might take place.

Jijo's in Galaxy Four. Except for official Institute ships, there aren't supposed to be any of our kind flying about these spiral arms right now. It's one reason Jijo was an attractive candidate for the Sooner Path.

One eye was still blurry, but he squinted with the other as the hydro-being slowed to a halt and flowed back into a roughly spherical shape.

Am I looking at their equivalent of a policeman? Or an immigration official?

A hollow-looking vacuole formed under the creature's surface. Bubbles escaped, glistening with strange surface tension. Lark thought of someone farting underwater, but for all he knew it was actually an eloquent lecture on fine points of interorder cosmic law.

Maybe it's demanding to know what I'm doing here. Requesting my passport and visa. Asking for my plea . . . or whether I want a blindfold . . .

The hollow space within kept growing as the creature grew distended toward Lark. Within the vacuole, he made out several floating objects—each one looking at first like miniature versions of the larger entity. These took up various positions in the void, then began to change, taking on new shapes and colors.

Well I'll be . . .

One turned a shade of blue somewhat deeper than the sky back home. It stopped rippling and seemed to harden an adamant shell, covered with symmetrical arrangements of bumps and blisters. Lark even saw a minuscule emblem take form—a rayed spiral insignia near the top of the oblate spheroid. He swiftly recognized a near perfect representation of the Jophur battleship *Polkjhy.*

I get it. Communication by sign and picture show. And that other glob . . . is that supposed to be a hydro ship?

The guess was soon confirmed as he watched a growing confrontation between two space behemoths, all played out within a space no larger than a traeki's topknot. Lark watched with transfixed fascination as the Jophur cruiser blasted away at the yellow globule. At first, its arrows were thwarted by swarms of sudden, flimsy balloons. But then more missiles and fire bolts got through, hammering the onrushing foe mercilessly, until the hydro vessel shredded into ragged pieces that flapped like tattered banners. Yet, several of these still managed to drape across parts of *Polkjhy*'s hard metal hull.

So that's how they boarded. It was combat unlike any he had read about, or dreamed of.

Now the blue shell expanded before him, and Lark saw the fight continue *within.* Yellowish beachheads spread from half a dozen points of insertion, advancing swiftly at first, then meeting stiffening resistance. Lark saw small glitters scurrying near the battlefront, probably representing individual Jophur and their fierce, slashing battle robots.

Sometimes, one or two of those sparks fell into a yellow stain. Instead of being extinguished they were swept toward collection points in the rear.

Captives. Prisoners of war.

When it happened to another pinpoint, Lark felt an abrupt surge of sensation sting his thigh.

That's me!

It also made him realize something else.

They aren't just communicating with me visually. There's a chemical component! Some of my understanding comes by watching the demonstration. But they must also be sending meaning down the nutrient tube directly, into my very blood.

Awareness of the fact might have sickened and repelled him . . . except that a strange calmness pervaded Lark's limbs. Another effect of molecular inducement, no doubt. As a biologist, he was fascinated.

Hydros must have over a billion years' experience dealing with us oxies. That doesn't necessarily make it easy to bridge the vast gulf between life orders, or else they'd be talking to me directly, in audible words. But they've accumulated tricks, I'm sure.

It put a new perspective on things. He had spent his entire professional life entranced by the wild diversity among just the few million oxygen-breathing species prevalent on one part of a single planet. Now he realized there were beings for whom the difference between a Jophur and a human must appear nearly inconsequential.

Have they ever beheld an Earthling before? It would seem unlikely. And yet they can play me like an urrish fiddle.

Lark felt humbled . . . and contemplated whether that was also a reaction imposed or suggested from the outside.

No matter. The important thing is that they want me to learn. They're interested in keeping me alive, and making me understand.

For the time being, at least, I can live with that.

EMERSON

He might not be an engineer anymore, but he could still appreciate good work.

With an excellent view of the vast repair project—from his own private little observation bubble, tucked behind *Streaker*'s bridge—Emerson could see nearly the whole vaulting edifice, from its central hearth-star all the way to the gaping laceration that now mangled the majestic sphere, exposing a wide swath of untamed stars. Despite frantic efforts by great machines to mend and patch, innumerable lumps of ragged debris still poured outward through the hole, crumbling to dust, vapor, and armadas of radiant comets.

The sphere's injury reminded him of his own maiming, which also had occurred in this very place.

Trembling, Emerson's hand raised toward the area near his left ear. A filmy creature quivered at his touch—the *rewq* symbiont he had brought along from Jijo. Together with unguents supplied by a traeki pharmacist, the rewq was partly responsible for his surviving an injury that should otherwise have left him dead or a living vegetable. The tiny thing released its gentle clasp on a surface blood vessel and rippled aside, letting Emerson stroke the scar tissue surrounding a hole in his head. Not an accidental lesion, but a deliberate hurt. This was where it happened, about a year ago.

Here—he recalled climbing into a small fighter craft, ready to sacrifice himself and cover *Streaker*'s desperate escape.

Here—he blazed forth in the little scoutship, shouting defiance at those hostile factions whose demands and extortions disproved their vaunted reputation for wise neutrality . . . cries that turned joyful when a *different* clique of Old Ones intervened, opening a door in the great shell to let Gillian and the others escape.

Here—exultation cut off as his tiny vessel was seized by slabs of force, hemming it in, then abrading and dissolving the armored scout like a skinned pineapple, yanking him to a captivity worse than any he could have imagined.

Emerson was still hazy on what followed. His captors used potent conditioning that made memory excruciating. For most of the last year, he had wandered in a fog of amnesia, punctuated by bouts of searing agony whenever he tried to recall.

Defeating that programming had been his greatest victory. Emerson's mind was now his own again—what remained of it, that is. Anguish-reflexes still tried to divert his roaming thoughts, impeding him from salvaging further recollections, but he had learned to fight back by not giving a damn about pain. Emerson knew each throbbing impulse meant he was putting another piece back in place, thwarting their purpose.

If only he knew what that purpose was.

Lacking important parts of his old brain, Emerson could not express in words the irony he felt, crouched in his secret little bubble niche, looking across the broad corrugated vistas of the Fractal World. Even mute, his emotions had a complex, fine-grained texture.

For instance, by all rights, he should be experiencing satisfaction from the rack and ruin tearing through this place. As swarms of huge robots poured in through the sphere's gaping wound, converging to shore up its unraveling rim, he ought to be hoping for them to fail. That would be vengeance—for his tormentors to be smashed, for all their hopes and works to fall like ash into an emancipated sun.

But there was something else inside him, older and stronger than wrath.

Love of a certain kind of beauty.

The gracefulness of artifice.

The glory of something well made.

He could still recall the day—ages ago—when *Streaker* entered this redoubt of the Retired Order for the first time, full of naive hopes that would soon be betrayed. Awed by the splendor, he and Karkaett and Hannes Suessi had argued ecstatically over the ultimate function of this titanic habitat—to cheat the eroding rub of time, taming the wasteful extravagance of a star. It seemed an engineer's paradise.

And he still felt that way! Remarkably, he cheered the robot workers on. Emerson figured he would have revenge on his tormentors, simply by surviving. So long as *Streaker* roamed free, frustration must surely fill those cold eyes he recalled peering down at him while cruel instruments reamed his mind, sifting and squeezing for secrets he did not have. . . .

Emerson shuddered. Why hadn't the Old Ones simply killed him when they finished trawling through his brain? Instead, they mutilated and cast his writhing body across space in some unknown manner to crash-land on lonely Jijo.

It seemed a lot of trouble to go to. In a strange way, the special attention bolstered Emerson's sense of worth and self-esteem.

So he was willing to be magnanimous. He rooted for the repair mechanisms as they spun vast, moon-sized spools of carbon fiber, weaving nets to catch and hold tottering fractal spikes, made of fragile snow and wider than a planet. He applauded the robot tugs, swarming like gnats to divert huge, drifting ruins away from collision paths that might wreak untold devastation. Emerson did not think of sapient beings living beneath those countless, glittering windows. Perhaps it was the lack of words, but to him, the Fractal World seemed not so much a habitat as a creature in its own right, self-contained, self-aware, and wounded, fighting for its life.

He used a pocket terminal to get close-ups. Unable to command by voice or keyboard, he found the little computer was conveniently programmed in other ways. It coaxed him to use a language of gestures that must have been developed for disabled aphasics on Earth, a handy mix of hand motions, eye flicks, and plain old pointing that usually conveyed what he wanted. It sure beat the clumsy, grunting efforts he used on Jijo, when communicating with poor Sara often reduced them both to tears of futility.

And yet . . . he recalled those months fondly. The sooner world had been beautiful, and the illegal colony of six allied races moved him deeply with their strangely happy pessimism. For that reason, and for Sara's sake, he wished there were something he could do for the Jijoans.

For that matter, he wished he could do something for *anybody*—Gillian, the Streakers . . . or even the hordes of hardworking robots, laboring to save an edifice that was built when early dinosaurs roamed Earth. Lacking useful work, he was reduced to staring at a great drama unfolding outside.

Emerson hated being a spectator. His hands clenched. He would rather be using them.

With a rapid set of winks, he called up the scene in the Plotting Room, where Gillian met with Sara and the youngsters from Wuphon Port. They were joined by a tall stack of fuming, waxy rings—Tyug, the traeki alchemist of Mount Guenn Forge, who filled out a quorum of Jijo's Six Races. Amid their animated discussion he saw the young centauroid *urs,* named Ur-ronn, gesture toward their small herd of glavers, mewling and licking themselves nearby. Beings whose ancestors had roamed the stars, but who since had reclaimed innocence—the method prescribed for winning a second chance.

Emerson wasn't quite sure of the connection, but apparently those reverted creatures had something to do with the huge, blobby star vessel that escorted *Streaker* here.

He was proud when a word came floating to mind. *Zang.*

Except to prevent *Streaker* from leaving, the great globule seemed indifferent at first, concentrating on the repair task, directing mechanical hirelings to weave vast nets of black fiber, bandaging cracks in the huge edifice. But after a day or so, the Zang were forced to pay attention when mysterious objects drifted toward the Earthship, approaching from various parts of the immense inhabited shell, nosing close to investigate.

The Zang drove each snoop away, keeping a cordon around the Terragens' cruiser. Yet, *Streaker*'s exotic guardians showed no interest in acknowledging Gillian's frequent messages.

Emerson recalled one of the few definite facts known about the mighty hydrogen breathers—they had different ways of viewing time. Clearly, the Zang felt their business with *Streaker* could wait.

Now he listened as Gillian consulted with the Jijo natives, trying to form a plan.

"What if we just herd the glavers onto a shuttle and send it over? Do we have a clue whether that would satisfy the Zang? Or if the glavers would be safe?

"Suppose the answer to both questions is yes. What does Galactic law say about a situation like this? Are we supposed to ask the Zang for a receipt?"

Out of the flood of words, only "glavers" and "shuttle" and "Zang" had any solid meaning to him. The rest floated just beyond clear comprehension. And yet, to Emerson, the rich sibilance of her voice was like music.

Of course he had always nursed a secret passion for Dr. Gillian Baskin, even when her husband, Thomas Orley, lived aboard *Streaker*—the sort of harmless infatuation that a grown man could control and never show. At least not crudely. Life wasn't fair, but he did get to be around her.

Alas the infatuation started affecting his judgment after Tom vanished heroically on Kithrup. Emerson started taking risks, trying to emulate Orley. Attempting to prove himself a worthy replacement in her eyes.

A foolish quest, but natural. And it paid off at Oakka, where minions of the Library and Migration Institute betrayed their oaths, conspiring to seize *Streaker's* cargo to benefit their birth clans instead of all civilization. There, Emerson threw himself into a wild gamble, and his boldness paid off, helping win a narrow victory—another brief deliverance—enabling *Streaker* to flee and fight another day.

But here . . .

He shook his head. In viewing tapes from *Streaker's* departing point of view, Emerson now realized that his sacrifice in the borrowed Thennanin scout had made very little difference. *Streaker's* escape path had begun opening even as he charged ahead, ignoring Gillian's pleas to return. He would have gone to Jijo anyway, and in more comfort, if he had just stayed aboard this ship and never fallen into the clutches of the Old Ones.

Scanning the near edge of the torn Fractal World, he immersed himself in the fantastic task of preservation. Numbers and equations were no longer trustworthy, but he still had an engineer's instincts, and these thrilled as he watched machines bolster vast constructions of ice and carbon thread. He had never seen cooperation on such scale among hydros, oxies, and machines.

That thought made the cosmos seem a nicer place somehow.

Time passed. Emerson no longer thought in terms of minutes and hours—or duras and miduras—but the uneven, subjective intervals between hungers, thirsts, or other bodily needs. And yet, he began feeling tensely expectant.

A bedeviling sense that something was wrong.

For a while he had difficulty placing it. The dolphins on duty in the bridge seemed unconcerned. Everything was calm. None of the display screens showed any obvious signs of threat.

Likewise, in the Plotting Room, Gillian's meeting broke up, as people dispersed to workstations or else observed the awesome vista surrounding *Streaker*. Nobody appeared alarmed.

Emerson conveyed to the little holo unit his desire to tap the ship's near-space sensors, scanning along its hull and environs. As he went through the exercise twice, the creepy feeling came and went in waves. Yet he failed to pin anything down.

Calling for a close-up of Gillian herself, he saw that she looked uncomfortable too—as if some thought were scolding away, just below consciousness. A holo image stood before her. Emerson saw she was examining the area around *Streaker's* tail section.

Signaling with a grunt and a pointed finger, Emerson ordered his own viewpoint taken that way. As the camera angle swept along the ship's outer hull—coated with its dense star-soot coating—he felt a growing sense of relief. If Gillian was also looking into this, it might not be just his imagination. Moreover, her instincts were good. If there were a serious threat, she would have taken action by now.

He was already feeling much better as the holo image swept past *Streaker's* rear set of probability flanges, bringing the stern into view.

That was Emerson's first clue.

Feeling better.

Ironically, *that* triggered increased unease.

Back on Jijo—ever since he had wakened, delirious, in Sara's, treehouse with a seared body and crippled brain—there had always been one pleasure that excelled any other. Beyond the soothing balm of secretions from the traeki pharmacists. Beyond the satisfaction of improved health, or feeling strength return to his limbs. Beyond the wondrous sights, sounds, and smells of Jijo. Even beyond the gentle, loving company of dear Sara. One bliss surpassed any competitor.

It happened whenever the pain stopped.

Whenever the conditioned agony, programmed into his racked cortex, suddenly let go of him—the abrupt absence of woe felt like a kind of ecstasy.

It happened whenever he *stopped* doing something he wasn't supposed to do. Like trying to remember. Any attempt at recollection was punished with agony. But the reward was even more effective, at first. A hedonistic satisfaction that came from not trying anymore.

And now Emerson sensed a similarity.

Oh, it wasn't as intense. Rewards and aversions manifested at a much subtler level. In fact, he might never have noticed, if not for the long battle he had fought on Jijo, learning to counter pain with obstinacy, by facing it, like some tormented prey turning on its pursuer . . . then transforming the hunter into the hunted. It was a hard lesson, but in time he had mastered it.

Not . . . there . . . he thought, laboriously forming the words one at a time, in order to lock in place a fierce determination.

Go . . . back. . . .

It felt like trying to fight a strong wind, or swimming upstream. Each time the holo scene made progress toward the ship's bow, he felt strange inside. As if the very *concept* of that part of *Streaker* was peculiar and somehow improper, like trying to visualize a fifth dimension.

Moreover, it apparently affected computers, too. The instruments proved balky. Once his view passed forward of the first set of flanges, the camera angle kept wandering aside, missing and curving back around toward the stern again.

A torrent of cursing escaped Emerson. Rich and expressive, it flowed the way *all* speech used to, before his injury. Like songs and some kinds of poetry, expletives were fired from a part of the brain never touched by the Old Ones. The stream of invective had a calming, clarifying effect as Emerson turned away from all artificial tools and images. Instead, he pressed his face close to the bubble window, made of some clear, incredibly strong material that Earth's best technicians could not imitate. He peered forward, toward *Streaker*'s bow.

It felt like trying to see through your own blind spot. But he concentrated, fighting the aversion with all the techniques he had learned on Jijo.

At last, he managed barely to make out glimmers of movement amid the blackness.

Sensing his strong desire to see, the *rewq* symbiont slithered downward, laying its filmy body over his eyes—translating, amplifying, shifting colors back and forth until he grunted with surprised satisfaction.

Objects swarmed around *Streaker*'s prow. Robots, or small ship-like things. They darted about, converging en masse near a part of the ship that everyone aboard seemed to have conveniently forgotten!

Emerson glimpsed a small, starlike flare erupt. Glints of actinic flame.

He wasted no more time cursing. On hands and knees, he scuttled out of the little observation dome, built by some race much smaller than humans that had once owned this ship long before it was sold, fifth-hand, to a poor clan of ignorant wolflings, freshly emerged from an isolation so deep they used to wonder if, in all the universe, they lived alone.

He had no way to report his discovery. No words to shout over an intercom. If he went to the Plotting Room, grabbed Gillian's shoulders, and *forced* her to look forward, she would probably respond. But how long might that take?

Worse, could it even risk her life? Whatever means was being used to cast this spell, it bore similarities to his own prior conditioning and Emerson recognized a special brand of ruthlessness. Those responsible might sense Gillian's dawning awareness, and clamp down harshly through her psi talent.

He could not risk exposing her to that danger.

Sara? Prity? They were his friends and dear to him. The same logic held for the other Streakers. Anyway, there was too little time to make himself understood.

Sometimes you had to do things yourself.

So Emerson ran. He dashed forward to the cavernous hangar—the Outlock—that filled *Streaker*'s capacious nose. All the smaller vessels that once had filled the mooring slips when they departed Earth were now gone. The longboat and skiff had been lost with Orley and the others at Kithrup. Even before that, the captain's gig had exploded in the Shallow Cluster—their first terrible price for claiming Creideiki's treasure.

Now the docks held rugged little Thennanin scoutboats, taken from an old hulk the crew had salvaged. It felt all too familiar, slipping into one of the tiny armored vessels. He had done this once before—turning on power switches, wrestling the control wheel built for a race with much bigger arms, and triggering mechanisms to send it sliding down a narrow rail, into a tube that would expel it. . . .

Emerson quashed all memory of that last time, or else courage might have failed him. Instead, he concentrated on the dials and screens whose symbols he could no longer read, hoping that old habits, skills, and Ifni's luck would keep him from spinning out of control the moment he passed through the outer set of doors.

A *song* burst unbidden into his mind—a pilot's anthem about rocketing into the deep black yonder—but his clenched jaw gave it no voice. He was too busy to utter sound.

If it were possible to think clear sentences, Emerson might have wondered what he was trying to accomplish, or how he might possibly interfere with the attackers. The little scout had weapons, but a year ago he had not proved very adept with them. Now he could not even read the controls.

Still, it could be possible to raise a ruckus. To disrupt the assailants. To dash their shroud of illusion and alert the Terran crew that danger lurked.

But what danger?

No matter. Emerson knew his brain was no longer equipped to solve complex problems. If all he accomplished was to draw the attention of the Zang—bringing their protective wrath down on the trespassers—that might be enough.

The wounded Fractal World turned before him as the airlock closed and he gently nudged the boat's thrusters, moving toward the interlopers. Waves of aversion increased in strength as he drew nearer. Pain and pleasure, disgust and fascination—these and many other sensations washed over him, rewarding Emerson each time his eyes or thoughts drifted away from the activity ahead, and punishing every effort to concentrate. Without the experience on Jijo, he might never have overcome such combination. But Emerson had learned a new habit. To *seek* discomfort—like a child pressing a loose tooth, attracted by each throbbing twinge, teasing and probing till the old made way for the new.

The little rewq helped. Sensing his need, it kept ripple-shifting through various color spectra, conveying images that wavered elusively, but eventually resolved into discernible shapes.

Machines.

He realized at least a dozen spindly forms had already latched themselves to *Streaker*'s nose. They clambered like scavenging insects probing the eye of some helpless beast. If the goal were simple destruction, it would all be over by now. Their aim must be more complex than that.

He recognized the hot light of a cutting torch. Either they were trying to burn their way into the ship, to board her, or . . .

Or else their effort was aimed at cutting something off. A sample, perhaps. But of what?

Emerson pictured *Streaker* in his mind, a detailed image, unimpaired by his aphasia with sentences. The memory was wordless, almost tactile, from years spent loving this old salvaged hull in ways a man could never love a woman, supervising so many aspects of its transformation into something unique—the pride of Earthclan.

All at once he recalled what lay beneath that bitter, flickering glare.

A symbol. An emblem supposedly carried by all ships flown by oxygen-breathing, starfaring races.

The rayed spiral crest of the Civilization of Five Galaxies.

Incongruity stunned Emerson. At first he wondered if this might be yet another trick, deceiving his perceptions once again, making him *think* that was their target. All this seemed an awful lot of effort to expend simply defacing *Streaker* of its bow insignia.

Anyway, the machines were clearly having more trouble than they had bargained for. The dense carbon coat burdening the Earthship was obdurate and resistant to every attempt by Hannes Suessi and the dolphin engineers to remove it. As he drew closer, Emerson saw that only a little progress had been made, exposing a small patch of *Streaker*'s original hull.

He almost laughed at the aliens' discomfiture.

Then he looked beyond, and saw.

More machines. Many of them, swarming darkly, converging from the starry background. Almost certainly reinforcements, coming to make short work of the job.

It was time to act. Emerson reached for his weapons console, choosing the least potent rays, lest he damage *Streaker* by mistake.

Well, here goes nothing, he thought.

I sure hope this works.

So intent was he on aiming—carefully adjusting the crosshairs—that he never noticed what had just happened *within* his crippled mind.

His use of two clear sentences, one right after another, smoothly expressing both wryness and hope.

GILLIAN

Realization crackled through her consciousness like pealing thunder. She cried out a shrill command.

"Security alert!"

Klaxons echoed down the Earthship's half-deserted halls, sending dolphins scurrying to combat stations. The ambient engine hum changed pitch as Suessi's crew increased power to shields and weapon systems.

"Niss, report!"

The spinning hologram spoke quickly, with none of its accustomed snideness.

"We seem to have been suborned by a combined psi-cyber stealth attack, with an aim toward distracting *Streaker*'s defenders, both organic and machine. The fact that you and I roused simultaneously suggests the emitter source has been abruptly destroyed or degraded. Preliminary indications suggest they used a sophisticated logic entity whose memic-level was at least class—"

"What's our current danger?" Gillian cut in.

"I detect no immediate targeting impulses or macroweaponry aimed at this vessel. But several nearby automatons show latent power levels that could turn dangerous at close range.

"So far, it seems they are content to fire away at each other."

She stepped toward the display showing a camera view of the ship's bow . . . exactly opposite from the region she had been inspecting, suspicious of some unknown menace. Her heart pounded as she saw how close it had been. All might have been lost, if the intruders had not fallen to fighting among themselves. Sharp flashes surged and flared as spiderlike shapes lashed at each other, casting battle shadows uncomfortably close.

"Where the hell are the Zang?" Gillian murmured under her breath.

Scanning the area of space where the hydrogen entities had been, her instruments showed no sign of the big globule-vessel . . . only a disturbing, elongated cloud of drifting ions. *Perhaps it's only backwash from their engines, when they departed on an errand. They may be back at any moment.*

Her mind quailed from the other possibility—that some weapon had removed the Zang from the local equation. A weapon powerful enough to leave barely a smudge of disturbed atoms in its wake.

Either way, the psi attack kept us from noticing our guardians were gone. Someone went to a lot of trouble making sure we'd sit still for a while.

She felt Suessi's engines dig in as Kaa started backing away from the combat maelstrom. But the pilot only made a little headway before the swarm of conflict followed, as if tethered to *Streaker* by invisible cords.

"Do you have any idea who—"

"None of the combatants has identified itself."

"Then what were they trying—"

"It appears that some group was attempting to steal *Streaker*'s WOM archive."

"*Streaker*'s. . . ?"

Her question froze in her throat. Gillian's mouth closed sharply as she understood.

By law, each Galactic vessel was supposed to carry a "watcher" . . . a device that would passively chronicle the major features of its travels. Some units were sophisticated. Others—the sort that a poor clan could afford—were crude mineral devices, capable only of recording the ship's rough location and identifying any ships nearby. But all of them fell into the category of "write-only memories" . . . designed to store knowledge but never be read. At least never within the present epoch. Eventually, each was supposed to find its way into the infinite archives of the Great Library, to be studied at leisure by denizens of some later age, when the passions of this one had faded to mere historical interest.

At once, the stratagem behind this attack made sense to her.

"The Old Ones . . . they must have found the codes, enabling them to read our WOM. It would tell them where *Streaker*'s been!"

"Enabling them to backtrack our voyage and find the Shallow Cluster. Indeed."

Gillian's reaction was strangely mixed. On the one hand, she felt angry and violated by these beings who would meddle in her mind and rob *Streaker* of its treasure. Information her crew had guarded for so long, and Tom and Creideiki paid for with their lives.

On the other hand, it might solve so many problems if the thieves succeeded. Some mighty faction would then have the secret at last, perhaps using it to dominate the next age. Battles and great conspiracies could then surge onward, perhaps letting Earth and her colonies drift back into the side eddies of history, neglected and maybe safe for a while.

"I'm surprised no one tried this before," she commented, wary as she watched the minibattle follow *Streaker*'s retreat across the vast interior of the Fractal World. The Niss answered.

"Indeed, it seems a logical ploy to try seizing the watcher from our bow. I can only hazard that our prior enemies lacked the means to read a coded WOM."

It spoke well for the neutrality of the Library Institute, that even the richest clans and alliances could not break the seals. That made Gillian wonder. Might the betrayals at Oakka have been an aberration? Perhaps it was just *Streaker*'s run of typical bad luck that put it at the mercy of rare traitors. Institute officials might be more honorable elsewhere.

If so, should we try again? Gillian wondered. *Maybe head for Tanith and try surrendering ourselves to the authorities one more time?*

Meanwhile, the Niss whirled thoughtfully. The Tymbrimi-designed software entity flattened into a planate whirlpool shape before speaking once again.

"It must have taken them much of the last year, using their influence as elder members of the Retired Order, to access the keys. In fact . . ."

The mesh of spinning lines tightened, exhibiting strain.

"In fact, this casts a pall across our earlier miraculous escape from this place."

"What do you mean?"

"I mean that we thought we were being aided by altruistic members of the Retired Order, benevolently helping us elude persecutors in the name of justice. But consider how conveniently easy it was! Especially the way we stumbled on references leading to the so-called Sooner Path—"

"Easy! I had to squeeze our captured Library for it, like pressing wine from a stone! It was—"

"It was easy. I now see that in retrospect. We must have been infected by a lesser meme parasite, conveying the attractive notion of fleeing to Jijo. A nearby sanctuary with just one way in and one way out. A haven whose only exit would lead us right back here again."

Gillian blinked, abruptly seeing what the machine was driving at.

Suppose one faction hoped to seize *Streaker*'s WOM, but knew it would take a while to access the right codes for reading it? Fugitive wolflings could not be left just hanging around in the open till then. Someone else might snatch the prize!

What better way to stash the memory unit for safekeeping than by sending it into hiding, guarded by the self-preservation skills and instincts of tested survivors? The Earthship's own crew.

"If we had not turned up about now, no doubt they would have sent word to Jijo luring us back. Indeed, the plan has earmarks—patience and confidence—that resonate of the Retired Order.

"Only now this failure to seize the object of their desire shows that their scheme broke down. Not everything is going their way. This faction still has enemies. Moreover, note how dismal the state of their power has become, under these conditions of calamity!"

"Calamity" was right. As Gillian watched, fighting seemed to ripple outward around them. Tactics sensors showed signs of conflagration spreading toward the nearest ragged edge of the wounded criswell structure.

"At this rate," she mused, "someone's gonna get fed up and use one of those big disintegrator rays. Maybe on *us*. We better think about getting out of here."

"Dr. Baskin, while we have been talking I've thought of little else. For instance, I have endeavored to call our captor-protector, the Zang ship entity, to no avail. A leading hypothesis must be that it was destroyed."

Gillian nodded, having reached the same conclusion.

"Well, if it ain't coming, I don't care to hang around waiting."

She raised her voice toward the intercom.

"Kaa! Give it a full effort. Let's make a break for t-point!"

The pilot acknowledged with a click burst of assent.

• *Cornered by orcas,*
    • *With our backs against sharp coral,*
        • *Watch them eat plankton!* •

As *Streaker* started pulling away, the battle storm followed. Detectors showed still more machines converging from all sides. Still, a gap slowly began to grow.

Then the Niss interrupted again.

"Dr. Baskin, something else has come to my attention that I know will concern you.

"Please observe."

The main viewer zoomed toward one corner of the fiery brawl—a scrap far smaller than some other battles *Streaker* had observed, though nearness made the flashes and explosions seem more garish by far. Rapid glimpses revealed that most of the fighters were machines, lacking any boxy enclosures to protect protoplasm crews. Clearly, the varied factions of "retired" races preferred doing combat by proxy, using mechanical hirelings rather than risking their own necks.

Then one object loomed into view, more squat in profile than any other—a tubby dart, rounded and heavily armored. Gillian recognized the outline of a Thennanin scoutcraft.

"Ifni!" she sighed. "Has he done it again?"

"If you mean Engineer Emerson d'Anite, I can tell you that interior scans show no sign of him within this ship. I surmise it is him out there, unleashing weapons with quite futile abandon, missing nearly everything he shoots at. Organic beings really should not face mechanicals in close combat. It is not your forte."

"I'll bear that in mind," Gillian murmured, deeply torn over what she could or should do next.

EMERSON

When he realized he wasn't hitting anything—and no one was shooting back—Emerson finally shut down the fire controls. Apparently, nobody thought him worth much worry, or effort. It felt irksome to be ignored, but at least no faction seemed bent on avenging the robots he had taken out with those first few lucky shots, igniting this fury.

Combat surged around him. There was no making sense of the shadowed struggle as machines flayed other machines.

Anyway, it soon dawned on him that something else was going on. Something more important and personal than events taking place outside.

Waves of confusion swept through Emerson's mind.

Nothing unusual about that. By now he was quite used to feeling befuddled. But the *type* of disorientation was exceptional. It felt like peering past dark clouds of delirium. As if everything till then had been part of a vivid dream, filled with perverted logic. Like a fever-racked child, he had made no clear sense of anything going on around him for a very long time. But in a brief instant light seemed to pierce the mist, limning corners that had been shrouded and dark.

Like a hint, or a passing scent, it lasted but a moment and was gone.

He suspected a trick. Another psi distraction . . .

But the light must have been more than that! The joy it brought was too intense. The sense of loss too devastating when it vanished.

Then, without warning, it was back again, much stronger than before.

Something he had been missing for a long time.

Something precious that he had never fully appreciated until it was taken from him.

I . . . I can think . . .

. . . can think in words again!

Not just words, but sentences, paragraphs!

I'm piloting a Thennanin war dart . . . Streaker *lies behind me . . . Over there, and across nearly the whole of heaven, I see the blemished sky arch of the Fractal World . . .*

At once an overwhelming flood of understanding filled Emerson. Things he had seen on Jijo and since. Concepts that had eluded him because they could not be shaped with images and feelings alone, but needed the rich subtlety of abstract language to shape and anchor them with a webbery of symbols.

Sadness flooded him when he thought of all the things he had wanted to tell Sara during their long journey together across the Slope. And to Gillian, after he returned home a devastated cripple. Two different kinds of love he could never express—or sort out—until now.

How is this possible? My brain . . . they destroyed my speech centers!

For some reason, after the Old Ones finished interrogating him, they had decided to let him live, but in silence. The means to do this they found simply by reading his own memories of poor wounded Creideiki. When they mimicked giving him the same injury, the resulting cruel mutilation had left him half dead . . . and less than half a man.

That much he had already worked out laboriously on Jijo, even without putting it in words. But the answer was never satisfying. It never explained the brutal logic behind such an act.

That was when it came to him.

A voice. One he had forgotten till that moment.

One he identified with chill, unblinking eyes.

"INACCURACY. WE DID NOT DESTROY THOSE PORTIONS OF YOUR ORGANIC BRAIN. WE BORROWED/TOOK/EXPROPRIATED A FEW GRAMS OF TISSUE FOR USE IN A GREAT GOAL. OUR NEED WAS GREATER THAN YOURS."

The effrontery of that claim nearly made Emerson howl with rage. Only by fierce discipline did he manage to form a reply, shaping it through pathways he had not used in too long a time. His voice sounded unpracticed, with an odd nasal twang.

"You bastards maimed me so I'd never talk about what you did!"

A sensation of aloof amusement accompanied the response.

"THAT WAS BUT A MINOR SIDE BENEFIT. IN FACT, WE DESIRED/NEEDED THE TISSUE ITSELF. IF TRUTH BE TOLD, IT SEEMED FAR MORE VALUABLE TO US THAN YOU EVER WERE LIKELY TO BE, AS A WHOLE ENTITY . . . ALTHOUGH IT MIGHT HAVE BEEN BETTER IF YOU WERE OF A SLIGHTLY DIFFERENT SPECIES. BUT WE HAD PHYSICAL POSSESSION

OF JUST ONE EARTHLING, SO IT WAS ORDAINED THAT YOU WOULD BE OUR DONOR."

The explanation left him more befuddled than ever.

"Then how come I can talk now?"

"IT IS A MATTER OF LINKAGE AND PROXIMITY. WE LEFT QUANTUM RESONATORS LINING THE CAVITY IN YOUR BRAIN, WHERE THE EXCISED TISSUE ONCE RESIDED. THESE HAVE CAUSAL CONNECTIONS WITH OTHER RESONATORS COATING THE SAMPLE WE TOOK AWAY. IF YOU ARE CLOSE ENOUGH, UNDER THE RIGHT CIRCUMSTANCES, YOUR NEURAL PATHWAYS MAY RESUME THEIR FORMER FUNCTION."

Emerson blinked. Leaning toward the scoutship's curved window, he peered at the dark skyscape, flickering with silent explosions.

"YES, THE CAPSULE IS NEARBY, BROUGHT CLOSE TO YOU BY A WORKER DRONE. ONE THAT SEEMS INNOCUOUS, EVADING ATTENTION FROM THE FACTIONS BATTLING AROUND YOU.

"IN FACT, THE DRONE CAN COME MUCH CLOSER STILL. THE TISSUE MIGHT BE YOURS AGAIN, UNDER CERTAIN CONDITIONS."

He wanted to scream at his former captors, declaring that they had no right to bargain with him over something they had stolen in the first place. But they would only dismiss that as whimpering over wolfling standards of fairness. Anyway, Emerson's mind was racing now, covering a great deal of territory in parallel, using both the old logic tracks and new techniques he had picked up during exile.

"If I serve you, then I'll get my speech centers back? What's the matter? Did your former scheme fail?"

"SOME OF US STILL HAVE FAITH/CONFIDENCE IN THAT PLAN. THOUGH AT BEST IT WAS ALWAYS A GAMBLE—AN ATTEMPT TO BRIBE ONE WHO IS/WAS FAR AWAY FROM HERE.

"BUT NOW, DEFYING ALL EXPECTATION, YOU ARE NEAR US ONCE AGAIN. IT PRESENTS ANOTHER POSSIBILITY FOR SUCCESS."

"Oh, I just can't wait to hear this," Emerson commented, but he had learned the first time that sarcasm was wasted on the Old Ones.

"THE CONCEPT SHOULD BE SIMPLE ENOUGH FOR YOUR LEVEL OF BEING TO UNDERSTAND. IF YOU HURRY, YOU CAN REBOARD THE EARTHSHIP AND FIND/RETRIEVE. INFORMATION WE DESIRE. A SIMPLE TRADE WOULD FOLLOW, AND WHAT YOU DESIRE MOST WILL BE YOURS."

Emerson clamped down, refusing to put in words some of the thoughts glimmering at the back of his mind. Whatever he expressed that way—even subvocalizing—must pass through a lump of protoplasm that lay out there somewhere, carried by a machine drifting amid the slashing rays and bursting mines. A piece of himself that others could sieve at will.

"So now you want to make a deal. But a year ago you thought you didn't need my useless carcass anymore. Why did you send me to Jijo, then? Why am I still alive?" The voice seemed resigned about providing an explanation.

"THERE ARE BOUNDARY CONDITIONS TO THE UNIVERSAL WAVE FUNCTION, AFFECTING WORLDLINES PROPAGATING IN ALL

DIRECTIONS. YOUR PHYSICAL EXISTENCE IN A FUTURE TIME IS ONE OF THESE BOUNDARY CONDITIONS. OUR ACTIONS MUST BE COMPATIBLE WITH KNOWN FACTS.

"HOWEVER, THERE IS LOOSENESS IN THE SLIP AND PLAY OF WORLDLINES. NUMERICAL CALCULATIONS SHOWED THAT IT WAS ONLY NECESSARY TO PUT YOU CLOSE TO YOUR PEERS, ALIVE, AT A CERTAIN PLACE AND TIME, IN ORDER FOR ACCOUNTS TO BALANCE. PLACING YOUR BODY ON JIJO, WITHIN ACCESSIBLE RANGE OF YOUR COLLEAGUES, APPEARED ADEQUATE."

He stared, appalled at both the power and the callousness implied by that statement.

"You . . . you'd call that hellish journey I went through *accessible?*"

The voice did not reply to that. Emerson's question might as well have been rhetorical.

His eyes skimmed the scout's displays. Now the letters and glyphs made instantaneous sense, indicating *Streaker*'s growing speed and distance. Clearly, Gillian was making another run toward the stars.

"THAT'S RIGHT. YOU HAVE ONLY A FEW DURAS TO ACT. IF YOU DO NOT REBOARD AND ACCEPT OUR OFFER, WE WILL BE FORCED TO DESTROY THE EARTHSHIP AND ALL YOUR COMRADES."

Emerson laughed.

"That assumes your enemies will let you! They almost grabbed *Streaker*'s WOM, before your faction interfered. They might have something to say about your plans, in turn.

"Besides, I'm an important boundary condition, right? You gotta help me live into the future, alongside my friends, or your whole cause-and-effect thingamajig falls apart!"

"THE DEMANDS OF CAUSALITY ARE NOT AS STRICT AS YOU IMPLY, HUMAN. DO NOT TEST YOUR QUESTIONABLE VALUE, OR TAUNT US WITH DISRESPECT."

He laughed aloud.

"Or what? You'll punish me? You'll inflict *pain*?"

Silence greeted his challenge, but he could tell the scorn had had an effect, this time. Contempt was a slim weapon, but they weren't used to it. The words stung them.

On the other hand, the Old Ones knew Emerson had little choice. Remaining behind was not an option, if he could avoid it. His hands decided for him, nudging to the scout's throttle, sending it accelerating after *Streaker* . . . though he felt a rising sense of dread.

What would happen when he left the vicinity of the robot carrying the missing piece of himself? Would it follow? Lurking nearby so he could continue to think?

When the voice spoke again, it seemed cool and distant.

"WE NOW SUPPLY YOU WITH A CODE TO USE IN CONTACTING US, WHEN YOU ARE READY TO ACT ON OUR OFFER."

A series of *colors* filled Emerson's mind—a simple sequence that seared its way into memory. He could not forget it if he tried.

Then his former captors offered a parting comment.

"CLEARLY WE MISESTIMATED YOUR LEVEL OF SAPIENCY, IN BELIEVING THAT SIMPLE AVERSION CONDITIONING COULD SWAY YOU EARLIER. CONGRATULATIONS ON YOUR APPARENT TENACITY AND FLEXIBILITY.

"NEVERTHELESS, WE HAVE CONFIDENCE IN THE EFFECTIVENESS OF OUR FINAL INDUCEMENT."

With that, the voice cut off, though Emerson wasn't done with them yet.

"Well let me tell you what you can do with your Ifni-damned offer, you gorslucking spawn of retard slime molds! Go seek redemption up your own cloacas, you jef-eating, dirt-licking, damned-to-Gehenna—"

Emerson's stream of invective went on while he sped after *Streaker*, hurrying past robot combatants that grappled and slashed one another, but never laid a claw or ray on him. He cursed on and on, enjoying the rich flood of invective and the feel of words spilling from his mouth, keeping it going for as long as he could. Each added second of crass language seemed a victory.

Swearing was his touchstone. Filling the small cabin with hoarse noise, he clung to the knack of speech, fiercely refusing to let distance—or the enemy—rip it away.

Soon he noted that *Streaker* was slowing down, pausing in its flight to let him catch up. The act of loyalty warmed him as the docking tunnel opened, spilling a welcome glow. But Emerson kept shouting his opinion of the Old Ones—their ancestry, their character, and their likely destiny on the great pyramid of existence.

Only when he finished latching to *Streaker*'s guidance beam did Emerson pause long enough to remember something.

Cursing didn't count.

He could do that even on Jijo. Like singing and sketching, profanity did not use the part of his brain that was stolen.

Emerson tried to say something else—to comment on the battle, the sky filled with shattered debris, or his own growing fear—and failed.

Desperately, his thoughts whirled, rummaging through his tormented brain, seeking an aptitude that had seemed so fluid and natural just moments before. A lifelong skill that villains had robbed from him, then briefly returned, but for too short a time.

It felt like trying to extend an amputated limb. The ghost was still there. A hint of volition. *Meanings* filled his mind, along with a readiness to act, to prompt sentences. To speak.

But some key element was gone again, and with it all the things he had hoped and planned saying to Sara. To Gillian.

Emerson slumped in a seat that had been built for a much larger pilot, a creature of great physical power, respected across the Civilization of Five Galaxies. His arms sank from the massive controls and his chin met his chest as tears streamed from eyes suddenly too foggy for seeing. He felt helpless, like an overwhelmed child. Like an ignorant wolfling.

Till that moment, Emerson had thought himself familiar with loss. But now he knew.

There was always someplace deeper you could go.

GILLIAN

Lieutenant Tsh't reported from the bridge. Turbulent bubbles fizzed as her tail slashed through oxywater.

"Engineer d'Anite is back aboard. Sh-shall we accelerate again?"

Gillian felt indecision like a heavy beast, clawing and dragging at her arms, her shoulders.

"Have sensors picked up any sign of the Zang?"

The Niss hologram expressed worry with taut lines.

"The hydrogen-breathing entities may be destroyed, along with their vessel. But even if the Zang are preoccupied elsewhere, some of these battling factions will surely unite to prevent our departure."

"We don't know their motives, or even how many cliques—"

"By appraising tactical patterns I count at least five different groups. Their forces are mostly robots of the sepoy-soldiery type, receiving instructions from various sectors of the Fractal World, working for local associations of the Retired Order."

The Niss paused for a moment, then resumed.

"Let me revise. I perceive SIX battle patterns. One seems aimed toward opening an escape path for us. So it appears we do have allies among the combatants."

"It appeared that way last time, too," she replied. "These helpers—are they strong enough to protect us?"

"Doubtful. The crucial moment will come when we pass through the narrowest part of the gap that's been torn in the Fractal World. Any group might choose to destroy us at that point, using the defense beams we saw earlier."

That was a cheery thought to dwell on as *Streaker* reentered the gaping corridor filled with evaporating debris and shimmering artificial comets. Only this time a sparkle of battle also followed the Earthship, ebbing and surging around it.

Gillian had Kaa steer just half a million kilometers from one ragged edge of the great wound, threading a path between the stumps and stark shadows of titanic, brittle spires.

"Maybe someone will think twice about shooting at us with those big guns, if we're so close to the shell itself."

From here they could make out some of the giant machines striving to shore up the torn criswell structure, using nets woven from great spools of carbon thread to arrest its decay. These were a completely different order of mechanism, autonomous and sapient—hired workers, not slaves.

In fact, though, most of the supply spools looked nearly empty.

They are running short of raw materials, Gillian thought. *All their efforts may fail if this keeps up . . . especially if bands of Old Ones fight instead of helping.*

A dolphin's joyful shout erupted behind Gillian. She turned in time to see Emerson d'Anite enter the Plotting Room, his head and shoulders slumped in apparent depression.

"Well, there's our hero—" Gillian began. But Sara Koolhan rushed past with a glad cry to embrace her friend. The little neo-chimpanzee, Prity, leaped among them, and soon Emerson was enveloped. Dolphins gathered around, clicking excitedly while their walkers hissed and clanked. The Jijoan youngsters—Alvin and his friends—slapped Emerson's back, shaking his hand and telling him how wonderful he was.

Even if their words made no sense to him, the air of approval seemed to wash away some of the man's dour mood. His eyes lifted to meet Gillian's, and she returned his tentative smile with one of her own. But then the Niss cut in.

"Two new swarms are approaching, Dr. Baskin."

She turned to look. "More sepoy robots?"

"No . . . and it worries me. These fresh arrivals are much more formidable beings, Gillian. They are independent constructor-contractors. Autonomous members of the Machine Order of Life."

"Show me!"

The fresh arrivals were already near, coming in crowds of about a dozen each from opposite directions—one depicted as a cluster of red dots, the other green. Each group swept imperiously through the battle zone. As evidence of their status, none of the combatant robots fired on the newcomers. Instead, most scurried out of their way.

This looks bad, Gillian thought as the fierce green sparkles entered visual range. Each of the leaders resembled a giant spiny sea urchin, almost a tenth as long as *Streaker,* though most of that was in spindly leg-appendages that writhed as the mechanism flew toward *Streaker*'s tail.

"Impact-t in thirty secondsss!" called Tsh't from the bridge. "Shall we open fire?"

"Negative!" Gillian shouted. "No one has used a beam or particle weapon on us yet. I'm not about to start. Let's see what their business is first."

One swarm converged near *Streaker*'s aft end. Several of the big, spiky mechs clamped on. Soon, a bright, shimmering glow began to float around them.

"They are dissolving the ship!" the Niss cried out. "Matter removal rates exceed thirty tons per second . . . and rising. We must fight them off!"

Tsh't reported targeting one of the machines with a laser turret, but Gillian countermanded the fire order.

"Don't do a thing till I say so! Akeakemai, give me a zoom focus on the machines that are still floating out there, *behind* the ones that landed!"

It was hard to peer past the fog that was being kicked up. But Gillian thought she made out a giant cylinder. A hooplike shape.

"It's a spool! Like the ones they unreel when they weave repair nets." She turned her head and cried, "Quick. What is the spectral signature of the removed material? Is it pure carbon?"

A brief pause. When the Niss spoke again, it sounded subdued.

"Carbon it is."

"How pure?"

"Very. The vapors contain no metal from Streaker's true hull. How did you know?"

Gillian's throat still felt as if her heart was beating there. But some of the panicky feeling ebbed.

"These big guys don't give a damn about petty bickering among hot-tempered oxy-life-forms. They have a job to do, and they're running out of raw materials. Their best supply of carbon was already disrupted when the Jijoans somehow triggered flares on Izmunuti. But *we* carry layers of the same material sought by the harvester sail-ships! This work team must have sensed us passing nearby and sent machines to fetch more for repairs."

"Confirmed," said the Niss. "As they move slowly along the hull, evaporated material is being sucked up and spun into polycarbon fiber, leaving the fuselage beneath intact."

Hannes Suessi called jubilantly from Engineering, clearly delighted to learn how the machines swiftly removed a coating that had stymied him for months.

"At this rate, we'll shed several megatons in no time," he added. "It's gonna make us much more nimble."

By now the second swarm—shown as red pinpoints—arrived in the vicinity of *Streaker*'s nose. Another set of enormous mechanisms clamped onto the bow. These huge visitors showed no special interest in the area around the rayed spiral symbol.

Gillian nodded.

"I guess they'll strip us from both ends now. Let's pray this really does leave the hull itself intact. If our luck has turned, their presence may deter anyone else from shooting at us till we're near the t-point."

The Niss whirled thoughtfully.

"Of course, there is another danger. If law and consensus are totally broken throughout the Fractal World, nothing prevents the various 'retired' factions from getting in touch with their younger cousins, via hyperwave or time drop."

"In other words, we might see battlefleets of Soro, Jophur, or Tandu come boiling through at any minute. Great." She sighed. "All the more reason to get the hell—"

The spinning moiré patterns suddenly ballooned outward—an expression of surprise.

"Something is different," the Niss announced. "The group at the bow . . . it is not doing the same thing as those at the stern."

Gillian took a step forward.

"Show me!"

At first the scene looked similar. Several long-legged machines clung to *Streaker*'s soot-covered hull, plying the black surface with shimmering rays. Only this time no milky haze of vapor poured toward mouthlike collectors.

No streams of dark fiber spun out the machines' back ends, to collect on huge spools. Instead, something weird happened to the dense coating *Streaker* had picked up during its passages through Izmunuti's atmosphere. A rainbowlike sheen rippled and condensed slickly behind the great mechanisms as they marched a spiral pattern along the hull.

No one spoke for several minutes. So unexpected and unexplained was this behavior that Gillian had no idea how to react.

"They're . . . not taking the carbon away. They are—"

"Transforming it, somehow," agreed the Niss.

At last, Suessi called. The chief engineer's cyborg image appeared on a secondary screen. Although his head was now a mirrored dome, Gillian could tell from the old man's body language that he had a theory.

"The soot poured out by Izmunuti . . . the phases that condensed on us were mostly carbon, all right. But a large fraction consisted of fullerenes—so-called 'buckeyballs' and 'buckeytubes.' There were a lot of Penrose diamond states, too. The material had some mighty strange properties, as we found when we tried cutting it, back on Jijo. All sorts of caged impurities give it traits like a high temperature superconductor, plus an altered coefficient of friction—"

"Hannes!" Gillian interrupted. "Please get to the point."

The silvery dome nodded.

"I've scanned the surface these new machines are leaving behind. The coating is far more uniform than raw star soot. The buckey states intermesh with each other in ways I've never seen. I'd have to guess the properties we observed before would be enhanced by many orders of magnitude."

One of the dolphins muttered.

"Oh great-t. Now it will be even harder to ssscrape off!"

Gillian shook her head.

"But what are they trying to accomplish? To seal us inside?"

If so, there might still be time to evacuate the ship, sending the crew scrambling for airlocks at the stern. Perhaps they might find shelter among the first group of machines.

"Our forward laser turret has a clear line of fire," announced Tsh't.

Gillian motioned with her right hand, restraining any action for now.

One of the kids from Jijo spoke up then. The little wheeled g'Kek, who called herself Huck made a good lookout, since she was able to scan four screens at once with her waving eyestalks.

"Uh-oh," she remarked. "It looks like our new visitors are gonna start fighting, too."

She pointed to where support vessels from both groups could be seen drifting toward each other. Barely constrained energies crackled as a showdown developed.

Scanners showed that many of the lesser war machines were withdrawing from this confrontation.

They'll use us as a battleground. How could things possibly get any worse?

Gillian knew it was a mistake to put it that way. One should not tempt Ifni, the goddess of luck, who could always come up with one more ratcheting of fate.

The Niss hologram coiled nearby. Its voice was low, resigned.

"Now we are being scanned from the Fractal World itself. Those controlling the great disintegrator beams have turned their targeting apparatus our way. We may soon go the way of the late Zang."

"They'll risk hitting the habitat, right where it's most vulnerable!"

"Apparently, some think it worth the risk, in order to intimidate us. Or else they would destroy what they cannot keep."

Gillian had seen those shafts of annihilation in action. *Streaker* could be vaporized in seconds.

LARK

These were hellish circumstances, and yet, for a biologist, it might be heaven. While his body endured cramped confinement in a stinking plastic bag, Lark's mind sped through lessons expanding his parochial view of the vast panorama of life.

He grew deft at a new form of communication, receiving visual images that came enhanced by meanings and connotations sent through a tube directly to his bloodstream. A language of hormones and mood-tweaking peptides. And it went both ways. Whenever Lark understood something new, he did not have to speak or even nod his head. The mere act of comprehending had metabolic effects—a familiar endorphin burst of satisfaction—that his alien tutor quickly detected.

Likewise, confusion or frustration brought rapid changes.

The globule-teacher kept revising its presentation until Lark grasped what he was being shown.

It was a strangely active kind of passive study.

Would you call this a form of telepathy? he wondered.

Yet, the method also seemed slow and crude. As visual lessons, the demonstrations were a lot like puppet shows. Physical portions of his instructor would bud off the parent body to float within a vacuole cavity, twisting and transforming themselves into living models or mannequins to play out a little scene. The same images might have been presented far swifter, and more vividly, using one of the computerized display units he had seen Ling use, on Jijo and in the Jophur ship.

Inefficient or not, Lark eventually realized why his captors used this approach.

It's fundamental to the difference between hydrogen-and oxygen-based ways of looking at the universe.

At a glance, the two worlds seemed utterly unalike.

While both biologies were based on carbon molecules, one used the reactive chemistry of oxidizing atmospheres, with liquid water serving as the indispensable solvent. Only narrow circumstances of temperature and pressure could nurture this kind of life from scratch. Normally, it arose in filmy skins of ocean and air, coating Earthlike worlds. Venturing beyond these lean oases, oxy-life must carry the same rare conditions with them into space.

"Reducing" environments were far more abundant, covering cold, giant planets like Jupiter, Saturn, Uranus, or Titan—and even the broad, icy domain of comets. Some of these worlds soaked in abundant hydrogen, while others featured methane, ammonia, or cyanogen. But most shared a few common features—enormous, dense atmospheres and turbulent convecting layers, somewhat like the roiling strata of a sun. Life-giving heat often flowed *upward,* from a hot planetary core. Sometimes there was no solid "surface" at all.

Because of this, most hydros were creatures of a vast, boisterous sky. Up and down became *tall,* unlimited, almost coequal with the other two dimensions. Nor was travel a matter of exertive *flying,* by defying gravity with flapping wings, but of adjusting buoyancy and propelling through fogs so dense the pressure was like the bottom of Earth's sea.

In such a realm, there were advantages to size. Big creatures cruised with languid grace, sifting for organic food. When caught in strong downdrafts, only a giant could fight free and keep from being hauled to searing, crushing depths. So huge did some hydro-beings grow, they could be viewed from space, resembling titanic, self-contained clouds.

And that was where organic chemistry—the Designer's Assistant—might have left things, if not for action by another party.

The Critic.

Evolution.

Inevitably, the logic of reproduction and advantage took hold on reducing worlds, as it did on oxidizing ones like Earth . . . though in different ways.

Oxy-life counted on liquid water to carry out the complex colloidal chemistry of proteins and amino acids. Yet, too much watery flow would dilute those same processes, making them useless. Even in the warm sea, this meant crafting compact packages—cells—of just the right size to evolve life's machinery. For two billion years, the limit of biological accomplishment on the early Earth had been to spread single-celled organisms through the ocean, soaking up sunlight and devouring each other while slowly improving their molecular techniques.

Until one day a cell consumed another—and let it continue living. A primitive eukaryote took in a blue-green alga and gave it a home, exchanging safe living quarters for sugars produced from photosynthesis. This act of cooperation gave the combined team a crucial edge in competition with other cells.

Nor was it the only joint venture. Soon, cells paired up in quantity, amassing and colluding, forming temporary or permanent associations to gain advantage over other teams. Complex organisms flourished, and evolution accelerated.

Some call it the food chain, or the Dance of Life. I've seen it played out on Jijo, in so many subenvironments and ecosystems. Plants use photosynthesis to store food energy in carbohydrates. Herbivores eat plants. Carnivores prey on herbivores, completing the cycle by returning their own substance to the ground when they defecate or die.

It looks like a well-tuned machine, with each part relying on the others, but paradoxes abound. Everything that seems at first like cooperation has its basis in competition. And nearly every act of competition takes part in a bigger, healthier system, as if cooperation were inherent all along.

Of course that oversimplified matters. Sometimes the balance was thrown off kilter—by some environmental change, or when one component species escaped natural controls keeping it in check. Like a cancer, it might "compete" out of existence the very eco-network that had enabled it to thrive in the first place.

Still, the basic pattern was nearly always the same on millions of fecund little worlds. Take compact bags of protein-laced water. Provide sunlight and minerals. Get them busy vying in life-or-death rivalry. Over the long run, what emerges will be ever-greater and more complex alliances. Cooperative groups that form organs, bodies, packs, herds, tribes, nations, planetary societies . . . all leading to the fractious but astounding Civilization of Five Galaxies.

The story of hydrogen-based life had similarities, but the plot took a different twist.

On Jovian-type worlds, size emerged from the start. Simple beings of vast extent flapped and fluttered across skies broad enough to swallow several hundred Jijos. Evolution caused such creatures to improve, though more slowly at cooler temperatures. Indeed, change did not always come about through reproduction and inheritance. More often, some *part* of a huge, drifting beast might stumble onto a new chemical trick or behavior. That portion would spread laterally, consuming and replacing the flesh next to it, gradually transforming the whole entity.

Death was still part of the process, but not quite in the same way it occurred on Earth.

To us, dying is a quantal thing. An individual may succeed in having offspring, or not. But either way, personal extinction stalks you all your life, and must eventually win, however hard you struggle or however much you innovate.

But to hydros, everything is murky, qualitative. Without such clear lines, death is relative. So long as a transformation happens slowly and smoothly, you look at it with no more dread than I fear cutting my hair.

Instead of building up through hard-won cooperation among tiny cells, life on Jupiter-type worlds was large from the start. It did not revolve as much around cooperation-competition. *Self* and *other* were known concepts, but distinguishing between the two had less central a role in existence than it did to oxy-beings.

Then how do you organize yourselves? Lark thought at one point, wrestling with frustration. *How do you recognize objects, goals, opponents, or ideas?*

Lark's tutor could not read his mind, or perceive his questions as discrete sentences. But clearly some kind of meaning entered his bloodstream, secreted by Lark's brain when he posed a query. It was a slower, less efficient process than speech, involving many iterations. But he wasn't going anywhere.

Objects throbbed within the vacuole, budding off the parent body, pulsing as they crossed the open space, then merging together or recombining with the greater whole. For quite some time, Lark had watched these little forms writhe into subtly formed shapes that performed for his edification. Now, all at once, he realized the deep truth underlying it all.

These little subselves. They are . . .

A throbbing wave penetrated his thigh, swarming down a leg then up his torso. The sensation was unlike any other, and Lark abruptly realized he had been given a *name.*

A name he could not repeat aloud in any language, or even in his thoughts—so he translated as best he could.

Deputies.

In their native environments, hydrogen-breathing entities did not tend to look outward for learning or fulfillment. If one huge beast encountered another, it might lead to combat, or predation—or peaceful intercourse—but little chance of permanent companionship. The vast winds of a Jovian sky soon scattered all acquaintances. A return visit or rendezvous was next to impossible.

Growth requires challenge, however. So, for conversation, appraisal, or understanding . . . they turned *within.*

Contained by spacious membranes, the core of a natural hydro-being was an oasis of calm amid planet-sized storms. Sheltered chambers could be fashioned at will, and small subunits budded to float freely for a while, engaging others in myriad ways. Like a human's internal thoughts and fantasies, these deputies might cluster, converse or clash, working out countless scenarios for the good of the greater whole.

Simulations.

Lark glanced at the globule-creature floating just outside his membrane enclosure. It had seemed autonomous, but now he knew the hydro was a mere "deputy" of something larger still—perhaps the huge ship-entity that had sacrificed itself under withering Jophur fire in order to penetrate this place.

Lark abruptly recalled something he had read once, in a rare galacto-xenology text, about a type of hydro-life called Zang.

Their great passion is simulating the world . . . the universe . . . but not through math or computers. They do it by crafting living replicas, models, mimicries, inside their own bodies.

In an odd way, it seemed familiar.

Like the way we humans explore future possibilities with our imaginations.

But there was more.

Because we start life as little bags of water—as cells—we oxies must work our way from the ground up, by a complex, bootstrapping dance of competition and cooperation, building coalitions and societies, gradually becoming creatures capable of taking the process in hand, through Uplift. For all its faults, our galaxy-spanning civilization is the culmination of all that.

From many . . . one.

Hydros do it differently. They begin large, but loneliness forces them to subdivide, to seek diversity within.

From one . . . many.

The insight filled Lark with sudden heady pleasure. To behold both differences and similarities with an entirely different empire of life was a gift he had never imagined receiving. One beyond his ability to ask or anticipate.

He yearned to share it, to tell Ling everything, and hear her own enthralled insights. . . .

Sadness was an abrupt flood, equal to the pleasure of moments before. Both emotions meshed and swirled, a mixture that poured into his veins, driven by his pounding heart. In moments it reached the tube in his leg, and then—

The tutor-entity floating nearby gave a sudden jerk.

The globule quivered, as if contemplating the chemicals given off by Lark's body during his epiphany, when everything became clear.

At least a hundred tiny vacuoles opened throughout its bulbous body. In each of these, a froth of nearly microscopic animalcules suddenly burst forth and interacted, frenetically merging, bouncing, and dividing. Lark stared, fascinated to watch a Zang "think" right in front of him. In practice, it was complex and blurringly fast.

The fizzing commotion ended as quickly as it had begun. All the little openings collapsed and the minuscule subdeputies resorbed into the main body. Lark's tutor throbbed—

He felt another wave of stimulation penetrate his leg, a warm sensation that spread quickly through his guts and arteries—a form of communication so intimate that it transcended any thought of embarrassment. It simply was.

Appreciation.

At least that was how Lark interpreted the molecular wave—hoping that it was not wishful thinking.

Appreciation is welcome.

Appreciation is reciprocated.

A short time later, he lost consciousness. A sudden drowsiness told Lark that his hosts wanted him to sleep—and he did.

No longer did a spacious chamber surround him, filled with other prisoners and visibly noxious fumes. Awareness returned nearly as swiftly. He had no idea how much later it was, only that he had been moved.

Instead, his transparent cocoon had been transplanted to a much smaller room. And there were other changes, too.

The membranes surrounding him had shrunk to form-fit against his body, like a baggy suit of clothes. Lark found that he was *standing up.* Perhaps they had even walked him here, prompting his body to move like a marionette. The notion was unpleasant, but freedom to stretch out from a cramped fetal position more than made up for it.

He still could not breathe, and relied on the thigh catheter for life support, but Lark's surroundings looked less hazy and there was not as great a sensation of nearby cold.

Carefully, tentatively, he shuffled his feet to turn around.

One of the Zang hovered nearby, though whether it was his erstwhile tutor he could not tell. Probably not. This one resembled the warrior-globule he had encountered in the halls of *Polkjhy*—the being that had burst through a wall, frightened Rann away, and rushed forward to take Lark captive. On close inspection, it was possible to see some of the adaptations necessary to shield hydrogen-breathing envoys against a caustic oxygen environment. Thick protective layers glistened, and it maintained a spherical form, ideal for minimizing exposure.

So, we're both suited up. Girded to meet each other halfway. Except that I'm still anchored by an umbilicus, and you fellows can shut me off like a light, anytime you want.

Lark raised his eyes beyond the Zang, and saw a feature of the room that had escaped his notice till now.

A window . . . looking outside!

Careful not to trip, he shuffled close, eager to see the stars. It would be his first direct view of space since he and Ling were trapped aboard the Jophur vessel when it took off from Jijo.

But instead of strange constellations, his attention was riveted at once by something vastly more strange—an object, floating against blackness, that somewhat resembled a spiny hedge anemone you might find behind a rock in an alpine meadow back home. Except his impression this time was of incredible size. Somehow, he felt the prickly thing might be as large as Jijo . . . or bigger still.

Soon, he could tell one more thing. The dark object was damaged. Glimmering sparks could be seen, twinkling in dim reddish light that poured through a jagged opening, torn across one hemisphere.

Polkjhy appeared to be heading toward that gaping hole, at a very rapid clip.

Earlier, the Zang seemed to say they had not succeeded in taking over the ship. Maybe their resources are stretched too thin. From simulated charts, it appeared that the Jophur still command the engines, weapons, and life support.

Perhaps they are speeding to a place where they can get help ridding the ship of infestations like the Zang . . . and me.

Or else, maybe the Jophur think this is where they'll find the "prey" Rann spoke of—the Earthship everyone's been searching for.

Lark turned his head to regard the warrior-globule. Did it have a purpose in bringing him here, and showing him this scene? Perhaps the Zang had figured out that Lark was no friend of the Jophur. Maybe they wanted an alliance. If so, he would gladly comply . . . on one condition.

You must help me find and release Ling. Give us a lifeboat, or some other way out of here, either back to Jijo or someplace else safe.

You do that, and I'll act as your hound, sniffing out and hunting down my "own kind."

Lark was being intentionally wry in his thoughts, of course. Only compared to hydrogen breathers could *Jophur* possibly be called his "kind." But sardonicism was probably far too subtle for the Zang to read by sifting his blood.

If we're going to team up, we'll need much better communications.

He watched the globule for any sign of an answer, or even comprehension. But instead, a few moments later, it seemed to *jump* in sudden agitation and surprise. Waves of nervous excitement entered Lark's body from the catheter.

What? What is it!

Spinning around, he sought a reason. Then his gaze passed through the window once again.

Oh, Ifni . . .

The battleship had already plunged much closer to the great corrugated ball, clearly aiming for the hole in one side. Lark noted at once that it seemed *hollow,* and glimpsed a compact round flame glowing within. Lark had no idea what to make of the scene, or what the flame could be. Anyway, something else quickly caught his attention.

Sparkling explosions rippled along one edge of the wide cavity. He watched several of the giant quills or spikes break off and drift in slow motion, already dissolving as the aperture widened destructively.

Most of the havoc seemed to be wrought by sharp needles of light, generated somewhere deep inside the great shell. A dozen or so rays converged on a single point, a speck, near a rim of the great wound, creating a painful mote of brilliance. Reflections off this target did most of the glancing damage to the nearby shell.

The speck darted about, sometimes evading the shafts completely, leaving them to hunt as it fled outward from the gap at a rapid clip. Whenever a pursuing ray caught up with it, the distant spark glared so brightly that Lark had to blink and avert his gaze.

What's going on? What is happening out there?

Once again, he felt like the ignorant savage that he was. Wisdom hovered nearby—the Zang no doubt understood these strange sights. But it might take several miduras of patient puppet shows to explain even the simplest aspect.

An abrupt thrumming vibration shook the floor beneath Lark's feet. The masters of *Polkjhy* were doing something.

He recognized the grating tempo of weapons being fired.

Soon, a double handful of glittering objects could be seen darting away from this ship, tracing an arc across space, hurtling at fantastic speed toward the sundered ball-of-spikes.

Are those missiles?

Lark recalled how the Commons of Jijo surprised the Jophur by attacking this very ship with crude chemical rockets. He had a feeling the bright arrows out there were more deadly, by far.

At first, he thought the weapons might be joining the attack on the bright speck. But their glitter swept on past it, following each of the cruel rays toward its source.

Another swarm of emotion-laden connotations swept through Lark's body. This time it was easy to interpret the Zang's critical commentary.

Hasty.

Unwise.

Self-defeating.

His tutors did not approve of the Jophur action. But there was nothing to be done about it now. The missiles had already vanished into the great cavity.

For lack of anything better to do, Lark nervously watched and waited.

A short time later, the bright beams began winking out, one by one.

Still glowing, their target kept darting toward deep space, while *Polkhjy* plunged to meet it.

EWASX

Calmness, my rings.

Cultivate serene reflection, I urge you.

Stroke the wax.

Respect the wisdom of our captain-leader.

TRUE, that august stack has not been itself lately. Some of its component rings suffered wounds when human vermin infiltrated our control center, using a crude bomb to attempt sly sabotage.

TRUE, a far worse shipboard infestation has now driven our proud crew from several decks, forcing us to abandon and quarantine portions of our dear *Polkjhy* vessel to the Zang blight.

TRUE, our leader's rings-of-command have fumed odd-smelling flavors and scents lately, prompting a few priest stacks to vent mutinous steam, fomenting rebellious vapors among the crew.

NEVERTHELESS, be assured that I/we shall remain loyal to our commander. After all, was not *this* conjoined pile of ill-fitting rings put together as an experiment, designed and implemented at the behest of our captain-leader? If another chief takes charge, the new leader might order our/My swift disassembly into spare parts!

MY RINGS, SOME OF YOU DO NOT SEEM ADEQUATELY OUTRAGED AT THAT PROSPECT.

Therefore, as your beloved Master Torus, let Me remind you (with jolts of electric pain/affection) that a Jophur is not the same sort of composite being as the one you composed on feral Jijo, when together you made up the traeki sage, Asx.

We/you/I are much greater now.

Ever since the gracious Oallie intervened, rescuing our race from placid unassertiveness, the Jophur clan has risen to power and eminence among vigorous competing races of the Civilization of Five Galaxies. This is not a destiny to be given up lightly. Especially with signs and auguries now pointing to an onrushing Time of Changes. With each passing jadura it grows clear that fortune may turn around, presenting us with the clues/hints/coordinates/relics carried by the dolphin-wolfling ship.

HENCE, MY/OUR AGREEMENT WITH THE CAPTAIN-LEADER'S DECISION TO INTERVENE!

Let the senior priest stack rant about law and decorum. Should we stand back and allow the Earthlings to be incinerated? After all we have been through, chasing them across vast reaches and five levels of hyperspace, with our prey/prize finally in sight, should we now let panicky members of the Retired Order lash out and destroy the greatest treasure in the known cosmos?

TRUE, we have no legal standing here in Galaxy Four. No formal right to fire missiles into the fractal sanctuary just ahead. But it is their own fault that we were forced to act! The Earthship and its contents are of rightful interest to *our* life order—we descendants of the Progenitors who still cruise star-speckled lanes. Retirees should mind their own business, contemplating deep thoughts and obscure philosophies, preparing their genetic lines for transcendence, not meddling in affairs that are no longer their concern!

One by one, our superlight projectiles strike their targets on the habitat's inner shell . . . and one by one, disintegrator beams flicker out.

BEHOLD! The last one goes dark, leaving the Terran vessel still driving ahead under its own power.

Success!

Now the wolflings sprint with alarmed speed toward the transfer point, hoping to escape this trap toward some unknown sanctuary beyond. But their hope is forlorn.

We are here, in good position to pounce.

[But how is it possible?]

Our second stack of cognition makes this query, venting steam-of-curiosity.

[Truly, we/I are glad to see the Earthlings survive those terrible, destructive rays. But how was it achieved? Should they not have vaporized during the first moments they fell under attack by such voracious beams?]

* * *

The same question travels in muted tones among Jophur stacks responsible for tactical evaluation. Pastel shadows of troubled concern flash across light-emitting ring flanks, while a worried mist wafts over that portion of the control center. Specialist toruses grow hot as they interact with computers, laboring to solve this quandary.

How *did* the Earthship survive such a fierce assault?

Is this yet another insidious wolfling trick?

Are they still receiving protection from the meddling Zang, in violation of the basic rule that each life order should mind its own business?

Are the hydrogen breathers truly willing/ready to risk Armageddon over matters they could not care about, or comprehend?

Now the senior priest stack ventures to challenge our captain-leader openly.

Striding forward on its ring of legs, that illustrious/sacred composite being nods its oration peak in a circle of righteous accusation.

"This Is Intolerable! By Sending Those Missiles, You/We Have Surely Alienated Any Affection This Colony Of Retirees Might Have Nurtured For Our Race, Clan, And Alliance!"

The captain-leader, perhaps sensing a precarious situation, replies in calmer tones, venting aromas of sweet confidence.

"Of Repercussions There Will Be Few.

"Of Legal Fault, We Have None, Since Those Directing The Rays Were Clearly Outlaws, According To The Codes Of Their Own Life Order.

"We Acted To Protect A Treasure Sought By All Oxygen-Breathing Civilization."

Many crew-stacks vent agreement. But the priest-stack is in no mood to be mollified.

"Few Repercussions? Even Now, Explosions Continue Rocking The Habitat Where Our Missiles Fell! The Entire Great Structure Is In Jeopardy!"

No denying that it is a serious matter. Lawsuits may result, dragging through the courts for thousands, or even millions of years. Nevertheless, confident-soothing aromatics swell from our glorious commander.

"The Social And Physical Fabric Of This Habitat Was Already Torn Apart By The Mere Presence Of Pathogenic Terrans. Now, All Stacks Take Note: Our Onboard Library Has Downloaded Population Data From This Macrohabitat. Regard How A Majority Of Occupants Has Already Departed!

"Some Fled To Other Retirement Homes, Farther From The Dangerous Passion-Waves Of Younger Races.

"Others Have Chosen To Abandon Retirement! Even Now, They Rejoin Our Life-Order, Seeking Companionship Among Their Former Clients, Becoming Active Once Again In The Flux-Turmoil Of The Civilization Of Five Galaxies.

"A Third Portion Of Refugees Has Moved On. Ahead Of Schedule, They Depart, Aimed For Transcendent Realms."

Reverent silence greets our commander's news. Within this very stack—among our/My own conjoined rings, there is brief unanimity of spirit. From Master Torus all the way to the humblest greasy remnant of old Asx, there is agreement about one thing—I/we/you are privileged to live in such times. To take part in such wonders. To see/observe/know events that will be legendary in eras beyond the morrow.

Our captain-leader continues.

"So, Like The Empty Shell Of An Ouiut Egg, This Habitat Is Less Important Than It May Appear. A Mere Few Trillions Remain In Those Tortured Precincts. For That Reason, Let Us Concern Ourselves No More With Its Fate. Any Reparations Adjudged Against Us Can Be Paid Trivially Out Of Our Reward, When The Earthship Is Safely In Custody, Sealed By Jophur Wax!"

The captain-leader's supporters cheer loudly, emitting joyful scent clouds. And yet, our/My contribution to the acclaim seems weak, lacking enthusiasm. Some of you rings, as tender and compassionate as a traeki, dwell dismally on the bad luck of those "mere few trillions."

Relentlessly, the priest-stack maintains its indictment.

"Such Foolishness! Had You Forgotten Our Own Difficulties? We Had Expected/Hoped To Find Aid Here, In Ridding Dear *Polkjhy* Of Its Human-Plus-Zang Infestations. Now Such Help Will Not Come At Any Price!"

Our captain-leader hisses, rearing higher upon the command dais, clearly losing both temper and patience.

Underlings quail back in dismay.

"That Situation Is Under Control. Zang Pests Are Isolated. While The Quarantine Holds, No Priority Exceeds That Of Capturing The Earthling Ship!"

Others may be impressed, but the priest-stack is not intimidated by shouting or physical gestures. Instead, that revered ring pile moves closer still.

"And What Of Communications? We Had Planned Using Local Hypermail Taps To Contact Our Clan/Alliance. Now Those Services Are Ruined. How Shall We Inform Superiors Of Our Discoveries/Opportunities On Jijo? Or Seek Aid In Pursuit Of These Earthlings?"

Subordinate ring piles scurry away from this confrontation between tall, august stacks, who now stand nearly close enough to press their gorgeous, fatty toruses against each other. Dense, compelling vapors clash and swirl around them, driving to confusion any lesser Jophur who happens to get caught in a backdraft. Stretching higher, each great lord tries to overawe the other.

From a privileged point of view, clockwise and slightly behind, I/we perceive the captain-leader using an arm-appendage to draw forth a hidden sidearm. Nervous tremors surge down our fatty core.

MY RINGS, WILL HE SHOOT?

Suddenly, the taut tableau is interrupted. Word-glyphs from the ship's chief tactics officer cut through the acrimonious stench like an icy wind, reminding us of our purpose.

"The Earthship comes within range! Soon it will pass nearby, on its way to the transfer nexus. Interception/opportunity will maximize in ninety duras."

Like two antagonistic volcanos deciding not to erupt—for now—our great lords back off from the precipice. Their stacks settle down and cease venting odious vapors.

Some things need not be said. If we succeed now, no reward will be denied this crew or its leadership. No forgiveness will be withheld.

* * *

Scans show that nearby space is filled with debris from the great calamity. Innumerable *ships* can also be seen peeling off the retirement habitat, seeking to escape toward the local transfer point.

Warily, we search among these sensor contacts for possible threats—for warships or other entities that might interfere, the way Zang globules hindered us, last time the Earthlings seemed within our grasp. Each vessel receives scrutiny, but none seems to be in range this time, or of a class strong enough to obstruct us.

Nor do the wolflings try to hide among these refugees, using them as decoys. Unlike at Jijo, the trick would not/cannot work, for we have kept them in sight ever since the disintegrator beams shut off. Clearly they know it, too, for their sole aim appears to be speed. To outrace us. To find sanctuary in the knotty worldlines of the transfer point.

But to get there, they must pass us. Logically, there seems to be little going in their favor.

And yet—(points out our/My second ring of cognition)—for three years the wolflings and their clients have proved slippery. Ever ready to spring devil-tricks befitting Tymbrimi, they have thwarted efforts by all the grand military alliances.

Now we face rumors that the sluggish forces of 'moderation' have begun to rouse, here and there, across the Five Galaxies. If that happens—if the Earthers manage delay after delay—there is no telling what the Pargi and other cautious fence-sitters might bring about!

Yes, My rings. Our wax overflows with disquieting worries. And yet, won't all that simply make our glory greater, when we Jophur succeed where others failed!

From *Polkjhy,* an ultimatum goes forth, similar to one the Terrans spurned before, when we sought them with beams and bombs under Jijo's ocean waters.

Surrender and give over your treasures. In return, our mighty alliance will safeguard Earth. The dolphin crew will be interned, of course. But only for a thousand years of frozen sleep. Then, at expiration time, they will be released into a new, reshaped Civilization of Five Galaxies.

Again, our only answer comes as insolent silence.

We prepare weaponry.

"The Earthship's dynamics are inferior-degraded," explains a tactical crew stack. "It still carries excess mass—hull-contamination acquired from multiple exposures to the sooty red giant star."

Polkjhy, too, passed through that polluting fog. But Earthlings can only afford lesser starship models, while our fine vessel is of a superior order, field-tuned to shed unwelcome atoms.

{Indeed?}

{Then how were the Zang able to board us?}

HUSH, MY RINGS!

I send coercive electric bursts down tendrils of control, reminding our second cognition ring to mind its own business.

* * *

Degraded or not, the preyship darts nimbly and appears well piloted. Our first warning shot misses by too wide a mark, and is not taken seriously.

Meanwhile, tactician stacks have been debating as to why the Earthship exists at all.

One faction insists the onslaught we saw—by planet-scale disintegrator rays, converging on a tiny ship—must have been a ruse! A garish light show, meant to make it seem the Earthlings were doomed, and persuade other assailants to back off while it accelerated away! Indeed, this astounding suggestion is now the majority opinion among *Polkjhy*'s tacticians—although it makes our missile attack seem foolish in retrospect.

{Behind us, the great habitat still shudders from those impacts. Other wounds are self-inflicted.}

This explanation seems evident from the fact that the dolphin-crewed ship endures. Yet, a minority suggests caution. We may have witnessed something real. Something true. An event worthy of alarm.

Our second warning shot lashes forth and is more accurate. It passes but a ship length from the quarry's nose.

"There Is A Worrisome Difference."

Thus announces a stack whose duty it is to monitor enemy conditions.

"The Target Resonates Strangely. Its Hypervelocity Profile Is Not The Same As It Was Before, Near The Red Giant Star. And There Are Unusual Reflections Off The Hull."

At our captain-leader's behest, deep scans are made, confirming that the preyship is the same model and type. Engine emanations are identical. Psi detectors sift for faint leakage through its shields, and sniff a telltale Earthling spoor.

Then, at high magnification, we/I view the hull at last—

My rings, how it shines!

No longer sooty and black as space, it gleams now with a slick perfection that one only sees on vessels newly minted from their yards.

More perfect, for when starlight reflects off the curved surface, each warped image seems brighter than the original!

What can this mean?

Our senior priest-stack fumes.

"After All We Have Been Through, And All That We Have Seen, Only A Composite Fool Would Not Have Expected Further Tricks/Exploits/Miracles.

"Only A Misbegotten/Misjoined Stack Would Not Have Called For Help."

Our captain-leader shivers, settling cautiously onto the command dais. Streams of worried smoke trickle from its wavering topknot.

Finally, gathering rigidity among its constituent rings, the august commander-stack orders a targeted strike, at one-tenth potency, meant to disable the Earthship's power of flight.

Humming a finely tuned battle song, *Polkjhy* lashes out, transmitting rays of formidable force, aimed toward severing three of the quarry's probability flanges. Fierce energies cross the narrowing gap between our vessels to accurately strike home—

* * *

DO NOT ASK QUESTIONS, MY RINGS. JUST DO AS I SAY.

Move gently, innocuously toward the door.

That's it. Tread quietly, without undue sound. Flash no color-shadows. Vent no anxious steam.

Now, while the rest of the crew is distracted by drama/tragedy, let us make silent departure, like the humble traeki you/we/I once were.

Responding to our passkey scent, the armored hatchway rolls aside, opening a way out of the control chamber. With rearward-facing eyebuds, we/I watch crowds of our fellow Jophur mill in a fog of fear/distress toxins.

The worst fumes rise from a puddle of burning wax and grease—the flaming remains of our former captain-leader.

The priest stacks had very little choice, of course. When our weapon-beam failed . . . when its energies vanished, absorbed somehow by the Earthship's glistening new skin . . . a change in administration-command was certain.

As inevitable as the spreading of space metric in an expanding universe.

Of course the chase is not over. Our position is favorable. The Earthship cannot evade us and we are capable of maintaining contact wherever it goes. Meanwhile, *Polkjhy* has a capacious onboard branch of the Galactic Library. In its wise memory, we shall plumb and doubtless find this trick they used—and the drawback that will help us neutralize it.

Alas, My rings, that will do little good for this mongrel stack of ill-matched parts.

While *Polkjhy* proceeds on nimble autopilot—shadowing the Earthship as we both plunge toward the transfer point—the realignment of executive power commences among crew-stacks who proved poor judgment by remaining excessively loyal to our former commander. Demotion and reassignment will suffice for some. Replacement of the Master Torus will do for others.

But as for poor Ewasx—you/we were the inspired invention of the old captain-leader. At best, our rings will be salvaged as replacements for soldiers wounded in combat against the Zang. At worst, they will be mulched.

Now am I grateful for the feral skills you learned as a sooner/savage/traeki. Your movements are admirably stealthy, My rings. Clearly, you know better than a Jophur how to hide.

As the hatch rolls smoothly back to place, let us quickly move in search of some quiet, sheltered place where we may contemplate the wax . . . pondering the dilemma of survival.

ALVIN'S JOURNAL

"You'll get used to this sort of thing after a while."

Those words, spoken by Gillian Baskin, still seem to echo down my hollow spines as I write down a few hasty impressions of our final moments near the Fractal World.

I had better hurry. Already I can feel the pressure on my hoonish nerves increase as the *Streaker* swoops and plunges along the threadlike "domain boundaries" that curl inside a transfer point. Soon, this awful kind of motion sickness will make it futile to work. So let me quickly try to sort among the terrible things I have lately experienced.

Strangest of all was Dr. Baskin's voice, filled with such a deep resignation that she seemed more *Jijoan* than star god. Like one of our High Sages reading from the Sacred Scrolls—some passage foretelling inevitable tribulation. Somehow she made the impossible sound frighteningly plausible.

"You'll get used to this sort of thing . . ."

While the transfer fields close in around me—as nausea sends chills and frickles up and down my shivering skin—I can only hope that never happens.

She said it less than a midura ago, while gazing back at our handiwork.

An accomplishment none of us sought.

A disaster that came about simply because we were there.

In fact, those milling about the Plotting Room watched *two* views of the Fractal World, depicted on giant screens—both of them totally different, and both officially "true."

Speaking as a Jijo savage—one who got his impressions of spaceflight by reading Earthling books from the pre-Contact Twentieth through Twenty-Second Century—I found things rather confusing. For instance, many of those texts assumed Faster-Than-Light travel was impossible. Or else, in space-romance yarns, authors simply took FTL for granted. Either way, you could deal with events in a simple way. They happened when they happened. Every cause was followed by its effects, and that was that.

But the screen to my left showed time going backward!

My autoscribe explained it to me, and I hope I get this right. It seems that each microsecond, as *Streaker* flickered back into normal space from C Level, photons would strike the ship's aft-facing telescope, providing an image of the huge "criswell structure" that got smaller and dimmer as we fled. The pictures grew *older*, too, as we outraced successive waves of light. By the contorted logic of Einstein, we were going back in time.

I stared, fascinated, as the massive habitat seemed to get healthier before my eyes. Damaged zones reknitted. The awful wound grew back together. And glittering sparks told of a myriad converging refugee ships, apparently coming home.

The spectacle provoked each of my friends differently.

Huck laughed aloud. Ur-ronn snuffled sadly, and Pincer-Tip kept repeating "gosh-osh-osh!"

I could not fault any of them for their reactions. The sequence was at once both poignantly lamentable and hilariously absurd.

Over to the right, Sara and Gillian watched a different set of images, caught by hyperwave each time we flickered *into* C Level. Here my impression was of queasy simultaneousness. This screen seemed to tell what was happening *right now*, back at the Fractal World. Time apparently moved forward, depicting the aftermath of our violent escape.

The effects flowing from each cause.

Of course, things are really much more complicated. That picture kept wavering, for instance, like a draft version of some story whose author still wasn't sure yet what to commit to paper.

Sara explained it to me this way—

"Photons haul slow truths, Alvin, while speedy hyperwaves carry *probabilities*."

So, this image represented just the most *likely* scenario unfolding behind us. However slim, there remained a chance it wasn't true. Things might not be happening this way.

By God, Ifni, and the Egg, I still pray for that slim chance.

What we saw, through rippling static, was a harsh tale of rapid deterioration.

More than a single great laceration now maimed the great sphere. Its frail skin peeled and curled away from several newly slashed wounds. These fresh cracks spread, branching rapidly as we watched, each one spilling raw sunlight the color of urrish blood.

Hundreds of exterior spikes had already broken loose, tumbling end over end as more towering fragments toppled toward space with each passing moment. I could only guess how much worse things were *inside* the great shell. By now, had a million Jijo-sized windows shattered, exposing forests, steppes, and oceans to raw vacuum?

The hyperwave scene updated in fits and starts, sometimes appearing to backtrack or revise a former glimpse. From one moment to the next, some feature of devastation that had been *here* suddenly shifted over *there*. No single detail seemed fixed or firmly determined. But the trend remained the same.

I felt claws dig into my back as little Huphu and the tytlal, Mudfoot, clambered onto opposite shoulders, rubbing against me, beckoning a song to ward off the sour mood. Partly from numb shock, I responded with my family's version of the Dirge for an Unremarked Passing—an umble so ancient that it probably predates hoonish Uplift, going back to before our brains could grasp the full potential of despair.

Roused by that low resonance, Dr. Baskin turned and glanced at my vibrating throat sac. I am told that starfaring humans do not like hoons very much, but Sara Koolhan whispered in her ear and Gillian nodded approvingly.

Clearly, she understood.

A few duras later, after I finished, the little spinning Niss hologram popped into place, hovering in midair nearby.

"Kaa reports that we are about ten minutes away from t-point insertion."

Dr. Baskin nodded.

"Are there any changes in our entourage?"

Her digital aide seemed to give a casual, unconcerned twist.

"We are followed by a crowd of diverse vessels," the machine voice replied. "Some are robotic, a majority house oxygen-breathing refugees, bearing safe-passage emblems of the Retired Order of Life.

"Of course, all of them are keeping a wary distance from the Jophur battleship."

The Niss paused for a moment or two, before continuing.

"Are you absolutely sure you want us to set course for Tanith?"

The tall woman shrugged.

"I'm still open to other suggestions. It seems we've tried everything else, and that includes hiding in the most obscure corner of the universe . . . no offense, Alvin."

"None taken," I replied, since her depiction of Jijo was doubtless true. "What is Tanith?"

The Niss Machine answered.

"It is a planet, where there exists a sector headquarters of the Library Institute. The one nearest Earth. To this site Captain Creideiki would have taken our discoveries in the first place, if we had not fallen into a cascade of violence and treachery. Lacking other options, Dr. Baskin believes we must now fall back on that original plan."

"But didn't you already try surrendering to the Institutes? At that place called Wakka—"

"Oakka. Indeed, two years ago we evaded pursuit by merciless battle fleets in order to make that attempt. But the madness sweeping our civilization preceded us there too. Sworn monks of the monastic, bureaucratic brotherhoods abjured their oaths of neutrality, choosing instead to revert to older loyalties. Motivated in part by ancient grudges—or else the huge bounties offered for Streaker's capture by various fanatical alliances—they attempted to seize the Earthship for their blood and clan relations."

"So, the Institutes couldn't be trusted then. What's different this time?"

Dr. Baskin pointed to a smaller display screen.

"*That* is what's different, Alvin."

It showed the Jophur battleship—the central fact of our lives now. The huge oblate warship clung to us like a bad smell, following closely ever since their earlier assault failed to disable *Streaker.* Even with Kaa at the helm, the dolphin crew thought it infeasible to lose them. You'd have better luck shaking off your shadow on a sunny day.

"Our orders are clear. Under no circumstances can we let one faction snatch our data for themselves."

"So, instead we shall go charging straight into one of the busiest ports of Galaxy Two?"

The Niss sounded doubtful, if not outright snide. But Dr. Baskin showed no sign of reacting to its tone.

"Isn't that our best chance? To head for a crowded place, with lots of traffic and possibly ships big enough to balance that imposing cruiser out there? Besides, there *is* a possibility that Oakka was an exception. An aberration. Maybe officials at Tanith will remember their oaths."

The Niss expressed doubt with an impolite sound.

"There is a slim chance of that. Or possibly sheer surprise might prompt action by the cautious majority of Galactic clans, who have so far kept static, frozen by indecision."

"That's been our dream all along. And it could happen, if enough synthians and pargi and their allies have ships in the area. Why wouldn't they intercede, in support of tradition and the law?"

"Your optimism is among your greatest charms, Dr. Baskin—to imagine that the moderates can be swayed to make any sort of decision quickly, when commitment may expose them to mortal danger. By now it is quite clear to everyone that a Time of Changes is at hand. They are pondering issues of racial survival. Justice for wolflings will not take high priority.

"Far more likely, your abrupt appearance will provoke free-for-all combat above Tanith, making Kithrup seem like a mere skirmish. I assume you realize the armadas who are currently besieging Terra lie just two jumps away from Tanith? In less than a standard day they would likely converge—"

"Abating the siege of Earth? That sounds worthwhile."

The Niss hologram tightened its clustered, spinning lines.

"We are dancing around the main problem, Dr. Baskin. Our destination is moot. The Jophur will not allow us to reach Tanith. Of that you can be sure."

Sara Koolhan spoke up for the first time.

"Can they stop us? They tried once and failed."

"Alas, Sage Koolhan, our apparent invulnerability cannot last. The Jophur were taken by surprise, but by now they are surely scanning their onboard database, delving for the flaw in our wondrous armor."

They referred to the gleaming mantle now blanketing *Streaker*'s hull. As an ignorant Jijoan, I couldn't tell what made the coating so special, though I vividly recall the anxious time when swarms of machine entities sealed it around us—dark figures struggling enigmatically over our fate, without bothering to seek consent from a shipload of wolflings and sooners.

The final disputants were two sets of giant repair robots, those at the stern trying to harvest carbon from *Streaker*'s hull for raw materials, and the other team busy transforming the star soot into a layer that shimmered like the glassy Spectral Flow.

Lightning seemed to pass between the groups. *Meme-directive impulses,* the Niss identified those flickering bursts, advising us not to watch, lest our brains become somehow infected. In a matter of duras, the contest ended without any machines being physically harmed. But one group must have abruptly had its "mind changed."

Abruptly united in purpose, both sets of robots fell to work, completing *Streaker*'s transformation just in time, before the first disintegrator ray struck.

"Who says there has to be a flaw?" Dr. Baskin asked. "We seem to be unharmable, at least by long-range beams."

She sounded confident, but I remember how shocked Gillian, Sara, Tsh't, and the others had seemed, to survive an instant after the attack began. Only the crippled engineer, Emerson d'Anite, grunted and nodded, as if he had expected something like this all along.

"There are no perfect defenses," countered the Niss. "Every variety of weapon has been logged and archived by the Great Library. If a technique seems surprising or miraculous, it could be because it was abandoned long ago for very good reasons. Once the Jophur find those reasons, our new shield will surely turn from an advantage into a liability."

The humans and dolphins clearly disliked this logic. I can't say I cared for it myself. But how could anyone refute it? Even we sooners know one of the basic truisms of life in the Five Galaxies—

if something isn't in the Library, it is almost certainly impossible.

Still, I'll never forget that time, just after the big construction robots finished their task and jetted away, leaving this battered ship shining in space, as uttergloss as any jewel.

Streaker turned to flee through the great hole in the Fractal World, and suddenly great spears of destructive light bathed her from several directions at once! Alarms blared and each ray of focused energy seemed to shove us outward with titanic force.

But we did not burn. Instead, a strange noise surrounded us, like the groaning of some deep-sea leviathan. Huck pulled in all her eyes. Pincer withdrew all five legs, and Ur-ronn coiled her long neck, letting out a low urrish howl.

All the instruments went crazy . . . and yet we did not burn!

Soon most of the crew agreed with the initial assessment of Hannes Suessi, who decreed that the disintegrator beams must be *faked.*

A showy demonstration, they must be meant to frighten off our enemies and let us escape. No other answer seemed to explain our survival!

That is, until the Jophur pounced on us a short time later, and *their* searing rays also vanished with the same mysterious groan.

Then we knew.

Someone had done us a favor . . . and we didn't even know who to thank. Or whether the blessing cloaked more misfortune, still to come.

A voice called over the intercom.

"Transfer point insertion approaching in . . . thirty ssseconds."

Those in the Plotting Room turned to watch the forward viewer, looking ahead toward a tangled web of darkness—first in a series that would carry us far beyond Galaxy Four to distant realms my friends and I had barely heard of in legend and tales about gods. But my hoonish digestion was already anticipating the coming nausea. I remember thinking how much better it would suit me to be aboard my father's dross ship, pulling halyards and umbling with the happy crew, with Jijo's warm wind in my face and salt spray singing on the sails.

Back at the hyperwave display, I found another person less interested in where we were going than the place we were leaving behind. Emerson, the crippled engineer, who wore a rewq over his eyes and greeted me with a lopsided human smile. I answered by flapping my throat sac.

Blurry and wavering, the image of the Fractal World glimmered like an egg the size of a solar system, on the verge of spilling forth something young, hot, and fierce. Red sunlight shot through holes and crevices, while cruel sparks told of explosions vast enough to rock the entire structure, sending ripples crisscrossing the tormented sphere.

Emerson sighed, and surprised me by uttering a simple Anglic phrase, expressing an incredible thought.

"Well . . . easy come . . . easy go."

Mudfoot chittered on my shoulder as *Streaker*'s engines cranked up to handle the stress of transfer. But our attention stayed riveted on the unlucky Fractal World.

The globe sundered all at once, along every fault line, dissolving into myriad giant curved shards, some of them tumbling toward black space, while others glided inward to a gaudy reunion.

Unleashed after half a billion years of tame servitude, the little star flared exuberantly, as if celebrating each new raft of infalling debris—its own robbed substance, now returning home again.

Free again, it blared fireworks at heaven.

My throat sac filled, and I began umbling a threnody . . . a hoonish death requiem for those lost at sea, whose heart-spines will never be recovered.

The chilling words of Gillian Baskin haunted me.

"You'll get used to this after a while."

I shook my head, human style.

Get used to this?

Ifni, what have the Earthers already been through, to make *this* seem like just another day's work?

To think, I once gazed longingly at the stars, and hankered for adventure!

For the very first time, I understood one of the chief lessons preached by Jijo's oldest scrolls.

In this universe, the trickiest challenge of all is survival.

PART THREE

THE GREAT HARROWER

To our customers across the Five Galaxies—

The Sa'ent Betting Syndicate has temporarily suspended accepting wagers concerning the Siege of Earth. Although we still predict imminent collapse by the affiliated forces defending that wolfling home world, conditions have once again become too fluid for our dynamical scrying engines to project reasonable odds.

For those already participating in a betting pool, the odds remain fixed at: twenty-to-one for the planet's conquest within one solar orbit (three-quarters of a Tanith year); fourteen-to-one for surrender within one-quarter orbit; five-to-two in favor of a "regrettable accident" which may render the ecosystem unstable and lead to effective organic extinction for the wolfling races; seven-to-two in favor of humans and their clients being forcibly adopted into indenture by one of the great clans currently besieging the planet, such as the Soro, Tandu, Klennath, or Jououroouou.

Despite these deceptively steady odds, several fluctuating factors actually contribute to a high level of uncertainty.

1) Betrayals and realignments continue among the mighty clans and alliances now pressing the siege. Their combined forces would have easily overwhelmed the Human, Tymbrimi, and Thennanin defenders by now, if they could only agree how to distribute the resulting spoils. But instead, violent and unpredictable outbreaks of fighting among the besiegers (sometimes incited by clever Terran maneuvers) have slowed the approach to Earth and made odds-scrying more difficult than normal.

2) Political turmoil in the Five Galaxies has continued to flux with unaccustomed speed. For instance, a long-delayed assembly of the Coalition of Temperate Races has finally convened, with a remarkably abbreviated agenda—how to deal with the unbridled ambition shown lately by more fanatical Galactic alliances. Having dispensed with preliminary formalities, the League may actually file official warnings with the War Institute within a Tanith year! Assembly of their coordinated battle fleet may commence just a year after that.

In addition to the League, several other loose confederations of "moderate" clans have begun organizing. If such haste is maintained (and not disrupted yet again by Soro diplomacy) it would demonstrate unprecedented agility by the nonzealous portion of oxy-society.

Naturally, this will come about too late to save Earth, but it may lead to rescue of some residual human populations, after the fact.

3) No one has reported sighting the infamous dolphin-crewed starship for half a Tanith year. If, against all odds, the fugitives were somehow to safely convey their treasures to an ideal neutral sanctuary—or else prove the relics to be harmless—this crisis might abate before igniting universal warfare throughout oxygen-breathing civilization. This would, of course, end our present policy of accepting bets only on a cash-in-advance basis.

4) Commercial star traffic, already disrupted by the so-called "Streaker Crisis," has lately suffered from "agitated conditions" on all interspacial levels. At least thirty of the most important transfer points have experienced thread strains. While the Institutes attribute this to "abnormal weather in hyperspace," some perceive it as yet another portent of a coming transition.

5) The continued upswell of socioreligious fanaticism—including sudden resurgence of interest in the Cult of Ifni—has had a deleterious effect on the business of bookies and oddsmakers all across the Five Galaxies. Because of added expenses (defending our own settlements from attack by fleets of zealous predeterminists) we have been forced to increase the house cut on all wagers.

Even the Sa'ent Betting Syndicate cannot continue business as usual in the face of a prophesied Time of Changes. . . .

HARRY

Uh-oh, he thought. *This is gonna be a rough one.*

Harry nulled the guidance computer in order to protect its circuits during transition. Window covers snapped into place and he buckled himself in for the shift to another region of E Space. One that had been declared "off-limits" for a very long time.

Well, it serves me right for volunteering. Wer'Q'quinn calls this a "special assignment." But the farther I go, the more it seems like a suicide mission.

At first nothing seemed to be happening. His official instruments were useless or untrustworthy, so Harry watched his own little makeshift *verimeter.* It consisted of an origami swan that shuddered while perched on a tiny needle made of pure metal that had been skimmed directly from the surface of a neutron star. Or so claimed the vendor who sold it to him in the Kazzkark bazaar. Nervously, he watched the scrap of folded paper twitch and stretch. His mind could only imagine what might be going on outside, with objectivity melting all around his little survey ship.

Harry's jittery hands scratched the fur of his neck and chest. The swan quivered, as if trying to remember how to fly. . . .

There came a sudden dropping sensation. The contents of his stomach lurched. Several sharp bumps followed, then violent rocking motions, like a boat swept by a storm-tossed sea. He gripped the armrests. Straps dug fiercely into his lap and shoulders.

A peculiar tremor jolted the deck under his bare feet—the distinct hum of a reality anchor automatically deploying. An unnerving sound, since it only happened when normal safety measures were strained near their limits. Sometimes an anchor was the last thing preventing random causality winds from flipping your vessel against shoals of unreified probability . . . or turning your body into something it would rather not be.

Well . . . *sometimes* it worked.

If only there was a way to use TV cameras here and see what's going on.

Alas, for reasons still not fathomed by Galactic savants, living beings entering E Space could only make sense of events firsthand, and then at their own considerable risk.

Fortunately, just as Harry feared his last meal was about to join the dishes and cutlery on the floor, the jerky motions began damping away. In a matter of seconds things settled to a gentle swaying.

He glanced again at the improvised verimeter. The paper swan looked steady . . . though both wings seemed to have acquired a new set of complex folds that he did not recall being there before.

Harry cautiously unbuckled himself and stood up. Shuffling ahead with hands spread wide for balance, he went to the forward quadrant and cautiously lifted one of the louvers.

He gasped, jumping back in fright.

The scout platform hung suspended—apparently without support—high over a vast landscape!

Swallowing hard, he took a second look.

His point of view swung gently left, then right, like the perspective of a hanged man, taking in a vast, blurry domain of unfathomable distances and tremendous heights. Gigantic spires, sheer and symmetrical, could be dimly made out beyond an enveloping haze, rising past him from a flat plain far below.

Harry watched breathlessly until he felt sure the surface was drawing no closer. There was no sense of falling. Something seemed to be holding him at this altitude.

Time to find out what it was. He worked his way around the observation deck, and at the rearmost pane he saw what prevented a fatal plummet.

The station hung at one end of a narrow, glowing thread, extruded from a hull orifice he'd never seen before. But a familiar, blue-striped pattern suggested it must in fact be the reality anchor, manifesting itself this time in a particularly handy way.

At the other end, high overhead, the anchor seemed to be hooked into the lip of a flat plane stretching away horizontally to the right. To his left, an even greater expanse of open sky spread beyond the half-plane. He had an impression of yet more linear boundaries, far higher still.

At least the station hadn't changed much in physical appearance during passage. Metaphorical stilt legs still hung beneath the oblong globe, waving slowly in space. Something seemed to be wrong with *vision,* though. Harry rubbed his eyes but the problem wasn't there. Somehow, all features beyond the windows *appeared* blurred. He couldn't recognize the mountainous columns, for instance, though the grotesque things felt somehow familiar, filling his mind with musty impressions of childhood.

This place was unlike anything he'd experienced since personality profile machines on Tanith had selected him to be the first neo-chimpanzee trained as a Navigation Institute Observer. He knew better than to ask any of the onboard programs for help figuring it out.

"The region of E Space where you'll be heading is seldom, visited for good reasons," Wer'Q'quinn had said before Harry set off this time. "Many of the traits that patrons instill in their clients, through Uplift—to help them become stable, rational, goal-oriented starfarers—turn into liabilities in a realm where all notions of predictability vanish."

Recalling this, Harry shook his head.

"Well, I can't say I wasn't warned."

He turned his head to the left and commanded—

"Pilot mode."

With a faint "pop" the familiar rotating *P* materialized nearby.

"At your service, Harvey."

"That's Harry," he corrected for the umpteenth time, with a sigh. "I'm getting no blind spot agoraphobia, so you might as well open the shutters the rest of the way."

The ship complied, and at once Harry winced at a juxtaposition of odd colors, even though they were muted by the strange haze.

"Thanks. Now please run a scan to see if this metaphorical space will allow us to fly."

"Checking."

There followed a long silence as Harry crossed his fingers. Flight made movement so much easier . . . especially when you were hanging by a rope over miles and miles of apparently empty space. He imagined he could hear the machine click away, nudging drive units imperceptibly to see which would work here, and which were useless or even dangerous. Finally, the rotating *P* spun to a conclusion.

"Some sort of flight appears to be possible, but I cannot pin it down. None of the allaphorical techniques in my file will do the trick. You will have to think of something original."

Harry shrugged. That made up a large part of why he was here.

"Have you located our watch zone?"

"I sense a narrow tube of normal space not far away from us, in figurative units. Subjectively, you should observe a glowing Avenue 'below' . . . somewhere in the fourth quadrant."

Harry went to the window indicated and looked down among the blurry, giant shapes.

"Ye-e-es, I think I see it." He could barely discern a faint, shining line. "We better try to get closer."

"Assuming you find a way."

"Aye," he agreed. "There's the rub."

Harry anxiously ran his fingers through his chin fur and scalp, wishing it hadn't been so long since he had had a good grooming. Back on Horst, where he and his distracted parents were the only chimps on a whole planet, it had always seemed simply a matter of personal hygiene to keep the insidious dust out of your pelt. Only during school days on Earth did Harry learn what a sybaritic art form it could be, to have one or more others stroke, comb, brush, and tease your hair, tugging the roots *just* right, till the follicles almost screamed with pleasure. Looking back on those days, the warm physical contact of mutual grooming was the one thing he missed most about his own kind.

Too bad his partners also *talked* so much—from banter and gossip to inquiries about every personal foible—the sorts of things Harry could never be comfortable discussing. His awkward lack of openness struck Earth chims as aloof, even condescending, while Harry found them overly prying. Invariably, he remained an outsider, never achieving full entry or intimacy in the college grooming circles.

Harry knew he was procrastinating, but he felt uncertain where to start.

"So, you are concerned about rumors of unusual detours in hyperspace and disturbed transfer points," Wer'Q'quinn had replied, after Harry returned from his last mission. "These phenomena are well outside your jurisdiction. But now it seems that a confluence of factors makes it necessary to confide in you."

"Let me guess," Harry had asked. "The disturbances are so bad they can be observed even in E Space."

"Your hunch is astute," Wer'Q'quinn agreed, snapping a GalTwo approval-punctuation with his beak. "I can see your recruitment was not a forlorn gamble, but rather evidence of my own deep insight, proving my value to the Institute and my worthiness of rapid promotion.

"Your next patrol begins in one-point-three standard days."

After allowing for briefings, that left just enough time for a bath and a good sleep in his barracks cubby. He had hoped for a longer rest. There was a foruni masseuse in the bazaar whose instinctive understanding of other species' musculoskeletal systems made the agile creature expert at loosening the kinks in Harry's spine. . . . Alas.

While nervously combing his chin, a frayed fingernail yanked some gnarly hair, making Harry twinge. He held the strand up for a close look.

It's a good thing chimp hair doesn't keep growing longer, like on the faces of human males who don't depilate. Back on Horst, he had seen Probsher shamen whose patriarchal beards lengthened over the years till they stretched nearly all the way . . .

Harry blinked, realizing what his subconscious was driving at. He turned quickly and pressed against the rearmost window, peering at the blue cable—which dangled the station over an immeasurable drop. Stretching upward, it seemed almost to disappear, aiming toward one edge of that far-off horizontal plane.

"Pilot," he said. "I want to see if we can play out the pseudolength of our reality anchor. Can we unreel any more?"

Harry's subconscious chortled at the pun, but he ignored it.

"It is already at maximum extension," came the reply.

Harry cursed. It had seemed a good idea. . . .

"Wait a minute," he muttered. "Don't be too literal. Try it another way. All right, so maybe we can't feed the anchor *out* any more. But tickle the damn thing anyway, will you? Maybe we can change its length some other way. By stretching it, maybe. Or causing it to *grow*."

He knew he was being vague. Flexible thought sometimes meant working your way around an idea's blurry outlines.

"I will try, and let you know," the computer replied. There followed a series of faint humming sounds, then a sudden jar as the platform dropped, weightless again just long enough to make fear erupt in his chest. It jerked short abruptly, sending Harry staggering against his command couch, feeling his stomach keep falling.

"H-h-h-" He tried again. "W-Well?"

"The rules of topology here seem to allow a wide range of flexible conformal mappings. Practically speaking, this means the cable can stretch, adjusting to any length, at almost any speed desired. Congratulations, Commander Harms. You seem to have found a way to maneuver in the subjective vertical."

Harry ignored the suspicion of sarcasm, which might he imagined. At least this trap had proved easier to escape than the banana peel mesa.

Still, I'll only feel safe after learning the metaphorical rules that apply here. There were reasons why patrol craft seldom entered this region. Many that tried never returned.

"Start lowering us then," he commanded. "Gently."

The flat half-plane overhead receded as the "ground" approached at a steady clip, reminding him of something—either the inexorable nature of destiny . . . or else an oncoming train.

While at Kazzkark, there had been time to enquire about the Siege of Earth.

He shouldn't be interested. Having dedicated his life to the monastic Navigation

Institute, Harry was supposed to forsake all prior loyalties of kinship or patron line. But few sophonts could ever transfer natural sympathies completely. Institute workers often discreetly sought news of "home."

When Harry found himself with an extra hour between briefings, he ventured to the bazaar, where a Le'4-2vo gossip merchant accepted his generous fee and showed him to an osmium-lined room containing a masked Library tap.

It didn't take long to find the topic—which had risen three more significance levels since the last time he checked—under the heading: "Major News—Quasi Current Events." The latest word from Galaxy Two was dire.

Terran forces and their few allies had been forced to retreat from the Canaan colonies, which were now provisionally ruled by a Soro admiral.

The beautiful dolphin-settled world of Calafia had been invaded. A third of that water-covered globe was taken over by a mixed squadron led by one faction of the Brothers of the Night, while a different clique from that same race of fanatical warriors fought bitterly to "liberate" the rest.

Earth itself was enveloped and frail Terragens forces would have crumbled by now, but for help from the Tymbrimi and Thennanin . . . and the way enemies kept fragmenting and fighting among themselves. Even so, the end seemed near.

In a footnote, Harry saw that the tiny Earthling leasehold on Horst had been occupied . . . by the horrible Tandu.

Shivers ran down his spine. There was mention of an evacuation by the local staff, so perhaps Marko and Felicity had time to flee with the other anthropologists. But somehow Harry doubted it. His parents were obsessive. It would be just like them to stay, assuming that the invaders would never bother a pair of scientists doing nonmilitary work.

Even if all the technicians and Terraformers left, where would that leave the natives? Human tribes that had turned their "probationary" mental status into license to escape the rigors of modern society, experimenting instead with countless diverse social forms—many of them imitating one totem species or another. Some groups purposely modeled themselves on the matriarchal hive societies of bees, while others mimicked wolf packs, or the lion's pride, or marriage patterns found only in strange, pre-Contact novels. Most of the little Probsher bands had little interest in technology or Galactopolitics.

They would be helpless meat to predatory warriors like the Tandu.

Fleeing the gossip merchant's shelter, Harry had tried to wipe the news from his mind. Soon victorious *eatees* would be scrapping over the remains of fallen Earthclan. With neutral governance dissolving all over the Five Galaxies, it should be simple to coerce the Uplift Institute, getting humans, chims, and dolphins declared open for adoption. All three races would be parceled out like spoils of war, each to a new "patron," for genetic-social guidance across the next hundred thousand years.

That is, if we don't "accidentally" die off during the confusion. It had happened before, nearly every time a wolfling race appeared, claiming to have raised itself to sapience without help from any other. The amazing thing was that Earthclan had lasted this long.

Well, at least gorillas are safe. The Thennanin aren't bad masters . . . assuming you must have a master.

I wonder who will get us chims, as part of the bargain?
Harry's teeth bared in a grimace.
They may find us more trouble than we're worth.

During his next briefing with Wer'Q'quinn, he had blurted a direct question. "All these hyperspatial anomalies and disturbances . . . are they happenin' on account of the war over Earth?"

Instead of rebuking Harry for showing interest in his old clan, the Survey official waved a suckered tendril obligingly.

"Young colleague, it is important to remember that one of the great mentational dangers of sapient life is egotism—a tendency to see all events in the context of one's own self or species. It is natural that you perceive the whole universe as revolving around the troubles of your former clan, little and insignificant as it is.

"Now I admit recent events may appear to support that supposition. The announcement of possible Progenitor relics—discovered in a secret locale by the infamous dolphin ship—precipitated open warfare among the most warlike oxygen-breathing clans. Trade patterns unravel as some alliances seize control over local transfer points. However, let me assure you that the energy fluxes released by the battles so far have been much too small to affect underlying cosmic links."

"But the coincidence in timing!"

"You mistake cause for effect. The angst and fury that now swirl around wolflings had been building for centuries before humans contacted our culture. Ever since the Fututhoon Episode, a nervous peace has been maintained mostly by fear, while belligerent parties armed and prepared for the next phase. Alas for your unlucky homefolk, it is an inauspicious time for innocents to stumble onto the star lanes."

Harry blinked for several seconds, then nodded. "You're talkin' about a Time of Changes."

"Indeed. We in the Institutes have known for almost a million years that a new era of great danger and disruption was coming. The signs include increased volatility in relations between the oxygen and hydrogen life orders . . . and there were outbreaks of spasmodic exponential reproduction within the Machine Order—violations requiring savage measures of suppression. Even among clans of our own Civilization of Five Galaxies, we have seen a rise of religious fervor."

Harry recalled the proselytes swarming the main avenues of Kazzkark, preaching diverse obscure interpretations of ancient prophecy.

"Bunch of superstitious nonsense," he had muttered. To his surprise Wer'Q'quinn agreed with an emphatic snapping of his beak.

"That which is loudest is not always representative," his boss explained. "Most species and clans would rather live and let live, developing their own paths to wisdom and allowing destiny to take its own time arriving. Who *cares* whether the Progenitors are going to return in physical form, or as spiritual embodiments, or by remanifesting themselves into the genome of some innocent presapient race? While fanatical alliances clash bitterly over dogma, a majority of oxygen breathers just wish to keep making steady progress toward their own species-enlightenment. Eventually all answers will be found when each race joins its patrons and ancestors in retirement . . . and then transcendence . . . following the great ingathering Embrace of Tides."

There it was again—Harry thought at the time. The basic assumption underlying nearly all Galactic religious faiths. That salvation was attainable by *species*, not individual organic beings.

Except for that Skiano missionary—the one with the parrot on its shoulder. It was pushing a different point of view. A real heresy!

"So, young colleague," Wer'Q'quinn had finished. "Try to picture how disturbing it was—to fanatics and moderates alike—when your hapless dolphin cousins broadcast images that seemed to show Progenitor spacecraft floating through one of the *flattest* parts of Galactic spacetime! The implications of that one scene appeared to threaten a core belief-thread shared by nearly all oxygen breathers. . . ."

At that point Harry was riveted and attentive. Only then, as luck had it, an aide barged in to report that yet another t-point was unraveling in the Gorgol Sector of Galaxy Five. Suddenly Wer'Q'quinn had no time for abstract discussions with junior underlings. Amid the ensuing flurry of activity, Harry was sent to the Survey Department to finish his briefing. There was never a chance to ask the old snake about his intriguing remark.

What core belief? What about the Streaker's *discovery has everybody so upset?*

At last the platform settled down to "earth."

The surface was relatively soft. His vessel's spindly legs took up the load with barely a jounce.

Well, so far so good. The ground didn't swallow me up. A herd of parasitic memes hasn't converged yet, trying to take over my mind, or to sell me products that haven't been available for aeons.

Harry always hated when that happened.

He looked warily across a wide, flat expanse covered with limp, fluffy cylinders. They looked like droopy, slim-barreled cactuses, all jumbled loosely against each other as far as the eye could see. He took over manual controls and used a stilt-leg to prod the nearest clump. They squished underfoot easily, rebounding slowly after he backed off.

"Can we retract our reality anchor now?" he asked the pilot.

"No need. The anchor is restored to its accustomed niche."

"Then what is that?" Harry asked, pointing to the blue cable, still rising vertically toward the sky.

"The ropelike metaphor has become a semipermanent structure. We can leave it in place, if you wish."

Harry peered up the stretched cord, rubbing his chin.

"Well, it might offer a way out of here if we have to beat a hasty retreat. Just note this position and let's get going."

The scout station set out, striding across the plain of fuzzy tubes. Meanwhile, Harry kept moving from window to window, peering nervously, wondering how this region's famed lethality would first manifest itself.

Rearing up on all sides, at least a dozen of the slender, immensely tall towers loomed in the background. Some of them seemed to have square cross sections while others were rectangular or oval. He even thought he perceived a rigid *formality* to their placement, as if each stood positioned on a grid, some fixed distance apart.

Harry soon realized the strange blurriness was not due to any obstructing "haze" but to a flaw in vision itself. Sight appeared to be a short-range sense in this patch of E Space.

Great. All I need is partial blindness in a place where reality literally can sneak up on you and bite.

It should be a short march to where he last saw the Avenue. Awkwardly at first, Harry accelerated his station across the plain of fluffy growths, all bent and twined like tangled grass. These "plants" didn't wave in a breeze, like the saw-weed of Horst. Still, they reminded him somehow of that endless steppe where dusty skies flared each dawn like a diffuse torch, painful to the eyes. The sort of country his ancestors had sniffed at disdainfully before returning to the trees, ages ago on Earth. Sensibly, they left scorching skies and cutting grass to their idiot cousins—primates who lacked even the good sense to escape the noonday sun, and later went on to become humans.

According to the Great Library, Horst had been a pleasant world once, with a rich, diverse ecosystem. But millennia ago—before Earthlings developed their own starships and stumbled on Galactic culture—something terrible had happened to quite a few planets in Tanith Sector. By the ancient Code of the Progenitors, natural ecosystems were sacrosanct, but the Civilization of Five Galaxies suffered lapses now and then. In the Fututhoon Episode, hundreds of worlds were ravaged by shortsighted colonization, leaving them barren wildernesses.

Predictably, there followed a reactionary swing toward manic zealotry. Different factions cast blame, demanding a return to the true path of the Progenitors.

But *which* true path? Several billion years would age the best-kept records. Noise crept in over the aeons, until little remained from the near mythical race that started it all. Speculation substituted for fact, dogma for evidence. Moderates struggled to soothe hostility among fanatical alliances whose overreaction to the Fututhoon chaos now promised a different kind of catastrophe.

Into this delicate situation Earthlings appeared, at first offering both distraction and comic relief with their wolfling antics. Ignorant, lacking social graces, humans and their clients irked some great star clans just by existing. Moreover, having uplifted chimpanzees and dolphins before Contact, humans had to be classified as "patrons," with the right to lease colonies, jumping ahead of many older species.

"Let them prove themselves first on catastrophe planets," went the consensus. If Earthlings showed competence at reviving sick biospheres, they might win better worlds later. So humans and their clients labored on Atlast, Garth, and even poor Horst, earning grudging respect as planet managers.

But there were costs.

A desert world can change you, Harry thought, recalling Horst and feeling abruptly sad for some reason. He went down to the galley, fixed a meal, and brought it back to the observation deck, eating slowly as the endless expanse of twisted, fuzzy tubes rolled by, still pondering that eerie sense of familiarity.

His thoughts drifted back to Kazzkark, where a tall proselyte accosted him with strange heresies. The weird Skiano with a parrot on its shoulder, who spoke of Earth as a sacred place—whose suffering offered salvation to the universe.

"Don't you see the parallels? Just as Jesus and Ali and Reverend Feng had to be martyred in order for human souls to be saved, so the sins of all oxygen-breathing life-forms can only be washed clean by sacrificing something precious, innocent, and unique. That would be your own homeworld, my dear chimpanzee brother!"

It seemed a dubious honor, and Harry had said so, while eyeing possible escape routes through the crowd. But the Skiano seemed relentless, pushing its vodor apparatus, so each meaningful flash of its expressive eyes sent a translation booming in Harry's face.

"For too long sapient beings have been transfixed by the past—by the legend of the Progenitors!—a mythology that offers deliverance to *species,* but nothing for the *individual!* Each race measures its progress along the ladder of Uplift—from client to patron, and then through noble retirement into the tender Embrace of Tides. But along the way, how many trillions of lives are sacrificed? Each one unique and precious. Each the temporal manifestation of an immortal soul!"

Harry knew the creature's eye twinkle was the natural manner of Skiano speech. But it lent eerie passion each time the vodor pealed a ringing phrase.

"Think about your homeworld, oh, noble chimpanzee brother! Humans are wolflings who reached sapience without Uplift. Isn't that a form of *virgin birth?* Despite humble origins, did not Earthlings burst on the scene amid blazing excitement and controversy, seeing things that had remained unseen? Saying things that heretofore no one dared say?

"Do you Terrans suffer now for your uniqueness? For the message that streams from that lovely blue world, even as it faces imminent crucifixion? A message of *hope* for all living things?"

Even as a crowd of onlookers gathered, the Skiano's arms had raised skyward.

"Fear not for your loved ones, oh, child of Earth.

"True, they face fire and ruin in days to come. But their sacrifice will bring a new dawn to all sapients—yea, even those of other life orders! The false idols that have been raised to honor mythical progenitors will be smashed. The Embrace of Tides will be exposed as a false lure. All hearts will turn at last to a true faith, where obedience is owed.

"Toward numinous Heaven—abode of the one eternal and all-loving God."

In response, the bright-feathered parrot flapped its wings and squawked *"Amen!"*

Many onlookers glowered upon hearing the Progenitors called "mythical." Harry felt uncomfortable as the visible focus of the proselyte's attention. If this kept up, there could be martyrs, all right! Only the august reputation of Skianos in general seemed to hold some of the crowd back.

In order to calm the situation, Harry wound up reluctantly accepting a *mission* from the Skiano, agreeing to be a message bearer . . . in the unlikely event that his next expedition brought him in contact with an angel of the Lord.

It was about an hour later—subjective ship time—that a blue **M** popped into place a little to his left.

"Monitor mode engaged, Captain Harms," the slightly prissy voice announced. *"I take pleasure to announce that the Avenue is coming into range. It can be observed through the forward quadrant."*

Harry stood up.

"Where? I don't . . ."

Then he saw it and exhaled a sigh. There, emerging out of the strange haziness, lay a shining ribbon of speckled light. The Avenue twisted across the foreground like a giant serpent, emerging from the murk on his left and vanishing in obscurity to his right. In a way, it reminded Harry of the undulating "sea monster" he had witnessed during his last survey trip, near the banana-peel mesa. Only that had been just a meme creature—little more than an extravagant idea, an embodied notion—while *this* was something else entirely.

From a distance, it looked like a pipeline whose cylindrical cross-section varied gradually as it stretched left-to-right . . . now straight and then curving gently. Still, the conduit—roughly as thick as Harry's station was tall—seemed ineffably more *solid* than its surroundings. As was only to be expected. Approaching the great tube, already he could tell that its interior was made of vaccum blackness, punctuated by glittering things called *stars.*

The Avenue did not conform to the allaphorical rules of E Space, because—strictly speaking—it consisted of everything that was *not* E Space.

Because of that, cameras might perceive it. The tech people at NavInst had loaded his vessel with sensor packages to place at intervals along the shining tube, then retrieve later on his way back to base. Ideally, the data might help Wer'Q'quinn's people foretell hyperspatial changes during the current crisis.

He pressed a button and felt a small tremor as the first package deployed, resembling a kind of tick, and approached the gently curving tube.

Now, should he turn left, and start laying more instruments in that direction? Or right? There seemed no reason to choose one way over the other.

Well, he was still an officer of the law. Harry's other job was to patrol E Space and watch for criminal activity.

"Computer, do you detect signs anybody's been through this area lately?"

"I am scanning. Interlopers would have to travel alongside the Avenue in order to reach an intersection with Galaxy Four. Any large vessel piercing the tube, or even passing nearby, would leave ripple signs, whatever its allaphorical shape at the time."

The platform nosed closer to the shining tube of brightness. Harry had glimpsed the Avenue many times while on patrol, but never this close. Here it appeared rather narrow, roughly the width of the station itself. The tube shone with millions of tiny sparks, set amid a deep inner blackness. The narrow, snakelike volume was filled with stars . . . and much more. Within that twisty cylinder lay the entire universe Harry knew—planets, suns, all five linked galaxies.

It was a topological oddity that might have looked, to its long-extinct first discoverers, like a wonderful way to get around relativity's laws. All one needed was an intersection near the planetary system one was in, and another near one's destination. The technique of entering and leaving E Space could be found in any Galactic Library branch.

But E Space was a world of unpredictability, meta-psychological weirdness, and even representational absurdities. Keeping the Avenue in view until you came to some point near your destination could entail a long journey, or a very short one. Distances and relationships kept changing.

Assuming a traveler found a safe exit point, and handled transition well, he might emerge where he wanted to go. That is, if it turned out he ever left home in the first place! One reason most sophonts hated E Space was the screwy way causality worked here. You *could* cancel yourself out, if you weren't careful. Observers like Harry found it irksome to return from a mission, only to learn they no longer existed, and never really had at all.

Harry didn't much approve of E Space—an attitude NavInst surely measured in his profile. Yet, they must have had reasons to train him for this duty.

The platform began zigging and zagging alongside the Avenue, occasionally stopping to bend lower on its stilts, bringing instruments to bear like a dog sniffing at a spoor. Nursing patience, Harry watched strange nebulae drift past, within the nearby cylindrical continuum.

A bright yellow star appeared close to the nearby tube edge, against a black, star-flecked background. It looked almost close enough to touch as his vessel moved slowly past. *I guess there's a finite chance that's Sol, with Earth floating nearby, a faint speck in the cosmos. The odds are only about a billion, billion to one against.*

At last, the station stopped. The slanted letter M seemed to spin faster.

"I note the near passage of three separate ship wakes. The first came this way perhaps a year ago, and the second not long after, following its trail."

"A pursuit?" This caught his interest. For the spoor to have lasted so long testified how little traveled this region was . . . and perhaps how desperate the travelers were, to pass this way.

"What about the third vessel?"

"That one is more recent. A matter of just a few subjective-duration days. And there is something else."

Harry nervously grabbed his thumbs. "Yes?"

"From the wake, it seems this latter vessel belongs to the Machine Order of Life."

Harry frowned.

"A machine? In E Space? But how could it navigate? Or even see where it . . ." He shook his head. "Which way did it go?"

"To the figurative left from the way we are now facing."

Harry paced across the floor. His orders from Wer'Q'quinn were clear. He must lay the cameras where they might peer from E Space back into more normal continua, offering NavInst techs a fresh perspective on the flux of forces perturbing the Five Galaxies. And yet, he was also sworn to check out suspicious activities. . . .

"Your orders, Captain Harms?"

"Follow them!" he blurted before the decision was clear in his own mind.

"Sorry. I am not programmed . . ."

Harry cursed. "Engage pilot mode!"

Almost before the cursive *P* popped into place, he pointed.

"That way. Quickly! If we hurry we still might catch them!"

The platform jerked, swinging to the left.

"Aye aye, Hoover. Off we go. Tallyho!"

Harry didn't even grimace this time. The program was irritating, but never at the expense of function. Even Tymbrimi usually knew where to limit a joke, thank Ifni. The station jogged onward in a quick eight-legged lope across the savannah of fuzzy, cactus-like growths.

To his left the Avenue swept by, a glittering tube containing everything that was real.

SARA

Things got pretty complicated right after *Streaker* began navigating the snarled innards of the transfer point.

From his liquid-filled chamber next door, Kaa thrashed muscular flukes, churning a foamy froth while protesting aloud.

"It'sss too damned crowded in here!"

Sara knew he wasn't complaining about *Streaker*'s cramped bridge, but the twisted labyrinth outside the ship—a maze of stringlike interspatial boundaries, looping and spiraling through every possible dimension, like the warped delirium of some mad carnival ride designer.

The t-point nexus *was* rather crowded, at least compared to the teaching vids Sara had watched in recent days. During any normal transfer, one might glimpse a few distant, glimmering dots amid the gnarled threads, and know that other ships were plying the same complex junction linking far-flung stars. But this time it felt like plunging through a tangled jungle, with countless fireflies strung out along every branch and vine.

Instrument panels flared amber warnings as Kaa repeatedly had to maneuver around large vessels moving ponderously along the same slender path. Margins were narrow and the dolphin pilot skimmed by some giant cruisers so closely that Sara caught brief, blurry glimpses in a viewer set to zero magnification. Turbulent ship wakes made *Streaker* buck like a skittish mount. Her straining engines moaned, gripping the precious thread for dear life.

Sara overheard Gillian's awed comment.

"All these starcraft *can't* be running away from the Fractal World!"

The Niss Machine answered, having managed to regain some of its accustomed saucy tone.

"Obviously not, Dr. Baskin. Only about a million other vessels are using trajectories similar to ours, fleeing the same catastrophe that drove us into panicky exodus. That is but a small fraction of the population currently thronging this dimensional matrix. All the rest entered from other locales. Library records show that this particular thread-nexus accepts inward funnelings from at least a hundred points in normal space, scattered across Galaxy Four."

Sara blinked at the thought of so many ships, most of them far bigger than poor *Streaker,* all in an Egg-blessed hurry to get wherever-whenever they were heading.

"I—I thought Galaxy Four was supposed to be deserted."

That was the image she had grown with. An entire vast galactic wheel, nearly void of sapient life. Hadn't her own ancestors come slinking this way in camouflaged sneakships, evading a fierce quarantine in order to settle on forbidden Jijo?

"Deserted, yes. But only by two of the great Orders of Life, Sage Koolhan. By machine intelligences and oxygen-breathing starfarers. The migrational treaty did not require evacuation by members of other orders. And yet, from what we are witnessing right now, it would not be far-fetched to suggest that a more general abandonment has commenced."

Sara let out a soft grunt of comprehension.

"The inhabitants of the Fractal World—"

"Were officially members of the Retired Order, basking in the gentle tidal rub of their carefully tended private sun, quietly refining their racial spirits in preparation for the next step.

"A step that some of them now seem ready to attempt."

"What do you mean?" asked Gillian.

"It is best illustrated visually. Please observe."

One of the major screens came alight with a wavering image—greatly magnified—of several dozen ragged-looking vessels flying in convoy formation, skating along the shimmering verge of a transfer thread. As the telescopic scene gained better focus, Sara noted that the ships' rough outlines resulted from their jagged coverings—a jumble of corrugation and protruding spikes. The very opposite of streamlining.

So, the fractal geometry of the fallen criswell structure carries on, even down to the small scale of their lifeboats, she realized. I wonder how far it continues. To the flesh on their bodies? To their living cells?

The portrayal magnified, zooming toward the bow of the lead vessel. There, Sara and her companions in the Plotting Room saw a glyphic symbol that seemed to shimmer in its own light—consisting of several nested, concentric rings.

Even a Jijoan savage quickly recognized the sigil of the Retired Order.

"Now watch what I have observed several times already. These refugees from the Fractal World are preparing to declare a momentous decision."

Sara felt Emerson approach to stand close by. Quietly unassuming, the tall wounded man took her left hand while they both stood watching a fateful transition.

The foremost craggy-hulled ship appeared to shudder. Wavelets of energy coursed its length, starting from the stern and ultimately converging toward the bright symbol on its prow. For a few moments, the glare became so intense that Sara had to shield her eyes.

The glow diminished just as rapidly. When Sara looked again, the glyph had been transformed. Gone were the circles. In their place lay a simple joining of two short line segments, meeting at a broad angle, like a fat triangle missing its connecting base.

"The sign of union," pronounced the Niss Machine, its voice somewhat hushed. "Two destinies, meeting at one hundred and five degrees."

Gillian Baskin nodded in appreciation.

"Ah," was all the older woman said.

Sara thought, *I hate it when she does that.* Now it behooved her to ask for an explanation.

But events accelerated before she could inquire what the mysterious change in emblems meant. As the camera shifted, they witnessed several more refugee ships undergoing identical transformations in rapid succession, joining the leader in assuming the two-legged symbol. All these separated from their erstwhile companions to form a distinct flotilla that began edging ahead, as if now eager to seek a new destiny. At the next transfer thread junction, they flared with ecstatic levels of probability discharge and leaped across the narrow gap, bound for Ifni-knew-where.

The remaining refugees weren't finished changing and dividing. Again, ripples of light shimmered along the hulls of several huge ships, which began losing some of their jagged outlines. Hulls that had been jumbles of overlapping spikes seemed to melt and flow, then recoalesce into smoother, more uniform shapes . . . the familiar symmetrical arrangement of hyperdrive flanges used by normal vessels in the Civilization of Five Galaxies.

Like before, each metamorphosis concluded in a dazzling burst at the foremost end. Only this time, when the glare faded, Sara saw another symbol replacing the nest of concentric rings—a rayed spiral glyph. The same one *Streaker* carried on her bow.

"These others, apparently, do not consider their racial spirits advanced enough yet for transcendence. They, too, have chosen to surrender their retired status, but this time in order to rejoin the society of ambitious, fractious, starfaring oxygen breathers.

"Perhaps they feel there is unfinished business they must take care of before resuming the Embrace of Tides."

Gillian nodded soberly.

"That unfinished business may be us."

She turned toward the bridge. "Kaa! Be sure to stay away from any ship bearing a Galactic emblem!"

From the water-filled control room came a warbling sigh in complex Trinary—the expressive, poetical language of neo-dolphins that Sara had only just begun to learn. Rhythmic squeals and pops seemed to voice resigned irony, and several of those in the Plotting Room chuckled in appreciation of the pilot's wit.

All Sara made out was a single elementary phrase—

* *. . . except the one biting our tail!* *

Of course. There was already one ship—bearing the rayed spiral crest—that wouldn't be shaken easily. Sticking to the Earthling vessel like a shadow—far closer than most navigators would call safe—the Jophur dreadnought loomed in the rear-facing viewer. Without the new, dense layers coating *Streaker*'s hull, Kaa might have unleashed his full suite of tricks, evading the battle cruiser in a mad dash among the twisting threads. But that wasn't possible with *Streaker* weighed down this way, maneuvering as sluggish as an ore freighter.

Well, without the coating, we would have fried the first instant those disintegrator beams struck, Sara thought. *And we'd be easy prey for the Jophur. So maybe it evens out.*

Turning back to the main magnifier screen, she watched the refugee flotilla break up once more. Those that had reclaimed the spiral galaxy symbol began peeling off, aimed toward heading back to the vigorous goals and passions of a younger life phase.

"From this t-point nexus, there are several routes leading eventually to the other four galaxies. The beings piloting those vessels are no doubt planning to rendezvous with former clan mates and clients."

Gillian sniffed.

"Like Grandpa and Grandma coming home from Happy Acres to move back in with the kids. I wonder just how welcome they'll be."

The whirling hologram halted briefly, its expression perplexed.

"I beg your pardon?"

"Never mind." Gillian shook her head. "So, we've seen a retirement home shatter before our eyes, and its residents divide in three directions. What about those?" She pointed to the craggy ships remaining in the flotilla, the ones who retained their original emblem of concentric circles. "Where will they go?"

The Niss resumed spinning.

"Presumably to another criswell structure. Truly retired species cannot long abide what they call the 'shallow realm.' They dislike space travel and crave instead the feel of solar tides. So they prefer hunkering deep within a gravity well, next to a tame star.

"In fact, I am picking up considerable short-range traffic right now . . . intership communications . . . inquiring if anyone in the area knows another fractal community that has spare volume and insolated—"

"In other words, they want to find out which other retirement homes have vacancies, to replace the digs they just lost. I get it."

"Indeed. But it seems they are having little luck. A majority of the vessels we glimpse now, streaking across the nexus, are asking the same question!"

"What? The ones coming from other entry points? They're also looking for a place to live? But I thought there were tens of thousands of other retirement habitats, each of them huge enough to—"

"Please hold awhile. Let me look into this."

Silence reigned while the Niss delved deeper, coiling its mesh of spinning lines ever tighter as it listened acutely. When it finally reported again, the synthetic voice was lower, sounding somewhat astonished.

"It seems, Dr. Baskin, that the catastrophe we observed at the Fractal World was not an isolated incident."

Another long pause followed, as if the Niss felt it necessary to check—and then double-check—verifying what it had just learned.

"Yes," the machine resumed at last. "The bizarre and tragic fact is confirmed. Criswell structures appear to be collapsing all over Galaxy Four."

It was hard for Sara to imagine. The devastation she had witnessed—a fantastically enormous edifice, an abode to trillions, imploding before her eyes—that could not possibly be repeated elsewhere! And yet, that was the news being relayed in sputtery flashes by refugee ships blazing past each other along the Gordian twists and swooping arcs of the transfer point nexus.

"But . . . I thought all that fighting and destruction happened because of us!"

"So I also believed, Sage Koolhan. But that may be because my Tymbrimi makers filled my personality matrix with some of their own exaggerated egotism and sense of self-importance. In fact, however, there is another possible interpretation of events that took place at the Fractal World. We may have been like ants, scurrying beneath a burning house, convincing ourselves that it was happening because our queen laid the wrong kind of egg."

Sara grasped what the Niss was driving at, and she hated the idea. As awful as it felt to be persecuted by mighty forces, there was one paranoiac consolation. It verified your importance in the grand scheme of things, especially if all-powerful beings would tear down their own great works to get at you. Only now the Niss implied their suffering at the Fractal World was *incidental*—a mere sideshow—spilling from events so vast, her kind of entity might never understand the big picture.

"B-but . . . b-but in that case," asked the little, crablike qheuen, Pincer-Tip. "In that case, who *did* wreck the Fractal World?"

Nobody answered. No one had an answer to offer—though Sara had begun ruminating over a possibility. One so disturbing that it came to her only in the form of mathematics. A glimmering of equations and boundary conditions that she kept prim and passionless . . . or else the implications might rock her far too deeply, shaking her faith in the stability of the cosmos itself.

Tsh't, the dolphin lieutenant, intervened with a note of pragmatism. "Gillian, Kaa reportsss we're nearing a junction that might take us to Galaxy Two. Is Tanith still your aim?"

The blond woman shrugged, looking tired.

"Unless anyone sees a flaw in my reasoning."

A sardonic tone once more filled the voice of the Niss Machine.

"There is no difficulty perceiving flaws. You would send us charging toward violence and chaos, into the one part of the universe where our enemies are most numerous.

"No, Dr. Baskin. Do not ask about flaws.

"Ask instead whether any of us has a better idea."

Gillian shrugged.

"You say the Jophur could figure out how to defeat our new armor at any moment. Before that happens, we must find sanctuary somewhere. There is always a slim hope that the Institutes—"

"Very well, then," Tsh't cut in. "Galaxy Two is our goal. Tanith Sector. Tanith World. I will tell Kaa to proceed."

In theory, clients weren't supposed to interrupt their patrons. Though Tsh't was only trying to be efficient.

At the same time Sara thought—

We're heading toward Earth. Soon we'll be so near that Sol will be a visible star, just a few hundred parsecs away, practically round the corner.

That may be as close as I ever get.

Gillian Baskin answered with a nod.

HARRY

About one subjective day after setting forth, pursuing the mysterious interlopers, Harry learned that an obstacle lay dead ahead.

Hurrying across a weird province of E Space, he dutifully performed his main task, laying instrument packages for Wer'Q'quinn alongside a fat, twisty tube that contained the entire sidereal universe. All the galaxies he knew—including the complex hyperdimensional junctions called transfer points—lay circumscribed within the Avenue. Whenever he paused to stare at it, Harry got a unique, contorted perspective on constellations, drifting nebulae, even whole spiral arms, shimmering with starlight and glaring emissions of excited gas. It seemed strange, defying all intuitive reason, to know the domain inside the tube was unimaginably more vast than the constrained realm of metaphors surrounding it.

By now he was accustomed to living in a universe whose complications far exceeded his poor brain's ability to grasp.

While performing the job assigned to him by Wer'Q'quinn, Harry kept his station moving at maximum prudent speed, following the spoor left by previous visitors to this exotic domain.

Something about their trail made him suspicious.

Of course, what I should be doing is lying low till Wer'Q'quinn's time limit expires, then collect the cameras and scoot out of here before this zone of metareality transmutes again, melting around my ship and taking me with it!

So dangerous and friable was the local zone of eerie shapes and twisted logic that even meme creatures—the natural life order of E Space—looked sparse and skittish, as if incarnated ideas found the region just as unpleasant as he did. Harry glimpsed only a few simple notion-beasts grazing across the prairie of fuzzy, cactus-like trunks. Most of the mobile concepts seemed no more complex than the declarative statement—*I am.*

As if the universe cared.

His agile vessel made good time following the trail left by prior interlopers. Objects made of real matter left detectable signs in E Space. Tiny bits of debris constantly sloughed or evaporated off any physical object that dared to invade this realm of reified abstractions. Such vestiges might be wisps of atmosphere, vented from a life-support system, or clusters of hull metal just six or seven atoms wide.

The spoor grew steadily warmer.

I wonder why they came through here, he thought. The oldest trace was about a year old . . . if his Subjective Duration Meter could be trusted, estimating the rate at which protons decayed here, converting their mass into microscopic declarative statements. From dispersal profiles, he could tell that the small craft in front—the earliest to pass by—was no larger than his mobile station.

They must have been desperate to come this way . . . or else terribly lost.

The second spoor wasn't much younger, coming from a bigger vessel, though still less massive than a corvette. It had nosed along in evident pursuit, avidly chasing after the first.

By sampling drifting molecules, Harry verified that both vessels came from his own life order. *Galactic* spacecraft, carrying oxygen-breathing life-forms—active, vigorous, ambitious, and potentially quite violent.

The third one had him confused for a while. It had come this way more recently, perhaps just days ago. A veritable cloud of atoms still swirled in its wake. Sampling probes waved from Harry's station, like the chem-sense antennae of some insect, revealing metalloceramic profiles like those associated with mech life.

As an acolyte of the Institutes, Harry was always on the lookout for suspicious behavior by machine entities. Despite precautions programmed into mechs for billions of years, they were still prone to occasional spasms of uncontrolled reproduction, grabbing and utilizing any raw materials in sight, making copies of themselves at exponentially increasing rates.

Of course, this was a problem endemic to all orders, since opportunistic proliferation was a universal trait of anything called "life." Indeed, oxygen breathers had perpetrated their own ecological holocausts in the Five Galaxies, sometimes overpopulating and using up planets much faster than they could restore themselves. Hence laws of migration that regularly set aside broad galactic zones for fallow recovery. But machine reproduction could be especially rapid and voracious, often beginning in dark corners where no one was looking. Once, a wave of autonomous replicators had built up enough momentum to seize and use up every small planetoid in Galaxy Three within the narrow span of ten million years, converting each gram into spindly automatons . . . which then began disassembling *planets.* The calamity continued until a coalition of other life orders intervened, bringing it to a halt.

Nor were machines Harry's sole concern. At times like this, when oxygen-breathing civilization was distracted by internal struggles, it was important to keep watch lest the rival culture of hydrogen breathers take advantage.

Still, the traces Harry picked up seemed more strange than dangerous. The lavish amount of metallic debris suggested that this particular mech could be damaged. And there were other anomalies. His sensors sniffed amino acids and other organic detritus. Perhaps small amounts of oxy-life were accompanying the machine-vessel. As cargo perhaps? Sometimes mechs used biological components, which were more resistant than prim logic circuits to damage by cosmic rays.

At the stroke of a midura, he had to halt the pursuit in order to lay another of Wer'Q'quinn's packages, aligning it carefully so the cameras peered straight into the Avenue, collecting data for NavInst technicians. Harry hoped it would prove valuable.

Of course his boss had plenty of measurements already, from probes that laced each transfer point, as well as hyperspatial levels A, B, and C. Moreover, travelers routinely reported conditions they encountered during their voyages. It seemed obscure and unconventional to send Harry all this way gathering information from such a quirky source. But who was he to judge?

I'm near the bottom of the ol' totem pole. I can just do my job as well as possible, and not try to second-guess my chief.

In pre-mission briefings, Harry had learned that strain gauges were showing increased tension along nearly every navigable route in the Five Galaxies. Ruptures and detours had grown routine as commerce began suffering noticeably. Yet, when Wer'Q'quinn made inquiries to high officials at Navigation Institute headquarters, the response consisted of little more than bland, reassuring nostrums.

These events are not unexpected:

Provisions have been made (long ago) for dealing with the phenomena.

Agents at your level should not concern themselves with causes, or long-term effects.

Perform your assigned tasks. Protect shipping. Safeguard the public. Continue reporting data. Above all, discourage panic. Hearten civil confidence.

Maintain your equipment at high levels of readiness.

Cancel all leaves.

It wasn't the sort of memorandum Harry found exactly relaxing. Even Wer'Q'quinn seemed disturbed—though it wasn't easy to read the moods of a land-walking squid.

The situation prompted Harry to wonder again about his current mission.

Perhaps Wer'Q'quinn didn't clear my trip with his bosses. He may have sent me to get a look at things from a perspective that no one at HQ could co-opt, anticipate, or meddle with.

Harry appreciated his supervisor's confidence . . . while at the same time worrying about what it implied.

Could everything be falling apart? he pondered. *Maybe the Skiano proselyte is right. If this is the end of the world, what can you do but look to the state of your own soul?*

Just a midura before taking off on this mission, with some mixed feelings and trepidation, he had accepted an invitation from the Skiano missionary to visit its small congregation of converts. Entering a small warehouse bay in one of the cheaper quarters of Kazzkark, he found a motley assortment of creatures following the strange new sect.

There had been a pair of portly synthians—creatures traditionally friendly to Terran customs and concepts—along with several little wazoon, a goggle-eyed pring, three por'n'aths, a striped ruguggl, and . . .

Harry recalled rocking back in surprise, dismayed to see a cluster of terrifying Brothers of the Night! With muscular, streamlined arms and shark-like faces, Brothers were famed for their intense though fickle religious impulses, sampling different creeds and pursuing them fanatically—until the next one came along. Still, it shocked Harry to see them in such a gregarious setting, worshiping alongside beings who had no relationship at all with their race or clan.

The variegated faithful had gathered before a symbol that Harry found at once both quaint and unnerving . . . a holo portrait of *Earth,* homeworld to his neo-chimpanzee line, depicted with cruciform rays of sacred illumination emanating outward. As the hologram turned, the planet seemed to swell . . . then burst apart, donating its own substance to the brilliant rays, enhancing the gift of enlightenment with an act of ultimate self-sacrifice.

Then, moments later, the world recoalesced in a feat of miraculous resurrection, beginning the cycle once more.

"We are taught that the aim of life is its own perfection," preached the Skiano, speaking first in a flashing dialect of Galactic Two, with glitters from its lower pair of eyes, then almost simultaneously via audible GalSeven through a vodor held in one hand.

"This wisdom is true, beyond any doubt. It crosses all boundaries of order or class. Once sapiency is achieved, life must be about more than mere self-gene-ego continuation. Long ago, the Progenitors taught that our highest purpose is to seek a sense of purpose. For existence to have meaning, we need a goal. A target at which to aim the projectile of our lives.

"But what in the universe is perfectible? Surely not matter, which decays, eventually reducing even the greatest artifacts and monuments to a dim glow of heat radiation. Any individual organism will age and eventually die. Some memories may be downloaded or recorded, but true improvement grinds to a halt.

"Even the cosmos we perceive with our senses appears doomed to entropy and chaos.

"Only *species* seem to get better with time. First blind evolution prepares the way on myriad nursery worlds, sifting and testing countless animal types until precious presapient forms emerge. These then enter a blessed cycle of adoption and Uplift, receiving guidance from others who came before, accelerating their refinement over time.

"Up to this point, the way taught by the Progenitors was good and wise. It meant that nursery worlds would be preserved and sanctified. It ensured that potential would be preserved, and wisdom passed on through an endless cycle of nurturing.

"And when an elder species has taught all it can, reaching high levels of insight and acumen? Then its own turn comes to resume self-improvement, retiring from the spacefaring life, seeking racial perfection within the loving Embrace of Tides.

"Down that route, into the snug clasp of gravity, the Progenitors themselves are said to have gone, waiting to welcome each new gene line that achieves ultimate transcendence."

The Skiano pressed its sucker-tipped hands together, leaning toward the congregation.

"But is that the sole route to perfection? Such a farsighted, species-centered view of salvation seems cold and remote, especially nowadays, when there may be very little time left. Too little for younger races to refine themselves in the old-fashioned way.

"Besides, where does this leave the *individual?* True, there is real satisfaction from knowing your life has been well spent helping the next generation be a little better than yours, and thus moving your heirs a bit closer to fulfillment. But is there no reward for the good, the honorable, the devoted and kind *in this life?*

"Is there no continuity or transcendence offered to the self?

"Indeed, my friends and compeers, I am here to tell you that there is a reward! It comes to us from the most unlikely of places. A strange little world, where wolflings emerged to sapiency whole and virginal, after a long hard struggle of self-Uplift with only whale songs to ease their lonely silence.

"That . . . and a comforting promise told to them by the one, true God.

"A dreadful-beautiful promise. One that the little world called Earth will soon fulfill, as it suffers martyrdom for all our sins. Yea, for every solitary individual sapient being.

"A promise of salvation and everlasting life."

With the last instrument packages deployed, Harry had time to kill before they must be retrieved, so he set out again after the interlopers.

All three had stuck close to the Avenue . . . a wise precaution, since conventional starcraft were scarcely built to navigate in E Space. This way there was always a chance of diving back into the real universe if things went suddenly wrong here in the empire of memes.

Of course, "diving" into the Avenue held dangers of its own. For instance, you might emerge in one of the Five Galaxies all right, with every atom in the right position compared to its neighbors . . . only separated by meters instead of angstroms, giving your body the volume of a star and the density of a rarefied vacuum.

Even if your ship and crew held physical cohesion, you could wind up in a portion of space far from any beacon or t-point, lost and virtually stranded.

By comparison, Harry's vessel was a hardy beast, flexible and far more assured for this quirky kind of travel. Designed specifically for E Space—and piloted by a trained living observer—it could find much safer points of entry and egress than the Avenue.

Of the vessels he was following, the machine entity worried him most, provoking something almost like pity.

It's really vulnerable here. The poor mech must be feeling its way along, almost blind.

Harry accelerated the station's bowlegged gait, curious to see what would drive such an entity to invade E Space, following the spoor of two oxy-life vessels. Soon, he began detecting traces of digital cognizance, a sure giveaway that high-level computers were operating, continuously and unshielded, somewhere beyond the haze.

It's like the thing's broadcasting to all the carnivorous memes in the neighborhood. Yoo hoo! Beasties! Come and eat me!

Harry peered through the murk to make out a fantastically sheer *cliff ahead*—grayish off-white—covered with symmetrical reddish splotches. The abrupt barrier reared vertically, vanishing into the mist some number of meters—or kilometers or astrons—overhead, and the shining, tubelike Avenue seemed headed straight for it!

The red-orange blemishes were arrayed in strict geometrical rows, like endless ranks of fighting ships. Harry eyed them dubiously, till the pilot called them two-dimensional discolorations. Nothing more.

The station marched on, stilt-legs swinging across the fuzzy steppe, and Harry soon realized there was a *hole,* just wide enough to admit the Avenue, with some room to spare on either side to admit the scout platform or a small starship.

"I believe somebody has used energy weapons here," the pilot mode murmured speculatively.

Harry saw the cavelike opening had been widened by some tearing force. Cracks ran away from the broken entrance. Crumbled fragments of wall lay among the fuzzy cylinders.

"Fools! Their ship was too bulky to fit. So instead of trying to find a metaphor that'd get them through, they just blasted their way!"

Harry shook his head. It was dangerous to try altering E Space by force. Far better to get your way by following its strange rules.

"This apparently happened a year ago, when the larger vessel tried following the smaller. Do you wish me to engage observer mode to find out what types of weapons were used?"

Harry shook his head. "No time. Clearly we're dealing with idiots . . . or fanatics. Either way it means trouble."

Harry looked into the blackness surrounding the Avenue as it passed within. No doubt this was another transition boundary. Once he moved inside, the metaphorical rules must change again.

Wer'Q'quinn would not like it. There was no absolute guarantee Harry could backtrack once he entered. The instrument packages were supposed to be his first priority.

After a long pause—spent largely scratching himself, neo-chim style—he grunted and decided.

"We're going in," Harry ordered. "Prepare for symbol shift!" He took his command seat and buckled in. "Close the blinds and . . ."

The cursive *P* whirled faster.

"Warning! Something is coming!"

Harry sat up and looked around. The sheer cliff took up half his field of view. On the other side, the glowing tube of the Avenue stretched back the way he came, across an open plain of fuzzy tubes as far as the haze would let him see.

Yanking on both thumbs, he recalled the first rule of survival in E Space. When in doubt about a stranger, be quiet and find out what it is, before it finds out about you.

"Identification? Can you tell where it's coming from?"

The pilot program hesitated for only a moment. *"The object is unknown. It is approaching from within the transition zone."*

From the dark cave in front of him! That ruled out ducking in there to hide. Harry whirled, looking desperately for an idea.

"We need to get out of sight," he muttered. "But where?"

"I cannot answer; unless we fly. Have you worked out a way yet, Harvey?"

"No I haven't, damn you!"

"The bogey is getting closer."

Harry brought his fists down on the armrests. It was time to try something, anything.

"Go to the wall!"

The station responded with an agile gallop. Thrusting his arms and legs into the manual control sleeves, Harry shouted.

"I'm taking over!"

As the platform reached the sheer cliff, he made two stilt-legs reach out, slapping their broad feet against the smooth surface.

Harry held his breath. . . .

Then, as naturally as if it had been designed for it, the station reared up and began climbing the wall.

ALVIN'S JOURNAL

I must hurry through this journal entry, no time for polishing. No asking the auto-scribe to fix my grammar or suggest fancy words. We've already boarded one of *Streaker*'s salvaged Thennanin boats, and our deadline to cast off comes in less than a midura. I've got to get this down fast, so a duplicate can remain behind.

I want Gillian Baskin to keep a copy, you see, because we don't have any idea if this little trip of ours is going to work. We're being sent away in hopes the boat will make it to safety while *Streaker* enters a kind of peril she's never seen before. But things could turn out the other way around. If we've learned anything during our adventures, it's that you can't take stuff for granted.

Anyway, Dr. Baskin gave me a promise. If she makes it, and we don't, she'll see about getting my journal published on Earth, or somewhere. That way even if I'm dead at least I'll be a real author. People will read what I wrote, centuries from now, and maybe on lots of worlds.

I think that's so uttergloss, it almost makes up for this separation, though saying good-bye to the friends we made aboard ship is almost as hard as it was leaving my family behind on Jijo.

Well, one of the crew is going with us, to fly the little ship. Dr. Baskin is giving us her own best pilot, to make sure we get safely to our goal.

"It doesn't look as if we'll need a crackerjack space surfer where we're going," she told us. "But you kids must have Kaa, if you're to stand a chance."

Huck complained of course, waving all her eyestalks and protesting with that special whining tone that only an adolescent g'Kek can fine-tune to perfection.

"We're being *exiled*," she wailed. "Just when *Streaker*'s going someplace really interesting!"

"It's not exile," Gillian answered. "You're taking on a dangerous and important mission. One that you Jijoans are well qualified for. A mission that might make everything we've gone through worthwhile."

Of course, they both have it right. I have no doubt we're being sent away in part because we're young and Gillian feels guilty about keeping us aboard where there's danger every dura, sometimes from a dozen directions at once. Clearly, she'd like to see the four of us—especially Huck—taken somewhere safe as soon as possible.

On the other hand, I don't think she'd part with Kaa if it weren't for important reasons that'd help her accomplish her mission. I believe she really does want us to make our way in secret through the Five Galaxies, and somehow make contact with the Terragens Council.

"We couldn't do it before," Dr. Baskin explained, "with just humans and dolphins aboard. Even sneaking into some obscure port, we'd have been noticed the second any of us spoke up, to buy supplies or ask directions. Earthlings are too well known by now—too infamous—for us to go anywhere incognito these days.

"But who will notice a young urs? Or a little red qheuen? Or a hoon, walking around one of those backspace harbors? You'll be typical shabby starfarers, selling a few infobits you've picked up along the way, buying fourth-class passages and making your way to Tanith Sector on personal business.

"Of course, Huck will have to stay secluded or disguised—you may have to ship her in an animal container till you reach a safe place. The Tymbrimi would protect her. Or maybe the Thennanin—providing she'd accept indenture and their pompous advice about a racial self-improvement campaign. Anyway, too much is riding on her to take any chances."

Gillian's reminder silenced Huck's initial outrage over being "shipped" from place to place. Of all us voyagers, my friend has the biggest reason to stay alive. She's the only living g'Kek outside of Jijo, and since the Jophur might annihilate all the g'Keks back home, it seems that motherhood, not adventuring, will be her calling now. A change she finds sobering.

"What about Kaa?" asked Ur-ronn, waving her sleek, long head, speaking with a strong urrish lisp. "It will ve hard to disguise a vig dolphin. Shall we carry hin in our luggage?"

Ignoring urrish sarcasm, Dr. Baskin shook her head.

"Kaa won't be accompanying you all the way to Tanith. He'd be too conspicuous. Besides, I made him a promise, and it's time to keep it."

I was about to inquire about that . . . to ask what promise she meant . . . when Lieutenant Tsh't entered the Plotting Room to say that she'd finished loading the boat with supplies for our journey.

My pet noor, Huphu, rode my shoulder. But her sapient relative, the secretive tytlal named Mudfoot, licked himself on a nearby conference table, resembling that Earth creature, an otter, but with white bristles on his neck and an expression of disdainful boredom.

"Well?" Gillian asked the creature, though he'd refused to speak since we left Jijo. "Do you want to go see the Tymbrimi, and report to them about matters on Jijo? Or will you come with us, beyond anything our order of life normally gets to see?"

When she put it that way, I think Gillian expected one answer from the curious tytlal. But it didn't surprise me that she got the other.

A tytlal will bite off its own tail for a joke.

I guess I ought to update how we got to this point—hurrying to pack a small boat and send it off toward a place where *Streaker* had expected to be going.

The reason is that Gillian seems to have gotten a better offer.

Or at least one she can't refuse.

How did we get to this parting of the ways?

Where I last left off, *Streaker* was swooping along the complex innards of a transfer point, just a couple of thousand arrowflights ahead of a Jophur battleship that clung to us the way a prairie-hopper holds on to its last pup. It seemed there'd only be one way to shake our enemy, and that was to head straight for one of the huge headquarters worlds of the Great Institutes, where there'd be lots of traffic and other warships around. If everything worked just right, an Institute armistice might be issued in the nick of time and protect us before a free-for-all firestorm blasted *Streaker* to kingdom come.

All right, it was a flaky plan, for sure, but the best one anybody thought of. And it beat letting the Jophur capture *Streaker*'s secrets to use against all other clans in the Five Galaxies.

So, there we were, darting along a t-point thread, dodging refugee traffic from hundreds of broken fractal worlds that were falling apart all over Galaxy Four. . . .

Don't ask me how or why *that* happened, because it's way beyond me. But at least one of us Jijoans had a clue to what was going on. Sage Sara seemed to grasp the meaning when a number of those giant spaceships changed their shape right before our eyes, as well as the symbols on their bows.

As I understand it, some of the refugees were looking for new retirement homes, to resume their quiet lives of contemplation. (Though it seems vacancies were hard to find.)

Others decided to abandon that comfortable existence and head back to rejoin their old oxy-life cousins during the present time of crisis. Dr. Baskin thought we'd slip in among this mob, flooding through the crowded transfer point on their way to populated zones of the Five Galaxies.

There was a third option, being chosen by a smaller minority—those who thought themselves ready to climb the next rung on the ladder of sapiency, rising out of the Retired Order to a much higher state. But we didn't think that group could possibly concern us.

Boy, were we wrong!

So, there we were, diving into the heart of the t-point—a looping, knot-like structure Kaa called a *transgalactic nexus*—that would send us out of old Galaxy Four altogether . . . when it happened.

Alarms blared. We swerved around another loop-de-loop, and there it was.

At first, I saw just a floating cloud of light, shapeless, without a hint of structure. But as we drew near, this changed. I got an impression of a tremendous *creature* with countless writhing arms! These appendages were reaching down to the converging transfer threads and *plucking starships off like berries from a vine!*

"Uh . . . is that normal?" Huck asked . . . unnecessarily, since we could see the looks on the faces of our Earthling friends. They'd never seen anything like it before.

Pincer-Tip stammered in awe.

"Is it a go-go-go-god?"

No one answered, not even the sarcastic Niss Machine. We were heading right for the giant thing, and there wasn't any possible route to jump away in time from the entity, plucking ships off transfer threads and popping them into pools of brilliance.

All we could do was stare, and count the passing duras, plunging toward the brilliance till our turn came.

Light flooded the sky. A tremendous arm of light came down upon us . . . and suddenly things began moving v-e-r-y s-l-o-w-l-y.

Queasy sensations flowed outward from my gut while my skin felt a strange kind of spreading numbness. As *Streaker* was lifted bodily off the transfer thread, her roaring engines muted to an idle whisper. All view screens filled with whiteness, a glow that did not seem to carry any heat. Paralyzed with fear, I wondered if we were about to be consumed by some kind of hungry being, or a dispassionate natural phenomenon. Not that it made the slightest difference which.

The illumination was so perfect in its hue, and resplendent texture, that I felt suddenly sure it could be nothing other than pure and distilled death.

How long the transition lasted, I have no idea. But eventually the brilliant haze diminished and all the visceral sensations ebbed. *Streaker*'s engines remained damped, but time resumed its normal pace. At last, we could see clearly again.

Sara was holding Emerson tightly, while the little chimp, Prity, hugged them both. Ur-ronn was huddled next to Huck and Pincer, while Huphu and Mudfoot clung with eight sets of claws to my tingling shoulders.

We all looked around, amazed to be able to do so.

The screens flickered back on, showing that we were still inside the tangled, twisted guts of the t-point . . . only we weren't in contact with a thread anymore! There seemed to be a fair-sized bubble of true space surrounding *Streaker.*

And not only *Streaker.* On all sides of us, arrayed in long neat rows, were ranks of other starships! Most of them much larger. All apparently waiting in still silence for something to happen.

Belatedly, the Niss hologram finally popped back into existence among us. Its mesh of fine lines looked tense, anxious.

"I see just one common feature among all these vessels," it said. "Every one of them bears the Sign of Unity. The symbol consisting of two line segments, joining at one hundred and four-point-five degrees. The Emblem of Transcendence."

Now, looking at the white glow, we could tell that it was somehow *sorting* through the vessels that it plucked up from the travel threads. Some—a majority—were conveyed around its shimmering globe and set back on their way. These vanished swiftly, as if eager to make good their escape to other galaxies.

But every hundredth or so vessel was pulled aside. The white glow seemed to examine each of these closely, then brought most of them over to join our phalanx of selected . . .

Selected what? Prisoners? Samples? Candidates? Hors d'oeuvres?

To our relief, that last notion was disproved when we saw a nearby starship abruptly pulse with soft fire, undergoing a reversal of its earlier transformation. In moments, the two-legged symbol had changed back into a nest of concentric circles. At once that vessel began slipping out of formation, wobbling as it jetted toward the flow of departing refugees.

"Chickening out," diagnosed Huck, as always charitable in her evaluation of others. The same thing happened several more times, as we watched. But the white glow kept adding new members to our ranks.

Emerson d'Anite began fiddling with the long-range display, and soon grunted, pointing to his discovery—that our bubble of local spacetime wasn't the only one!

There were at least a dozen other assembly areas, and perhaps a lot more. Some of them contained spiky, fractal-shaped spacecraft, like those nearby. Others seemed filled with blobby yellow shapes, vaguely spherical, that sometimes merged or separated like balls of grease.

"*Zang*," identified Emerson, clearly proud to be able to name the lumpy objects aloud, as if that single word helped clarify our confusion.

"Um . . ." Sage Sara asked. "Does anyone have any idea what *we're* doing here? Have I missed something? Have we just been mistaken as members of the *transcendent order of life?*"

Lieutenant Tsh't tossed her great, bottle-nosed head.

"That-t would be q-quite a promotion," she commented, sardonically.

"Indeed," added the Niss. "Most oxygen-breathing species strive for many hundreds of thousands of years—engaging in commerce, Uplift, warcraft, and starfaring—before at last they feel the call, seeking a tame star near which to wallow in the Embrace of Tides. Having joined the Retired Order, a species then may pass another million years until they feel ready for the next step."

Ur-ronn made a suggestion.

"Should we consult the Livrary Vranch you have avoard this shif?"

The whirling Niss shivered.

"The Galactic Library does not contain much information about the Retired Order, since our elders often say that such matters are none of our business.

"As for what happens beyond retirement . . . well, now we are talking about realms of religion. Most of the great cults of the Five Galaxies have to do with this issue—what it means for a race to transcend. Many believe the Progenitors were first to pass this way, bidding all others to follow when they can. But—"

"But that doesn't answer Sara's question," finished Gillian Baskin. "Why have *we* been plucked out to join this assembly? I wonder if—"

She stopped, noticing that the mute former engineer, Emerson d'Anite, was gesturing for attention again. He kept tapping his own nose, then alternately pointing forward, toward the window separating the Plotting Room from *Streaker*'s bridge. For a few moments, everyone seemed perplexed. Then Tsh't made a squeal of realization.

"The nose of our sh-ship! Remember how a faction of Old Ones and machines reworked our hull, giving us our strange new armor? What if they also changed the WOM watcher on our bow? None of us has had a good look since it happened. Maybe the symbol is not a rayed ssssspiral anymore! Maybe it'ssss . . ."

She didn't finish. We all got her drift. Perhaps *Streaker* now wore an emblem identifying its inhabitants as something we're definitely not.

Others seemed to find this plausible . . . though no one could imagine why our benefactors would want to do such a thing. Or what the consequences might be, when we're found out.

Toward the front of the crowd, I watched Gillian Baskin's face and realized she wasn't buying that theory. The woman obviously had another idea in mind. Perhaps a different explanation of why we were here.

I was probably the only one close enough to overhear the one word she spoke then, under her breath, in a tone I took to be resigned sadness.

I'm writing the word down now, even though I have no idea what it means.

Here was all she said.

"Herbie . . ."

So, that's how we wound up parting company.

It looks as if *Streaker* may have found sanctuary after all . . . of a sort. At least the Jophur battleship is no longer in sight, though who knows if it might show up again. Anyway, Dr. Baskin has decided not to fight this turn of destiny's wheel, but instead to ride it for a while and see where it may lead.

But we Wuphonites won't be going along. We're to climb aboard an old Thennanin star boat—which still has the rayed spiral symbol on its prow—and have Kaa pilot us to safety in Galaxy Two. It'll be hard, especially having to latch on to a rapid transfer thread from standstill in this weird space bubble. And that will be just the beginning of our difficulties as we try to find a backwater port where no one would much notice us slipping into the Civilization of Five Galaxies.

Once there, if Ifni's dice roll right, we'll endeavor to act as Gillian's messengers, deliver her vital information, and then maybe see about finding something to do with the rest of our lives.

Like Huck, I have mixed feelings about all this. But what else can we do, except try?

Tsh't has finished loading all our supplies in the hold. Kaa is in the dolphin-shaped pilot's saddle, thrashing his flukes and eager to be off. We've all received hugs and good-luck wishes from those we're leaving behind.

"Make Jijo proud," Sage Sara told us. I wish she was coming along, so we'd have her wisdom, and so our group would have a representative from all Six Races of the Slope. But if anyone from our little hidden world ought to go see what *transcendent creatures* are like, and have a chance of understanding, it's her. Things are the way they are, I guess.

Tyug, the traeki alchemist, is venting sweet steam. The aroma soothes our fears and qualms at parting. I guess if a traeki can be serene about entering a universe filled with Jophur, I should be open-minded about meeting long-lost cousin hoons—distant relatives who've spent all their lives with the power and comforts of star gods, but who've never read Conrad, Ellison, Butler, or Twain. Poor things.

"We need to name this thing," Pincer-Tip insists, banging the metal floor of the boat with his claw.

Ur-ronn nods her sleek urrish head.

"Of course, there can ve only one that fits."

I agree with a low umble. So, we turn to Huck, whose eyestalks shrug, conveying some of the unaccustomed burden of responsibility she now carries.

"Let it be *Wuphon's Dream*," she assents, making it unanimous.

Gillian Baskin waits by the hatch for me to hand over the copy disk from my autoscribe. So I must now finish dictating this entry—as unpolished and abrupt as it is.

If this is where my story ends, dear reader, it means *Streaker* somehow made it, and we didn't. I have no complaints or regrets. Just remember us, if it pleases you to do so.

Thanks, Dr. Baskin. Thanks for the adventure and everything.
Good luck.
And good-bye.

HARRY

Something was terribly familiar about this region of E Space, ever since he first stared across the prairie of twisted, fuzzy growths toward narrow spires that climbed to meet a vast, overhanging plane. The back of Harry's neck kept *tickling* unpleasantly—the way a neo-chimpanzee experiences déjà vu.

Now he regarded the same scene from another vertiginous angle, as his scout vessel clung to a gigantic sheer cliff amid a blurry haze. Innumerable reddish blotchy patterns repeated symmetrically across the smooth vertical surface, like footprints left by an army of splayfooted monsters.

"Well," he commented, his voice scratchy with surprise. "I never did *this* before. Who'd've thought the rules here would let a big machine climb straight up, like a spider on a w—"

Harry stopped. Realization left him mute as his jaw opened and closed.

It can't be!

He stared at the cliffs repetitious markings, then the distant spires, nearly lost in shrouding mist. A mental shift of scale made it all clear.

I . . . would've sussed it earlier, but for the blurry vision in this crazy place.

He felt cosmically stupid. Harry moaned aloud.

"By Cheetah's beard an' Tarzan's hernia . . . it's a *room.* A room, in somebody's goddam house!"

Awareness lent focus to his tardy perception.

The prairie of fuzzy-floppy cylindrical growths?

Carpet!

The tall, narrow spires?

Furniture legs.

And that huge flat plane I fell from before . . . it must be a table.

The blotchy pattern on this "cliff' was probably *wallpaper,* or some tasteless counterpart. From this close, he had no clue if the motif was Earthling or alien.

This zone of E Space has so few visitors, it was probably in a raw, unmanifested state when I dropped in. The whole megillah may have coalesced around some image from my own subconscious mind!

He had been thinking about the station format, equipped with long legs from his last mission, comparing it to a spider. Perhaps that thought helped precipitate this eerily personal subcosmos.

Unless I'm actually dreaming it all, and my body's really lying in crumpled delirium somewhere, smashed under tons of debris where the station fell, an instant after I arrived.

Either way, it showed just why most sophonts thought this part of E Space especially dangerous.

Perhaps this was how insects saw things inside a house—everything a blur. Harry wondered if there were pictures on the walls, a bowl of fruit on the table, and a humongous kitten purring on some sofa, just across the way.

Maybe it was better not to know, or force E Space to reify too much.

Just one thing spoiled the impression of a quaint, gigantic drawing room—the *Avenue*—a slender, sinuous tube of radiance that emerged from the misty distance, wound its way across the floor, then pierced the wall below Harry's vantage point. A place called Reality, dominated by matter and rigid physical laws.

"I sense vibrations approaching," the station announced. *"From the point of connection-rupture."*

In other words, from a mouse hole below, where the Avenue plunged toward through the wall another zone of E Space. Three interlopers had taken that route before, leaving distinct traces. A small vessel squeezed through first, about a year ago . . . followed by a pursuer who carelessly blasted a wider path. Both left spoor signs of oxy-life. A third, more recent craft, shed mixed clues before entering the narrow route.

Now something was coming the other way.

Harry checked the station's weaponry console and found several panels lit up . . . meaning they were able to function here, though in what fashion remained to be seen.

"Let's see if we can try that other trick again," he murmured.

Taking manual control, he sealed the station's reality anchor to the adjacent wall with an audible "thunk." Then, nervously, he detached each clinging foot from the wall, until his vessel dangled high above the ground. "Lower away!" he said, causing the cord to stretch, halting just two ship lengths above where carpet met wall. The Avenue lay just a little to his left.

Whatever's coming out . . . it can't be much bigger than this station. And most starships that visit E Space aren't well designed for it. I've got advantages, including surprise.

It seemed logical. Harry almost had himself convinced.

But logic was a fickle friend, even back in his home universe. In E Space, it was just one of many games you could play with symbols and ideas.

One of many ways to fool yourself.

"Here it comes!" announced pilot mode, as something began nosing out of the dark tunnel.

It looked pathetic—absurdly long and barely narrow enough to fit through the tunnel. The intruder comprised a chain of hinged segments carried on stiff, articulated legs. It scuttled out of the dark passageway rapidly, then swerved aside, crouching along the wall as tremors ran from section to section. Watching from above, Harry's impression was of something wounded and frightened, cowering as it tried to catch its breath.

He did not have to engage observer mode to know at once, this entity was a machine. Its rigid formality of movement was a dead giveaway. More significant was the fact that it did not *change* very easily. Upon entering a new region of E Space, any other kind of life-form would already have flexed and throbbed through some sort of transition, adjusting its self-conception, its *gestalt,* to suit the new environment.

In this realm, believing often made things so.

Yet, by their very natures, machines were supreme manifestations of applied physical law. Consistency was a source of their power, back in Reality. But here it had crippling effects. Faced with an imperative need to adjust its form, a machine could only do so by carefully evaluating the new circumstances, coming up with a design, then implementing each change according to a plan.

Zooming in with a handheld telescope, Harry saw the mech's body swarm with smaller motile objects—repair and maintenance drones—laboring frantically to alter its shape and function by cutting, moving, and reattaching hunks of real matter. In the process, bits and pieces kept falling off, crumbling or dissolving into big strands of carpet. Harry's atom sensor showed a veritable cloud of particles billowing outward . . . debris that would start attracting scavenging memes before long.

Clearly, this thing had once been a spacefaring device, a dweller in deep vacuum and darkness. It was amazing the machine could adapt to this environment at all.

A sensor flashed anomaly readings. Some of the pollution consisted of oxygen, nitrogen, and complex organic compounds—telltale signs of quite another order of life.

Wait a minute.

Harry had already been suspicious. Now he felt sure.

This was the third entity he had been tracking.

"Must've bumped into something it disagreed with," he surmised. "Something scary enough to make it run away."

Pilot mode soon confirmed this.

"I am detecting more bogeys, approaching the rupture boundary from the other side, following this one at a rapid pace."

Harry narrowed down the source of the abnormal gas emissions to a sealed swelling near the middle of the caterpillar-shaped machine. *A habitat.* A container for atmosphere and other life-support needs. Some glassy shimmers might be windows, though the interior was too dim to see anything.

Clearly the machine knew time was short. Reconfiguration work accelerated, but little drones broke down from the frantic pace, overheating and tumbling to the carpet, which began waving toward the commotion, showing unnerving signs of animate hunger. Atoms were rare in E Space, and did not last long. Many simple, meme creatures found bits of matter useful as trace nutrients, lending a bit of reality to living abstractions.

"Thirty duras until arrival of the newcomers," confirmed pilot mode.

Though its work was unfinished, the caterpillar-machine decided there was no more time to spare, and began hurrying away next to the glowing Avenue.

I wonder why it doesn't try a dive back into normal space by jumping into the Avenue. Sure, it might emerge almost anywhere, and need centuries to find its way to a decent hyperspatial shunt, but don't machines have plenty of time?

He could think of several possibilities.

Perhaps it's too badly damaged to survive reentry.

Or maybe its organic cargo can't afford to spend centuries drifting through space.

The awkward machine suffered dire problems. Metal-hinged legs began freezing in place, or snapping and falling off. Harry pictured a wounded animal, struggling on with its last strength.

He turned to watch for the pursuers. A burst of light heralded their emergence, shining from the tunnel. Carpet strands quailed in response. Then the first creature appeared.

Harry's impression was of an armored earthworm, with a glistening head consisting of shiny plates. A beast of dark holes and airless depths. But this quickly changed. In a speedy metamorphosis, the entity adjusted to this different realm. Eyelike organs sprouted above, while pseudopods erupted below, until it stood gracefully atop myriad delicate tendrils, like a millipede.

Or megapede, Harry decided.

Only one kind of creature could adjust so quickly in E Space. One that was native to it. A sophisticated meme-carnivore. An idea—perhaps *the* very idea—of predation.

As the first one transmuted to fit the ad hoc rules of a gigantic parlor room, several more crowded from behind, members of a hunting pack, eager for a final dash after their helpless prey.

It's none of my business, Harry thought, pulling anxiously on both thumbs. *My first duty is to collect Wer'Q'quinn's instruments. My second is to track and deter interlopers . . . but the memes will take care of this one by themselves.*

But Harry's indecision was stoked by a sudden memory of the last time he had listened to the Skiano missionary preach its strange creed from a makeshift pulpit, beneath a slowly turning hologram of crucified Earth. With both light and sound, the evangelist sermonized that each sapient individual should look to the deliverance of his or her own soul.

"Although our sect has burst only recently upon the boulevards and byways of the Five Galaxies, we are already seen as a threat by the old faiths. They try to limit our message through regulations and legal harassment, using unscrupulous means to undermine our emissaries. Above all, they claim that we teach *selfishness.*

"If the Abdicators, Awaiters, Transcenders, and other traditions agree on one thing, it is that salvation must be achieved by *species* and *clans,* perfecting themselves to follow our blessed Progenitors into the Embrace of Tides. Each generation should work selflessly to help their heirs move farther, step by step. How terrible, then, if individuals, in their trillions and quadrillions, start thinking of themselves! What if redemption could be achieved by each thinking being, through faith in a God who is above and beyond all known levels of universal reality?

"What if the Embrace of Tides might be *bypassed* by achieving a heavenly afterlife, described in the sacred works of Terra? Would everyone then cease trying for racial progress? Abandoning posterity in favor of spiritual rewards *now*?"

The Skiano's lower set of eyes had flashed.

"There is an answer. The answer of Buddo, Moshé, Jesu, and other great prophets who taught during Earth's era of glorious loneliness. Their answer—our answer—is that salvation's greatest tool has always been compassion."

Even days later, Harry's thoughts still roiled around the incredible, many-sided incongruity of the Skiano's message.

Chewing his lip, he turned to address the floating **P** symbol.

"How many hunters are there?"

"The memoids number five," answered pilot mode. *"Two are now fully transformed and have resumed pursuing the mech interloper. Two are still shifting. One remains inside the tunnel, awaiting its turn."*

He saw a pair of meme-carnivores accelerating across the pseudo-carpet, each propelled by a million rippling tendrils, rapidly overtaking the decrepit machine. Two more finished transforming while Harry paced, wishing he had never attended the Skiano's revival meeting.

In fact, he could not be sure what motivated his decision to act. Compassion might have been part of it. But Harry preferred blaming it on something else.

Curiosity.

I'll never find out what the clumsy-fool machine is carrying, if it gets gobbled up by a bunch of ravenous opinions.

The fifth memoid emerged and began its metamorphosis.

Harry let out a cry of resolution and punched a button, releasing the reality anchor, causing the station to plummet straight down with all eight legs deployed like claws.

His first opponent fell easiest.

A memoid is defenseless during transition, while reformatting its conceptual framework for a new environment. "Paraphrasing itself into another idiom," as Wer'Q'quinn had explained during Harry's training.

During that time, its self-assured cohesion wavered, making it vulnerable to external points of view.

This one reacted quickly when the plummeting station pierced its spine in several places, injecting some critical notions.

INTERRUPTION

HESITATION

DOUBT

In E Space, an idea can hold together without a brain to think it. But only if the proposition is strong enough to believe in *itself.* To such a self-sustaining concept, uncertainty was worse than a toxin, especially if inserted at the right place and time. Unable to cope, this complex meme faltered and quickly dissolved, allowing its component propositions to be gobbled up by the surrounding carpet. That left Harry free to amble quickly after its peers.

Be like a spider, he thought, preparing the weapon console for action. His advantages were now stealth and speed . . . plus the fact that this entire subdomain of E Space must have coalesced a while ago around some seed-image from his own mind—probably a childhood memory of somebody's Brobdingnagian parlor.

Approaching the next two memes rapidly from behind, he chose to snare them with an entanglement ray. It seemed ideal for attack in E Space, shooting finely woven arrays of syllogisms—logical arguments collected from digests of the Great Galactic Library going back over a billion years.

Well, here goes nothing.

Harry aimed and fired.

The weapon was contingent, meaning that its appearance and form varied depending on local conditions. In other zones of E Space, he had seen it lash out beams of caustic light, or discharge glowing disproofs like fiery cannonballs. *Here,* streams of distilled argument seemed to spiral out from the station like webs of sticky silk, flying over and beyond the next pair of memic carnivores.

One of them stumbled instantly, snarling its abundant legs in viscous cords of ancient persuasion, tangling its torso amid strands of quarrelsome reasoning, rolling to a jumbled ball, then rapidly dissipating into vapor.

Its partner was luckier. While cornered by surrounding webs, the predator managed to stop just in time. Wherever a line of caustic contention did make contact, burning its flanks, rebuttals flowed from the wound like fervent antibodies.

The creature turned its metaphorical gaze, and proceeded to spit poison. Gobbets flew toward the station—presumably cogent explanations meant to convince Harry's vessel not to exist anymore. He might have tried shooting them down, or swatting them, or even enduring the assault. But Harry had already chosen another tactic. Taking advantage of his knowledge about the local zone, he made the station flex all eight legs, then *leap,* soaring above the acrid missiles and beyond, over the pair of trapped allaphors.

For several long seconds he flew, watching a sea of carpet pass below . . . so high that he began worrying about the descent, especially when his path seemed headed dangerously close to the glowing Avenue.

I'm not ready for reentry here! The odds of surviving a random collision were not good.

Fortunately, by making the station writhe to one side, he managed to just miss the shining tube. But landing came unbalanced and hard. Harry flew against the nearest bulkhead, taking a painful blow to his right shoulder. Worse, the cabin filled with sounds of something shattering. An alarm blared. Red lights flashed.

Wincing, he scrambled back to the control panel, where he learned that two legs had snapped in the fall and a third was badly twisted. His trusty vehicle limped badly as it stood to meet new challenges.

Still, Harry felt aflame with adrenaline, baring his teeth and loosing a savage, chimpanzee snarl.

Three down. Two to go, he thought, hopefully.

Unfortunately, the next fight wouldn't be as easy.

One of the remaining predators could be seen just ahead, already pouncing on its hapless prey, tearing metal pieces off the giant machine, dismembering it with happy abandon. The other memoid turned to face Harry. Alert and fully prepared, its form had fully adjusted to this realm, and now resembled just the sort of feral insectoid you'd most hate to find crawling under the furniture—something many-clawed and stingered. He got an impression of savage joy, as if the adversary facing him was the essence of combativeness.

Dribbles of foamy disputation frothed at the memoid's mouth, then flew toward Harry.

Leaping out of the way was impossible this time, so he tried to dodge left, then right. But despite desperate zigzagging, one of the blobs struck his forward window pane, spreading to coat it with a glimmering slime.

Harry averted his gaze, but not before waves of apprehension flooded.

What the hell am I doing here? I could be safe in bed. If I stayed on Earth, I might've had the company of lovers, friends, instead of coming all this way to die. . . .

Regret caused bitter pangs, even though he knew the source was an alien assault. Fortunately, the emotion was diffuse, generalized. The memoid didn't know what kind of creature he was, so its thought-poisons weren't specific. Not yet. Alas, predators at this level of sophistication had remarkable sensitivity, adapting quickly to their victims' weaknesses.

Harry didn't plan on giving it the chance. He triggered another entanglement ray, and once more his station flung webs of gooey argument. This time, however, his target agilely evaded the trap—perhaps by assuming some unique and unrelated axioms. The few strands that touched just slid off, unable to impeach exotic postulates. Only briefly inconvenienced, the memoid flexed its back and charged—flowing toward Harry so fast he could never hope to retreat.

Its maw gaped, but instead of teeth there gleamed rows of pointy, spiraled *screws,* turning rapidly as the creature rushed to attack. The sight was fearsome and unnerving.

It's gonna board me!

Harry reached for the weapons console, stabbing a button labeled DISTRACTION FLARES. They had saved his hide on other missions, creating dazzling displays of confusing data, like floating clouds of chaff, enabling his escape from even bigger monsters.

Only this time the effect was disappointing. Clouds of mist erupted before the charging predator, but it barely slowed.

When in doubt, get physical, he thought, activating the minigun. Vibrations rattled as high-velocity bullets launched toward the attacker, who reared back, bellowing and clawing at the air. But hope soon crashed as Harry realized the impacts weren't doing harm. Rather, the creature seemed to snatch and grab at the projectiles, incorporating the material into its information-based matrix! The rotating screws changed color, from a simulated pastel blue to a dark, metallic gray.

Harry shut the gun down, cursing. He had just *improved* the enemy's chances of getting at him.

The station barely shuddered when the memoid struck, clambering on top for a close embrace. A complex rarefied idea had little weight or momentum. But ideas *could* wear at you, and this one did so pointedly, chomping with those spinning drill bits, tearing through the vessel's hull.

Harry tried other buttons and levers, but nothing worked. Each weapon was dead, or else reformatted in some way the adaptable memoid shrugged off.

In E Space, an object made solely of atoms could not stand for long against living ideas.

Several dimples appeared in the walls . . . which then burst inward as whirling conical blades drilled through. Moments later, the screws began changing shape, taking form as little creatures. *Mites,* Harry thought, knowing that even little insects and spiders had parasites. The predator had figured out an excellent trick, using the logic of this subrealm against Harry.

He stabbed a final button, meant for desperate situations like this one.

Instantly, the control room filled with holographic images, a crowd of milling beings, mimicking various kinds of oxy-, hydro-, and machine life. A few slithered. Others walked, or rolled, or stomped, resembling some pangalactic, cross-temporal, omnireality cocktail party.

A dozen or so mite-like invaders spread out, seeking the station's conceptual core—Harry himself. The nasty little things flashed horrid pincers, while sniffing through a crowd of imitation sophonts. One of them chose an ersatz Zang to attack, hurling itself at a floating yellow blob that shivered when struck. At once, the hologram collapsed inward around the mite, enveloping it in a crushing layer of antimemes. The resulting implosion finished with a burst of light, followed by a thin trail of dust falling to the deck.

They contain some real matter, Harry realized. These things are freaking dangerous!

If one bit him, it might not just assail his mind. It could also chew away at his real body.

Two more times, invaders got suckered into attacking wrong targets, and were destroyed. But Harry could tell they were growing more cautious. Gradually, the mites learned to ignore hydro-and machine forms, and began zeroing in toward his type of oxy-based organism.

I've got to act first. But how? What can I do to fight my way out of this mess?

If he ever made it back to base, he'd have suggestions for the crews who maintained the weapons systems. But for now, Harry saw just one hope . . . to shake the parent memoid off, breaking its control over the mites. That would also leave holes in the station's hull. But one problem at a time.

He didn't dare take up manual controls which would give him away. So instead he called up pilot mode.

"Yes, Herman?" the floating *P* answered.

"Don't hover close to me!" Harry whispered through gritted teeth. "Keep your damn distance and listen up. I want you to send the station jiggling and swerving about . . . random action . . . try to shake the Ifni-cursed alien off our hull!"

"That would violate safety parameters."

"Override!" Harry growled. "Emergency protocols. Do it now!"

The scout platform began moving. Though hampered by two broken legs, it was not much burdened by the big memoid, whose total real mass was probably only a few hundred grams, even after eating Harry's bullets. The limp even helped a bit, getting a swaying motion started as the station began shifting left, right, forward, and then spinning around, commencing a drunkard's walk across the carpeted landscape.

Despite its low inertial mass, the big memoid clearly did not like this. After all, movement was a form of information. Harry heard faint mewling sounds as it scrambled for a better grip, holding on to keep contact with its mites.

Unfortunately, the zigzagging also affected *Harry*, pushing him to and fro. The holograms automatically emulated his movements, but he knew this would give him away soon.

Through one window, he caught a blurry glimpse of the metallic machine entity, the big interloper he had followed earlier, who had no business coming to a realm where *thinking* made things so.

It had already been dismembered, carved into several chunks by the last predator, which was now working its way toward the habitat bulge—

A rolling motion yanked Harry from that dolorous scene, throwing him against another window. The one still coated with tincture-of-regret.

Oh, I regret, all right.

I regret not coming here armed with some real memic weapons! True wolfling brain poisons. Sick-sweet incantations that hypnotized millions, fixating them on just one view of reality, making flexible minds as rigid as stone.

Harry felt sure of it. Even these local predators—lithe and supple in abstraction space—would turn conceptually brittle if exposed to the seductive reasonings of Plato or Marx or Ayn Rand . . . Freud or Aquinas . . . Goebbels or Hub—

The station braked with a shuddering jar, splitting Harry's thought and sending him slamming against a storage cabinet. He turned frantically in time to see several of the mites also come flying—propelled by their real-mass components. Two of them collided with holograms and were instantly destroyed.

But two others survived to smack the wall near Harry. As he gathered his balance, he could sense their regard swiveling his way.

Uh-oh.

They had him cornered, with his back against the lockers. As the station resumed its wild movements, the mites approached from two sides across the bucking deck, snapping jaws and waving scorpion-like tails.

Harry tried clearing his mind. Supposedly, if you practiced mental discipline, you could make your intellect impervious to toxic notions.

Unfortunately, beings who were that disciplined made lousy E Space observers. He had been recruited for his credulous imagination—a trait these parasites would use to demolish him.

"Uh . . . could I maybe, interest *you* guys in entertaining an idea or two?" He spoke quickly, breathlessly. "How about—this sentence is a lie!"

Their reaction, a snapping of pincers, seemed amused.

"Well then . . . how do you know you exist?"

Total contempt.

Shucks, it worked in some old tellie shows.

Of course, sophisticated memes would dismiss such cliches like flint-tipped arrows bouncing off armor. But what about a concept they might not have met before?

"Uh, has anyone ever told you about something called *compassion*? Some think it's the surest route to salv—"

The mites prepared to spring.

The station swerved again as the autopilot threw another gyration.

Suddenly, a radiant glow flooded the window opposite Harry, filling the control room with torrents of *starlight.*

Harry sighed.

"Well, I'll be a monkey's unc—"

Before he could complete the phrase, several things happened at once.

Both parasites leaped.

The big meme predator clinging to the outer hull screeched dismay.

His wildly gyrating station collided with the Avenue, a glancing blow, with the big memoid pressed between, giving it a taste of the Reality Continuum.

Tormented ululations filled Harry's brain as the predator burst asunder, spilling its complex conceptual framework in explosive agony.

Deprived of its parent, one of the mites shattered just before reaching his throat. But the other held cohesion long enough to strike him from behind.

It was Harry's turn to scream. He howled as something fluxed into his body. Pain yanked away all rational thought, piercing his buttocks and spine, then coursing along his outer flesh like searing fire. Meanwhile, deep within, qualms and uncertainties began attacking every belief, every assumption he ever held dear.

Suns and galaxies loomed around Harry as the station leaned into the Avenue, pushing against the membrane separation, threatening to trigger an unplanned, uncontrolled and certainly lethal reentry transition.

Machinery wailed, joining his bellow of despair.

All the memes and holograms had vanished. Air leaked out of the station through a dozen small holes. But he never noticed. Teetering between one realm of living ideas and another of harsh, universal rules, Harry fought to hold on to something. His essence. His sense of inner being.

Himself.

EWASX

This is not the best of all possible hiding places.

Then why did we/I choose it, my rings?

Out of all the twisty crannies that make up the great battleship, why did we take shelter in this chamber of glass-sealed walls and bubbling incubation cells?

Because it is home? The place where we began?

Our second torus of cognition refutes this with a reminder that *most* of our component rings had their origins elsewhere—in pungent mulch pits filled with delicious rotting vegetation, at a crude settlement called Far Wet Sanctuary, on lonely Jijo.

It is true. Only three present members of our shared stack started here, aboard the *Polkjhy,* in this sterile nursery, where infant rings are nurtured to perfection with computer-controlled drips of synthetic nutrients. But they are three of our most important parts, yes?

- Our muscular torus-of-movement, with agile legs.
- Our donut-of-smells, making us recognizable to the Jophur crew.
- And, of course, your Master Ring, most precious of all. The essential (Me) ingredient, needed to transform modestly diffuse traeki into gloriously focused Jophur.

Is that not reason for nostalgia? Enough to call this darkened chamber home?

(Though it appears to have suffered damage recently, and been repaired with hasty patching.)

Yes, go ahead. You may stroke the wax of memory. Recall the way things used to be on Jijo, before the change. Recollect how we/I learned to understand *alien* forms of parenthood, from close association with five other races.

During our prior incarnation, as the beloved traeki sage, *Asx*, we/I used to hold qheuen grubs and g'Kek larvae in our gentle tentacles, as well as hoon and human babies, rocking them, or spilling sweet aromatic mist-lullabies, crafted to bring happy dreams.

These recollections are preserved, not melted by our violent transformation into *Ewasx*. And yet, I am confused.

What point are you trying to make, my rings?

That we should be jealous?

That no ring stack—traeki or Jophur—can ever know a parent's love?

We are piled up from parts. Assembled. *Made,* like some machine. Perhaps that is why other races hate/envy us so.

What? You say there is no such hatred on Jijo? Ah, but consider the price you colonists paid for likability! To live in brute ignorance. Worse yet, afflicted to remain placid traeki, almost inert with lack of ambition. Won't you admit, at last, that life was never this vivid when you comprised poor compliant Asx?

You will? You will? You'll concede that much?

Well, then. Perhaps we are making progress.

WHAT? WHAT'S THAT?

You would have *Me,* the Master Torus, confess something in return?

You wish me to admit that we have lately, also seen some drawbacks—some disadvantages—to the monomaniacal way Jophur behave.

No, you needn't stroke recent wax, or replay those horrid events we observed before fleeing the control room. Foul-tempered, aggrieved and violent, the actions of our leaders were hardly inspiring. They don't exhibit great progress toward enlightenment.

But what choice is there? We of *Polkjhy* must pursue the dolphin-crewed ship! Its secrets may shed light on a time of changes, now convulsing the Five Galaxies. If Earthlings truly did find Progenitor Relics in a shallow globular cluster, what might that say about the way Galactic Civilization has been run for a billion years? Could it imply that our entire religious-and-genetic hierarchy is upside down?

WHAT IS THAT YOU SAY?

Our second ring of cognition asks —*so what?*

- *so what* if ancient beliefs about the Progenitors prove wrong!
- *so what* if we were lied to about the Embrace of Tides!
- *so what* if some other clan manages to seize *Streaker,* and read its information first! Why should any sensible sapient get into a grease-lather over matters so obscure and trivial?

– ——

– ——

– ——

I . . . hesitate to answer.

The question seems so jarringly incomprehensible . . . like asking why we breathe oxygen, or metabolize food, or procreate, or express loyalty to kindred and posterity! It disturbs Me gravely that you/we could even raise such doubts!

PERHAPS I/WE SHOULD NOT HAVE FLED THE CONTROL ROOM, AFTER ALL.

(Seeking sanctuary in this dim/familiar hiding place.)

Indeed, our shared core roils with mad, provocative thoughts, questioning central Jophur beliefs. Moreover, since becoming a fugitive, I no longer seem to have the Masterful force of will that once let me squelch such ponderings.

PERHAPS IT WOULD HAVE BEEN BETTER TO LET THE FOLLOWERS OF THE HIGH PRIEST DISASSEMBLE US/ME FOR SPARE PARTS.

That might have been My greatest service to desperately beset *Polkjhy,* and to the great Jophur clan as a whole.

The chief advantage of this refuge is that ship sensors will be unable to detect our body traces, masked by row after row of transparent growth cabinets, filled with juvenile rings of all types. Of course, there are robot nurses here, tending the young. These slave-drones would report me, but only if someone on the bridge *asks.* Unless or until a specific enquiry is made, I/we can probably remain safe here, emitting authority pheromones, giving the machines orders, pretending to be in charge of the caretaking facility.

There is another danger. At random intervals, various Jophur ring piles come to the door demanding spare parts.

Mostly, these are soldiers. Tall, formidable warrior stacks, bearing wounds and horrid stains from their ongoing struggle to expel Zang invaders from the battleship. That infestation currently blights a third of *Polkjhy*'s decks and zones. Some recent progress has been made against it, but our fighters show the cost, seeking replacements for rings damaged in close combat with the hydrogen breathers.

Fortunately, none of their caste seems inclined to question our/My presence here . . . and we mostly stay out of sight.

Yes, my rings. It is only a matter of time till we/I are caught. Soon we will face disassembly. I wonder if they will bother salvaging any of our toruses or waxy memory beads for use elsewhere.

Probably not.

During long, idle moments, we/I linger before vision-odor displays, captivated by events that have enveloped *Polkjhy* since our captain-leader was killed.

Do you recall, my rings, how our great ship swooped through the twisted bowels of the transfer point, following the Earthship so closely, and with such skill, that they could never get away?

From the Research Department, crew-stacks reported progress understanding the *Streaker*'s strange protective layer—the coating that prevented our rays from stopping the dolphins earlier. That veneer seemed to offer invincibility, but according to our onboard Library we learn the technique was abandoned by most Galactics long ago! The tactic is quite easily defeated, once an opponent knows how. Only surprise made it effective back at the Fractal World.

The librarians promised a recommended countermeasure, shortly.

Meanwhile, the transfer nexus grew crowded with refugee ships, not only from the dissolved retirement community behind us, but from hundreds of others! Each emigrant vessel decided among three choices—to remain in Galaxy Four and seek room in some other cloistered shelter, or else to change life orders—going back to the starfaring Civilization of Five Galaxies . . . or possibly forging deeper into the Embrace of Tides, seeking transcendence. It was enthralling, and a great honor, to watch so many exalted Old Ones make this fateful judgment, though it did not affect our tenacious pursuit of the Earthlings.

That was when we encountered *the Harrower.*

A thing of legend.

A rare phenomenon of destiny.

A cloud of light that sorted through the agitated, thronging vessels. Choosing some. Sending others along their assigned ways.

DO YOU RECALL OUR SURPRISE, MY RINGS, WHEN THE HARROWER PLUCKED UP THE EARTHLING SHIP, AND GENTLY PLACED IT AMONG THOSE AIMED FOR TRANSCENDENCE?

Stunned amazement filled *Polkjhy*'s halls and chambers.

Who could have imagined this would happen? Dolphins are the youngest licensed sapient race in the Civilization of Five Galaxies. Whether by trickery or merit, this was the last thing any sane entity would expect!

At that point, our new captain-leader gave in to the inevitable. Commands were given. *Polkjhy* must give up the chase!

Instead, we would aim for Galaxy One, toward a Jophur base, to be cleansed of infesting Zang, and to report all we had learned. Even without the Earthship in our grasp, we would be able to tell its fate, and that data should be valuable.

Moreover, there is *Jijo,* an excellent consolation prize! When we reveal its location to the home clan, that little sooner world will make an ideal outpost for genetic experimentation/exploitation. A source of wealth for the race. Final destruction of the g'Kek, alone, would make our travails worthwhile.

Perhaps the clan would be so joyful over those achievements that allowance would be made for *this* crude, hybrid stack—for this Ewasx—if we/I manage to avoid capture-disassembly till then.

Thus the crew rejoiced, despite apparent failure of our central mission. Although the *Streaker* had escaped, it seemed to be no fault of our own. We had accomplished more than any other ship in known space. Now we could go home.

Only then the truly unexpected happened.

Do you recall, my rings? Or is the wax-of-surprise still too fresh and runny for true-memory to congeal?

We faced our own turn before the Harrower, expecting to be conveyed routinely, like so many others, on a swift path toward Galaxy One.

Strange light filled the ship, and we/I felt *scrutinized.* Some of our/My rings—former parts of Asx—compared it to communing with Jijo's wonder stone, the Holy Egg.

Then, to our/My/everyone's amazement, *Polkjhy* was lifted off the transfer thread and placed amid a row of the elect! The chosen! Those whose emblems marked them for great honor and enlightenment, far down amid the Embrace of Tides.

Thus we learned the wondrous glory of our new honored state . . . and the pain yet to be endured.

What no one could explain, from our senior priest-stack on down to the lowest warrior, was *why?*

Why were we chosen for this honor?

One we never sought.

One that brings no gladness to any Jophur stack aboard this noble ship.

I/we stand corrected.

ONE STACK EXPERIENCES GLADNESS.

Some of the cognition rings left over from Asx rejoice at the news!

They think this means *Polkjhy* may never report on Jijo. The weird, miscegenist society of sooner races might yet be left in peace, if this battleship never makes it home.

Is that what you hope/believe, my rings?

I would discipline you now, with jolts of loving pain, to drive such disloyalty out of our common core, except—

Except that now the Harrower appears to have finished its task! The armadas it collected in pockets of coiled space have begun moving at last . . . in rows, columns, regiments . . . all pouring along special transfer threads that glow hot with friction.

Vibrations and sudden swerves shake *Polkjhy so* powerfully that swaying motions penetrate even our mighty stabilizing fields.

And now, as if none of that were enough, the sequence of upsetting surprises continues.

Robots continue tending the incubators, wherein juvenile rings of many shapes, attributes, and colors thrive on distilled nutrients, growing into components to make new Jophur stacks.

Soldiers keep coming for repairs, seeking to replace damaged walker-rings, sword-manipulators, chem-synth toruses, and even mortally wounded Master Rings. Clearly, the battle against the Zang rages on with deadly fury.

Meanwhile, on monitors, I/we watch *Polkjhy* emerge in some far star system, part of an orderly swarm of transcendence candidates—ranging from conventional-looking starships and spiky fractal shapes all the way to quivering blobs that appear horridly Zangish before our appalled gaze!

For several jaduras, this bizarre armada uses B-Level hyperspatial jumps to cross a gap of several paktaars, skirting around a vast glowing nebula in order to reach the next transfer point. Finally, the convoy dives into this nexus and another thread-ride commences, swooping along multidimensional flaw boundaries where space itself condensed long ago from the raw essence of an expanding universe.

While all this activity continues, we/I remain in a dim corner of the nursery chamber, hiding from our/My own crewmates . . . until the unexpected once again forces its way into our shock-numbed consciousness.

We stare at a new interloper.

A recent arrival, standing before our disbelieving senses.

The strangest being that I/we/I have ever seen.

It came just moments ago, arriving via an unconventional route—by supply tube—conveyed to the nursery in a slender car designed for transporting raw materials and samples, not sapient beings!

Crawling out before we could react, it unfolded long limbs, revealing a shape with proportions like a *Homo sapiens.* Indeed, the head protruding atop looked completely human. And familiar.

I/we stared, did we not, my rings? Several of our cognition-memory toruses exclaimed, releasing recognition vapors and causing words to vent from our shared oration peak.

"Lark! Is . . . it . . . really . . . you?"

Indeed, the face cracked open with that unique human-style smile. When it/he spoke, the voice was as we knew him from olden days, on Jijo.

"Greetings, reverend Asx . . . or shall I say *Ewasx*?"

While several of our components wrangled over an appropriate reply, others stared at the transformed body below the neckline. Lark's bipedal stance was similar, striding on stiff, articulated bones. Only now translucent film enveloped his flesh, ballooning outward like profoundly baggy garments, billowing and throbbing with a sick, semiliquid rhythm that sent quivers of nausea down our/My central core. An especially large bulge distended from his back, like a tumor, or a great burden he showed no sign of resenting.

Our chem-synth rings detected several awful stinks, such as methane, cyanogen, and hydrogen sulfide gas.

Sure stench-signs of Zang!

Surprise made our reply somewhat disjointed, to say the least.

"I/we . . . cannot say what . . . *name* . . . would best apply to this stack . . . at this time. Voting commences/continues on that point . . . And yet . . . it can be said in truth that certain parts of us/Me/I/we recognize certain . . . *parts* . . . of you/You . . ."

Our shared voice trailed off. Neither Anglic nor GalSix seemed well suited to convey appropriate/accurate levels of astonishment. Emotional pheromones vented . . . and to our surprise, the "Lark/Zang" entity answered in kind!

Molecular messages puffed from his new outer skin, triggering instant comprehension by our/My pore receptors.

MUTUAL RECOGNITION
AMICABLE INTENT
WILLINGNESS TO FIND RESOLUTION

Seeking the source of these scent messages, our/My sensors now locate a toroidal-shaped bulge, situated near Lark's chest.

Purple colored.

A traeki ring, incorporated in the group entity across from us!

At once, we/I recognize one of the small rings Asx secretly created, without knowledge of the Ewasx Master, to help Lark and his human companion escape bondage several jaduras ago.

Stroking memory wax from that time, I/we now realize/recall—there had been a *second* cryptic ring.

"I left the other one here," Lark explains, as if reading My/our thoughts. "It was wounded. Ling hid it in this nursery, to get care and feeding. That's one reason I came back. My new associates want to find the little red ring. They want to know its purpose."

He does not have to explain his "associates." A Jophur instinctively knows—as most unitary beings do not—that it is possible to blend and mix and match disparate components to make a new composite being. In this case, the chimera is an amalgam of human, traeki, and Zang . . . a terrifying union, but somehow credible.

"You . . . wish to have our/My help recovering the red ring?" I ask.

Lark nods.

"Its powers may bring peace to this vast vessel. . . ."

He pauses for a moment, as if communing with himself, then goes on.

"But there is something else. The price I demanded for cooperating in this mission.

"We're going to rescue Ling."

HARRY

Voices encroached on his latest nightmare, pushing past a delirium of jibbering clamors and scraping agonies.

"I think he's coming around," someone said. Harry thrashed, shaking his head from left to right.

For what seemed an eternity, his mind had felt stripped, laid bare to E Space, fertile ground for colonization by parasitic memes—intricate, self-sustaining symbolic entities unlike anything conceived on Earth, invading to expropriate his incoherent dreams. Even now, as something like consciousness began to dawn, eerie shapes still thronged and cackled, more bizarre than anything born in an organic mind.

Somehow—perhaps by force of will, or else plain obstinacy—he pushed most of them aside, clawing his way toward wakefulness.

"Are you sure we oughta let him get up?" asked another, higher-pitched voice. "Look at those teeth he's got. He could be dangerous!"

The first speaker seemed calmer, though with a touch of uncertainty.

"Come on. You've seen chimps before. They're our friends. We couldn't be luckier, after everything we've been through."

"You call *this* a chimp?" the other rejoined. "I never spent as much time around 'em as you have, or read as many books, but I bet no chimp ever looked like this!"

That comment, more than anything, spurred Harry to fight harder against the clinging drowsiness.

What's wrong with the way I look? I'll match my face against a hairless ape's, any day!

Of course the voices were human. He recognized the twangy overtones, despite a strange accent.

How did humans get into E Space?

Painful brightness stabbed, the first time he tried cracking his eyelids. A groan escaped Harry's lips as he raised a heavy forearm over his eyes.

"I—"

His throat felt parched. Almost too scratchy to speak.

"I could use . . . some water."

Their reaction surprised him. The higher voice squawked.

"It talks! You see? It *can't* be a chimp. Clobber it!"

Harry's eyes flew open, this time to a world of glare and blurry shadows. Struggling upward, he sensed a pair of nearby figures backing away quickly. Young humans, he perceived—male and female—filthy and disheveled.

"Hey!" he croaked. "What d'you mean I can't be a—"

Harry stopped suddenly, unable to move further or speak. He could only stare at the arm in front of him. His own arm . . . covered with sparse fur.

Glossy *white* fur.

His hair was the color of frost on a windowsill during winter mornings on Horst.

Harry's chest pounded. Worse, a sharp pain stabbed his spine, just above the buttocks, like a numbed hand or foot coming back to life.

"Watch out," the young female cried. "It's gettin' up!"

Fighting panic, Harry scrambled to his feet, clutching at his body, checking it for wounds, for missing parts. To his great relief, all the important bits seemed still attached. But his eyes roved wildly, out of control, seeking to find out what else was wrong.

White fur . . . white fur . . . I . . . I can live with that . . . assuming it's the only thing that's changed. . . .

One of the humans reentered his fear-limned field of vision. The male, wearing tattered rags, with several weeks' stubble on his chin. Mixed up by anxiety and confusion, Harry could only snarl reflexively and back away.

"Hey there," the youth said in soothing tones. "Take it easy, mister. You asked for water. I've got some, in this here canteen."

There was an object in his hand. It looked like a dirty gourd or pumpkin, stoppered with a cylinder of wood.

What is this, Harry thought. *Some sorta joke? Or more E Space mind garbage?*

Still retreating across the deck of his battered scout station, he glimpsed through a window that the scenery outside had changed. The vast plain of fuzzy carpet was now yellow, instead of beige, and the mist had grown thicker, obscuring everything except a nearby mound of metal rubble, smoldering as it slowly dissolved into the surrounding greedy strands. He wanted to ask what had happened, how long he had been out, where these humans had come from, and how they had gotten inside his ship. Perhaps he owed them his life. But caught in a flux of near hysteria, it was all he could do right now to keep from screeching at them.

White fur . . . but that's not all. Something else is wrong! Those mites did more to me than that, I know it!

Now both humans were in clear view. The female—not much more than a girl—had a nasty scar down one side of her face. She gripped a crowbar, brandishing it like a weapon. The boy held her back, though he too was clearly dismayed and confused by Harry's appearance.

"We're not gonna hurt you," he said. "You saved us from the monsters. We came over and patched your hull for you. Well, we plugged the holes at least."

"—and it wasn't easy!" the young woman declaimed, ending sharply as the man waved sharply.

"Look, my name is Dwer and this is Rety. We're humans . . . Earthlings. Can you tell us who—and what—you are?"

Harry wanted to scream. To ask if they were blind! Shouldn't patrons know their own clients? Even with white fur, a chimp was still—

He felt a sudden tickle behind him. Of course the bulkhead was back there and he could back up no farther. But the sensation came just an instant too soon, in too strange a fashion, as if the wall was brushing an extension of his spine.

My spine.

That was where—the last thing he recalled—a little predatory memoid had attacked and chewed its way into his flesh, filling his mind-body with waves of turmoil and disorientation.

"I mean . . . you *look* like you might be some sort of a relative," the youth went on, babbling nervously. "And you spoke Anglic just now, so maybe . . ."

Harry wasn't listening. Nervously, with a rising sense of dread, he groped around behind himself with his left hand, brushing the bulkhead, then moving downward.

Something started rising up to meet the hand. He sensed it clearly. Something that was part of himself.

A snakelike tendril, covered with hair, planted itself assuredly into his palm. It felt as natural as scratching his own ass, or pulling on his thumb.

Oh, he thought, with some relief. *It's just my damned tail.*

His mouth went round.

Breath froze in his throat . . . then whistled out with a long, mournful sigh.

The two humans edged away nervously as the sigh underwent a metamorphosis, transmuting like some eager meme with a mind all its own, turning into coarse, hysterical laughter.

The effect, when he finally got around to examining his reflection calmly, wasn't half as bad as he had feared. In fact, the white fur seemed rather—well—charismatic.

As for his new appendage, Harry was already resigned to it.

Surely it must have uses, he thought. *Though I'm not looking forward to the tailoring bills.*

Things could have been much worse, of course. The memoid parasite that invaded his body had been dying, moments after its parent exploded from brief contact with Material Reality. With a final gasp, it must have latched on to some random thought in Harry's mind, using that to force a quick shift in self-image. In

E Space, the way you pictured yourself could sometimes have dramatic effects on who and what you became.

One thing was certain—he could never go to Earth looking like this. To be called a "monkey" would be the last insufferable humiliation.

When I joined the Navigation Institute, I figured it meant I'd probably live the rest of my life apart from my kind. Now I belong to Wer'Q'quinn more than ever.

At his command, the station was now striding alongside the great, shining Avenue, limping at maximum safe speed, retracing its earlier path to pick up the instrument packages and finish this assignment before anything else went wrong.

One good thing about Wer'Q'quinn. The old squid will hardly notice any difference in my looks. All he cares about is getting the job done.

That left him with one more problem.

The young humans.

Apparently, Rety and Dwer had been the "organic cargo" carried by the hapless machine entity. Their little habitat was about to be attacked and torn open by a ravenous meme-raptor when Harry arrived. From their point of view, he was like the proverbial cavalry. A knight from some storybook, galloping to the rescue just in the nick of time.

They later returned the favor, after the final memoid fled the scene, bloated on stolen atoms. After talking the dying mech into using its last resources to build an airlock bridge, they boarded Harry's station, saving him from asphyxiation while he sprawled on the deck, stunned and unconscious.

The mech then expired, contributing its mass as temporary fertilizer to this matter-parched desert.

"We never could figure out where we were, or why it took us here," Dwer explained, while wolfing down a triple helping of Harry's rations. "The machine never spoke, though it seemed to understand when I talked in GalTwo."

Harry watched the boy, fascinated by Dwer's mixture of the savage and gentleman. He never denied being a sooner—descended from criminal colonists who had abandoned technology over two centuries ago. Yet, he could read half a dozen Galactic languages, and clearly grasped some implications of his situation.

"When the mech took us aboard, near the red giant star, we thought we'd had it. The scrolls say machines that live in deep space can be dangerous, and sometimes enemies to our kind of life. But this one made a shelter for us, improved our air, and fixed the recycler. It even asked us where we wanted to go!"

"I thought you said it never spoke," Harry pointed out.

Rety, the teenager with the scarred cheek, shook her head.

"One of its drones came aboard with a piece of metal that had words scratched on. I dunno why it used that way to talk, since we had a little tutor unit that could've spoken to it. But at least the robot seemed to understand when we answered."

"And what did you say?"

Both humans replied at the same time.

Dwer: "I asked it to take us home."

Rety: "I told it to bring us to the most important guys around!"

They looked at each other, a smoldering argument continuing in their eyes.

Harry pondered for a long moment, before finally nodding with understanding. "Those sound like incompatible commands. To you or me, it would call for making a choice between two options, or negotiating a compromise. But I doubt that's what a machine would do. My best guess is that it tried to combine and optimize both imperatives at the same time. Of course its definition of terms might be quite different from what you had in mind at the time."

The young humans looked confused, so he shook his head.

"All I can tell for sure is that you were definitely *not* heading back toward your sooner colony when I found your trail."

Rety nodded with satisfaction. "Ha!"

"Nor were you aimed at Earth, or a base of the Great Institutes, or any of the mighty powers of the Five Galaxies."

"Then where—"

"In fact, the mech was taking you—at lethal risk to itself—into dimensions and domains so obscure they are hardly named. It seemed to be following the cold trail of two—"

A warning chime interrupted Harry. The signal that another of Wer'Q'quinn's little camera packages lay just ahead.

"Excuse me awhile, will you?" he asked the humans, who seemed to understand that he had a job to do. In fact, even Rety now treated him with respect that seemed a little exaggerated, coming from a member of Harry's patron race.

He got busy, using the station's manipulators to recover the final probe, then spraying it with a special solvent to make sure no memic microbes clung to the casing, before stowing it away. Nearby, the Avenue gleamed with starlight. The realm of material beings and reliable physical laws lay just a few meters away, but Harry had no intention of diving through. His chosen route home was more roundabout, but also probably much safer.

While finishing the task, he glanced back at Dwer and Rety, the two castaways he had saved . . . and who in turn had rescued him. They were fellow descendants of Earthclan, and humans were officially Uplift-masters to the neo-chimp race. But legally he owed them nothing. In fact, as an official of one of the Great Institutes, it was his duty to arrest any sooners he came across.

And yet, what good would that accomplish? He doubted they knew enough astrodynamics to be able to tell anyone where their hidden colony world lay, so nothing could be gained by interrogating them. From what they had said so far, their settlement was highly unusual, a peaceful blending of half a dozen species that were mostly at each other's throats back in civilization. It might be newsworthy, in normal times. But right now, with all five galaxies in a state of uproar and navigation lanes falling apart, they seemed likely to fall between the cracks of bureaucracy, at Kazzkark Base.

Anyway, Harry was surprised to learn how pleasurable it felt to hear voices speaking native wolfling dialects. Though a loner most of his life, he felt strangely buoyed to have humans around, who were very nearly his own kind.

The camera slipped into its casing with a satisfying clank. Checking his clipboard, Harry felt a glow of satisfaction.

The last one. I know some other scouts were betting against my ever returning, let alone achieving success. I can't wait to rub their noses—and beaks and snouts and other proboscides—in it!

With a heavy limp, his battered station turned away from the Avenue at last, heading toward a cluster of slender towers that he now knew to be legs of several huge, metaphorical chairs and a giant table. His best route home.

I wonder how long this zone will stay coalesced around my viewpoint seed. Will it melt back into chaos when I'm gone? Or is that a symptom of what Wer'Q'quinn keeps warning me against—an inflated notion of my own self-importance?

In fact, Harry knew he wasn't the first material outsider to pass through this zone in recent times. Before he came, and before the hapless mech, two other spacecraft had passed through—one chasing another.

Could all of this—he looked around at the vast furniture and other tchotchkes of an emblematic parlor—have already taken shape before I arrived? I sure don't consciously recall ever being in a room like it before, even as a child. Maybe one of those vessels that preceded me provided the seed image.

It bothered him that he still had no idea why the mech had brought Dwer and Rety here.

Combining two request-commands. Taking the humans "home," and bringing them to "the most important guys around."

He shook his head, unable to make sense of it.

One thing, though. I know the Skiano missionary is gonna plotz when he sees the three of us Earthlings—two actual living humans and a transformed chimp—striding along the boulevards of Kazzkark. It oughta make a sensation!

A table leg loomed just ahead, the one Harry hoped to ascend back toward his chosen portal, assuming it remained where gut instinct told him it must . . . And if the station was still capable of climbing. And if . . .

Pilot mode popped into space nearby, a cursive *P* rotating in midair.

"Yes?" Harry nodded.

"I am afraid I must report movement, detected to the symbolic left of our present heading. Large memoid entities, approaching our position rapidly!"

Harry groaned. He did not want another encounter with the local order of life.

"Can we speed up any?"

"At some modest increased risk, yes. By twenty percent."

"Then please do so."

The station began moving faster . . . and the limp seemed to grow more jarring with each passing step. Harry glanced at Rety and Dwer, who as usual were bickering in a manner that reminded him of some married couples he had known—inseparable, and never in accord. He decided not to tell them quite yet. *Let 'em think the danger's over, for a while longer at least.*

Stationing himself near a portside window, Harry peered through the murk.

We only need a few more minutes. Come on, you memoid bastards. Leave us alone just that long!

Harry's back itched, and he started reaching around with a hand to scratch it . . . but stopped when the job was handled more conveniently by his new appendage. His tail, lithely curling up to rub and massage the very spot. At once, it felt both natural and surprising, each time it moved to his conscious or unconscious will.

He caught the two young humans staring at him. Dwer at least had the decency to blush.

Eat yer hearts out, Harry thought, and used the tail to smooth his pelt of sleek, ivory fur. Poor humans. Stuck with those bare skins . . . and bare butts.

Then he had no more time for whimsy.

Out there amid the haze, he spied movement. Several dark gray entities. Huge ones, far larger than the megapedes he had fought before. Through the mist, these looked sleek and rounded, nosing along the vast carpet like a herd of great elephants.

Then Harry realized. That was the wrong metaphor. As they drew nearer, he recognized their rapid, darting motions, their earlike projections and twitching noses.

Mice . . . goddamn giant mice! Ifni, that's all I need.

He felt a shiver of dismay as he realized—they had spotted the station.

To the pilot mode, he gave an urgent, spoken command. "Increase speed! We've got to climb the leg before they reach us!"

Amber and red lights erupted across the control board as the jarring pace accelerated. A great woodlike pillar loomed before them, but Harry also sensed the memes scurrying faster in pursuit. Self-sustaining conceptual forms far more sophisticated and carnivorous than any he had seen. It was going to be tight. Very tight indeed.

God. I don't know how much more of this I can take.

PART IV

CANDIDATES FOR TRANSCENDENCE

Our universe of linked starlanes—the Five Galaxies—consists of countless hierarchies. Some species are ancient, experienced in the ways of wisdom and power. Others have just begun treading the paths of self-awareness. And there are innumerable levels in between.

These are not conditions in which nature would produce fairness. There would be no justice for the weak, unless some code moderated the raw impulses of pure might.

With this aim, we inherit from the Great Progenitors many traditions and regulations, formalizing the relationships between patrons and their clients, or between colonists and the nonsapient creatures that inhabit life-worlds. Sometimes these rules seem so complex and arbitrary that it taxes our patience. We lose sight of what it is all about. Recently, a savant of the Terran starfaring clan (a dolphin)—suggested that the matter be viewed quite simply, in terms of respect for the food chain.

Another Earthling sage—(a human)—put it even more simply, expressing what he called the Meta Golden Rule.

"Treat your inferiors as you would have your superiors treat you."

FROM THE JOURNAL OF GILLIAN BASKIN

I wish Tom could have been here. He would love this.

The mystery.

The terrifying splendor.

Standing alone in my dim office, I look out through a narrow pane at the shimmering expanse of raw *ylem* surrounding *Streaker*—the basic stuff of our continuum, the elementary ingredient from which all the varied layers of hyperspace condensed, underpinning what we call the "vacuum."

The sight is spine-tingling. Indescribably beautiful. And yet my thoughts keep racing. They cannot settle down to appreciate the view.

My heart's sole wish is that Tom were sharing it with me right now. I can almost feel his arm around my waist, and the warm breath of his voice, urging me to look past all the gritty details, the worries, the persisting dangers and heartaches that plague us.

"No one said it would be safe or easy, going into space. Or, for that matter, rising from primal muck to face the heavens. We may be clever apes, my love—rash wolflings to the end. Yet, something in us hears a call.

"We must rush forth to see."

Of course, he would be right to say all that. I've been privileged to witness so many marvels. And yet, I answer his ghost voice the way a busy mother might chide a husband so wrapped up in philosophy that he neglects life's messy chores.

Oh, Tom. Even when surrounded by a million wonders, someone has to worry about the details.

Here aboard this frail dugout canoe, that someone is me.

Days pass, and *Streaker* is still immersed in this remarkable fleet. A vast armada of moving receptacles—I hesitate to call the spiky, planet-sized things "ships"—sweeps along, sometimes blazing through A- or B-Level hyperspace, or else turning to plunge down the throat of yet another transfer point . . . an immense crowd of jostling behemoths, racing along cosmic thread paths that correspond to no chart or reference in our archives.

Should I be surprised by that? How many times have I heard other sapient beings—from Soro and Pila to Synthians and Kanten—preach awe toward the majestic breadth and acumen of the Galactic Library, whose records encompass countless worlds and more than a billion years, ever since it was first established by the legendary Progenitors, so long ago.

We younger races feel the Library must be all-knowing. Only rarely does someone mention its great limitation.

The Library serves only the Civilization of Five Galaxies. The ancient culture of oxygen-breathing starfarers that we Earthlings joined three centuries ago.

To poor little Earthclan, that seemed more than enough! So complex and overpowering is that society—with its mysterious traditions, competing alliances, and revered Institutes—that one can hardly begin to contemplate what else lies beyond.

But more does lie beyond. At least seven other orders of life, thriving in parallel to our own. Orders that have wildly different needs and ambitions, as well as their own distinct kinds of wisdom.

Even the ever-curious Tymbrimi advised us to avoid contact with these ultimate strangers, explaining that it's just too confusing, unprofitable, and dangerous to be worth the trouble.

To which I can only say—from recent experience—*amen.*

Of course, it's common knowledge that the oldest oxygen-breathing races eventually die or "move on." As with individuals, no species lasts forever. The cycle of Uplift, which stands at the core of Galactic society, is all about replenishment and renewal. Pass on the gift of sapiency, as it was passed to you.

Being new to this game, ignorant and desperately poor, with our own chimp and dolphin clients to care for, we humans focused on the opening moves, studying the rules so we might act as responsible patrons, and perhaps avoid the fate that usually befalls wolflings.

Beginnings are important.

Yet, each alliance and clan also speaks reverently of those who came before them. Those who, like venerated great-grandparents, finished their nurturing tasks, then turned their attention to other things, maturing to new heights and new horizons.

After we fled treachery at Oakka World, I decided not to trust the corrupted Institutes anymore and to seek advice instead from some of those learned, detached elders we had heard about. Beings who had abandoned starfaring for a more contemplative life in the Retired Order, cloistered near the fringes of a dim red star.

Events at the Fractal World soon taught us a lesson. Aloofness does not mean impartiality. The so-called Retired Order is, in fact, only a vestibule for oxy-races that can no longer bear the rigors of flat spacetime. Though they huddle like hermits in a gravity well, 'embracing tides' as they seek to perfect their racial souls, that doesn't necessarily make them tolerant or wise. After our travails with the Old Ones, I was willing to head back into the Five Galaxies, and risk contact with oxy-civilization once more.

Only now we find ourselves, against all logic or reason, adopted willy-nilly into the Transcendent Order!

At least that is what the symbol on our prow seems to mean. Somebody, or something, planted a single wide chevron there—perhaps as a very bad joke.

An emblem signifying high spiritual attainments, plus readiness to abandon all temporal concerns.

In effect, it says—Hey! Look at us. We're all set for godhood!

Sheesh, what a situation. I feel like a street kid with a stolen tuxedo and fake ID, who somehow managed to bluff her way into the Nobel Prize ceremony, and now finds herself sitting next to the podium, scheduled to give a speech!

All *this* street kid wants right now is a chance to slink away without being noticed, before the grown-ups catch on and really give us hell.

Getting away won't be easy. A kind of momentum field rings this huge flotilla, carrying us along helplessly amid the horde of giant transports. Moreover, our navigation systems are haywire. We've no idea where we are, let alone where to go.

At one point, during an especially smooth transit through B Space, Akeakemai reported that the surrounding field seemed weak. I had him nudge *Streaker* to the edge of the swarm, hoping to slip out during one of the cyclical jumps back to normal space. But as we prepared to break free, Olelo thrashed her flukes with a whistle warning. We were being scanned by hostile beams, cast from an enemy ship!

Soon we spied the Jophur dreadnought, working its way through the throng of giant arks.

Once, the battlewagon had seemed omnipotent. Now it looked minuscule compared to the surrounding behemoths. Stains marred its once shiny hull in places where the skin seemed to *throb*, like infected blisters. Still, the crew of egotistic sap-rings had great power and determination to pursue *Streaker*. They would pounce whenever we left the convoy's safety.

We fell back amongst the titans, biding our time. Perhaps whatever ills afflict the Jophur will eventually overcome them.

The universe may produce another miracle.

Who knows?

Perhaps we will *transcend*.

The Niss Machine plumbed our stolen Library unit, researching data about the strange layer covering *Streaker*'s hull, both shielding her and weighing her down. It began as a thick coat of star soot, amassed in the atmosphere of a smoldering carbon sun. Later, some mysterious faction transformed the blanket—beneficently, or with some arcane goal in mind—creating a shimmering jacket that saved our lives.

"It is a form of armor," the Niss explained. "Offering tremendous protection against directed energy weapons—as we learned dramatically at the Fractal World. Trawling for records, I found that the method was used extensively on warships until approximately two hundred million years ago, when a fatal flaw was discovered, rendering it obsolete."

"What flaw?" I asked. Naturally, something so convenient must have an Achilles' heel.

The Niss explained. "Much of the soot pouring out from Izmunuti consists of molecules you Earthlings call fullerenes—or buckeyballs—open mesh spheres and tubes consisting of sixty or more carbon atoms. These have industrial uses, especially if gathered into sheets or interlocking chains. That's why robot harvesters visited Izmunuti, acquiring material in their futile effort to repair the Fractal World."

"We already knew the stuff was strong," I answered. "Since Suessi had such trouble removing it. But that's a far cry from resisting Class-Eight disintegrator beams!"

The Niss explained that it took special reprocessing to convert that raw deposit into another form. One with just the right guest atoms held captive inside buckeyball enclosures.

"Atoms of strange matter," the disembodied voice said.

I confess I did not understand at first. It seems that certain elements can be made from ingredients other than the normal run of protons, electrons, and neutrons, utilizing unusual varieties of quarks. Such atoms must be kept caged, or they tend to vanish from normal space, hopping off to D Level, or another subcontinuum where they feel more at home.

It felt weird to picture *Streaker* sheathed in such stuff.

Then again, I guess it would be weirder to be dead.

I well remember expecting to be vaporized when those fierce beams struck. But our surprising new armor absorbed all that energy, shunting every erg to another reality plane, dissipating it harmlessly.

"Sounds like a neat trick," I commented.

"Indeed, Dr. Baskin," the Niss answered, with a sardonic edge. "But a few hundred aeons ago, someone discovered how to render this fine defense useless by reversing the flow. By turning this wondrous material into a huge antenna, absorbing energy from hyperspace—in effect cooking the crew and everything else inside."

So, that was why no one in the Five Galaxies had been stupid or desperate enough to use this kind of armor for a long time. It worked at first, because the Jophur were taken by surprise. But they have their own Branch Library aboard the *Polkjhy,* every bit as good as ours. By now they must surely have caught on and prepared for our next encounter.

Somehow, we've got to get rid of this stuff!

I assigned Hannes Suessi to puzzle over that problem. Meanwhile, my plate is full of other troubles.

For one thing, the glavers howl, night and day.

Before leaving aboard Kaa's little boat, Alvin Hauph-Wayuo instructed us in the care and feeding of those devolved descendants of mighty starfarers. There wasn't much to it. Feed them simulated grubs and clean their pen every few days. The glavers seemed stolid and easy to please. But no sooner did Kaa depart, taking Alvin and his friends to safety, than the filthy little creatures started moaning and carrying on.

I asked our only remaining Jijo native what it could mean, but the behavior mystifies Sara. So I can only guess it has something to do with the changing composition of the huge migration fleet surrounding us.

As we move across vast reaches of space and hyperspace, more globule-like vessels keep joining the throng, jostling side by side with jagged-edged arks of the former Retired Order. *Zang* . . . plus other varieties of hydrogen breathers . . . now make up roughly two-thirds of the armada, though their vessels are generally much smaller than the monumental, fractal oxy-craft.

Our glavers must be sensing the Zang presence somehow. It makes them agitated—though whether from fear or anticipation is hard to tell.

They aren't the only ones feeling edgy. After leaving so many crewmates behind on Jijo, *Streaker* seems haunted and void . . . a bit like a wraith ship. Mystery surrounds us, and dangerous uncertainty lies ahead.

Yet, I can say without reservation that the dolphins left aboard this battered ship are performing their tasks admirably, with complete professionalism and dedication. After three years of winnowing, we are down to the last of Creideiki's selected crew. Those who seem immune to reversion or mental intimidation. Tested in a crucible of relentless hardship, they are pearls of Uplift—treasures of their kind. Every one would get unlimited breeding privileges, if we made it home.

Which doubles the irony, of course.

Not one of the fins believes we'll ever see Earth again.

As for Sara, she spends much of her time with the silent little chimp, Prity, using a small computer to draw hyperdimensional charts and complex spacetime matrices.

When I asked the Niss Machine to explain what they were doing, that sarcastic entity dismissed their project, calling it—*"Superstitious nonsense!"*

In other words, Sara still hopes to complete the work of her teacher, combining ancient Earthling mathematical physics with the computational models of Galactic science, trying to make sense out of the strange, frightening disruptions we have seen. Convulsions that appear to be unsettling a large fraction of the universe.

"I'm still missing some element or clue," she told me this morning, expressing both frustration and the kind of heady exhilaration that comes with intense labor in a field you love.

"I wonder if it may have something to do with the Embrace of Tides."

The Niss seems all too ready to dismiss Sara's efforts, because they have no correlation in the Great Library. But I've been impressed with her gumption and brilliance, even if she does seem to be bucking long odds. All I can say is more power to her.

Always hovering near Sara—with a distant, longing expression in his eyes—poor Emerson watches her tentative models flow across the holo display. Sometimes he squints, as if trying to remember something that's just on the tip of his tongue. Perhaps he yearns to help Sara. Or to warn of something. Or else simply to express his feelings toward her.

Their growing affection is lovely to behold—though I cannot entirely deflect pangs of jealousy. I was never able to return Emerson's infatuation, before his accident. Yet he remains dear to me. It is only human to have mixed feelings as his attention turns elsewhere. The stark truth is that Sara now has the only virile male human within several megaparsecs. How could that not make me feel more lonely than ever?

Yes, Tom. I sense you are still out there somewhere, with Creideiki, prowling dark corners of the cosmos. I can trace a faint echo of your essence, no doubt making, and getting into, astonishing varieties of trouble. Stirring things up even more than they already were.

Assuming it isn't wishful thinking—or some grand self-deception on my part—don't you also feel my thoughts right now, reaching out to you?

Can't you, or won't you, follow them?

I feel so lost . . . wherever "here" is.

Tom, please come and take me home.

* * *

Ah, well. I'll edit out the self-pity later. At least I have Herbie for company.

Good old Herb—the mummy standing in a corner of my office, looking back at me right now with vacant eyes. Humanoid but ineffably alien. Older than many stars. An enigma that Tom bought with more than one life. A treasure of incalculable value, whose image launched a thousand Galactic clans and mighty alliances into mortal panic, shattering their own laws, chasing poor *Streaker* across the many-layered cosmos, trying to seize our cargo before anyone else could wrap their hands-claws-feelers-jaws around it.

My orders sound clear enough. Deliver Herbie—and our other treasures—to the "proper authorities."

Once, I thought that meant the Great Library, or the Migration Institute.

Sorely disappointed and betrayed by those "neutral" establishments, we then gambled on the Old Ones—and nearly lost everything.

Now?

Proper authorities.

I have no idea who in the universe that would be.

Till this moment, I've put off reporting my most disturbing news. But there's no point in delaying any longer.

Yesterday, I had to put a dear friend under arrest.

Tsh't, my second-in-command, so competent and reliable. The rock I relied on for so long.

It breaks my heart to dial up the brig monitor and see her circling round and round, swimming without harness in a sealed pool, locked behind a coded door plate.

But what else could I do?

There was no other choice, once I uncovered her secret double dealings.

How did this happen? How could I have been blind to the warning signs? Like when those two Danik prisoners "committed suicide" a couple of months ago. I should have investigated more closely. Put out feelers. But I left the inquest to her, so involved was I with other matters.

Finally, I could no longer ignore the evidence. Especially now that she helped another, far more dangerous prisoner to esc—

I had to interrupt making that last journal entry, several hours ago. (Not that I was enjoying the subject.) Something intervened, yanking me away.

An important change in our state of affairs.

The Niss Machine broke in to say the momentum field was collapsing.

The entire huge armada was slowing at last, dropping from A Level down to B, and then C. Flickers into normal space were growing longer with each jump. Soon, long-range sensors showed we were decelerating toward a brittle blue pinpoint—apparently our final destination.

Olelo's spectral scan revealed a *white dwarf star,* extremely compact, with a diameter less than a hundredth that of Earth's home sun, consisting mainly of ash from fusion fires that entered their last stage of burning aeons ago. In fact, it is a very massive and old dwarf, whose lingering furnace glow comes from gravitational compression that may last another twenty billion years.

We began picking up nearby anomalies—spindly dark objects revolving quite close to that dense relic star. Massive structures, big enough to make out as black shadows that sparkled or flashed, occulting the radiant disk whenever they passed through line of sight. Which they did frequently. There were a lot of them, jammed so close that each circuit took less than a minute!

Soon we verified they were orbiting artifacts, jostling deep inside the sheer gravity well.

Of course, the concept was familiar, reminding me of the Fractal World, crowding and shrouding its small red sun—a contemplative sanctuary for retirees. Indeed, this place bears a family resemblance to that vast habitat. Only here the distance scales are a hundred times smaller. Tremendous amounts of matter abide in that curled well, crammed into a tight funnel of condensed spacetime.

Whoever lives down there must not value elbow room very much.

They belong to an order of life that craves a different kind of dimensionality. A squeezing clasp—an 'embrace'—that older races interpret as loving salvation.

Joining others in the Plotting Room, I watched this new variation on an old theme gradually loom before us.

"There are tens of billionsss of white dwarves per galaxy," commented Akeakemai. "If even a small fraction are inhabited like this, the p-population of transcendent beings would be staggering. And none would've been detectable from pre-Contact Earth!"

Sara held the hand of Emerson, whose eyes darted among the surrounding vessels of our convoy, perhaps fearing what they might do, now that we'd arrived. I sympathized. We're all waiting for the other shoe to drop.

Deceleration continued through normal space, as the Niss Machine rematerialized to report. It had finished researching the symbol on our prow—the broad chevron representing our counterfeit membership in a higher order of sapiency.

"Let me conjecture," I said, before the whirling hologram could explain. "The emblem stands for a *union of the hydro-and oxy-life,* coming together at last."

One of my few remaining satisfactions comes from surprising the smug machine.

"How . . . did you know?" it asked.

I shrugged—a blithe gesture, covering the fact that I had guessed.

"Two line segments meeting at an angle of one hundred and five degrees—and it's actually one hundred and four point five—that can only represent the *bonds of a water molecule.*"

"And that symbolizes. . . ?" Sara Koolhan asked.

"Hydrogen plus oxygen, combining to make the fundamental ingredient of all life chemistry. It's not so mysterious."

The spinning lines seemed to sway.

"Maybe for you," the Niss replied. "Earthling preconceptions are not as fixed, perhaps. But to me this comes as a shock. After all the warnings, the endlessly repeated stories about how dangerous the hydros are . . . how illogical, touchy, and inscrutable they can be . . ."

I shrugged.

"Young boys call little girls names, and vice versa. Often, they can't stand each others' company. At least, till they grow up enough to need one another."

It was a facile analogy. And yet, the comparison made sense!

I used to wonder about the oxy-hydro antagonism. How, if they are so fundamentally different, so explosively hostile and incompatible, did the Zang and their brethren manage to keep peace with the Civilization of Five Galaxies for so long? Why hasn't one side wiped out the other, instead of grudgingly cooperating in complex feats of migration and eco-management, sharing spiral arms and space lanes with a relative minimum of violence?

How, indeed? It seemed improbable.

That is, unless the whole thing was already worked out at a higher level! A level where both life orders at last matured enough to find common ground.

A consummation, with each side providing what the other lacks.

So.

Here we are, at a place of fusion and consolidation.

A union forged amid strong gravity currents, deep within the Embrace of Tides.

We seem to be invited.

That leaves just one question.

Why?

HARRY

He expected to be welcomed home with congratulations, perhaps by Wer'Q'quinn himself, or at least the old squid's senior aides, eager to receive Harry's data and hear about his successful mission.

A damned difficult mission, if truth be told. An epic voyage to one of the worst parts of E Space, where he had prevailed against horrible odds, and even picked up a couple of human-sooner castaways for good measure!

Anticipating acclaim, what he found at Kazzkark Base was chaos.

All the north pole docking bays were full, except a few set aside for official use. Approaching one of those, Harry had to shout his priority code, adding threats until a surly Migration Institute monitor-drone finally vacated a slot reserved for NavInst craft.

Beyond the starlit scaffolding, he glimpsed a myriad sleek refugee ships, tethered in layers from one end of the planetoid to the other, creating a dense, confusing snarl of shadowy forms and glinting strobe lights.

"Ain't it excitin', Dwer?" murmured the girl with the scarred face—Rety—whose eyes gleamed at the sight. "Didn't I promise ya? Stick with me an' I'll get you to civilization! That's what I said. Good-bye smelly ol' Jijo, and hello galaxy! We'll never be dirty, hungry, poor, or bored again."

Harry exchanged a glance with the other human, the tall male. Both young savages were clearly out of their depth. But unlike Rety, Dwer seemed to know it. His eyes expressed worried awe at the view outside.

Kinda like the way I feel, Harry pondered. Starships were packed together like shattered murvva trunks after a bad windstorm on Horst.

The disruptions must've got a lot worse since I left . . . especially if folks are choosing dumpy old Kazzkark as a place to run away to!

Magnetic grapples settled snugly around his battered survey station, which at last powered down with a relieved groan as repair bots automatically converged to plug holes and fix other damage. Harry, too, exhaled the tension he had carried in his spine ever since departure, sighing deeply.

Home again . . . such as it is.

Downloading Wer'Q'quinn's data to a portable wafer, he turned and ushered his guests toward the airlock. In normal times, returning from any other mission, this pair would have stirred a sensation at the sleepy base. Hints at a newly discovered sooner infestation would spread quickly, and make the arresting officer famous.

Residual loyalty tugged at Harry. Humans were patrons to his own race, after all. Ostensibly, he wasn't supposed to care about that anymore. But habits were hard to break.

Besides, Dwer and Rety saved my life.

The conflict left him feeling more ambivalent than triumphant as they passed through a short tunnel into the planetoid.

With everything in an uproar, maybe my report about them will just be overlooked.

He decided he could live with that.

The Ingress Atrium was filled with noise and commotion as a mélange of races pushed and jostled, ignoring the delicate rhythms and rituals of racial seniority and interclan protocol as they pressed for admission, hoping for sanctuary from an increasingly unreliable cosmos. Harry's Institute credentials got him through several gates, moving to the front of the queue with his two humans in tow. Still, it took most of a midura to reach the final portal labeled IMMIGRATION AND QUARANTINE. Along the way, he overheard some of the worry and panic fluxing through the Civilization of Five Galaxies.

"—three out of four transfer points in Lalingush Sector show dislocations, or catastrophic domain recombinations," hissed a tunictguppit trader in GalSeven, exchanging gossip with a rotund p'ort'l whose chest-mounted eye blinked furiously.

The p'ort'l snorted in reply—a rich sound, with multitoned harmonies. "I hear most of the remaining transfer points have been seized by local alliances, who are exacting illegal taxes on any ship attempting to enter or leave. One consequence is vast numbers of stranded merchants, students, pilgrims, and tourists with no way to get home!"

To Harry's surprise, the two young humans didn't seem at all panicky or intimidated by the crowd. Rety grinned happily, stroking the neck of her little urrish "husband," while Dwer stared at the diversity of sapient life-forms, occasionally leaning over to whisper in the girl's ear, pointing at some type of alien he recognized—perhaps from legends told around a campfire, back on his tribal homeworld—a more cosmopolitan attitude than Harry would have expected.

Nevertheless, Dwer betrayed underlying nervousness in the way he clutched his bow and arrows tightly under one arm.

Harry had considered confiscating the crude archery equipment. In theory, prisoners weren't supposed to go around armed. Still, he doubted even the most stickling Galactic bureaucrat would recognize the assortment of twigs, strings, and bits of chipped stone as a weapon.

Speaking of rule sticklers, he thought, on reaching the main desk. The same sour hoonish official was on duty as last time, and just as obnoxious as ever. Despite the declared state of emergency, Twaphu-anuph flapped his richly dyed throat sac at anyone who showed even the slightest irregularity of documentation, ignoring their protests, sending them back to the end of the line. The hoon seemed frazzled from overwork and strain when Harry stepped up to the desk.

Get ready for a surprise, you gloomy old bureaucrat, Harry thought, relishing how his new tail and fur color would shock Twaphu-anuph.

To his disappointment; the hoon barely regarded Harry with a quick scan before looking back down at his monitor screens. Apparently, the pale fur coloration did not alter the official's gestalt of a Terran chimpanzee.

"Ah, *hrr-rrm.* So it is Observer Harms, once again inflicting his unwelcome simian visage on my tired sensoria," Twaphu-anuph commented in snidely accented GalSix. "Only this time—equally noxious—he brings along two of his grubby Earthling masters. Have they come to take you home at last, like a truant child?"

Harry sensed Rety and Dwer stiffen. He hurried to respond with more firmness than he might have otherwise.

"Twaphu-anuph, you exceed your prerogatives, which do not include heaping personal abuse on a fellow acolyte of the Great Institutes. However, if you pass us through at once, I may refrain from lodging a formal protest."

Perhaps it was fatigue from a long, successful mission that gave Harry's voice a more confident tenor. To his surprise, the big hoon seemed unmotivated to continue his traditional derisive taunting. Twaphu-anuph held out a giant hand.

"Hr-rr-r. Show me the humans' identification tags. *Please.*"

Harry shook his head.

"They are specimens claimed for observation by the Navigation Institute, entering Kazzkark under my own credentials. You may image both humans and do a bio scan before letting us through. That should take about thirty duras to accomplish. Regulations do not allow a longer delay. Or shall I complain to Wer'Q'quinn?"

Their eyes met. A low, rumbling sound fluttered from below Twaphu-anuph's chin as the throat sac drummed. Harry knew he was being roundly cursed in a semiprivate racial dialect. Formal insult could not be taken, since no official Galactic language was involved, but several onlookers seemed to grasp the cutting remark, expressing agreement or amusement in their own ways. Ever since the debacle at the NuDawn Colony, centuries ago, malevolence from hoons had been a tedious fact of life to members of beleaguered Earthclan.

Dwer Koolhan abruptly burst out laughing, a sound that cut through Twaphu-anuph's hostile umble, causing it to trip and founder. The hoon gave up a surprised stare as the young human responded in Anglic—also an unofficial tongue, but one that many sophonts understood these days.

"Ouch, what a good cut! Hold on there a dura, while I explain to this poor chimp what you just said about his body type, his ancestors, and all that!"

Leaning toward Harry, Dwer offered a quick wink and whispered.

"Smile and pretend you're tellin' me something to say back at the fool."

Harry blinked.

"What do you think you're trying to—"

Dwer stood up straight again, guffawing loudly and pointing at Harry. He made as if to say something to Twaphu-anuph, but was unable to get by gasps of laughter.

"He says . . . the chimp says . . ."

Rety wore a sour expression, rolling her eyes. But Harry could only stare in amazement as Dwer gathered a deep breath, looked straight at Twaphu-anuph . . . and began approximating a deep hoonish umble!

A kind of ferocity seemed to flash in Dwer's eyes as he threw a belch-like groan at the officious inspector, whose throat flapped with astonishment and dismay.

Abrupt silence reigned when Dwer took a breath and switched to Anglic.

"There, wasn't that clever? Where I come from, any chimp who said something like that would be called a real—"

Harry grabbed Dwer's arm and squeezed. The young man was wiry for a human, but no match for chim strength. Obediently, Dwer cut off at once, smiling amiably at the crowd. None had ever heard an Earthling umble before. It sure was a first for Harry!

Then, as if for good measure, Rety's little "husband" stuck his little urrish head out from her pouch, giving the tall hoon a hiss of raspberry scorn, prompting still more surprised shouts from the throng.

"Enough!" Twaphu-anuph cried, slamming his heavy fist on a switch, causing the portal to fly open. "Hoon-talking humans? Earth-talking hoons? *Has the whole cosmos gone crazy?* Get out of here! Go!"

While the bureaucrat buried his massive head in his hands, Harry kept his grip on Dwer's arm, pulling until all of them passed safely onto the covered avenues of Kazzkark, letting go only when the Ingress Atrium was far behind them.

Stepping back, he regarded the sooner boy, as if for the first time.

After a long pause, Harry grunted with a brief nod.

"I got just one question for you."

"Yes?" Dwer replied, clearly expecting to be chided.

"Can you teach me how to do what you did back there?"

There are ways of reporting an event that make it seem uneventful.

While waiting in Wer'Q'quinn's lobby for his boss to see him, Harry quickly modified his written account of meeting Dwer and Rety in E Space, removing his surmise that they came from a sooner world. It wasn't necessary to hide any actual facts. Who else but another Earthling would recognize Dwer's handsewn buckskins and neolithic weaponry for what they were?

He could rationalize that he wasn't really breaking his oath. Sort of.

"Your ship broke down and you lost all personal effects before the machine craft picked you up," he coaxed the pair. "You also suffered brain damage, resulting in partial amnesia. That should qualify you for basic aid, under the Traveler's

Assistance Tradition. Maybe enough to pay for air, water, and protein till you find a way to earn your keep. Got that?"

While Dwer nodded soberly, Rety murmured to the little male urs.

"You hear that, yee? Brain damage? I bet Dwer can fake *that* real good."

Her "husband" responded by aiming a swift nip at her left hand, which she yanked back just in time. All at once, Harry decided he liked the small creature.

"I know some people in Low Town," he said. "Maybe they can find the two of you some jobs you're suited for. Meanwhile, here's a data chip with standard information about Kazzkark and the surrounding sector," he continued, handing over a clear rod, which Rety slid into her prize possession—a rather beat-up-looking tutorial computer of Terran design. "Study hard while I'm inside. When I finish, I'll take you someplace safe. But in return I'm gonna want your story—the *whole* story, you understand? About your home and everything."

Both humans nodded, and Harry felt sure they meant it.

A musical chime seemed to fill the air—a unique rhythm and melody that Harry had been taught to recognize more surely than his own name.

A summons. Wer'Q'quinn's staff must have finished going through his data, taken by instruments that had peered at the Real Cosmos from the outside.

At last, he thought, standing up. Already the two young humans were immersed in images from the teaching unit, so he left without a word. Hurrying toward his boss's office, Harry felt growing excitement. With this recent success, he had earned some consideration from the Navigation Institute. Perhaps enough to be let in on the big secret.

Maybe now someone will tell me what in Ifni's Probabilistic Purgatory is going on!

Several miduras passed before he emerged at last from Wer'Q'quinn's sanctuary, feeling rather dazed.

He had hoped for an explanation.

Now Harry wondered if it was such a good idea, after all.

Ain't it always like this? The gods warn us to be careful what we wish for. Sometimes it comes true.

There was good news, bad news . . . and tidings that were downright terrifying.

First came congratulations on surviving a hard voyage. The changed fur coloring—plus addition of a new body appendage—seemed relatively mild compared to the afflictions that some other observers came home with. He was given a generous personal compensation allowance, and the NavInst staff said nothing more about it.

As for the mission, Wer'Q'quinn could not be more pleased. Using the peculiar perspectives of E Space to gaze in at the sidereal universe, Harry's cameras had measured a progressive *stretching* of the underlying subvacuum. A process that was rapidly nearing rupture. Thanks to his bold mission, Wer'Q'quinn's local savants knew almost as much about this process as their august superiors, back at Quadrant HQ.

That was also the bad news.

Those superiors must have known for some time what was going on. Yet they had delayed declaring an emergency till the last moment. Even now they were downplaying public fears.

"Could it be a conspiracy?" Harry had asked Wer'Q'quinn, at one point.

The squid-like being thrashed several tentacles. "If so, Observer Harms, this conspiracy includes the topmost beings-in-authority of *all* major institutes, plus most elder races, as well. In fact, now that we have fresh facts, my staff has been able to coerce better infolink references from our Kazzkark branch of the Great Library, revealing something so remarkable that we are stunned nearly breathless from the news."

Harry swallowed, hard. "What is it?"

"Apparently, this is not the first time events such as these have occurred! A lesser version of the same phenomena took place about one hundred and fifty million years ago, associated with the permanent or temporary dysfunction of seventy percent of all transfer points! Then, too, society was racked by massive social disruptions and genocidal wars. Galaxy Three, in particular, suffered terribly."

"But . . . how could such things be hidden? The Library—isn't it supposed to be . . ."

Wer'Q'quinn waved the objection away, as if it were naive. "Few facts were suppressed, per se. Rather, the cover-up was executed more subtly, by emphasizing the significance of some events, and minimizing others out of all proportion."

Harry felt glad of his fur, covering a blush of embarrassment. This was exactly what he had done, burying the truth about Dwer and Rety under mounds of detail.

"The chaos of that epoch has always been attributed to widespread inter-clan warfare, which turns out to have been a symptom, rather than the cause," Wer'Q'quinn continued. "Anyway, people are accustomed to finding historical records murky, clouded by uncertainty, the farther back you go. That may be why a far more crucial event—the *Gronin Collapse*—gets so little attention."

"The . . . what?"

"The Gronin Collapse. Forgive me, you are a wolfling, and your education is deficient. But most Galactic schoolchildren know that the Progenitors returned, in spirit form, approximately two hundred and thirty million years ago, to guide and protect oxy-life during one of its worst crises. Interstellar navigation became tortuous. Conflicts slashed populations. Only a small number of starfaring clans survived to begin renewing the Cycle of Uplift with a fresh generation."

"I . . ." Harry frowned. "I think I heard of it. Weren't *machines* and *Zang* supposed to be responsible, somehow?"

"A superficial explanation that most accept without further probing. In truth however, the answer was something else. Something more grand . . . and far more frightening."

Which brought Harry to the third, and most worrying, bit of news.

"Apparently, these recent convulsions are part of a *natural catastrophe* whose proportions have not been seen since the Gronin Collapse. And we will face far worse calamities during the duras and piduras to come."

"H . . . how much worse?"

Wer'Q'quinn twisted several long, suckered tendrils around each other in a grasp strong enough to bend steel. The elderly sophont, normally as unshakable as a neutron star, seemed to shiver, as if it took strong will to utter the next words.

"It seems that our civilization may be about to lose a galaxy."

Harry reached the anteroom still in a daze.

Wer'Q'quinn had indicated that he already had an assignment planned for Harry, whose promotion would take effect along with those new duties, starting tomorrow.

Something about a message, just recently broadcast from besieged Earth. A warning, aimed at all Institute outposts. Senior officials have squelched it, wherever possible, but rumors of its content were already spreading panic through several quadrants.

It all sounded fascinating. But right now Harry's exhaustion showed even to his normally oblivious boss. His head was in a muddle, and Wer'Q'quinn had ordered him home for some well-earned rest before starting anew.

Entering the richly paneled outer chamber, Harry stood for a long time, blinking, wondering what was missing.

Dwer and Rety, he realized at last.

They were supposed to stay here, waiting for me.

He peered left and right.

They were gone!

Hurrying through the far portal, he stood on the topmost step of Navigation Institute headquarters, staring at the teeming crowds, wondering where the two humans might have run off to. Humans never before exposed to the intricate dangers of Galactic culture, with no idea what hazards lurked out there among several hundred temperamental species . . . many of whom hated Earthlings on sight.

SARA

It all boiled down to a matter of language.

You can only contemplate what your mind is able to describe, she thought.

The system of organized Galactic dialects had helped oxy-races communicate with minimal misunderstanding for two billion years—a primly logical structure of semantics, syntax, grammar, and meaning. But now she figured it had a double purpose—*to obscure.* A sophisticated culture of technically advanced and deeply intelligent beings was channeled away from pondering certain topics. Certain possibilities.

This could be the real reason wolfling races wind up being annihilated, she thought. They may more readily look past the blind spots. See what mustn't be seen.

That cannot be allowed.

* * *

Through a crystal pane, Sara glanced at swarms of gigantic, needle-shaped habitats orbiting a dense relic star at furious speed. Lined up along the radial path followed by escaping rays of light, their inner points seemed almost to brush the intensely bright surface. Anyone living down there—perched deep within the white dwarf's steep gravitational well—would experience profound tidal forces, tugging and stretching—'embracing'—every living cell.

Of course, that was the whole point of living here.

Unlike the Fractal World, mere hydrogen metal could not survive the glare or tortuous strain of this place. Hannes Suessi had tried to explain what kinds of field-reinforced materials might withstand such forces, but Sara's mind only reeled at his cascade of obscure terms. The technology, far beyond her barbarian education, seemed altogether godlike.

Ah, but *math* . . . that was another story. Even back home, with just pencil and paper as her only tools, she had learned all sorts of clever shortcuts to describe the countless ways that *space* might fold, flex, or tear—*analytical* methods, like calculus, that lay outside the normal Galactic tradition.

Now, with some of *Streaker*'s onboard wizard machines to assist her, Sara found herself performing extravagant incantations. By word and gesture, she caused glorious charts and graphs to appear in midair. Tensors cleaved before her eyes. Tarski transforms and Takebayashi functions dealt handily with transfinite integrals at her merest whim, solving problems that no mere numerical processor could calculate by brute force alone.

Her little chimp assistant, Prity, helped by silently molding shapes with agile hands, fashioning outlines that became equations.

Equations portraying a cosmos under stress.

I wish Sage Purofsky could have seen this.

It was as if both calculus and computers had been waiting to achieve their potential together. Joined now under her direction, they were already making her old teacher's dream come true, proving that the ancient concepts of Einstein and Leibniz and Lee had relevance, after all.

Perhaps experts on Earth had already accomplished the same thing, either openly or in secret. Still Sara felt as if she were exploring virgin territory. Those concepts cast light upon the future—revealing a calamity of untold magnitude.

Well, at least now we know—we weren't at fault for what happened to the Fractal World. Gillian will find that comforting, I guess.

Dr. Baskin clearly felt guilty over contributing to the havoc that had struck the vast, frail shell of hydrogen ice, crushing billions of inhabitants when it collapsed. It had seemed to be a direct result of *Streaker*'s presence—like a snake corrupting Eden. But Sara's evidence now pointed to natural phenomena, ponderously inevitable, as impersonal as an earthquake. Far more unstoppable than a hurricane.

No wonder so many other refugee arks joined our convoy. Delicate criswell structures must he shattering all over the Five Galaxies, forcing members of the Retired Order to choose quickly whether to rejoin oxy-civilization or transcend to the next level . . . or else stay where they are, and die.

Unable to bear even a brief separation from the Embrace of Tides, many chose to remain huddled next to their little red suns, even as the continuum shivered around them, crushing their brittle, icy homes into evaporating splinters.

Looking down at the brilliantly compact white dwarf, Sara wondered. Would the same worsening conditions also affect this crowded realm—where sparkling needle shapes whirled quickly around a superdense star? It was a far mightier place than the Fractal World, occupied by revered races even more ancient than the 'Old Ones,' combining the best of hydrogen and oxygen cultures.

Surely members of the Transcendent Order must know what's coming. We are like ants compared to such wise beings. They'll have means of protecting themselves during the Time of Changes.

It was a reassuring thought.

Unfortunately, Sara could not keep from worrying.

She worried about the Buyur.

Her news got a sober reception at the next staff meeting. Even when Sara exonerated *Streaker* from the Fractal World tragedy, Dr. Baskin seemed more concerned with understanding what might happen next.

"You're saying that all these disruptions are a natural result of the *expansion of the universe*?"

"That's right," Sara replied. "The spacetime metric—including the underlying ylem—stretches and weakens, eventually reaching a fracture point. Domain boundaries abruptly snap and reconnect. A bit like pressure building underground for release in a quake. So-called threads, or flaws in the original matrix, can be pinched off, turning transfer points into useless maelstroms, isolating whole sectors, quadrants, or even galaxies."

The older woman shook her head. "Cosmic expansion has been going on for fourteen billion years. Why should all this come to a sudden head now?"

The Niss Machine interjected at that point.

"The simple answer to your question is that this occurrence . . . is not unique."

"What do you mean?"

"I mean this sort of thing has happened before.

"Let me illustrate by asking a question, Dr. Baskin. Does this symbol have any meaning to you?"

Sara watched an image take shape above the conference table—a complex form with thirteen spiral rays and four ovals, all overlaid.

Gillian blinked for a moment. Then her mouth pinched in a sour expression. "You know damn well it does. Tom found it engraved on those strange ships we discovered in the Shallow Cluster . . . the so-called *Ghost Fleet* that got us in trouble the minute we laid eyes on it."

Bowing its funnel of nested lines politely, the Niss Machine continued.

"Then surely you recall one possibility we discussed—that the Ghost Fleet might represent emissaries from an entirely different civilization? One completely apart from our five linked galaxies. Perhaps an expedition that had crossed hundreds of megaparsecs of flat, open space to reach us from a quite different nexus of life?"

The Niss waited for Gillian to nod.

"Well, I can now refute that guess. It is not true.

"Rather; those ships come from our past . . . a past when *more* than five galaxies made up this nexus-association."

A water-filled tube ran along one wall of the conference room, where Akeakemai slashed his broad tail, causing a storm of bubbles to swirl around his sleek gray body. With Lieutenant Tsh't under arrest, he was now the senior dolphin aboard—an honor that clearly made him nervous.

"M-mo-more? You mean there were once—*sssseventeen* galaxiessss?"

"Seventeen, aye. Of which several were elliptical types, as well as thirteen spirals. However, a while later—(the records are vague on exact timing)—there appear to have been eleven . . . and then seven . . . and finally the five we know today."

Silence reigned. Finally, although his cyborg visage remained mirror smooth, Hannes Suessi stammered.

"But—but how could we not already know about something so . . . something so . . ."

"Something so huge? So epochal and traumatic? I believe your own state of shocked surprise is a clue. Each such loss would have struck hard at the normally placid, deeply conservative society of the time. In fact, the waves of disruption that Sage Koolhan just described must have been even worse in those earlier episodes, wreaking untold havoc and ruin. Survivors would have been busy for ages, picking up the pieces.

"Now suppose older, wiser spirits asserted themselves during the aftermath, taking control over the Great Library through those crucial centuries, it would not require much effort to erase and adjust appropriate archive entries . . . or divert blame for the chaos onto more mundane culprits. Say, the Zang, or criminal oxy-clans, or a breeding-explosion by machine life-forms."

"But how could they conceal the loss of whole galaxies!"

"That may have been easier than it seems. The last time this happened on a large scale—the Gronin Collapse—there followed hardly any mention of lost territories, because the Migration Institute had already prepared by—"

Sara stood up.

"By evacuating them!"

She turned to address Gillian and the others.

"The Transcendents must have known in advance, two hundred thirty million years ago. They ordered abandonment of the two galaxies they were about to lose, before the rupture took place." She stared into space. "This explains the mystery about Galaxy Four! Why *all* of that spiral was recently assigned fallow status, forcing all oxygen-breathing starfarers to depart. It wasn't for reasons of *ecological management,* but because *they sensed another split coming!*"

The Niss hologram shrugged, as if it all seemed obvious now. The entity made no apologies for taking so long to catch on.

"Clearly, the higher orders of life have either confided in or manipulated senior officials of the Great Institutes, so the governing bodies of oxy-civilization would make preparations."

"But there's so much we still don't understand!" Sara objected. "Why must the affected galaxy be emptied of starfarers? How does all this affect the other life orders? What does it—"

Gillian Baskin interrupted.

"I'm sure you will help us pierce those veils as well, Sage Koolhan. Meanwhile, this news is disturbing enough. When you said a galaxy was about to split off, I thought you meant the one containing Earth—the Milky Way. That might help explain why our planet was isolated for so long. And why we created such commotion when we finally made contact."

The Niss answered with some of its old patronizing tone.

"With all due respect, Dr. Baskin, do curb your innate human tendency toward solipsism. Despite some petty excitement caused by this little ship, the universe does not revolve around your kind."

Sara found the rebuke snide and unfair. But Gillian accepted it with a nod.

Suessi reported on efforts to cast off the ship's transparent sheath, an armor layer that once had protected it against devastating weapons, but now seemed a death shroud. It had proved nearly fatal just two hours ago, when *Streaker* tried to depart the white dwarf's funnellike gravity well, sneaking away from the swarm of "candidates for transcendence."

Unfortunately, the Jophur battleship, *Polkjhy*, lay waiting just above, swooping in to launch a new form of attack. Emitting complex pulses on a hyperspatial resonance band, the enemy stroked a response from the strange atoms locked in *Streaker*'s outer shell, turning the throbbing layer into a huge antenna, drawing a flux of energy from D Space! As the Niss predicted, temperatures soon climbed. The deck plates warmed steadily, with no apparent way to slough the mounting heat.

Lacking any effective means to fight back, *Streaker* could not even tear free of *Polkjhy*'s grasping fields to dive back amid the mob of craggy arks, spiraling inexorably toward the white dwarf star. If the assault continued, the Earthlings would have to surrender . . . or else broil.

Then, abruptly, a Zang globule approached from the swarm, beaming a recognition code that set the herd of Jijoan glavers baying loudly in the hold. With evident frustration, the *Polkjhy* released its grip and backed away as "deputy" vessels budded off the giant Zang, moving toward *Streaker*.

Relieved, the Terrans rendezvoused with the rescuing globules.

"I guess it's time to say good-bye to our little friends," Gillian Baskin had said. The glavers were about to meet a destiny mapped out for them long ago.

Willingly, the small troop of quadrupeds clattered to the airlock, where Sara bid them farewell.

May this bring the redemption that your ancestors sought, when they came to Jijo. A strange, but honorable goal. To unite what had been distinct. To bridge the gap, helping oxygen and hydrogen meld as one.

At last she understood how both civilizations had been able to coexist for so long, despite a fractious antipathy during their youthful, starfaring phase. Because they were fated for each other, like preordained mates, who only discover affinity on their wedding eve.

Moreover, this union explained why the known cosmos was never overwhelmed by *machines*. United, the hydro-and oxy-orders were more than a match for silicon and metal, preventing digital sapience from taking over and exploiting every scrap of matter in all five linked galaxies.

It seems so tidy, so perfect—even romantic, in a way. Almost as if the universe were designed with this in mind.

Watching the glavers go—carried by translucent, glowing bubbles—she envied their clear-cut role. Their obvious importance. At that moment, they were Jijo's great success, valued participants in something inarguably noble, contributing their wise simplicity to help bring about glorious fusion.

Streaker seemed emptier when they were gone.

Suessi reported failure. The material covering the hull proved impossible to scratch by any means at his disposal.

"Whoever gave *Streaker* this coating not only saved our lives, back at the Fractal World. They also made sure we must stay with this convoy, all the way to the bottom."

With *Polkjhy* orbiting above, ready to pounce if *Streaker* tried leaving, there seemed no choice but to accompany the candidates' armada, spiraling toward the great, javelin-shaped habitats. Akeakemai sighed a resigned Trinary haiku.

• *Are we ready? Or not?*
• *Yanked from blissful dreaming,*
• *Hear the call of depths!* •

Emerson D'Anite laughed aloud, despite his crippled brain. But Sara had to consult her portable computer for a translation. Even so, she probably missed nuances of the quirky, intuition-based language.

Am I ready? To become transcendent?

Sara wondered what that meant, but all she could picture was an image of vast, cool intellects, in hybrid bodies stretched thin by tides, contemplating ornate wisdom that would make her beloved equations seem like the flagella flailings of some crude bacterium. Even if such beings found a way to incorporate humans and dolphins into their composite mind, she scarcely found the prospect attractive.

Anyway, this is probably just a trick played on us by the Old Ones—like reaming Emerson's brain, or turning Hannes into a cyborg. A joke we'll only get when we reach those glittering needles.

Accepting Suessi's report, Dr. Baskin concentrated on practical matters.

"What physical threats do we face, as we approach the white dwarf?"

"There is strong ultraviolet radiation," answered S'tat, one of Suessi's engineers, from atop a walker unit at the far end of the conference table. "But our armor seems to handle it without t-trouble."

"How about the intense gravity down there? Will our clocks slow?"

"Yessss. The field is intense enough to make a difference in the flow of t-time." Akeakemai nodded, bubbles rising from his blowhole. "By lessss than one percent."

Gillian nodded. "And the gravitational *gradient*?"

Sara had done the research.

"The tides are several orders bigger here than at the Fractal World. You'll feel a tugging sense along the length of your body. I don't expect them to be pleasant—though they say that older sapients find it irresistibly attractive. Even addictive."

Gillian nodded.

"The famed *Embrace of Tides*. The more advanced a sophont species becomes, the more they crave it, and the less they can bear traveling where space is flat. That's why we see little of transcendent life-forms. No wonder they're considered a separate order."

"Separate," Suessi agreed. "But still ready to meddle in the affairs of younger races."

Sara watched Gillian shrug, appearing to say—*Why worry about things we can never change?*

"So this is transcendence. Each uplifted species that survives starfaring adolescence eventually winds up in such a place. Both oxies and hydros. From across the linked galaxies, they converge at white dwarf stars in order to achieve . . . what? Niss, do you know?"

The spinning lines whirled, a maze of shifting patterns.

"Your question is the same one that obsesses theologians, back in the 'adolescent' culture we call home.

"Some believe transcendent beings find renewed youth in the Embrace of Tides.

"Others say the elders pass through a mystic portal, following the blessed Progenitors to a better realm. As you well know, minor differences over such details can rouse strong tempers among hot-blooded clans, such as the Soro, or Tandu—"

"Tell me about it!" Hannes muttered sourly. "Ifni-cursed fanatics."

"So it seems to you—and my Tymbrimi makers, and other moderate clans who feel the affairs of the Transcendent Order are rightfully none of our business. We will find out the truth, when our own turn comes.

"But need I remind you those 'fanatics' you mention are powerful among the races who swarm flat spacetime in a myriad starships? They wield great influence, and act more swiftly than the moderates. Their fleets presently lay siege to Terra, and have hounded this crew ever since we escaped the Shallow Cluster."

Sara watched Gillian lean forward, her cheekbones stark in light from the whirling hologram. "You're building up to some point. Get on with it."

"My point is that this ship, Streaker, has suffered terrible persecution because it represents a danger and an affront to reverent tradition all across the Five Galaxies.

"The relics and data you carry appear to threaten deeply held creeds."

"We already knew that much," Gillian replied. "Can I assume you've finally figured out why?"

The Niss broadened its spiral of lines, spreading and almost brushing the blond human's face.

"Indeed, I think that I have.

"It seems your discovery resurrects an ancient heresy that had been considered dead for millions of years.

"A heresy claiming that everything our civilization believes is wrong."

LARK

Deep within the Jophur battleship, things had changed yet again.

The last time Lark visited the *Polkjhy*'s Life Core, the place resembled a dense but orderly forest grove—a farm in three dimensions—featuring lush green rows and columns of vegetation neatly organized on metal scaffolding to purify the great vessel's air and water, serving the Jophur crew efficiently, like any other machine.

Now it was a tangle of riotous growth, a jungle where plants and autotrophs from a myriad worlds had broken out of their assigned places, curling round the disappearing latticework, intermingling in a bedlam of anarchic biogenesis.

Amid the profuse, growth, he glimpsed skittering little things—animals of varied types that surely had not been here before. Did they escape from some onboard lab-menagerie during the crash and confusion of battle? Or did caretaker computers deliberately thaw and release them from storage, in some vain effort to regain control over a miniature ecosystem that grew more complex and wild with each passing midura? Moving deeper, he even spied little scavenger organisms that looked like individual Jophur rings, writhing and twisting as they made their way along branches, seeking rotten matter to consume. Their pale colors expressed innocence and simplicity of purpose. None appeared eager to seek sophistication, or to gather sapiency by combining into stacks.

Lark found the Life Core's new look an improvement. He came from a world where nature was allowed to find its own equilibrium—a complex balance, invariably messy, that worked better than any plan. Even when many participants of a planetary biosphere were foes, preying on each other with tooth and claw, the overall result wound up looking like cooperation, giving each individual and species a role to play, helping the whole system thrive.

Kind of like our own little group of strange allies, he thought, *pondering the curious expedition that had made its way to the heart of the Jophur warship. We may not trust each other, but lacking any other choice, we work together.*

Pushing through the rank overgrowth, he paused near a vine that hung heavy with ripe clamber-peaches, popular on more oxy-worlds than anyone could count. Lark plucked one and brought it to his mouth, but then had to wait for rippling layers of membrane to creep out of the way, until there was room enough to take a good bite out of the fruit. Red juice sprayed around his tongue and between several teeth, dribbling down his chin, assailing taste buds with pleasure. Greedily, he consumed several more. It was Lark's first decent meal in days.

The passenger—a modified Zang globule that spread its bulk across his body like a cumbersome second skin—seemed to catch some of Lark's complaint. A tendril presented itself before his left eye, and a vacuole opened inside that gelatinous mass. Tiny subdeputy blobs popped forth, performing a microscopic drama, communicating in the Zang manner, by simulation.

Lark shook his head.

"No, I'm not ungrateful. I realize you've been feeding me from your own body mass, so we could get this far. But forgive me if I prefer something that doesn't stink of rotten eggs, for a change!"

He was fairly sure that his actual words—sonic vibrations in the air—had no meaning to the alien. That type of language, abstract and structured, was as foreign to such bubble-beings as the notion of walking around on stilt-limbs, stiffened by rigid bones. Lark's best guess was that the creature/entity tracked his eye movements instead, somehow gleaning import from *which* little speck or simulated blob he chose unconsciously to look at, in which order. The result was a crude form of telepathy, unlike any he had ever heard or read about.

Subdeputies whirled some more, inside their vacuole-theater.

"Yeah, okay," he answered. "I know. Gotta keep moving. There isn't much time."

A rustling commotion disturbed the dense foliage just ahead. Lark reached warily for his best weapon, the purple ring which sprayed message chemicals on command, sometimes overcoming Jophur guards or battle-drones. Although its effectiveness had declined, the tricky little torus still reduced the number of times they had to fight, making possible this journey deep behind enemy lines.

A bulky form pushed through the jungle. Wide at the bottom and tapered on top, it had the ominous shape of a Jophur.

Or a traeki, Lark reminded himself, crouching amid shadows. Even when the figure drew near enough to identify by its stained contours, he still wasn't sure which word should apply. The composite being had once been *Asx,* a beloved traeki sage, then became haughty *Ewasx* of the Jophur.

Now it would answer to neither name. Ripples coursed up and down its waxy pyramid of greasy donuts, while segments vied and debated among themselves. Inside that fatty tower, new arrangements were being worked out, with the Master Ring no longer in complete control.

Quite possibly—at any moment—the issue might be decided in favor of resuming loyalty to *Polkjhy*'s captain-leader, or reporting Lark's presence to the embattled crew. But not yet. Meanwhile, there continued a strange, tentative partnership of Zang, human, and ring stack. A loose coalition of collective beings. Lark decided to call the confused creature "X"—at least till it made up its minds.

Waves of shadow and color flashed briefly, while the stack whistled breathy Galactic Six from its oration peak.

"I/we/I managed to accomplish the intended feat—accessing a terminal at the agronomist's workstation. (The agronomist erself was elsewhere, having been reassigned to combat roles during the emergency.) My/our appointed task of discovering news—this proved possible to achieve."

"Yes?" Lark took a step forward. "Did you learn where they took Ling?"

He had hoped to find her in the Life Core, near the nest where they had been happy—all too briefly.

The composite creature twitched and shuddered. Across its corrugated, waxy flesh there crawled dozens of small rings, crimson in color, feeding on its secretions. To the *Polkjhy* crew, those innocuous-looking toroids were carriers of a plague, more horrid than the Zang infestation.

"Of the remaining humans—Ling and Rann—there are no recent reports. As to their last known position, I/we narrowed it down to a quadrant of the ship . . .

one that became cut off twenty miduras ago, when fresh incursions of Zang-like entities apparently penetrated the hull."

News of hydrogen-breathing reinforcements did not affect Lark's passenger as expected. The globule-entity quivered, indicating a strong desire to avoid contact with the newcomers until they could be viewed from a safe distance.

So, there are factions, nations, races . . . or whatever . . . among hydros, too. Like us, they fear their own relatives more than the truly alien. I guess that shouldn't surprise me.

During their long, circuitous journey from the nursery chamber, all three odd allies had stopped to watch images on terminal screens, broadcast by the Jophur crew to keep their soldiers informed of what was going on outside. While X tried to describe a white dwarf star and explain what was known about transcendent life, the Zang seemed upset. What disturbed it was mounting evidence that hydro-and oxy-orders eventually merged, blending together in a steep mixing bowl of gravitational tides. Apparently, Lark's passenger found the news unnerving.

You are in way over your depth, just like me, aren't you? he asked the Zang at one point. It took several tries to get the question across—he was still learning this quirky mode of conversation. But eventually, after trembling violently for a while, it calmed down and meekly indicated assent.

Even hydro-entities must have trouble dealing with their gods. It seemed to be a law of nature.

"But you have Ling's last coordinates?" he asked X.

"Indeed. It should be possible to approach that sector . . . if we dare."

Lark nodded. Somehow he must persuade his companions that the risk was worthwhile. "And the other matter you were going to look into?"

The pile of greasy toroids flashed a series of shadows—flickering patterns-of-regret that seemed so deeply Jijoan that the creature felt more like Asx than ever. In speaking, it switched to GalSeven.

"Alas, the news is dire from your perspective . . . and perhaps ours/mine. During this ship's long journey, from the ill-fated retirement habitat to this indrawing of transcendent races, there were several moments when the *Polkjhy* got a fix on local star groups, ascertained its position, and managed to fire off message capsules. Of these attempts, at least three show high likelihood of escaping the convoy-swarm and making their way to chosen sites in the Civilization of Five Galaxies.

"In other words, the Jophur have succeeded in reporting to their home clan all about Jijo.

"All about the forlorn g'Kek.

"About traeki refugees who for so long escaped dominance by master rings.

"And about humans and other races, ripe for secret experimentation/manipulation, out of sight from law or any other restraint."

Lark's shoulders slumped. His heart felt so heavy that flashes of concerned inquiry came from the Zang passenger, worried about his metabolic state.

Jijo is lost, he realized.

Of course that had always been in the cards, one way or another. But *Polkjhy*'s troubles had made it seem possible—just barely—that the great battleship might meet a gruesome end before reporting what it had discovered in Galaxy Four. For this reason, he and Ling had abandoned the safety of their little nest, hoping to sow confusion in the enemy HQ.

I guess we should have just stayed here, making love and eating fruit till they found us, or till the universe came to an end.

Now he had nothing left, except a desire to free Ling for as long as they might have left together . . . And to hurt the enemy, if possible.

Fortunately, a weapon lay at hand. A gift from the crafty old traeki sage, Asx.

The red ring. The one Ling hid in the nursery, before she was captured. It must have been programmed by Asx as a predator, spreading and reproducing through the incubators, filling a wide range of niches. When combat with Zang invaders brought Jophur soldiers to the infirmary, seeking spare parts, they were given descendants of that original ring.

A mutated form of Master-type torus, with differences that only a wise old pharmacist-sage could have come up with, applying lessons learned by the traekis during two thousand years of exile. Tricks that Jophur sophisticates would never have encountered on the space lanes.

Soon, the fortunes of war shifted once again. Instead of beating back the hydros, Jophur forces resumed losing ground. A strange epidemic seemed to afflict many of the troops. Fits of self-doubt, or traeki-style multiple thinking, beset those who had formerly been egotistically self-centered and assured. Some suffered stack dissolution—breakdown into individual components that then crawled off, each seeking its own way. Others grew contemplative, or went catatonic, or began ranting and reeking madly.

A few started entertaining new and unusual notions.

If only we had first spread the disease close to the command center, before they could react.

But the Jophur were quick, clever, and resilient. Retreating and establishing lines of quarantine, they managed to retain control over vital ship functions.

Just barely. For most of *Polkjhy,* the overall result was chaos. A traveler could not know in advance what the next deck or corridor would be like. Weakened by struggle, no party to the conflict seemed able to do more than hold its home enclaves while anarchy spread everywhere else.

"One additional point merits discussion," continued X. "I/we picked up information by eavesdropping on the command channel. Reports indicate deep concern on the part of the bridge crew. The captain-leader and priest-stack have been debating the significance of a message, recently received."

"A message?"

"A *warning,* recently beamed across the Five Galaxies. If true, this alert bodes ill for a great many races and clans, but especially for this ship and all its varied occupants."

"Who sent this warning?" Lark asked.

"The homeworld of your own race, Lark Koolhan. Beleaguered Earth, surrounded and threatened by annihilation.

"Apparently, feeling that they have little to lose, the Terragens Council recently broadcast an iconoclastic theory to explain recent disruptions racking the Five Galaxies. A hypothesis derived by some of their sages, after secretly combining wolfling mathematical incantations with Galactic science. So provocative is this concept—so disturbing and frightening its implied accusations—that the Great Institutes have been moved to issue frantic denials. So frantic, in fact, that Earthlings have attained fresh credibility in many quarters!

"Indeed, the reaction has been profound enough that some clans now send armadas to help lift the siege, while others converge bent on wrathful genocide! The fleet battles near Terra have intensified tenfold."

Lark listened, at first unable to react except by blinking—at least a dozen times—in numb surprise.

"But . . . what . . ."

He shook his head, provoking a squishy, nervous response from his blobby passenger.

"But what was the warning?"

The creature he called X puffed colored steam, expressing nervous awe in the manner of a Jijoan traeki.

"They claim that the Great Institutes have been concealing a terrible danger. That most of the links uniting our Five Galaxies may soon dissolve, unleashing turmoil and desolation on the unprepared. In the ensuing violent backlash, many great and noble things may be lost.

"Moreover, if the Earthlings are right—(and not perpetrating a desperate hoax)—we aboard the *Polkjhy* are in the greatest danger of all. Here, at this sacred locale, where transcendent beings seek enlightenment within the Embrace of Tides."

DWER

At first, he expected the hunt for Rety to be easy.

How could a human hide in Kazzkark? Everywhere Dwer went, people turned and stared with a variety of sensory organs. Diverse limbs and tendrils pointed, while susurrant comments in a dozen Galactic dialects followed him down every lane. Apparently, Earthlings were infamous.

Even if no one in Kazzkark had any idea what kind of smelly biped Rety was, the girl would draw attention to herself, as surely as stars were fire. In all the time he'd known the young sooner, that trait had never failed.

Dwer's instincts were more reticent. He preferred slinking quietly through this bizarre noisy place—spacious as a canyon, yet claustrophobic as a boo forest, with a slim roof to keep precious air from blowing into space. The environment would be unnerving enough without throngs of aliens loudly arguing or gesticulating, then lapsing to hushed murmurs as he passed.

I always hated crowds. But according to Harry Harms, this is just a tiny outpost! I can't imagine a real city.

Dwer tried not to stare, partly because it was impertinent, and to keep from looking like a total rube. Among the bedtime stories his mother used to read aloud, a standard plot told of some rustic innocent coming to a metropolis, only to be fleeced by urban predators.

Fortunately, I don't have much to covet or steal, he thought, *counting blessings.*

At a busy intersection, Dwer paused to consider.

If I were Rety, where would I dash off to?

None of this would have happened if he'd been vigilant. While waiting for Harry at Navigation Institute HQ, Dwer had left Rety to visit the toilet. It took some time, as he studied the strange array of mechanisms designed to remove waste products from many species. Emerging—mussed and damp from several near accidents—he cursed to find Rety gone and the front door gaping to a busy street.

Harry's gonna be mad, he thought, plunging outside, hoping to catch sight of her. Dwer briefly glimpsed a short bipedal form just turning a corner, and sped in pursuit, but soon lost the dim figure in a maze of side avenues.

He needed a plan. Carefully, Dwer ran through a list of Rety's priorities.

Number one—get away from Jijo and make sure no one ever takes her back again.

To Dwer, that seemed pretty much a done deal. But *she* might worry that Harry Harms knew too much. Conceivably the chimp might gather enough information to figure out Jijo's location, and even insist they return with him. Rety might not want to take the chance.

Number two—make a living. Become invaluable to somebody powerful, so she'll never be hungry again.

That left Dwer at a loss. The girl had her computerized tutor unit, plus the data on Kazzkark that Harry provided. Could she have figured out a scheme while Dwer was in the toilet?

Number three—get rid of her scars. Rety had always been self-conscious about the weals that marred one side of her face, caused by cruel bullies who had tormented her back in the Gray Hills Tribe. Personally, Dwer did not much notice the marks. He had seen worse on Jijo. Besides, anyone who ever loved or hated Rety would do so because of her powerful presence and force of will.

Still, she would want to take care of that as soon as possible.

Was it possible, on Kazzkark? With no resident human population, would there be proficiency to perform repairs on Earthling flesh?

Why not? Computers can store the expert knowledge of countless skilled workers. And medicine would get top priority. You never know which species will visit an outpost, so you'd best be prepared for all of 'em.

Dwer knew he was reasoning from a slim base of information. Since infancy, he had heard stories about the radiant civilization his ancestors left behind. Now he felt numbed and dazzled by the reality.

Maybe I should've waited for Harry. I know Rety and he knows Kazzkark. We'd do better together than separately.

Preparing to head back, Dwer suddenly experienced a strange, disquieting sensation. It took moments for him to find a word to describe it.

I'm . . . lost.

It had never happened to him before! Not back home. Always there had been the sure draw of north, and a sort of internal map that unreeled each time he made a turn or took a step. But here on a drifting planetoid, his brain must lack some necessary cue. Dwer had no idea where he was!

He stood near a stony wall, trying to get bearings while streams of varied, bizarre life-forms swept past. Ignoring them, he fought to concentrate but was blocked by a rising sense of panic.

After E Space, I figured I could adjust to anything. I may be a sooner, but I'm not a savage. I grew up with other races around me. But this . . . all this . . .

The noise, bustle, smell, and grating *presence* of so many types of sapient minds—some of them brimming with hostility toward his kind—made him want to duck into the nearest hole and not come out again.

How long the funk would have lasted, Dwer had no idea. But it cut short abruptly when a large, fuzzy figure barged into his field of view, shorter and much rounder than a human, with whiskered cheeks and a pelt of bristly brown fur. A stout biped, vaguely mammalian, it displayed sharp teeth in a grimace that Dwer took as a deadly threat—until it boomed eager greetings in Anglic!

"As I live and breath mints! A human?

"Well, well! Indeed a human, here in the booney tunes! I have not this pleasure had since past times . . . before crisis times, when peace was! Shake?"

The creature held forth a meaty paw, from which retractile claws kept popping in and out, unnervingly. Dwer blinked, remembering vaguely about an old Earthling tradition of touching and clasping palms that had largely been abandoned long ago, since most aliens disliked it. Nervously, he extended his left hand—the one he would miss a little less if the creature snapped it off. "Shaking" felt awkward, and they were both clearly glad when it was over.

"Forgive my ignorance," Dwer said, attempting to mimic the formal, interspecies bow he had seen used a few times on Jijo. "But can you tell me who . . . or what . . ."

His voice trailed off as the rotund figure opposite him grew flushed. Sallow skin reddened underneath the streaky brown fur. Dwer feared he must have given offense—until the creature began huffing in a rhythmic manner, clearly trying to imitate human-style laughter.

"Is true? You recognize me not? *A Synthian?* Among the best of friends we have been to you humans! *Very* best! Well, well. Until this cursed crisis, that is. I admit. Friendship is tested, sorely, when death flows like starlight. I admit this. I, who am called Kiwei Ha'aoulin. This I admit. You will not hate me for it?"

Dwer nodded. A Synthian? Yes, he had heard of them . . . and vaguely recalled seeing pictures in an old folio, when Fallon taught him a little Galacto-xenology in the Biblos archive. Indeed, the race had been known for good relations with Earth, back in the early days before starship *Tabernacle* fled to Jijo. Though a lot might have changed since then.

"It is my turn to apologize, Kiwei Ha'aoulin," he said, mimicking the name as well as he could. "I kind of suffered a little . . . er, brain damage in deep space. An accident where all my possessions were lost."

The Synthian's eyes swept across Dwer's ragged clothes before settling on the qheuen-made bow and quiver of arrows.

"*All* possessions? Then this lovely proto-aboriginal archery set . . . it is not thine to display, or possibly to sell?"

Dwer stared for several seconds. According to Harry Harms, no Galactic should even recognize the finely carved wooden implements for what they were. Yet this one knew the primitive weapon on sight, and clearly desired it! Covetous eagerness seemed to crackle from its bunched-up muscles.

A hobbyist, Dwer realized. *An enthusiast.* He had met the type, even back on Jijo. For some reason, his instincts as a tracker and hunter abruptly kicked in. Commerce, after all, followed many laws of the jungle. Panic fled as familiarity took its place.

"Well, well," he said, slipping into a soft semblance of the other person's speech. "Perhaps I exaggerated. I admit that I managed to hold on to a thing or two from the shipwreck. A few special things."

"*Treasures,* no doubt," the Synthian replied, while avid tremors coursed its hunched spine. "Well. I am one, among my kind, known as a *fishy-naddo* of things Terran-earthly. I would help you find a market for such things. And thus? From poor castaway to enabled starfarer you might become! Enabled enough to buy a ticket in comfort from this miserable un-place to a somewhere-else-place, perhaps?"

Not waiting for an answer, the Synthian slipped an arm around Dwer's.

"Well, well. Shall we talk more? Kiwei Ha'aoulin knows very nice meal-site nearby. Good food! Good talk about treasures and news from the stars! Come?"

Dwer's right hand stroked his bow. On Jijo it was, indeed, valuable. Beneath his foolish demeanor, Kiwei Ha'aoulin must have a keen eye for quality. Who knew what an *aficionado* of primitive Earthling tools might pay?

I'd hate to part with it, but how much use is it here, as an actual weapon? Anyway, this could help me learn more, and maybe find Rety.

Driven as much by hunger as curiosity, Dwer nodded. "I accept your hospitality, Kiwei Ha'aoulin. Let's go and talk of many things."

Ignoring hostile stares and murmurs from all sides, he accompanied his new friend, hoping for the best.

EMERSON

Gazing from a secret crystal sanctuary, he watched countless stars roll by . . . along with just as many glittering lights that were actually huge vessels. In fact, nearby space had grown so crowded that a single sweep of the naked eye made out hundreds of shining snowflakes, or bubbles, liquidly shimmering. Fractal arks jostled past globule-forms in an ever-tightening throng, spiraling toward their common goal—a white-hot disk surrounded by swarms of giant, glittering needles that almost grazed its surface.

Emerson chose not to look that way. Just thinking about the destination was as painful as its glaring image.

He knew what must happen soon, before *Streaker* arrived. He had worked hard to prepare.

Crippled without speech, Emerson had only a rudimentary grasp of why

Streaker was here, or what it meant for Zang vessels to mix amicably with some of the same oxygen breathers they used to shun . . . or sometimes fought bitterly. Watching Gillian and Sara converse, their brows furrowed with a blazing intensity of focused thought, he had tried to sift amid the "wah-wah" sounds for hints of meaning. But many of their oft-repeated phrases—like "the Embrace of Tides"—evoked no response from his wounded mind. Unless it had something to do with the increasing tendency of his body to twist and stretch in a preferred direction, with his feet aimed toward the white dwarf star.

At least some individual words seemed to resonate, just a little.

"Embrace," he whispered, relishing its sensuous quality.

A few hours ago Emerson had been sitting beside Sara, with her head resting against his shoulder while they enjoyed a quiet moment together. Stroking her hair had become his normal way to help ease the tension of her daily struggle—Sara's ongoing effort to wrestle truth out of the universe by sheer mathematical force. His duty was a pleasant one. He would gladly provide anything she needed or wanted.

That is, except for the one thing she desired this time.

With gentle hints, Sara had shyly made known her willingness to reach new intimacy . . . but he was forced to turn her down. Peeling away from her warm clasp, Emerson saw questions in her eyes. Worry that he might not find her arousing. Worry that his wounds had robbed him of manly desires. Worry that there was so little time left for two to become one.

How could he explain? It would take words, sentences, volumes to justify thwarting such a natural desire, for bodies to follow where hearts already had gone. Frustrated, he sifted memory for a *song* that might suffice, but came up empty. All he could do, before fleeing to his star-covered sanctuary, was touch Sara's cheek and let his eyes express the trueness of his love.

In fact, there was nothing wrong with Emerson's sexuality. He longed to prove it to her. But not now. A confrontation loomed, and he needed every resource. Strong animal cravings might help keep him anchored through the coming showdown, reminding him of priorities that more advanced minds had forgotten.

His plan was necessarily crude, since thinking came so hard without words. By visualizing certain acts, body movements, emotions, and images, he had a general idea what to expect, and how to react when the time came.

It must be soon. Emerson could still discern meaning from a spatial diagram, and one truth grew plain as *Streaker* gyred into the white dwarf's gravitational funnel. A point of no return would come when the convoy of immense spacecraft got so closely packed that no single ship could escape on normal engine power. Gillian would have to break out before then, or risk forever abandoning the outer cosmos—the realm of open vacuum where young races thrived. Where blazing spaceships crossed star-speckled skies.

The same logic applied to the secret faction of Old Ones.

They have to act soon, or else be trapped along with . . .

Emerson stopped short—then resumed his thought, warily.

. . . or . . . else . . . be . . . trapped along with us, down among the Transcendent habitats, unable to intervene any longer in the affairs of the Five Galaxies. . . .

A low grunt escaped his throat. Despite expecting it this time, the sudden return of speech filled him with aching mixtures of sorrow, joy, and fear.

The words . . . the words are back again!

At least Emerson was better prepared now. For many days he had been storing memories, laboriously freezing snippets of speech that others said, in hope of fitting the pieces when this moment came.

"Let me conjecture. The emblem stands for a union of hydro-and oxy-life, coming together at last. . . ."

". . . those derelict ships we found in the Shallow Cluster must have come from our past . . . when more than five galaxies made up this nexus-association."

". . . suppose older, wiser spirits asserted themselves after each disruption . . . controlling the Great Library . . . to erase and adjust archives . . . or divert blame . . ."

". . . So, this is transcendence. Every species that was uplifted . . . and survives to adult phase . . . winds up in such a place. . . ."

"Whoever gave Streaker this coating not only saved our lives . . . they made sure we must stay with this convoy, all the way to the bottom . . ."

". . . no way to get rid of the heat . . ."

So many ideas, converging at once! It might seem like this for a blind man to have cataracts removed from his eyes, revealing vistas of utter clarity where there had been fog. And yet, many concepts also felt somehow familiar! As if they had been lurking close to comprehension for quite some time, massaged and predigested by undamaged portions of his brain, awaiting only clear sentences to make it all come together.

Emerson would gladly have spent hours just standing there, letting gravitational tides align his head toward the heavens while he grabbed and combined notions from cascades that seemed to roar through his mind like a pent-up flood. But he was not given the leisure.

A voice interrupted—at once both remote and mocking. Distant, yet derisive.

"WE NOTE THAT YOU DID NOT CALL. US, DESPITE HAVING BEEN SUPPLIED WITH A CODE TO USE, WHEN READY TO ACT ON OUR OFFER."

Emerson scarcely bothered peering amid the glittering lights outside. A dark ship must have drawn nearby in cloaked secrecy, and trying to spot it would be futile. Instead, he went into rapid motion, squeezing his body out of the narrow crystal dome, then sliding down the rungs of a ladder designed for another race, in a far different time.

"I was curious to see just how badly you want the goods you asked for," he replied in a low mutter under his breath. *Sound* wasn't the medium of communication here. Rather, the Old Ones were monitoring a stolen plug of his own gray matter they had somehow kept in quantum contact to the rest of his brain. When brought close enough, it flowed with words. *His* words.

Words they could instantly read.

"WE DO NOT HAVE TO EXPLAIN TO THE LIKES OF YOU. IT IS ENOUGH THAT WE SEEK, AND YOU SHALL PROVIDE."

Jogging down a hallway, Emerson pulled from his pocket a small handmade instrument with a flashing indicator. No words had been needed to construct the simple tool, nor did he contemplate its meaning.

"Aren't you guys running out of time?" he asked his tormentors—members of the Retired Order, whose homes had vanished in the ruin of the Fractal World. Retirees whose vaunted *detachment* had failed under testing.

"If you wait much longer, you'll transcend, whether you like it or not. The data you seek won't do you any good. There'll be no way to tell your friends, back in the Five Galaxies."

Icy tones echoed in his head.

"WE HAVE SPENT AEONS CULTIVATING PATIENCE. ALL THIS RACING ABOUT, TAKING FIERCE ACTIONS . . . IT IS UNPLEASANT WE HAD FORGOTTEN HOW QUICKLY DEEDS ARE FOLLOWED BY EFFECTS."

Emerson rounded a corner and passed through a hatch, guided by the telltale marker.

"Yeah, all the uncertainty must be driving you nuts. So tell me, how does it feel to *almost* gain entry to the Transcendent Order, your goal for a million years, only to sneak away at the last moment, just to carry off a few bytes of data stolen from a miserable Earthship? Aren't you tempted just to let go of all those old obsessions? To give in and embrace the tides?"

The reply came only after a long pause, while he raced down *Streaker*'s long, almost-deserted hallways.

"YOU HAVE NO IDEA HOW DIFFICULT IT IS TO HOLD BACK.

"THE GRAVITATIONAL TUG AND STRETCH ARE VOLUPTUOUS IN A MANNER THAT NO WORDS—NO MERE PHYSICAL SENSATION—CAN DESCRIBE."

"Go ahead and try," Emerson urged. "What *is* the big deal about the Embrace of Tides?"

"YOU ARE TOO YOUNG TO UNDERSTAND. WITHIN THE EMBRACE, ONE FEELS UNION WITH THE WHOLE COSMOS. IT IS COMFORTING PHILOSOPHICALLY, AS WELL AS ON THE LEVEL OF FAITH. THERE IS WISDOM HERE, AND KNOWLEDGE VASTLY BEYOND THE GREAT LIBRARY, OR EVEN WHAT WE KNEW IN THE FRACTAL WORLD."

"Really? Then why not just go?" Vehemence filled his voice, now echoing off the pale walls. "Do the wise and noble thing. Accept your diploma. *Graduate*, dammit! Gimme back my brain. The life you stole from me. Go down to your paradise with clean karma and a clear conscience!"

When the meddlers replied, there seemed almost to be a note of contrition.

"UNDER NORMAL CIRCUMSTANCES, YOUR PLEA MIGHT HAVE ETHICAL MERIT. BUT NOW FAR GREATER ISSUES ARE AT STAKE THAT FORCE US . . ."

There was another pause.

"JUST A MOMENT. WE DETECT SOMETHING IN YOUR EMOTIVE TONE. IN YOUR MANNER . . ."

Emerson felt strange, tickling sensations, as if the left side of his brain were being scraped or probed. When the voice resumed, it had a new, resentful tone.

"YOU HAVE LEARNED TRICKS OF DECEPTION AND DISTRACTION. CLEARLY, IT IS NO LONGER POSSIBLE TO SCAN YOUR THOUGHTS SIMPLY BY MONITORING WORDS AND GLYPHS. THE THINGS YOU SAY APPEAR ARGUMENTATIVE, BUT IN TRUTH THEY ARE MEANT TO DEFER. TO DELAY.

"REVEAL WHAT YOU ARE HIDING! REVEAL, OR EXPERIENCE PAIN!"

Emerson gritted his teeth as he ran, trying hard not to laugh out loud or show the depth of his contempt. But a little leaked out as blankets of concealment were assailed by ancient skill. While the Old Ones could not draw facts out of his reluctant mind, they got a good picture of his attitudes.

"WE PERCEIVE THAT ALL FORMS OF BASIC COERCION ARE OBSOLETE OR INAPPLICABLE IN YOUR CASE. YOU HAVE GONE PAST PAIN, A LESSON THAT MANY RETIREES SPEND AGES OVERCOMING. NOR DO YOU WHIMPER AND CLASP AFTER WHAT WAS TAKEN FROM YOU. NO INDUCEMENT OR BRIBE WILL CAUSE YOU TO BETRAY FRIENDS AND CLAN MATES. YOU HAVE NOT EVEN TRIED TO STEAL THE DATA WE ASKED FOR.

"ALL OF THIS MAY BE ADMIRABLE, ESPECIALLY IN A WOLFLING. INDEED, UNDER OTHER CIRCUMSTANCES, WE MIGHT TAKE PLEASURE IN COMPENSATING YOU FOR YOUR TRIALS, AND CONVERSING FURTHER ABOUT THE VIRTUES OF UNCERTAINTY.

"BUT THE ISSUES WE FACE ARE TOO DIRE, AND TIME IS SHORT. THE INFORMATION MUST BE OURS!"

The telltale in Emerson's hand flashed a new direction. *Up.* He halted below a ceiling hatch that lay cracked open. Light streamed from within.

Still hoping for delay, he blurted aloud.

"Let me guess. You had a backup plan, in case I wouldn't do as you asked."

"CALCULATIONS BASED ON EARLIER NEURAL SCANS PREDICTED ONLY A MODEST CHANCE YOU WOULD COOPERATE. SURELY YOU DON'T THINK WE WOULD COUNT ON SUCH A SLENDER HOPE.

Letting the voice jabber on, Emerson slipped his tracker in a pocket and leaped, catching the rim of the hatch and writhing his legs to haul himself into a maintenance conduit. Silently blessing the low ambient gravity, he consulted the device again before heading aft along a tube lined with ducted cables.

". . . NATURALLY WE WERE NOT SO FOOLISH AS TO RELY ON YOU ALONE."

Fearing the Old Ones were about to break contact, he blurted.

"Wait! I still may be able to help you. But you gotta understand . . . we humans hate being kept in the dark. Can't you tell me *why* you need *Streaker*'s data? What's so damn special about that stupid fleet of ancient ships we found?"

That was the chief perplexing quandary dogging the fugitive Earthlings for three long, hellish years.

Oh, the superficial answer was easy. When Creideiki and Orley beamed images from the Shallow Cluster, they triggered religious schisms across the Five Galaxies. Rival clans and alliances, who had controlled their feuding for ages, sent battle fleets to secure *Streaker*'s samples—and especially the coordinates of the derelict fleet—before their rivals could acquire them.

Some said the Ghost Armada might be blessed Progenitors, returning to survey their descendants after two billion years. But if so, why react violently? Wouldn't all dogmatic differences be worked out, once truth was shared by all?

Emerson sensed hesitation. Then a faint perception of agreement, as if the voice was waiting for something *else* to happen. Meanwhile, it might as well converse with a bright wolfling, to pass the time.

"ALL OF THIS HAS TO DO WITH THE EMBRACE OF TIDES. THE DELICIOUS TUG THAT EACH OLDER RACE BEGINS TO FEEL AFTER LOSING INTEREST IN DASHING ABOUT ON MANIC STARSHIPS.

"WE ALL FOLLOW THIS ATTRACTION, DROPPING OUR FORMER DIFFERENCES TO ASSEMBLE TOGETHER NEXT TO LITTLE RED SUNS, WHERE OUR MINDS MAY GROW AND PURIFY.

"THEN, FROM SUCH PLACES OF RETIREMENT, MANY PROCEED TO SITES LIKE THIS ONE, WHERE OXYGEN AND HYDROGEN MERGE PEACEFULLY, UNITING IN COMMON APPRECIATION OF THE STRENGTHENING EMBRACE, PROVING THAT A PLAN IS AT WORK, MAGNIFICENT AND BEAUTIFUL. . . ."

Emerson heard a low clattering, coming from somewhere just ahead. Softly, he laid the tracker down, then hurried toward the rustling sounds. From another pocket, he pulled a slim device—one he had stolen days ago from Gillian Baskin's office.

". . . THOUGH WHERE THE COMBINED RACES GO FROM HERE—TO WHAT DESTINY—HAS ALWAYS BEEN A MYSTERY. YOUNGER CLANS DEBATE IT ENDLESSLY, BUT TRANSCENDENT LIFE-FORMS NEVER EXPLAIN WHAT HAPPENS NEXT. ALL WE HAVE ARE HINTS AND STRANGE EMANATIONS FROM . . ."

Concentrating hard to blank his thoughts, Emerson rounded a corner and abruptly saw *starlight* ahead, glimmering through a crystal pane. He knew this place. It housed the main communication laser, a wide-barreled tube occupying most of the available volume, aimed through a broad window.

Streaker's magical coating lay beyond, a meter thick but utterly transparent, covering nearly all of the ship in a layer that was both miraculous and deadly.

A figure stood nearby, working at an open access panel. Emerson recognized the fluid skill of those hands, using tools to perform rapid modifications on the laser system. One arm was clearly artificial, while remnants of the head lay encased in a mirrorlike dome. Cyborg components like these had saved the life of *Streaker*'s chief engineer, back at the Fractal World. Generosity, from a different, more kindly faction of Old Ones—or so the crew thought at the time.

Next to Suessi lay a large data reader and several crystalline knowledge cells—enough to hold all of *Streaker*'s hard-won discoveries.

"Hello, Hannes," Emerson said aloud.

The instant he spoke, several things happened at once.

Servos whined as the figure spun around, raising a cutter torch whose short flame burned blindingly hot. Without his old friend's face to look at, Emerson could only assume the man meant to use it.

Meanwhile, the voice interrupted its explanation with a hiss of surprise that seemed to shoot through Emerson's head like an electric jolt. He cried out, instinctively grabbing at his temples. But that reaction lasted just an instant. Gritting his teeth, he aimed the stolen plasma pistol past Suessi's shiny dome.

"Stop it, or I shoot the laser right now! You know pain won't work on me."

The lightning ceased at once.

"IN TRUTH, WE NOW BELIEVE IT, HAVING FOOLISHLY REPEATED THE ERROR OF TAKING YOU FOR GRANTED. OUR COMPUTER MODELS CONSISTENTLY UNDERESTIMATE YOUR FERAL CLEVERNESS. COULD THIS ADAPTABILITY HAVE BEEN FOSTERED DURING YOUR EXILE ON THE SOONER WORLD?"

"Flattery'll get you nowhere. But yeah, I learned some new ways of thinking, there. You should hear me curse, sometime. Or sing."

"IN ANOTHER LIFE, PERHAPS. SO YOU FIGURED WE WOULD HAVE AN ALTERNATE AGENT. DID YOU ATTACH A TRACER, TO FIND HIM THE MOMENT WE ARRIVED?"

Emerson nodded. "Something like this seemed likely. The one person you might have altered would be Hannes."

"WE DID NOT ALTER THE HUMAN ARTIFICER. THOSE WHO REPAIRED HIM WERE SINCERE. BUT WE LATER INCORPORATED THAT FACTION, AND THUS GAINED THE ACCESS CODES. SINCE IT CLEARLY MATTERS TO YOU, BE ASSURED HE HAS NO PAIN. HE PERCEIVES THIS AS JUST A BAD DREAM."

"How considerate of you!" Emerson snapped.

"YOU THINK US CALLOUS. YET, WITH THE DESTINY OF MANY RACES AND TRILLIONS OF LIVES AT STAKE, WE HAD REASONS—"

"I see only that you're cowards! You feel drawn by the Embrace of Tides, yet you fear to go in. You worry it may be a mistake!"

"AN OVERSIMPLIFICATION, BUT TRUE ENOUGH.

"THE STORY IS SO BEAUTIFUL, SO PERFECT—WITH OXY AND HYDRO LIFE ORDERS COMBINING IN ELEGANT PEACE, MERGING AMID A GLORIOUS FUNNEL OF TRANSCENDENCE—THAT HARDLY ANY CANDIDATES EVER QUESTION THE GENERAL ACCEPTANCE OF THIS PATH, FOLLOWED BY THEIR ANCESTORS SINCE TIMES IMMEMORIAL.

"THE EMBRACE IS ALMOST IRRESISTIBLE. DARING TO TRANSCEND IS AN ULTIMATE ACT OF TRUST. OF FAITH.

"BUT THEREIN LIES THE RUB! TO SOME OF US, FAITH IS NOT ENOUGH. THERE WAS ONCE A MINORITY VIEW, A HERESY THAT LOOKED ON THE EMBRACE OF TIDES, AND CALLED IT SOMETHING ELSE."

Emerson nodded.

"A recycling system. You're worried that this white dwarf is just like the oceanic trench on Jijo . . . the Great Midden. A graceful way to clear away the old and make way for the new! Yeah, that makes just as much sense as a mystical portal to some higher layer of reality!"

Deep sadness filled the alien presence—a fretful brooding that seemed poignant in a species so ancient and learned.

"THE DISCOVERY MADE BY YOUR DOLPHIN-CREWED SHIP IN THE SHALLOW CLUSTER . . . THE REAL REASON IT CAUSED SUCH CONSIDERATION . . ."

Abruptly the voice stopped. Emerson crouched nervously as the deck shuddered beneath his feet. Tremors accelerated, growing in pitch and intensity.

"You're attacking us!" he accused. "All your talk was just to humor me until—"

The voice interrupted.

"YOU ARE RIGHT THAT I WAS PERFORMING A DELAYING TACTIC. BUT FOR A DIFFERENT REASON. THE SHOCKS YOU FEEL ARE FROM STRAIN FRACTURES IN THE VERY FABRIC OF THE COSMOS, CONTINUING THE SAME PROCESS THAT DEMOLISHED OUR HOME THAT YOU CALLED THE FRACTAL WORLD.

"THESE FRACTURES ARE SPREADING AT AN ACCELERATING RATE."

"Sara thinks—"

"WE HAVE FOLLOWED HER WORK WITH INTEREST. SHE APPEARS TO KNOW WHAT THE TRANSCENDENTS COVERED UP—THAT FATE SEEMS BOUND TO SMASH THE TIES BINDING OUR GALAXIES . . . INDEED, THE NETWORKS THAT MAINTAIN CIVILIZATION."

It was an awesome statement. Yet, something else the voice had said bothered Emerson.

"A . . . delaying tactic? Why? I already stopped Hannes from—"

He shouted an oath.

"*Of course.* You Old Ones wouldn't leave anything to chance. You'd have a third option. A backup for your backup! What is it? Tell me!"

"OR ELSE WHAT? WILL YOU SHOOT YOUR FRIEND? WE COULD HAVE SENT HIM CHARGING AT YOU, SEVERAL DURAS AGO. WITH CYBORG STRENGTH AND SPEED, WE CALCULATE THIRTY PERCENT ODDS HE WOULD HAVE PREVAILED BEFORE YOU PUT HIM OUT OF ACTION. A WORTHWHILE GAMBLE, FROM OUR POINT OF VIEW.

"EXCEPT THAT BY NOW OUR THIRD AGENT HAS ALREADY DEPARTED YOUR SHIP."

"Your . . . third agent?"

"WE MADE A BARGAIN WITH A YOUNG WOLFLING. IN EXCHANGE FOR COPIES OF YOUR SHIP LOGS, WE WILL TAKE HER AWAY FROM THIS PLACE. "FROM HERE TO SEE HER GODS."

Darting past immobile Suessi, Emerson pressed against the laser-window and peered outside.

Streaker's nose lay to his left, where just one of the airlocks had been cleared of the magic coating to allow egress. Emerson could not see that aperture. But a few hundred meters outward, he glimpsed a stubby vessel—a little escape pod, puffing as it turned toward a dark patch of space.

A black patch that blocked a swath of stars.

Emerson's brain seemed to spin. His thought processes were much quicker than they had been before his mutilation. Still, it took moments to realize—

"Lieutenant Tsh't! You sprang her from the brig and helped her escape!"

"A SIMPLE MATTER OF MEME-INFECTING YOUR SHIPBOARD COMPUTERS. MUCH HARDER WAS THE PHYSICAL EFFORT, HELPING HER ENTER PLACES WHERE GILLIAN BASKIN HAD HIDDEN THE SECRETS, WORKING WITH A MIND-CONTROLLED SUESSI TO STEAL THEM, THEN HAVING BOTH AGENTS SMUGGLE OUT THE MATERIAL BY SEPARATE ROUTES.

"AND NOW AT LAST, DESPITE YOUR INTERFERENCE, WE ARE ABOUT TO POSSESS THE DATA NEEDED TO MAKE CORRECT DECISIONS AFFECTING MULTITUDES.

"THIS PUTS US IN A GENEROUS MOOD TO REDRESS YOUR MANY INCONVENIENCES. OUT OF RESPECT FOR YOUR FERAL INGENUITY, LET US MAKE AMENDS. IN DEPARTING WE SHALL LEAVE BEHIND SOMETHING YOU'LL BE GLAD TO HAVE BAC—"

The voice cut off abruptly as another wave of spacetime tremors struck. This one made Emerson's skin crawl with tingling sensations. Pulsations coursed the length of his digestive system, producing several loud eruptions.

The stars outside wavered, and the vague black patch he had glimpsed before started to shimmer, revealing a familiar outline.

A Galupbin-class sneakboat, he identified. An expensive, but conventional Galactic design.

"Wha—?" uttered a nearby voice. Hannes Suessi groaned, recovering consciousness. "What'm I doin' here? What's happening?"

Emerson had other things to worry about than updating a friend. Spatial fluctuations had confused the enigmatic Old Ones. With their cloaking mask disrupted, they dropped all pretense at stealth and made speed toward the little life pod, in order to pick up Tsh't and the information they prized. But the same tumult that made *Streaker*'s hull vibrate was causing them trouble, too.

Indeed, the surrounding vast armada of "transcendence candidates" seemed to be breaking up! Wavelets of compressed metric tore through their crowded ranks, pushing one phalanx of great ships toward another. Emerson saw collisions—and sparkling explosions—ripple from one area to the next, as jagged oxy-vessels merged prematurely with hydro-globules, releasing convulsions of raw energy.

Amid all this chaos, something far more disconcerting was going on. At least from Emerson's perspective. His power of speech kept fading, then surging back again, briefly enhanced beyond all natural ability, causing countless strange associations to spill forth.

The voice was absent, yet he continued getting impressions from the beings he called Old Ones. Sensations of deep concern. Shifting toward worry. Followed by desperation.

Moving in fits and starts, their sneakboat approached the little pod carrying Tsh't, fighting chaotic disruption waves all the way. While the heavens coruscated with dire accidents—and untold populations died just short of their transcendent goal—Emerson's erstwhile tormentors struggled to dock with the renegade dolphin lieutenant.

"I feel . . . like somehow I been *used*," murmured Suessi, moving alongside to peer out the window. "I sure wish you could talk, lad. I could do with some light put on the subject."

Emerson glanced at Suessi, then at the shadowy sneakboat . . . and then rapidly from his friend to the big comm laser.

"Hannes . . ." he began, then had to wait till another wave of fluency passed through his mind. He knew that each time might be the last.

"Hannes, we gotta use the comm laser to burn those two boats, now!"

Suessi stared in surprise at the brief, unexpected eloquence. His dome-covered head turned to follow Emerson's pointing finger. "What, those? Why not call Dr. Baskin and use real combat beams—"

The quantum link to Emerson's speech center flickered out, leaving him shrouded in dull muteness, unable to explain that the foe would surely have meme-disabled the fire-control systems of any formal weapons in order to guarantee their safe escape.

He managed to force a few words out by sheer will power.

"No . . . time! Do! Do it!"

The shiny dome nodded. Both shoulders lifted in a true Suessi shrug.

"Okay! You gotta help me, though. This thing ain't exactly meant for frying spaceships."

They set to work at once, sharing a rhythm long familiar to engineers laboring through a shipboard emergency—from Roman trireme, to ancient submarine, to the first sluggish starcraft Earthlings once hurled toward the Milky Way, filled with hopes for a friendly universe. Emerson found that speechlessness did not hamper him as much if he let his hands and eyes work together without interference. Somehow, they knew which connections to shift. Which adjustments to make. When Hannes spoke, the hands responded as if they understood.

It left his mind free to observe with strange detachment, even as *Streaker*'s hallways started clamoring with alarm signals, sending crew rushing to battle stations. Clearly, Suessi yearned to go join his engine gang, but so great was their mutual trust, the fellow took Emerson's word that this was more important.

It made Emerson doubly glad he hadn't been forced to shoot his friend.

"Okay," Suessi announced. "Here goes nothing."

The laser throbbed, and the air temperature in the little chamber abruptly *dropped* several degrees as pulsating energy flooded into space.

Instantly, he could tell that the first pulse missed its target, disappearing among the flashes of coruscating catastrophe that surrounded *Streaker*, growing more garish and terrible by the minute.

Cursing roundly, Emerson stabbed several control buttons, bypassing the computer, then began slewing the laser by hand, aiming by sight alone.

Meanwhile, the sneakboat kept fighting waves of spacetime backwash to finally make contact with the little craft carrying Tsh't. Impact wasn't gentle. Hull panels crumpled on one side, but the sturdy, Thennanin-built pod held together. Soon, the larger vessel's surface melted to envelop the escape capsule, drawing it inside.

Tsh't and her purloined cargo were safe in the grasp of those who wanted it so badly.

Emerson had mixed feelings while struggling to adjust the balky laser. Though he hated the Old Ones for their callousness—especially the way they had mutilated him and others for their own purposes—he also understood, just a little, their rationale. Without words, he could picture the panicky background for their actions.

Ultimately—after passing through the young, hot-tempered, starfaring stage—each race had to choose whether to continue down a comforting funnel that appeared to welcome all whose souls were ready. A place of union, where the best of hydro and oxy cultures merged, preparing to move on.

But move on to what?

The vast majority felt it must be something greater and more noble than anything in this cosmos. The place where blessed Progenitors had gone so long ago.

But there was another, minority opinion.

On Jijo, Emerson had learned something deep and gritty about the cycle of life. A metaphor that he held in his mind, even after speech had gone away.

An image of the deepest part of the sea.

And a single word.

Dross.

He jabbed the firing button.

Once again, the laser moaned a cry, deeper than a hoonish umble and more combative than the war shout of a desert urrish warrior, accompanied by a sudden wave of cold.

Something flared in the night! A sparkle of destruction. Fire illumined one end of the sneakship, outlining its aft segment, which now shimmered with devastating explosions.

All at once, words returned to Emerson's life. The voice reentered his mind, in tones that conveyed hurt perplexity.

"DO YOU KNOW WHAT YOU HAVE DONE?

"ONCE ON OUR WAY, WE PLANNED SENDING YOU THE CYLINDER. THE PLUG OF TISSUE THAT YOU CRAVE. AFTER WE HAD NO FURTHER NEED OF IT, OR OF YOU.

"NOW YOUR TREASURE WILL BE LOST, ALONG WITH US, AS WE FALL INTO A DYING WHITE SUN."

Already the mortally wounded sneakboat could be seen tumbling along a plummeting trajectory, while *Streaker*'s engines cranked to push the other way.

"I know that," Emerson sighed. So many hopes had turned to ash when he fired the laser bolt. Especially his dream of talking to Sara. Of telling her what was in his heart. Or even holding on to thoughts that right now seemed so fluid and natural, so easy and fine. Smooth, graceful thoughts that would become hard again, moments from now, when what had been stolen, then restored, would finally be lost forever.

"BUT WHY?

"IN YOUR CRUDE WAY, YOU UNDERSTAND OUR WORRY. YOU SYMPATHIZE WITH OUR MISGIVINGS ABOUT THE EMBRACE OF TIDES. YOU EVEN SUSPECT WE MAY BE RIGHT! WOULD IT HAVE BEEN SO BAD TO

LET US HAVE THE CLUES WE NEED? TO LEARN THE TRUTH ABOUT DESTINY? TO KNOW WHICH WAY TO CHOOSE?"

The plaint was so poignant, Emerson weighed explaining, while there was time.

Should he talk about orders from the Terragens Council, that secrets from the Shallow Cluster must be shared by *all* races . . . or none?

A raging corner pondered telling the aliens that this was Pyrrhic revenge, getting even for things they had done to him—no matter how well justified they thought they were.

In fact, though, neither of those reasons excused his act of murder. While *Streaker* shuddered under ever more intense spacetime waves—climbing laboriously through a maelstrom of colliding transport arks and flaming Zang globes—he found there was only one answer to give the Old Ones.

The right answer.

One that was both logical and entirely just.

"Because you didn't ask," he explained, as the quantum links began flickering out for the last time.

"You . . . never once said . . . please."

HARRY

The search went badly at first.

Kazzkark was a maze of tunnels where sophonts could all too easily disappear—whether by choice or mischance.

And matters only worsened as the placid lifestyle of an Institute outpost vanished like a memory. More refugees poured in, even after the planetoid started quivering in response to waves of subspace disturbance. Tempers stretched thin, and there were more than enough troubles to keep police drones of the Public Safety Department busy.

When it came to looking for a pair of lost humans, Harry was pretty much on his own.

His first good lead came when he overheard a Synthian chatter to comrades in a space merchants' bar, bragging about a sharp business deal she'd just made, acquiring some first-rate wolfling relics for resale to the collectors' trade.

"Mild guilt—this I experience, concerning the meager price that I paid for such marvelously genuine handcrafted items," prated the husky creature in Galactic Six.

"Of their authentic, aboriginal nature, I have no doubt. Evidence of this was overwhelming, from the moment I programmed my scanner with appropriate archaeological search profiles, checking for tool marks, use patterns, and body-oil imbuements. The result?

"Absolute absence of techno-traces, or other signs of forgery! A bona-fide aboriginal tool/weapon, weathered and worn from the primitive fight for survival under barbaric circumstances!

"What? What is that you say? You would view this marvelous acquisition? But of course! Here it is. Behold the elegant sweeps and curves, the clever blending of animal and vegetal materials, revealing non-Galactic sapiency in its full, unfettered glory!

"The shipwrecked human who formerly owned these artifacts—his reported brain damage must have undermined all sense of value! His recovery from space amnesia—it will not bring pleasant realizations for the poor young wolfling, when he realizes how much more he might have charged for his precious archery set, which will now garner me great profit on the aficionado circuit.

"Especially now that the chief source of all such relics—planet Earth—will surely vanish under cascades of fire, within a few jaduras."

Harry was not present where these words were spoken. He was halfway across Kazzkark, searching for Rety and Dwer in a poor refugee encampment, when those snatches of dialogue were sent to his earpiece by a clever spy program.

Using his new rank-status, he had ordered a scan of all sonic pickups, scattered throughout the planetoid, sifting countless conversations for certain rare key words. Till now, the computer had just found trivial correlations. But this time, the Synthian went through half the list in a few duras, covering all but Dwer's name!

Racing across town, Harry sent a priority call for backup units to join him. Perhaps it was the new golden comet on his collar, or just a sense of urgency, but Harry plunged through the crowd, ignoring shocked looks from senior patron-class beings.

He arrived to find several proctor robots already hovering menacingly near a bar advertising a range of intoxo-relaxants. A throng gathered to watch.

"The rear exit is secured, Scout-Major Harms," reported one of the bobbing drones. "The denizens within seem unsuspecting. Several fondle concealed weapons, of types we are equipped to counter, with moderate-to-good probability of success."

Harry grunted.

"I'd prefer a guarantee, but that'll do. Just stay close. Let everyone see you as we enter."

He was tempted to draw his own sidearm, but Harry preferred to handle this courteously, if possible.

"All right. Let's go."

Half a dozen Synthian traders sat in a booth, looking alike in grayish brown fur with dark facial streaks. Thickset, their heavy shoulders and bellies draped with pouched bandoliers. Harry soon found the one he wanted. A sleek bow and quiver of arrows, made from finely carved wood and bone, lay on the table. When a merchant reached for these, Harry bore in, asking where she got them.

Kiwei Ha'aoulin reacted with combative relish, striking an indignant, lawyerly pose. After listening to the Synthian complain loudly for more than twenty duras—vociferously denouncing "illegal eavesdroppers and bureaucratic bullies"—Harry finally broke in to remind Kiwei that Kazzkark was sole property of the Great Institutes, and lately under martial law. Moreover, would the merchant *like* to unpack her ship's hold, comparing each smig and dram meticulously to the official cargo manifest?

All bluster quickly faded from the raccoonlike countenance. Harry had never met a Synthian, but they were familiar figures on daytime holodramas back on Earth, where Synthian characters were stereotyped as jovial, enthusiastic—and relentlessly self-interested.

This one took a long pause to evaluate Harry's proposition, then switched to rather good colloquial Anglic.

"Well well, Scout-Major. You had only to ask. Shall I lead you to where I last saw Dwer Koolhan. Yes! But be warned, he may not look the same! *If* you find him. For as we parted, he was making enquiries. Asking questions about cosmetic surgery. As if his intent was to go into hiding!"

While they hurried together along the main boulevard, Harry muttered into his cheek microphone, inquiring if any local body-repair shops had done custom work on humans during the day and a half since Kiwei Ha'aoulin last saw Dwer.

He also checked in with HQ. Wer'Q'quinn had scheduled yet another emergency meeting of the local NavInst planning staff in four miduras.

What was left of the staff, that is. Most scouts and senior aides had already departed, scurrying across the quadrant on urgent rescue missions, commandeering vessels of all sizes to evacuate isolated outposts, setting up buoys to divert traffic from destabilized transfer points, and tracking the advance of chaos across this portion of the Five Galaxies.

Especially troubling were reports of violent outbreaks among oxy-clans, or between various life orders. An uncommonly furious confrontation had flared in Corcuomin Sector between one of the more reclusive hydrogen-breathing cultures and a vast swarm of machine entities, whose normal home-domain in deep space had grown so ruptured that vast numbers of unregistered mechs began migrating into rich territory forbidden to them by ancient treaties. So frenzied and brutal was the resulting clash that weapons of unprecedented force had been unleashed, tearing through walls separating various levels of spacetime, causing vortices of A and B hyperlevels to come swirling into the "normal" continuum, wreaking havoc everywhere they touched. There were even reports that *memetic* life-forms seemed to be involved as allies of one side or another—or perhaps taking advantage of the confusion to spread their ideogrammatic matrices into new hosts—filling the battlefield with riotous sensory impressions, fostering ideas that were too complex and bizarre for any organic or electronic mind.

Amid all this, Wer'Q'quinn kept delaying Harry's next assignment. Too inexperienced and undiplomatic to be entrusted with a big command, Harry was also apparently too valuable to waste on some futile errand.

"Keep in touch," Wer'Q'quinn kept telling him. "I suspect we will need your expertise in E Space before we're done."

The Synthian merchant motioned toward one of the side streets selling clothing and personal accoutrements of all kinds.

"Here is where I last saw the human, bidding me farewell as he clutched a purse filled with GalCoins from our transaction, appearing eager to rush off and spend his new fortune as quickly as possible."

"GalCoin?" Harry asked. Far better if Dwer had been paid in credits or marks, which could be traced across the Commercial Web. "How much did you pay?"

Kiwei Ha'aoulin tried to demur, claiming commercial privilege, but soon realized it would not avail.

"Seventy-five demi units."

Harry's fists clenched and he growled. "Seventy-five! For genuine Earth-autochthonous handicrafts from a preindustrial era? Why you unscrupulous—"

He went on cursing the Synthian roundly, since the merchant clearly expected it. Anything less would have insulted her pride. But in fact, Harry's mind was already racing ahead. He had no intention of informing Kiwei Ha'aoulin that the precious bow and arrows were far more recently made than she thought. They were, in fact, contraband from an illegal sooner settlement, carved by qheuen teeth and burnished at an urrish forge.

He was interrupted by a computer message. Apparently one of the body shops had been visited lately by a young Terran, who paid cash for a quick cosmetic overhaul. Nothing fancy. Just a standard flesh-regrowth profile that the shop had in its panspecies file.

"Let's go!" he told the Synthian. She resisted momentarily, then caught the fierce look in Harry's eyes. Kiwei Ha'aoulin gave an expressively Earth-style shrug.

"Of course, Scout-Major Harms. Well, well. I remain perpetually at your service."

Unfortunately, the repair shop in question lay some distance beyond the Plaza of Faith. To reach the other side, they would have to work their way past a host of missionaries and zealots, all fired up by the steady unraveling of order throughout the Five Galaxies.

Much had changed since Harry last visited this zone, where elegant pavilions had been tended by neatly robed acolytes, politely pontificating their ancient dogmas in the old-fashioned way, with traditional rhythms of surety and patience. Since most Galactic sects aimed to persuade entire races and clans, the emphasis had always been on relentless repetition and exposure—to "show the flag" and let other sapients slowly grow accustomed to a better view of destiny. Individuals mattered only as vehicles to carry ideas home, spreading them to family and nation.

This atmosphere of tranquil persistence had already begun wearing thin during Harry's last visit. Now, as intermittent subspace tremors made the stony walls shiver, it seemed to be unraveling completely.

Crowds filled the once placid compounds of several religio-philosophical alliances—the Inheritors, Immersers, and Transcenders. Immaculate fabric partitions got trampled as listeners pushed toward shouting deacons dressed in gaudy silver gowns, perched on ridiculously elevated platforms that teetered near the high ceiling. Their amplified and translated words boomed or flashed, transmitting stridency in at least a dozen Galactic dialects, as if persuasion could be bought through sheer volume. Each side fought so hard to drown out the others that Harry could hardly make out anything beyond a head-splitting roar. That did not deter the crowds however, whose urgency seemed to make the air crackle with supercharged emotion.

This place must be swarmin' with invisible psi waves and empathy glyphs, Harry realized, glad that his own mental talents went in other directions, leaving him blissfully insensitive to such scraping irritations. *A Tymbrimi who got caught in this mob would prob'ly fry his tendrils on all the crazed vibrations.*

There were other changes in the Plaza. Platoons of Inheritor and Immerser acolytes could be seen carrying staffs, cudgels, utility cutters, and other types of makeshift weaponry, eyeing each other with distrustful wrath. Beyond one translucent curtain, Harry even thought he glimpsed several sharply angled figures moving about—huge and mantislike.

He shuddered at the unmistakable silhouettes.

Tandu.

Next Harry and Kiwei Ha'aoulin passed pavilions of the Awaiters and Abdicators . . . or rather, their remnants. Tattered banners lay charred on the ground—silent testimony to how vehement the ancient rivalries had become. Their differences of opinion were no longer even ostensibly patient, or theoretical, now that a day of reckoning seemed near.

A few soot-covered Awaiters—mostly spidery guldingars and thick-horned varhisties—picked warily through the ruins, protected by drones they had hired from some local private security service. The varhisties, in particular, looked bitterly eager for revenge.

Meanwhile, every side avenue seemed filled with clamor and speculation. A formation of cop-bots swept eastward at top speed, rushing around the next corner toward some noisy emergency. Duras later, Harry glanced down an alley and thought he glimpsed some shabby scavengers stripping a corpse amid the shadows.

Along the main north-south Way, preachers stood on rickety pulpits, shouting for attention. The dour-looking Pee'oot proselyte was still where Harry remembered, stretching out its spiral neck and goggle eyes, jabbering in obscure dialects about the need for all species to return to their basic natures—whatever that meant.

Harry also spotted the Komahd evangelist, whose deceptive smile split even wider upon meeting Harry's gaze. Its rear tripod leg thumped loudly for emphasis.

"*There!*" the Komahd shouted, pointing with bony digits. "Perceive how yet another Terran passes by, thus proving that this vile infection will not be rubbed out when their homeworld is finally invaded and brought to justice. No, friends. Not even when Earth is sequestered, and its rich gene-pool is divided up among the righteous. For they have spread among us like infecting viruses!

"Have you all not seen, this very day, copious evidence for their malignant influence? Even here on far Kazzkark, wolflings and their insane followers spew vile lies and calumny, reviving ancient selfish heresies, undermining our shared vision of destiny, debasing the foundations of society, and depicting our revered ancestors as little more than fools!"

While shouting hatred of Harry's clan, the Komahd kept "smiling" and batting deceptively beguiling eyelashes, creating a misleading expression that clearly meant something quite different wherever the creature came from. It seemed noteworthy that the proselyte's ire, previously directed paranoically toward hydrogen breathers, now seemed centered wholly on poor little Earthclan.

That struck Harry as rather unfair and overwrought, since everyone was betting on the fall of Terra in a matter of weeks or days, if not hours. Nevertheless, he sensed danger from the Komahd's small band of followers. The emblems of his Navigation Institute uniform might not offer protection if he stayed.

"Wait," Kiwei Ha'aoulin murmured as Harry tugged her arm. "I find this sophont's argument cogently enticing! His rhetoric is most appealing. The logic seems unassailable!"

"Very funny, Kiwei." Harry growled. "Come on. *Now*."

Clearly delighted with her own wit, the Synthian chortled happily. Kiwei's people were enthusiasts, but pragmatists above all. Like many races in the "moderate majority," they cared little about obscure religious arguments over the nature of transcendence, preferring to go about their business, leaving destiny to take care of itself. All else being equal, they would happily have shared the infamous "*Streaker* discovery" openly, and even paid the Terragens a nice finder's fee, to make it all worthwhile.

Alas, the moderate majority was also famous for dithering and indecision. Eventually, they might finish their endless deliberations over whether to save Earth, though by that time help would come too late to accomplish anything but stir the ashes.

Speaking of going about one's business, Harry hoped this would be the last of the religious swarms. But no sooner did he and Kiwei push around the next bend than they found the way completely blocked by the biggest mass gathering yet! Crowds extended far ahead and to both sides, filling a domed intersection that had formerly been a market for selling organonutrient supplements.

The mélange of sapient species types dazzled him with its sheer variety—from willowy, stalk-like *zitlths* to a pair of hulking *brmas*. Indeed, an amazed scan took in many races that Harry had only vaguely heard of before. The veritable forest of strange limbs, heads, torsos, and sensory organs mingled and merged till his confused eyes found it hard to tell where some creatures finished and others began.

Smell alone was so dense and complex, it nearly made him swoon.

Many onlookers used portable devices to monitor what was being said by the distant missionaries—who could only be made out from here as dim silvery glints on an upraised stage. Others tilted their varied eyes toward a dozen or so large vid screens, mounted high along the stone walls, each one emanating a different dialect.

A fraction of the crowd pressed forward, seeking something ineffable from direct experience.

"Curious," Kiwei Ha'aoulin commented. "I count several racial types that are not normally prone to religious fervor. And quite a few others whose clans are in deep ideological conflict with each other. Note over there! A tourmuj Awaiter and a talpu'ur Inheritor, standing enraptured, side by side. I wonder what conceptual magic has them so captivated."

"Who cares?" Harry groaned impatiently. He wanted to reach the body shop before closing time, so the trail would not go cold. "Ifni! We'll never get around this mess."

He was about to suggest turning around and taking a long detour, when the sound of his Anglic cursing attracted attention from a tall, camellike being, who turned to regard Harry with coal-black eyes.

It was a j'8Iek, whose starfaring nation had such a long history of antipathy toward Earthlings that Harry's right hand twitched, seeking comfort from the touch of his sidearm.

Only this particular j'8Iek did something unexpected. After staring at Harry for several duras, it abruptly swept its long neck downward, *bowing* in a gesture of deep respect! Applying force with all four powerful legs, the creature pushed against the crowd, opening the beginnings of a path for Harry and his companion.

Somewhat amazed, the two of them moved forward, only to have the same thing happen again! Time after time, some onlooker would notice Harry, then hurriedly nudge those in front, clearing a path. No one objected or demurred. Even high-ranking beings from senior patron lines made way graciously, as if to an equal.

The experience was all the more daunting and strange to a chimp who stood less than a meter and a half high. It felt as if some force were dividing a sea of tall aliens before him, creating a narrow lane that he could not see beyond, leaving him with no idea what to expect at the other end. The whole thing would have felt just a bit unnerving, if everybody didn't seem so damned friendly.

That made it *totally* unnerving!

He was too immersed in the crowd to catch anything but an occasional glimpse of the big display screens. But soon the preacher's voice came through in clear Galactic Seven, causing him to stumble with sudden recognition.

"*. . . anyone can understand why the great and mighty religious alliances have been driven to a frenzy by this news, broadcast recently from the sacred martyr world. This gift sent to us from wonderful doomed Earth.*

"A gift of truth!

"By combining Galactic science with their own ingenious mathematics, the wolflings have uncovered a secret that high officials of the Institutes tried for many aeons to conceal—a secret also known by majestic beings of the Retired and Transcendent orders—that the convulsions presently racking the Five Galaxies are part of a natural process! One we should embrace, rather than dread!"

At once Harry recognized the manner of speech, as well as the strange message.

It was the Skiano proselyte! The one who used to sermonize in the street, unable to afford even a sidewalk pulpit. Given to extravagant metaphors, it had compared humanity's "wolfling" nature—supposedly arising to sapience without intervention by a patron race—to legends of "virgin birth." Harry vividly recalled the great prow-shaped head with twin pairs of inset, flashing eyes, uttering a chilling prophecy that Earth would suffer a kind of crucifixion, gloriously dying for the sake of others, before rising again, in spirit.

Now he understood why the crowd parted for a Terran—even a mere chimpanzee. (One with a tail that twitched nervously!)

Alas, that knowledge came as slim comfort. Clearly, the Skiano was riding a wave of public hysteria. Harry had walked into a revival meeting for one of the most bizarre heresies ever to strike the Five Galaxies!

Entranced and thoroughly amused, Kiwei Ha'aoulin began leading the way, forging ahead eagerly, as if to compensate for Harry's growing reluctance, acting like a strutting majordomo, alerting one and all that an *Earthling* was coming through!

In a whispered aside, she urged him to enjoy the special treatment while it lasted.

"Well well. Maybe you should buck up, little furry fellow! With the whole cosmos shaking apart, we might as well have some fun."

Not a typically Synthian attitude. But then, fatalism can be a strong antidote to cowardice.

This time, Harry decided to accept Kiwei's reasoning. He squared his shoulders back, trying for the full bipedal dignity that human patrons had imbued into his ancestors while also giving them the gifts of speech and sapiency. He smoothed down the hackles in his pale fur, and even allowed the anomalous tail to rise up, in pride.

Abruptly, the throng ended. He and Kiwei found themselves at a raised platform where visiting dignitaries could sit and watch the spectacle in comfort.

Harry wanted only to get away and resume his earlier business, searching for the wayward sooners. But the only path available aimed straight up a ramp to the reserved area. As he climbed alongside Kiwei, the Skiano missionary's strange dogma resonated.

". . . *why do the mighty alliances and Old Ones so oppose the idea of a God who loves each person? One who finds importance not in race or clan, but in every particular entity who is aware and capable of compassion?*

"Could it be because they fear such an idea might bring an end to Uplift or species improvement?

"Nonsense! Those things would still take place, undertaken by free individuals! By sovereign souls who have faith in themselves and a personal redemption—when each honorable sapient will meet the Creator of All, finding utter fulfillment at the Omega Point."

Harry had heard it all before—a strange blending of ancient Earth beliefs—many of them mutually incompatible—upgraded to address the mass fears of a Galactic civilization where the accustomed certainty was melting on all sides. The Skiano's brilliant added touch—portraying the wolfling planet in the role of glorious, redeeming martyr—took advantage of Terra's plight . . . while doing little to help save it from wrathful battle fleets.

If Harry thought the sermon bizarre, something more interesting awaited him among the varied dignitaries—none other than his old antagonist, the port inspector, who slouched as low as possible, clearly wishing to be elsewhere.

Harry loudly greeted the big hoon, calling out his name.

"Twaphu-anuph! Is that really you? Come to expand your horizons a bit, have you? Decided it was time to see the light?"

Upon spying Harry, Twaphu-anuph recoiled. With his elegantly dyed throat sac flapping miserably, he gestured lamely toward a young female hoon sitting next to him.

"My presence here . . . it was not voluntary. My . . . hr-rrm . . . *daughter* made me come."

Harry barely stifled a guffaw. If hoons had one appealing trait, it was how they doted on their offspring. Harry still found it mystifying why this charming attribute nevertheless resulted in a race of dour, prudish, inflexible bureaucrats.

While Harry savored Twaphu-anuph's discomfort, the Skiano kept preaching.

"Today we see the great powers striving to suppress truth—even as they vie to rain ruin down on Blessed Earth. Why? Because they worry about the Big Mistake.

"Long ago, a so-called 'heresy' was quashed. But truth can only be hidden, never destroyed.

"Now they fear all sapients will see at last—"

The prow-headed missionary paused dramatically.

"—that the vaunted 'Embrace of Tides' may be an embrace of lies!"

The crowd must have already known the gist of this message. Yet a moan coursed the vast hall when it was said aloud.

It gave Harry a chance to torment the port official some more.

"How 'bout that, old fellow?" he murmured. "Generation after generation, workin' and slaving and havin' no fun, just so's your distant smart-aleck descendants will get to jump through a black hole to paradise. But what if there's nothing down there, at the other end of the singularity? What if it's all for nothin'?"

While Twaphu-anuph slumped miserably, his daughter leaned forward eagerly, peering with excitement toward the dais, where the Skiano paced back and forth under spotlights.

". . . but there is another kind of salvation! One that needn't dwell on far horizons of space and time. One that comes to each of us, if we just open up . . ."

Twaphu-anuph's daughter turned to her other companion, a sturdy-looking young male hoon, whose arm she held with evident affection. A slender rousit perched on her shoulder, staring at a black, ferretlike creature lounging on the male's back. Another inexplicable irony was that animals tended to like hoons, something that sapient beings seldom did.

Both youths were clearly well embarked on a bonding cycle—a scene that might have looked fetching, except the inevitable outcome would be yet another generation of sullen oppressors.

Why would hoons attend this bizarre rally? It runs counter to everything they stand for!

Harry jerked reflexively, reacting to a nudge from his Synthian companion.

"Over there!" Kiwei Ha'aoulin pointed. "Is that possibly one of the Earthlings you seek?"

Harry peered toward one end of the glare-lighted stage, where the Skiano's attendants swarmed in flowing robes of blue and gold. In their midst stood a smallish human figure, similarly attired, who made commanding gestures, sending acolytes fanning through the congregation, armed with collection plates.

Harry blinked in surprise.

Rety!

A bath alone would have transformed the sooner girl. Resplendent garments took things further. But Harry saw that her *face* had also changed. Where scar tissue once puckered her cheek and jaw, smooth pink skin now glistened.

The customer at the body shop wasn't Dwer, after all. *I should've guessed.*

Rety must have nosed around Kazzkark till she found the one group that would find her invaluable—a cult whose icon was the blue wolfling planet. Indeed, from the looks of things, she had risen to some prominence. A survivor, if Harry ever saw one.

"And now," Kiwei Ha'aoulin murmured. "We complete the circle. You are about to be reunited in full, and I will take my leave."

Harry reached out to stop the Synthian . . . then noticed that the audience was rippling once again. Like the Red Sea, parting. Emerging from a morass of beings who shuffled, slithered, flopped, or crawled out of the way, there strode a slim figure dressed in dun-colored clothing that seemed blurry to the eye. With the hood of his homespun garment thrown back, Dwer Koolhan's shock of unruly hair seemed to gleam in contrast, like his dark eyes.

Well, he must've spent some of the seventy-five coins, Harry thought, noting that the young man held a small electronic tablet and was using it the way natives on Horst would hold a dowsing rod, searching back and forth for water. On the back of one arm, Dwer also wore a makeshift arrangement of bent metal tubes and elastic bands that no Galactic would see as a weapon, but Harry recognized as a vicious-looking wrist catapult—more useful at close urban quarters than any bow and arrows. At his waist, the human wore a long knife in a sheath.

To anyone but another Earthling, he might have seemed completely calm, oblivious to the crowd. But Harry read tension in Dwer's shoulders as the living aisle spilled him toward the dignitaries' ramp. Kiwei had begun edging away again, but now the Synthian's curiosity overcame caution and she stayed to watch the young sooner approach.

"Well, well. . . . Well, well . . ." Kiwei said, over and over, licking her whiskers nervously.

Dwer acknowledged Kiwei with a nod, showing no sign of any rancor over being cheated—much to the Synthian's obvious relief.

Approaching Harry, he turned off the small finder tool.

"Smart of you to set up a personal beacon, Captain Harms. I bought some lessons on how to set this tracker onto your signal. We use sniffer-bees for the same purpose, back home."

Harry shrugged. He hadn't expected it to work. But clearly, wherever these sooners came from, their schooling included resilience.

"I'm just glad you two are all right," he replied gruffly, nodding toward Rety.

Dwer scanned the scene onstage, where Rety could now be seen with the Skiano's parrot on her shoulder, leading the audience in a strangely compelling psalm, merging contributions from at least half a dozen Galactic dialects with slow, sonorous Anglic. Though his pupils dilated, Dwer's face showed no surprise.

"Shoulda figured," he commented with a terse head-shake. "So, how d'you suggest we get her out of there without startin' a riot among these—"

The young man stopped abruptly. His jaw dropped . . . then snapped shut again.

"I don't believe it," he murmured. Then, with an expression of grim determination, he added, "Excuse me, Cap'n Harms. There's something I got to do right now."

Harry blinked. "But . . . what—"

Dwer moved past him, quickly and silently slipping off his outer tunic. With rapid, agile motions, he tied the arms and hooded neck, creating a makeshift bag which he grasped in his left hand. Creeping in back of the first row of dignitaries, Dwer ignored protesting grunts from those seated in the second rank. The crowd's continued chanting covered all complaints as he sidled behind Twaphu-anuph and the inspector's daughter, making straight for the third hoon—the young male, whose ferret-like pet seemed at last to sense something. Though it faced the other way, spiny hackles on its neck lifted from the mass of black fur. It started to turn, bringing both glittering eyes around. Eyes that flared with shocked realization the same moment that Dwer lunged.

Well I'll be shaved, Harry thought as the creature writhed in Dwer's hard grasp, snapping and hissing furiously until it was swallowed by the improvised sack. Even then, the fabric container bulged and jerked as the beast fought confinement.

That was a tytlal! He had thought there was something familiar about the lithe creature—but the size had seemed wrong. *A miniature tytlal . . . riding the shoulder of a hoon!*

No wonder recognition was slow. Tytlal normally massed nearly as much as a chimpanzee. Far from being mere pets, they were intelligent, articulate starfarers, well known and admired on Earth. Also, like their Tymbrimi patrons, they thoroughly disliked hoons!

Possible explanations occurred to Harry. Was Dwer rescuing a captive tytlal *child* from captivity?

That theory vanished when the third hoon turned around, saw Dwer, and cried out an umble of delighted surprise. While the bag kept quivering, onlookers were treated to a sight unprecedented in the annals of the Civilization of Five Galaxies—a human and hoon embracing each other joyfully, like long-lost cousins from the same hometown.

They found a place to talk, assembling in the lattice space supporting the dignitaries' platform. Harry watched in amazement as Dwer's huge alien friend spoke colloquial Anglic perfectly, though with an archaic accent.

"Alvin" also exuded an enthusiasm—a joie de vivre—that seemed totally natural, though Harry had never seen anything like it in a hoon before.

"Hr-rr. The last time I saw you, Dwer, you were dangling under a *hot-air balloon,* preparing to take on a Jophur battleship single-handed. How did you wind up here?"

"It's a long story, Alvin. And we'd never have made it without Captain Harms, here. But what about you? Does this mean the *Str—*"

Dwer stopped abruptly and shook his head, amending what he had been about to say.

"Does this mean our *friends* escaped to the transfer point all right?"

For the first time in his life, Harry saw a hoon shrug—a surprisingly graceful and expressive gesture for such an uptight species.

"Yeah, they did. That is, sort of. In a way." The tattooed throat sac fluttered and sighed. "For now let's just say it's also a long story."

Kiwei the Synthian had a suggestion.

"I know a very nice establishment where they offer free food and drink to tellers of fine tales, no matter how long. Shall we all go—"

Dwer ignored Kiwei.

"And your pals? Ur-ronn? Huck? Pincer? Tyug?"

"They are well—along with the *friend* who brought us here. You can imagine that some of us find it easier to get around in public than others do."

Dwer nodded, and Harry saw that levels of meaning passed between the two.

Wait a minute, he pondered. *If Dwer and Rety are sooners, from some hidden colony world, but they know this hoon, then that must mean—*

He lost the thought as Alvin responded to something Dwer said by umbling with jovial tones that sounded uncannily like laughter.

"So, you finally got the drop on old Mudfoot."

The young human held up the now quiescent bag. "Yeah, I did. And he doesn't come out till I get some answers, at long last."

Alvin laughed again—making Twaphu-anuph shiver with visible confusion. But the bureaucrat's daughter seemed to adore the sound. With a second show of rather unhoonish enthusiasm, she introduced herself as Dor-hinuf, and surprised both Earthlings by offering to shake their hands.

"Ever since he arrived, Alvin has been telling us about your wonderful world of Shangri-la," she told Dwer. "Where so many races live together in peace, and where hoons have learned to *sail!*"

Her infectious excitement seemed as strange as the sudden bizarre image filling Harry's mind—of hoons braving sea and spume in spindly boats.

Shangri-la? Harry noted.

Of course he'd mask the true name of the sooner planet. But why under that particular name? Why a Terran literary reference?

For that matter, how did a hoon ever come to be called Alvin?

From the sound of things behind them, the Skiano's heretical rally was starting to break up at last. Harry brought this to the others' attention.

"For once, I agree with Kiwei. We should go someplace private and talk further, before I have to report back to headquarters. But first let's collect Rety—"

He stopped then, sensing that something was changing. Through the soles of his feet, Harry felt another of the tremors that had made Kazzkark tremble intermittently for several jaduras. Only this time a new rhythm seemed to take over.

A rising intensity.

Others sensed it too. The hoons splayed their shaggy legs and a soft mewling escaped the bag where Dwer kept his tytlal prisoner. The viewing stand rattled unnervingly, and dust floated downward from the stony ceiling—the only barrier between living creatures and the sucking vacuum outside.

Things are getting worse, Harry thought.

When a crack appeared in the nearby wall and began to spread, he revised his estimate again.

This one is bad. Real bad.

KAA

"Pilot, wake up! Come quickly, you are needed!"

Like a fish with a hook in its jaw, tugged out of the sea by a cruel line, Kaa felt brutally *yanked* as intruding words pierced his dream, shattering a sonic phantasm of Peepoe.

She had been swimming beside him. Or rather, a pattern of echoes and sonar shadows, reflecting off his cabin, had coalesced as a likeness of her graceful form, undulating happily nearby, almost close enough to touch. Jijo's gentle sea had surrounded their bodies as they plunged ahead, naked and free.

Dolphins sleep just one hemisphere at a time. But this episode had the full flux and power of the Whale Dream, enveloping him in the presence of his beloved, and the planet where they had hoped to spend their lives together.

When the noisome voice broke in, shattering that blissful illusion, he felt the loss of Peepoe all over again, finding himself once again stranded in harsh metal purgatory, megaparsecs away from her.

In frustration, Kaa thrashed his flukes on the flotation bed of his walker unit. Bleary from fitful sleep, his right eye focused at last to regard the strange figure of *Huck,* a creature whose physical form seemed like an improbable swirl of organic and mechanical parts. Rolling on twin jittery wheels, the young g'Kek waved all four eye-stalks in frantic agitation, jabbering rapidly about something that had her terribly upset.

Anglic speech patterns came slowly to waking neo-dolphins, especially after immersion in the Whale Dream, but this time Kaa's anger bulled through, driving a hot response.

"I sssaid I wasn't to be disturbed . . . except in an emergency!"

Huck's frantic words penetrated at last.

"This *is* an emergency!" she wailed. "I j-just woke up and found Pincer-Tip—"

"Yeah?" Kaa asked, sending a signal down his neural tap to power up the walker. "What about him?"

The g'Kek was already rolling swiftly out of the little cabin, two eyes aimed ahead and two back at Kaa.

"Come quick! Pincer's *dying*!"

The little red qheuen lay collapsed near the airlock—a crablike figure with five legs splayed outward symmetrically, like an ailing starfish. Several claws still shuddered and snapped reflexively, but there was no other sign of movement. When Kaa brought his walker unit closer, aiming its forward camera for a close look, he saw trails of ugly-looking substance—like ichor—dribbling from beneath the wide chitin carapace.

"What-t happened?" he asked anxiously.

Huck snapped back.

"How should I know? I told ya, I was in that little cabinet you assigned me as a hiding place, tryin' to sleep, since you won't let me leave the ship. When I came out, he was like this!"

"But-t . . . don't you know what's wrong with him? Can you do anything?"

"Hey, just because I'm a g'Kek, that don't make me a doctor, any more'n every dolphin is a pilot. We've got to call for help!"

Kaa listened to the sick qheuen's ragged breathing. Whatever the nauseating substance was, it came from all five armpits, where the delicate air vents lay. Clearly, the poor thing was nearing total collapse.

"We . . ." He shook his sleek gray head left and right. "We can't do that."

"What?" Huck rocked back so hard that both rims bounced off the floor. Her spokes hummed and she stared with all four eyes. "We're not in a wilderness anymore, fish-head. We're at *civilization*! They got all sorts of things out there, beyond that airlock. Stuff we Jijoans only read about in books, like *hospitals* and *autodocs*. They might save him!"

Kaa felt the young g'Kek's wrath and outrage. The heat of her devotion to a friend. He sympathized. But there could only be one answer.

"We can't call attention to ourselves. You know that. If anyone here even suspected that a dolphin was aboard this ship, they'd cut it apart to get at me. And the same holds for a g'Kek. We'll just have to wait for Alvin and Ur-ronn to get back. They can move about without attracting attention. Or better yet, when Tyug returns, the alchemist can try—"

"That could take miduras! You know Alvin's got himself a star-hoon girlfriend. Tyug's spying on the Jophur, and Ur-ronn stays out longer and longer each time, talking to engineers!"

That was the plan, of course, for that trio to act as spies and envoys, getting to know the nature of things within Kazzkark Base, and in the Five Galaxies at large. If possible, they would make contact with some of Earth's few allies, or else look for some way to buy passage toward Galaxy Two. While attempting to deliver Gillian Baskin's message to the Terragens Council, they would also try to learn about their own kind, finding some way of securing future livelihoods, for themselves and their friends.

Huck was right. Alvin and Ur-ronn might stay out for hours longer. Pincer would not last that long.

"I'm sssorry," Kaa said. "We can't risk throwing everything away for just a sssslim chance of—"

"I don't *care* how slim it is, or about the risk! It doesn't matter!"

Her eyestalks waved and twined in furious anger. But while she cursed him roundly, Kaa knew he must be firm for her sake, even more than his own. With all the g'Keks of Jijo now in peril of genocide—deliberate extinction by wrathful Jophur, bent on satisfying an ancient vendetta—this one little female might be the sole hope of her entire species. Along with a tube of seminal plasm, stored in the scoutboat's refrigerator, she might possibly reestablish her posterity in some safe hiding place, protected by sympathetic guardians.

Although it was not a role the adventurous Huck relished, she had claimed to see its importance. Until now, that is, when she would toss it all away for friendship.

Personal loyalty. Love. These are supposed to outweigh all other considerations, Kaa thought, wallowing in misery, even as the young g'Kek railed at him, demanding over and over that he open the door.

Raised on Earthling novels, she feels the same way about it that I do. That only the worst sort of person would put stark pragmatism above intimate devotion, abandoning someone you care about to certain death . . . or something worse . . . even if it is logically the "right" thing to do.

So Kaa silently derided himself while Huck did it aloud, making the small control room echo with her wails.

Yet, he would not relent.

Anyway, the issue was settled soon. Just a few duras later, Pincer-Tip was dead.

Huck lacked both strength and will to help dispose of the body. That chore was left to Kaa, using the mechanical arms of his walker to heave the bulky qheuen toward the recycler. Huck turned three eyes away from the gory scene, but the remaining stalk quivered and stared, as if dumbly transfixed.

How could this happen? Kaa worried as he sent control messages down his neural tap, causing the machine to move like an extension of his body. *Did someone attack the ship? Or was this caused by the disease we heard about . . . the one that slaughtered many qheuens back on Jijo?*

If so, how was Pincer exposed?

Abruptly, Huck let out an amazed cry. Her whistling shouts brought Kaa spinning around, stomping back from his grisly task. He looked down where she pointed, at the bloody deck where Pincer had lain.

There, partly masked by gruesome liquids, both of them now made out a *design* of some sort, carved deeply into the metal deck.

"He . . . he . . ." Huck stammered. "He musta cut it with his teeth, while he was dying! Poor Pincer couldn't walk or talk, but he could still move his mouth, as it lay against the floor!"

Kaa stared, in part amazed by the slicing power of qheuen jaws, and by the acute—even artistic—rendering that had been the poor creature's final act.

It showed a face, vaguely humanoid, but somewhat feral looking, with lean, ravenous cheeks and a small, bitter mouth. He recognized the shape at once.

"A Rothen!"

The race of sneaky criminals and petty connivers, who had persuaded a cult of humans to believe they were patrons of all Earthclan, and rightful gods of Terran devotion.

Then he remembered. There had been such a creature aboard *Streaker*! A prisoner, brought aboard in secret at Wuphon Port. A Rothen overlord named *Rokenn*, mastermind of many felonies against the Six Races of Jijo.

"He musta stowed away aboard this ship!" Huck cried. "Stayed hidden till we docked, then came out an' killed poor Pincer to get at the door!"

Kaa's mind roiled over the disastrous implications. No matter how capable, Ro-kenn could not have managed such an escape all by himself. He must have had help aboard *Streaker*. Moreover, if this Rothen made it into Kazzkark, all their plans might be in jeopardy.

Stay calm, he told himself. Ro-kenn can't go to the authorities. The crimes he committed on Jijo are worse than anything the sooners did.

Yes, but he might hurry to one of the big fanatic clans or alliances, and try to sell them information about *Streaker* and Jijo. At the very least, he'll send word to other Rothen.

"We had better try to contact Alvin and Ur-ronn." Kaa said. And for once he could tell that Huck agreed.

Only that was far from easy. It seemed that all available telecomm lines were jammed with frantic traffic. And things only got worse as another wave of subspace disruptions hit. causing the planetoid to shake and rattle, resonating like a great, hollow bell.

FROM THE JOURNAL OF GILLIAN BASKIN

The universe is awash in tragedy. Yet, only now, as it seems to be falling apart, have I finally begun to see some of the ironic, awesome beauty of its cosmic design.

As happened at the Fractal World, we find ourselves surrounded by sudden devastation, orders of magnitude greater than I ever imagined.

Far below us, whirling near the condensed core of a massive ancient star, we see vast needle-shaped habitats—each one longer than the moon is wide—made of superstrong godstuff, built to withstand fierce tidal strains. Only now those habitats of the Transcendent Order show signs of terminal stress, shedding their outer skins like brittle slough—quivering as wave after wave of spatial convulsions surge through this part of Galaxy Four.

According to both Sara and the Niss Machine, these are symptoms of a fantastic rupture, beyond anything seen in a quarter of a billion years.

The effects have been even worse on the huge armada of "candidate ships" accompanying *Streaker* converging on multiple, crisscrossing downward spirals toward those needle monoliths. What had been a stately procession, triumphant and hopeful, wedding two of life's great orders in a great and glorious union, is swiftly dissolving into chaos and conflagration.

So closely were the giant arks and globules packed together—in dense, orderly rows—that each wave of hypergeometric-recoil throws one rank against another. Collisions produce blinding explosions, slaughtering untold millions and throwing yet more vessels off course.

Yet, despite this awful trend, only a few other craft have joined *Streaker* in attempting to escape, climbing laboriously outward through the maze, seeking some relative sanctuary of deep space. It seems that the addiction of tides cannot easily be broken, once sapients have tasted its deeper pleasures. Like rutting beasts, irresistibly drawn toward mating grounds they know to be on fire, a majority continue on course, accelerating into the funnel, bound for the Embrace they so deeply desire.

Is this the ultimate destiny of intelligent life? After striving for ages to become brainy, contemplative, wise (and all that), do all races wind up driven forward by ineffable instinct? By a yearning so strong they must plunge ahead, even when their goal is falling apart before their eyes?

At last, for the first time in three long years, I begin to understand the persecution we Streakers have suffered—and Earth, as well. For our discovery of the Ghost Fleet truly does present a challenge, a shocking heresy, that strikes at the very heart of Galactic belief systems.

Most of them—and the hydrogen breathers, as well—maintain that true transcendence is the ultimate destiny of those who merge within the Embrace of Tides. *Something* must lie beyond . . . or so they've reasoned for countless ages. Why else would the universe have evolved such an elegant way of focusing, gathering, and distilling the very best of both life orders?

Surely, this must be the great path spoken of by the Progenitors, when they departed two billion years ago.

Ah, but then what of the Ghost Fleet, with its haunting symbols and glimmering hints at ancient truth?

Where did we find it?

In a "shallow" globular cluster, dim and nearly metal-free, drifting lonely toward the rim of Galaxy Two. A place where spacetime is so flat that even young races experience a faint, nervous revulsion. A kind of creepy agoraphobia. Such locales are seldom visited, since they contain nothing of interest to any life order, even machines.

(In which case, what clue . . . what hunch . . . drew Creideiki there? Did he set Streaker's course for the Shallow Cluster because it seemed neglected by the Great Library, with an entry as skimpy as the one about Earth?

(Or was there something more to his decision? A choice that seemed so strange at the time.)

Now, at last, I see why our enemies—the Tandu and Soro and Jophur and the others—got so upset when *Streaker* beamed back those first images of the Ghost Fleet . . . and of Herbie and the rest.

If these truly are relics of the great Progenitors, sealed away in field-protected vessels for countless aeons, what does that imply about the Embrace of Tides? Did the founder race—earliest and wisest of all—seek desperately to avoid the attraction? Did they shun the deep places? If so, might it be because they knew something terrible about them?

Perhaps they saw the Embrace as something else entirely. Not a route to transcendence, but a trash disposal system. A means for recycling dross, like the Great Midden on Jijo.

Nature's way of siphoning away the old in order to make room for the new.

Standing in his glass case, Herbie smiles at me across my desk. The mummy's eerie humanoidal rictus has been my most intimate companion, ever since Tom went away. Sometimes I find myself talking to him.

Well, old fellow? Is this the big joke? Have I at last figured out why you've been grinning all this time?

Or are there more layers yet to peel away?

More terrible surprises to come.

It isn't easy trying to work our way out of this trap with our two best pilots gone. The swarm of arks and globules appears to extend endlessly above us, reaching far out beyond the range of any solar system. The sheer amount of mass involved approaches macroplanetary scales! Like the accretion disk surrounding a newborn star.

Where could all these "candidates" have come from?

Might the same thing be happening elsewhere? A lot of elsewheres? If even a small fraction of older white dwarves are home to such convergences, that would mean millions of sites like this one, surrounded by migrants eager to enter paradise, despite a growing gauntlet of collision and fire.

On a practical level, *Streaker* cannot attempt any hyperspace jumps till we're clear of all these massive ships, and the rippling effects of their mighty engines.

Even if we do succeed in working our way outward, the Jophur dreadnought is still out there. We detect it from time to time, tracking us like some tenacious predator, crippled and dying, with nothing else to live for anymore beyond finishing the hunt. If we make it to open space, there will be that peril to contend with.

If only we could rid ourselves of this deadly coating and restore Streaker to her old agility!

Hannes has been working on a new idea about that, alongside Emerson D'Anite. Something involving the big Communications Laser.

Poor Emerson struggles to explain something to us—humming melodies and drawing pictures, but all we can tell so far is that he managed to defeat yet another meme-attack on *Streaker* a while back, and destroyed the renegade—Tsh't—in the process.

I cannot help it. I grieve for my friend. The sweet comrade who was by my side through crisis after crisis. Poor Tsh't only thought she was doing the right thing, seeking help and succor from her gods.

Now another wraith follows through the night, surging like a porpoise through my restless dreams.

The big news is that the Niss Machine lately made a breakthrough. It managed at last to tap into what passes for a communications network among the Transcendents.

As one might expect, it is a dense, complex system, as far beyond Galactic-level technology as a hand computer exceeds an abacus. It was invisible for so long because only small portions on the fringes use classical electronics or photonics. The core technique appears to be quantum computing on a scale so vast that it must utilize highly compressed gravitational fields.

"Such fields are unavailable here," *commented the Niss.* "Even among the needle habitats, whirling just above the compact star core, the potentials are many orders of magnitude too small.

"We must be picking up the margins of something much greater. Something with its center located far away from here."

Of course it occurred to us that this might be our chance. Our hope of communicating with "higher authorities," as ordered by the Terragens Council. The creatures who betrayed us at the Fractal World—those so-called Old Ones—were like infants in comparison to the minds using this new network. Indeed, all signs suggest they are the pinnacle that life achieves.

Yet, I'm reluctant to just hand over our data from the Shallow Cluster. We've been disappointed too many times. Perhaps the Transcendents also suffer from the same fear—that a deadly trap underlies the Embrace of Tides.

If it entered their thoughts to be vengeful toward us, we'd have all the chance of a hamster against a bolo battle tank.

"Let's ask simple questions, first," I said. "Any suggestions?"

Sara Koolhan burst forth.

"Ask about the Buyur! Are they down there? Did the Buyur transcend?"

Lately, she's grown obsessed with the last species to have leasehold over Jijo. A race of genetic manipulators, who seemed to know in advance that sooners would invade their world, and about a coming Time of Changes.

"Even such a simple query will be hard to translate. It may be impossible to slip within the matrix in such a way that anyone will notice, or bother answering," warned the Niss. "But I will try."

Of course, we risk drawing the attention of even more powerful enemies. But with the odds already against us, it seems a worthwhile effort.

Meanwhile, our dolphin astronomer, Zub'daki, has more bad news to report about the swarm of incoming Candidate vessels.

He knows and cares little about hyperspatial disruptions tearing the fabric of reality. That is Sara's department. Zub'daki's interest lies in the white dwarf itself, and the sheer amount of matter approaching it like flotsam in a whirling drain.

"What if most of the arks misssss their target?" he asked. "What if they fail to rendezvous with the needle-gatewayssss?

"What if the needles are no longer there to collect them?"

I fear that my initial response was callous, asking why we should care if a stampede of giants go tumbling into a grave of their own making. As mere ants, it is our duty to escape. To survive.

But I will go and hear what he has to say.

What will one more worry matter? I've long passed the point where I stopped counting them.

LARK

The reunion was bizarre, joyous, and rather unnerving.

Having long dreamed of this moment—being reunited with his lover—Lark now stared at Ling across a gulf far wider than the few meters separating them.

She floated in a blobby stew, a dense swarm of writhing, pulsating objects that moved languidly within a vast, transparent membrane—a bloated mass that filled most of this large chamber and extended through several hatchways into more of the ship beyond.

In addition to Ling's human form, he glimpsed at least one wriggling qheuen larva, plus several animal types from Jijo and other worlds. Lark recognized a multitude of traeki rings, plus countless twining green things that must have once been plants.

Bubblelike forms also crowded throughout the teeming life-brew, rippling like amoebae, or bobbing gelatinous balloons. Though colored and textured differently than the Zang creature he carried about like a suit of clothes, Lark could tell they were related.

Despite the family resemblance, his passenger reacted violently to sighting these "cousins." The Zang tried to make him flee. But Lark was adamant, willing both stiff legs to stride forward, to Ling.

Her naked form was draped with various throbbing creatures. *Symbionts,* Lark thought. Some of them covered her mouth and nose, while others penetrated flesh directly to the bloodstream. Weeks ago, the sight might have sent chills down his spine, but by now the concept was familiar as breathing. Simply a more extensive version of the arrangement he had made with the Zang.

Moving closer, he sought Ling's eyes, trying for contact. Had this vast cell simply incorporated her for some crude biochemical purpose, as an *organelle,* to serve a minor function for the whole? Or did she retain her essence within?

Lark's passenger extended a pseudopod over his left eye, creating a vacuole in front of his field of view. Inside that small space, hundreds of tiny "deputies" budded and performed gyrations, mimicking shapes and playacting a suggestion that Lark should turn around and get the hell away from here!

"Oh, stop bellyaching, you coward," he replied with disgust. "On Jijo we learned you can make friends out of old enemies. Besides, have you got anything better to do right now?"

His meaning somehow got through, causing the Zang to retract its deputies, resorbing them into its body and pulling back sullenly.

Indeed, there would be no going back to the creature's base, on the opposite side of the battleship. In between them lay a huge wilderness. *Polkjhy* now swarmed with *things,* crawling through the hallways, chewing through compartments and walls, transforming them into grotesque shapes and outlandish forms. So far, essential systems seemed to have been spared. Those were still under control of the remaining Jophur crew—who seemed to grow ever more shrill and panicky in their communications—but for how much longer?

He felt a large presence come up alongside. The third member of their party.

"You are right, Lark," murmured the stack of glistening rings, whose throbbing mass quivered as its components debated among themselves.

"This vast macro-entity appears foreordained to expand until it fills *Polkjhy* entirely. We might flee, but to what end? Our trail has brought us here. Our/My/your/our destiny clearly lies within. Let us find out what it wants. What are its aims. What it came here to accomplish."

Within the gelatinous mass, Lark saw signs of change. Ling's eyes, which had been dismayingly vacant, now seemed to clarify, gradually focusing past the membrane, toward him.

All at once, a light of recognition shone! Though her mouth was covered by a symbiont, the squint of a smile was unmistakable, and her arms moved forward, reaching out. Joyful at the sight of him. Reaching in welcome.

"Well, look at the bright side," he commented, although the Zang passenger shivered with fearful resignation. "It looks kinda interesting in there. Maybe we'll learn a lot, eh?"

The giant membrane did not try to grab or seize them when they approached. Rather, it recoiled a bit, then seemed to sniff cautiously, as if deigning to be wooed. Lark extended his arm, brushing the surface. It felt chilly, and yet electrically pleasant in a way he could not quite fathom.

The Zang quivered, then seemed to change its mind. Lark had an impression of surprise. This was not the deadly foe it had expected, but a distant relative, greater and more kindly.

Decision came. A cavity formed, shaped like a tunnel, or a doorway.

Lark didn't hesitate. He strode forward, to his love.

It seemed that his instinct was correct. There was something deeply natural about this merging.

In theory, the hydro-and oxy-orders were incompatible, using disparate chemistry, different energetics and existing at widely distinct temperatures. But life is very good at problem solving. *Symbiosis* enables two or more organisms to pool abilities, accomplishing what one alone never could. It happened when early cells joined together in Earth's oceans, creating unions that were more competent than their separate parts.

Lark soon got used to the idea that this could take place on a much more sophisticated level, especially when guided by sagacious intelligence.

Anyway, while a teeming swarm of other "organelles" surrounded him, he cared about just one, whose caress made him feel more at home in this strange place than he ever had in his bed, on Jijo.

I'm glad we're still functional in all the ways that really matter, he commented.

Ling curled alongside, maximizing contact between their drifting bodies. Her answer came not as sound, but directly, as if conveyed by the fluid surroundings.

Typical male. Nothing else matters, as long as your sexual organs are satisfied.

He blinked.

Weren't yours?

She replied with a languorous squeeze, evidently content. Her skin still trembled slightly with the rhythms of their intense lovemaking.

A part of Lark—the restless thinker—wondered what possible use the macro-being could make of human sexual passion. Not that he was ungrateful for this new phase of existence. But once his thoughts began spreading outward, they would not stop.

Whatever happened to Rann? he inquired.

The one other human aboard, a fierce Danik warrior, had turned his talents to helping the Jophur. Lark would not relax knowing that enemy was out there, somewhere.

Don't worry about Rann. He won't be bothering us.

When he glanced at her, Ling shrugged, causing bubbles to flurry off her shoulders.

He was absorbed also. Mother must not have liked how he tasted. But she doesn't waste good material, so she put him to work in other ways. I saw a couple of Rann's parts a while ago—a leg and a lung, I think—incorporated in some organelle.

Lark shivered, feeling grateful that his "taste" met the macrobeing's approval.

You call it Mother?

She nodded, not having to explain. The name made as much sense as any other. Though nurturing kindliness was clearly just one aspect of its nature. There was also a brutally pragmatic side.

He sensed agreement from the Zang, his longtime companion, who now existed as a compact globule, floating nearby. Their sole remaining link was a narrow tube connected to his left side, and even that might dissolve soon, as they learned their separate roles in this new world. The Zang was still deeply uncertain, though one might have expected it to be more at home in this world of drifting shapes, where bulbous deputies swam back and forth, performing gaudy simulations.

In the murky distance, he saw that someone else was having a better time adjusting. The stack of waxy traeki rings—who had once been Asx, and then the Jophur called Ewasx—stood planted on the floor, surrounded by clusters of bubbles, membranes, and crawling symbionts. From waves of color that coursed across its flanks, Lark could tell the composite creature was having the time of its life. What could be more essentially *traeki* than to become part of something larger and more complex, a cooperative enterprise in which every ring and particle played a part?

Lark still wondered about how it all was organized. Did there exist an overall controlling mind—like a Jophur master ring? Or would every component get a vote? Both models of symbiosis existed in nature . . . and in politics.

He had a feeling such details were yet to be worked out. "Mother" wasn't finished taking form.

Come along, Ling urged, taking his hand. I want to show you something.

Lark needed a little while to get used to locomotion in this new medium. Much of the time, it involved movements akin to swimming, though in other locales the surrounding density changed somehow and their feet met the floor, allowing a more human mode of walking. There were no clear transitions, as between sea and shore. Rather, everything intermingled and merged, like the thoughts he and Ling shared.

Guiding him along, she finally pointed to a vast nest of tendrils that spread outward from a central point, waving and twisting. Many were linked to wriggling forms—Lark saw another larval qheuen, a couple of traeki stacks . . . and a form that resembled a centauroid urs, curled in a fetal ball, protected by something like an embryonic sac. He did not recognize the tawny figure, though urrish "samples" had been taken by the Jophur, on Jijo. Its flanks heaved slowly, as if calmly breathing, and Lark saw intelligent clarity in the triple set of eyes.

There were other oxy creatures. Some he identified from images on paper textbooks he had skimmed long ago, back home in the Biblos archive, while others he did not recognize. All were entangled with symbionts linking them to hydroglobules and other blobby things. The most eerie thing about it was that none of them seemed particularly to mind.

Mother taps the data mesh here, Ling explained, pointing to where the tendrils converged. Peering to look past the murk, he made out one of *Polkjhy*'s main computer panels.

Ling reached for three writhing tentacles, offering one each to Lark and the Zang.

Let's take a look at what's happening elsewhere.

It was a strange way of taking information. Partly neuronal and partly visual, it also involved portions of the mind that Lark customarily used for imagination, picturing an event with that tentative *what-if* sensation that always accompanied daydreams.

That made sense. For all hydro-beings, thinking was a process of simulation—spawning off smaller portions of themselves to play roles and act out a scenario to its logical conclusions. Helped by his prior experience with the Zang, Lark soon caught on, learning how to reach out and pretend that he *was* the object of his attention.

I am Polkjhy . . . once a proud battleship of the haughty Jophur nation.

Now I am divided . . . sectioned into many parts. My Jophur crew—doughty but distraught—have cleverly sealed off what they consider to be the most essential areas . . . engines, weaponry, and basic life support.

Driven by single-minded, purposeful Master Rings, they prepare for a last stand against loathsome invaders . . . while continuing to pursue their grudge hunt. Chasing the Earthling ship, whether pursuit leads them to Hell, or Heaven itself.

Lark felt a wash of strange emotion—grudging respect for the dauntless Jophur. Their resilience, in the face of one catastrophe after another, showed why their kind had gained power and influence among the vigorous, starfaring oxy-clans. That they could manage, even temporarily, to stave off powers much older and stronger than themselves was an impressive accomplishment.

Even so, Lark hoped they would fail soon.

Ling guided his attention, nudging it gently outward, beyond the battered hull.

He briefly staggered at a sudden impression, like that of an immense tornado!

A giant cyclone surrounded them, a swirling crowd of massive objects, sparkling and flashing while they spiraled down a condensing funnel toward the dim white fire of a tiny star.

Lark quickly found that his knowledge base was no longer limited to the narrow education of a Jijoan sooner—a rustic biologist, weaned on paper-paged books. It took only a slight effort of will to slip into Ling's mind and *perceive* facts, correlations, hypotheses explaining what they now saw. And beyond Ling, there were other archives—less familiar, but equally available.

Abruptly, he reached outward to the immense cyclone of descending spacecraft, identifying with them.

I am the Candidates' Swarm, a migration of the elect, chosen from among retirees of both oxygen-and hydrogen-breathing civilizations.

Elated to be here, at long last.

Fatigued by the pointless struggles and quandaries of flat space and real time.

Lured and allured by the seductive enchantments of the Embrace of Tides.

Fully aware of the disruptions now coursing through the Five Galaxies.

Cognizant of dangers lying ahead.

Nevertheless, I draw inward. Merging my many subunits. Creating unique blendings out of what was merely promising raw material. Integrating the best of hydrogen and oxygen.

Hoping and wondering what comes next . . .

Lark now saw a context for what had befallen *Polkjhy.* It was part of a much larger process! The same blending of life-forms must be happening on each of the millions of huge vessels out there . . . only perhaps more peacefully, with less resistance by the resident crews, who would be much better prepared for it than the poor Jophur.

And yet, he could not help but grasp a background tone of desperate worry. This majestic ingathering of transcendence candidates should have been smooth and ordered, as it was for ingatherings during more 'normal' times.

Only now instead, it grew more ragged and disrupted with each passing dura. The sparkles that had looked so gay earlier were now revealed as fiery impacts. Violent death spread ever more rapidly among the converging ships.

Again, Ling pointed and his mind followed. Instead of outward, their shared attention plunged *down,* toward the source of gravity and light, where immense slender edifices whirled in tight orbit around a compact star.

To initial appearances, the needle-habitats were also suffering severe strain. As he and Ling watched, chunks larger than mountains shattered or fell off, dissolving under the shear force of intense tides.

And yet, Lark felt no anguish, worry, or sense of imminent danger.

No wonder! he realized. The needles aren't habitats at all! They are gateways to another place!

Ling nodded.

Actually, it is predictable, if you think about it.

Lark sent his mind swooping like a hawk toward one of the fast-revolving structures, long and narrow, like a javelin. Though portions of its skin were flaking off—torn loose by chaotic hyperwave disturbances—he somehow knew those portions were unimportant. Mere temporary abodes and support structures. As these sloughed away, they revealed a shimmering inner core, each one a needle-opening, luminescent and slippery to the eye.

His image-self arrived just as one of the "candidates"—a fully merged and transformed globule-ark—finished its long spiraling migration and approached the needle at a rapid pace, skimming just above the white dwarf's licking plasma fire. The great hybrid vessel—now a completely blended mixture of hydrogen and oxygen civilizations—fell toward the exposed gateway, accelerating as if caught in some strongly attractive field.

Abruptly, the globule-ark seemed to slip *sideways,* through a narrow incision that had been cut in space-time.

The opening lasted but a few moments. But it was enough for Lark to perceive.

His first impression from the other side was of dense spinning blackness. A dark ball that glimmered with sudden, bright pinpoints. Somehow he could sense the twist and curl of vacuum as space warped around the thing, distorting any constellations that lay beyond.

It is a neutron star, Ling commented. *Long ago it used up or expelled any fuel it had left. Now it has self-compressed down to a size far smaller than a white dwarf—less than ten kilometers across! The gravitational pressure is so great below the surface that atomic nuclei merge with their surrounding clouds of electrons, forming "degenerate matter."*

Those sparks you see below are gamma ray flashes—translated into visible range by the transcendent mesh for our convenience. Each flash represents a grain, perhaps as small as a bacterium, that quickened up to near the speed of light before striking the surface.

There are half a billion of these dense relics in any galaxy . . . and a new one produced every thirty years or so. But only a few neutron stars have the narrow range of traits needed by the Transcendent Order. Well behaved. Rapidly spinning, but with low magnetic fields.

Lark overcame his surprise.

I get what's going on. The process continues!

How could a growing appetite for tides be satisfied by a mere white dwarf star? *Of course, they'll migrate to a place where the fields are even more intense.*

So, the myriad candidate vessels surrounding Polkjhy right now were only passing through! They use the white dwarf as an assembly area—a place to merge and transform, getting ready for the next phase.

The next time a slit-passage opened, Lark once again cast his thoughts through, riding the carrier wave of a vast information-handling system, like a sea flea surfing atop a tsunami, seeking to learn what kind of life transcendent beings made for themselves in such a strange place.

A *fog* seemed to envelop the neutron star, like a dense haze, whirling just above the surface.

Habitats, Ling identified.

Lark tried to look closer, but was stymied by how fast the objects sped by, just above the sleek black surface.

Each orbit took minuscule fractions of a second, racing around a course where gravity was so intense that tidal forces would rip apart any physical object more than a few meters across. Even with his perceptions enhanced by Mother, there were limits to what his organic brain could grasp.

But. . . . Mentally, he stammered. When hydro-and oxy-life merge, the result is still organic . . . based on water. Bodies with liquid chemistry. How can beings like us survive down there?

As if his question were a command, the focus of their attention shifted outward, to surrounding regions of space, further from the neutron star, where an enormous throng of dark, spindly objects could now be made out, parked in stately rows.

Lark sensed *metallic* presences, each waiting its turn with a patient silence that could only originate in the vast depths of interstellar vacuum.

Realization struck.

Machines!

A third life order had arrived. Answering some compelling call, the best and highest of their kind assembled to participate in a new union.

Another kind of marriage.

A narrow slit appeared in space, allowing ingress from a white dwarf assembly zone. One more globule-ark popped into the twisted sky, bringing its cargo of merged organic life-forms.

Several dozen of the waiting mechanicals converged around it, weaving a cocoon of fibrous light.

There was no resistance. Lark's expanded empathic sense picked up no dread, or resignation. Only readiness for metamorphosis.

The biologist in him recognized something elegant and natural looking about the process, although soon the details grew too complex and blurry even for his enhanced perceptions to follow.

All at once, amid a burst of actinic flare, everything was transformed. Consumed.

What fell away from the flash seemed like no more than a rain of glittering specks, plummeting eagerly toward the comforting squeeze—the intense embrace—of gravitational fields just above the neutron star.

Lark's head whirled in awe. He pulled back his attention, anchoring it to the real world by riveting on the soft brown eyes of Ling.

Is that it? Is that where everything culminates? With hydros, oxies, and machines merging, then orbiting forever next to a dense black sun?

Ling shook her head.

That's as far as I've been able to probe. But logically, I'd guess otherwise.

Think about it, Lark. Three life orders coalesce. The three who are known as the fiercest. The most potent at manipulating matter and energy. At last we know why hydros, oxies, and mechs have been able to coexist for so long . . . since they share a common destiny, and none can thrive without the others.

But there are more orders. More sapient styles than just those three! Quantals and Meta-memes, for instance.

And rumors of some that have no mention in the Great Library. Simple logic—and aesthetics—make me imagine that the process continues. Others must join as well. At some level beyond the one we just saw.

Lark blinked.

Some level beyond?

But what could lie beyond. . . ?

Then, all at once, he knew.

Sharing his realization, the little Zang next to him vented foul-smelling bubbles—the equivalent of a dismayed wail—and shrank inward. But Lark only nodded.

You're talking about black holes.

An unbeckoned flood of information crowded his thoughts, revealing many different types of "holes" known to science—sites where the density of matter passed a point of no return, wrapping gravity so tightly that no light, or information of any kind, could escape. Only a few of the deep singularities would do for the purpose Ling described. Smaller ones, mostly—massing up to just a few dozen times a typical sun. Bottomless pits, whose steep fringes would have the greatest tides of all . . . and where time itself would nearly stand still.

In such a narrow zone, just outside the black hole's event horizon, distinctions of matter and energy would blur. Causality would shimmer, evading Ifni's grasp. Under the right conditions, all of life's varied orders might merge, creating a pure sapiency stew. Intelligence in its most essential form.

If everything worked.

You're right, it's logical and aesthetic. Even beautiful, in its own way.

But I have one question, Ling.

Where do we fit in this grand scheme of things?

I mean you and I!

All the beings on these arks and globules surrounding us may be ready for such a destiny . . . assuming they survive the disruptions and chaos in order to reach the next level. After all, they've spent ages refining their souls, getting ready for this transformation.

But you and I were caught up in it by accident! Because we're in the wrong place at the wrong time. We don't belong here!

Ling's hand slipped into his, and Lark felt her warm smile inside his mind.

You don't like our new nest, love?

He squeezed back.

You know I do. It's just kind of hard to look forward to the next step—being "merged" with some star-computer mechoids, then squished down to the size of a pea, and finally—

She stopped him with a light mental touch, a calming stroke that brushed away incipient panic.

It's all right, Lark. Don't worry about it.

I very much doubt we're going to proceed much farther down that path.

Not if the Jophur have anything to say about it.

SARA

Getting an answer to her question did not settle any of the worries plaguing Sara.

While the Niss hologram gyred nearby, her forehead creased with concern.

"Damn! I hoped to learn the bastards had transcended."

The computerized voice replied with puzzlement.

"Might I ask why you are concerned about the fate of any one particular elder race?"

Her frown deepened. "The Buyur weren't just any race. Back when they held the lease on Jijo, they were renowned for cleverness and wit. You might say they were the Tymbrimi of their time, only far subtler at playing games of manipulative politics and power . . . and they had a much longer view of what it took in order to execute a good joke."

"In the name of my Tymbrimi makers, thanks for the compliment," the Niss replied sarcastically. But Sara had learned to ignore its feigned moods, designed to irk people in the short term. She was concerned about a race of jesters whose notion of a punch line could easily span a million years. Patient comedians whose intended victims might include her own folk—the Six Races of the Commons of Jijo.

"Are you sure the Transcendents keep such good records?" she asked. "Maybe the Buyur passed through a different white dwarf—a different merging-funnel—when they graduated to the next level."

"You misunderstand the nature of quantum computing," commented the Niss, dryly. "Every part of the Transcendent Mesh is in local contact with all others. There are no distinctions of space, or even time. All Transcendents know what the others know. We are talking about the closest thing to what you humans used to call the Omniscient Godhead . . . on this side of the Omega Point."

Sara grunted, slipping into the thick accent of a Dolo Village tree farmer.

"So far, I seen about a dozen levels o' so-called star deities, and I ain't been impressed with a one of 'em. Pettiness seems to follow life, no matter how high it climbs."

"So young to be so cynical," the Niss sighed. "Be that as it may, the query you sent into the Mesh did receive an answer. Assuming the Transcendents are not lying, we can be fairly certain that the Buyur have not joined them yet."

Sara glowered at the news. It had seemed the best possible solution to a problem gnawing at her lately. The deeper she went into the equations—modeling the violent convulsions now racking the cosmos—the more one fact became clear.

The math was just too elegant, too beautiful for *all* of Galactic society to have missed the correlations. No matter how hidebound and narrow-minded the majority were, *some* others must surely have come up with similar, revealing shortcuts. Similar ways of seeing past the blinders.

Anyone who did so would have pierced the veil of secrecy, and known far in advance that a spatiotemporal crisis was coming. A time when all hyperspatial paths would undergo upheaval, and confusion would reign.

Mounting evidence convinced Sara that the Buyur must have known. They knew that the the cryptic top entities running the Galactic Institutes would prepare for the coming Time of Changes by ensuring that Galaxy Four was declared fallow and evacuated. Only then the Buyur embellished, fiddling with Jijo and its surroundings.

They arranged for one of two nearby transfer points to go dormant, leaving only one way in and out, and then for Izmunuti to enter carbon-giant stage, creating the perfect lure for sooners. A perfect bottle for whatever specimens came nosing into the trap.

And there are more coincidences, she pondered. Like why all the squatter groups settled only on the Slope, despite our initially warring natures. Supposedly that was because of the Sacred Scrolls, but I figure there was another force at work.

The Egg. Silently influencing our ancestors, even two millennia before it burst up through the ground.

Indeed, why stop there? Might the Buyur have chosen *which* races should send sneakships to Jijo, seeding the illicit colony with just the right mix?

Did they manipulate the g'Kek, for instance, driving those happy, prosperous space dwellers into a hopeless vendetta with the Jophur, just so that a small remnant would have to flee, seeking shelter beneath Izmunuti's stark, unblinking eye? Did they then liberate some Jophur from their master rings, creating a shipload of restored traeki who must take shelter on Jijo and befriend the g'Kek?

The problem with thinking about plausible conspiracies was that the mind quickly gorged on every correlation, turning each one into a glaring likelihood . . . such as blaming the Buyur for all that had happened to Earth during the last several thousand years. Because the darkness, ignorance, pain, and isolation helped make humans what they were, eventually forcing them to dispatch sneakships toward far corners of space. Sending out lifeboats—such as the sneakship *Tabernacle*—in hope of preserving small samplings of humanity against the coming deluge.

Did the Buyur set all that up, just in order to have the right ingredients for their masterpiece on Jijo?

Sara shook her head. If she followed that road—extending her theory far beyond available proof—it would end in paranoia. But the first parts. The parts that got set up half a million years ago? Those parts just fit too well.

"We have learned another thing, by tapping the Transcendent Mesh," the Niss explained. "A titanic space battle has been going on for weeks near the outskirts of your home Solar System. Even augmented by some recent brave allies, Earth's defenses are now verging on collapse. Soon, fanatics will have the path open before them.

"When they finally converge on the blue homeworld of your race, Sara, it would be unrealistic to hope for mercy."

While she probed for answers, the escape attempt was going slowly.

With its outer flanges still mired by the "magic" coating, *Streaker* was nowhere near as nimble as before.

Without Lucky Kaa at the helm, it taxed Akeakemai and the other dolphins to pilot the ship slowly outward, away from the white dwarf star.

All around them spun the worst traffic jam of all time, a high-speed vortex of riotous confusion, peppered with debris from violent explosions. While most of the candidate globes tried to keep on course—doggedly continuing their downward spiral, despite collisions and chaos waves—a small minority were attempting to flee, like *Streaker*. Enough of them to disrupt the ranks, shredding any remaining semblance of order. Getting through such a maelstrom would take more than Ifni's luck. It would take a miracle.

Even if the Earthship made it to open space, there would be the Jophur battleship to contend with. And the old problem of finding a safe place in the universe to hide.

Sara glanced across the Plotting Room at Gillian Baskin. The older woman stood in conference with a sleek, blue-gray figure who floated beyond a glass barrier, in the flooded half of the chamber. It was the dolphin astronomer, Zub'daki, explaining something in a dialect of Anglic that was too high-pitched for Sara to follow. But from the hunch of Gillian's shoulders, it could not be good news. Her face was pale and drawn.

These moments may be our last. I should spend them with Emerson, not wallowing in theories about ancient crimes, or analyzing cosmic calamities no one can do anything about.

Alas, Emerson was never around. Despite his handicap, the brain-damaged engineer had commandeered all the technicians that Hannes Suessi could spare. They had given up trying to scrape away *Streaker*'s dangerous, cloying outer layer, and were working instead on the communications laser. Though Emerson's idea was still unclear to most of the crew, Gillian had approved the project, partly in order to give off-duty personnel something to do, keeping their minds occupied.

I wish I had such a refuge . . . a way to stay busy, pretending I was making a difference. But the only technology I know anything about is how to make paper, using crude pulping hammers and power from Nelo's little water-driven mill. Beyond that, I'm just a shaman. A spinner of incantations. A practitioner of the quaint Earthling art of calculus.

Prity came alongside carrying several sheets covered with perspective renderings—representing hyperspatial pathways, tormented and stretched almost to the breaking point. Sensing her mistress's mood, the little chimp assistant put the papers aside and climbed into Sara's lap.

Dear sweet Prity, Sara thought while stroking her. *You are mute, while Earth's chimps have progressed to speak and fly starships. And yet, how I would have loved to show you off! You would surely have amazed them, if we ever made it to Terra.*

Continuing her conversation with Zub'daki, Gillian used quick hand gestures to conjure up holographic images of several other dolphin faces, including Akeakemai and the chief astrogator, Olelo, who listened for a few moments, then protested loudly enough for Sara to overhear snatches of bubbly Trinary-Anglic.

". . . we are proceeding as fast as prudently possible, under the circumstancessss. It would be foolhardy and recklessss to just charge ahead through this chaotic traffic jam!"

She could not make out Dr. Baskin's reply, but it had considerable effect on Akeakemai, whose eyes bulged with an almost human look of surprise. Chagrin overcame the perpetual "smile" that neo-dolphins always seemed to wear.

Sara gently lifted Prity from her lap and put her on the deck. She stood up and began moving toward the conversation, whose intensity grew with each passing dura.

"But-t-t-t—" Akeakemai sputtered. "What about the *Transcendentsss*? Surely they would never allow such a thing to happ-p-pen!"

Allow what to happen, Sara puzzled as she approached. *Oh, what is it now?*

Abruptly, the Niss Machine manifested its holo presence, spinning in midair near Gillian Baskin.

“I have bad news,” it announced. “The gateways have shut down. They are accepting no more candidates from this ingathering swarm.”

“I was afraid of this,” Gillian said. “The subspace disruptions have overcome the gateways’ ability to function. Now the arks will have nowhere to go, piling up just above the surface of the dwarf.”

“The pileup is already taking place, as ever larger numbers of candidate vessels finish their transformations and settle into that low, crowded orbit. However—” The hologram twisted and bowed. “You are wrong about the gateways. They are not dysfunctional. True, they appear to have stopped sending more candidates through to realms beyond. But this is because they now have other tasks in mind.”

“Show us!” Sara demanded, intruding on Gillian’s authority. The older woman nodded, and a multidimensional image sprouted. All objects were represented on a logarithmic scale, allowing events to be seen in vivid, compressed detail.

Down near the white dwarf, giant vessels thronged like a teeming herd of restless beasts, circling ever more tightly around a blazing fire. More streamed in steadily as Sara watched, contributing to a disk that kept spreading and thickening. Each new arrival came seeking passage to the next level. To a fabled place, next to some deep gravity well, where they might transform yet again, and bask in the embrace of mighty tides.

Only the conduits were gone! The needlelike structures had been busily occupied, just moments ago, passing candidates toward their goal. But now the immense devices deserted their stations and could be seen climbing away, abandoning the latecomers to their fate!

The gateways shimmered with inconstant colors that made them seem slippery to the eye, reminding Sara of the *spectral flow*—the desert of psi-active stone, back home on Jijo—where even a single glimpse could send a mind reeling.

Rising steadily away from the dwarf star, each needle plunged through the funnel of descending arks, forcing countless many of them to maneuver wildly out of the way, leaving behind swirls of confusion. Whatever order had remained in the mass pilgrimage swiftly vanished. Massive explosions glittered behind each behemoth, like phosphorescent diatoms, churned in some dark sea when a great beast comes rushing through.

“One of those things is headed almost straight for ussss!” the astrogator cried.

Gillian snapped an order. “Get us out of here, and to *hell* with prudence! Maximum inertial speed!”

Akeakemai responded with an emphatic tail slash. *“Aye!”*

Almost at once, *Streaker*’s engines began groaning with urgency. Sara felt ominous vibrations underfoot, along with a strange tension in her spine as compensating fields struggled to match acceleration.

“You know this is ffffutile, of course,” commented Zub’daki. “Even if we avoid collisions and the Jophur, we still aren’t going to make it-t. *Streaker* would have to be several light-years away in order to escape the coming calamity.”

“What are you talking about?” Sara asked. “What’s coming?”

Before the dolphin astronomer could answer, she stepped back with a gasp.

In the holo display, one of the huge, javelin-shaped gateways could be seen rising rapidly, leaving roiling chaos in its wake, on a course that seemed destined to pass nearby. While trillions died from crashes or fiery detonations, the "gateway" surged blithely onward and upward.

Only now Sara also observed—

"It's *shooting* at some of the ships!"

Indeed, the needle-artifact was apparently not content with disrupting the migration with its backwash. It also flailed out with beams of force, like cruel, glowing lariats, aiming at specific targets as it climbed.

This was no anomaly. All the other gateways were behaving the same way as they hurried away from the white dwarf.

Sara felt Prity take her right hand. Aghast at the orgy of destruction—vastly more bloody and devastating than what had happened at the Fractal World—she could only stare and wonder.

I wish Emerson were here, so we could watch the end together.

Amid the advancing wave of blinding outbursts and detonations, she had time for one more thought before the shimmering monster lashed one more time, reaching toward *Streaker,* with dazzling rays of light.

Forgive me for thinking it—but God . . . it's beautiful . . .

ALVIN'S JOURNAL

How can I express the joy I feel? Or the sorrow that simultaneously fills my tense and throbbing spines?

Sometimes life seems just too ironic. The universe may be shaking apart around us, and yet I've been blessed by Ifni's own good fortune, to find love and strange-warm acceptance among my own kind. Meanwhile, poor old Pincer—whose idea it was to undertake the adventures that eventually brought us here from our wilderness home—met an untimely death at the very threshold of civilization, because he happened to be in the wrong place at the wrong time.

Scout-Major Harry Harms wanted to put out a police alert for the murderer, but Pilot Kaa begged him not to. A full investigation would blow our cover, revealing the presence of dolphins and sooners at Kazzkark. Above all, *Huck* must be protected, as the only living g'Kek survivor outside of Jijo—though she chafes at being put in such a position. Indeed, Huck is the angriest among us, shouting to avenge Pincer, whatever the cost!

I was forced to agree with Kaa. With law and order starting to crumble, it is doubtful that a "full investigation" would amount to very much, anyway.

"I'll put out some feelers," assured Scout-Major Harms. "And unleash ferret programs to look for any Rothen-like images on the monitors, in case Ro-kenn is careless enough to stroll openly along the avenues. But I'll wager he's gone underground. Rothen are notoriously clever at disguises and that sort of thing."

"Or else he may have already taken shelter with one of the great clansss," added Kaa. "Perhaps he is dickering with them right now, to sell out *Streaker* and Jijo."

Against that possibility, Harry asked Kaa to move our little starship over to the docks of the Navigation Institute, sheltering it behind his own, odd-looking craft.

"You must understand, I'd never do this under normal circumstances," he explained. "I took an oath. My first loyalty is to the Institute, and to the Civilization of Five Galaxies." Then Harry shrugged expressively. "But right now it's unclear what that means anymore."

I confess, it was hard at first to watch him speak without umbling out loud! I know it shouldn't surprise me so much to see a chimpanzee talk with sober eloquence. Especially one who stood so straight and tall, with elegant white fur and an enviably agile tail. Clearly, his race has benefited from several more centuries of genetic Uplift since the Tabernacle departed Earth, bringing his mute cousins to Jijo.

"In any event," Major Harms continued. "You have a full set of bio identifications on Ro-kenn, contained in that report you're carrying for the Terragens Council. Perhaps they'll put some of their notorious *interstellar agents* on his trail. I'm sure the bastard will get paid in full for what he's done. Don't you worry."

A bold reassurance. Even Huck seemed a little mollified.

And yet, given what we've heard about the Siege of Terra, how likely is it to come true?

Even before Pincer's death, our glorious fellowship was breaking up.

Last week, Ur-ronn met up with the *p'un m'ang* owners of a freighter—birdlike creatures with bristles instead of wings and no manipulative organs to speak of, except for their beaks. This crew was in a real fix. Their "hired hand" had left them in order to head home during the crisis. They seemed delighted by the chance to hire an urrish replacement, even when Ur-ronn told them her technical education was somewhat lacking.

Since piloting is mostly automatic along the main trade routes, and robots take care of most ordinary tasks, what the crew really needs is someone with intelligence and tactile agility, to pick up stuff, run errands, and pull levers whenever the machines prove too inflexible. That sounds easy enough for a tireless worker like Ur-ronn, whose nimble hands can wrap around any task. It should be like child's play, after slaving away for Uriel, back at Mount Guenn Forge.

I asked Twaphu-anuph to look over the contract with a hoonish bureaucrat's eye for detail, and he declared it satisfactory. The p'un m'ang will drop Ur-ronn off at their third stop, a port where urrish ships stop frequently, and she can make contact with her own kind. Along the way she'll gain experience while earning some credits to spend.

I hope she doesn't hector her poor employers to death with questions.

"At least the ship is warm and dry," Ur-ronn said, after visiting her new employers. "There's none of the Ifni-cursed humidity I had to put up with on the way here! And the p'un m'ang don't smell as bad as Earthlings, either!"

Kaa answered with an amiably derisive spitting sound. The two of them had spent a lot of time together during the journey from Galaxy Four, talking about technology and diverting each other's worries. I doubt I'll ever see a stranger-looking friendship than a water-loving dolphin and a hydrophobic urs, getting along famously.

"I'll keep all three eyes open for an Earthling or Tymbrimi ship to pass this on to," she continued, patting the pouch under her left arm. Inside lay a copy of Gillian Baskin's report, deep-quantum coded for decipherment by the Terragens Council.

(I have another hidden duplicate. Who knows which of us will get through first. Assuming the cosmos cooperates . . . and that Earth survives.)

I felt sad when Ur-ronn set off to depart with the p'un m'ang. Bidding our dear comrade farewell, I wanted to pick her up till all four hooves left the ground, and squeeze her in a full hoonish hug. But I know that our races view such things differently. Urs are not a nostalgic or sentimental people.

Of course Ur-ronn loves Huck and me, in the manner of her kind. Perhaps she will think about us, now and then, with passing fondness.

But her life will soon be busy and focused.

She will never miss us nearly as much as we already miss her.

Such is the world.

As Ur-ronn departed, another companion returned to me.

After miduras of intense questioning, Dwer finally got what he wanted from Mudfoot. At last the little noor *spoke,* confessing the truth of what we had supposed all along—that centuries ago some Tymbrimi planted an illicit colony of their beloved clients on Jijo. Although most noor are born silent and partly devolved, a secret group among them retained fully uplifted mental powers. They are *tytlal.*

Mudfoot agreed to provide Dwer with code words and phrases that will bring the secret ones out of hiding. This was Dwer's price for letting the creature go. Mudfoot's aim now is to make contact somehow with the Tymbrimi and inform them what's happened on Jijo. Since that goal is compatible with my own, the little fellow will accompany me when I journey onward.

Dwer seems satisfied. Indeed, I think his chief aim was to get the best of Mudfoot, just once, before he and Kaa set course on their long voyage back to Jijo.

Before everything comes apart.

The Five Galaxies rock and shudder as the moment of sundering approaches.

With space quakes intensifying, and cracks spreading through the ancient planetoid's walls, it grows apparent that even isolated Kazzkark will be no refuge against the coming convulsions. Already the refugee flow has reversed, as more ships and sapients leave than arrive.

With half the normal space lanes already disrupted, many folks are using the remaining stable routes to head home, while there's still time. Or else a life sustaining planet to land upon, and live, even if the stars of heaven recede out of reach.

Among those departing, the most singular looking are acolytes dressed in robes of blue and gold, spreading the gospel of a bizarre faith—one that focuses on salvation for *individuals,* not races. A creed in which *Earth* plays the central dramatic role, as *martyr planet.*

A sect that proclaims love for Terra, while joyous over its crucifixion.

I have no idea if the same message has been preached in a million other locales, or by just the one Skiano apostle. Either way, the cult seems to have struck a chord that resonates in these troubled times. Fanning across space to spread the word, these missionaries seemed eager to take advantage of the chaos, and the shakiness of more ancient faiths.

At the center of it all, acting as the Skiano's chief aide and majordomo, is *Rety,* the young human female who once seemed such an untamed savage, even on remote Jijo. Transformed by surgery and new garments, she beckons and commands the converts—even sophisticated starfarers—like some haughty lord of an ancient patron clan.

And they take it! Bowing respectfully, even when the parrot on her shoulder squawks irreverently caustic remarks.

I've never seen a human act more confident, or more arrogantly assured of her status.

Meanwhile, the Skiano himself paces slowly, an eerie light flickering in one set of eyes, while the other pair appears to stare at distant horizons.

Naturally, Dwer has failed persuading Rety to leave this fanatical group. She would not even budge when Harry Harms offered a transit pass to one of the most secure Earthling colonies, a place called Garth, located far from the current troubles, where she might possibly find safety and comfort with her own kind.

Harry and Dwer both express frustration. But frankly, I find Rety's adamant resolution understandable. She has learned how pleasant it can be to find a sense of importance and belonging among people who value you.

So have I.

It's nearly time to put down my journal. Dor-hinuf expects me at her parents' dwelling, where members of the local hoon community will gather again for an evening of dinner and poetry. A normal enough occurrence, back home on Jijo, but apparently quite daring and new among my star-god relations.

I must paw through the box of books I brought from Jijo and select tonight's reading. Last time, we had some Melville and Cousteau, but it seems that human authors are a difficult reach for many of these civilized hoons. I expect it will take a while for me to teach them the merits of Jules Verne and Mark Twain.

Mostly, they want me to umble from the odes of Chuph-wuph'iwo and Phwhoon-dau, singing melodramatically about taut sails straining against sturdy masts, defying wind and salt spray as a knifelike prow cleaves bravely through some gale-swollen reach. My father would be proud to know that the hoonish literary renaissance of Jijo, so long eclipsed by Earthling authors, is at last finding an eager audience among our distant, starfaring cousins.

It is most gratifying. And yet, I wonder.

How can this be?

Consider the irony! Huck and I always dreamed of how romantic and wonderful it would be to go flitting about in spaceships. But these civilized hoons only see starcraft as conveyances—dull and uncomfortable implements for travel between assignments—as they plod through the routine destiny assigned to our kind long ago by our Guthatsa patrons.

So what makes them receptive *now,* to umbles of hope and joy? Is it the growing chaos outside? Or was something lying in wait all along, sleeping underneath a dark shell of oppressive, bureaucratic unhappiness?

Can it really be the simple image of a sailboat that triggers an awakening, a stirring deep inside?

If so, the elation might have lain buried forever. No *civilized* hoon would willingly risk life and limb at sea, chiding their children to reflexively avoid such places. The mere thought would be dismissed as absurd. The accounts would not balance. Averse to risk, they would never give it a try.

Besides, what hoon can swim? Nothing in our ancestral tree would logically suggest the way hoonish spines frickle at the sight of wintry icebergs on a storm-serrated horizon, or the musical notes that rope and canvas sing, like a mother umbling to her child.

Only on Jijo was this discovered, once our settler ancestors abandoned their star-god tools, along with all the duties and expectations heaped on us by the Guthatsa.

In fairness, perhaps our patrons meant well. After all, we owe them for our sapient minds. Galactic society sets a stern standard that most elder races follow, when uplifting their clients toward sober, dependable adulthood. The Guthatsa took our strongest racial traits—loyalty, duty, devotion to family—and used them to set us down a single narrow course. Toward prudent, obsessive responsibility.

And yet, only now are Dor-hinuf and her people learning how our patrons cheated us. Robbing our greatest treasure. One that we only recovered by playing hooky . . . by ditching class and heading for the river.

To Jijo, where hoons at last reclaimed what had been stolen.

Our childhood.

LARK

The transcendence gateways appeared to have finished their migration, climbing outward from their former position near the surface of a white dwarf star. Now all the huge, needle-shaped devices glistened in much higher orbits, beyond the outer fringes of the candidates' swarm.

The distance traveled was a short one, as space journeys went. But in crossing it, they created murderous bedlam.

Below lay a roiling cauldron of fire and confusion, as millions of vast spacecraft fought desperately for survival. Already disordered by chaos waves, all the prim spiral traffic lanes were now completely unraveled, curling and splitting into myriad turbulent eddies. Engine resonances intersected and interfered, creating mutual-attraction fields, yanking vessels suddenly toward each other. When one giant ark-blob veered to avoid a neighbor, that brought yet another hurtling toward explosive impact.

Eruptions seemed to coruscate up and down the densely packed funnel, converting what had formerly been sentient matter into white plasma flame.

As if intending to make matters worse, each of the titanic needles also *lashed out* during its brief voyage, using beams of fierce brightness to seize several dozen spacecraft, chosen apparently at random, dragging them like calves at the end of a lariat.

Among the unchosen, those who brushed accidentally against the tendril-beams were instantly vaporized.

Why? Lark asked, appalled by the sight. *Why did they do it?*

He was counting on Ling for an explanation, since she had once been a starfarer and had spent more time exploring the Transcendents' Data Mesh. But on this occasion, she was equally astonished and aghast.

I . . . cannot begin to guess . . . Unless they already had their quota of candidates, and decided that any more would he superfluous . . . Or else maybe the chaos waves are getting too strong, and they had to give up trying to send more nominees through to the next level.

He shook his head, dislodging one of the symbionts that had taken residence there recently, devouring his last hair follicles.

But that doesn't explain the callous disregard for life! Those are sapient beings down there! Quadrillions of them! Every one was a member of some ancient race that had studied and improved itself diligently for ages just to get here. . . .

Ling took his arm and stroked it, pressing herself against him for the warm comfort it provided them both.

Even so, Lark, they were still like animals, compared to the Transcendents. Expendable. Especially if their destruction might serve a higher purpose.

He blinked several times.

Higher purpose? What purpose could possibly justify—

He cut off as a new presence began making itself known, groping toward them across the mental byways of the mesh. Soon, Lark recognized a familiar presence—one that had formerly been his teacher . . . then an enemy . . . and was now simply a friend.

"X," the modified traeki, had been doing some independent exploration, and now wanted to report its findings.

The Jophur have despaired of ever returning to their clan, or accomplishing their mission. Moreover, they realize they have very little time. Soon, the macroentity that we now are part of—what you call "Mother"—will complete its conquest of the Polkjhy by breaking into the engineering section, where the former crew have made their last redoubt. When that happens, they will cease to be Jophur—at least by their own narrow definition.

Before that happens, they have decided to embark on a dramatic and conclusive course of action. A final act of vengeance.

Lark cast his mind outward, visualizing the once mighty battleship and its surroundings. Whether by luck or by dauntless piloting skill, *Polkjhy* had apparently succeeded in escaping the candidates' swarm. Only tattered outskirts of the whirling disk lay between them and deep space—a starry night sky that *rippled,* every now and then, with shivering waves of chaos. The prospect of flight beckoned, now that a getaway path seemed clear. But *Polkjhy*'s remaining crew members knew it could never be. Mother would absorb them into the new hybrid existence, long before they reached the first transfer point. Assuming the t-point was still usable.

Engine noises rumbled through the liquid environment, carrying notes of deep resolve. Lark sensed *Polkjhy*'s trajectory—and realized it was aimed almost straight toward one of the gleaming needle-gateways!

Throughout all this struggle and confusion, the Jophur kept tenaciously—even single-mindedly—to their original purpose. They never lost track of the Earthling ship.

Now it lay dead ahead, ensnared by the Transcendents in a webbery of light.

Casting his viewpoint outward, Lark verified that each great needle was now surrounded by clusters of captive starcraft, wrapping them in layer after layer of lambent windings. No reason or purpose for this strange activity could be learned by sifting the mesh, but soon Lark noticed that a faint resonance seemed to echo from one of the confined vessels.

Something familiar.

Ling joined his efforts and together they focused closer, until something *clicked* and the circuits abruptly filled with jagged sonic patterns.

A *human voice,* somber but grimly determined.

". . . we repeat. This is not a destiny of our choosing. We are not legitimate members of the candidate swarm. Nor are we part of the retired life order. We have no business in the Embrace of Tides, nor do we wish to experience any form of transcendence at this time.

"Duty calls us back to Galaxy Two. Please let us go! We humbly request that you let us flee this doomed place, while there is still time.

"Again, we repeat. This is not a destiny of our choosing. . . ."

Lark felt the traeki's mental touch, sharing thoughts that seemed to slither, like smooth rivulets of dripping wax.

How interesting. Apparently the Terrans have been selected to perform some honored task. Some chore or service deemed worthwhile by the highest overminds. Yet, they petition to escape this distinction, resuming their forlorn plight in a world of danger and sorrows!

Meanwhile, the remaining Jophur send Polkjhy charging ahead with but one thought in mind—to deny the Earthlings any taste of a transcendence they have not earned!

A confrontation looms. One that should prove interesting to observe.

Lark appreciated the traeki's sense of detachment, even though the most likely outcome was for *Polkjhy* to be swatted aside—vaporized—like some irritating gnat, by powers unimaginably more powerful.

He considered ways to avoid this undesired end.

I wonder if it might be possible for us to communicate with Streaker, via the mesh.

Ling nodded.

I don't see why not. If only for a few moments.

Their traeki friend also agreed.

i/we have our/my own reasons to wish this. Let us work together and strive to achieve that connection.

HARRY

When one of the big South Pole galleries suddenly collapsed—blowing several thousand gasping tenants into deadly vacuum—the high officials in dominion over Kazzkark finally gave in to the inevitable. They issued the long-awaited directive.

Evacuate!

"My research—sifting through the oldest, most ambiguity-protected archives in the Great Library—indicates that conditions were probably similar during the Gronin Collapse," Wer'Q'quinn explained when Harry reported for his last assignment.

From a high balcony at Navigation Institute HQ, they watched as crowds thronged down the main arcades toward various egress ports, streaming to reclaim the starships that had brought them here. Meanwhile, Wer'Q'quinn waved a languid pseudopod and continued contemplating the past.

"Then, as now, the Institutes went into denial at first. Later, under instructions from higher life orders, they concealed the truth from most of our civilization until it was too late for any concerted preparation. Indeed, an identical scenario would have repeated this time, if not for the recent warning that was broadcast from Earth. Without it, most of the races in the Five Galaxies would have had scarcely any chance to get ready."

"A lot of clans chose to ignore the warning," Harry groused. "Some are too busy *attacking* Earth to listen."

After a gloomy silence, he went on.

"I don't suppose there's any chance that all these spatial disturbances will affect the Siege of Terra, is there?"

Wer'Q'quinn swiveled a squidlike gaze toward the chimpanzee scout, as if scrutinizing him for any sign of wavering loyalty.

"That seems unlikely. We estimate that up to thirty percent of the t-points in Galaxy Two will remain at least partly functional. Of course, during the worst part of the crisis, metric backlash will convulse every level of hyperspace. Woe unto any vessel that tries to undergo pseudoacceleration while *that* is going on! But this should scarcely inconvenience the great battleships presently surrounding your ancestral solar system. They will be safe, so long as they remain in normal space, and refrain from using probability weapons until the rupture is over.

"Naturally, we expect the effects will be far more severe in Galaxy Four."

Harry nodded. "Which is exactly where you're sending me."

"Would you withdraw? I can send another."

"Oh, yeah? *Who* else are you gonna find who's willing to enter E Space at a time like this?"

Wer'Q'quinn's answer was eloquent silence. Of his remaining staff, only Harry had the experience—and talents—to hold any hope of success in that bizarre realm of living ideas.

"Well," Harry grunted. "Why the hell not, eh? You say I should have time enough to lay down new instrument packages along the Path, from here to Galaxy Four, and still make it back before the crisis hits?"

"It will be close," Wer'Q'quinn averred. "But we have supplemented our traditional calculations with new estimates, utilizing wolfling techniques of mathematical incantation that were contained in the message from Earth. Both methods appear to agree. The main rupture should not take place till after you safely return."

Another long silence stretched.

"Of course, I would've gone anyway," Harry said at last, in a gruff voice.

A low sigh. A nervous curling of tentacles.

"I know you would."

"For the Five Galaxies," Harry added.

"Yes." Wer'Q'quinn's voice faltered. "For the Civilization of . . . Five Galaxies."

Down on the boulevards of Kazzkark, the worst of the exodus appeared to be over. While gleaners sifted through dross and wreckage from so many hurried departures, Harry strode along with a floating donkey-drone, bearing capsules to deposit in E Space for Wer'Q'quinn. Telemetry from these packages might reveal more about the strains now pulling apart the connective tissue of space. Perhaps next time—in a hundred million years or so—people might understand things a little better.

And there *would* be a next time. As the universe expanded, ever more of the ancient "flaws" that linked galaxy to galaxy would stretch, then break. After each sundering transition, the number of surviving t-points would be smaller, their connections less rich, and the speedy lanes of hyperspace become that much more inaccessible.

As it ages, the cosmos is becoming a less interesting, more dangerous place. Everything must have seemed so close and easy in the Progenitors' day. A time of magic, when it was almost trivial to conjure a path between any two points in seventeen linked galaxies.

He squared his shoulders back.

Oh, well. At least I get to take part in something important. Even if Wer'Q'quinn is exaggerating my chances of getting home again.

Kazzkark had seemed so immaculate when he first arrived here from training school. Now a dusty haze pervaded the corridors, shaken from the walls by quakes and chaos waves, which rattled this entire sector at ever narrower intervals. They had grown so frequent, in fact, that he hardly noticed most of them anymore.

It just goes to show, even the abnormal can get to seem normal, after a while.

Approaching the dockyards, he witnessed a large party of hoonish clerks and their families, carrying luggage and tugging hover-carts, preparing to board a transport for one of their homeworlds. The queue was orderly, as you would expect from a hoonish procession. Yet, something appeared different about this group. They seemed less dour, more animated, than others of their kind.

It's their clothes! Harry realized, all at once. *Alvin's got them wearing Hawaiian shirts!*

Indeed, roughly a third of the hulking bipeds had set aside the more typical robes of boring white or silver and draped themselves instead with tunics bearing garish prints of flowers and tropical ferns—split down the back to leave room for their craggy spines. Umbling as they waited patiently in line, the group made every nearby corridor reverberate with tones that seemed far livelier than the dirge-like chants usually heard from hoons.

One GalSix trill-phrase, in particular, caused Harry to stumble.

If I didn't know better, I'd swear that translates into Anglic as "heigh ho!"

Some of the older hoons looked on all this with perplexed—even miffed—expressions. But toward the front there stood a crowd of youths—*teenagers,* he noted—who boomed out the refrain with enthusiastic bellows of their bulging throat sacs.

A cheerful ballad about transition, and eagerness for new vistas.

Over in a corner, shuffling behind the hoons, stood a strange figure, looking like a short, shabby Jophur. It was *Tyug,* the traeki alchemist from Jijo, accompanying Alvin on the next phase of his adventure.

Harry tried to catch Alvin's eye as he walked past, but the lad was fully immersed, enjoying his role as the out-of-town boy who had come to stir things up. With Dor-hinuf close to his side, and a pair of mini-tytlal lounging on his broad shoulders, Alvin leaned against a loosely wrapped shipping crate, feigning nonchalance while keeping a close vigil over its contents.

One edge of the tarpaulin shifted as Harry watched. From the darkness within, a single *eye* drifted upward at the end of a waving stalk. Another tried to follow, squeezing through to twist and stare at the surroundings.

Without pausing in the umble song, Alvin silently used one burly hand to grab both wayward eyes and cram them back inside. Then he tied the tarp down firmly. The crate shuddered, as if someone inside were rolling back and forth in protest. But Alvin only leaned harder until things settled down.

"Ahoy!" shouted a hoon at the front of the queue, when the portal opened at last, leading to their ship. "Avast back there. Here we go!"

Harry tried holding it in. He struggled hard and managed to make it fifty meters farther along before his splitting sides could take it no longer. Then he ducked around a stony corner, sagged against the nearest wall, and guffawed.

The Official Docks were nearly deserted. Dignitaries of the Library, Migration, Commerce, and War Institutes had already scurried off, leaving empty moorings. Only Wer'Q'quinn's busy teams remained on duty, rushing forth on rescue missions, or using beacons to guide traffic around danger zones. Noble work. Harry's own days might be better spent that way, helping save lives and patching the raveled skeins of Galactic society. After the main rupture event, NavInst must promote recovery by getting trade going again.

But Wer'Q'quinn saved me for this mission. I guess the old octopus knows what he's doing.

Ahead lay Harry's venerable observation platform, designed for cruising the memic jungles of E Space. Although this mission was bound to be the most dangerous yet, Harry found his footsteps speeding up, drawn by strange eagerness.

Humming under his breath, he recognized the same melody Alvin's new in-laws had been umbling as they prepared to depart.

It seemed a catchy tune.
Good for traveling.
A song of anticipation.

More chaos waves struck the planetoid while he was busy loading Wer'Q'quinn's instruments into the hold. Ancient stone walls groaned with resonant vibrations, causing the ship's decks and bulkhead to vibrate violently. Harry had to scoot out of the way when an unsecured crate toppled from an upper shelf. Thanks to Kazzkark's slight pseudogravity, he managed to avoid getting crushed, but the box smashed hard, spilling delicate parts across the floor.

While sweeping up, he listened for the wailing siren to announce a vacuum breach. Only after several duras passed did his fur settle down. Apparently, the dock seals were holding—for now.

Harry stepped outside to visit the stocky little Thennanin-built star cruiser that lay parked behind his station. Stepping through its airlock, he shouted for the pilot.

"Kaa! You ready to ship out? I'll be outta here in less than a midura, if you're still thinking of tagging along."

The sleek gray dolphin emerged from his control cubicle, riding atop a six-legged machine. Kaa was starting to look weary. It had been weeks since he'd had a swim. Aside from rest periods in a narrow water tank, he'd spent most of that time lying on the float bed of a walker-drone.

"It'sss not soon enough for me," the pilot hissed. "Alassss, I'm stuck waiting here till Dwer returns."

Harry glanced around.

"Aw hell," he grunted. "*Now* where's Dwer gone off to?"

Another voice spoke up from a rear doorway, uttering Anglic words with unctuous, almost seductive tones.

"Well, well. I would surmise that the young human is trying—yes, one more time!—to persuade his female counterpart—Rety—to come along. Would you not guess it so?"

Kiwei Ha'aoulin emerged from one of the tiny cabins, working past a pile of supplies tied down by cargo netting. The Synthian had pressed to accompany Kaa, despite warnings that it would surely be a one-way trip. In fact, each admonition just heightened her resolve. Kiwei even offered to finance all the food and other items needed for Kaa's voyage.

She did not believe that a so-called "great rupture" was imminent.

"These disturbances will pass," she had blithely assured. "I am not saying everything will go back to normal. While the Institutes and great clans spend centuries sorting things out, they will be lax about enforcing minor rules against little sooner colonies—or against smuggling! Can't you scent business opportunities in this? I shall serve as Jijo's commercial agent, yes! In utter secrecy and confidence, as off-planet liaison for the Six-or-Seven Races, I will market primitive autochthonous implements on the collectors' market, and make us all quite rich!"

Harry had watched greed battle typical Synthian caution. Eventually, Kiwei resolved the conflict by entering a state of pure denial, blithely rejecting any notion that upheavals might change the cosmos in fundamental ways. Harry felt guilty about giving in to her request. But a Synthian trader could be obstinately tenacious, wearing down all opposition. Besides, Kaa needed the supplies.

Kiwei stepped over the crude caricature that Pincer-Tip had carved in the metal deck—a chilling image of the qheuen's murderer, who had probably departed Kazzkark by now, plotting more mischief.

"Indeed, Dwer went after Rety. I was monitoring comm channels, moments ago, when an urgent message came through from the boy."

Kaa thrashed his tail. "You didn't t-tell me!"

"Pilot, you seemed well occupied with pre-takeoff checklists and such. Besides, I had it in mind to go now and help the young human, myself! Generous, yes? Would you care to come along, Scout-Major Harms?"

Harry squirmed. His launch window would be optimum in a midura. Still, if the boy was in trouble . . . "Did Dwer say what's the matter?" The Synthian rubbed her belly—a nervous gesture.

"The message was unclear. Apparently, he feels urgent action is needed, or the girl will not survive."

They tracked the young Jijoan to a nearby warehouse chamber, crouching behind a pile of abandoned crates.

Wearing a dark cloak and a frustrated expression, he gazed at a gathering of sapients, about forty meters away.

Empty cargo containers had been festooned with blue and gold draperies, a convivial backdrop for the big Skiano missionary, who stood surrounded by about two dozen acolytes from almost as many races. The Skiano's head jutted above most followers, resembling a massive ship's prow. One pair of eyes gleamed ceaselessly, as if lighting the way into a warm night.

Most of the proselytes had already dispersed to far reaches of civilized space, spreading their exceptional message of personal salvation, but this remnant group remained by their leader, chanting hymns that chilled Harry's spine.

"What's up?" he asked Dwer, stepping past him. Harry quickly spotted Rety, a small human figure, sitting apart from the others, her face lit by the glow of a portable computer.

"Watch out!" Dwer snapped, seizing Harry's collar and yanking him back hard.

"Hey!" Harry complained—till several small projectiles pelted a nearby crate, sending splinters flying.

He blinked. "Someone's shooting at us!"

Dwer hazarded a glimpse back around the corner, then motioned it was okay for Harry and Kiwei to rejoin him. He pointed toward a pair of blue-clad acolytes—a *gello* and a *paha*—standing protectively near the dais, glaring with expressions of clear warning. Both races had been uplifted to be warriors, with innate talents for violent conflict. Though now dedicated to a religion of peace, these individuals had been assigned a task worthy of their gifts. While the gello brandished a metal-tipped staff, the paha sported a simple device on one arm—a wrist catapult, like the one Dwer was seen wearing earlier.

"Interesting," Kiwei said. "Disallowed more sophisticated weaponry, they swiftly caught on to the advantages of wolfling arts. No doubt Rety taught them. Perhaps their new faith disposes them to be more open-minded than most."

Harry shrugged aside Kiwei's foolish commentary.

"They don't want us comin' any closer. Why?" he asked Dwer.

"I was warned not to bother Rety anymore. They said I was *distracting* her. They can't bring themselves to kill a sacred Earthling. But since 'it is the Terran destiny to suffer for us all,' they won't mind shattering a bone or two. I'd be careful, if I were you."

Harry's frustration flared.

"Look, Dwer, we don't have much time. Rety's decided to stay with folks who'll love an' take care of her. That's a lot more than most folks have in this universe, and better odds than she'd have coming with us! It's time to let her make her own choices."

Dwer nodded. "Normally, I'd agree. Rety's been a pain. I'd like nothing better than to see her make it on her own. There's just one problem. Things may not be quite the way you just described 'em."

Harry's eyebrows arched.

"Oh? How's that?"

In reply, Dwer pointed.

"Look to the right, beyond the platform. See something there? Beyond that curtain?"

Blowing another sigh, Harry peered toward a flowing veil of colorful fabric between two massive pillars, just past the Skiano's meditating followers. "What're you talkin' about? I don't get . . ."

He paused. Something *moved* back there. At first, the outlines reminded him of an angular machine, with sharp edges for cutting, slicing. Then an errant gust blew the drapes harder against the object, revealing a stark, mantis-like outline.

"Ifni's boss . . ." Harry murmured. "What's a Tandu lurking back there for?"

Of one thing he felt sure—no Tandu would ever join the Skiano's heresy! Immortality of some abstract "soul" could not appeal like a chance to crush enemies or impose their racial will on a recalcitrant cosmos. Till now, constraints of ritual and law kept such impulses in check—Tandu seldom killed openly without a veneer of Galactic legality. But what if civilization collapsed? There were rumors of secret bases, filled with countless warrior eggs, ready to hatch at a moment's notice.

"Why are the paha and gello just standing there?" he wondered aloud. "They must not realize—"

Kiwei interrupted.

"They do realize. Note how they keep their backs toward the curtain, as if to ignore what's beyond. Clearly, they have orders. The Tandu is here for some approved purpose!"

Purpose? Harry tugged nervously on his thumbs . . . till he had an idea.

"Kiwei, hand me your data plaque. I want to try something."

The Synthian complied, and Harry started mumbling commands into the handheld unit. Using his authority, he ordered ferret programs to search for transmissions emanating from Rety's computer. With luck, he would soon—

"Got it!" he announced, while his companions crowded close. On a split screen, the left side abruptly revealed the young Jijoan woman, her visage smoothed by recent surgery. On the right, they saw copies of the charts that had her attention transfixed.

"What now?" Dwer asked. "Use this link to speak to her? I guarantee she'll just get angry and cut us off."

Harry shrugged. "I was hopin' to spy a little first." He studied the image on the right. "It looks like a list of planets where their cult recently sent missionaries. Most are trading worlds, with good spatial contacts and cosmopolitan cultures that don't oppress odd points of view. These folks are clever. But I don't see what this has to do with—"

He cut off as an expression of smug pleasure crossed Rety's face. She spoke with clear satisfaction.

"This one's perfect!"

The picture jiggled as she stood, slinging the computer under one arm. Harry caught blurry glimpses of blue draperies, and the faces of squatting acolytes, staring at some far horizon. The scene steadied when Rety came to a halt and spoke loudly, to be heard above the murmuring chant.

"Master, I've chosen my own place. See? I have it listed right here!"

The camera view swung around to face upward, briefly catching the image of a colorful Earthling parrot, pacing on a massive shoulder. Then Rety corrected her aim, facing the screen straight at the Skiano's imposing head. Beyond the ram-like chin, its upper brace of eyes shone like headlamps, aimed at posterity, while the lower pair roved in search of final truth.

Rety continued. "It's Z'ornup! I'm sure you've heard of the place. It has just the right atmosphere and all that stuff, so's I can stay healthy. There's also a human trading post, in case I ever need others of my kind—which ain't likely, but I guess it's better not to close off all my options, right?

"Anyway, you already sent a small mission there, but I see the planet sits in a good spot, with lots of space trails leading in all directions, where we can send any new converts we recruit. With all that going for it, I figure Z'ornup needs a higher-level apostle, right? That's someone like me! I'll use the last commercial shuttle headin' for Galaxy Three. It leaves in half a midura, so with your permission—"

The Skiano's unwavering stare dimmed at last. The bottom set of eyes turned down to regard Rety.

"Such a posting is beneath you, my dear wolfling child. I will not have you sullied by mundane chores, proselytizing and breathing the same air as unbelievers."

"But I—"

"There is a reward that awaits the worthy," the missionary continued, intoning with a remote, pontifical voice. "It was alluded to by your own saints and prophets, long ago. By Jesus and Isaiah and Mohammed and Buddha . . . in fact, by all the great sages of your blessed-cursed race, whose suffering in darkness allowed them to see what remained hidden to all those living in the light."

"I know that, Master. So let me go forth and spread the word to—"

"Of course, those prophets made errors in recording what they saw. How could they accurately chronicle such glory with crude ink and paper, using languages that were little more than animal-like grunts? Nevertheless, destiny has spoken. The beacon they lit will ignite other pyres, spreading the heat of truth everywhere, even as ruins topple around us."

"I agree! So now let me—"

"But alas, I will not see that promised land, that apotheosis. Like Moses, I must halt before entering a mere temporal Valhalla. My labors have exhausted this poor flesh. It is time to seek the recompense that I was offered in a dream. To bypass the routine of Purgatory and proceed directly to Paradise!"

Rety's response was quick and restless.

"That's great. Happy travelin'. Now about Z'ornup—"

"My reward beckons," the Skiano went on, ponderously. "A personal salvation much finer than the Embrace of Tides. And yet . . . I cannot shake an uneasy premonition. Have I done everything required? What if I arrive only to learn the heavenly gatekeepers do not recognize my strange face and body? After all this time devoted only to Earthlings, are they quite ready to receive nonhuman souls in Heaven?"

The prow-shaped head rocked from left to right.

"It occurs to me that the gatekeepers will be more accommodating if I arrive escorted, with an entourage of those who will testify on my behalf . . ."

The image on the screen wavered, as if the hands holding it suddenly trembled from realization, even as the rhythmic chanting reached its final climax and faded into echoes. Rety's voice came hoarse and nervous.

"This 'trip' you've been talkin' about . . . it's not to another preaching mission, is it? You're plannin' to die!"

The answer made Harry shiver.

"To abandon this shell, yes. Accompanied by converts, to demonstrate my worthiness . . . plus a human; a true wolfling from the martyr world, to vouch for me in front of all the angels and saints."

Harry's shoulder was jogged, so hard that he nearly fell over. Dwer clutched his arm, squeezing with great force. He pointed.

"The curtain . . ."

Kiwei uttered a low moan as the shrouding drapes fell, revealing a regal Tandu warrior, painted and accoutered for ritual slaughter, advancing toward the acolytes with six arms upraised, brandishing glinting blades.

Instead of leaping to defense, both of the soldier-disciples—the gello and paha—joined their fellow converts in a crescent-shaped formation, waiting quietly with their leader centered before them.

Rety, now struggling in the Skiano's adamant embrace, abruptly stiffened and let out a soft cry, staring upward in aghast awe while the parrot squawked, flapping overhead.

"Summon police drones!" Kiwei urged. "This ceremony is not entirely voluntary. I will attest to it!"

As if that'd do any good, Harry mused as he ran forward, following Dwer's more rapid footsteps. *The law is crumbling. Anyway, help would never get here in time.*

Worse, Harry realized, groping at his hip where his sidearm sometimes lay holstered. *Sure enough. Left it on the station.*

In which case, a mighty good question would be exactly what he and Dwer hoped to accomplish by rushing toward the debacle, except to join the Tandu's ceremonial mincing session!

The Jijoan youth slid to a halt just twenty meters from the assembled devotees. Flinging his cloak aside, Dwer lifted the compound bow he had brought from his faraway home, with an arrow nocked and ready.

"Those are mine!" the Synthian shrieked from far behind, more offended by theft than ritual murder-suicide. "You stole them from my compartment. I demand they be returned at once, or I shall file a complaint!"

In the time it took Kiwei to babble that absurd threat, the Tandu finished approaching its scheduled victims, lifting several blades high—and Dwer loosed three arrows in rapid succession.

Harry reached out for the young hunter.

"You can't harm a Tandu that way! It has no single weak spot to disable—"

He stopped as the little missiles seemed to veer off course. Instead of hitting the executioner, they missed by a wide margin and struck the Skiano instead! Two dark eyes were extinguished by plunging bolts of wood and stone. A third arrow vanished down the missionary's throat, when he opened it to scream.

The Skiano's white arms convulsed. For an instant, only one of the four clutched Rety—and she chomped down on the remaining hand with her teeth. Slipping free of his spasmodic grasp, she ducked down to avoid being seized by the paha, then swerved in an unexpected direction, *under and between the Tandu's spiky legs!*

Harry waved his arms.

"Over here! Run!"

A terrifying noise escaped the Tandu. Hired under certain conditions, it had come armed only with weapons appropriate for a formally pious sacrifice. Resistance was not part of the bargain. This amounted to breach of contract!

Its bellow resonated down the hallways of Kazzkark, calling for comrades to come avenge this insult. Meanwhile, one blade flicked to remove the paha's head.

The husky gello warrior reacted impulsively by swinging its metal-edged staff, crushing one of the Tandu's forelegs, then another, before its own turn came for skewering upon a scalpel-like edge. Meanwhile, two more acolytes—a flying *glououvis* and claw-footed *zyu8*—also lost sight of the purpose of the gathering. Responding to ancient loathings, they launched themselves at the Tandu, to peck at it from above and below while dodging its flailing knives.

Amid this pandemonium, Dwer kept firing arrows, taking out the giant mantis-like creature's sensory stalks, one at a time.

Harry thought of telling Dwer to save his ammo. That tactic seldom worked against Tandu. But then Rety finally broke free of the melee and bolted toward the edge of the raised platform. Sensing freedom just ahead, she took two long steps, making ready to leap.

Harry's throat caught as he saw the Tandu reach after her. The razor-sharp sword already dripped with multicolored gore.

A new swarm of chaos waves struck. The floor convulsed, bucking like a wounded animal. Dust clouds poured from shuddering walls and gay banners billowed before a rising wind. In the distance, a siren wailed.

Harry staggered, watching helplessly as Rety teetered at the rim of the heaving platform, then sprawled over the edge amid a flailing of frantic arms and legs.

He tried rushing forward to catch her—knowing he would be too late.

Till the moment her head struck pavement, Rety was defiant. She neither cried out nor moaned, refusing to give the universe any satisfaction—least of all by whimpering about bad luck.

GILLIAN

Lucifer means "Light bearer."

The thought came unbeckoned, while shimmering luminance poured in through a nearby window, playing across her face.

Angels are bright . . . though not always good. The sight before her reminded Gillian how many beautiful and terrifying sights she had witnessed during recent months and years. And how many deep assumptions she'd been forced to revise.

For instance, she recalled that time, deep within a twisty transfer point, when the Earthling crew had confronted the *Great Harrower* as it sifted among countless starcraft, choosing a fraction to aim toward transcendence. That huge glowing specter had reminded Gillian of some mighty seraph, culling the virtuous from the wicked, on Judgment Day. No one was more surprised than she when the blinding ball of energy seemed to identify *Streaker* amid a crowd of passing vessels, plucking the Earthship and setting it aside for some purpose the Harrower never bothered to explain.

Perhaps now we'll find out, she thought. Indeed, there appeared to be a definite family resemblance between that earlier "angel" and the giant needle-gateway now holding *Streaker in* thrall, spinning out radiant tendrils that snaked amorously around several dozen selected spacecraft. The behavior reminded Gillian unpleasantly of a spider, busy wrapping living morsels, preserving them for later.

All the other ensnared ships parked nearby were vast arks filled with merged hydro-and oxy-life-forms—true transcendence candidates—yanked from the maelstrom surrounding the white dwarf. *Streaker* was minuscule by comparison—a tiny caterpillar next to oversized beach balls. Yet, she now wore her own blanket of shiny, billowing strands.

"The material is unknown," commented Hannes Suessi. "I cannot even get a decent reading with my instruments."

The Niss Machine hazarded a guess.

"Someone may have had this in mind for us all along. Even back at the Fractal World. The coating we received there could be meant to serve as a buffer—or perhaps glue—between our fragile metal hull and this new substance . . . whatever it is."

Gillian shook her head.

"Perhaps it's another kind of protective armor."

Silence stretched for several seconds as they all turned to look at the rearward-facing view screen. Everyone clearly shared the same dour thought.

Something was about to happen soon. Something that called for "protection" on a scale formerly unimaginable.

At least the earlier orgy of destruction appeared to be over, down below where millions of space vessels once cruised in prim columns and well-ordered rows, like polite pilgrims seeking redemption at a shrine. That procession had been smashed, crushed, pureed. Now, only an occasional flash told of some surviving "candidate" finally succumbing to forces that had already pulverized millions of others, leaving a turbid stew of gas, dust, and ions.

A roiling funnel now surrounded the ancient stellar remnant, shrouding its small, white disk beneath black streamers and turbulent haze.

According to Zub'daki, that whirling cloud had special dynamical properties. It would not orbit for long, or even spiral inward gradually, over the course of weeks or years.

"The debris storm has almost no net angular momentum," the dolphin astronomer announced. "As collisional mixing continues, all the varied tangential velocities will cancel out. When that happens, the whole mass will collapse inward, nearly all at once!"

Asked when this infall might occur, the dolphin scientist had predicted.

"Sssoon. And when it does, we'll be at ground zero for the greatest show in all the cosmossss."

Staring at that murky tornado—comprising the pulverized hopes of countless races and individual beings—Gillian's crewmates knew the show would begin shortly. Akeakemai whistled a dubious sigh, getting back to Gillian's original question.

"Protective armor . . . againsssst what's coming?" The dolphin switched languages to express his doubts in Trinary.

• *When the great gods,*
    • *In their puissance,*
• *Start believing,*
    • *Their own slogans—*

• *Or their wisdom,*
    • *Omniscient,*
• *Or their power,*
    • *Invincible—*

• *That's when nature,*
    • *Wise and patient,*
• *Teaches deities,*
    • *A lesson—*

• *That's when nature,*
    • *Keen and knowing,*
• *Shows each god its*
    • *Limitations—*

- *Great Dreamers must*
    - *Ride Tsunami!*
- *For Transcendents?*
    - *Supernova!* •

Gillian nodded appreciatively. It was very good dolphin imagery.

"Creideiki would be proud," she said.

Akeakemai slashed with his tail flukes, reticent to accept praise.

• *Irony makes for easy poetry.* •

Sara Koolhan commented, "Forgive my ignorance of stellar physics, but I've been studying, so let me see if I get this right.

"When that big, whirling cloud of dross and corpses finally collapses, it's going to dump a tenth of a solar mass onto the hot, dense surface of that white dwarf star. A dwarf that's already near its . . . *Chandrasekhar limit.* The weight of new material will overcome the heat and other forces that till-now were keeping the dwarf expanded, compressing the core to incredible density . . . which causes . . ."

Sara flushed, as if fearing she was only embarrassing herself with words and concepts learned only in the last hour. Gillian smiled, encouragingly. "Which causes that core to suddenly undergo superfast nuclear fusion, triggering further collapse into—"

"What Earthlings used to call a 'type one' supernova," the Niss Machine cut in, unable to resist an inbuilt yen to interrupt. "Normally, this happens when a large amount of matter is tugged off a giant star, falling rapidly onto a neighboring white dwarf. In this case, however, the sudden catalyzing agent will be the infalling flesh of once living beings! Their body substance will help light a pyre that should briefly outshine this entire galaxy and be visible to the boundaries of the universe."

Gillian thought she detected hints of hysteria in the voice of the Tymbrimi-built machine. Though originally programmed to seek surprise and novelty, the Niss might well have passed the limit of what it could stand.

"I agree, there doesn't seem much chance of surviving such an event, no matter how fancy a coating we are given. And yet, the coincidence seems too perfect to ignore."

"Coincidence?" Suessi asked.

"The cancellation of angular momentum is too perfect. The Transcendents must have meant this to happen. They slaughtered the remaining candidates for a purpose—in order to trigger the coming explosion."

"So. Yes? Then the big question is—why aren't we down there now, mixing our atoms with all those other poor bugs, beasties. and blighters?"

Gillian shrugged.

"I just don't know, Hannes. Obviously, we have a role to play, but what role? Who can say?"

Zub'daki didn't expect mass collapse to occur for twenty hours, at least. Possibly several days.

"The infall may be disssrupted by outward radiation pressure, as the star heats up," the dolphin scientist explained. "It could make the whole process of ignition messsssy. Unless they have a solution to that problem, as well."

He didn't have to explain who "they" were. The shimmering needle-gateway throbbed nearby, as long as Earth's moon, spinning webs of mysterious, translucent material near several dozen captive ships.

Assured that the crisis would not come for a while yet, Gillian headed to her quarters for some rest. Upon entering. she glanced across the dimly lit chamber at an ancient cadaver, grinning away in a glass cabinet.

"It seems our torment won't go on much longer, Herb. The end is coming at last, in a way that should erase all our troubles."

The gaunt corpse said nothing, of course. She sighed.

"Ah well. Tom had a favorite expression. If you've really got to go you might as well—"

Baritone words joined hers.

"You might as well go out with a bang."

Gillian swiveled around, crouching slightly, her chest pounding from surprise. Something—or someone—stood in the shadows. The figure was tall, bipedal, with the shoulders and stance of a well-built human male.

Who . . . who's there?" she demanded.

The answering voice came eerily familiar.

"No one you should fear. Dr. Baskin. Let me move into the light."

As he did so, Gillian's heart sped instead of slowing down. She stepped back with her right hand pressed midway between throat and sternum. Her voice cracked on the chisel-like wedge separating hope from dread.

"T-Tom. . . ?"

His ready smile was there. An eager grin, always a bit like a little boy's. The stance, relaxed and yet ready for anything. Those well-known hands, so capable at a thousand tasks.

The head—black haired with a gray fringe—tilted quizzically, as if just a little disappointed by her response.

"Jill, are you so credulous, to believe what you see?"

Gillian struggled to clamp down her emotions, especially the wave of desperate loneliness that flooded as brief hope crashed. If it really were Tom, she would already know in several ways, even without visual sight. And yet, the careworn face seemed so real—fatigued by struggles that made her own trials pale by comparison. Part of her yearned to reach out and hold him. To soothe those worries for a little while.

Even knowing this was just a lie.

"I'm . . . not that naive. I guess it's pretty clear who you really are. Tell me . . . did you take Tom's image from my mind? Or else—"

She swiveled to glance at her desk, where a holo of her husband glowed softly, next to a picture of Creideiki, along with others she had known and loved on Earth.

"A bit of each," came the answer while Gillian was briefly turned away. "Along with many other inputs. It seemed a useful approach, combining familiarity with tension and regret. A bit cruel, perhaps. But conducive of concentration.

"Are you alert now?"

"You have my attention," she replied, turning back to face her visitor . . . only to be rocked by a new surprise.

Tom had vanished! In his place stood *Jacob Demwa,* elderly master spy of the Terragens Intelligence Service, who had lobbied hard for the commissioning of a dolphin-crewed ship. *Streaker* was just as much his doing as Creideiki's. Dark, leathery skin showed the toll of years spent cruising deep space, among Earth's many outposts, fighting to stave off the fate suffered by most wolfling races.

"That's good," her visitor said, in a voice much like old Jake's . . . though it lacked some overtones of crusty humor. "Because I can spare only a small part of my awareness for this conversation. There are many other tasks requiring imminent completion."

Gillian nodded.

"I can well imagine. You Transcendents must be frightfully busy, slaughtering trillions of sapient beings in order to set off a brief cosmic torch. Tell me, what purpose did all those poor creatures die for? Was it a religious sacrifice? Or something more practical?"

"Must one choose? You might say a little of both. And neither. The concepts are hard to express, using terms available in your discursive-symbolic language."

For some reason, she had expected such an answer.

"I guess that's true. But thanks anyway, for not using terms like 'crude' or 'primitive.' Others, before you, made a point of reminding us how low we stand on life's pyramid."

The image of Jake Demwa smiled, with wrinkles creasing all the right places.

"You are bitter. After suffering through earlier contacts with so-called Old Ones, I can hardly blame you. Those creatures were scarcely older than you, and hardly more knowledgeable. Such immature souls are often arrogant far beyond their actual accomplishments. They try to emphasize how high they have risen by denigrating those just below. In your own journal, Dr. Baskin, you say they snubbed you like 'ants scurrying under the feet of trampling gods'

"In fact, though, any truly advanced mind should be capable of empathy, even toward 'ants.' By deputizing a small portion of myself, I can speak to you in this manner. It costs little to be kind, when the effort seems appropriate."

Gillian blinked, unable to decide whether to be grateful or offended.

"Your notion of selective kindness . . . terrifies me."

The Demwa replica shrugged.

"Some things cannot be helped. Those composite beings who died recently—whose stirred mass and other attributes now form a dense cloud, hovering at the brink of oblivion—they will serve vital goals much better with their deaths than they would as junior Transcendents. Here, and at many other sites across the known cosmos, they will ignite beacons at just the right moment, when destiny opens a fleeting window, allowing heavens to converse."

Her brow grew tense from concentration.

"Beacons? Aimed where? You Transcendents are already masters of everything within the Five—"

Abruptly, Gillian hazarded a guess.

"*Outside?* You want to contact others, *beyond* the Five Galaxies!"

Demwa seemed to croon approvingly.

"Ah, you see? Simple reasoning is not so difficult, even for an ant!

"Indeed, an aim of this vast enterprise is to shine brief messages from one heavenly locus to another. A greeting can be superimposed on the blaring eruption of light that will soon burst from this place, briefly achieving brightness greater than a whole galaxy."

"But—"

"But! You are about to object that we can do this anytime! It is trivial for beings like us simply to set off supernovas, flashing them like blinking signal lights.

"True! Furthermore, that method is too slow, and too noise-ridden, for complex conversation. It amounts to little more than shouting 'Here I am!' at the universe.

"Anyway, the vast majority of other galactic nexi appear to be mysteriously silent, or else they emanate vibrations that are too cryptic or bizarre for us to parse, even with our best simulations. Either way, the puzzle cannot be solved by remote musing on mere sluggish beams of light."

Avoiding the false Demwa's scrutinizing gaze, Gillian stared at a far wall, deep in thought. At last she murmured.

"I bet all this has to do with the *Great Rupture* that Sara predicted. Many of the old connective links—the subspace channels and t-point threads—are snapping at last. Galaxy Four may detach completely."

Her hands clenched.

"There must be some *opportunity.* One that only takes place during a rupture, when all the hyperspace levels are convulsing. A window of time when . . ."

Looking back at her visitor, Gillian winced to find it transformed yet again. Now Jake Demwa was replaced by the image of *Tom's mother.*

May Orley grinned back at her, bundled in thermal gear against a Minnesota winter, with a ski pole in each hand.

"Go on, my dear. What else do you surmise?"

Such rapid transfigurations might once have unnerved Gillian, before she had departed on this long, eventful space voyage. But after years spent dealing with the Niss Machine, she had learned to ignore rude interruptions, like rain off a duck's back.

"A window of time when spatial links are *greater* than normal!" She stabbed a finger toward the Transcendent. "When physical objects can be hurled across the unbridgeable gulf between galactic clusters, at some speed much greater than light. Like tossing a message in a bottle, taking advantage of a rare high tide."

"A perfectly lovely metaphor," approved her ersatz mother-in-law. "Indeed, the rupture is like a mighty, devouring wave that can speedily traverse megaparsecs at a single bound. The supernova we set off shall be the arm that throws bottles into that wave."

Gillian inhaled deeply as the next implication struck home.

"You want *Streaker* to be one of those bottles."

"Spot on!" The Transcendent clapped admiration. "You validate our simulations and models, which lately suggested a change in procedure. By adding *wolflings* to the mixture, we may supply a much needed ingredient, this time. Perhaps it will prevent the failures that plagued our past efforts—those other occasions when we tried to send messages across the vast desert of flatness between our nexus of galaxies and the myriad spiral heavens we see floating past, tantalizingly out of reach."

Gillian could no longer stand the unctuous pleasantness of May Orley. She covered her eyes, in part to let the Transcendent shift again . . . but also because she felt rather woozy. A weakness spread to her knees as realization sank in.

Instead of imminent death by fiery immolation, she was being promised an adventure—a voyage of exploration more exceptional than any other—and Gillian felt as if she had been punched in the stomach.

"You've . . . been trying this a long time, have you?"

"Ever since recovering from the earliest recorded crisis, just after the Progenitors departed, when our happy community of *seventeen* linked galaxies was torn asunder. Across the ages since then, we have yearned to recontact the brethren who were lost then."

The voice was changing, mutating as it spoke, becoming more gruff. More gravelly.

"It is a pang that hurts more deeply than you may know. For this reason, above all others, we made sure that starfarers would abandon Galaxy Four, in order for the loss to be less traumatic, this time."

Uncovering her eyes, Gillian saw that the transcendent now resembled *Charles Dart,* the chimp scientist who had vanished on Kithrup, along with Tom and Hikahi and about a dozen others.

"You can truly remember that far back?"

"By dwelling deep within the Embrace of Tides—skim-orbiting what you call 'black holes'—we accomplish several ends. In that gravity-stressed realm we can perform quantum computing on a measureless scale, combining the insights of every life order. With loving care, we simulate past events, alternate realities, even whole cosmic destinies."

Gillian quashed a manic surge of hysterical laughter. It was awfully posh language to come from the mouth of a chimp.

She fought for self-control, but the Transcendent did not seem to notice, continuing with its explanation.

"There is yet another effect of living near an event horizon, where spacetime curls so tightly that light can barely struggle free."

"Time slows down for you."

"Exactly, while the rest of the universe spins on madly. Others plunge past us into the singularities, diving headlong toward unseen realms, pursuing their own visions of destiny—but we remain, standing watch, impervious to entropy, waiting, observing, experimenting."

"Others plunge past . . ." Gillian repeated, blinking rapidly. "*Into* the black holes? But who. . . ?"

A grim smile spread slowly, with her growing realization.

"You're talking about other Transcendents! By God, you aren't the only high ones, are you? All the life orders merge next to black holes—first hydros and oxies and then machines and the rest—gathering near the greatest tides of all. But that's not the end of the story for most of them, is it? They keep going, *into* the singularities! Whether it takes them to a better universe, or else eliminates them as dross, they choose to keep going while *you guys* stay behind.

"Why?" she asked, pursuing the point. "Because you're afraid? Because you lack enough guts to face the unknown?"

This time the transformation took place before her eyes. A whirl of painful color that seemed somehow *vexed.* An instant later it resolved in the shape of her own father, long dead, but now restored to his appearance at the end, lying in a hospital bed, emaciated and bitter, regarding her with grim disapproval.

"I would ponder, Dr. Baskin, whether it is wise or justified to taunt powerful beings whose motives you can scarcely comprehend."

She nodded.

"Fair enough. And I humbly apologize. Now will you please choose another form? This one—"

In another flashy pirouette, the visitor reformed as a *Rothen,* one of those scoundrels who claimed to be Earth's patron race, gathering around themselves a cult of human thieves and cutpurses. Gillian winced. It served as a reminder of the messy situation faced by all her kind back home, where threats and dangers piled up faster with each passing year, month, and day.

"Now that I have explained your role, there are further matters to discuss," continued the ersatz Rothen. "A few details have been entered into your computer—some precautions you should take, for comfort during the coming transition. But the new coating we are spinning around your ship is quite intelligent and capable. It will protect you when the star explodes, escaping most of the heat and shock as the gravitational backlash throws you into a hyperlevel far beyond—"

Gillian cut in.

"But what if we don't *want* to go?"

The Rothen-shaped being smiled, a friendly gesture that brought her only chill.

"Are glory and adventure insufficient motivations? Then let's try another.

"Even now, the defenses surrounding Earth are collapsing. Soon, enemies will own your homeworld, then all its colonies, and even the secret refuges where Terrans stashed small outposts for desperate safety. Only you, aboard Streaker, have an opportunity to carry seeds of your species, your culture, beyond reach of the schoolyard bullies who would kill or enslave every human and dolphin. Do you not owe this to your ancestors, and descendants? A chance to ensure survival of your line, somewhere far from any known jeopardy?"

"But what chance is that?" she demanded. "You admit this never worked before."

"Simulations show a much better chance with revised techniques, and especially now that wolflings and sooners have been added to the recipe. I told you this already."

Gillian shook her head.

"Sorry. It's tempting, but I have orders. A duty . . ."

"To the Terragens Council?"

The Transcendent seemed dubious.

"Yes . . . but also to my civilization. *The Civilization of Five Galaxies.* It may be an anthill to you. And yes, it's in a nasty phase right now, dominated by those 'schoolyard bullies' you mentioned. But the Tymbrimi and some others think that may change, if the right stimulation is applied."

She nodded toward Herbie, the ancient relic of *Streaker*'s mission to the Shallow Cluster.

"Truth can have a tonic effect, even on those who are lashing out, out of fear."

The Rothen-figure nodded, even as its features began melting in another transformation.

"A laudable position for a young and noble race. Though, of course, our needs take higher priority than a civilization of fractious starfaring primitives.

"In any event, the time is nearly upon us . . . as you are about to find out."

The visitor's features remained murky, while Gillian puzzled over the meaning of its last remark.

Abruptly, the comm line on her desk chimed. A small holo image erupted. It was Zub'daki. The dolphin astronomer's gray head looked agitated and worried. He did not seem to realize Gillian had company.

"Dr. Bassskin!"

"Yes? What is it, Zub'daki."

"Events are accelerating in ways I hadn't anticipated. You might want to come up and have a look-k!"

Gillian's guts churned. Normally, she would respond quickly to such a summons. But right now, it was hard to imagine anything in the universe more important than this conversation she was having with a transcendent deity who controlled all their lives.

"Can it wait a bit? I'm kind of busy right now."

The dolphin astronomer's dark eye widened, as if he could not believe what he was hearing.

"Doctor . . . let me explain. Earlier I said the infall of the debris cloud might be delayed by light pressure. As the white dwarf heats up, its increasing brightness pushes back against the collapsing disk, slowing the arrival of more matter. It could make for a sloppy, uneven supernova.

"But-t something's changing! The gas and sooty dust are starting to *clump*! All the mass is consolidating into little dense ballsssss! Trillions and gazillions of dense *marbles,* all at once!"

"So?" Gillian shrugged. She was distracted by the sight of her visitor, who now stood in front of the glass display case, gazing at Herbie. The Transcendent's outline kept rippling as it tried adjusting its form. She realized that it must be attempting to simulate Herbie's original appearance, before the mummy spent a billion years in desiccated preservation, back at the Shallow Cluster.

"So? You ask *ssssso?*" Zub'daki sputtered, aghast. "This means the debris cloud will be effectively transparent to light pressure! As it precipitates onto the star, nothing impedes the acceleration. The whole great mass plummets all at once, with tremendous speed!"

Gillian nodded.

"So the supernova will take place quickly and smoothly."

"And with unprecedented power!"

While she conversed with Zub'daki, her visitor seemed to be having trouble finding the right shape, as if there was something *slippery* about Herbie's figure. Or else the Transcendents were too busy with other matters right now to apply much computing power for such an unimportant task.

She shook her head.

"I expect we're just witnessing some more supercompetent technology at work, Zub'daki. Clearly, this was all arranged. Perhaps long before we were born. Tell me, do you have a new estimate for when infall-collapse begins?"

Frustration filled the dolphin's voice.

"You missssunderstand me, Doctor! Infall has *already—*"

The astronomer's voice cut short, interrupted by a shrill clamor of alarm bells. The dolphin's image swung around as shadowy figures rushed back and forth behind him, hurrying to emergency stations. Then Zub'daki's image vanished completely.

It was replaced by the whirling tornado of the Niss Machine.

"What is it?" Gillian demanded. "What's happening now?"

The Niss bent slightly, as if starting to note the presence of her visitor. Then the hologram shivered and seemed to forget all about the Transcendent.

"I . . . must report that we are once again under attack."

Gillian blinked.

"Attack? By whom?"

"Who do you think? By our old nemesis, the Jophur battleship, Polkjhy. Though clearly mutated and transformed, it is approaching rapidly, and has begun emanating vibrations on D Space resonance frequencies, once more turning our hull into a receiving antenna for massive flows of heat—"

"Stop!" Gillian shouted, waving both hands in front of her. "This is crazy! Do the Jophur know what's going on here? Or whose protection we're under?"

The Niss gave its old, familiar shrug.

"I have no idea what the Jophur know, or do not know. Such persistence, in the face of overwhelming power, would seem to verge on madness. And yet, the fact remains. Our hull temperature has started to rise."

Gillian turned to her visitor, whose face was coalescing into a visage of humanoid-amphibian beauty, almost luminous in its color and texture. At any other time, it would have been one of the most transfixing sights of Gillian's life—and she barely gave it a second glance.

"Well?" she demanded.

"*Well what, Dr. Baskin?*" the Transcendent asked, turning toward her. There was still a tentative, uncertain quality to the reconstruction, a near resurrection of her longtime companion, the antediluvian cadaver.

"Well . . . are you *going* to protect us?"

"Do you ask for our protection?"

In amazement, she could hardly speak.

"I thought . . . you put so much effort into choosing and preparing us . . ."

The Niss Machine whirled in-perplexity. "Are you talking to me? Is someone in there with you? My sensors seem unable to—"

With an irritated hand gesture, Gillian caused her artificial assistant to vanish from sight. She gazed in wonder as the Transcendent seemed to shimmer, growing brighter by the instant.

"Such investment merits confidence, Dr. Baskin. Can wolflings survive the vast gulf between heavens? Have you the fortitude to endure all the cryptic challenges that await you? And the denizens you'll meet, when you arrive at some distant galactic realm?"

Her guest became radiant, completing the transformation from cadaverous mummy into something truly like a god.

"It occurs to us that one final test might be called for in the interest of verifying your mettle."

Gillian covered her eyes, and yet the glare soon grew too bright to endure, outlining the bones of her hand. The visitor's words pierced her skin, vibrating her soul.

"One more trial to pass . . . in the slim moments that remain . . . before our universe changes."

LARK

Despite occasional gaps, a distant voice came through clearly, resonating in his mind.

"A few details have been entered into your computer—some precautions you should take, for comfort during the coming transition. But the . . . coating we are spinning around your ship is quite intelligent and capable. It will protect you when . . . star explodes, escaping most . . . heat and shock as the gravitational backlash throws you into a hyperlevel far beyond—"

Working together with Ling and other members of the Mother Consortium, he had labored hard to achieve this—sifting through the incredible complexity of the Transcendent Mesh for something simple enough for mere organic life-forms to understand. After all their efforts, this was the best result so far, eavesdropping on a conversation between a human and her transcendent visitor. An explanation, in plain Anglic, of what the great ones hoped to accomplish from all the recent violence and turmoil.

Apparently, they would take advantage of rare cosmic conditions to launch specially modified ships, sending messenger-envoys hurtling on one-way voyages across the immense gulf separating clusters of galaxies.

"By adding wolflings and sooners to the mixture, we may . . . prevent the failures that plagued past efforts . . . when we tried to . . . cross the vast flat deserts between our galactic nexus and the myriad spiral heavens we see floating past, tantalizingly out of reach . . ."

Lark felt growing agitation in the surrounding watery medium, where he and Ling floated amid a jostling throng of symbiotic organisms. "Mother" was clearly both excited and worried by this news. He knew this, in part, because his own fretful thoughts helped shape the overall mood.

Ling's presence made itself known. Turning around, he saw her swim toward him through the living murk, reaching out to clasp his hand. At the instant of contact, he felt her mind stroking his own, bringing dire news.

Can you feel it? The Jophur master rings have decided to assail and destroy *Streaker*, no matter what the repercussions!

Lark blinked in surprise. Putting out his own mental feelers to probe the data network of starship *Polkjhy*, he tapped the Jophur command frequencies and soon confirmed the worst.

The priest-stack and the new captain-leader were in complete accord. With stark decisiveness, they had sent *Polkjhy* careening on a new, deadly course. Attacking, heedless of the consequences.

What can they hope to accomplish? Interfering with the Transcendents will only invite those mighty ones to swat this ship—and all of us aboard—out of the sky like annoying insects!

Ling nodded, and Lark saw that he had just answered his own question. From the Jophur leaders' point of view, this offered a last chance to wipe out the hybrid oxy-hydro superorganism that had taken over most of their ship. Apparently, the Jophur would rather go out in a blaze of glory than surrender.

The suicidal decision saddened Lark. If only they would simply wait for the supernova! He had a hankering to watch the run-up to that gaudy event. To feel the first hyperdense flux of neutrinos sleet through his body, heralding a crackling dawn. One that would illumine night on a myriad worlds.

Of course, Mother wasn't about to take this lying down. With approval of every sapient member, the community launched an immediate, all-out assault against the remaining vital strongholds held by unconverted Jophur. Soon Lark began sensing the fractious fury of combat, as both sides flung deadly bolts along stained corridors, further melting *Polkjhy*'s already tortured inner walls. Lark's nerve endings responded, turning each injury or death into a pang, physically painful. Personally intense.

Mother is about to break into the engine compartment, Ling noted. But we may not be able to cut power in time to save the Earthlings . . . or to prevent angering the Transcendents.

Indeed, resistance was bitter as ring stacks and robots stubbornly held their ground against the costly assault. But Zang globules and other members of the Mother Consortium kept up the pressure, storming Jophur defenses with spendthrift courage.

We'd better go help, Lark thought, and Ling nodded. They both had a sense of how drained Mother's reserves were. This was no time to hang back.

And yet, even as they made ready to join the fray, something restrained both of them. A resistance that stopped Lark in his tracks.

Not a *command,* as such. More like a consensus decision—a general feeling among other components of the symbiosis. An agreement that the two humans should not be risked right now.

They would better serve the whole with their intelligence and knowledge, by probing through the Mesh, trying once more to communicate.

With some reluctance, Lark accepted the wisdom of this. Together with Ling, he went back to work, reopening the channels they had discovered before.

"It occurs to us that one final test might be called for . . . verifying your mettle.

"One more trial . . . before our universe changes."

Lark exhaled a sigh that formed bubble trails in the frothy medium.

So. The Transcendents were still tinkering, trying to optimize their experiment till the very last moment. Or else the "gods" were amusing themselves at the expense of those poor Earthlings. Either way, they weren't about to defend *Streaker* with omnipotent power. Instead, they would let *Polkjhy* attack, evaluating the results.

There wasn't much time left *for* exploration. With one part of his mind, Lark tracked the great mass-infall of collapsing debris.

Already the white dwarf surged and boiled as the cloud's inner fringes struck its surface at high velocity. Concentric waves of actinic blue fire crisscrossed the ancient, tormented surface, spouting gaudy flares of plasma back toward space, hinting at far greater fireworks to come.

Meanwhile, uncoded insults hurled from *Polkjhy*'s bridge, taunting *Streaker*'s crew as their hull was turned into a betraying antenna, forced to siphon heat from other folded layers of space.

At that point a familiar voice joined in.

It was Lark's old friend, the traeki from Jijo who had once been *Asx*, then *Ewasx*, and now was a wise, multicomponent being, simply called "X."

i/we have finally made full contact with the Earthship's computer, the hybrid creature announced.

Congratulations, Lark replied. Have you transmitted the information you wanted to send?

With a sense of waxy satisfaction, X confirmed it was done. Everything that had been learned about Jophur master rings was now copied into *Streaker*'s onboard storage system, including the knack for growing red toruses—the kind that had proved so potent against egocentric dominance.

And yet, what good would the information do? Even if *Streaker* survived the present attack, *and* the coming stellar explosion, the Transcendents would only hurl it away from the Five Galaxies, riding a cosmic tidal wave, careening toward starscapes where no Jophur ever lived.

X showed no sign of recognizing any inconsistency.

You might be interested in something else I have learned. There is a passenger aboard the Earthship. Someone now counted among its honored leaders. A human person, familiar to us both.

Lark sensed anguished irony behind the words. Bending his will toward the indicated path, he finally gained access to *Streaker*'s housekeeping files and discovered the datum X referred to.

Sara!

A spasm rocked him, from sheer surprise. Eddies tugged Lark's body, while Ling grasped his right arm, to help him get over the shock.

What is my sister doing out here . . . so far from Jijo? How did she wind up in such a mess!

The blow was made worse when Mother came up with an estimate of heating rates aboard *Streaker.* At this pace, the influx would reach critical levels in less than half a midura.

Soon after that, all the water aboard the dolphin-crewed ship would start to boil.

EMERSON

The alarm seemed to take everyone in *Streaker*'s control center by surprise.

The others had been so intent and worried about the engorged, enraged star—and about mysterious actions of the nearby needle-gateway—that they seemed to forget about danger from mundane enemies.

But he had not.

Emerson knew better. He had dealt with Jophur before and understood their tenacity—a single-mindedness that had been grafted into their race by careless Uplift consorts, who had failed to grasp the basic value of moderation. When the assault came, he was ready.

Lacking speech or literacy, Emerson could not read the flashing monitor screens or figure out the exact nature of their weapon. Details did not matter. He understood that it somehow had to do with making *Streaker hot.* Already the walls and floor plates were emanating uncomfortable warmth. Large amounts of energy poured in, even though the small sun was still not ready to explode.

Sara reached for his hand, and he felt guilty putting her off with a mere loving squeeze, before dashing away. But Emerson figured that a chance of saving her life was worth more than staying by her side and roasting together.

Running down a torrid hallway, he kept shouting, in hopes that the automatic intercoms would pass on his simple message.

"Suessi! . . . Karkaett! . . . Now, now, now!"

Would they come? So much labor had gone into making his idea a reality, applying a two-hundred-year-old technology to new problems in survival. And yet, he worried. They might have simply been humoring him, working together as a way to stay busy till the end. . . .

Clambering through a maintenance tube, Emerson hurried till he reached the small chamber where his last, triumphant encounter with the Old Ones had taken place—and breathed relief when he saw that Hannes and a couple of dolphin engineers were already there, gathered around the big laser. They babbled to each other in the sweet dialect of engineering. Emerson could no longer parse the quick, efficient meanings, but their speech sounded like music, nevertheless.

The graceful lyrics of competence.

Hannes turned his mirrorlike dome to ask Emerson a question. One that was simple enough for his frail remaining language centers to grasp.

"Yes!" He nodded vigorously. "Do . . . it!"

Hannes pushed a switch and the laser abruptly bucked in its mounting brackets—hissing and straining like some great beast, snorting as it sprang into action.

Emerson shifted position in order to sight along the massive barrel, curious to see where massive amounts of energy were now pouring.

He saw nothing but stars.

Sure enough, a nearby view screen showed a red dot, representing the Jophur vessel *Polkjhy*, approaching *Streaker*'s other side.

Of course he had been lucky with the Old Ones. It would have taken another unlikely stroke of extreme good fortune for this enemy to be within reach. Anyway, a battleship's defenses might deflect even such a potent beam.

He shrugged. It didn't matter. He and the others did not have to smite the Jophur in order to defeat them.

Emerson felt a chill draft. He shivered, and soon noticed a distinct fog begin to form above each dolphin's blowhole, like individual fountains of frost. His own breath began condensing, too. In moments, the small chamber became noticeably colder, and Hannes shouted for everyone to evacuate. It was time to leave, allowing the machine to perform as planned.

Still, Emerson hung back, relishing a flow of icy air that gushed through ducts to far corners of the ship. He visualized the laser beam acting as a great pump, sucking heat as fast as other forces drew it in, then shooting it forth toward the cosmos. Grinning, he took satisfaction in the way an ancient Earthling technology thwarted Galactic foes—as it had once before, a long time ago, aboard a crude, wolfling vessel braving the maw of a torrid sun.

I . . . still . . . have it . . . He pondered, glancing down at his hands.

When his grin became noisy—a chattering of clenched teeth—Emerson finally let Hannes and the others tug him back toward habitable areas.

Anyway, Sara was waiting for him.

Now at least they would have a few moments together.

Until the star exploded.

GILLIAN

"You never asked for volunteers," she told her visitor accusingly.

The transcendent being returned to her office, assembling itself out of dust motes and particles of air—perhaps in order to resume their conversation, or else to congratulate Gillian for the clever trick worked out by *Streaker*'s engineering crew—creating a *refrigeration laser,* a device for dumping heat overboard, spraying it garishly skyward as fast as energy flowed into the ship from D Space.

Few Galactics had ever needed such a crude, gaudy, *wolfling* device. It would seem preposterously primitive, like rockets, or propeller-driven aircraft. But when humans began exploring the depths of their own sun two centuries ago—going there out of pure curiosity—the trick of laser-cooling had proved both useful and fateful, in several ways.

Shortly after reappearing, the visitor seemed to float before Gillian, an entity with lustrous gray skin and a short, powerful tail whose flukes actually stirred a breeze, kicking up midget whirlwinds, rustling the papers on her desk. Coalescing further, it started taking a resemblance to Gillian's dearest dolphin friend, Lieutenant Hikahi, one of those who had been left behind on Kithrup, along with Tom and Charles Dart.

Before the Transcendent could speak, Gillian completed her accusation.

"You say you need wolflings, to add as *ingredients* for your message-probes to other galaxies. Did it ever occur to you to ask? I know my fellow Earthlings. You'd have gotten thousands, *millions* of volunteers for such a trip! Even knowing in advance that it would involve merging with hydros and machines and other creepy things. There have always been enough weirdos and adventurers. People who'd pay any price, just to be the first to see some far horizon."

The ersatz dolphin rolled on its side, almost languidly, as if relishing a new experience.

"We shall make note of that-t," crooned a close approximation of Hikahi's voice, causing Gillian a lonely pang. "Perhaps we'll take your advice . . . next time the question comes up."

She stared for a moment, then gave a low, dry laugh.

"Right. When another rupture comes, in a hundred million years!"

"That's not so very long, for those of us who make our true homes next to ssssingularities. We who you called 'cowards' for biding our time in a black hole's stretched borderline, rather than plunging into the unknown."

"Look," she raised a hand. "I already apologized for that. Right now, though, I think we'd better cut to—"

"*The chasssse?*" Her visitor rolled the simulated body in a loop.

Gillian raised an eyebrow. "Do you already know—"

"What you are going to say? Your surface thoughts are trivial to read. But even without using psi, we can make good estimates, based on appraisal of your past behavior under varied circumstances. These models were recently revised. Would you like to know what our latest simulations foretell?"

She answered, guardedly.

"I'm listening."

The imitation Hikahi brought one dark eye toward Gillian.

"You were about to decline the honor of being our emissariessss. You would claim that urgent obligations beckon you elsewhere. Obligations that cannot be ignored."

Gillian shrugged.

"Anyone could've guessed that, after our last conversation. Assuming I did decline, how would you have replied?"

"I would have said that you have no option. A conveyance and shield have already been woven around your ship, ready to clasp the opportunity when a space-time rift opens nearby. With luck, it might carry you safely beyond the limits of known civilization. That kind of investment is not given up lightly. Your request would be refused."

With her next breath, Gillian exhaled a bitter sigh.

"I guess that answer's inevitable. So. How do your simulations predict I'd respond next?"

The dolphin-shaped being sputtered laughter.

"With threatsssss!

"You would claim readiness to blow up your ship . . . or to interfere with the mission in some other way."

Gillian felt her face grow warm. That really had been her next move. A desperate ploy. But no other tactic came to mind in the short time available.

"I guess it is a bit of a cliché."

"Naturally, all such possibilities have been taken into account. In this case, our analyses show you would be bluffing. Given a stark choice between adventure, on the one hand, and assured extinction on the other, you could be relied upon to choose adventure!"

Gillian's shoulders slumped. The Transcendents were quick learners, and with awesome computational power they could simulate whole alternate realities. Small wonder they outmaneuvered any plan she came up with, using her limited human brain.

"Then that's it?" she asked. "We have no choice. We head for some far galaxy, like it or not."

"Your linear guess is only partly correct. Indeed, you have no choice. That part of it you have right, Dr. Basssskin. We can compel you and your crew to depart, and that-t would be that."

The visitor shook its sleek gray head as it began yet another transfiguration. Hikahi's outlines grew blurry. Her simulated body started stretching.

"But our simulations did not stop with your behavior today. They scrutinized what you might do later . . . during the weeks, months, and years that stretch ahead, until your people arrive at some distant realm."

Gillian blinked. "You worked it out that far ahead?"

"To a high degree of probability. And that is where a problem keeps cropping up in our models. Given enough time, something else will occur to you. You will realize that it is possible to have your adventure, plus revenge as well! A way to visit far-off realms, and also retaliate against those who thrust you on so great a voyage, against your will."

She could only stare, blinking in confusion as the Transcendent finished converting to a different body shape . . . another dolphin image, a bit longer and stronger looking than Hikahi, with scar tissue covering a savage wound near the left eye.

Creideiki, she realized, with a faint shiver.

"I . . . don't . . . I don't know what you mean. Unless . . ." Gillian swallowed, and tried concentrating. It was difficult, under that strangely powerful cetacean gaze.

"Unless you're concerned about what we'd *say* about you, to whatever high minds we meet on the other side."

This time, the visitor did not respond in Anglic. Rather, the facsimile of *Streaker's* old commander lifted that tormented head and cast a spray of squealing clicks, filling her office with couplets of ornate Trinary verse.

• *What revenge is*
  more long-lasting
• *Than the cruelty*
  of slander,
• *Spoken by outraged*
  descendants,
• *Defaming their*
  distant parents?

• *Would you escape*
  time's death sentence?
• *Or entropy's*
  cruel erosion?
• *We know just one*
  surefire method
• *To succeed and*
  be immortal—

• *If you want to*
  live forever,
• *First earn love and*
  fierce devotion
• *From those who will*
  carry onward,
• *They will speak your*
  name resounding
    Even when the stars grow cold. •

Gillian squinted at the replica of her old comrade and leader. The dolphin captain looked so genuine, so tangible, as if she could reach out and stroke his warm gray flank—battered, yet unbowed.

"That's . . . the first truly wise thing I've yet heard from you gods," she said. "It's almost . . . as if you really *are Creidei—*"

The Transcendent interrupted. Its sleek form began dissolving, folding inward toward a ball of light.

"Are you . . . entirely sure . . . that I am not?"

She blinked, unsure what to make of the non sequitur.

"Wait!" she cried out. "What's going to happen? What are you going to—"

The visitor vanished silently. But in her mind a soft presence lingered for another moment, whispering.

We have much to do . . . and very little time. . . .

A shrill whistle filled the air. A holo image of Akeakemai burst in, calling from *Streaker*'s bridge.

"Gillian! Zub'daki says that mass infall is speeding up! The explosion's just minutes away!"

She nodded, feeling tired and altogether unready to witness the end of the universe. Or any part of it.

"I'll be right up," she said, turning toward the door.

But the pilot's voice cut her short.

"That's not all!" he added, with frantic tones. "The big needle-gateway . . . it's—"

There followed a noisy clatter. Gillian saw a blur of motion on the bridge, as officers dashed in all directions, propelled by agitated tails.

"Niss!" she called out. "Show me what's going on out there!"

Abruptly, a new holo display opened, presenting a view of nearby space. The planet-sized Transcendent needle took up most of the scene. One of its flanks was now almost too bright to look at, reflecting angry light from the dwarf star—a fuming conflagration, rapidly heating toward Armageddon. Already, deep within, new pressure-driven fusions were using up the star's final stores of hydrogen and helium, then carbon and oxygen, then . . .

Gillian quickly saw what had Akeakemai upset. The needle was *splitting open.* Moreover, as it broke apart, beams of light reached out to seize three nearby objects.

Flashing labels identified the targets.

Streaker was the first. Gillian felt its hull shudder as the beam struck.

The Jophur battleship was next.

Finally—one of the globelike "candidate vessels," now wrapped in a fuzzy mass of special fabric.

All three were being drawn inward.

Then, as if with a surgeon's delicate lancet, the light beams started carving all three vessels apart.

"X"

Can you feel it now, my rings? and my other little selves?

How about you, Lark?

And you, Ling?

Can you sense how *Mother*—the macro-entity we all joined—writhes with uncertain fear as blades of force cut through *Polkjhy*'s hull? Can you sense distant walls and bulkheads separate, spilling air, liquid, and creatures into vacuum? For a few moments, it seems our time of destruction has arrived.

Our/my/your end has come, at last.

ONLY NOTE! Can you sense a sudden change in mood?

Mother rejoices, as we/i/all realize the truth.

These are *scalpel rays,* slicing rapidly, selectively. Only a few small segments are being removed from *Polkjhy*!

Likewise, instruments tell us that just one or two prim holes are being drilled in the Earthship *Streaker.*

But the third victim seems less lucky!

The nearest mighty globule-vessel—a giant candidate-craft, already prepared for its epic journey—has been torn open and gutted! Horrified and awed at the same time, all our rings and segments watch as the contents are sacrificed . . . thousands of sapient-hybrid beings, cast aside like the entrails of some fresh-caught fish . . . leaving behind only a lambent shell of glimmering tendrils.

A living shell that now moves rapidly toward *Polkjhy*!

AND NOW, ATTENTION TURNS TO THE LIVID SUN.

How long did it spin in peace? A remnant of this galaxy's earliest days, the dwarf star had long ago finished its brief youth and settled down to placid retirement. Left alone, it might have spent another twenty billion years slowly shrinking as it eked out a flickering white surface flame. Lacking a nearby stellar companion, it would never obtain the sudden infusion of mass required for a more ecstatic death.

Only now that mass infusion comes!

Like pilgrims to a shrine, millions of starships recently answered the Great Harrower's summons. They came to this place, arranging themselves in polite, crisscrossing spiral queues, seeking redemption and advancement . . . only to find death on the very threshold of transcendence. Their corpses, compressed into compact balls, now rain upon the star, inciting new ferment, taking its matter/energy balance close to a special value.

An acute point of no return.

MY RINGS . . . MANY OF YOU ONCE WERE MEMBERS OF ASX, THAT WISE OLD TRAEKI SAGE.

Back on Jijo, you had no need to contemplate such things. Instead of Chandrasekhar limits and radiative opacities, we/you/i used to adjudge disputes among local villages and tribes. We offered marriage counseling to fractious urrish, human, and qheuen families. We would squat for days on some aromatic mulch pile, happily arguing among ourselves.

Now, Mother obligingly makes available vast stores of information, offering free access to *Polkjhy*'s onboard Library, lately captured from the remnant Jophur.

So it is that i/we/you know all about *critical thresholds* and the *catastrophic collapse* that will soon occur, followed by a tremendous "bounce," expelling much of the poor star at high fractions of lightspeed.

First will come a burst of neutrinos. Not so many as in a "type two" supernova. But enough so that those phantom particles will impart heat and momentum into any body within ten Jijoan orbits. (We are much closer than that!) X rays and gamma rays will follow . . . and then other forms of light. So much that the wavefronts will carry their own palpable gravitational fields as they plunge through this point in space with the brightness of one trillion suns.

Finally, if anything remains of poor *Polkjhy,* it will be struck by the shock wave of protons, neutrons, electrons, and newly-created massive ions, imparting accelerations of one hundred thousand gravities.

No wonder the Transcendents feel this event will rip holes in the cosmic *ylem.* Apparently, that is their desire. To kindle a pyre. One bright enough to propel seeds across the greatest desert of all.

DO YOU HEAR THE LATEST, MY RINGS?

Lark and Ling report what they have learned by tapping into the Transcendent Mesh.

An explanation of the recent violent surgery by flashing scalpel rays!

Apparently, the high ones have decided on a last minute change in plans.

Quick improvisation is not their normal habit, but now they labor furiously, redesigning. Reconfiguring.

AND WE ARE OBJECTS OF THEIR SUDDEN INTENT!

Transfixed, we all watch as two slim plugs of matter slide smoothly out of the Earthship and head this way, leaving holes that seal quickly behind them. These slender tubes race toward *Polkjhy* . . . even as the gutted shell of the third vessel approaches us from the other side, shimmering and alive.

Dolphins, Ling says, identifying the contents of the cylinders taken from Streaker. About a dozen of them. Volunteers, coming to join us, along with some gene stores, and cultural archives . . .

With breakneck speed, the tubes slide into slots prepared for them. *Just in time,* as the rippling shell wraps around *Polkjhy* and seals shut with a blaze of energetic union.

All of Mother's components—even the newly captured Jophur officers—stagger briefly from psychic shock as that mass of luminous tendrils takes hold of our transformed vessel—bonding and penetrating—turning it into a throbbing, vibrating whole.

Something eager. Coiled and ready for what comes next.

CAN YOU SENSE THE NEARBY AGONY OF DYING GODS?

The needle-gateway writhes and flickers as it draws *Streaker* toward it. Glowing and collapsing inward, the transcendent nexus *flexes,* creating powerful fields, causing space to warp straight through its innards, generating a tunnel. A lean passageway.

An improvised escape route for the Terrans to strive for.

Will they make it in time?

AND NOW COMES IGNITION OF THE BRIGHTEST COMPACT DETONATION IN THE UNIVERSE.

Perhaps it will not be our knell of extinction, after all.

A poll has been taken, among Mother's many members. Nearly all agree.

This is what we would have chosen if the Transcendents had asked. (Indeed, with their mighty simulations, perhaps they did.)

Our merged union is a distillation. A combination of life orders. A mélange, filled with hybrid vigor. Laced with special flavors from Jijo and Earth, our community may have the right mix that it takes to succeed at last, where so many others failed.

To bridge what was unbridgeable.
To help unite what was separate.
To bring the cosmos more diversity . . . and make it one.

We can feel *Polkjhy*'s new tendrils reaching out, clasping the fabric of space, awaiting the moment when a chaos wave next strikes.

The biggest chaos wave of all.

The Great Rupture.

Have the Transcendents timed things right? Do they really have the skill to trigger their explosion at precisely the moment, so *Polkjhy* can catch that wave?

Yes, my rings and other selves.

i/we/I/you can hardly wait to find out.

THE WHITE DWARF TREMBLES.

It is just ten thousand kilometers across. Ignition will flow at the speed of sound—a few thousand kilometers per second. That means it should take less than a dura. . . .

STREAKER LABORS MIGHTILY, STRIVING TO REACH THE ESCAPE TUNNEL.

Go, Sara!

You can make it.

Go!

Each passing second seems an eternity, as the Earthship struggles toward that flickering sanctuary.

ABRUPTLY, OUR SUNWARD SENSORS CATCH A BRILLIANT LIGHT!

A blinding flare that flows and ripples with mad speed across the tormented stellar surface, like the sudden striking of a match.

Then—

CAN YOU FEEL THEM, MY RINGS?

Neutrinos in the wax.

What a strange sensation! Like remembering tomorrow.

And now, here we go—

PART V

THE TIME OF CHANGES

Some life orders are more communicative than others.

Members of the Quantum Order have no sense of either place or time. At least, none corresponding with the way we view those properties. Though willing to exchange information, they generally make no sense of our queries, nor do we comprehend most of their answers. There must be some commonality of context in order for the word "meaning" to have any significance. Compared to the Quantum Order, it is almost trivial to converse with hydrogen breathers, machines, or even the most coherent sapient memes.

Once, however, a member of the touvint client race presumptuously interrupted its elders at a D-Space rendezvous, and confronted one of the quantals with a naively simple question.

"What can we expect?"

The answer has puzzled scholars for a million years.

Without hesitation, the strange being replied—

"Everything."

GALAXIES

The supernova's photon front caught *Streaker* just short of a swirling black tunnel—the escape path promised by cryptic Transcendents.

Alarms wailed and dolphins squalled as waves of searing energy struck from behind, crushing the normal protective fields, slamming each square meter with more heat than a normal sun would over the course of its lifespan. The blast would have evaporated the *Streaker* of old almost instantly.

But the Earthship was like a whale whose skin was coated with hard-shell barnacles, *Streaker* toiled under layers of strange stuff—coatings that shimmered in the heat, as if *eager* for the ruinous light.

Sara held Prity and Emerson. A rumbling vibration rattled her bones and the marrow inside. Blinding turmoil swamped every outside camera, but sensors told of staggering photon and neutrino fluxes as the star passed its limits of endurance . . . or perhaps ecstasy. In real time, the eruption took milliseconds, but *Streaker*'s duration-stretched field let the crew witness successive stages, in slow motion.

"Our magic coating's impressive," commented Suessi. "But these're just photons. No way it can handle what's next. More than a solar mass of real matter . . . protons and heavy nuclei . . . leapin' this way at a good share of lightspeed."

Sara had learned enough practical physics to know what fist was about to smite them. Each atom of oxygen and carbon in my body passed through a convulsion like this one . . . cooked in a sun, then spewed into great clouds, before condensing to form planets, critters, people.

Now her own stardust might return to the cosmic mixing bowl, perhaps joining the life cycle of a new world, yet unborn. It seemed a dry consolation. But she knew another.

Lark.

I got his message—just as that shell closed around the *Polkjhy*, spreading its lambent tendrils, preparing to catch waves of hyperreality, the very moment when galaxies part company forever.

By now, his ship must already be punching through, catching a great tide of recoiling metric. Outward bound on a great adventure.

Ironies made her smile. Among the three children of Nelo and Melina, Lark alone never dreamed of leaving his beloved Jijo. Yet now he would see more of the cosmos than even the great Transcendents! An avowed celibate, he and his mate could sire a whole nation of humanity in some far galaxy.

Good-bye, brother. May Ifni's Boss keep an eye on you.

Have fun.

Their escape tunnel loomed, a cave filled with eerie, unnerving spirals. She looked up at Emerson. Moments ago, as a final hail of crushed Old Ones fell on the white dwarfs tormented surface, he had barked a single word—

"Dross!"

—and smiled, as if watching a deadly foe collapse in failure.

Someone counted subjective seconds till the matter-wave would hit. ". . . fourteen . . . thirteen . . . twelve . . ."

Meanwhile, Akeakemai crooned. "Almost there . . ."

The pilot's flukes thrashed, urging *Streaker* along to the refuge. "Almossssst . . ."

The suspense was so awful, Sara's mind reflexively fled to a domain where she had some control. Mathematics. To a problem she had discovered recently—while Gillian dickered with the Transcendents to take *Polkjhy as a replacement,* and let *Streaker* go.

Amid a maze of transfinite tensors, Sara had found a renormalization quandary that simply would not go away.

In fact, it seemed *essential, in order* to describe the chaos waves they had seen. And yet, according to the Transcendents' own models, it made no sense!

I thought I knew the whole truth when I foresaw the galactic breakup, arising from the expansion of the universe. But now I can tell—some added force is driving things faster than expected.

It only made sense if she made a peculiar conjecture.

Something is coming in. Something titanic.

Details were vague, but she knew one thing about the intruding presence.

It won't be found in any gravity well. We must look elsewhere, in flat space. Far from the Embrace of—

Streaker shook suddenly. Vibrations leaped in force and volume, shuddering her spine. Someone screamed.

"Matter wave!"

For an instant, time seemed to flicker—

Then, across the span of an eyeblink, Sara was surrounded by leaping, yelling figures. Emerson squeezed her as if it were the end of the world. And briefly, she thought it was.

Then she knew Prity's gleeful screech, the dolphins' whistled raspberries of joy, and her lover's gasping laughter. Amid the tumult and confusion, Sara noticed—all the ominous rumblings were gone. Vanished! Replaced by a happy roar of unleashed engines.

The view screens were back on, showing vistas of strangely distorted *ylem*—the walls of a weirdly beneficent tunnel, sweeping them along.

"We made it!" Suessi's amplified voice exulted.

We . . . did?

Sara realized with some chagrin that her math-trance had kept her from witnessing the moment of triumph and salvation.

Well, damn me for a distracted nerd, she thought, and threw herself into kissing Emerson with all her might.

E SPACE

Harry's profession always seemed a lonely one.

Now I know why Wer'Q'quinn sent solitary scouts on missions to E Space. Too many minds can be dangerous here. And embarrassing.

During earlier trips to the kingdom of living ideas, he sometimes entered a new territory only to find the local matrix crystallizing around symbols that leaked from his own mind. Since there was seldom anyone else around but herds of local memoids, it hardly mattered what the shapes revealed about his subconscious.

This time, the station carried *five* strong-willed personalities, from four different races. Harry worried from the moment his vessel emerged through a drifting purple haze, striding on long, spidery legs.

The initial fog shredded, as if blown aside by his passengers' curious scrutiny. Dwer and Kaa and Kiwei Ha'aoulin pressed the windows rimming the control chamber. Dwer had been in E Space before. The others were transfixed by their first visit to this famous, mythical province.

You wouldn't peer about so eagerly if you'd seen what I have.

Still Harry refrained from closing the louvered blinds. This would be the last chance of their lives to see E Space.

And maybe my last trip, as well.

Soon, the mist cleared to reveal a vast landscape of cubes, pyramids, tilted planes, and other more complex geometric forms. At least, that was how the objects began.

The first time he looked closely at one, it started *melting,* congealing, taking on new, rounded contours. Soon he saw protrusions on both sides that resembled . . . ears! Then a flared nose. Moments later, a mouth full of yellowed teeth grimaced back at him, both unappealing and familiar.

He checked instruments. The memic-monolith stood over thirty pseudokilometers away! Apparently, he had just triggered the manifestation of a gigantic sculpture representing his own head, towering higher than the largest structures on Earth. Glancing left and right, he saw that Synthian, dolphin, and human-shaped statuary were coagulating in all directions. Replications of Kaa, Dwer, and Kiwei soon stretched as far as the eye could see.

"Well, well," commented the delighted Synthian trader, with both hands folded across her belly. "Should someone wake Rety, so she might also partake in this opportunity for megascale immortalization?"

Harry shook his head while a mammoth sculpture mimicked his expression of piqued irritation.

"The poor kid is sleeping off a concussion. Anyway, this sort of thing generally doesn't last. Most of these gross memes just fade back into the ylem, soon as the stimulating host mind leaves."

"But occasionally they *don't* fade? There is a chance this will be permanent?"

Harry shrugged, wondering why Kiwei cared.

"I've seen things—crypto-shapes and frozen images from the distant past. Wer'Q'quinn says reified meme-stuff can sometimes get more rigid than anything made of true matter, like the ideas that become permanently fixed in some living brains. I guess there are concept-objects in E Space that may outlast all the protons an' quarks, an' the whole sidereal universe."

Kiwei gazed at a range of hillocks and mountains, most of them wearing her own smug, rounded countenance.

"Really?" Her sigh was wistfully hopeful.

Dwer and Kaa both chuckled. But Harry shook his head.

"Let's get moving," he said. "Before something else goes wrong."

So far, little had gone according to plan.

First came that riotous muddle at the Kazzkark warehouse. While Dwer covered their retreat with a hail of arrows, Harry and Kiwei had managed to grab the unconscious Rety and carry her off without being ripped to shreds by the angry Tandu warrior. Nearby hallways clamored with sounds of reinforcements—more of the vicious creatures—charging to help their comrade wreak havoc while chaos waves shook the little planetoid from end to end.

With a backward glance, Harry caught the final moments of the Skiano missionary—spreading his arms in rapture as the Tandu hurled him into a globe-icon of Earth that shattered into jagged shards, merging his shredded body with the blue "martyr planet."

Troubles followed them to the Institute Docks, where slabs of rock wall were already coming loose, toppling to crush vehicles parked at nearby wharves. Screeching alarms warned that a vacuum breach was imminent. Harry hurried everyone aboard and got his station under way—with Kaa's little corvette towed behind—just before the ceiling started collapsing. By the time he reached the main airlock, there wasn't much point going through emigration protocols. The obstructing wall *dissolved,* revealing fields of weirdly twinkling stars.

It took a while to dodge swarms of hazardous debris before they could make even a simple, short-range hyperjump. Meanwhile, chaos waves rocked the planetoid. *Even if I make it back from this mission, there'd be no sense reporting here.*

There are other Institute bases.

Anyway, they say it's safer to be on a planet these days.

Finally, the chaos waves ebbed, though he knew worse was to come. As Kazzkark vanished from sight, Harry hoped Wer'Q'quinn, the old squid, would make it somehow.

Things got kind of blurry then. He gave coordinates to Kaa and let the expert space pilot take their co-joined vessels through a dozen B-Level jumps, then into a small t-point that was already declared dangerously unstable.

Kaa's innovative thread-jumping maneuvers somehow kept them from being torn, sliced, roasted, or vaporized. Still, it was a wild, nerve-racking ride. Harry spent half the time cursing cetaceans and their ancestors, all the way back to the Miocene.

At last, they reached his assigned entry point—a special place, darker than black, where the walls between reality levels were thin enough to pierce—and it was Harry's turn to take over. Soon, materiality shimmered and they underwent transition to a realm whose physics let ideas have a life of their own.

It gladdened Harry to depart the province of giant statuary, entering a terrain covered by endless swaths of undulating orange "grass"—each blade consisting of some basic concept that thrived free of any language or host mind.

On close inspection, the prairie looked eroded, discolored. Large patches seemed broken or seared, as if raked by quake and fire. Apparently, E Space wasn't immune to the tumult shaking five linked galaxies. Even the memoid herds were affected. He witnessed several great flocks darting to and fro, stampeding as both ground and sky rippled threateningly.

While his passengers stared in wonder, Harry set course for the Cosmic Path. He must find a portion that peered into Galaxy Four and set his instruments as soon as possible. Fortunately, these new devices were disposable. He could leave them in place till they were destroyed. Their death cries would give Wer'Q'quinn's people vital data about the Great Rupture. This time, his boss promised, the information would be broadcast widely, not kept in secret files for use by elder races and star gods.

That was the main reason Harry agreed to this mission. It might seem odd to worry about events a hundred million years from now. But for some reason he identified with people in that distant era. Maybe his efforts would spare those folks some of the ignorant terror now sweeping Five Galaxies. Even if, by then, the "gods" were distant heirs of chimpanzees, and the Navigation Institute of that future age was staffed by descendants of today's lice. The kind infesting his fur right now, making him constantly yearn to scratch his—

"Captain Harms," said a whirling circular shape that appeared uncomfortably near his nose. *"I have news! Your goal should now lie in view. Congratulations! And may I add that it has been a real—"*

Harry cut off observer mode holo with a curt head-shake. Hustling to a bank of windows, he peered past the ever-present E Space haze . . . and caught sight of a sinuous glow, twisting across the countryside just ahead. "Well, something's going right, for a change," he murmured.

While laying his instruments, he would find an appropriate site along the Path, put Kaa and the others in the corvette, and shove the little vessel into normal space—hopefully within reach of their destination. Harry might then have barely enough time to get back home to civilization before the whole place rocked and rolled.

Rety was adamant.

From the moment she got up—stumbling into the control chamber with a hand pressed to her head and the other stroking her little urrish "husband"—Rety made one fact abundantly clear.

She was *not* returning to Jijo with Dwer and the others.

"*You* may be homesick for filth an' a bunch of low-tech barbarians, but if I never hear o' that place again, it'll be too soon! I'm going back with Harry."

That was it. No gratitude for saving her life. No mention of her erstwhile religion, or inquiries about her late guru. Just a fierce determination that defied all argument.

Even so young, she is formidable. I've met some humans with personalities this strong. All were world-shifters—for well or ill.

But most had one trait Rety lacked. They knew the pragmatic value of tact. Of course, she'd been raised by savages. In civilization, she might learn social skills, forge alliances, achieve aspirations, and possibly even be liked.

There was just one problem with her plan.

"I'll be honest, miss. There's a good chance I can get you all to the right quadrant of Galaxy Four. Maybe even the sector. But my own odds of survival after—"

Rety laughed. "Don't tell me odds! I ain't worried 'bout odds since I was gored by a gallaiter, and given up by my own tribe for dead. Yee an' I are gonna stick right by your furry side, if you don't mind. And even if you do."

The others were no help.

Once Harry verified this length of Avenue looked into Galaxy Fours, Kaa used a spectral analyzer to peer into the path—filled with dark nebulae and glittering stellar clusters—searching for the telltale blush of a particularly stormy red-giant star. Kiwei occupied herself staring at the plain of memes, apparently trying to impose her will again, causing more shapes to appear.

Dwer's sole response was a rolling of eyes. He had no aim to intervene in Rety's life again.

"Oh, all right." Harry sighed. "Just promise you'll stay out of the way. And no whining about where you finally wind up!"

Rety nodded. "So long as it ain't Jijo. And there's plumbing. And beds with—"

A buzzer announced the dropping of another instrument package along the curving Path. With luck, Wer'Q'quinn's devices would be positioned well before the biggest chaos wave of all. Then it would be a matter of dropping Kaa and the others off near a mapped t-point and wishing them luck.

He offered Kiwei another chance to withdraw.

"You don't have to enter Galaxy Four. After the links snap, there'll be no more travel between—"

She raised a meaty hand, chuckling. "Not more fairy tales about a permanent 'rupture' please! Scout-Major, you've been misled. The Five Galaxies have always been—"

The station abruptly jolted to a halt. A shrill squeal made everyone turn as Kaa used his tail flukes to thump the pad of his walker.

"C-come!" the dolphin urged. "Come and see thissss!"

Harry and Kiwei hurried to join him at a bank of windows. Kaa used his neural tap to create a pointer ray, aimed toward the glittering Avenue.

"*There it iss!*" The pilot hissed clear, moist satisfaction. "I found it!"

Dwer asked—"Izmunuti?"

"Yesss! Just past that oblong cloud of ionized hydrogen. The spectral match is perfect. So are surrounding star formationssss."

"Wow," Dwer said. "I think I can even make out a familiar constellation or two. All twisted, of course."

Kaa raised a sleek gray head, chattering happily. And though Harry's Trinary was rusty, he caught the gist.

- *It would be enough to do my duty,*
    - *having helped the cause of Earthclan.*

- *It would be enough to rescue Peepoe,*
    - *and to spend a lifetime with her.*

• It would be enough to help save Jijo,
• and to taste those silky waters.

• All those things and many others,
• would have let me face death happy.

• But among those counted pleasures,
• this means I reclaim my nickname! •

Kiwei peered toward the vast sprawl of pinpoints.

"Then Jijo's sun. . . ?"

"Is right th-there!" Kaa turned a dark eye toward Harry. "Major Harms, if you insert us here, how many paktaars would that leave us from—"

A sudden jab on the shoulder diverted Harry's attention. He swiveled to see Rety, holding her urrish companion in the crook of one arm. The little creature—her "husband"—craned its long neck, peering at the Path.

"Uh, Major Harms, could we ask you a question?"

"Not right now, Rety. We're making an important decision."

She nodded. "I know. But yee just saw something you oughta look at." She pointed along the sinuous tube, back the way they'd just come. "There's stuff goin' on in there."

Harry straightened. "What do you mean?"

"I mean in the last few duras there's been three or four really bright . . . There goes another one!" She winced as a sudden glare hit her eye. "Is that normal? Can stars get so shiny, all of a sudden? I figure you'd want to—"

"Observer mode!" Harry shouted. "Scan the Avenue for sudden stellar bursts. Are they E-Space illusions, or is something real happening in Galaxy Four?"

The hovering symbol whirled for only a moment.

"The outbursts have spectra and brightness profiles of unusually energetic, type SN1a supernovae. Such explosions are known to affect the interfacial membrane that you call the Avenue."

"I can see that!" Harry snapped. The mammoth tube's stable sinuosity had started to move. It shivered and heaved near each sudden point of aching brightness.

"Safety parameters deem it prudent to retreat now from the boundary."

Kiwei protested. "But supernovas do not happen this way! Each is an isolated astrophysical event!"

"I don't like this," Dwer added.

"Maybe we oughta do what the voice says," Rety suggested. "Back off. Head for civilized space. Take shelter on some planet till all this blows ov—"

"Forget it-t!" Kaa squalled. "Harms, keep your promissss!"

Harry nodded. "Okay. Everyone who's going to Jijo, move through the airlock to the corvette. We'll need a few duras—"

His sentence cut off as another little blue star abruptly flared—this time just to their left, almost adjacent to the boundary—expanding its effulgence a billionfold, filling the cabin with blinding glare.

Lightspeed was no impediment to the causality disruption that followed. Some kind of metric wave hammered the fleshy inner surface of the Path, making it buck and heave like a tortured snake. The perimeter warped into E Space, discoloring horribly as new bulges formed, flailing like agonized pseudopods. Several of these curled around the station, lashing spasmodically.

It seemed a rather personal way to be assailed by a supernova. But Harry had no time to dwell on ironies of scale. "Prepare for transition!" he croaked in a terrified voice.

All at once, the entire Path seemed to *shimmer,* and Harry knew that the estimates had been wrong.

The rupture is coming.

His passengers had just moments to grab some nearby object before the sidereal universe seized Harry's vessel with a horrid moan, yanking them all back into a realm of atoms.

SOL SYSTEM

Gillian knew just two living pilots who might stand a chance of maneuvering swiftly through spacial conditions like these.

Keepiru, and Kaa. Both had started out three years ago with Creideiki's carefully picked crew.

Now, both were gone. Each to where he was needed most.

Each to where he belonged.

Fly true, Keepiru. She cast the wish outward, past a myriad random glimmering stars. *Wherever Tom and Creideiki decide to go, please guide them through to safe harbors.*

As for Kaa, she had felt guilty since pulling him away from Jijo, where Peepoe needed him. According to Sara's calculations, the route back to Jijo would be perilous, demanding all his skill, as well as a generous helping of his famous luck.

Soon—upon emerging into the hyperspatial byways of Galaxy Two—*Streaker* began picking up news casts. Amid frenzied reports of local calamities and rescues came a few notes—barely mentions—about the severing of all contact with Galaxy Four. Praise be to the wise and sagacious Migration Institute's decision, a mere half a million years ago, to evacuate all of that vast region's starfaring clans! Of course, the disruptions were likely to be temporary. So, everyone remain calm.

Gillian knew better.

So, that's done. The end of an age . . . and a smaller cosmos for us all.

But I know you'll make it, Lucky Kaa. May you swim with Peepoe soon and remain Ifni's favorite all your life.

Conditions in the other four galaxies weren't quite as bad. Yet, the remainder of civilized space was raucous and high-strung. The Navigation Institute kept posting detours till it ran out of buoys, then stationed gallant volunteers along every known route, shouting themselves hoarse over subspace frequencies, diverting traffic to a few safe paths. Flotillas set out from countless planets on daring mercy missions, braving maelstroms to rescue lost ships and stranded crews.

It was Galactic Civilization at its best—the reason it would almost certainly survive this chaos, and possibly emerge stronger than ever. After things settled down, that is. In a few thousand years.

Alas, while many clans and races dropped their petty squabbles to lend a hand, others took advantage of the disorder to loot, extort, or settle old grudges. Religious schisms spread like poisonous ripples, amplifying ancient animosities.

And where is Streaker *heading, right now? Straight for the worst site of fanatical warfare, praying we get there before the fighting's over. Talk about jumping from the frying pan into the fire.*

At least Gillian had no complaints about *Streaker*'s rate of speed. Right now, she probably had the fastest ship in all of oxygen-breathing civilization.

Not to put down Akeakemai, but without Keepiru or Kaa, this trip would have taken months, following the marked detours. *We'd arrive at our destination only to find ashes.*

So, it's a good thing we had outside help.

That "help" embraced the Earthship's bristly cylinder like a second skin—a blanket of shimmering tendrils that reached out to stroke the varied metric textures of the cosmic continuum, sensing and choosing course, speed, and level of subspace in order to make the best possible headway. Undaunted by warning buoys and danger signs, the semi-sapient coating steered *Streaker* along routes that flamed and whirled with tempests of unresolved hypergeometry, making snap transitions that would have taxed even Keepiru at his best.

The great Transcendents might hate leaving their comfortable Embrace of Tides, seldom venturing from their black hole event horizons to meddle in the destiny of lesser races. But their *servants* sure knew how to fly.

Perhaps this special treatment balanced some of *Streaker*'s awful luck during the last three years. But after narrowly escaping a supernova explosion, Gillian gave up tallying miracles—good, bad . . . and simply weird.

Just get us home in time, she thought, whether or not a Transcendent might still be listening.

By the time *Streaker* passed the triple beacons of Tanith, Gillian knew the impossible was about to happen.

We're going to see Earth again . . . though perhaps only from afar. And it may be the last thing we ever do.

When golden Sol became the brightest glitter in the view screen, they began encountering new warning buoys, laid down by a different bureaucracy. The audio version in Gal Seven carried the officious, rumbling tones of a dour, hoonish civil servant.

> **BEWARE TRAVELERS!**
> **YOU ARE ENTERING A CONFLICT ZONE**
> **DULY REGISTERED UNDER THE RULES OF WAR!**
> **YOU ARE ADVISED: RETURN TO TANITH AT ONCE!**
> **IF YOU HAVE BUSINESS HERE,**
> **INQUIRE WITH REPRESENTATIVES OF**
> **THE INSTITUTE FOR CIVILIZED WARFARE**
> **ABOUT A SAFE-CONDUCT PASS,**

OR ELSE REGISTER AS YET ANOTHER
CO-BELLIGERENT FORCE
EITHER ALIGNED AGAINST THE
TERRAN DEFENDERS
OR FOR THEM.
THE FOLLOWING RACES/NATIONS/
CLANS/ALLIANCES
HAVE DECLARED VENDETTA- ENFORCEMENT CAMPAIGNS
AGAINST THE OXY-LINEAGE KNOWN
AS EARTHCLAN . . .

It went on like that for a while, listing some of the factions who had laid siege to Gillian's homeworld—a long, intimidating roll call. Apparently, after years of bickering over who should get the privilege of conquering Earth, the Soro, Tandu, Jophur, J'8lek and others had agreed to join forces and divide the spoils.

On the defending side, a tally of humanity's allies remained depressingly sparse. The Tymbrimi had remained true, at great cost. And the doughty Thennanin. Material aid—arms, but not fighters—had been smuggled in by p'ort'ls, Zuhgs, and Synthians, as well as a faction of the Awaiter Alliance. And a new group, calling itself the *Apostles,* had lately sent shiploads of volunteers.

The War Institute message went on to describe a long chain of protests, filed by the Soro and others, complaining about "wolfling tricks" that had stymied several successive attempts to bring their warships within firing range of Earth, resulting in massive casualities and the loss of several dozen major capital vessels, all caused by weapons and tactics not found in the Galactic Library, and therefore suspiciously improper ways for folks to slay their own would-be killers!

That part made Gillian chuckle proudly . . . though apparently the Terragens Council was running out of "tricks." In fact, their forces were now reduced to a fiery ring, marked by Luna's orbit.

The Institute buoy finished by officially attesting that the rules of war had largely been adhered to as this conflict wound down to its inevitable conclusion.

"Some rules!" sniffed Suessi. In some other eras, the War Institute had formalized combat to a relatively harmless sport, pitting professional champions, or strictly measured fleets, against each other for privilege or honor. But under today's loose strictures—made almost unenforceable by recent chaos—the battle armadas infesting Earth could do almost anything. Gas its cities. Capture and "adopt" its citizens. Anything except harm the planet's fragile biosphere. And even that might be overlooked as society unraveled.

There was some good news. Apparently, the so-called Coalition of Moderate Races had finally declared open opposition to the siege, gathering forces to compel a cease-fire. The first units might arrive in a few weeks, if they weren't held up by traffic snarls.

We've heard such promises before, Gillian thought bitterly.

The Niss reported that oddsmakers and bookies (who hardly paused doing business, despite the Great Rupture) gave Terrans little hope of lasting that long.

"Well, a lot has changed lately," she told *Streaker*'s crew as they plunged toward the shell-of-battle surrounding their home star. "Let's see if we can make a difference."

Her plans remained flexible, depending on what conditions were like near Earth.

Perhaps it might be possible to break the siege by causing a distraction. After all, her ship was the great prize everyone had been chasing for so long. Word of *Streaker*'s discoveries in the Shallow Cluster had set off all this frenzy in the first place. Nor would that passion have abated, with the Great Rupture fresh in memory and apocalyptic prophecies crisscrossing civilization, more disruptive than chaos waves. While tumult still rattled every sector and quadrant, each dogmatic alliance would feel more anxious than ever to solve the Progenitors' Riddle before its rivals.

What if *Streaker* suddenly appeared before the besieging forces, confronting the attackers, taunting them, and then turning to flee across a turbulent galaxy? Might that draw the battle fleets away, buying Earth much-needed time? With luck, it could reignite strife between the Tandu and other radical factions, winnowing their ranks so the timid "moderates" might at last intervene.

Such a move might seem to conflict with Gillian's orders from the Terragens Council. Those instructions had been to hide. Above all, not to let Creideiki's data fall into the wrong hands. *Streaker* should surrender the information only to qualified impartial agencies, or else when the people of the Five . . . rather, *Four* Galaxies, could agree how to share it.

Well, I've taken care of that! What agency could be more "qualified and neutral" than the merged community that took over the former Jophur battleship, *Polkjhy*? A consortium of emissaries from several life orders, picked by the transcendents to represent our entire macroculture to some far-distant realm?

All the Ghost Fleet samples, including Herbie the enigmatic cadaver, were now aboard that transformed starship, racing far beyond reach of even the most dogged zealot. Perhaps some far-distant alien civilization would be suitably impressed, or even be able to answer questions about the enigma.

All that remains from the Shallow Cluster is a set of coordinates. And those are in a safe place.

Heady sensations filled Gillian's chest. She recognized the source.

Freedom.

Along with *Streaker*'s remaining crew, she now felt liberated of an awful burden. A weight of *importance* that used to hang on them all like a shroud, requiring that they slink and hide, like prey. Too valuable to be brave.

But that had changed.

We are soldiers now. That is all.

Soldiers of Earthclan.

HYPERSPACE

Everything unraveled after the great rupture. All the wonderful structure—the many-layered textures of spacetime—began coming apart.

Wer'Q'quinn's experts had warned Harry. Recoil effects would be far worse in Galaxy Four, when all its ancient links to other spirals snapped and most transfer points collapsed. Additionally, all the known levels of hyperspace—A through E—would come more or less unfastened, like skins sloughing off a snake, and largely go their own way.

Not only have I lost any hope of going home, he thought during the wild ride that followed. *We may all be stuck forever in some pathetic corner of a single spiral arm. Perhaps even a solar system!*

That assumed they even made it safely back to normal space.

Harry's station shuddered and moaned. All the louvered blinds rattled in their frames, while unnerving cracks began working their way through the thick crystal panes. Just outside, a maze of transfer threads churned like tormented worms, whipping in terminal agony, Spaciogeometric links, robbed of their moorings, now snapped violently, slicing and shredding each other to bits.

This seemed a frightfully bad time to try evading the speed of light with shortcuts that had been routine for aeons. Cheating Einstein had become a perilous felony.

It might have been safer simply to drop to normal space and ride out the aftershocks near some star with a habitable fallow planet. Worst case—if FTL travel became impossible—at least they might have a place to land. But Kaa would have none of that. Almost from the moment they dropped out of E Space, the dolphin took over control, ditching the now useless corvette, and sent Harry's station careening through a nearby transfer point—a dying maelstrom—desperately scouring for a route to the one place he called home.

Harry had never seen piloting so brilliant—or half so mad. His stubby station was hardly a sport-skimmer, yet Kaa threw the vessel into swooping turns, hopping among the radiant threads like some doped-up gibbon brachiating through a burning forest, throwing its weight from one flaming vine to the next. Kaa's tail repeatedly slapped the flotation pad. The dolphin's eyes were sunken and glazed while floods of information poured through his neural tap. A ratchet of sonar clicks sprayed from the high-domed skull, sometimes merging to form individual words.

Peepoe was one Harry heard often. Having done his duty for *Streaker* and Earth, Kaa had just one priority—to reach his beloved.

Harry sympathized. I just wish he asked me before taking us on this insane ride!

No one dared break Kaa's concentration. Even Rety kept silent, nervously stroking her little urrish husband. Kiwei Ha'aoulin crouched, muttering to herself in a Synthian dialect, perhaps wishing she had listened to the inner voice of caution rather than greed.

Only Dwer seemed indifferent to fear. The young hunter braced his back against the control console, and one foot on a nearby window, leaving both hands free to polish his bow while a Gordian knot of cosmic strings unraveled spectacularly outside.

Well, I guess anything can seem anticlimactic, Harry thought. *After watching a whole chain of supernovas go off at once—and having the Avenue seize you like some agonized monster—one might get jaded with something as mundane as a conflagration in hyperspace.*

Kaa pealed a yammering cry, sending the station plunging toward a huge thread whose loose end lashed, shuddering and spraying torrents of horrid sparks! Rety shouted. Vertigo roiled Harry's guts, threatening to void his bowels. He covered his eyes, bracing for impact . . .

. . . and swayed when nothing happened.

Not even a vibration. Around him stirred only a low chuckle of engines, gently turning over.

Both fearful and curious, Harry lowered his hands.

Stars shone, beyond the pitted glass. Patterns of soft lights. Stable. Permanent.

Well, almost. One patch twinkled oddly, as a wave of warped metric rippled past. Tapering chaos disturbances, still causing the vacuum to shiver. Still, how much better this seemed than that awful pit of sparking serpents!

Behind the station, receding rapidly, lay the transfer point they had just exited, marked by flashing red symbols.

DO NOT ENTER, blazoned one computer-generated icon.

NEXUS TERMINALLY DISRUPTED.

CONDITIONS LETHAL WITHIN.

I can believe that, Harry thought, vowing to embrace Kaa, the first chance he got . . . and to *shoot* the pilot if he tried to enter another t-point like that one.

In the opposite direction, growing ever larger, stood the red disk of a giant star.

"Izmunuti?" Harry guessed.

Kaa was still chattering to himself. But Dwer gave an emphatic nod.

"I'd know it anywhere. Though the storms seem to've settled since the last time we passed this way."

Rety reacted badly to this news.

"No!" Her fists clenched toward Harry. "You promised I wouldn't have to go back! Turn this ship around. Take me back to civilization!"

"I don't think you grasp the problem," he replied. "At this rate, we'd be lucky to reach *any* habitable world. Clearly, the nearest one is—"

The young woman covered her ears. "I won't listen. I won't!"

He looked to Dwer, who shrugged. Rety's aggrieved rejection of reality reminded Harry of a race called *episiarchs,* clients of the mighty Tandu, who could somehow use psi—plus sheer force of ego—to change small portions of the universe around them, transforming nearby conditions more to their liking. Some savants theorized that all it took was a strong enough will, plus a high opinion of yourself. If so, Rety might hurl them megaparsecs from this place, so desperate was she *not* to see the world of her birth.

Kaa lifted his bottle-nosed head. The pilot's black eye cleared as he made an announcement. "We c-can't stay here. Jijo is still over a light-year away. That'll take at least a dozen jumps through A Space. Or fifffty . . . if we use Level B."

Harry recalled predictions made by the Kazzkark Navigation staff—that the rupture would make all hyperlevels much harder to use. In Galaxy Four, they might detach completely and flutter away, leaving behind the glittering blackness of normal space, an Einsteinian cosmos, where cause and effect were ruled strictly by the crawling speed of light.

But that peeling transition would not come instantly.

Perhaps the rapid layers could still be used, for a while at least.

"Try B Space," he suggested. "I have a hunch we may need to drop out quickly and often along the way."

Kaa tossed his great head.

"Okay. It's your ship-p. B Space it issss. . . ."

With that hiss of finality, the pilot turned his attention back through the neural tap, to a realm where his uncanny cetacean knack might be their only hope.

Harry felt the station power up for the first jump.

I'd pray. If creation itself weren't already moaning in pain.

Almost from the start, they saw disturbing signs of ruin—debris of numerous space vessels, wrecked as they had tried following exactly the same course, flicker-jumping from Izmunuti toward Jijo.

"Some folks passed this way before us," Dwer commented.

"And quite recently, by all appearances." Kiwei's voice was awed. "It seems that an entire fleet of large vessels came through. They must have been caught in hyperspace when the Rupture struck."

The results were devastating. As Izmunuti fell away behind them, and Jijo's sun grew steadily brighter, Harry's instruments showed appalling remnants of a shattered armada, some of the hulks still glowing from fiery dismemberment.

"I make out at least two basic ship types," he diagnosed, peering into the analytical scope. "One of 'em might be Jophur. The other . . . I can't tell."

In fact, it was hard to get a fix on anything, because their own vessel kept heaving and shuddering. Kaa yanked the station back into normal space whenever his fey instincts told him that a new chaos wave was coming, or when a flapping crease in B Level threatened to fold over itself and smash anything caught between.

Crossing this unstable zone of hyperreality—a rather short span by earlier standards—became a treacherous series of mad sprints that got worse, dura by dura. Each flicker seemed to take greater concentration than the last, demanding more from the gasping engines. And yet, there could be no pause for rest. It was essential to reenter hyperspace as soon as possible, for at any moment B Level might detach completely, leaving them stranded, many light months from any refuge. Food and air would give out long before Harry's small group might traverse such a vast distance of flat metric.

Too bad we Earthlings never pursued our early knack at impulse rocketry, after making contact with the Civilization of Five Galaxies. It seemed the most ridiculous of all wolfling technologies, to make ships capable of brute-force acceleration toward lightspeed. With so many cheap shortcuts available from the Great Library, who needed such a tool kit of outlandishly extravagant tricks?

The answer was apparent.

We do. Anyone who wants to travel around Galaxy Four may need them. Perhaps temporarily. Or else from now till the end of time.

At least there were clear signs of progress. Each jump brought them visibly closer to that warm, sturdy sun. Yet, the tense moments passed with aching slowness, as they followed a rubble-strewn trail of devastated starcraft.

"I guess that Jophur battleship must have got word to their headquarters, while it was off chasing *Streaker*," Dwer concluded. "Their reinforcements arrived at the worst moment, just in time to be smashed by the Rupture."

"We should rejoice," mused Kiwei. "I have no wish to live in a Jophur satrapy."

"Hmph," Harry commented. "That assumes all of their fleet was caught in hyperspace during the worst of it. For all we know, a whole squadron may have made it safely. They could be waiting for us at Jijo."

It was a dismal prospect—to have endured so much, only to face capture at the end by humorless stacks of uncompromising sap-rings.

"Well," Dwer said, after a few more edgy jumps, when the yellow star was already looking quite sunlike. "We won't have long to wait now."

He pressed close to the forwardmost window, as eager to spy Jijo as Rety was to evade the verdict of destiny.

EARTH

The solar system was littered with wreckage from more than two years of seesaw fighting—shattered reminders of stiff wolfling resistance that surely came as a rude shock to invaders expecting easy conquest. Fourth-hand tales of that savage struggle had reached *Streaker*'s crew, even at the remote Fractal World. Apparently, that defense was already the stuff of legends.

Ion clouds and rubble traced the inward path of that fighting retreat . . . vaporized swathes in the cometary ice belt . . . still-smoldering craters on Triton and Nereid . . . and several asteroid-sized clumps of twisted metal, tumbling in orbit beyond Uranus.

It must have been quite a show. Sorry I missed it.

More debris was added recently, when the Great Rupture struck. Ships that tried any kind of FTL maneuvering during the causality storm had been lucky to reach normal space again with more consistency than an ice slurpie. Saturn's orbit was now a glittering junkyard, soon to become a vast ring around the sun.

Unfortunately, long-range scans showed more than enough big vessels left to finish the job. Scores of great dreadnoughts—several of them titans compared to the enormous *Polkjhy*—gathered in martial formations along the new battlefront, all too near Earth's shimmering blue spark.

The first picket boats hailed *Streaker* well beyond the orbit of Ceres. A bizarre, mixed squadron consisting of corvettes and frigates from Tandu, Soro, and gorouph navies, joined in uneasy federation. They were alert, despite the havoc that residual chaos waves still played on instruments. When *Streaker* ignored their challenge and kept plunging rapidly sunward, the nearest ships raced closer to open fire with deadly accuracy.

Blades of razorlike force scythed at the Earthship—only to glance off its transmuted hull. Heat beams were absorbed quietly, with no observable effect, dissipating harmlessly into another level of spacetime.

If these failures fazed the enemy, they did not show it openly. Rushing closer, several lead vessels launched volleys of powerful, intelligent missiles, hurtling toward *Streaker* at great speed. According to Suessi, this was the worst threat. Direct energy weapons had little effect on the Transcendent's coating. But *physical shock* could disrupt anything made of matter, if it came hard and fast enough, in a well-timed sequence of shaped concussions.

As if aware of that danger, *Streaker*'s sapient outer layer suddenly became active. Tendrils fluttered, like cilia surrounding a bacterium. Swarms of tiny objects flew off their waving tips, darting to meet the incoming barrage. Under extreme magnification, the strange interceptors looked like tiny pockets of writhing protoplasm, jet-black, but disconcertingly alive.

"Reified concepts," explained the disembodied Niss Machine, sounding awed and unnerved. "Destructive programs, capable of making a machine terminally self-hostile. They don't even have to enter computers as data, but can do so by physical contact."

"You're talking about freestanding memes!" Gillian replied. "I thought they can't exist here in real space, without a host to carry—"

"Apparently, we're wrong about that." The Niss shrugged with its funnel of spinning lines. "Remember, Transcendents are a melding of life orders. They are part meme, themselves."

She nodded, willing to accept the incredible.

The expanding memic swarm collided with the incoming barrage, but effects and outcomes weren't evident at first. Tension filled *Streaker*'s bridge, as the missiles continued on course for several more seconds . . .

. . . only to veer abruptly aside, missing the Earth ship and spiraling off manically before igniting in flashy torrents of brilliance, lighting up the asteroid belt.

The dolphins exulted, but Gillian quashed any celebratory thoughts as premature. She recalled a warning, from the Transcendent being who had visited her office.

"Do not be deceived by illusions of invulnerability. You have been given advantages. But they are limited.

"It would be wise to recall that you are not gods.

"Not yet, that is. . . ."

Indeed, Gillian wasn't counting on a thing. After all, hadn't the Jophur found a countermeasure to their earlier "miraculous" coating, just by consulting the Library? Soon the enemy would learn not to send mere robots against a ship defended by hordes of predatory ideas. Or else they would attack with overwhelming numbers.

Still, I guess the ends justify the memes, she thought, raising a brief, ironic smile. Tom would have liked the pun—a real groaner.

Right now, in the heat of battle, she missed him with a pang that felt fresh, as if years and kiloparsecs meant nothing, and their parting had been yesterday.

This would have been the moment he was born for.

The next line of ships—destroyers—had little more effect. A few of their missiles managed to detonate nearby, but not in a coordinated spread. *Streaker*'s protective layers dealt with the flux.

When Akeakemai asked for permission to fire back, Gillian refused.

"We might damage a few," she said. "But they'd notice our offensive capacity is tiny, compared to defense. I'd rather leave them guessing we're equally formidable, both ways. *So* formidable, we can afford to ignore them."

Of course, it was all part of a bluff she had worked out. Her greatest one yet.

A new force rose to meet *Streaker*—this time consisting of sleek, powerful cruisers. Meanwhile, the giant dreadnoughts near Earth began changing formation, arranging themselves into a hollow shell, its cusp aimed toward Gillian's ship. Loudspeakers groaned, twittered and beeped in several formal languages, as commanders of the united fleet beamed a final warning.

IDENTIFY YOURSELF, OR BE DESTROYED.

She wondered.

After all this time, hounding us to every far corner of the Five Galaxies, have we really changed so much that you don't recognize your intended prey—coming now to beard you in your den?

Gillian decided.

It's time to end the silence. Answer their beamed challenge with one of our own.

Pressing a lever, she unleashed her pre-recorded message—one that had drawn her entire concentration ever since *Streaker* dived into that cool black tunnel milliseconds ahead of a supernova's fist. It was inspired partly by her own interview with the transcendent being.

More than one can play games of illusion, she had thought. Of all the tricks pulled by her godlike visitor, the one that impressed her *least* had been that showy series of visual poses, mimicking everyone from Tom and Jake Demwa to Hikahi and Creideiki.

Mirages are a dime a dozen.

If Earthlings possessed any creative craft that was equal to the best Galactic technology, it lay in the art of manipulating optic images. The play began with one of her oldest disguises—one she routinely used to fool *Streaker*'s stolen Library unit.

Appearing suddenly in the holo tank, a stern Thennanin admiral strode forth, preening his elbow and shoulder spikes, puffing up his extravagant head-crest, and clearing his vents with a deep *harrrumph,* before commencing to speak in stately, formal Galactic Six, addressing his remarks to those besieging Earth.

"Brethren! Fellow high patrons of starfaring civilization and descendants of the Great Progenitors! I come before you now at a crucial juncture of choice. You, along with

all your clients and clan mates, may profit or suffer because of decisions made during this nexus of opportunity.

"The time has come to look past blinders of false belief. Your aggression here (which my clan had the great wisdom to resist) is anathema to destiny. It brings you nothing but cascading sorrow, replenished from an inexhaustible supply of hardship that the universe willingly provides the obstinate!"

It really was a very good Thennanin, quite pompous and credible. But credibility—even plausibility—wasn't the point here.

No, it was the sheer *effrontery* of this ruse that should gall them.

Her ersatz admiral continued.

"Consider the facts, misguided brethren.

"Number one.

"To whom did the Progenitors reveal relics of great-and-profound value?

"To you? Or even to the Old Ones you revere?"

While speaking those words, the Thennanin started to *melt*, shifting and reconfiguring in a much more gaudy and disturbing manner than the Transcendent had. (Her visitor's intent had been to focus Gillian's thoughts, while her aim right now was to frighten . . . then enrage.)

The big admiral finished transforming into a quite different entity that now floated in midair, glossy and gray, resembling Captain Creideiki at his most handsome and charismatic, before an accident permanently scarred that handsome, sleek head.

"No, they did not! The Progenitors did not disclose hidden truths to you, or to any noble clan or alliance!

"In fact, the Ghost Fleet was revealed to one such as this!"

Creideiki's image thrashed its tail flukes for emphasis.

"A member of the youngest of all client races. A race whose talents would have made any senior patron eager to adopt them, yet who proudly call themselves members of wolfling Earthclan!

"Next, consider yet another fact. The way the Earthship, Streaker, evaded all your searches and clever schemes to capture it! Even when you bribed and suborned the Great Institutes, did such acts of treasonous cheating avail you at all?"

The figure began shifting again, continuing, sotto voce, with teasing GalSix undertones.

("Tell me, brethren. Have you begun to guess the identity of the vessel now plummeting toward you, laughingly defiant of your vaunted power?

"Do you need more clues? You shall have them!")

A male human shape replaced Creideiki. She had tried using Tom as a model, but that proved too hard. So, she settled on old Jake Demwa . . . which was probably a good idea anyway. The Soro would instantly recognize him from two centuries of frustration, when he had proved their bane on numerous occasions.

"Fact three: Despite great wealth and innumerable lives spent subduing the Terrans' homeworld, what have you accomplished here, except to make their legend grow? Even on the verge of apparent success, can you be certain this is not yet another ruse? A trick, meant to draw in your reserves? To make their unexpected triumph seem all the greater in others' eyes?

"Even if you win, and the last human lies dead—with every dolphin and chimp readopted by some humorless clan—will you withstand the vengeance others may then take upon you, in the name of martyred Earth?

"Ask yourselves this. Might these wolflings rise even stronger, out of death? Either in fact, or else in a flood of new ideas? Ideas that will span the New Era to come, diverting Galactic culture down paths you can't imagine?"

Streaker shuddered. The lights flickered. On other screens, Gillian glimpsed a brief, violent, one-sided battle, as the cruiser flotilla fired volleys while sweeping past. Either they were getting a knack for using dumbed-down brains in their missiles or there were simply too many, this time. For whatever reason, about a dozen got through, detonating uncomfortably close.

Suessi gave a thumbs-up sign, indicating the pattern wasn't focused enough to be dangerous. But it showed the limits of their defense.

Just so long as the enemy can't tell. Let them think we're just shrugging it all off, for a bit longer.

In the holo tank, Jake Demwa faded into another shape—one of the elder races *Streaker* encountered at the vast, chilly habitat called the Fractal World. Without pause, that stark visage continued the soliloquy.

"Or take fact number four. Did any of you foretell the Great Rupture? So conservative were you all, so trusting of your own elders, that you had no idea that Old Ones were manipulating the Great Library, and the other Institutes! For their own reasons, they kept the Civilization of Five Galaxies ignorant. We had no inkling to prepare, or that this sort of massive spatiotemporal breakup has happened before!

"Yet, a warning did come. Even while beset by attackers, the Terrans did their citizenly duty, broadcasting an alert based upon their alternative mathematics.

"Is it a coincidence that great harm befell those who ignored the warning? Those blinded by their contempt for wolfling science. Those who chose obstinate ideology over pragmatism? While those who heeded remained safe?"

("Have you guessed yet, brethren? Have ye figured out who streaks toward you now? Insolent. Heedless of the reverence you feel yourselves due? Can you sniff/sense/feel/grok the very thing you covet . . . and secretly fear?")

Cruisers fell in behind *Streaker*, cutting off retreat. Looming just ahead, the unified armada of capital ships left their siege positions to meet this challenge, spreading to envelop and enclose the impudent newcomer in an inescapable mesh of fire.

"They're talking to each other," informed the Niss Machine. "From battleship to battleship. A lot more discussion than you'd expect for warships going into a fight. It's coded, but I can tell it is pretty heated.

"Is it possible they don't understand your hints and clues, Dr. Baskin? Perhaps you've been too coy. Shall we go ahead and tell them who we are?"

She shook her head.

"Relax. They're probably just arguing over how best to kill us."

Streaker had one hope. This kind of envelopment pattern meant the enemy must concentrate their volleys into a very narrow zone, or else risk damaging each other. If the Earthship could create *uncertainty* over its exact position, that might result in a focused blast that was offset just enough, so their Transcendent-shell would not be overwhelmed. Then, amid the blinding aftermath, *Streaker* would swerve away and run for it! With any luck, this amazing survival would make the enemy pause long enough for a good head start . . . before the entire fleet came baying after her.

The aim was simple: to buy time, giving Earth a brief respite—a chance to quickly rearm the Luna fortresses—and possibly get a few mothers and children away before the end.

"They are p-preparing to fire!" announced the detection officer, who then squealed a warning in Primal Delphin. *"Here come sharkssss!"*

Gillian felt palpable twinges go off in her mind as several hundred speedy missiles leaped from launching tubes, arming themselves as they raced toward *Streaker.* At this range, many would carry psi and probability warheads, as well as annihilation charges.

Streaker's protective shell cast forth swarms of countermemes and some sent missiles astray. But this time the effort would clearly be inadequate.

"You know what to do," she told Akeakemai, trusting her life to his skill. This was not a job for a pilot but for a gifted geometrodynamics engineer.

Lacking anything else to do while waiting for obliteration, Gillian turned back to the scene playing out within the holo tank—the same message being watched on the command deck of every battleship.

The last of her simulated Old Ones started to dissolve. And yet—(copying tricks she had learned from the Transcendent)—the voice went on, using tones that were intentionally infuriating, patronizing, and serenely confident.

"Can you see the symbol on this vessel's prow? Is it the familiar emblem of five spiral rays? Or has something else taken its place? Can you recognize the nature of our new shell?

"And yet, by now your scans also show the ancient, mundane hull within. The Earthling figures of our crew.

"Well? Can your minds resolve this anomaly? This dissonance? Is there an explanation?"

The image in the tank reformed at last, taking a shape she had recorded during her interview with the Transcendent. A form that was sure to spoil the enemy's composure.

If just one glimpse of Herbie—a billion-year-old mummy—had thrown half the fanatics in five galaxies into a tizzy, what would the mummy's reconstructed likeness do? Emulated in apparently living flesh, the faintly amphibian humanoid now offered an enigmatic smile that broadened to uncanny width, conveying a touch of cruel empathy.

"Come now, foolish youngsters. Surely you can draw conclusions from what lies before your very—"

Akeakemai interrupted with a squeal.

"Impact in ninety secondsss! Let's do it-t!"

Gillian blinked as *Streaker*'s engines let out a wail of exertion, yanking the ship out of normal space.

Too bad, she thought, regretting that it had happened quite so soon.

I wanted to watch the show once through, all the way to the end.

In theory, you could dodge enemies by jumping into hyperspace.

Unfortunately, that idea was older than a lot of stars.

The arts of war had long ago adapted to such tactics. When *Streaker* jumped, so did the pack of onrushing missiles, which had no trouble sensing which way she headed.

Akeakemai played the engines swiftly, sending their old Snark-class survey ship leaping *laterally* among the known strata that still overlay Galaxy Two.

Unlike Galaxy Four, the varied levels of hyperspace were still accessible here, though with greater difficulty than before. Gillian was counting on that difference now to disrupt the timing of the incoming barrage. With any luck, there might also be chaos waves—aftershocks from the Great Rupture—to warp space and confuse the death machines.

Alas, it did not take long to realize—she had committed the worst sin of any commander. Assuming her enemies were stupid.

In B Space, where all stars turned into midget rainbows, the detection officer yelled dismay.

"Mines! They've filled the place with—"

Akeakemai was swift, triggering a second jump, but not before several nearby objects detonated, slamming *Streaker* with shock waves, even as the ship flickered over to A Space.

The strange-familiar sensations of that speedy realm crowded around Gillian, as if each direction she turned became a *tunnel,* offering a shortcut beyond some far horizon. Down each of those tubes, there glowed the disk of a single majestic, spinning sun.

"Fifty seconds," murmured Hannes Suessi, mostly to himself.

"More mines!" came the rapid cry . . . unneeded, as a drumbeat of savage thuds rocked the ship, straining the energy-absorbing power of *Streaker*'s new shell. Excess heat brought sweat popping from Gillian's skin.

In our old form, we'd be vapor by now, she thought during the agonized moment it took to flick into D Space.

It was a lousy place to look for shortcuts. Everything looked *far away,* as if you were peering through the wrong end of a telescope.

Unfortunately, D Space was also inhabited, by members of the Quantum life order—glimmering half-shapes whose outlines grew more vague the closer you looked at them. A multitude of these amorphous beings suddenly converged on *Streaker* the moment she appeared.

"Our enemies must have hired local allies to guard this back door." The Niss Machine sounded bemused by such clever thoroughness.

Gillian saw chunks of the transcendent coating evaporate under this new attack.

"Get us *out* of—"

Anticipating her wishes, Akeakemai yanked *Streaker*'s laboring engines one more time . . . the same moment the converging missiles struck.

JIJO

Kaa eked out one last jump before B space disappeared.

The wrenching leap peeled every nerve in Harry's body, forcing air from his lungs in an agonized scream.

Even when transition finished—and the shuddering passengers of Harry's station found themselves miraculously back in the normal continuum—a plague of scraping irritations kept their skins twitching. Rubbing tears from his eyes with quivering hands, Harry *knew,* with vivid certainty, the exact moment that B Space finished detaching completely from Galaxy Four, to float away on its own, leaving the domain of atoms to spin on, bereft and alone.

It felt as if something had been amputated. A presence that had been in the background, unnoticed, for his entire life. Now it was gone forever.

We got out just in time, he thought as vision cleared. Then he turned to marvel at what Kaa had accomplished with that final display of piloting skill.

There, glowing just ahead, lay a blue globe, wearing a slender skin of moist air. Continents—mottled brown and green—bulged between arcs of ocean. Along the sweeping terminator, lightning could be seen dancing atop clouds and mountain peaks.

"Jijo, I presume," Harry murmured, silently adding—*my new home.*

"Yeah," answered Dwer. "Welcome. It's good to be back."

Judging by his taut stance, the young man was eager to reclaim the forest trails he loved. Apparently, there were women waiting for him down there, in a feral forest, who considered themselves his "wives." Dwer seemed loath to explain the situation, but he felt anxious to get back. That much was clear.

And what about me? Harry pondered. *A career with the Navigation Institute doesn't offer much promise now. Even if Galaxy Four retains a few hyperspatial links, nobody's gonna want to hire an E Space scout.*

He eyed the blue world, which crept closer at a snail's gait—the relative velocity determined solely by hard momentum and kinetic energy. Without microjumping to fine-tune the approach, landing could be difficult and dangerous.

They had a pretty good pilot, of course. So that part didn't worry Harry, much. But once the station was down, it might never leave again. Antigravity relied on tricks that involved balancing forces from several layers of hyperspace. With most of those layers gone, the field generators would probably never be able to push hard enough to climb free of Jijo's heavy pull.

Most likely, it's a planet-bound life from now on.

Heck, at least it's a life.

Jijo sure looked a whole lot better than dusty Horst. Even prettier than Terra, in fact.

And there are neo-chimps here . . . though of an earlier breed that couldn't talk yet. Other than that, Dwer says they're pretty civilized.

He sighed.

I guess being the "ape that speaks" should set me apart.

That . . . and my white fur . . .

. . . and my . . . tail.

It was enough to make him chuff dry laughter. What an ironic reversal of his time on Earth, where the chatty, sophisticated chims found him taciturn and slow. Here, his mates and grooming partners would scarcely bug him with irritating gossip.

For conversation, I'll have six other sapient races in the "Commons of Jijo"—or eight, if you include dolphins and tytlal. And soon, chimps will make nine.

He glanced at Kaa, whose brilliant piloting had brought them here, safe and mostly sound. So anxious was the dolphin for those warm coastal waters—and to find his Peepoe—that it might take some persuasion to get him to land ashore first and let everyone else debark.

"Well, well. It is a winsome little place," commented Kiwei Ha'aoulin. "I suppose it should do for a spell, while I assess the commercial possibilities."

Harry shook his head. The Synthian had apparently retreated into her former madness, assuming that everything would soon return to normal. For her sake, Harry hoped Kiwei remained cheerful and crazy for the rest of her life, because she would spend it all here, in a small corner of Galaxy Four.

Kaa tossed his dark gray head, emitting a worried sputter.

"I'm detecting shipssss!"

Harry rushed to his instruments.

"I see 'em. They're *behind* us. Your last couple of crazy jumps took us past 'em! We'll reach Jijo weeks before they do."

Peering closer at the readout, he went on.

"They're mostly small craft—lifeboats, scouts, shuttles. Survivors, I guess, from those fleets who got torn up in B Space, during the Rupture." He paused, pulling nervously on both thumbs. "They're headin' for the only refuge in sight. The same place we are."

Dwer blew a long sigh. "So, even if the Commons managed to get rid of the Jophur garrison while we were away, the danger isn't over."

Harry nodded. By standards of his former civilization, the oncoming forces were pathetic and weak. Some of the lifeboats would not make it. Others would burn in Jijo's atmosphere. Still, the remnant would be far more than his little station could stave off. Soon, the Jijoans would face real troubles.

And, he realized, the coming confrontation could have long-lasting repercussions.

Unless there were other sooner outposts, hidden on fallow planets elsewhere in Galaxy Four, this might be the one place where oxygen breathers existed with knowledge and experience of starfaring.

Even if hyperspace is completely cut off, a culture will someday expand outward from Jijo. That culture may fill this entire galaxy, starting a new tradition of Uplift when it comes across promising species along the way.

The implications chilled Harry.

Whoever won control of Jijo, this year, might establish the morality—the whole social ethos—of that star-spanning civilization to come.

Harry had already been willing to give his life for one community. Now, it seemed there would be no rest. Before even partaking of Jijo's food and air, he must decide to become part of this new world and take on its troubles as his own.

From what I've heard, this Commons of Six Races was a pretty impressive bunch. If Dwer and Rety—and Alvin and Ur-ronn—are any indication, the Jijoans will put up a stiff fight.

He patted the console of his trusty old station.

Maybe we can help just a bit, eh?

Their approach spiral took them over Jijo's dark side, below a big moon that Dwer identified as "Loocen." Harry exclaimed when he spied a line of bright sparkles along the day-night boundary. Glistening *cities* shone in a long crescent across the airless surface. Then he realized.

Reflections. Sunlight, that's all it is, caught at an angle as dawn creeps across the lunar surface. The domes are silent, lifeless. They have been ever since the fabled Buyur departed—how long ago? Half a million years?

Still, he admitted. *It is a pretty sight. And maybe someday—*

A piping cry made Harry turn around.

Rety was standing by a far window, obstinately refusing to look at the soft beauty of her homeworld.

Sullen, with arms crossed, she ignored repeated calls from her "husband," the miniature male urs called yee. The little centauroid stood on the windowsill, prancing with all four delicate feet, reaching out with his long neck to nip Rety's shoulder, then gesture at the view outside.

"look, wife! look at this sight!"

"I seen it before," she muttered sourly. "Scenery. Mountains an' bushes an' dirt. Lots of dirt. No 'lectricity or computers, but all the *dirt* you could ever want to—"

"not scenery!" yee interrupted. "turn and see fireworks!"

Rety stayed obdurate. But others hurried to find out what the little fellow meant. "Douse interior lights," Harry ordered so glare from the observation deck would not drown the view outside.

Jijo's night stretched below, a dark coverlet that might come ablaze with city lights within a few generations, no matter who won the coming battle. Now, though, the expanse showed no visible sign of sapience that Harry could detect, even with instruments. *Well, the Six Races have been hiding for a long time,* he thought. *They must be good at it by now.*

It was interesting to imagine what kind of starfaring civilization might arise out of the Jijoan Commons, with its fervent traditions of environmental protection and tolerance, and yet an easygoing individualism when it came to endeavor and new ideas. Something pretty interesting, assuming it survived the coming crisis.

At first, Harry saw nothing to justify yee's excitement. Then Dwer nudged him, pointing to the right.

"Look. A spark."

"How pretty," Kiwei commented.

It *did* look like a flickering ember, blown upward from a campfire, wafting—gently and very slowly—out from that thin film of atmosphere into the black sky above.

"Observer mode," Harry commanded. "Zero in on the anomaly I'm looking at and magnify."

The computer scanned his eyes, judged the focus of his attention, and complied. A holo image erupted, showing the strangest object Harry had ever seen, despite years spent exploring the weird memic corners of E Space.

A long, slender tube hurtled upward, pointy-end first. And from its tail poured gouts of white-hot fire.

"It . . . looks like a burning *tree.*" Kiwei murmured in amazement.

"Not a tree," Dwer corrected. "It's boo!"

Curiosity finally overcame Rety, who turned around at last—barely in time to see the flame go out. While the slim missile coasted for several seconds, Harry's instruments measured its size, which was many times bigger than his station!

Abruptly, the pencil-shaped object split in half. The rear portion tumbled away, still smoldering, while the front part erupted anew from its aft end.

Kiwei uttered hushed perplexity.

"But, what natural phenomenon could—"

"not natural, silly raccoon!" yee cried. "boo *rocket* made by urs-hooman-traekis! shoot rocket high to welcome Rety-yee home!"

Harry blinked, twice. Then he grinned.

"Well, I'll be. That's what it is, all right. A multistage rocket made of hollowed-out tree trunks . . . or whatever you call 'em, Dwer."

He called again to the computer. "Zoom in at the front terminus. The part that's farthest from the flames."

Like the tip of a spear, that end flared a bit before tapering to a point. It rotated slowly, along with the rest of the crude rocket.

A brief glint told them everything. A pane of some kind of glass. A pale light shining from within. And a pair of brief silhouettes. A snakelike neck. A crablike claw.

Then Harry's station swerved, making everyone stumble. Kaa reported they were entering the planet's atmosphere.

"T-time to buckle up-p!" the pilot commanded. Soon, a different kind of flame would surround them. If they survived the coming plummet, it would not be long before their feet stood on solid ground.

Yet, Harry and the others remained transfixed for a moment longer, watching the rocket for as long as possible. The computer calculated its estimated trajectory and reported that it seemed aimed at Jijo's biggest moon.

At last, Rety commented. She stomped her feet on the deck, but this time it was no tantrum—only an expression of pure joy.

"Uttergloss!" she cried. "Do you know what this means?"

Harry and Dwer both shook their heads.

"It means I'm not trapped on Jijo! It means there's a way *off* that miserable dirt-ball. And you can bet your grampa's dross barrel that I'm gonna use it."

Her eyes seemed to shine with the same light as that of the flickering ember, till their orbital descent took it out of sight. Even when Harry ushered her to a seat and belted her in for landing, Rety's wiry frame throbbed with longing, and the grim inexorability of her ambition.

"I'll do whatever it takes.

"I'm headin' *out* again, just as fast an' as far as this grubby ol'universe lets me."

Harry nodded agreeably. One of the last things he ever wanted to be was some-one standing in Rety's way.

"I'm sure you will," he said without the slightest doubt or patronizing tone of voice.

Soon the windows licked with fire as Jijo reached out to welcome them.

HOME

Terrible wounds marred the haggard vessel as it prepared to drop back into normal space. Most of *Streaker*'s stasis flanges hung loose, or had vaporized. The rotating gravity wheel was half melted into the hull.

As for the protective sheathing which had safeguarded the crew—that gift of the Transcendents now sparked and unraveled, writhing away its last, like some dying creature with a brave soul.

Gillian mourned for its lost friendship. As she had mourned other misfortunes. And now, for the loss of hope.

Our plan was to avoid destruction, leading the enemy on a wild chase away from Earth.

Our foes planned to thwart and destroy us.

It looks like we each got half of what we wanted.

Suessi was down in the engine room, working alongside Emerson and the rest of their weary team, trying to restore power. As things stood, the ship had barely enough reserve energy to reach the one level of space where there weren't swarms of mines—or other deadly things—converging from all sides.

No, we're headed back to face living enemies. Oxy-beings, just like us.

At least it should be possible to surrender to the battleships, and see her crew treated as prisoners of war.

Assuming the victors did not instantly start fighting over the spoils.

Of course, Gillian couldn't let herself be captured. The information in her head must not fall into enemy hands.

She let out a deep sigh. The ninety-second battle had been awfully close. Her tactics had almost worked. Each time a mine went off, or a quantum horde attacked, or a chaos aftershock passed through, it disrupted the neat volley of converging missiles, shoving their careful formations, reducing their numbers, until the detonation—when it occurred—was off center. Inefficient.

Even so, it was bad enough.

As *Streaker* finished its last, groaning transition into the normal vacuum of home space, surrounded by clouds of blinding debris, she knew the grand old vessel could not defeat a corvette, or an armed lifeboat, let alone the armada awaiting them.

"Please transmit the truce signal," she ordered. "Tell them we'll discuss terms for surrender."

The Niss Machine's dark funnel bowed, a gesture of solemn respect.

"As you wish, Dr. Baskin. It will be done."

While the hardworking bridge crew worked to replace burned-out modules, all the monitors were blinded by a haze of ionized detritus and radiation. The first objects to emerge from the fog were a pair of large gravity wells—modest dimples in spacetime.

Earth and Luna . . . she realized. *We came so close.*

Soon other things would show up on the gravity display, objects rivaling moons, majestic in power.

The tense moment harkened Gillian back across years to the discovery of the Ghost Fleet, so long ago, when she and Tom had been so young and thrilled to be exploring on behalf of Earthclan, in company with their friend Creideiki. It had looked a bit like this. A haze surrounded them as *Streaker* worked its way slowly through a dense molecular cloud, in that far-off place called the Shallow Cluster.

An interstellar backwater, gravitationally flat. A place where there should not have been anything to interest starfaring beings.

Yet, the captain had a hunch.

And soon, emerging through the mist, they glimpsed . . .

Nothing.

Gillian blinked as stark, astonishing reality yanked her back to the present. A nervous murmur crossed the bridge as crew members stared in disbelief at emptiness.

Laboring mightily, *Streaker*'s wounded engines managed to pull the ship free of its own dross cloud, clearing the haze far enough to reveal more of nearby space.

There was no sign of any vast, enclosing formation.

No fleet of mighty battleships.

"But . . . I . . ."

Gillian stopped, unable to finish the sentence. Someone else had to complete the thought.

"Where did everybody go?" asked Sara Koolhan, whose hand clutched Prity's with a grip that looked white and sweaty.

No one answered. How could they? What was there to say?

Silence reigned for several minutes while sensors probed gradually farther.

"There's a lot of debris, but I don't see any big vessels within a cubic astron of here," ventured the detection officer at last. "Though I guess they could be hiding behind Luna, getting ready to pounce!"

Gillian shook her head. That armada of giant dreadnoughts would scarcely *fit* behind the moon's disk. Besides, why set a trap for prey that lies helpless, already in your grasp? *Streaker* could not run, and a puppy would beat her in a fair fight.

"I'm detecting a lot of fresh hyper-ripples in the ambient background field," added Akeakemai. "Engine wakes. Some really big ships churned things up hereabouts just a little while ago. I'm guessing they tore outta here awful damn fasssst!"

While *Streaker*'s crew continued laboring to repair sensors, the Niss Machine remanifested its whirlpool shape near Gillian.

"Would you care for a conjecture, Dr. Baskin?"

"Conject away!"

"It occurs to me that your little holographic message might have had unexpected consequences. It was meant to enrage our enemies into following us as we fled, but please allow me to submit another possibility.

"That it scared the living hell out of them."

Gillian snorted.

"That crock of bull-dross I cooked up? It was sheer bluff and bluster. A child could see through it! Are you saying that a bunch of advanced Galactics, with all their onboard libraries and sophisticated intelligence systems, couldn't penetrate to the truth?"

The Niss spiral turned, regaining a bit of its former insouciance.

"No, Dr. Baskin. That is not what I am saying. Rather, I am insinuating that a primitive wolfling like yourself, caught up in the emotions of a transitory crisis, cannot see the essential truth underlying all your 'bluff and bluster.'

"The Galactics did perceive it, however. Perhaps only instants after they fired upon Streaker. Or else later, when they sensed we were returning, having survived the unsurvivable . . . and began broadcasting a simple offer to discuss surrender."

"But that was—" she stammered. "I didn't mean *their*—"

"You gave your command in Anglic. And the inbuilt ambiguity of that language gave our foes leeway to interpret the offer either way. An ambiguity they cannot abide."

"So, they took it as a demand for *their* surrender." Gillian blinked rapidly. "I would never . . . could never attmpt such a bluff."

"And hence the alliance shattered. Perhaps all it took was one defector—and the coalition flash-evaporated, as each squadron fled for home."

She stared. "You're guessing. I don't believe it."

The Niss shrugged, a twisting of its dark funnel.

"Fortunately, the universe doesn't much care whether we believe. The chief question now is whether our foes were sufficiently terrified to completely abandon their goals, or if they have merely withdrawn to reassess—to consult their own auguries and prepare fresh onslaughts.

"Frankly, I suspect the latter. Nevertheless, it seems that something noteworthy happened here, Dr. Baskin.

"By any standard, you must accept history's verdict.

"The word has a strange flavor, spoken aboard this ragged vessel. So, I can understand if you have trouble speaking it aloud.

"Let me coax you, then.

"It is called Victory."

The forces of Terra emerged, climbing slowly, tentatively from their last redoubts, as if suspecting some deadly trick. Out of seared mountain peaks and blasted lunar craters, stubby ships nosed skyward, bearing scars from countless prior battles. Together they cast beams of inquiry toward every dark corner of the solar system. Distrustfully, they threw intense scrutiny toward the one remaining intruder, whose tattered outlines were not at first familiar.

"Keep well back," Gillian ordered her pilot. "Make no sudden moves. Let's be patient. Let them get used to us."

Akeakemai agreed. "We're emitting *Streaker*'s transponder code. But it'll take a while to get other messages out. Till then, I'd rather not make those guys nervoussss!"

It was an understatement. Those tattered-looking units had managed to keep the terrifying Tandu, and many other allied warrior clans, at bay for two years. All told, Gillian would rather not be fried by her own people, just because they had jittery trigger fingers.

After all this time, she could wait just a little while longer.

Jake Demwa isn't going to be happy with the condition I'm bringing Streaker home in, she mused. *Without two-thirds of its crew, or the Shallow Cluster samples. He'll grill me for weeks, trying to figure out where Creideiki and Tom went off to, and what strange matters may have kept them busy all this time.*

On the other hand, she did come back to Earth bearing gifts.

The secret of overcoming Jophur master rings, for instance.

And information about the Kiqui of Kithrup, whom we may claim as new clients for our growing clan.

And the rewq symbionts of Jijo, which help species understand each other.

Plus everything the Niss and I learned by interrogating our captured Galactic Library branch.

And there was more.

The Terragens Council will want to know about the lost colony on Jijo and the Polkjhy expedition. Both groups face great dangers, and yet they seem to offer something the council long sought to achieve—offshoots of Earthclan that might survive beyond reach of Galactic Civilization, even if Terra someday falls.

There were plenty of other things to talk about, enough to keep Gillian in debriefing for years.

Everything we discovered about other life orders, for instance. Especially the high Transcendents.

As powerful and knowing as those godlike beings appeared, Gillian had come away from her encounters with a strange sensation not unlike pity. They were, after all, not the eldest or greatest of life's children, only the ones who stayed behind when everyone else dived into one-way singularities, seeking better realms beyond.

Cowards, she had called them in a moment of pique. Not a fair characterization, she admitted now, though it held a grain of truth.

They seem trapped by the Embrace of Tides. And yet they are unwilling to follow its pull all the way—whether to a higher place or to some universal recycling system. So they sit instead, thinking and planning while time wafts gently by. Except when it seems convenient to sacrifice a myriad lesser life-forms in order to accomplish some goal.

All told, they weren't company she'd look forward to inviting over for dinner.

As the haze of battle cleared, Gillian ordered *Streaker*'s cracked and fused blast armor sloughed away from the viewing ports for the first time since Kithrup, allowing her to stand before the glittering Milky Way—a spray of constellations so familiar, they would have reassured even some cavewoman ancestor whose life was spent in hardship, grubbing for roots, a mere ten thousand years ago.

Lightspeed is slow, but inexorable, she thought, *gazing at the galaxy's bright lanes. During the next few millennia, this starscape will flare with extravagance.*

Supernovas, blaring across heaven, carrying the first part of the transcendents' message.

A simple message, but an important one that even she could understand.

Greetings. Here we are. Is anybody out there?

Gillian noticed Emerson—whose duties down in Engineering were finished at last—hurry in to embrace Sara. The couple stood nearby with their silent chimp companion, regarding the same great vista, sharing private thoughts.

Of course, the young genius from Jijo was another gift to Earth, a treasure who, using only mathematical insight, had independently predicted the Great Rupture. That alone was an impressive accomplishment—but now Sara was making further, startling claims, suggesting that the Rupture was only a *symptom.* Not of the expanding universe, as Earth's savants claimed, but of something more complex and strange. Something "coming *in* from outside our contextual framework" . . . whatever that meant.

Sara thought the mystery might revolve somehow around a race called the "Buyur."

Gillian shook her head. At last, there would be others to pass such problems on to. Skilled professionals from all across Earth—and dozens of friendly races—who could deal with arcane matters while she went back to being a simple doctor, a healer, the role she had trained for.

I'll never order anyone else to their death. Not ever again. No matter what they say we accomplished during this wretched mission, I won't accept another command.

From now on, I'll work to save individual lives. The cosmos can be somebody else's quandary.

In fact, she had already chosen her first patient.

As soon as the spymasters let me go, I'll focus on helping Emerson. Try to help restore some of his power of speech. We can hope researchers on Earth have already made useful breakthroughs, but if not, I'll bend heaven in half to find it.

Was guilt driving this ambition? To repair some of the damage her commands had caused? Or was it to have the pleasure of watching the two of them—Sara and Emerson—speak to each other's minds, as well as their hearts.

Watching them hold hands, Gillian relaxed a bit.

The heart can be enough. It can sustain.

Akeakemai called.

"We're back in two-way holo mode, Dr. Baskin. And there's a transmission coming in."

The big visual display erupted with light, showing the control room of an approaching warship. It had the blunt outlines of Thennanin manufacture.

The crew was mostly human, but the face in front of the camera had the sharp cheekbones and angular beauty of a male Tymbrimi, with empathy-sensitive tendrils wafting near the ears.

". . . that we must find your claims improbable. Please provide evidence that you are, indeed, TAASF Streaker. I repeat . . ."

It seemed a simple enough request to satisfy. She had spent hard, bitter years striving for this very moment of restored contact. And yet, Gillian felt reluctant to comply.

After a moment's reflection, she knew why.

To any human, there are two realms—"Earth" and "out there."

As long as I'm in space, I can imagine that I'm somehow near Tom. We were both lost. Both hounded across the Five Galaxies. Despite the megaparsecs dividing us, it only seemed a matter of time till we bumped into each other.

But once I set foot on Old Terra, I'll be home. Earth will surround me, and outer space will become a separate place. A vast wilderness where he's gone missing—along with Creideiki and Hikahi and the others—wandering amid awful dangers, while I can only try to stay busy and not feel alone.

Gillian tried to answer the Tymbrimi. She wished someone else would, just to take this final burden off her shoulders. The ordeal of ending bittersweet exile.

She was rescued by an unlikely voice. Emerson D'Anite, who faced the hologram with a smile, and expressed himself in operatic song.

"Let us savor our folly!
Man is born to be jolly!

"His idle pretenses,
and vain defenses,
trouble his senses, and baffle his mind.

"Leaner or fatter,
we cavort and flatter,
so let us be cheerful and let us pretend.

"*Fun* is the triumph
of mind over matter,
we'll all get home if we laugh in the end!"

DESTINY

The Zang components were better prepared to take all this in their philosophical stride. So were the machine entities who helped make up the macrocommunity called *Mother.*

In both hydro- and metal-based civilizations, there existed a widespread conviction that so-called "reality" was a fiction. Everything from the biggest galaxy down to the smallest microbe was simply part of a grand simulation. A "model" being run in order to solve some great problem or puzzle.

Of course, it was only natural for both of these life orders to reach the same conclusion. The Zang had evolved to perform analog emulations organically, within their own bodies. Machines did it with prim software models, carried out by digital cognizance. But ultimately, it amounted to the same thing. Joined at last, they found a shared outlook on life.

We—and everything we see around ourselves, including the mighty Transcendents—exist merely as part of a grand scenario, a simulacrum being played out in some higher-level computer, perhaps at another plane of existence—or else at the Omega Point, when the end of time brings all things to ultimate fruition.

Either way, it makes little sense to get caught up in feelings of self-importance. This cosmic pattern we participate in is but one of countless many being run, in parallel, with only minute differences from each to the next. Like a chess program, working out every move, and all possible consequences, in extreme detail.

That was how some of the other Mother-components explained it to Lark and Ling. Even the Jophur-traeki converts seemed to have no trouble with this notion, since their mental lives involved multiple thought experiments, flowing through the dribbling wax that lined their inner cores.

Only the human and dolphin members of the consortium had trouble reconciling this image—this idea that everything is a simulation—for different reasons.

Why? Lark asked.

Why would anyone expend vast resources doing such a thing? To calculate the best of all possible worlds?

Once they find it . . . what would they do with the result?

And what will they do with all the myriad models they have created along the way?

What will they do with us?

That question seemed to startle the Zang components, but not the machines, who answered Lark with strangely earnest complacency.

You oxies are so obsessed with self-importance!

Of course, all the models have already been run, evaluated, and discarded. Our feelings of existence are only an illusion. A manifestation of simulated time within one of those discarded models.

To Lark, this attitude seemed appalling. But Ling only chuckled, agreeing with the dolphins who had recently joined the onboard community, and who clearly considered this whole metaphysical argument ridiculous.

Olelo, a leader among that group of former *Streaker* crew members, summed up their viewpoint with a burst of Trinary haiku.

• *Listen to the crash*
• *Of breakers on yonder reef,*
• *And tell me this ain't real!* •

Lark felt glad to have the newcomers aboard, in several ways. They seemed like interesting folks, with a refreshing outlook. And they helped keep up the oxy side of the ongoing debate. There would be plenty of time for give-and-take discussions over the course of many subjective years, until the transformed *Polkjhy* finally reached journey's end.

With a flicker of awareness, he cast his remote senses through one of the external viewers, taking another look at the cosmos. Or what passed for one.

It was a perspective few others had ever witnessed. A *blankness* that was quite distinct from the vivid color, black. None of the great spiral or elliptical galaxies were visible in their normal forms—as gaudy displays of dusty white pinpoints. From this high standpoint, no stars could be seen, except as mere ripples, brief indentations that he could barely make out, if he tried.

Everything seemed flattened, ephemeral, tentative—almost like a crudely drawn rough draft of the real thing.

In fact, *Polkjhy* was no longer quite part of that universe. Gliding along just *outside* the ylem, the modified vessel rode atop a surging swell that was composed not of matter, or energy, or even raw metric. The best he could figure—having discussed it with others and consulted the onboard Library—*Polkjhy* was riding upon a swaying fold of *context.* A background of basic law, from which the universe had formed long ago, when a perturbation in Heisenberg's Uncertainty Principle allowed the sudden eruption called the Big Bang.

An emergence of Something from Nothing.

What he saw now was not things or objects but a vast swirl of causal connections, linking one set of potentialities to another.

Behind the hurtling ship, diminishing rapidly with each passing dura, several of these junctions could be glimpsed twisting away from a recent, shattering separation. A splitting apart of ancient ties.

He felt Ling's mind slip alongside his own, sharing the view. But after a while, she nudged him.

All of that lies behind us. Come. Look ahead, toward our destiny.

Though nothing tangible existed on this plane—not matter, or memes, or even directionality—Lark nevertheless got a sense of "forward" . . . the way they were headed. According to the Transcendents, it was a large cluster of galaxies, lying almost half a billion parsecs away from Galaxy Two. A place where enigmatic signals had been emanating for a long time, hinting at sapient activity. Perhaps another great civilization to contact. To share with. To say hello.

Its sole manifestation—to Lark's subjective gaze—was a swirl of faintly glowing curves and spirals. Vague hints that another domain existed where hyperdrive and transfer points and all the conveniences of spacefaring might be found in abundance.

We'll live to see that, Ling pondered. And much else. Are you glad we came?

Unlike the dolphins, no transcendent had ever asked Lark about his wishes. Yet, he felt pretty good.

Yeah, I'm glad.

I'll miss some people. And Jijo. But who could turn down an opportunity like this?

In fact, some already had. Gillian Baskin, striving to remain where her duty lay. And Sara, whose love he would carry always. In sending a dozen dolphin volunteers, Baskin had included other gifts to accompany *Polkjhy*'s voyage—*Streaker*'s archives, the genetic samples accumulated during a long exploration mission.

Plus another item.

Lark glanced at the most unique member of the Mother Consortium, encapsulated in a golden cocoon of *toporgic* frozen time. An archaic cadaver, possibly a billion years old, that had traveled with *Streaker*'s luckless crew ever since their fateful visit to a place called the Shallow Cluster.

Herbie was its name.

The mummy's enigmatic smile seemed all-knowing. All-confident.

"Isn't this your most precious relic?" Lark had asked during those frenetic moments leading up to the supernova explosion, as the *Streaker* samples were stowed and *Polkjhy*'s protective shell closed around it.

"Herb and I have been through a lot together," Gillian answered. "But I figure it's more important that he ride with you folks. He may tell some distant civilization more about us than a whole Library full of records."

The Earthling woman had looked tired, yet unbowed, as if she felt certain that her trials would soon end.

"Besides, even if *Streaker* somehow survives what's about to come, I figure old Herbie's not irreplaceable.

"I know where we can get lots more, just like him."

That cryptic remark clung to Lark as he and his mate let their senses roam, watching a soft luminance sweep by—the loose threads and stitching that always lay hidden, behind the backdrop of life's great tragicomedy. For some reason, it seemed to imply a story still unfolding. One in which he kept playing a part, despite an end to all links of cause or communication.

Someone could be felt sliding alongside the two floating humans. A dolphin—long, sleek, and scarred from many travails—jostled their bodies slightly with backwash from its fins, slipping a strong mental presence near theirs, sharing their view of the austere scenery beyond *Polkjhy*'s glimmering hull.

Soon, their new companion sang a lilting commentary.

• *Even when you have left*
  • *Old Ones, Transcendents,*
    • *and gods far behind,*

  • *Who can truly say they are*
    • *beyond Heaven's Reach?* •

Ling sighed appreciatively and Lark nodded. He turned to congratulate the cetacean for summing up matters so well.

Only then he blinked, for his eyes were staring at an empty patch in Mother's rich, organic stew.

He could have sworn that a big gray shape drifted right next to him, just moments before—glossy, warm, and close enough to touch! A dolphin he had not met, among the newcomers.

But no one was there.

It would be many years before he heard that voice again.

AFTERWORD

(. . . FOLLOWED BY A HOONISH DENOUEMENT!)

I feel it's bad practice for a writer to get stuck in a particular "universe," writing about the same characters or situations over and over again. To keep from getting stale, I try never to write two "universe" books in a row. And yet, clearly, the Uplift Storm Trilogy *(Brightness Reef, Infinity's Shore,* and *Heaven's Reach)* is an exception. I never deliberately set out to "go the trilogy route." But this work took off, gaining complexity and texture as I went.

Life can be that way. If you drop one stone into a pond, the ripples may seem clear. But start tossing in more than a few at a time, and those patterns take off in ways you never imagined. A realistic story is much the same. Implications and ramifications spread in all directions.

Many people have asked questions about my Uplift series. This is certainly not the first time an author speculated about the possibility of genetically altering non-sapient animals. Examples include *The Island of Dr. Moreau, Planet of the Apes,* and the *Instrumentality* series of Cordwainer Smith. I grew up admiring these works, and many spin-offs. But I also noticed that nearly all these tales assume that human "masters" will inevitably do the maximally stupid/evil thing. If we meddle with animals to raise their intelligence, it will be in order to enslave and abuse them.

Don't get me wrong! Those morality tales helped tweak our collective conscience toward empathy and tolerance. Yet, ironically, I feel it is now unlikely our civilization would behave in such a deliberately vile way toward newly sapient creatures, for one reason. Because those morality tales did their job!

The Uplift Series tries to take things to the next level. Suppose we genetically enhance chimps, dolphins, and others, with the best of motives, offering them voices and citizenship in our diverse culture. Won't there still be problems? Interesting ones worth a story or two? In fact, I expect we'll travel that road someday. *Loneliness* ensures that someone will attempt Uplift, sooner or later. And once an ape talks, who will dare say "put him back the way he was"?

It's about time to start thinking about the dilemmas we'll face, even if we're wise.

* * *

As *Glory Season* let me explore a range of relationships that might emerge from self-cloning, the Uplift Universe gives me a chance to experiment with all sorts of notions about starfaring civilization. And since it is unapologetic space opera, those notions can be stacked together and piled high! For instance, since we're positing Faster Than Light Travel (FTLT) I went ahead and threw in *dozens* of ways to cheat Einstein. The more the merrier!

One problem in many science fictional universes is the assumption that things just *happen* to be ripe for adventure exactly when *we* hit the space lanes. (For instance, the villains, while dangerous, are always just barely beatable, with some help from the plucky heroes.)

In fact, the normal state of any part of the universe, at any given moment, is equilibrium. Things are as they have been for a very long time. An equilibrium of *law* perhaps, or one of *death*. We may be the First Race, as I discuss in several stories, especially "Crystal Spheres." Or we could be very late arrivals, as depicted in the Uplift books and in *Existence* and "Lungfish." But we're not very likely to meet aliens as equals, or even near equals.

Another theme of this series is environmentalism. What we're doing to our Earth makes me worry there may have already been "brushfire" ecological holocausts across the galaxy, set off by previous starfaring races who heedlessly used up life-bearing planets as their "Galactic Empire" burned out during its brief reign of a few tens of thousands of years. (Note how often science fiction tales ring with the shout, "Let's go fill the galaxy!" If this already happened a few times, it might help explain the apparent emptiness out there, for the galaxy seems, at this moment, to have few, if any, other voices.)

A galaxy might "burn out" all too easily, unless something regulates how colonists treat their planets, forcing them to think about the long run, beyond short-term self-interest. The Uplift Universe shows one way this might occur. For all the nasty traits displayed by some of my Galactics—their past-fixation and prim fanaticism, for instance—they do give high priority to preserving planets, habitats, and potential sapient life. The result is a noisy, vibrant, bickering universe. One filled with more life than there might have been otherwise.

For the record, I don't think we live in a place like the wild, extravagant Uplift Universe. But it's a fun realm to play in, between more serious stuff.

Pile on those marvels!

Hang on. There's more to come.

Only now . . . a denouement!

I did it once before, following the afterword to *Earth*. And there's another . . . a *secret* lagniappe to *Foundation's Triumph,* where I tied together most – but not all of Isaac's loose ends.

So, then, here's a little denouement—a story-after-the-story—for those of you who hung around all the way through my final remarks.

It revisits one of our characters a year or so after the Great Rupture, and it attempts to tie off just a few (out of many) of my own loose ends.

Enjoy.

CIVILIZATION
[ALVIN'S DENOUEMENT]

The seas of Hurmuphta are saltier than Jijo's.

The winds don't blow steady, but in strangely rhythmic bursts, making it awkward and dangerous to sail a close tack.

That is, till you figure out the proper cadence. After that, you get a feel for the rolling tempo, sensing each gusty surge and tapering wane. With a light hand on the tiller, you can really crowd the breeze, filling the mains till you've heeled over with spars brushing the wavetops!

The first time I did that with Dor-hinuf aboard, she hollered as if Death itself had come up from the deep, to personally roar a Chant of Claiming. By the time we got back to the new dock, soaked from head to toe, she was trembling so hard I figured I must have really gone too far.

Boy was I wrong! The moment we stepped through the door of our little seaside khuta, she grabbed me and we made love for three miduras straight! My spines hurt for several days after.

(Soon I realized, civilized hoons seldom experience the stimulated drives that come from exhilaration! Back on Jijo, that was part of daily life, and served to balance a hoon's instinctive caution. But our starfaring relatives lead such sedate lives, except for once-a-year estrus, they hardly ever think of sex! Fortunately, Dor-hinuf has taken to this new approach, the way an urs takes to lava.)

Alas, we now have less time for romantic trips together. Business is picking up, as word spreads across the high plateau—where hoonish settlements huddled for a thousand years, confined to prim, orderly city streets, far from any sight of surf or tide. After all that time, I guess there's a lot of pent-up frustration. Or maybe it has something to do with the way the Five Galaxies have been shaken up lately. Anyway, lots of people—especially a younger generation—seem willing to consider something new for a change. Something our Guthatsa patrons never taught us.

Groups arrive daily, flying down to our lodge on the deserted coast, emerging from hovercars to stare at the glistening lagoon, nervous to approach so much water, clearly mindful of rote lessons that all hoons have been taught for ages—that oceans are *dangerous.*

Of course, any hoonish accountant also knows that risk can be justified, if benefits outweigh the potential cost.

It takes just one trip across the breezy bay to convince most of them.

Some things are worth a little jeopardy.

* * *

My father-in-law handles the business details. Twaphu-anuph resigned his position with the Migration Institute to run our little resort, meeting investors, arranging environmental permits, and leasing as much prime coastal land as possible, before other hoons catch on to its real value. He still considers the whole thing kind of crazy and won't step onto a sailboat himself. But each time the old fellow goes over the accounts I hear him umbling happily.

His favorite song nowadays? "What shall we do with a drunken sailor"!

I guess it bothers me a little that neither the haunting images of Melville, nor the Jijoan sea poetry of Phwhoon-dau, have as much effect on Twaphu-anuph as a few bawdy Earthling ditties. The rafters resound when he gets to the crude part about shaving the drunkard's belly with a rusty razor.

Who can figure?

I'm so busy these days—giving sailing lessons and reinventing nearly everything from scratch—that I have no time for literary pursuits. This journal of mine lies unopened for many jaduras at a stretch. I guess my childhood ambitions to be a famous writer will have to wait. Perhaps for another life.

In fact, I found a better way to change my fellow hoons. To bring them a little happiness. To change their reputation as pinched, dour bookkeepers. And perhaps help make them better neighbors.

Back on Jijo, all the other races *liked* hoons! I hope to see that come true here, as well. Among the star-lanes of civilization.

Anyway, the literary renaissance is already in good hands. Or rather, good *eyestalks*.

Huck gave in to half of the role assigned to her.

"I'll have babies," she announced. "If you guys arrange for hoonish nannies to help raise 'em. After all, *I* was raised by hoons, and look how I came out!"

I would have answered this with a jibe, in the old days. But without Pincer and Ur-ronn around, it just isn't the same. Anyway, I'm a married man now. Soon to be a father. It's time I learned some tact.

Huck may be resigned to staying pregnant, since she's the only one who can bring a g'Kek race back to life in the Four Galaxies. But she absolutely refused the other half of the original plan—to live in secrecy and seclusion, hiding from the ancient enemies of her kind.

"Let 'em come!" she shouts, spinning her wheel rims and waving her eyes, as if ready to take on the whole Jophur Empire, and others who helped extinguish her folk, all at the same time. I don't know. Maybe it's her growing sense of prominence, or the freedom of movement she feels racing along the smooth sidewalks of Hurmuphta City, or the students who attend her salons to study Terran and Jijoan literature. But she hardly ever comes down to the Cove anymore, and when she does, I just wind up listening to her go on for miduras at a stretch, saying little in response.

Maybe she's right. Perhaps I am turning into just another dull old hoon.

Or else the problem is that g'Keks seldom compromise—least of all Huck. She doesn't understand you've got to meet life halfway. For every change you manage to impose on the universe, you can expect to *be* transformed in return.

I brought gifts from Jijo to my spacefaring cousins—adventure and childhood. They, in turn, taught me what serenity can be found in home, hearth, and low, melodic rituals inherited from a misty past, before our race ever trod the road of Uplift or cared about distant stars.

Those stars are farther than they used to be. Ever since the Five Galaxies abruptly became four, half the transfer points and interspatial paths went unstable, and may remain so for the rest of our lifespans. Untold numbers of ships were lost, trade patterns disrupted, and worlds forced to rely on their own resources.

I guess this means it'll be a while before we get a letter from Ur-ronn. I'm sure she's having the time of her life, somewhere out there, consorting with engineers of all races, up to her long neck in pragmatic problems to solve.

Although urs aren't a sentimental people, I do hope she remembers us from time to time.

All I can say about poor Pincer is that I miss him terribly.

Sometimes you just have to let go.

Death has always been the one great, hopelessly impassable gulf. Now there is another. When Galaxy Four finally ripped loose, it seems every sapient being felt it happen, at some deep, organic level. Even on a planet's surface, it staggered many folks. For days, people walked around kind of numb.

Scientists think the recoil effects must've been far worse in Galaxy Four itself, but we'll never know for sure, because now that entire giant wheel of stars lies beyond reach, forevermore. And with it, Jijo. My parents. Home.

There are consolations. It feels nice to imagine dolphins, swimming with abandon through the silky waters off Wuphon, playing tag with my father's dross ship, then coming near shore each evening to discuss poetry by Loocen's opal light.

Of course, the Commons of Six Races can now tear up the Sacred Scrolls and stop hiding their faces from the sky. For the laws of the Civilization of Five Galaxies don't apply to them any longer. Perhaps Jijo's people have already dealt with the Jophur invaders. Or maybe they face even worse crises. Either way, the burden of guilt we inherited from our criminal ancestors can be shrugged off at last. The folk of the Slope aren't trespassers—or *sooners*—anymore.

Jijo is theirs, to care for and defend as best they can.

I have faith they'll come out all right. With a little help from Ifni's dice.

Speaking of strange colonists, I'm now being nagged by a little otterlike creature who wants yet another favor.

Ever since admitting he could talk, Mudfoot has been a real chatterbox, constantly demanding to know if Tymbrimi ships have come to Hurmuphta Port, or if any vessels are bound for the chaotic Tanith Sector in Galaxy Two, still picking up pieces from a shattering war. Mudfoot's impatience is characteristic.

Though Mudfoot now calls himself a *tytlal,* he'll always be a *noor* to me. I prove it by puffing my throat sac and humming a favorite umble. He joins my pet Huphu on my shoulder, and soon they're wrapped up together, dumb to the outside world.

"He will never leave," Dor-hinuf predicts. Indeed, Mudfoot seems to enjoy his daytime job on the yacht, scrambling among the sails and spars, chewing sourballs and muttering caustic remarks about the landlubber passengers.

Yet, I'm not so sure. A flame burns inside the small creature, like a human with a cause, or an urs with a gadget she wants to try. Mudfoot will never rest till he's taken care of unfinished business.

Knowing what I do about tytlal, it probably has to do with a joke. Something long range and desperately funny . . . unless you happen to be on the receiving end, that is.

Someday, I figure we'll wake up and find him gone—with all our lanyards tied in knots as his fond way of saying good-bye.

Mudfoot is reading over my shoulder as I write this, panting and grinning enigmatically, enjoying my speculations without offering a clue.

Enough. Come on, you little rascal. There are customers waiting.

The breeze is fine, and companies of clouds march in neat rows past a silver horizon.

Let's go give some stuffy old hoons the thrill of their lives.

TIMELINE OF THE UPLIFT UNIVERSE

NOTE: This is based on historical summaries offered by Earth's branch unit of the Galactic Library. For some reason this unit grows ambiguous and evasive as we look farther back in time, using language that becomes increasingly vague and oracular. Entries over 300 million years must be taken as only generally valid, and possibly mythological.

2.8-2.75 BYA: Scholars attribute Paean of Loneliness to this age. The Paean of Loneliness is an ode to Uplift, supposedly voiced by the Progenitors, themselves.

2.7 BYA: Institute for Foresight is created.

2.3 BYA: Progenitors retire, gradually separating themselves from affairs of lesser races, leaving behind laws and edicts regarding tradition of Uplift.

2.26 BYA: Progenitors physically leave the "Many Galaxies" (according to Inheritor legend), or transcend (by Awaitor lore) to another plane of reality.

2.22 BYA: Progenitors "pass on" (according to the Transcendor faith).

2.202 BYA: The Galactic Institute for Migration begins to take on its modern form.

2.1 to 1.9 BYA: Formative stages of present Galactic civilization.

1.9 BYA: Institute for Civilized Warfare formed. The Library records from this time forward are notably more complete than for earlier epochs.

1.4 BYA: Modern Library and Uplift Institutes reorganized, and essentially assume their modern forms. Eukaryotic organisms take sway in earth seas. Primitive life forms colonize land.

620 MYA: The ecologically insensitive "Lions" dominate the Galaxies. Ash spreads through vast parts of the Galaxies.

618 MYA: The Tarseuh forge a coalition with six other elder or retired Hero Races and overthrow the "Lions".

598 MYA: Ultraconservative Institute for Recovery of Honor, dedicated to repairing damage wrought by the "Lions," dominates Central Galaxies.

541 MYA: Diversity is artificially induced in many worlds, possibly including Earth [causing the Cambrian explosion]. This is the last reference to what might be Earth in the Galactic Library, before Contact.

400 MYA: Karrank% released from clienthood and granted the planet Kithrup as a "retirement home."

145 MYA: The quality of available Library data increases again on a scale even more dramatic that of the 1.9 BYA improvement. This relative improvement is tacitly recognized by most individual sapient scholars and intellectuals, but seldom acknowledged-let alone discussed-in official or academic circles.

60 MYA: A medium-scale "Time of Crisis." A zone of Ash forms in Earth-local space. Twelve-spin machine civilization is scapegoated and suppressed. Dinosaurs and many other life forms die off on Earth, making way for Age of Mammals.

52 MYA: The last recorded "wolfling" race, the Paranaj, is discovered; within a few hundred years it is extinct.

33 MYA: Thennanin uplifted by the Wortl; join Abdicators Alliance.

2.1 MYA: Soro uplifted by Hul

100 KYA: At about this time O-2 civilization begins to experience a wave of uplift atrocities and associated ecological disasters.

50 KYA: The Bururalli Holocaust wipes out most higher animals on Planet Garth; The Bururalli are destroyed as punishment. The Nahalli ulsu-Bururalli are reduced to clienthood and indentured to the Thennanin for rehabilitation. Humans on earth showing early signs of agriculture and control over domestic beasts.

1470 BC (~4000 BxY): Tymbrimi patrons, the Caltmour, wiped out in galactic war. The Institute for Civilized Warfare calls it an "unfortunate error." Time of the Egyptian Middle Kingdom on Earth.

1961 AD (251 BxY): First human spaceflight. 1969 (243 BxY): Humans land on the Moon and return.

2015 (197 BxY): Earth-based observers discover planets in the habitable zones of nearby star systems. These include what will later be called NuDawn.

2026 (186 BxY): First crude attempts in modifying Dolphins begin; these experiments were abandoned a few years later.

2046 (166 BxY): Near light speed probes sent to six planets orbiting nearby stars.

2100 circa (110 BxY): Earth controlled by the Bureaucracy—a despotic regime in response to the Time of Troubles.

2051 (109 BxY): Chimp uplift effort officially begins, after many amateur or secret false starts.

2055 (86 BxY): Dolphin uplift project resumes after protests and legal shut-downs.

2121 (151 BxY): First manned human STL interstellar travel.

2132 (80 BxY): The Hegemony, the second generation of the Bureaucracy, controls the Earth.

2154 (56 BxY): Helene DeSilva is born.

2187 (25 BxY): First modern probationary policies implemented.

2189–2192 (23–20 BxY): The Politburo of the Bureaucracy foolishly makes probationary criteria applicable to members of the General Assembly. This results in the wholesale replacement of Assembly members, and subsequent replacement of the Politburo.

2191 (21 BxY): Confederation of Nations founded. It will succeed The Bureaucracy in a bloodless revolution.

2198 (70 BxY): Humans establish their first interstellar colony, NuDawn.

2202 (10 BxY): Jacob Demwa born.

2211 (1 BxY): Earth has established four colonies beyond the Solar system and is actively exploring space using near-light-speed vessels.

2212 (0xY): First Galactic Contact. Human explorers aboard the Vesarius meet Tymbrimi traders.

2213 (1 AxY): Sequestration of NuDawn as sooner infestation by Galactic Institute of Migration. Earth learns of the incident two years later.

2213 to 2237 (1 AxY to 25 AxY): Terragen Confederation in constant conflict with the Galactic Institute for Migration over the three surviving pre-contact Terragen colonies.

2214 (2 AxY): The Confederation of Nations is reorganized and renamed The Terragens Confederation. New election rules allow far-flung communities to participate in a representative democracy.

2227 (15 AxY): Neo-Chimpanzees recognized as Stage Two Clients and Humans recognized as independent patrons of Neo-Chimpanzees and Neo-Dolphins.

2237 (25 AxY): A small branch Library is installed at La Paz, Earth.

2246 (34 AxY): *Sundiver* incident (January). Library at La Paz is upgraded through a GLI grant.

2263 (41 AxY): Humans awarded a sealed Library Patent related to stellar research.

2231 (119 AxY): Neo-dolphins recognized as Stage 2 clients.

2394 (182 AxY): Garth colonized by Terragens under a lease agreement from the Galactic Institute for Migration (G.I.M.)

2422 to 2487 (210 to 275 AxY): Human-Galactic relations stable. Clan Terragens now holds ten G. I.M. leases for Ecological Recovery Worlds, as well as a "home-world lease" on Earth. While spiteful clans hope Earthlings will fail, these recovery projects are goinf so well that the G.I.M. is pleased with Terragens custodianship on all lease-hold worlds. Terragens have now been on good terms with the G.I.M. for more than 225 years.

2489, May (277 AxY): Streaker encounters derelict fleet, sends psi-cast message, and the Five Galaxies go into turmoil.

ACKNOWLEDGMENTS

Some of the spectacles contained herein did not start in my own twisted imagination. First, my dear and recently (2020) departed friend Freeman Dyson ignited countless imaginations with his original notions of a Dyson Swarm or Dyson Sphere. But the Fractal World, that tremendous structure made of huge fluffy spikes, presenting far more surface area (for windows) than any Dyson sphere, was described by another friend, Dr. David Criswell.

I want to thank my insightful and outspoken pre-readers, who scanned portions of this work in manuscript form—especially Stefan Jones, Steinn Sigurdsson, Ruben Krasnopolsky, Damien Sullivan, and Erich R. Schneider. Also helpful were Kevin Lenagh, Xavier Fan, Ray Reynolds, Ed Allen, Larry Fredrickson, Martyn Fogg, Doug McElwain, Joseph Trela, David and Joy Crisp, Carlo Gioja, Brad De Long, Lesley Mathieson, Sarah Milkovich, Gerrit Kirkwood, Anne Kelly, Anita Gould, Duncan Odom, Jim Panetta, Nancy Hayes, Robert Bolender, Kathleen Holland, Marcus Sarofim, Michael Tice, Pat Mannion, Greg Smith, Matthew Johnson, Kevin Conod, Paul Rothemund, Richard Mason, Will Smit, Grant Swenson, Roian Egnor, Jason M. Robertson, Micah Altman, Robert Hurt, Manoj Kasichainula, Andy Ashcroft, Scott Martin, and Jeffrey Slostad. Professors Joseph Miller and Gregory Benford made useful observations. Robert Qualkinbush collated the glossaries. The novel profited from insights and assistance from my agent, Ralph Vicinanza, along with Pat LoBrutto and Tom Dupree of Bantam Books.

Special thanks to Lou Aronica, who encouraged and who recognized that this extended novel was . . . a *trilogy!*

Emerson's last song comes from the finale of Giuseppe Verdi's opera *Falstaff*.

As usual, this tale would have been a far poorer thing without the wise and very human input of my wife, Dr. Cheryl Brigham.

For the 2021 edition, I also want to thank Robert Pryor, Bonnie Hartmeyer, RM Harvey, Darrell Ernst, Matt Crawford, Jonathan Armstrong, David Ivory, Jenna Claver, Duncan Cairncross, Steve Jackson, Keith Halperin and others, especially Doug McElwain, for many kinds of help, including correcting OCR errors from translating original paper volumes—and some from the original text! And yet again, hardworking and long-suffering Cheryl. The TIMELINE OF THE UPLIFT UNIVERSE was compiled by Alberto Monteiro, based upon work done by Kevyn Lenagh and me in our book *CONTACTING ALIENS: A Guide to David Brin's Uplift Universe* . . . which in turn benefited from *GURPS Uplift* by Stefan Jones (Steve Jackson Games).

ABOUT THE AUTHOR

David Brin is an astrophysicist whose international-bestselling novels include *Earth*, *Existence*, *Startide Rising*, and *The Postman*, which was adapted into a film in 1998. Brin serves on several advisory boards, including NASA's Innovative Advanced Concepts program, or NIAC, and speaks or consults on topics ranging from AI, SETI, privacy, and invention to national security. His nonfiction book about the information age, *The Transparent Society*, won the Freedom of Speech Award of the American Library Association. Brin's latest nonfiction work is *Polemical Judo*. Visit him at www.davidbrin.com.

OPEN ROAD
INTEGRATED MEDIA